"CAPTURES THE MAJESTY
AND TURBULENCE OF THE AMERICAN
FRONTIER...COMBS IS A MASTER."
—*Publishers Weekly* *

"A GLORIOUS ADVENTURE."
—*The Neshoba Democrat* (Mississippi)

"STUNNING...BRILLIANT."
—*Sycamore Mohawk Leader* (Ohio)

"WONDERFUL...[A] SWEEPING STORY."
—*Southern Book Trade*

"For those who love Westerns, not just like them, but love them, there is a new writer whose words are superb, whose style is magnificent and whose story will endear him to everyone who feels the lure of the Old West. . . . Brules is a loner, a drifter and a man with a mission. He is UN-FORGETTABLE."—*Ocala Star-Banner*

"HUGE . . . SPRAWLING . . . this is one book that will absolutely enter your heart."
—*The Record-Chronicle* (Denton, Texas)

"A BIG, BOLD WESTERN."—*San Jose Mercury News*

"This wonderfully crafted story would make a classic Western movie, though Hollywood cinema would be hard-pressed to set the stage as well as Combs has."
—*Bangor Daily News*

"THE BEST WESTERN NOVEL OF THE YEAR . . . [Combs] dug deep, hitting primal bedrock on almost every page. The descriptions of the territory and lifestyles on the plains and in the mountains are so vivid that readers will be forced to catch their breath on more than one occasion."
—*Council Fires*, the Publication for Western American Enthusiasts

"A crossover novel that is both an epic western and a darn good story."—*Fort Worth Star-Telegram*

By Harry Combs:

BRULES
THE SCOUT

THE SCOUT

SCOUT

HARRY COMBS

A Dell Book

Published by
Dell Publishing
a division of
Bantam Doubleday Dell Publishing Group, Inc.
1540 Broadway
New York, New York 10036

ISBN: 0-440-21729-6

Reprinted by arrangement with Delacorte Press

Printed in the United States of America

Published simultaneously in Canada

June 1996

10   9   8   7   6   5   4   3   2   1

Contents

Prologue Statement of Steven Cartwright   1

1   Cloud Peak Camp   17
2   The Buffalo Hunt   38
3   Battle of the Rosebud   46
4   Run, Jupiter, Run   73
5   Conference on the *Far West*   104
6   The Rosebud and the Crow's Nest   119
7   High Noon and the Height of Land   136
8   The Battle of the Little Big Horn   142
9   Weir Point and Reno Hill   155
10   Like White Antelope on a Hill   171
11   Bouyer and the Deep Ravine   178
12   A Sad Journey   185
13   The Medicine Man   195
14   A Dismal March   220
15   Patrol on the Yellowstone   231
16   The Nez Perce   237
17   Tragedy at Bear Paw   244
18   Hard Ride at Hatch Gulch   282
19   Melisande   301
20   A Celebration   317
21   Duty   346
22   Escape   374
23   Honeymoon   389

24	Two German Knights	410
25	The Meeker Women	439
26	Winter Plans	464
27	Taos	489
28	Santa Fe and the Railroad	505
29	A Train to Denver	515
30	A Command Performance	544
31	Don't Cry, Alfred	565
32	Apache Country	583
33	Chaffee's Victory	625
34	General Crook Brings Order	637
35	Hell in the High Sierras	662
36	How Long Is Forever?	680

Prologue

Statement of
Steven Cartwright
BROKEN BOW RANCH
Norwood, Colorado
August 1919

I was born in 1898 on a ranch in the high country of southwestern Colorado. The ranch was dominated by a beautiful mountain, Lone Cone Peak, just to the south.

Lone Cone was my favorite mountain. Its northern slopes were the summer range of our ranch and so, as a boy, I rode over a great part of it. I recall that there was game everywhere, deer and elk and often bear.

It was still wild country in those days, although the Indians had been removed from the area some fifteen years before I was born. Like any boy I dreamed of the colorful tribes that once roamed through that country, and often liked to imagine, as I came around the shoulder of the mountain, that I could see some wandering Utes in the valley below looking for good hunting grounds, or perhaps a long line of Arapahoe warriors, bedecked with brilliant feathers and riding their painted horses, bent on serious business.

I explored the whole wild range as freely as an eagle wings through the clouds, in tune with it all—the bright greens of the quaking aspens in summer; their shiny gold in the fall; and in the winter the white crown of snow on Lone Cone, standing in all its majesty against the blue of the eastern sky.

I loved the dazzling sunsets of the desert country to the west; the shimmering mystery of the distant desert and the rumbling sound of the San Miguel River, rushing fresh born from the rock springs of the glacial basin far above Telluride.

The lower slopes of Lone Cone were covered in oak brush. Midway up the shimmering aspen trees skirted the mountain, and higher still the towering blue spruce trees cast their deep shadows—shadows of a mysterious forest that stretched up to timberline at almost thirteen thousand feet.

I often climbed above timberline on Lone Cone to what I thought was the greatest view in the world. Northwest of the mountain, some forty miles away, stood the snowcapped peaks of the La Sals—the Salt Mountains of Utah. Due west lay the Blues. To the southwest lay the red stone sculptures of Monument Valley, and to the south—the mummylike mountain called the Sleeping Ute. When I turned to the east, the giant peaks of the San Juans towered in their snow-clad vastness, beckoning to an adventurous heart.

It was a wonderful place for anyone to live, particularly a young boy. Indeed, even now I recall my youthful wanderings in that country with a joyous heart.

Yet, of all my adventures, the most exciting, mysterious, and wonderful experience was my friendship with old Brules. Old Brules was my hero, a mysterious mountain man, Indian scout, perhaps an outlaw. He lived all alone in a cabin high on the southwest shoulder of Lone Cone.

To me Brules was a fascinating, original source of information on the Old West. On those rare occasions when I was in his presence, I could hear the thunder of the buffalo herds, the voices of the prairie wind, the beat of war drums, and the wild, shrill cry of an Indian charge. He could convey all the excitement and turmoil of that irresistible force that moved the frontier westward, across half the continent, to the Pacific shores in less than fifty years. In fact, he was a part of that turmoil; he had seen almost all of it and drawn his own conclusions. He was fair and honest when it came to passing judgment on the natives who resisted that force to the best of their ability.

He was keen to observe the vast differences in character of one Indian tribe from another. He would describe what separated the cruel and the kind, the ugly and the beautiful, the cowardly and the brave; he knew, too, the different ways these peoples lived in the wilderness.

I first came to know Brules in the spring of 1909 when, as a boy of eleven, I helped with the branding of slick calves—weeners—high up on our summer range on Lone Cone. When it was over and we were headed home, I hit out alone to see for myself if I could find the cabin of the old mountain man. Sure enough, it was where I had heard it would be, and nearby there was the old man himself, panning for gold in the little stream that ran past.

He seemed quite disturbed when I rode up. Clearly strangers were not welcome, but when he saw that his visitor was only a boy, he seemed to grow easier. I felt uncomfortable and left quickly, but I had actually seen and spoken to the legendary mountain man—the outlaw.

That summer I managed to go by his cabin a few more times. I would just wave a greeting and pass by. He never made a sign of recognition, until the last time, at the end of the summer, he waved back.

By late summer of the next year I had got to know old Brules pretty well; I stopped at his camp whenever I could, and he became more friendly, and took an interest in me. He began to show me things about trapping and the use of firearms. Most dramatically, that summer when I was twelve and he was an old man past sixty, he gave me an exhibition of his shooting. I had been around firearms all my life and had lots of instruction on how to use a rifle and handgun, but I had never seen anything like the exhibition Old Man Brules put on that day with his 1873 Winchester and his Smith & Wesson .38-caliber revolver.

The guns were old and obviously had seen better days, but their action was smooth and clean. Brules was absolutely astounding—he never missed! Whether he set up a small target at long range for his rifle, or I threw cans or bottles into the air (sometimes two at once) for his revolver, he blasted them with deadly accuracy. I had seen men do that with shotguns but never with a rifle or pistol.

Even more impressive was his speed. He could fan his revolver so rapidly that all six shots went off in a steady roar. What's more, each one was accurately placed.

He would complain that his timing had slowed with age and that his eyesight was dimming, but I saw little evidence of either. I wondered what Brules's shooting had been like when he was really in his prime.

I knew that a great treasure of information about the Old West was locked up in his heart and mind, but as a boy I never quite had the nerve to start questioning. Our friendship was confined to a few meals around the campfire, and bits of instruction from him on the matters that I found to be not only fascinating and exciting, but invaluable.

My visits to Brules's cabin were performed at great risk, for I had been strictly admonished to stay away from the old outcast. My mother was particularly adamant on the subject.

During those years, because there were no schools in the vicinity, I was taught by my mother. She was a college graduate and had enough background to take me through an entire grammar-school education.

Studying with her was a glorious experience—she had the knack of making each subject a great compelling adventure. I'm sure I had one of the best fundamental educations that any boy could hope for.

My mother was a stately and beautiful lady with raven-black hair, high cheekbones, flashing black eyes, and a copper complexion that was something to behold. I loved her dearly. There was a deep bond between us.

When the situation demanded, however, she could be extremely severe. I remember very clearly when I let it slip that I had visited old man Brules. My mother reprimanded me sternly for having disobeyed her orders. That night, when my father got home, I was escorted to the woodshed. My father was a just and kind man, but he was a person of principle, and he demonstrated, very clearly, that when my mother gave an order it was to be obeyed. He delivered his message strong and well, and the whole ranch heard the results of his administrations. After that I visited old Brules only on very rare occasions.

After two more years of tutoring my mother decided that she had done the best for me in the way of a grammar-school education, and I was sent to Granville, Ohio, to live with a cousin of hers and attend high school for two years. In 1914 I entered Phillips Academy, Andover, Massachusetts.

I loved Andover and received a great education. I had lots of fun with athletics, making the football and track teams with considerable ease. I made friendships, some of them of lifelong duration, but I was aware that there was a gap between me and many of the eastern boys—our backgrounds were so completely different; they really had no comprehension of what I was talking about when I described life on the Broken Bow Ranch.

I graduated from Andover in 1916, and was accepted at Yale. That summer I insisted on coming home to Colorado. I had been away from the West for four years, and I recall very distinctly how exhilarated I was to find that beautiful country just as inspiring as I had remembered it. Somehow the East seemed very limited and unexciting.

Through a connection my father got me a job with a survey crew for the summer, working in the big goosenecks of the San Juan River downstream from Mexican Hat, Arizona. That was wild and in some ways unexplored country, and the experience was a fine adventure. I learned to keep a job, earn a living, and be very much my own man. I was eighteen years old and full of a lot of ideas about life in the future.

When the survey team broke up in the late summer, I pocketed my wages, saddled my horse, and headed out for the ride back to the ranch.

As I left the trading post at Mexican Hat, a fine Navajo blanket caught my eye. With my new-earned wages I felt wealthy beyond dreams and bought it for a ten-dollar bill. It was one of the most beautiful pieces of work I had ever seen, and I thought it would make a great contribution to the bedroll tied up in the slicker on the back of my saddle.

The ride from Mexican Hat to the Broken Bow was a

distance of about one hundred and twenty-five miles as the crow flies, and I made it easily in two and a half days. My horse and I were in great condition from working in the canyon country all summer.

The meeting with my mother and father was a joyous one, and two days later my father suggested that I might like to visit the upper cow camp where the boys were branding calves for the fall roundup. I jumped at the chance, especially when he offered me his favorite horse for the trip, a thing that he had never done before.

The steady climb brought me to the cow camp and a reunion with my old cowboy friends. They seemed glad to see me, but jokingly allowed that I had gone a little eastern. They were a great bunch of fellows and we had a wonderful time.

I left the roundup early and headed straight for Brules's cabin, hoping that nothing had happened to him in those four years, and that I would find him the same as I had left him. I was not disappointed. When I rode out of the timber, fifty yards east of his cabin, I saw him squatting down by the creek working his pan. When he saw me, he stood up, pushed his old hat back on his head, and said, ''Well, I'll be damned! Where in the hell have you been? By God, you done growed some since I last seen you!''

He received me with open arms, and was plainly touched by the fact I would come back to visit him.

At this time I stood about six foot two and weighed around a hundred and ninety-five pounds; I was lean, raw-boned, and didn't worry about encountering any kind of opposition or punishment when I got back to the ranch. I decided that I would stay with Brules long enough to have him tell me about his life in the Old West. If I could just get the old man talking, I thought that I would be in possession of a treasure.

I was desperate to get Brules going, because it might be my last chance. At the end of the week I would be leaving for college in the East, and it would probably be at least two years before I returned—old Brules might not be around then. I couldn't entertain such a thought.

By asking a series of provocative questions I finally managed to get Brules started talking. In the evening, as he gazed into the campfire with those strange piercing gray-green eyes with pupils that narrowed to cross slits in the light like a cat's, he began to tell me his life story.

This is what he told me.

In midsummer of 1867, as a youth of eighteen, Brules had started up the Chisholm Trail from Texas on a cattle drive. His trail boss was a tyrannical bully named McIntyre, for whom Brules, over the next three months, worked up a solid hatred. The drive ended in Hays City, Kansas, where cattle prices were reported to be higher. That was mid-October.

Hays City was a wide-open town, and his first night there, with pay from the cattle drive in his pocket, Brules met an attractive dance-hall girl, Michelle, in whom he immediately took an interest.

Brules was to meet his best friend, Pedro Gonzales, at a place called the Longhorn Saloon in Hays. Pedro was a Mexican, kin to a fine old Castilian family with vast horse-ranching properties in the state of Chihuahua. The two had met the year before in the borderland country of Texas and had several adventures together.

Brules described Pedro as a dashing fellow, who rode a magnificent black stallion, and wore a black sombrero, black vest, and black boots all trimmed in silver. Brules admired Pedro's bravado and the charm of his flashing smile.

When they met in Hays, Pedro had a surprising plan for the two of them to rob a bank in Taos. But before they got to it, Brules got into a fight with McIntyre over Michelle. McIntyre was killed, the hall burned, and Brules and Michelle escaped out onto the open prairies. They headed into Comanche territory to hide out, and were captured by the wild Quohadi Comanches. The Comanches were the cruelest and most ferocious of all the tribes—even buffalo hunters stayed clear of them. After a harrowing ordeal, Brules managed to escape, but not before the Indians had tortured Michelle to death before his eyes.

Escaping to Taos, Brules met up with Pedro again, and they decided to give up the idea of robbing the bank, and become buffalo hunters instead. It took them a while, but they were successful in getting many hides. Pedro was to take the wagon loaded with hides into Fort Union to sell them. But when he did not return after three weeks, Brules went off to see what had happened to him. What he found were Pedro's remains after the Comanches had finished with him. From that point on Brules hunted Comanches with a vengeance. In fact, he cleared the territory of them. He killed so many warriors, hunting them like big game, that he became a legend among the Indians. Because he left the sign of a cat whenever he did his killings, he was known as the Cat Man. The Comanches thought him supernatural. Eventually, they would not come near the area of the "spirit killer."

Satisfied at last that he had rid the world of enough Comanches, Brules went off to the La Sal Mountains far to the west to hunt grizzly, and was nearly killed by a bear. He was found and nursed back to health by a beautiful Shoshone girl, Wild Rose, with whom he fell in love. He courted her, followed her to her home in Wyoming, and finally won her with the help of his friend Wesha, son of Shoshone chief Washakie, and with the payment to her greedy father of a whole herd of horses captured from the fierce Blackfeet Indians.

Brules and Wild Rose were married, traveled far to the south again, and Brules built them a cabin halfway up Lone Cone Mountain. A few months later the pregnant Wild Rose was thrown and crushed by her horse, when a grizzly bear spooked it. Their daughter Morning Star was born prematurely, and Wild Rose died shortly thereafter. A despondent Brules buried his beloved wife and returned with Morning Star to the Shoshone reservation at Lander, Wyoming.

Brules and his baby daughter were kindly received by the Shoshone, especially Wesha and his family. As he had hoped, one of Wesha's sisters adopted Morning Star and agreed to bring her up along with her own young child, born two weeks before Morning Star.

Brules told me, at that time he was so low he didn't care if he lived or died. The loss of Wild Rose, and then having to give up their child, seemed unbearable.

Wesha then rose to the occasion. He informed Brules that the next day eighty Shoshone warriors were leaving Wind River to join General George Crook's forces at the foot of the Big Horn Mountains to fight against their blood enemies, the Sioux.

Wesha said what Brules needed to get out of this state of gloom was a good war. It didn't take Brules long to make up his mind. He left the next morning with the Shoshone contingent for the three-day ride to Cloud Peak Camp and the Sioux Wars.

Before Brules left the fireside that night, he spent a few minutes telling me how he felt about Lone Cone. He said when his Army discharge came through from Crook's cavalry in 1886 after the Geronimo wars ended in Arizona, he lingered around the southwest awhile, and then headed back to Lone Cone in the summer of '88. In all those years, Brules realized, he had grown more and more lonesome for his first love, Wild Rose. He just couldn't seem to be happy anywhere; he grieved for her often, and believed it was time that he went back to be near her.

When he finally returned to the Broken Bow, and saw the old cabin and visited Wild Rose's grave, he knew there was no other place in the world that he wanted to be. As he looked around, he saw that their painted horses had been long gone out of the pasture, running free somewhere up there in the mountains. He was glad for that. Twice he saw the band with a big stallion, and knew that they'd multiplied well during the time he was gone. But they were running wild, and that was what Wild Rose would wish for them.

Brules told me a strange thing. He said he had thought a lot about Wild Rose and mourned for her many times during the campaigns of the Indian wars, but he had actually seen her in his dreams only a few times. Yet the first night that he came back here and slept in the bunk where he and Wild Rose had spent so many happy nights, she returned to him in a dream. Even though it was twelve years later, she was just as young and beautiful as he'd ever seen her. She talked to Brules, but he couldn't hear her very well, though he could sense what she was saying. She said that she'd been watching him, and that she was glad to see him back. Her voice was very faint, and she smiled her sad smile and looked at Brules with her soft, doelike eyes.

Brules said he'd been back on Lone Cone now for twenty-eight years, and that Wild Rose came to him often in his dreams. He was an old man, and Wild Rose had been gone for forty years, but he said that she still came to him as a young woman. She was so beautiful. Oftentimes Brules would go out in the early morning or evening and sit by her grave. There was no marker, but you knew the place, because a deep bed of wildflowers grew over her grave in the spring.

Brules told me that he didn't want to go anywhere else now. He only wanted to stay here, and see Wild Rose when she felt like coming. At different times she would tell Brules that she was waiting for him to join her, and he knew it wouldn't be long. He wanted to be with her again too. So it was with real joy that he looked forward to the time when they would be together at last.

Then Brules told me something that was almost uncanny. I can remember the words practically as he said them. He started by saying, "Now let me tell you another strange thing. Maybe you won't believe me, but it's true. Many years ago I seen Wild Rose once and she was real. She weren't no spirit. It was down near the foot of the mountain in a big meadow, and she was gathering wildflowers. It was in the afternoon and it were no dream. I seen her! I absolutely seen her! Strange as it may seem, she weren't wearing her beaded headdress and her Shoshone buckskin skirt. She was wearing white woman's clothes. I think that was very strange. I called to her and she seen me, but she didn't want to speak with me. She just mounted her horse and galloped away. I ran after her, but I was old and on foot and had to let her go, my heart broken. I just dropped to my knees and put my head in my hands, and bawled.

"That was almost twenty years ago. I don't know why she run off, but I'll ask her when I go to her soon."

His story ended, Brules said nothing more.

I watched those strange eyes, which began to close, as if they were hiding the wounds of a soul, retreating into a private world.

I got into my bedroll, and my last recollection was of the old man's shaggy eyebrows and weathered face, turned red in the dying coals of the campfire, still carrying with him more secrets of the Old West, holding in his mind and heart the happenings of long ago.

The sun was shining brightly when I woke up, and the old man was gone. Perhaps he wanted to be alone, feeling he had unfolded his soul too much.

But I knew there was a vast amount more. I yearned to know about his time as a scout in the Indian Wars. They had to have been incredible adventures! I vowed someday I would come back and visit him again high up on this mountain.

I decided to take a look at his cabin; I had never been in it—only on the outside, sitting around the fire or walking over by the corral or by the creek. Gingerly, I went up to the door, opened it, and looked in.

I was immediately struck by its neat, clean appearance, and the sense of order that seemed to prevail in the small space. The floor was made of shining adobe that looked as if it had been swept and mopped a thousand times. Beside the old potbellied stove, with a bucket on top, was a bin for firewood. On the other side, against the wall, was a wide wooden platform made of planks laid over log supports. It served as both a storage shelf and a table. A wolf skin was hung on one wall and the only window gave a fine view of the distant Sleeping Ute Peak. An impressive set of full-curl mountain bighorns was nailed to one wall, and on the other the tines of a trophy elk horn served nobly as a gun rack for two old rifles: an 1873 Winchester and a big .50-caliber Buffalo Sharps, probably the one General Crook had given him in the spring of 1885.

A rim of low logs containing clean straw served as a bed in the corner. Spread upon it was a comfortable, well-cared-for buffalo robe, which clearly served as the only covering the old man had in the deadly cold of a Rocky Mountain winter, where, if the stove went out, the temperature inside could drop to forty below.

On the table was a piece of Indian pottery, a bowl of Shoshone pattern, and it contained late-summer wildflowers, whose beauty and brilliant colors were startling. Their significance was obvious.

I stepped out of the cabin and walked over to where my father's horse was tied. I undid the oilskin slicker from the back of the saddle and rolled out the Navajo blanket I had bought at Mexican Hat.

It looked fantastic in the bright sunshine. The red, blue, yellow, and brown—formed into the figure of the thunderbird—made it one of the best-looking man-made things I had ever seen. I hesitated a minute and then strode into the cabin, and spread the blanket on the bed. Like magic it brightened up the whole interior of that lonely mountain home.

Feeling immensely pleased, I stepped out and turned to take a last look at my farewell present to old Brules—my outlaw, the mountain man, the hero of my boyhood dreams.

In September 1916 I entered Yale University, where I studied, played some football, and fell in love with an airplane. It was a beautiful Curtiss flying boat that belonged to the Yale Naval Aviation Unit, which I soon joined. War was declared in April 1917, and our Yale unit was transferred to the jurisdiction of the U.S. Navy.

Of course we all knew there was a terrible war being waged in Europe, and felt somehow we might be caught up in it, but when war was actually declared on Germany by the United States, it still came as a bit of a shock.

Six months later we were loaded aboard a troop transport, and ten days later landed at Liverpool. After sixty days of additional training in England and Scotland, we found ourselves on the coast of France at the harbor town of Dunkirk, the western end of the long line that marked the ghastly front between the two struggling armies.

We could hear the thunder of the guns from our barracks,

but we were spared the horror and mud of trench warfare. We flew daily antisubmarine patrols in all kinds of weather over the English Channel. Some of our people did well using depth charges on enemy submarines. I wasn't one of those, but I can recall some pretty nerve-wracking experiences in the bad weather of early 1918 when the English Channel raged at its worst.

Armistice was declared in November 1918, and we were headed home. With so many hundreds of thousands of troops to move back from France we didn't get to the United States until the spring of 1919. We were mustered out at the Naval Air Station at Pensacola, in early May.

I returned home and once again hunted up old Brules. The closer I came to his cabin, the more apprehensive I grew that I would find it deserted, or something worse. When I burst out of the timber, it was with great joy that I saw the smoke of a campfire. Brules was not immediately present, so I waited a few minutes. I soon saw him coming up from the corral, walking the slow distinctive gait of an aging man.

Not wishing to startle him, I yelled hello and waved. He stopped, transfixed. As I rode slowly toward him and dismounted, the old man gave vent to the only extravagant emotion I ever saw him display. He let out a whoop, threw his hat into the air, and came trundling over to me with his arms wide apart.

I ran quickly to him and we embraced in a grand "abrazo." He began to pound my chest and beat my back, with tears in his eyes, treating me like a long-lost son.

I realized then that I had become so fond of the old man, in my own mind, that he was like another father to me, or perhaps a grandfather. In any case, I was delighted to see him and to see he was still reasonably firm and of sound mind, even if his body might be getting old and stiff.

I can't remember exactly what was said when we first met, except something about me being a real warrior now, back from the wars, and what's more, a "flying man."

Brules had never seen an airplane. In those days they didn't come around Colorado with great frequency and none came over the western slope or flew around the mountainous country. Yet Brules knew that flying machines did exist and that young men flew them, whirling about, high in the sky. He had heard somehow that I was a naval aviator, and that set me up high—in his estimation—in the category of a mountain man or Indian scout.

We sat around the fire that night like real old friends. He was no longer talking to a boy, and he knew it. He started asking the questions of me instead. I told him what I could about the war on the western front, my experiences in flying, looking for submarines in the dirty weather of the Channel, and what I had learned of aerial warfare. I was surprised at his interest, though to him it was still a great mystery how anything could fly that was big enough to carry a man.

He asked a lot of questions about how the world looked from up high, and how the clouds looked when the sun shone on them from above. He was amazed to learn that when we were in the clouds, we could lose all sense of equilibrium, often could not tell up from down, and might lose control of the aircraft. I told him some simple instruments for balance and direction were being devised.

All these things were great fun for me to talk about, but they weren't getting me any closer to his ten years in the Indian Wars. So I came right to the point.

"You know, Mr. Brules, those stories of yours were great companions of mine when I was on the Western Front. At times I was terribly frightened, but I recalled your stories about gathering yourself together for a matter of life or death and having the courage to go through with it. I have to tell you, sir, you were my hero."

With that the old man chuckled and bade me sit down by the fire, poking up the logs a little. "Well, son" (he used to call me "boy" instead of "son"; I had definitely been promoted), "if I'm your hero, I got to tell you, you got a bum one. Sure, I might have had some guts to fight Comanches and roam the West alone, but, by God, you'd play hell getting me in one of them flying machines."

I laughed along with him and, as I did so, I watched the

light on his strong, wrinkled face and in those amazing eyes that had given him the name of Cat Brules.

As I squatted by the fire I knew that now Brules would tell me whatever I asked him, but I needed to get him started. So I told him I wanted to hear about what he had done after he arrived at Crook's camp on Goose Creek.

1

Cloud Peak Camp

Brules started out,

Well, son, maybe you studied a lot about them Indian Wars, but let me tell you a couple of things that I'll bet you ain't never heard of. When I first met Baptiste Pourier, one of Custer's scouts, at Rawlins in 1874, Custer had just been up in the Black Hills and stirred up a hell of a rumpus. He'd led an expedition from Fort Abraham Lincoln on the Missouri to the sacred country of the Sioux—territory that had been promised them in a treaty they made in '68 with the government. Them Black Hills was to be theirs for a long time—and no white man was to come in there.

Custer was sent into that sacred country to protect the railroad surveyors of the Northern Pacific and also keep the miners out, but I think his real purpose was to find gold. If he started a gold rush there'd be no *keeping* the miners out and the cavalry would have to be called in. Then Custer would get his battle, where he could make a name for himself and advance his career.

Be that as it may, it sure stirred up a lot because he did find gold, and a big gold rush started. The Sioux begun attacking wagon trains and mining camps, and raiding ranches, with the usual horrible killings that them Indian raids produced. That made a lot of *talk* back east.

By the fall of 1875 a lot of them Indians on the Standing Rock and Pine Ridge and Red Cloud Reservations decided to leave and go out into the Big Horn country, which was really the country of the Crows. It was wild, free, and full of buffalo. The Sioux thought they'd live on their own and to hell with any treaties. They figured that the white man had broke 'em bad and they was gonna break 'em right back.

Of course, from a military standpoint, that couldn't be allowed. Wild Indians roaming the country, destroying wagon trains, murdering whites, would bring the wrath of the whole nation down, not just on the Sioux, but on the U.S. Army for not doing its job.

Anyway, the government, them damn fools, issued a statement to the reservation agents and others, to be spread among the Indians, telling them that if they wasn't back on the reservation by the first of January 1876, they'd be considered as hostiles and subject to attack.

Well, hell, a great many of the Sioux had already left the reservation and was way up, as I said, in the Big Horn country and never did get that message—especially 'cause it was wintertime and travel was damn near impossible.

Anyhow, what happened then was the big generals got together—Phil Sheridan, who was located in Omaha, and Tecumseh Sherman, whose headquarters was in Chicago. They cooked up a campaign that they figured would solve everything. It would put an end to the Sioux, stop all the murders and the fighting, and put them Indians back on the reservation. What's more, the army careers of a lot of officers would be helped by the promotions and all them things that go with being a soldier boy in time of war.

To make this campaign work they figured up a pretty good scheme. It was to go like this: Out of Fort Abraham Lincoln, at Bismarck, North Dakota, there was to come a big column of infantry and, along with the Seventh Cavalry, a supply steamer called the *Far West,* an old sidewheeler that could make it up the Yellowstone in good shape. It weren't no luxury Mississippi showboat but good enough for the expedition, and able to go in pretty shallow water. That expedition was to progress on up the Yellowstone to the mouth of the Tongue or the Rosebud rivers. Then, from Fort Ellis, up in Montana near Bozeman, a few companies of infantry under Colonel Gibbon was to come down the Yellowstone and meet with the command from Fort Lincoln.

The whole expedition was under General Terry. Custer was in command of the Seventh Cavalry and Terry was his boss. To make a kinda three-pronged stab at the Sioux, General George Crook, located in Cheyenne, was to work his way up the Bozeman Trail past Fort Laramie and on through the Badlands to Crazy Woman Creek, and from there to the foothills of the Big Horns.

Them military guys weren't so dumb that they didn't know the general whereabouts of the Sioux, but they didn't know their exact location. It was an area maybe two hundred by three hundred miles; an area of sixty thousand square miles that you had to cover on horseback. They knew that the hostiles was somewhere in the basin of the Rosebud or the Big Horn or the Tongue, and there was enough of them to be easily found once you crossed one of their trails.

The huge expanse of uninhabited country was laced with substantial rivers. At the southwest corner were the towering snow-clad peaks of the Big Horns, and to the northwest a fellow could see the snowy rounded tops of the Absaroka Mountains. Just south of where we was were the low but rugged Wolf Mountains, kinda stone ridges covered with timber. All the rest of the country was rolling grassland, dotted with small creeks that run into them big rivers. Wherever that happened there was usually a deep ravine with adobe buttes sticking up in different places. The creeks ran through the countryside so there was cottonwood trees and lots of them. In some places, such as the valley of the Little Big Horn, patches of pine timber were found along the river.

The early explorers and mountain men called that whole area "Big Sky" country, and it was sure well named. There was a dome of blue sky from one far horizon to another. You could have a whole cavalry regiment within your range of visibility and yet never see it! It would be too far away, even if it was kicking up a lot of dust.

Now let me give you some idea of what the difference was

between this and what I told you about fighting the Comanches. When I was down on the Canadian River and the Staked Plains of Texas and all that mesa country east of Raton, conditions was plumb different than it was with the Sioux.

True, the Comanche nation were numerous and tough fighters, but there was only about twenty thousand of them. Even at that they done held up the progress of the Spanish settlements for some two hundred years, and, by God, they held the Americans out of western Texas and southern New Mexico for almost forty years. They was tough and daring fighters and the cruelest, dirtiest bastards on earth, but not as numerous as the Sioux.

The Sioux nation was something like sixty thousand as far as the commander was concerned. And they was divided into a lot of different tribal circles. You remember, I done told you there was four different bands of 'em: the Peichkas, the Sata, the Co-cho, and finally the Quohadi, the last ones that was running free and the ones I'd done my fighting with?

Well, the Sioux nation had many, many more bands than that. There was the Teton, Oglala, Hunkpapa, Miniconjou, Santee, Sans Arc, and some others that I don't rightly remember. But, let me tell you, they was all tough fighters, all great warriors. And seemed like to me they was better looking than the Comanches, tall and straight, and plenty mean.

At any rate, for some reason the size of the Sioux nation was something even the government didn't understand. It was too hard to keep records or to keep track of them on the reservation.

On the Rosebud River the chief medicine man, Sitting Bull, got to beating the tomtom, giving lots of sun dances and all that stuff, to kinda churn 'em up. Hell, they just naturally gravitated toward this leader. Sitting Bull was quite a priest in his own right. I don't think he was much of a warrior, but he sure as hell could stir up the Sioux nation when he took a notion. Though Sitting Bull was a medicine man and kind of a prophet, there were some other chiefs in the Sioux nation that was awful good fighters—Crazy Horse, Gall, and Red

Cloud—and really they was just about as good generals as any of the white generals they was up against.

The Indians never did attack any situation unless they outnumbered the enemy several times to one. They never sustained an attack for long, they always got tired of things and run off. That give some white men the idea that the Indians was cowards, but that wasn't so at all. It was just that it wasn't the same discipline. A single Indian like a Sioux or Comanche was just as brave as the white man and more athletic—that is, with the exception of the hard-boiled mountain man, that's been out on the frontier for years and lives life just like the Indian. Them Indians was mostly able to outwrestle, outrun, or out-anything else your average white man.

But you hear a lot of white men brag about a few white soldiers could whip a whole bunch of Indians, how any white man could lick two or three Indians by himself. Well, it is more likely the other way around. The Indian was stronger and, in many cases, swifter, and could fight like a tiger if he wanted to.

The Indian had two problems, though. One of them was that he didn't have no wagon trains and supply system. He had to make his living off the land by hunting, so he couldn't keep a large number of people together at any one time for very long. He couldn't sustain nothing, couldn't hold a siege, couldn't keep up any kind of lengthy campaign.

The second thing was that he couldn't make ammunition. He had to go to the white man for ammunition and guns, otherwise the only weapons he could make out of his own supplies was bows and arrows, clubs and spears. They was pretty effective, but they sure as hell weren't in the class with a rifle, especially something like an 1873 Winchester repeater.

Another thing that held the Indian back was that he was a free spirit. He could go anywhere he wanted to, and the chiefs led their people not by discipline but just by influence. If the Indian decided to turn around and run, which was most likely the best way of doing things anyway, there was nobody going to stop him.

On the other hand, when a white cavalry outfit was ordered to dismount, they dismounted and they didn't run off unless the commanding officer gave the order to run off. If they disobeyed orders under combat, they could get shot. There was none of this stuff of going off and deciding that the war was getting too disagreeable or something, and that you was going home. The white man couldn't go home; he was enlisted in the service, and hard discipline kept him there.

That had been practiced over thousands of years by white soldiers, but the Indians never did get it. So, in the long run, they couldn't fight the white man and hope to win.

Some of them soldier fellows used to talk to me about military strategy, and once in a while they'd say something that would make a little sense.

They told me that the real purpose of a military force was to destroy the enemy's military force. Once that had been done, the whole country could be occupied very easy and controlled easy, but the Indian never did that—he fought hit and run, hit and run, all the time. Well, every time he run, he would give up some territory, and gradually the whites just advanced, having better supplies, ammunition, and all that.

Course, when the railroad came along, that really finished it because the army could haul big loads of ammunition, cannon, and horses, and a whole cavalry regiment could move across the country in two days. That made a lot of difference.

Still, it wasn't wise to fool around with a band of Sioux if you didn't know what you was doing, because when it came right down to hand-to-hand fighting, the real contest, they was damn good warriors and you better be ready to do what you had to do to stay alive.

Anyways, Sherman and Sheridan figured that they was really going to pulverize the hell out of the Sioux. They was just going to kind of crunch them redskins—or that's what they figured—between their advancing columns.

I think that I rightly recall that when you was here four years ago, I told you that I rode them three days with the eighty Shoshone warriors to Cloud Peak Camp on Goose Creek, where General Crook was gathering his forces.

I must say I was mighty proud to be with my friend

Wesha and them Shoshones. The Shoshone had enough intelligence to apply white man's cavalry tactics to their own maneuvers. They used bugles and whistles to signal different orders from their leaders, and they plumb obeyed those orders. A parade of Shoshone riding in columns of twos, with the American flag flowing in the breeze, was a sight to see, with them in their Indian splendor with colors and beaded and feathered war bonnets. They would cut right and left to a given command, and when Wesha brought 'em into Crook's camp at Cloud Peak, they wheeled and formed into maneuvers with a bugle call, like Crook's troops. Wesha led 'em up to Crook's tent and then dismounted and stood at attention with the smartness of the best troop.

It sure was an impressive sight. Still, I couldn't help wondering how their discipline would hold up in actual combat.

After we arrived and made camp, the first thing that happened was, I run into Baptiste. I hadn't seen him since 1874, when we met in Rawlins and he had tried to get me to go with Custer in the Black Hills campaign. He acted mighty glad to see me and steered me right. He took me to Major Randall, who was Crook's chief-of-scouts, and I was enlisted then and there in the Company of Scouts. I was right proud to be in that kind of company because those fellows knew their business.

I didn't know how to read and write too good, but I knew how to spell "Brules." I signed that on the muster. When they asked me my first name, I told 'em, "Some call me 'Cat' and some call me 'Deadeye' and some call me 'Cat Eye.' "

"All right," Major Randall said, kinda winkin' at Baptiste, "we'll put you down as C. Brules."

I told him it didn't make no difference to me, just as long as I got to go hunt Sioux.

I remember everybody laughed about that. I sure liked travelin' in the company of them men—Frank Girard, Baptiste Pourier, Louis Reichard, and that old mountain man, Bill Hamilton.

We hadn't been in camp more than two days, when Big Bapt come to me and said, "Me and Girard and Louis Reichard is going out on a scout to look for ze Crows, ze ones who is s'posed to be coming in to join Crook. General wants to know where is they? Maybe they is scared to come through the Sioux Country and meet us. Anyway, we go north, traveling at night, and we'll bring them back into camp."

"Fine, that suits me." I said, "Are we leavin' tonight?"

Baptiste shook his head. "No, thees time you are going to stay here—you and Bill Hamilton. Otherwise there weel be no scouts around. You weel stick with ze pack train and watch ze mules to see that they do not get run off by Indians."

That's a helluva thing! I thought. I come out to hunt Sioux and damned if they don't have me watchin' a pack train and a thousand lousy mules. I reckon right then I felt a little discouraged about the U.S. Cavalry.

I seen our campsite was in one of the most beautiful pastures in the world, although poorly located for Indian attacks—it bein' kinda down in a hollow and situated so that Indians could get as close as two hundred yards without bein' seen.

We didn't find General Crook at Cloud Peak Camp, but met him down on the Goose Creek, some miles below where that camp was supposed to be. When Crook came up, he didn't have no Indian guide and he hit Goose Creek too far down the river.

It was a big encampment. I think Crook had about twelve hundred men with him, counting the cavalry and companies of infantry. He had some damn good officers, if you like officers. They had Gatling guns and other heavy stuff, plenty supply wagons, and more mules than they needed to pull 'em. Damn if it didn't seem like almost a thousand mules.

The next day we was told we was going to a new camp on Goose Creek—the one where we was supposed to be in the first place. Everybody reckoned it was about ten miles north. With Girard and Baptiste gone there weren't nobody with Crook's columns that knowed the lay of the land for certain. Anyhow, we struck camp and set out till we come to a small creek, called Beaver Creek, and started down it. We never did get to Goose Creek Camp. Instead, we kept on and two days later finally ended up camped where the Prairie Dog Town Fork meets the Tongue River.

I heard lots of them officers complainin' that it weren't the best spot for defense, there bein' high bluffs around on either side of the river. Also there not bein' very good feed for the horses. Not understandin' anything about soldier boys at that time, I didn't enter into their discussion.

I ain't forgot nothin' about that campaign. It was sure a new thing to both me and them soldier boys! When we was on the march they would go dashin' up and down yelling, and there was buglers blowing the bugles. They would go in there with all the noise of the mules and the wagons. I never seen such a fuss in my life, and sure didn't understand it.

How are you going to sneak up on Indians that way? One old scout said that fighting Indians with the cavalry was just like going on a duck hunt with a brass band.

Anyhow, during that time that we come down the Beaver, I had made up my mind that I could never stand to ride with a column. It was too much dust and too much noise. So I told Major Randall, "Dang, if I'm going to be a scout, I gotta get off to the side." He laughed and agreed, "Yes, perhaps you're right."

Sometimes I'd ride only a mile off to the side of the column, or a mile ahead, and sometimes I'd ride twenty miles out. That was my way of doing it.

Major Randall was smart. Being chief-of-scouts he didn't try to use no discipline on me. I reckon he knowed scouts was made up of wild mountain men, and he wasn't gonna order them around like cavalry troops, or Fritzes. Them Fritzes was the German immigrant boys in the infantry. A scout was real free, and as long as he kept comin' into camp at night and reportin' what he seen, nobody much bothered him.

So, it was when we was comin' down the Beaver, headed for the Tongue River, I seen my first herd of buffalo since I'd hunted Comanches on the Staked Plains. To me them buffalo was a sight for sore eyes, and General Crook musta felt the same way, 'cause I seen him ride out with some of his staff and do some shootin'. Some said that this was his reputation—wantin' to always go off and hunt with a few officers a long ways from the column.

As it turned out, he was dang lucky that the Sioux didn't get his scalp. Trouble was, they did hit the column in force sometime later while he was away. Anyhow, it didn't make no difference to me just as long as I got to hunt. There bein' plenty of ammunition available for the scouts, I done right well. I killed quite a few antelope, and put down two buffalo and some elk, in the day and a half we was going down the Beaver. When we got to the Tongue we all ate mighty good.

While we was in camp there, I begun wanderin' around the country. Mostly I traveled at night and laid low in the daytime. Usually I left my horse on the picket line in camp— I'd druther do it on foot—it bein' easier to hide and me bein' one lone man.

Funny thing! About that time I begun keeping track of dates. I guess it was 'cause everybody laughed at me so much when I signed up with the scouts on the fourth of June. Eighteen seventy-six. When they told me what the date was, I couldn't believe it! Old Baptiste got to laughing so hard, and said, "Oh, boy, you really is a mountain man—you can't keep track of no dates."

Well, that was true. For a few weeks there I hit a bunch of unusual things—so I tried to keep 'em in order, and thinking about dates helped me a lot.

One afternoon, I guess it was early June, I was easin' my way along the Tongue River north and west of our camp, movin' through the cottonwoods real cautious-like, when I come across fresh tracks where a lot of ponies had crossed the river from somewhere southwest. They was headed northeast and I seen where their trail run up on the high buttes on the north side of the river.

Before I left the cover of the cottonwoods, I took a good look around. Seein' no motion where the trail run up over the top of the bluff, I hightailed it up there. It was a real steep climb and that alkali clay was kinda slippery and loose, but I made it up there in good time. I run hard mosta the way up without gettin' outta breath. When I got near the top, I lay down and crawled up to take me a look over the skyline.

I knowed them tracks had to be Indian ponies on account

of 'em not bein' shod, and judgin' by the trail, it looked like there was anywhere from fifty to a hundred of 'em. I figured it had to be a war party, 'cause there weren't no sign of travois, and if there'd been squaws along, they woulda never put the ponies to the steep clay cliffs.

Sure enough, when I eased my head up over the top, I seen 'em about a mile and a half away, goin' along the rim of the cliff in a kinda easy lope—a long line of Indians. They was in war feathers. The dress was considerable different than the Comanches, and I knowed with them bonnets they had to be Sioux. What's more, they was headed for Crook's camp at the junction of the rivers. I figured I'd better get a warnin' in as quick as I could.

I slid down off them clay bluffs and waded the chest-high river to the south side, holdin' my rifle and pistol outta the water, and then started down along the cottonwoods at a steady jog, hopin' to make it to the camp before them Indians got there. But I knowed it was pretty hopeless, me bein' on foot and them bein' on horseback and havin' a couple a miles' lead.

It was a good ten miles back to the camp, and when I was still a mile and a half away I started to hear shootin'. I knowed I was too late to give any warnin', but I kept on runnin' in hopes of gettin' in on some of the action. As I got to the camp all them Sioux was ridin' back and forth on the high bluff, shootin' down into the camp at the soldier boys.

The Sioux was quite a sight up against the skyline, just whoopin' and yellin' and ridin' up and down, showin' off their horses and occasionally pullin' up and firin' some shots. I could see that they was equipped with repeatin' rifles, no doubt Winchesters. It weren't till later that I learned they was usin' a better rifle than our troopers. Theirs was as good as mine, which was a 1873 repeatin' Winchester I got off the Blackfeet when I was courtin' Wild Rose. The Sioux got their 1873s off traders at the Red Cloud, Pine River, and Cheyenne agencies.

That sure was a sore point with the soldier boys—all them Indians havin' fine rifles that the government agencies had give 'em so they could do their huntin'. The soldiers only had them single-shot Springfield carbines, which most of the time jammed with them rimfired cartridges, so they'd have to stop and pull the cartridge out with a knife.

Well, like I said, I got to camp just in time to see all the confusion. Soldiers was runnin' around duckin' the heavy fire comin' from the Indians, and I figured there weren't no use of my lookin' for Major Randall to announce the comin' of the Indians—they'd already announced theirselves.

Some of them soldiers was fallin' into line and tryin' to look like they was waitin' for orders, which of course was the worst thing they could do. They could easy be picked off by the Indians up on the ridge, even though the range was a good five hundred yards. But them poor men was more scared of gettin' flogged for not obeyin' orders than they was of the Indians. I seen an officer standin' there and knowed right away that he was Colonel Mills, chief of the First Battalion, Third Cavalry.

Just then one of them young staff officers come ridin' into camp all excited and breathless, yellin', "Colonel Mills, Colonel Mills!"

"Here, sir," the colonel replied.

"General Crook desires you mount your men instantly, cross the river, and clear the bluffs of all Indians."

"All right!" barked Colonel Mills, and he give some orders.

All of a sudden four companies of the First Battalion was mounted and chargin' down the riverbank, jumpin' in and half wadin', half swimmin', and crossin' the river under heavy Indian fire. It seemed like a real brave effort, but it didn't make no sense to me. One good thing about it, at least when they got close to the other shore they had the cover of the cottonwoods. Off to the right was another company of the battalion firin' at the Indians, tryin' to keep 'em from doin' too much harm to the troopers crossin' the river.

I stood there watchin' awhile, sorta amused, as the line of blue-coated boys went scramblin' up the bluffs toward them Indians. The Indians was still whoopin' and hollerin' and ridin' around shootin' every now and then.

Suddenly the idea come to me—I might as well get me

some rifle practice right then. There was a ledge of rock to my left. I dropped down, rested my rifle on it, slammed a shell into the chamber, and took real careful sightin' on a big buck that was ridin' up and down, showin' off. His war feathers streamed clear down to his horse's flanks, and he was quite a sight. Instead of carryin' a lance and a shield like a Comanche, he was wavin' that repeatin' rifle and really whoopin' and hollerin'. He was a movin' target and a long ways away, but I decided to go to work on him.

I fired the first shot low on purpose, just to see where it'd kick up the dust. It puffed up a little bit ahead of his horse, low by about five feet. On the next shot I made the correction, and was real pleased to see them wavin' arms of his go up in a wild kinda spread. Then he fell off and bounced in the dirt as his horse shied away.

I went to work on two other Indians the same way. One cartwheeled off real slick-like and his horse run off, and the other kinda doubled up and hung on to his horse's mane. I reckon I cut him a little low, not quite hittin' him in the chest but maybe in the gut. What the hell, I figured he was gonna have a good bellyache for a spell, and wouldn't be back to do no more shootin' at our camp.

Them Indians begun to scatter right after that, and by the time the troopers got to the top of the hill, the Indians was plumb gone. Later on I heard Colonel Mills say that they seen 'em run off to a far ridge about three miles away and, it bein' toward evenin', there weren't no sense to pursue 'em.

Anyway, that was my first look at the Sioux and the first time I seen the way them soldier boys fought. I must say, them soldiers had plenty of guts, but didn't seem to me they had much brains. Sure weren't my idea of huntin' Indians.

Later that night when I reported to Major Randall's headquarters, I heard Colonel Mills and Colonel Henry and Major Randall all talkin' in Crook's tent. Either Colonel Mills or Colonel Henry—I don't know which—said somethin' to the other that tickled me.

"Must compliment you, Colonel, on the fine marksmanship of your men. You did a great job of covering us. We saw three of those Indians fall. Some troopers in your battalion were doing a fine job of shooting.''

It sure give me a chuckle, but I didn't say nothing. It was a damn cinch that them cavalry carbines wasn't accurate enough to do any four-hundred-yard job across the Tongue River and up to that bluff where them Indians was ridin'. I knowed who knocked them Indians off, but there weren't no point speakin' up.

Major Randall finally come outta General Crook's tent, and I got to report to him. I told him where I'd found the pony trail crossin' the river up above and how I'd tried to get to camp in time. He just grunted and said, ''All right, Brules, you keep on fanning out and report anything you see, only try to get here ahead of the Indians next time.''

I had to laugh at that a little bit, even though it irked me some. Sure I coulda got there ahead of them Indians, if I knowed how to fly! Other than that, his orders suited me just fine, and I kept workin' in about a twenty-mile circle all around the camp on both sides of the Tongue and Prairie Dog Town Fork.

This time I done it on Cimarron, reckonin' the speed of a horse was more advantage in scoutin' than bein' able to sneak in and out. I found it was plumb different than huntin' Comanches alone. Hell, there was no hidin' a whole regiment of soldier boys, so I come to realize I better not be on foot. I couldn't fly, but I could damn well ride, and on Cimarron it was pretty near the same.

Two days later Crook moved his camp back to where he shoulda been in the first place—on Goose Creek at the foot of the Big Horns. It was a much better camp, and there weren't no commandin' bluffs on every side. What's more, it was in the most beautiful horse country I'd ever seen. Green pasture meadows was everywhere, and Goose Creek itself was the clearest stream that come outta the Big Horn Mountains—all gurglin' and bubblin' and filled with trout.

We stayed in that camp for a while and it was there that I got to know a real interestin' feller. Strange enough, he weren't no soldier, but was what they call a correspondent, doin' an important job for a Chicago newspaper. I sure took a likin' to him. Like I said, I don't cotton to most folks and I'm generally slow to take up with anybody—but he was one of them men that I knowed right away I could really trust. His name was Jack Finerty.

He was an Irishman, a long stringbean of a fellow, thin, and maybe six foot three or four inches tall. He carried a notebook around with him and was always takin' notes and writin' things down. When he'd get to talkin', it'd always be in a real flowery language. There weren't no doubt when you was listenin' to him that he was an educated man, but that didn't seem to make no difference.

He was a regular fellow, and I seen that the soldier boys loved him—'specially the officers. What's more, the scouts took a real liking to him—them that I knowed. Frank Girard told me that he liked Finerty best of all of them newspapermen that come along on the campaigns.

Finerty and me had one thing in common—we sure liked that bottle of whiskey, and so we had plenty of good times together. He was real interested in the scouts and always tryin' to take down their names and learn all about 'em, like he was plannin' to write a history of 'em. He thought a lot of Frank Girard and Baptiste Pourier—you could tell that for sure by the way he talked about 'em.

When he'd get me a little bit drunk, he'd start pumpin' me for information. I didn't care to tell him too much, and used to leave out a lot about my past, things that I didn't think would do nobody any good. But one thing he got interested in was my huntin' Comanches.

I was never quite sure if he thought I was full of what the Irish called "blarney" when I told him about a few of my doin's down on the Canadian, but he'd take out his pencil and paper and write it in that notebook.

Another reason why the soldier boys liked him so much was they found out he had plenty of guts. It weren't till sometime after that I heard how he had rode in the charge Mills led goin' across the Tongue River and up the bluffs. I reckon

Finerty didn't have to do that, but he wanted to be in on the action to be able to tell about it firsthand.

It was him who told me that there was lots of folks wonderin' where the Crows was that was s'posed to come in and join Crook's troops. As a matter of fact, although I knowed that Frank Girard and Baptiste Pourier was about as good scouts as could be found in the western country, I was gettin' a little worried myself. From everything I'd heard, there was lots of Sioux between Crook's camp and the Crow agency in Montana. Even the best of scouts sometimes, by sheer bad luck, got theirselves in a jam.

Anyway, we was plenty glad when, about the time we'd give up ever seein' them scouts again, Frank Girard and Louis Reichard come ridin' into camp, along with the biggest Indian I'd ever seen.

He was a giant of a man—a Crow—and he sure looked the part of a blood enemy of the Sioux. Later, Baptiste come back and told us what the trouble was. The Crows had knowed we was s'posed to be camped at Goose Creek. When they didn't find no camp there, 'cause Crook had took the wrong road, they figured our group weren't the troops they was s'posed to join.

Only after our scouts found 'em did they make theirselves knowed and agree to go along. The Crows was afraid to come into camp for fear of bein' fired on. So Girard left Baptiste back with them to give 'em confidence, and brought the chief in. Then Major Burt and Louis Reichard went back to lead 'em in.

Along toward late afternoon we seen a lot of dust in the distance and here come a whole gang of Crows. There musta been near two hundred of 'em, along with the major and Louis Reichard and my good friend Big Baptiste. Them Crows rode right into camp, whoopin' and hollerin' and yellin', dashin' around with their lances wavin', showin' off all their paint and feathers and war bonnets, and puttin' their horses through their paces—all for amusement, I reckoned, and to show off to the soldier boys. Then they come around and started shakin' hands with everybody in the camp.

I never seen Crows before and I was surprised and pleased to see what good-lookin' people they was. They didn't seem to have the squat build and high cheekbones of the Comanches.

Them Crows done a good job settin' up their camp in a big hurry, and gettin' their fires goin' so they could cook their evenin' meal.

That night there was a big powwow with General Crook standin' in the middle of 'em all. There was a campfire, and lots of them Indians made speeches and said things that Frank Girard done the interpretin' for. I didn't hear all what was said and didn't much care. From what I heard of Indian powwows, they was mostly lots of flowery speeches and fellows tryin' to put on all kinda dignity, and lyin' to one another while they was doin' it.

After all the powwow war council, them Indians went around, dancin' their different dances and bangin' their drums. Although they had rode hard all day to get there, them crazies stayed up beatin' the drum and singin' their wild, weird chants. The din was horrible—they sure can do that when they set out to. I finally took my blanket, went off a piece, and rolled up in some brush so I could sleep.

The next day I watched the damnedest exhibition I ever seen in my life. General Crook had heard that there was a village of Sioux up at the headwaters of the Rosebud and he decided to go after them. He planned to leave his wagon trains behind and have the men carry their own beddin' on the back of their horses, with the grub to be carried by pack mules. On top of that he decided to mount the infantry on mules. This was kinda stupid, seein' as how them infantrymen—I reckon there was five hundred of 'em—never had rode a horse or a mule before.

Tom Cosgrove, chief of scouts in the Wind River Valley, was standin' near me. He says to the other scouts, "Watch this. This is gonna be a real show." It sure as hell was. Them poor infantrymen—most of 'em nothin' but a bunch of German or Irish immigrant boys that had just come over from the Old Country maybe three or four months before—had signed up for the army, been shipped out west, drilled around some parade ground or fort someplace, and then come out on this Sioux campaign. They was hardly fit to be doin' what they was doin' to begin with, let alone ridin' a bunch of unbroke mules.

The extra mules that Tom Moore, the chief packer, had been herdin' along wasn't used to this kind of stuff. Lots of 'em had never had nothin' on 'em from the time they was borned. It was his packer and the packer's men's duty to take them green mules along on a campaign and break 'em as they went. Whenever one was needed to carry a pack saddle, first he'd be loaded up, usually with somethin' that didn't make no difference if it got bucked off. After he was loaded a few times with wood and stuff like that and had got through buckin', he'd settle down and pull.

Of course, none of this figurin' included ever havin' foot-soldier boys climbin' on their backs. The way the mules could buck, it'd take a good horseman to sit on 'em, and that sure was a problem for some poor devil that'd never even sat on a milk wagon before.

What a day! It was the damnedest rodeo I ever seen. Five hundred all lined up, and one by one they got on them mules. Of course, some of the packers and officers that was supervisin' the job had sense enough not to saddle them mules, so that most of them boys rode bareback first. It was sure as hell they was gonna get bucked off, and it was better to get bucked off where you didn't get hung up in a stirrup or nothin'. On the other hand, some of the mules was ordered saddled, and when the poor boys tried ridin' 'em, a few of 'em got hurt real bad.

There was a couple of them mules that didn't do nothin' but hunch up a little, or maybe crow-hop some, and walk off stiff-legged, but the majority of 'em went to work really buckin' and brayin' like they was unbroke broncs comin' outta brandin' chutes. So mosta them soldiers kept gettin' bucked off, makin' big arcs in the air and landin' on their butts or on their hands and their heads, and everywhere else. There was dust everywhere and shoutin' and brayin' mules—plenty of cheerin' when one of them boys would hang tight.

The scouts and mounted troopers yelled, "Don't pull no

leather," "Hang on with your knees," and that kind of stuff. It didn't make no difference to the foot-soldier boys, 'cause they was so confused, they didn't know what was goin' on anyway.

Them that got the biggest kick out of it all was the Indians. Them Crows and Shoshones stood off to one side, laughin' themselves sick, thinkin' it was the funniest thing they ever seen. They're mighty good horsemen and it sure musta seemed ridiculous to them to see the palefaces gettin' bucked off so frequent-like. I didn't like to see it a'tall, 'cause it kinda run down the white man in front of the Indians. Maybe them Indians didn't have sense enough to know that them poor soldier boys had never done no riding before.

Finally, some of the young bucks among the Crows and Shoshones decided to show off. When a trooper'd get bucked off, one of them young braves would run out and tear up alongside of the buckin' mule, grab his halter rope, and leap on his back and put on a real exhibition of how to ride. That didn't do nothin' but make them poor infantrymen a little shamefaced, and prob'ly a little madder. I'll say this, though, every man kept climbin' back on his mule till the whole place finally settled down. I guess in the army that's what happens. You either follow orders, no matter how scared you are, or you get shot. Anyway, that was Crook's idea of doin' the job.

So, about June sixteenth, the general called for the march on the Tongue River with the whole outfit—maybe eleven hundred men plus scouts and Indian allies. We was goin' after the village of Sioux near the head of the Rosebud that he had heard about, and he was meanin' to move fast.

Crook's intentions was real simple. He knowed that if he took his supply wagons with him, he weren't never gonna catch up with the Sioux. His troops was gonna have to move faster'n that, and the only way to do it was to lighten up the load and move right out. That was behind his idea to mount the infantry on the mules, so they could move right along with the cavalry.

It was a great idea, but somethin' shoulda been done a long time before, in the trainin' at some parade ground or when Crook was out huntin' for grizzly bear or somethin'. Anyway, that's the way the army done things, and we headed off that mornin'. I remember the day, 'cause that day was the last good buffalo huntin' I ever done.

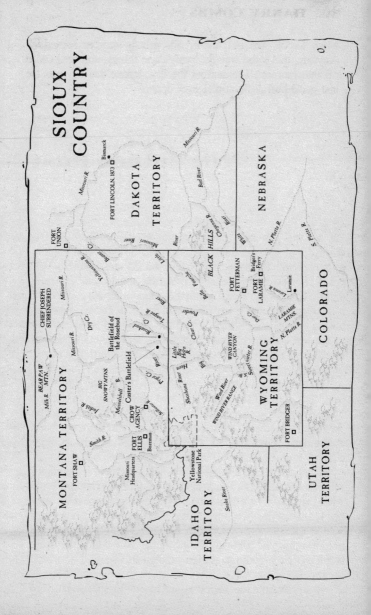

2

The Buffalo Hunt

We was marchin' toward the northeast away from the Big Horn Range into the finest game country in the world—rollin' grassland with plenty a good water. The sky was clear blue and prairie flowers everywhere perfumed the air. It bein' the middle of June, all the world seemed to be coming alive and turning green. When we got to the crest of a grassy slope we busted out on a sight that thrilled the whole command. As far as the eye could see, there stretched a herd of thousands and thousands of buffalo. It seemed like the whole earth was brown with 'em.

Some of them soldiers went frantic-like when they seen 'em, but the officers rode up and down the line, sayin', "Steady, men, keep your ranks." I could tell by the looks on the faces of some of them boys it almost killed 'em not bein' able to have 'em a real buffalo hunt. But not one of 'em made a move to disobey.

That's what the army discipline does for you. It sure don't set with me, although I reckon it's s'posed to win battles. From what I seen of it, it's about the only thing that keeps them poor boys alive. Mostly poor immigrants and farmhands, they couldn't shoot worth a damn. If it hadn't been for them always holdin' ranks and followin' their officers' commands, they sure woulda been wiped out. As it was, they still weren't no match for the Sioux.

I still wasn't too happy about havin' to stick with Tom

Moore and guard the pack train. But I done the best I could, considerin' it was goin' against my grain.

When we sighted the buffalo, I was ridin' two or three hundred yards out on the upwind side of the pack outfit and about even with the trail of the cavalry. It was a good place to be. It kept me away from the dust, and every now and then if I got the urge, I'd ride out five or ten miles and do a little scoutin'.

Well, while I was ridin' out there to the side with all them buffalo all around, I got a real hankerin' to do some huntin'. Then I heard the damnedest hollerin' and whoopin' from behind, and there come the Crows on the left of the column, and the Shoshone on the right, all stripped down for action and ridin' like furies. They started shootin' the herd and having' theirselves a helluva time.

That made General Crook fightin' mad. He was tryin' to keep the Sioux from knowin' we was comin' and here his Indian allies took off on a buffalo hunt. For me it was kinda amusin' to watch, and I learned a thing or two. Years later, when I heard all the stories about how the Indians never killed any game except for the food—that it was the white man that always shot out all the animals around 'em—I'd say, "I'm here to tell you that ain't so. *Them* Indians just killed for the fun of it. They was wastin' good ammunition that day, shootin' buffalo right and left for the howlin' fun of it."

General Crook said, "Well, better kill buffalo than let buffalo live to feed the Sioux." But that's a poor excuse for goin' out and eliminatin' a herd of buffalo. At least when Pedro Gonzales and me was killin' buffalo, we was killin' for the hides.

I couldn't see no use of me goin' in to shoot buffalo. The way the officers was stopping their men, I knew it woulda made me look kinda silly if I joined in. On the other hand, I must admit I was sure itchin' to do some buffalo huntin' again, and the memory of eight years before down on the Canadian with Pedro was strong in me.

Finally, I swung in close to the head of the column and spoke to Major Randall. I told him I'd like to head to the north

and see whether all the shooting' and yellin' had done anything toward attractin' the Sioux.

With a twinkle in his eye he said, "Sure, you go on out
and scout about twenty miles north, and come and meet the
column tonight. But don't do any shootin', otherwise there
won't be any buffalo left." Then he give me a big wink.

Well, that was a compliment all right. I moved off to the
left of the column and eased out across that rollin' country,
watchin' the buffalo in the distance stampedin' to the Indians'
whoopin' and hollerin'. I swung up over a rise of land outta
sight of the column, then I put Cimarron into a nice easy lope.
I used my field glasses in every direction, lookin' for signal
fires or other signs. In that country there weren't any cover and
I coulda seen Indians a long ways off.

I had a good horse and knowed he could make it back to
the column without gettin' trapped. After a spell we topped a
ridge and I looked down at the valley of the Rosebud. From
what I could see, it looked like a wonderful place to camp—
plenty of grass and water and the Rosebud windin' through the
sweetbriar patches that give the stream its name.

I could still hear the crackin' of the Shoshone and Crow
buffalo guns in the distance, but I couldn't see nothin' around
that looked like Sioux. I reasoned that if there was Sioux in the
country, they'd be huntin' buffalo, too, them bein' just as crazy
as the Shoshones and the Crows.

As it turned out, the Sioux heard the firin' from a long
way off, and was moving toward us to see what was goin' on.
When I got to that camp spot in the valley of the Rosebud,
them Sioux was still a good many miles down the creek, but
comin' up our way. There weren't no way I coulda knowed
that, though.

I sat there on my horse on the ridge, lookin' off in the
distance in order to see everything I could, and makin' up my
mind that Crook would camp in this spot that night, it bein' a
perfect site. At the speed his column was goin', he'd just about
get here in time to make camp.

I was kinda daydreaming, when I saw first one, then two
and three, and then a whole small herd of buffalo, trottin' over

the hill and down into the basin of the Rosebud. They was movin' at a right good pace, the cows and calves weavin' in and out as they poured over the ridge like a great big snake makin' its way along the land.

The thought went through my mind that here was supper meat for the whole command. So I slipped off my horse and knelt down and began sightin' careful along the barrel of my Winchester. I didn't wanta waste ammunition, but the excitement of the hunt was pretty great for me. I had to admit, in that way, I was kinda like the Indians.

I shot the lead cow first and she went over with a roll. The others split off in other directions, and there weren't no chance of my gettin' a stand. I knowed that, but I went to work on 'em while they was runnin', and when I got through, I'd put nine cows down before the herd got outta my range. They was strewed out over an area of about three hundred yards, and I hadn't wasted no bullets. That was a real satisfaction to me.

I led my horse on down to where the buffalo lay, got out my big knife, and started to go to work cuttin' some choice pieces. I knowed we wasn't gonna use hides nor nothin', so there weren't no use skinnin' 'em. We was on a military campaign, not no hide-collectin' expedition. It wasn't like when you shoot deer and elk now, and you take the whole carcass on into the ranch. We didn't do nothin' like that in them days. We couldn't bother to gut an animal, only took back straps and the haunch and the tongue and let the rest go.

I done some cuttin', layin' the meat aside. I'd been workin' for a couple of hours when the first batch of soldier boys rode down into the valley. They was some surprised when they seen me, a lone scout, with nine buffalo down, but they cheered when they saw they was gonna have a good meal that night. Pretty soon the rest of the whole column come along, and Frank Girard rode over to me and asked what the hell I was doin'.

I told him I figured the troops would need somethin' to eat, and I reckoned they was gonna camp in the valley that night so they might as well feed on buffalo, that bein' about the best eatin' there ever was. As far as I could see there wasn't no Sioux around, and if there was they woulda heard the shootin' the Shoshones and the Crows done. So my nine shots didn't make no difference.

Girard didn't say nothin', but him and Baptiste rode out and looked at every one of them buffalo while the column was filin' by a half a mile to the north. They stayed down by the last dead bull, walkin' around it two or three times and talkin'. Then they mounted up and rode back to where I was still cuttin' meat.

Both of 'em got down off their horses and I stood up. I could tell that they had somethin' important to say to me, them bein' important men, and I was ready to hear. Girard dropped down on his haunches, broke off a blade of grass, and started pickin' his teeth. Baptiste done the same thing, so I followed, all three of us sittin' there on the prairie alongside that dead buffalo, hunkered down holdin' our horses.

After a few minutes Girard said to Baptiste, "Pourier, you hired Brules. Maybe you'd better tell him."

Big Bapt grunted a couple of times and then said, "You know, Brules, me and Girard, we theenk you make one great scout someday. Damned good shot. Maybe ze best shot I ever seen."

With that he made a kinda big gesture with his arms toward them dead buffalo. "No, you don't waste ammunition. Every one of these is shot in ze neck. All dead right off. We see that. No blood. No drag tracks. They all fall dead. Damned good man with horse too. And you got eyes like ze eagle, good eyes to see at night. You got plenty of guts and you never talk too much."

He paused to think, then went on. "But there is one theeng, Brules, you know notheeng about. That is this army and how soldier boys think. Soldiers most of ze time is plenty damn fools. Crazy. Don't theenk like mountain man."

He smiled a little and shook his head. "We know this. All ze same, we are all now cavalry scouts and General Crook, he is commander of this campaign. Plenty good soldier, but no mountain man. Now, one theeng about a soldier boy. When General Crook geeve a command, soldier boy obey. This is plenty hard for scouts, 'cause scouts come from free men. But now you join with scouts that work for General Crook. And scouts do what he say. He tells soldier boys not to shoot guns at buffalo. Crazy Crows they no pay attention to Crook. They go out and shoot guns and kill lots of buffalo. Only theeng they do is let Sioux know we're in ze country."

He shrugged. "It is okay if you go away twenty miles to the north and maybe kill a couple of buffalo to take tongue. But when you come ahead, pick out campsite, kill nine buffalo for column to eat, you theenk you done pretty good, huh? For mountain man what you done is good. For soldier boy—no good." He stopped and looked at me to see if I understood things right.

I chewed my meadow grass a minute and then told him, "That seems kinda strange to me. There wasn't no Sioux within miles and if there had been, they woulda seen the columns of dust no matter how much shootin' me or them Shoshone and Crow did. Now, them soldier boys has been on short rations long enough. It's about time they had some good meat to eat."

Baptiste nodded, but for once he didn't laugh that big, hearty laugh of his. He said, "Yes, my friend, what you say is right. But what you and I think is right, that for ze army is always wrong. It is too bad, but I tell you what, none of them soldier boys is going to eat your buffalo tonight."

That sure made me boilin' mad. I looked him in the eye and said, "Whatcha mean? It's fresh meat. It's the best they could have!"

Baptiste stayed calm. "I know, my friend, but you not understand. What you theenk—they is going to eat the meat raw? That's why I say you don't understand army. Tonight, General Crook, he tell everybody 'no fires.' "

I guess my jaw musta dropped plumb open, 'cause both Girard and Baptiste began to laugh. I hollered, "No fires! He must be crazy. What does he think? By havin' no fires the Sioux ain't gonna see us?"

Girard and Baptiste both nodded.

"He's gotta be crazy. They don't have to see no fires at

night for their scouts to know where we are. Besides that, you got Shoshone and Crows ridin' all over the country, shootin' up the buffalo herds for sport, and I'll bet you when they come in tonight they'll have *their* fires. They're gonna cook their buffalo meat and eat it. They're gonna have one big feast and they're likely gonna have some dancin' too. What's Crook gonna do? Keep his whole command layin' there in the cold and the dark without anything to eat except the hardtack, while them savages that's s'posed to be our allies is cookin' fresh meat on big bonfires and dancin' around and makin' music?''

Baptiste and Girard was lookin' straight at me, and they was noddin' as if to say, ''Everything you say is true, Brules. We agree.''

But then Big Bapt shook his head. ''Brules, you got a lot to learn. You may theenk you done good, but General Crook is plenty mad that one of his scouts go out and disobey orders, and act just like ze Indians. All these dead buffalo weel do no good. Ze soldier boys cannot eat them raw and they're not going to have fires. So you see, my friend, all does not go ze way of good sense in ze army. And you is in ze army now.''

I asked him, ''Does that mean that I ain't allowed to have a fire tonight?''

Baptiste and Girard both nodded, lookin' at me sympathetic-like.

''Then I can do somethin' else, and the troops can too. We'll cut up this stuff, dry it out in strips, and make some pemmican out of it.''

Both Girard and Baptiste laughed and slapped their thighs. Baptiste said, ''You plenty nice young fool, all right. You can make pemmican, sure. But do you theenk the soldier boys know abut pemmican?''

With that he got up and slapped my shoulder to show we was still friends. Both of them got onto their horses and rode away, and I stood there alone on the prairie by the buffalo carcass with my pony reins in one hand and my bloody knife in the other. Those two was real scouts and real mountain men, and I had the greatest respect for 'em. For that very reason my heart was heavy, 'cause I knowed they was tellin' me the truth.

When them soldier boys finished settin' up, there was no fires. Later when I wandered close enough, I could hear them boys all bitchin' about Crook's orders. And soon them Shoshone and Crow come in all wore out from huntin'. Some of 'em was carryin' pieces of buffalo, and some of 'em even had their squaws packin' meat in behind 'em. It didn't take too long for them rascals to set up campfires, and they done just what I said—roasted buffalo meat, ate real good, and then sang and danced all night long.

Now, I ain't one for eatin' raw meat except when it's absolutely necessary, so durin' the night, I went over near them Shoshones and made me a little fire, and had me a good meal of buffalo meat. Then I went off a little ways from the noise, rolled up, and slept good for the night, so I was ready for anything that come in the mornin'.

3

Battle of the Rosebud

At first light Frank Girard come outta the camp, over to where the Indians was, and held a powwow with the chiefs. He passed along the orders of General Crook that the Shoshone and Crow scouts was to try to locate the Sioux.

I reckon by that time everybody felt we was gettin' close to where there was gonna be some action. We was right in the country where they had to be, and unless them Indians was wantin' to run away (in which case we couldn'ta done nothin' about it anyway), then they was bound to be tanglin' with us before long. The head of the Rosebud River looked like a good place for it to happen.

That's the way it worked out. I'll never forget the look on the faces of them Indians when they got orders to move out in the early dawn and to begin to make contact with the enemy. Durin' their buffalo hunt and all the dancin' around the fire-light, they was real brave, 'specially the Crows, which was much more numerous than the Shoshone, but when it come to daylight and time for them to go up against the Sioux, they sure changed color. It was real evident that they had a healthy respect for the Sioux nation. They wasn't about to get tangled up with their ancient enemy unless the odds was all in their favor, and that mornin' they didn't figure they was.

They knowed if they was away from Crook's column and had to do any fightin' on their own, they'd be outnumbered by maybe ten to one, and besides that, they'd be up against a tough enemy. Sure was funny seein' them Crows goin' around makin' all sorts of excuses and findin' all kinds of problems to keep 'em from goin'.

I'll say this for the Shoshone—they acted a whole lot better. There was only a small party of 'em, but they mounted their horses and looked to their war rig with what amounted to a reasonable display of speed. They was the first to move outta camp, although they wasn't doin' no gallopin' or shoutin' or yellin' around. They just went out in single file, real quiet, actin' like their hearts wasn't in it. Quite a while later the Crows went, and even then they moved slow and kinda dragged a little.

The pony soldiers got their horses saddled and their mules packed, and then the infantry moved out, too, on their saddle mules, just as if they was a cavalry outfit. By this time the green-broke mules had quieted down some and them foot soldiers rode along on 'em, though they looked more like sacks of grain settin' up top of the saddles than real horsemen.

The chief packer, Tom Moore, under orders, crossed the Rosebud with his pack train, along with Colonel Henry and Colonel Van Fleet's battalion. The Third Cavalry, Mills's, stayed over on the right bank, so I tagged along with Tom Moore's outfit, figurin' that stickin' near the packers was a good way to stay outta General Crook's sight.

Along about eight-thirty that mornin' it was gettin' warm, and the column come to a halt and dismounted. Some of the pony soldiers rested on the ground, takin' it easy, smokin' and talkin', and tryin' to stay in the shade of their horses. Then, all of a sudden we heard some shots just over the bluffs to the north of us. One of the officers said, "Sounds like our Indians are shootin' buffalo again over there."

But from the location of the shots and the way they seemed to be traded back and forth, that weren't my idea a'tall. Not bein' under any orders except to stay somewhere near old Tom Moore's pack train and also do a little scoutin', I lit out on a gallop for the bluffs and rode up near the crest. I'd just hit the top when here come a whole bunch of Crows on a dead gallop. They wasn't ridin' for fun. They was plumb scared to death.

They was in full retreat and went tearin' on past me yellin', "Heap Sioux! Heap Sioux!"

I rode on and just topped another ridge when I seen a whole line of Sioux warriors—a sight that'll curl your hair. I've seen lots of Comanche on the move—maybe as many as three hundred and fifty at a time—but I ain't never seen anything like that long line of gallopin' Sioux warriors, ridin' abreast and wearin' their feathers and warpaint, and most of 'em carryin' rifles instead of lances. Some of 'em had on war bonnets and was stripped to the waist, ridin' tight up on the withers of them little Indian ponies, just like they was runnin' in a horse race.

I took a good look before I turned around, and raced back to the column. Our Indian scouts had beat me to it and by this time all of our cavalry boys was mounted. Crook had lined up the foot soldiers on their bellies facin' north on the left bank of the Rosebud.

Tom Moore's pack outfit was back about three hundred yards behind the infantry. Between him and the infantry was Colonel Henry and Captain Van Fleet's battalion.

As I come dashin' in past the infantry skirmish line, I could see on the right bank across the creek that Colonel Mills's Cavalry was mounted. I reckon when they seen the Crow warriors come runnin' in, everybody had saddled up quick.

That was a good thing, 'cause right quick after I rode up, that line of Sioux warriors—and I'm gonna swear there was at least a thousand—topped the ridge. I've heard some people tellin' how the Sioux had twenty-five hundred warriors in that battle. That's what Jack Finerty said, but bein' a newspaper reporter he was prob'ly exaggeratin'.

They didn't charge down on us but stopped there and begun firin', most of 'em using new 1873 Winchesters. Pretty soon everything broke loose, 'cause Crook got sick of havin' them Indians shootin' at us with them long-range repeatin' rifles, when his troops only had single-shot carbines.

Crook's regimental adjutant, a fellow named Lemley, went dashin' and splashin' across Rosebud Creek, ridin' from Crook's headquarters across to Colonel Mills, who was on his horse at the head of his command. From where I was standin' over by the pack outfit, I could hear the voice of Lemley clear and plain.

He shouted, "The commandin' officer's compliments, Colonel Mills. Your battalion will charge those bluffs in the center."

Mills immediately swung his battalion into line, and I must say they looked mighty good.

Risin' in his stirrups ol' Mills shouted, "Charge!"

The whole damned bunch of them pony soldiers, as the Sioux called 'em, went chargin' straight down the right bank of the Rosebud and struggled up toward the center of the Sioux line. The Sioux kept up a rapid firin' and I seen many of the horses fall—some, I s'pose, 'cause of the rugged nature of the ground.

Things didn't look good. It was the same story all over again: lots of guts and no brains, but them cavalry boys sure had the guts. They kept right on goin', and by the time they got within fifty yards of the Sioux, them Indians—just like most Indians when they met with unexpected resistance—broke and run.

Mills got his troops to the top of the bluffs, dismounted, and began firin' from his position on foot. His horse holders hurried the horses back down the bluffs and outta the line of fire. At the same time this maneuver was goin' on, Crook's adjutant rode over to Colonel Henry on the left bank of the Rosebud, yellin' somethin' I couldn't hear. I guess he told 'em to charge the Sioux on the left, which Henry done. He made a good job of clearin' them Indians from the tops of the bluffs.

I seen right away that Crook was a good general, even though he might be dumb about lots of things, 'cause he kept five troops of the Second Cavalry under Captain Noyes in the rear as a reserve. He ordered forward just two troops of the Third, one under command of Captain Van Fleet and another under a young fellow named Crawford. They was to occupy the bluffs clear to the west, just to keep the Sioux from roundin' that point and comin' in on us from behind.

It began to be obvious from the heavy firin' that the Sioux was workin' harder on the left. So Crook detached a couple of companies of the cavalry under Mills to support Henry. It was a good thing he done it, 'cause a lot more Sioux come up and the fightin' got plenty heavy. When there come a lull, it looked like the line of Sioux was about half again as big, maybe even double the number that I first seen on the ridge.

Every so often some of them fool Indians would ride up and down makin' gestures to let you know just what they thought of you, and them thoughts wasn't complimentary. I remember there was one chief in the bunch that seemed to kinda stand out. He went ridin' back and forth like he owned the place, and later some of the officers said he was the famous Sioux chief, Crazy Horse. I ain't got no way of tellin' for sure. I'll say he was a brave Indian, but all that fightin' and shoutin' was plain new to me and not the kinda Indian fightin' that I'd knowed about.

It didn't make no sense to stand up there in plain sight and shoot at one another when, with a little careful trackin' and handlin', you could pick the enemy off one by one without 'em ever knowin' you was around. At least that's the way I woulda did it. But it was too late by that time for my kind of fightin'.

Well, I ain't goin' on to explain all about that battle. I reckon there's been a lot of folks told stories and wrote things about the famous Battle of the Rosebud who knows more'n I do about them cavalry tactics and everything that went on. To me it was just a great boilin' mess—lots of hollerin' and shootin' with big clouds of dust. There was lots of shoutin' by the officers and lots of stupid firing by the troops. Seems like mosta the time they was just makin' noise with guns to keep their courage up.

But I'll say one thing, they all had guts. While the Indians was movin' back and forth and formin' and re-formin' into groups that didn't seem to make no sense, the cavalry and infantry fellows was holdin' the line and obeyin' orders. I reckon that's what they call discipline, and that's the difference between the white man's army and a bunch of Indian braves. I reckon that's why in the end, along with a lot of other things, the white man came out on top, maybe not in this battle but in the winnin' of the West.

I heard some heavy firin' along the left side of the line, then some Indian war cries, and here come the Crows and this time the Shoshone with them who'd been rallied by Major Randall. I reckon the Crows finally got their courage back up when they seen how our cavalry and infantry was standin' up to the Sioux charge.

Anyway, by the time Randall got them Indian allies reorganized, our infantry had moved from the skirmish line to the top of the bluffs along with the cavalry. Them Crows and Shoshones come rippin' right through our lines and plunged straight into the Sioux, who was now formed on a second ridge just a little farther north.

When the Sioux seen their Indian enemies comin', that stirred 'em up and they rode right in there. It was the worst melee I ever seen—both outfits yellin' and shootin' with men and horses fallin' all over the place. Our men had to stop firin', afraid of hittin' their own Indians, and the way them warriors was millin' around in all the dust and confusion, you couldn't tell the difference.

When the fight finally broke off, there musta been a hundred dead horses layin' in that little swale, but I don't s'pose there was over twenty-five Indians killed. I reckon it shows that there's some point to the way they always fought, hangin' on to the off-side of their horse, usin' it as a shield between them and the enemy. When them Crows and Shoshones come out from tanglin' with the Sioux, they looked like they'd had enough, but don't forget that they was outnumbered plenty.

Every now and then some of them Sioux chiefs would ride back and forth, givin' a bravery run to show the men what great warriors they was. They sure looked fancy all made up in their war paint and feathers, but they also looked like real good targets. Finally, I decided I couldn't stand it no longer. I'd seen enough of that Indian show-off stuff and decided I'd take part in this fight and do it my own way.

I got down on my belly and crawled along behind some rocks and shrubbery, weavin' my way along till I was out a few yards in front of our infantrymen, but hid from 'em so they wouldn't shoot me by mistake. I didn't have enough confidence in their way of shootin' to think that my backside was safe. I found me a fallen log and a place that I could run my rifle underneath so the log would be a shield and I wouldn't have one of them Indian sharpshooters drillin' my skull.

I settled down then and went to work with the Winchester on some of them warriors that was runnin' up and down on the bravery runs. I'd heard a lot of times that General Custer said a Winchester weren't good at any long range, and that he always took along a Springfield huntin' rifle that'd reach out better. I don't know about that, but I can tell you that if you use a Winchester right, it'll kill as nice as can be at three hundred and fifty to four hundred yards.

I made a couple of shots just to get the range and the lead and then settled down and started killin'. I shot eleven warriors outta the saddle before them bravery runs stopped. After that, them Sioux used a little more caution about the way they handled theirselves.

When I ground out the last shot at a runnin' Sioux, I seen him spill from the saddle in a cloud of dust. His body jack-knifed a couple of times when it hit the ground and his horse kinda bucked and kicked away.

I heard one of the officers yellin', "By God, there's a scout up there that's doin' some real shootin'."

That made me feel right good, but after that there weren't much left for me to do. When the bravery runs quit it seemed, for a while, like the firin' in front of us eased, and the Sioux started fadin' away. It weren't that way over by Henry's command at our left. The firin' was rapid and steady there, indicatin' that the Indians was pressin' on pretty good.

Things went along that way for the most part of an hour, and I didn't see much to get off a shot at, nothin' that was worthwhile and in a sure range. I reckoned my sport was over and started crawlin' back real easy and slow-like to where the infantry was laying down.

Then Frank Girard come walkin' up fast from behind me and said, "Brules, General Crook is gettin' tired of this skirmishin', and he's ordered Mills to go down the Rosebud to strike the Indian village where the canyon comes out at its northern end. I'm to go with Mills, and Crook may need an extra scout. You're to report to his headquarters."

I looked up at Girard, feelin' kinda shocked. The Rosebud River run through a narrow gorge at the north end of our bowl-shaped valley. That gorge was called, for reasons not too hard to guess, Dead Man's Canyon. I just couldn't believe that any general in his right mind would send a squadron of cavalry through a narrow gorge like that with hostile Sioux all around. If there was ever a perfect place for an ambush, that canyon was it, and to send troops down there seemed to me to be askin' 'em to ride to their death. It was over and above the normal stupidity of army orders. I just shook my head.

For a minute I was so surprised, I couldn't say a word, and then finally I blurted out, "Hell, man, has the general lost his mind? He has to be plumb crazy to order a bunch of men down a canyon like that!"

Girard shrugged his shoulders. "He thinks if we hit the Sioux village it'll draw the pressure off of our front." He turned on his heel and started off in a jog to grab his horse that was picketed below. I watched him and the rest of Mills's men ease down off the slope and take off along the Rosebud to the mouth of the canyon, wonderin' all the time if it was the last I'd see of 'em.

Just before Mills's troops entered the mouth of the gorge a bunch of Sioux, maybe fifty in number, collected up on one of the bluffs on the west side of the canyon, lookin' right down to the gorge. Mills was smart enough to stop the command and detach two troops of cavalry to charge the Indians on the hill. The Sioux returned only scattered gunfire, then rode off like the wind and headed north along the canyon's rim. Obviously they was intendin' to set up a trap farther down the canyon.

That canyon was twelve miles long and Crook figured that the big Sioux village was at the north end where it opened up into a valley again. Well, I'd say that there just were no way that they was ever gonna work through that canyon without bein' shot to a man.

After a while even General Crook got the same idea. Maybe he felt nervous or guilty or sorryful, 'cause a little later he sent a troop of cavalry under Captain Noyes, to follow up Mills and give him a little help.

The withdrawal of so many troops from the skirmish line give the Indians encouragement they didn't need, least not when they outnumbered us by about three to one. Thinkin' that our troops was withdrawin' and runnin' off, they begun to increase their fire. It got 'specially heavy around where Colonel Henry was in position at our left.

I remembered Girard's orders, and although I didn't have any hankerin' to go near Crook's headquarters, I decided I'd better do it just in case there might be somethin' sensible connected with the whole scheme. Crook was standin' on the side of the hill, down a little ways from the right flank of the infantry line. The standard bearer was beside him, so he was easy to spot. Not knowin' just what was comin' next, but thinkin' I might be asked to do some scoutin' duty, I went first to get my horse. He was all saddled up and picketed a ways back from the line, but all the shootin' seemed to have made him a bit jumpy.

By the time I got to Crook's headquarters, I could see that all hell was breakin' loose around Henry's command, where the Sioux was pressin' in hard. I later learned that a German officer in Henry's battalion had moved hisself and his troop too far out in front and got surrounded. There was one big fight before he broke back through the Sioux lines and returned to Henry's command.

I drawed up in plain sight, about forty yards away from Crook's headquarters, and just stood there waitin'. I figured that if he needed me, one of his staff would see me and they'd tell me what to do.

The way Crook kept watchin' through his spyglass, 'specially over Henry's command, I knowed he was worried about the goin's-on. It didn't take no genius, with the dust and shoutin' and swirlin' of Sioux and heavy firin', to see that he had good reason. The firin' of the Sioux kept increasin', and ever so slow, parts of Henry's command was easin' back on down off the bluffs. Any fool could see it was gettin' critical, 'cause if the Indians ever got to the edge and started shootin' down, they'd massacre them that was below.

Crook seen that, 'cause he suddenly called for an officer, who come runnin' over leadin' his horse. He give him some orders, and then looked around and spoke to an adjutant, who come runnin' over to me. The adjutant pulled up, saluted, and said real short-like, "You! You're one of the scouts. Your name, sir."

"Brules."

"All right, Brules, you're to accompany Major Nickerson. He has an important message for Colonel Mills. You're to overtake the detachment before they get too far down the canyon. Mount up and ride alongside Major Nickerson and keep your eyes peeled for Sioux. Make sure the major gets through."

I had to stand there a minute and wonder whether I really heard this silly son of a bitch say that or not. When he told me to keep my eyes open for Sioux, it was like tellin' a man who was fallin' off a cliff to watch out for the ground that's comin' up. And then for Crook to tell me and Nickerson—two lone men—to ride down that canyon after Mills's and Noyes's squadrons, it was like askin' a man to fight a grizzly bear with his fists. I thought the general was plumb outta his mind, but I didn't say nothin'.

I just sorta stood there for a few seconds lookin' at this young peacock of an adjutant as if his head had been chopped off. Them high army boys was just like that. They'd try somethin' and if it didn't work, they'd shrug their shoulders and try somethin' else. Only, there'd be a whole hillside of dead men layin' there. I weren't aimin' to be one of 'em.

The adjutant looked at me funny, turned around, and trotted back where Nickerson was waitin' for a message to be wrote out for him by one of Crook's staff. The adjutant spoke to the major, and then another officer handed Nickerson a note, which he stuck in the gauntlet of his glove.

Nickerson whirled his horse around and come gallopin' up to me and said, "Brules, mount up immediately. We're carryin' an important message for Mills's command. It's your job to keep the Sioux off my back and to get me through at all costs."

When I just stood there gape mouthed, he yelled, "Come on, now! Mount up and move out!"

For a minute I didn't know what to do. Then I just automatically vaulted into the saddle and started my stallion downhill toward the mouth of the canyon after Nickerson, who was gallopin' along at a brisk clip.

"Keep the Sioux off my back," he'd said. How was I s'posed to keep a thousand Sioux off his back while he rode down that canyon? Sure as anything, Mills's and Noyes's squadrons up ahead had rode into a trap, and them Indians would soon be closin' around 'em. And for us two men to ride down the canyon was just like a human sacrifice.

I started off at a trot and then the more I got to thinkin' about it, the madder I got. I kicked Cimarron up to a gallop and took out after the major. It didn't take long to find out that Cimarron was a better horse than his, so by the time we got to the mouth of the canyon I'd moved up beside him.

With the wind in my teeth I yelled at him, "Major, this is crazy as hell. We ain't got no business—two lone men—ridin' down this canyon. The Sioux will blow our heads off! Rein up a little! If we have to go down there, let's split up and go along either wall of the canyon, each man coverin' the other. We can stay in the brush, and one of us might just get through."

"No," he shouted at me on a dead gallop. "We're going right down the flat of the canyon. We can't make it in good enough time on the side of the hill. We must catch Mills. General's orders."

That didn't make a bit of sense to me, either, but there weren't much I could do but stay at a dead gallop alongside Nickerson.

In the bottom of the canyon most places was pretty good goin', bein' gravel and hard-baked mud, but we had to cross the Rosebud a half a dozen times as we went, zigzaggin' back and forth from one side to the other. We rode through the water on a dead splash every time we crossed. Meanwhile, I kept cranin' my neck lookin' up at the walls of the canyon and behind every rock and tree, expectin' to get blowed clean outta the saddle at any minute.

Finally, I just crouched down on the side of my horse, makin' as small a target as possible. Nickerson didn't seem to have sense enough to do that and rode sittin' straight up facin' the wind. When I'd lean down, Cimarron would pick up speed and it weren't long before I'd be passin' Nickerson and have to rein back and wait for him to get even. Why I didn't just tell him to go to hell and go back myself, I'll never know. I guess somehow the whole business was so stupid that I couldn't think of nothin' better to do than to stay with him and try to help him get through.

We rode almost five miles at a full gallop and our horses, even Cimarron, who was in good condition, was flecked with foam when we begun to see the dust of Noyes's and Mills's columns just trottin' along ahead. Why they hadn't been attacked yet I didn't know.

When we was still about a quarter of a mile away, the troops come to a halt. We dashed by the rear of the column, passing 'em all, and rode right up to the front, drawin' everybody's attention. As we reached Mills at the head, our horses was flounderin' and soaked with sweat. What had happened was that Frank Girard had heard heavy firin' way outta the canyon to his left and rode up to tell Mills. Mills had reined up to listen and that's when Major Nickerson and me arrived. Nickerson pulled up his horse within ten yards of Mills and started bellowin', just as if Mills was a hundred yards away.

"Colonel Mills, Henry and Vroom are hard pressed and must be relieved. Henry's badly wounded and Vroom's troop is cut up. The general's orders are that you and Captain Noyes will file by your left flank out of the canyon up the nearest draw, and fall on the rear of the Indians that are pressing our units."

Just by luck the command had been halted where a cross valley intersected the main canyon of the Rosebud. The troopers didn't waste any time obeyin' that order. Most of 'em had been spooked about bein' in the canyon anyway. They filed out to the west on both sides of the cross valley. It was so rough that they had to dismount and lead the horses over deadfalls and rock piles till they broke out on top. I started to follow 'em and Nickerson turned to me and give me the strangest order.

"Brules," he said, "I'm accompanying Colonel Mills through this defile. You are to ride back up through the canyon and report to the general that his orders have been delivered to Colonel Mills and are being executed at this minute."

This mornin' I'd heard some of the dumbest orders that ever any man was to give. Now this fool was tellin' me to ride back up the canyon—five miles on a horse that was plumb wore out—with the whole country loaded with Sioux. The movement of Noyes's and Mills's troops had sure been noticed by the Indians and they didn't need me to tell them that back at headquarters.

There could only have been one reason why we was allowed to pass—all of us had rode into a trap. We was allowed to come on in, and now only by sheer luck was Mills and Noyes and Nickerson escapin' through the cross valley. The Indians would be closin' in from behind by now, and down ahead in the canyon there must be a real ambush waitin'.

I found out from Finerty, who visited the site later, that there was a thousand warriors waitin' just past the cross valley, ready to pounce on the column when it went through the canyon. Only the order turning 'em outta the canyon saved Mills's troops from a total massacre.

After givin' me them orders Nickerson rode up off the hill to the west along with the rest of 'em and I sat there plumb flabbergasted when the last of the cavalrymen passed. I still couldn't figure out what to do.

But havin' had sharp orders, my only choice was to ride back up the canyon. I got off and waited a few minutes for Cimarron to quit blowin', and then mounted and started back along the creek bed real slow. I was tryin' to figure out what to do.

Instinctively, I crossed to the east side of the Rosebud and begun workin' up through the heavy rocks and timber that give some cover. I figured unless I was really unlucky and rode right straight into a bunch of Indians, I'd have a better chance up there than to be down in plain view. At least I could see what was happenin' across on the west side of the canyon slope and high bluffs, and I was stayin' outta sight as much as possible from the walls above me on the east side.

My progress was painful slow. I had to go around a lot of deadfalls and in and outta some thick timber, so it took me almost an hour to work my way up the canyon. Meanwhile, I heard lots of firin' off to the west. That told me that Mills's troops had rammed into the Indians that was pressing Henry.

Several times I got off my horse and walked, weavin' in and outta tough places and only mounting again when we could move forward at a trot and still not be too exposed. I was nearin' the south end of the canyon, and beginnin' to think that maybe I was gonna luck through, when I come to a big dirt slide that I had to go across to get to the cover on the other side. I reckon that slide was a hundred and fifty yards across and I knew that when I started across there that I'd be in plain sight.

I hid behind a twisty ol' cedar tree for a few minutes and looked around the canyon. I couldn't see nothin' movin' on either side. Of course, that's just the time when Indians is usually around.

I looked real careful at the dirt slide and couldn't see no pony tracks or no sign of moccasins clear up to the top of the bluffs and clear down to where the slide touched the Rosebud. Yet somehow or other I felt like somethin' was watchin' me. I couldn't make it out. I musta stayed hid that way about ten minutes, which was a long time considerin' the hurry I was in to get myself outta the valley.

I was in real trouble, unless the hackles that was standin' up on the back of my neck was tellin' me wrong. I couldn't see no other way out, so I finally mounted the stallion and put the quirt to him. He started across that steep dirt slide as fast as he could go. We was about halfway there when I heard some whoopin' and a couple of shots that blew up the dirt in front of

Cimarron's head. He shied hard, and if I hadn't been well seated I mighta been left behind.

I knowed the shot had come from across the canyon, and when I looked up I seen about fifteen warriors at the base of the cliffs on the opposite side, tearin' down the slope on a dead run. About a quarter of 'em was mounted. I thought the best thing to do was to get to the timber ahead and then start up the slope to get cover under the east bluffs.

My horse had took about two more jumps when the whole skyline of the bluffs on the east filled up with mounted Sioux. They give one loud whoop and come over the bluffs down the dirt slide toward me. I reckon they wasn't over a hundred and fifty yards away and they was firin' as they come.

Their bullets was singin' all around, as I turned the stallion directly downhill and slashed him into a quick bunch of crow-hoppin' jumps. Somethin' like a hot iron creased my cheek, and right then and there I thought I was gone.

I didn't have time to think much about it, except to feel mad, and I laid the quirt on hard. Cimarron was takin' tremendous leaps goin' downhill, the dust bustin' up all around him, and I was leanin' as far back on his haunches as I could, to give him a chance to balance each time he come down to earth.

It sure wouldn't do to have him somersault forward. With them Indians tight on my back, that'd be the end of me. I'll say this for that horse: With the bullets singin' around him, he done that slope in good shape, although near the end I thought I felt him stumble and wondered if he'd been hit.

We reached the bottom of the canyon maybe sixty or seventy yards upstream from the Indians that was closin' in from the other side, and I was still leadin' the ones behind me by a hundred and fifty yards. The trail at the bottom of the Rosebud was wide and well packed from the cavalry having come down there an hour or so before.

I rode with my head down and only once in a while looked back to see whether they was gainin' or not. It seemed to me that we was about holdin' even and might make it outta the canyon after all—and then the worst happened.

One Sioux was ridin' high up on the hill and about three hundred yards behind. Outta the corner of my right eye I seen him jerk his horse to a stop and dismount, lay his rifle along the rock, and take careful aim.

That's the kind of shootin' I don't like to be in the way of. There's all the difference in the world between that and people ridin' on a dead gallop while they're shootin' at you. When somebody settles like that it shows two things: One, he's a pretty good shot, and two, he's using his head cool, not hurryin' himself. What's more, he's usin' a gun rest and your chances is gettin' tougher.

I seen the puff of smoke from his gun and a second later felt Cimarron stumble. He recovered for a minute and I figured he weren't hard hit. We was only about three hundred yards from the mouth of the canyon, and I was hopin' to keep him goin' till we got in the clear.

Then, after about ten more jumps, I seen from the foam of his mouth that he was fleckin' blood. Pretty soon he begun flounderin' and I could tell that he didn't have much left. I took a closer look and seen what plumb chilled me to the bone—streams of bright, frothy red was pourin' outta his mouth and nostrils. I knowed then that all his heart's blood was pumpin' out. The whole front of his chest and withers had turned bright red, and it was for sure that he wouldn't last another hundred yards.

I was ready for it. I was holdin' my Winchester in my right hand and when he went down, I landed runnin'. I sprinted my best the last fifty yards to the mouth of the canyon and run out into the open to where the Rosebud come flowin' in a sharp turn from the west. There was a slight embankment at the turn, and I dropped down behind it with the gun to make my last stand.

There was nothin' else for me to do but to crouch down there and fight it out. I was scared—yeah, so scared, I could hardly keep my breath. My tongue had gone dry and I felt like my very life was tryin' to ooze outta me. The only thing that kept me from panickin' total was that I was mad about the whole fix I was in.

I reckon I took it out on the Sioux. If I say so myself, I done some real fancy shootin' that day.

The Sioux come down that canyon in a big bunch, ridin' like hell and yellin'. They was about a hundred yards off. I knew I didn't have time to get off more'n three or four shots, so I just started shootin' the horses.

When I put the first one down, I seen it was the right thing to do, 'cause there was a great big pileup of Indians right behind it. I done that three times, and though I don't s'pose I killed an Indian in the bunch, there was lots of 'em hurt in the spills, and they made three big piles.

This split the bunch apart and they whirled past me on the bed of the Rosebud. Some of 'em rode down the stream and others jumped the bank to the west of me, firin' at me as they went, and circlin' around to come in behind. I quick crouched as low as I could against the bank, coverin' myself with a nearby bush, and begun firin' hard, this time aimin' at the Indians theirselves. I worked the lever just as fast as I could go and got off my shots in split seconds.

There's times in your life when things is real vivid and clear 'cause your senses is workin' at their best. This was one of 'em. Every time I glanced down them sights, there was a Sioux in line, and I touched off the trigger and slammed another shell in and drawed another bead and let go another shot.

I put five of 'em down in quick succession, and the Indians began to mill around to try to figure out just exactly where I was located and how to get at me. Then I heard a yell from the west, up the Rosebud, and seen a bunch more Indians ridin' down on me from that direction.

There is also times when a man gets hisself up against odds that's too great, and there ain't no use fightin' no more. I started to stand up and die quick in the hail of bullets, which I knowed was comin', when I seen the strangest thing ever. There was whoopin' and yellin' among the Sioux that was millin' around me, and they suddenly broke and started off toward the others that was comin' from the west. Then I seen, God bless 'em, them that was comin' wasn't Sioux, they was Shoshones!

Them two bands of Indians struck one another in a clash that was like the battles of them armored knights that my mama used to tell of. I never seen such millin' and bangin' around, horses pilin' up, guns firin' and tomahawks swingin'. It was the wildest thing you ever seen.

Them Shoshones sure was tough fighters and, like one of the officers said, "resolute men." They looked awful good to me.

The main part of the battle was ragin' about a hundred yards to the west, and the roar of it was deafenin'. I seen that I might have a chance to escape and I jumped up and started runnin' along the embankment of the creek bed, duckin' in and among every patch of brush around.

Suddenly, from all the melee in front of me, an Indian on a beautiful painted horse busted loose and come ridin' for me on a dead run. I knelt down and took careful aim and waited till he got real close. When he was about forty yards away I was just about ready to blow his brains out when I noticed, God Almighty, he was a Shoshone.

He was ridin' toward me with his right hand extended clear down, showin' me only too well the best thing that I wanted to see. It was my brother, Wesha. He come up alongside and I run with his horse and reached for his arm, grabbed it, and swung up behind him. By this time a bunch of the Sioux had broke loose and was followin' him, comin' from off the hill above. Besides that there was a couple of Sioux stragglers on the chase for me. They closed in around us and all the firin' felt like the blast of a hot furnace.

How the two of us got through that I'll never know, but Wesha put his pony right to the embankment and we busted out on the north side of the Rosebud. We rode right through them firin' warriors on the dead gallop to where Crook's infantry was lined up along the tops of the bluffs to the north.

Some of them soldier boys was lookin' behind and down into the valley of the Rosebud, and seen the whole fight between the Shoshone and the Sioux. When we come ridin' up on the ridge, with me hangin' on to Wesha's waist, both of us leanin' down hard on the horse's neck like we was carryin' the mail, the whole infantry put up a cheer.

Once we was safe among 'em, Wesha reined in, and I slid off in a hurry. I took one hard look at the man that had saved my life, and began to say something.

A few Sioux stragglers had followed us in close, but the infantry give 'em a volley that kinda reduced their enthusiasm. Sudden-like, Wesha whirled around on his horse, which was already foam flecked, and went chargin' right back out through the ranks of the infantry and into the melee. Then there was a lull in the infantry firin' 'cause the Indians had withdrawed to a second ridge. I found out that Mills and Noyes had struck 'em from the side when they filed outta that cross canyon.

I watched Wesha ride up and brain one of them retreatin' Sioux just as nice and neat as you'd bust a possum off a tree limb with a stick. And he didn't let up there. He kept chargin' around till I lost sight of him, but there weren't no doubt that he was makin' a good account of hisself.

There I stood, afoot, still hangin' on to my Winchester, and real downhearted about losin' ol' Cimarron, not to mention all my saddle gear.

Pretty soon a man on horseback come ridin' over from one of the dismounted cavalry units that was just to the west of us. When he come in close, I seen it was Tom Cosgrove, chief of the Wind River scouts. He come lopin' over to where I stood, and drawed up his horse.

He held out his hand and told me, "Let me shake the hand of a lucky man. I seen the whole show from up on the hill."

I ain't much for humor, but I took his hand and shook it and said, "Well, I reckon I would rather have your seat than mine."

Cosgrove laughed real hearty and it was easy to see why the Shoshone trusted him. "Yeah," he drawled, "if it hadn't been for Wesha you woulda never made it. He's a good man— as brave as a lion, and a fine warrior."

"I sure seen that."

I stood there kinda wonderin' about what had just happened to me, and havin' a whole different feelin' about lots of things, 'specially Indians. I don't make friends easy, and there ain't many men I like. It's seemed to me that most men's hands are turned against me, but once in a while, when one of 'em done me a friendly act, I weren't one to forget it. I'd say that savin' my life was downright friendly, and I decided right then and there that Wesha was not only my friend, he was the finest man I knew. I owed him somethin' and he sure would get repaid if there was any way that I could do it.

Cosgrove rode off and the battle was still whirlin'. The infantry was under orders to move forward across the ridge and follow where the Sioux had moved, one ridge farther north. The commandin' officer, Colonel Chambers, had held the troops there for a few minutes till he seen how it was going to come out between the Shoshone and the Sioux at the mouth of the canyon.

It weren't more'n ten more minutes before the Indians on both sides broke off, and the Sioux started up around us to the north, with the Shoshone whoopin' and yellin' and ridin' back toward us. Chambers then give the command for the infantry to advance north to the next ridge, which they done on the double, and me not knowin' what else to do, I trotted along right with 'em.

They formed a skirmish line on the second ridge and begun shootin' at the Sioux who was over on the third. Meanwhile, I'd reloaded my Winchester with some cartridges I had in my belt and walled up behind a kinda mud bluff and settled down to do some real shootin'. The way them soldier boys was bangin' away, I knowed they wasn't doin' much good, but the sound of the firin' heartened 'em a little, and they kicked up a lotta dust where the Indians was lined up back of the next ridge.

I reckoned if I stayed there a little bit and started some accurate shootin', I might do some good. I kept watchin' careful, and every time I'd see an Indian's head ease up over the ridge I'd draw a tight bead and lay right into him.

It wasn't much later that the Sioux broke off and rode away to the north, leaving long lines of dust climbin' up in the air behind 'em. The battle of the Rosebud was over—one of the most famous battles of the Indian Wars.

I reckon it was about four in the afternoon and the engagement had been goin' on since noon. Some of Crook's troops had took a mighty good beatin', and he weren't much for followin' up them Sioux on tired horses with beat-up soldiers. It's a good thing he didn't, 'cause the main camp of the Sioux weren't more'n five miles away. A hot pursuit woulda drawed him into as many Indians as Custer faced eight days later on the Little Big Horn, only eighty miles away.

Yes, sir, it was a tough battle, and I reckon Crook was outnumbered maybe two and a half to one—maybe three to one—but he sure didn't win no victory, although the Sioux rode off first.

I went over near Colonel Henry's infantry to report to Major Randall. He seemed glad to see me and said from where he'd been on the ridge he'd looked back over his shoulder and seen the whole incident at the mouth of the canyon. He congratulated me, and told me I was a lucky man.

I come back at him with "That depends on how you look at it." When he asked me what I meant, I told him I was unlucky to have had the misfortune of servin' under an officer as brainless as that Nickerson, stupid enough to send a man back alone up through the canyon with a useless message. I allowed as how Crook hadn't acted too bright either.

Randall, bein' an old army man hisself, just kinda grunted and didn't say nothin'. That's the way it is with them soldier boys. They got some fool code or somethin' that says it ain't theirs to reason why, it's but to do and die.

If that ain't a jackass way of goin' about fightin' Indians, I'd like to know what is. It sure ain't my code, and I weren't interested in havin' somebody be real wasteful with my life.

He seen I was a bit stirred up, so I reckon he thought it best to ease off. "Brules, you lost a fine horse today, and you need another. We'll certainly furnish you with another good animal."

He meant well, but I was still sore over the death of Cimarron, so I said, "Major, I'm right grateful to you for makin' the offer, but from the cavalry horses I seen and the condition of 'em in this command, I ain't lookin' forward to ridin' any horse I can pick from what's left over.''

He laughed a little bit and told me, "Suit yourself, but they sure beat walking. Check with Captain Bowman at the remount squadron.'' He throwed me a friendly salute and rode off.

But I knowed a better way than that. I went on down to where the infantry was gatherin' up their gear and found Tom Moore, and told him the fix I was in.

Moore just nodded. "I know what you mean, Brules. Ain't none of them cavalry horses, except the officers' thoroughbreds, that's worth anything. And you ain't got no chance of layin' your hands on one of them. But there is some horses assigned along with the mules to the pack train, and maybe we could get you somethin' outta that bunch. There's prob'ly a geldin' or two that'll carry you through the rest of the campaign.''

I grunted a little. "A geldin'—Christ!''

We went down into the valley where the packin' stock was tethered. I picked a young bay geldin' who looked like he'd be all right to carry me on a nice afternoon ride, but he sure weren't no warhorse. Since all the Sioux had rode off, it was quiet around the mouth of the canyon and I took the bay horse back down there to where ol' Cimarron's carcass lay. I was sure gonna miss him. I'd expected to find my saddle and bridle and the rest of my things gone, as Indians usually don't leave much on the battlefield if they can help it. But them Sioux musta left in a big hurry, 'cause everything was still there.

I worked my rig off the stallion's body and resaddled and bridled the bay. At least I was mounted again, although you wouldn't hardly call it that if you was proud of your horseflesh. I had my own plans, though. I knowed that if I could find the right situation, I'd kill a Sioux and take his horse. From what I seen of them horses, they'd do all right, 'specially the painted ones. All I needed was time, and I reckoned I'd get that before too long.

Crook had retired back to the campground on the Rosebud, and set up there for the night. Some tents were raised in the cottonwood trees by the sluggish stream where the army surgeons had started workin' on them poor wounded soldiers. Most of 'em was brave, but once in a while you'd hear 'em moan or even scream. I figured that meant they was diggin' a bullet outta someone.

There was wounded Shoshones and Crows in there too. Some of 'em was really bad hit, and I recall pretty clear watchin' the surgeons dig around in their innards just like they done with the pony soldiers, but there weren't a moan out of 'em.

Funny thing about Indians. They can't or won't admit that they feel any pain. I reckon this is why they're so expert on the torture and why they don't have much respect for the white man, who, when he's bein' tortured to death, does all that screamin' and cryin'. In any case, I had to hand it to them Shoshones and Crows. They didn't do no complainin' when they was bein' tortured by the army surgeons.

The next mornin' we started back up the Rosebud toward the camp on Goose Creek, draggin' the wounded along on travois. Them travois sent up a cloud of dust, and when they started goin' over rough ground, the jerkin' and joltin' and bangin' musta really raised hell with the wounded men who had to ride that way or not a'tall. On our departure we looked up at the distant bluffs all around and seen outlines of small bunches of Sioux warriors watchin' our retreat.

Crook didn't call it a retreat. I heard afterward he told how he'd defeated the Sioux on the Rosebud, but it sure didn't look like that to me. Yeah, he'd run 'em off from the fight, but there was lots more of 'em still there when we was pullin' out. Victors don't usually leave.

We couldn't travel too fast with the wounded, so we didn't make it back to the wagon train the next night, but camped in a good place on the upper part of Rosebud Creek. Both nights after the battle we heard the damnedest howlin' from our Indian camp, although I guess as far as Indian battles went, their losses wasn't too heavy. Still, you knowed they was wailin' for their dead, and it weren't a pleasant sound for white men to hear.

The only time I liked it was when I was huntin' Comanches on the Canadian River. After I'd made a few kills, I'd listen to 'em howl. That was music to my ears in them days, but hearin' it now from the Shoshones, my wife's people, didn't make me feel worth a damn.

It was a long night, June 18, 1876, that night after the Battle of the Rosebud and I can't forget it, not only because it was the end of the battle, but because it was one of the longest and most dreaded nights that I ever spent in my life.

While the wailin' was going on, I had business to attend to, and I went looking for Tom Cosgrove. I found him with his mule men, and asked him to come along with me, that I was looking for Wesha up in the wailin' camp.

Cosgrove told me, "Wesha won't be there—the top warriors or the chiefs don't engage in the wailin'. They think that it's women's work and for young boys that don't know much about battle. It's plum undignified for a chief to show any emotion like that. Wesha has gone off with his brother, Nawkee, and they're camped outside the circle, maybe two to three hundred yards away, but I think that we can find them. I reckon that you want to thank him personal for saving you."

"Yes, I do," I said, "and I've got a few other things to say to him too. My Shoshone ain't all that good. I could speak with Wild Rose, all right, but she learned English so much faster than I could learn Shoshone, that we kinda leaned on the English language. So I don't trust myself to say things the right way, 'special if they're different kind of sensitive things that you don't want to make no mistake about. Wesha saved my life today at great risk of his own, and I don't take that lightly. If you will help me where my Shoshone falls down, it will mean a lot and I would kinda like to have a witness along."

Well, in a way Tom Cosgrove was a real friend, although he and I had never said much about it before. I knew that he liked me and I knew that he was real fond of Wesha, and he liked the idea of two men gettin' together, as brothers, especially after combat. It means a lot to young men.

So he gladly went along. Sure enough, just as he'd said, we found Wesha and Nawkee were camped off maybe a quarter of a mile from the wailin' camp.

When we walked up to the fire both of them rose in a real graceful and dignified fashion. They knowed Tom, of course, and he said in Shoshone that he was comin' along with me to witness what I had to say. They both nodded to me polite-like and waited.

I told them, in the best Shoshone I could, that I weren't as a rule beholden to most men, and that I kinda counted on myself for the livin' of my own life and defendin' of it, but there weren't no doubt in my mind that Wesha had saved my life that day there on the Rosebud and I weren't forgettin' it. Someday I hoped that I'd have the chance to do the same for him, but in the meantime he could count on me for anything he needed that I could give him.

All the time Tom was listen' and helpin' me out where I would stumble. I could see Wesha lookin' straight at me with his keen dark eyes flashin' in the firelight. You could tell he was pleased to see me, his ol' huntin' buddy, but mostly he was lookin' me straight in the eyes and that's somethin' few men can do.

When I had finished talkin', them two Shoshone brothers just stood there for a minute. Then Wesha turned to Cosgrove and started talkin' as if he were referring to me in a dignified manner and in praise in front of a witness.

Even though I couldn't speak Shoshone good, I could understand it most of the time. This is about what he said:

"When I rode among the Sioux to save this man, my brother, I did so because he is one of our friends showing bravery, and because the Sioux are our blood enemy. I thought it to be a great shame upon all of us if one lone warrior, any one of us white or red, should be allowed to fall under the blows of so many Sioux without any friend to help him. Because he is my brother, I felt even stronger this way. Now my heart is glad that I have saved him, for I look upon him and I see that my brother is not as most men.

"You can see for yourself that he has the body and the

face of a mighty warrior. He has the fearless eyes, the eyes of a panther. I have known that such eyes have strange powers, and it is well believed that this man is better than all other men with the rifle. I know, for I have been with him. I know that his aim is true and straight as a sunbeam, and that when his rifle speaks, it speaks with the tongue of death. My heart is glad because this man is my friend and my brother. I should not like to think of him as an enemy. He would be a terrible enemy. "Now," he said as he turned toward me, "my brother for many moons, you have been my friend, you shall now be my blood brother."

Wesha then turned toward the fire and stuck out the palm of his right hand. With his left hand he drawed a knife from his belt and, in a quick motion, cut two sharp gashes in a cross on his palm. The blood flowed almost in a spurt as he turned and knelt down in front of me. Takin' his knife by the blade, he handed it to me across his bleedin' palm, handle first.

I knew what he meant, but Cosgrove said quickly out of the side of his mouth, "You do the same, Brules. He's gonna make a blood brother of you. Kneel down and face him."

Well, I never kneeled to no man, but when this Indian friend of mind, a friend of many hunts, a friend who had helped me attain the bride price for my darling Wild Rose, and a friend who willingly saved my life at the risk of his own, it seemed only right that I should kneel with him and before him. It was a small price to pay for what he had done for me, and I was honored.

With one swift motion I cut my right hand the same way he'd done his. Normally it would cause a lotta pain to cut your hand deep till the blood flowed, but this time I didn't feel no pain, just a sense of pride 'cause I knowed what was comin' next.

I returned the knife to the Shoshone and held out my palm. Wesha took my hand, wet with blood, in his and clasped it in the firelight in front of Tom Cosgrove, chief of the Shoshone Scouts, and Nawkee, Wesha's brother. It was a true ceremony, and now I was not only a brother of the Shoshones, but the true blood brother of my noble friend Wesha. To be real honest with you, that was just exactly the way I wanted it.

If there's anything that makes two men closer than bein' blood brothers, I don't know what it is. As far as I was concerned, Wesha was my real friend and brother and he could count on me clear to the death if need be. That's the way he'd offered his life to me, without me even askin', when he dragged me out from sure death among the Sioux, riskin' his own scalp to save mine. It would be little enough for me to pay him back, if necessary, with my life.

After that ceremony it didn't seem like there was anything that we could say that would be dignified enough to have a meaning and so, with as graceful a bow as I could muster, Tom Cosgrove and I stepped away from the fire and walked back toward the cavalry camp.

I was too full of emotion to talk, and Tom Cosgrove was too sensitive to bother me. We walked in silence.

4

Run, Jupiter, Run

When we arrived back where Tom's men were camped, one of them came up quickly and said, "Tom, there's an officer from Crook's headquarters has come looking for the scout Brules. They want him to report right away to General Crook's tent."

Tom kinda raised his eyebrows and said, "Well, Brules, maybe you got your work cut out for you. Looks like you are gonna be doing something important."

I went up to the sentries at Crook's tent and told them I was the scout Brules, obeying the orders of the general. The message was relayed inside, and out of the tent burst my old friend Baptiste.

"My God, Brules, where ze hell have you been? We been looking for you all over. You been needed bad. General he wants to see you, come in right away."

He ushered me in to meet the great General Crook and I stood at attention, facing that gentlemen, who was standing with his hands behind his back, looking down at a table where he had a lot of maps spread out. He looked up at me, with keen eyes, and smiled a little. Right away, I liked the man.

The general started out by saying, "Brules, you come to me with very high recommendations. Pourier here thinks that you're the finest shot in the West. That is hard to believe, but I take Pourier's word anytime.

"Brules, I want to tell you that we are having real trouble.

I think that you know that this campaign has been planned on a three-pronged operation to trap the Sioux—wherever we find them, at the head of the Tongue or the Rosebud or the Bighorn. We know that the biggest part of the Sioux nation is in there somewhere. We tangled with some of them this afternoon. We don't know where their village is and what is even more difficult, I don't know the exact location of General Terry, who has come up the Yellowstone with the Seventh Cavalry and some infantry battalions, nor the present location of Colonel Gibbon, who has come down from Fort Ellis in Montana to join Terry somewhere along the Yellowstone.

"What makes matters worse, they don't know where I am! We had agreed at the early part of the campaign that we would send out scouts to keep one another informed. But quite early on the contact through scouts evaporated. That can only mean one thing. Every scout that has tried to go between Gibbon's camp and mine, or between mine and Terry's, somehow have been intercepted and destroyed. Our Indian scouts have reported finding courier scouts in both of those commands lying beside their dead ponies, riddled with arrows. The Sioux have probably found our scouts too. So we are operating absolutely in the blind.

"I don't know when Custer is going to attack, Gibbon doesn't know where I am, nor does Terry, and I have received no information from either of them. I'm waiting here now for the Fifth Cavalry as a reinforcement, which I have been informed arrived in Cheyenne ten days ago from Fort Hays, Kansas, and has started up the Bozeman Trail to join me.

"It is most important for Terry to know where I am located, and to know that I have made contact with a very strong force of Sioux, far stronger than anybody who planned this campaign had in mind when they planned it. I don't begin to have enough troops to handle the situation and he doesn't either. It will be necessary for us to combine our forces, and be joined by Gibbon and his infantry battalion, in order to face the Sioux nation in the numbers that I suspect are located in this area.

"Therefore, it is of the utmost importance to get a message to the commanding officer, Terry. I think he can communicate with Gibbon satisfactorily by the waterway. It is hard to see how there could be enough Sioux to block that. He has a supporting river steamer called the *Far West*. I have no doubt that if we can reach Terry with a message reporting to him what we have encountered, the nature and strength of these forces, as well as the fact we're waiting for the Fifth Cavalry to arrive as reinforcements, he can plan a much better approach to this problem.

"Pourier said that not only are you a formidable rifleman, but you have the instinct of an Indian, that you can travel at night and avoid detection or capture. I understand that you conducted a campaign all by yourself against the Comanche nation in New Mexico. Is that true?"

"Well, General," I said, "I done some huntin' there, took my toll of Quohadi Comanches, and I'm still here to face you. It don't seem likely that I could have done that without my having some of the same instincts they do. At least enough to beat them at their own game."

"Yes," said General Crook, with a twinkle in his eye. "I'm inclined to agree with you. I think that you're probably the only man we have in this entire command that could make your way down through all this country to find General Terry.

"My intention, Brules, is to have you leave tonight, bound straight for the Yellowstone to find General Terry, wherever he may be along that watercourse, and deliver him a message my adjutant has prepared. Brules, you are a fine man and I know you are equal to the task."

"General, I ain't gonna do that. Sir, I ain't equal to that."

General Crook's jaw dropped like he'd been punched in the belly. Here was a smart-aleck young scout standing there in front of him, declining to accept his order, right in the middle of a campaign where we'd faced the enemy in combat that very day. At a time like that, refusing to obey an order can cost you your head.

"General, I know it's plumb important to get this message through to General Terry and I think I can do it, but there ain't no way that anybody can go down directly to the Yellowstone, when the country is crawling with Sioux.''

General Crook's face turned from flushed anger to a kind of a mild curiosity. ''Well, Brules, what do you propose?''

''Well, sir, I propose to go west instead of east. I'm gonna cross the Big Horn Mountains by going through Bear Tooth Pass and then I'll drop down into the Big Horn Basin and cross the Big Horn River. From there I'll head for the southeast corner of the Absaroka Range, hit Shoshone River, and cross over to Red Lodge Creek. I'll go up northwest till I hit the head of the Stillwater. I know that country well, havin' raided Blackfoot villages up that way for horses.

''I'll follow the Stillwater down to the Yellowstone and once I'm there, I'll go down the Yellowstone some way or other if I have to cut a log and ride it. That way I won't miss General Terry no matter where he is. Whether he is at the mouth of the Big Horn, the Rosebud, or the Tongue. I'll find him somehow, General. I'll give him your message and I think I can do it without getting shot full of arrows.

''There will be the odd Sioux hunting here and there, but after this battle it's my best guess they'll move their villages farther down the Rosebud, maybe even cross over to the Little Big Horn to get the women and children away from the troops. If that's the case, I won't be meeting many of the hostiles. I'll travel at night, and if I'm gonna get there and do you any good, General, I better get started right now.''

Honest, it was wonderful to see the expression on General Crook's face. It turned all the way from fierce anger at my refusal to accept his order to deep curiosity and then, finally, to a welcome smile, as if I'd solved his whole problem.

''Young man, I think that you have brains as well as guts,'' he said to me. ''That is a fine plan, and I approve of it this moment. Adjutant, see that the message for Terry is wrapped in waterproof oilskin, provide Brules with a bag so he can carry it under his clothes and next to his skin. I want it to get there even if it has to float down the Yellowstone on Brules's carcass.''

With that the staff officers laughed and I had to grin too. I liked the general right away. I had heard things about him, some good, some bad. Folks had said that he was a fine gentlemen, but the kinda guy who would go huntin' rather than pay attention to a campaign. He sure did love huntin', but that didn't spoil my feelings toward him a'tall.

Lots of people said that he was the most overrated officer in the service, a dilettante, he was too easygoing and pleasure loving. Maybe, but I can tell you one thing about Crook: I know that he was a gentleman and liked to have some fun in life, but he knew a hell of a lot more about Indians than any other military man I met in the West. I can tell you that I served him for ten years from that time on, and was even with him down in Arizona when he was shagging Geronimo around. He understood the problems far better than any of the other officers in the army.

Well, things happened fast. Crook immediately gave an order that I was to get the best racehorse on the place. I could see a couple of them young staff officers kinda gulp, 'cause they thought each one of their own horses might be taken.

"General," I said, "I will take a Shoshone with me."

"Shoshone?" said the general. "We have no Shoshone scouts."

"No, sir, this is no scout, this is a Shoshone warrior, my blood brother. He's subchief of the Shoshones." I then extended my bloody hand, and General Crook's eyes opened wide.

"Yes, I see." He was no fool, and he knew the customs of the Indians.

"Yes, yes, he is that fine warrior that rode to your rescue. I saw the whole thing. It was a mighty brave and skillful act. You will have a fine companion and brave bodyguard to go with you. I approve."

I nodded. I was glad to hear that. I hadn't asked him for permission, I just told him I was going to take Wesha. Instinctive-like, he knew that I wasn't going to go without him. He was experienced enough to know that scouts were hard to handle. If you got real good ones, you better give them a little leeway.

He continued by saying, "Brules, you're the luckiest man I know. I have never seen anyone so near death come out with only a scratch. There must have been a hundred Sioux around you."

"That there was, General," I said. "But, General, I wasn't lucky, I was damn unlucky."

"What do you mean by that, Brules?"

"I mean that I was sure as hell not lucky to have some damn fool officer like Major Nickerson give me an order to ride back up that Dead Man's Canyon with a message for you which was way out of date. By the time I got it to you, hell, General, I didn't need to tell you we had engaged the enemy! You could hear the firing long before I'd even reached you. It was only by God's grace and the strength of Wesha's arm that I made it, General. It ain't lucky to have a commanding officer that gives you that kind of instructions."

For a moment Crook flushed, but didn't say anything. He just put his head down, his hands behind his back, and walked back and forth, behind the table.

"Young man, I know how you feel. The scout is a man born to the freedom of the plains and the mountains. It is hard for you to see why discipline is so necessary. But without discipline we would lose this Indian war, just as surely as with discipline we will win it. Four thousand years of military history tells us that wars are not won by the brave deeds of individual men, but by disciplined troops who follow orders of competent commanders and are staunch to the command regardless of how stupid it may appear.

"Any other course of action results in a rout like the Indians do when the going gets tough. They turn around and run. That is why they will be defeated. Discipline is a harsh mistress. The exacting toll of men often seems hard and merciless and without reason. This is the price of superior military action. Unfortunately, commanders do give stupid orders—they are only human. All commanders make mistakes and the subordinates pay for these mistakes with their lives. This is the sad heritage of military discipline, but without this discipline system we would be the slaves of other nations."

He paused and walked up and down for a minute with his head down in thought and his hands clasped behind him. Then he spoke again. "Brules, you are a crack shot and a great tracker, obviously a strong man in the peak of your youth. You and your blood brother, Wesha, are two of the finest men that we can pick in this whole command to carry out this job. You are not born into the military tradition, and we do not exact that from you. I only give you one command. You get that message to General Terry without fail any way you see fit." Crook put out his hand to shake, patted me on the back, and said, "Good luck, son, and get going right now."

Well, I couldn't argue with what the general had to say. I seen then what made a commander. He was a great man in many ways. I was inspired in his presence, and I must say, his little lecture on military history took some of the anger out of my brain. I began to see what he was talking about and what he was up against.

I'll have to say another thing: I was proud to serve under a general officer of his type—you see, he weren't stupid like that Nickerson, he was going to put the right man in the right place. For that kind of man you would cut off your right arm. I would say today if he told me to charge a Sioux or an Apache position, I would do it without hesitation, 'cause I'd know he knew it had to be done and he wouldn't have chosen me if I hadn't been the kind of man that he thought could do it. He was the kind of leader men follow!

When I went out of Crook's tent I grabbed Tom Cosgrove, who was waiting outside, and told him, "Tom, go get Wesha and tell him to bring his best horse. Then get me the best horse in the camp. I'll meet you both right back here. Tell Wesha that we have a long, tough mission and to take as much pemmican as he can get ahold of, and to be ready for a hard ride.

"Say to him that he will tell the sons of his sons that he rode ahead of the pony soldiers to seal the fate of his blood enemies the Sioux. The whole Shoshone nation will know that he is a hero and a mighty warrior from this time on. He is already the best-thought-of man in his nation, but this time he will be like a god. Go, Tom, go quickly, please. Get him here just as quick as you can.''

At that moment the adjutant came out of the tent and said, ''Oh, I am glad to see that you haven't run off yet, Brules. We've got to find you the right kind of horse.''

I said, ''That you do, sir. That horse is going for one hell of a ride.''

The adjutant turned to several lieutenants who were standing nearby, a part of Crook's staff, and cracked out some orders. These fellows left on the dead run. The adjutant said, ''Wait here, Brules, they'll bring their horses up and you can take your pick.'' A few minutes later I heard the hoofbeats of several horses and up come riding these young lieutenants of the cavalry. Lots of those men were from good families who gave a good horse to their favorite son. There weren't any one of them that wanted to give their horse over to a scout, 'cause they knew what was going to happen—they was never gonna see that horse again. That scout would either ride him to death or the Indians would get him. But when a general said bring your horses, not one lieutenant asked why, they just said, ''Yes, sir.'' Well, that was one moment that I could appreciate discipline. I wasn't gonna have to haggle and argue over what kind of horse I was gonna have for the ride that I knew was comin' up. I had a pretty good eye for horseflesh and it didn't take me long to settle on a big black stallion with white stockings. I reckoned he was damn near seventeen hands. He reminded me a lot of Pedro's Blackie; I guess that fact was what made me make the final choice. Any way you looked at him, he made one hell of a horse.

If you could see the sad look on that young second lieutenant's face when I picked that horse. I said to him, ''Mister, I know how you feel. I'm gonna bring this horse back to you if I can, but you might as well know that the mission I'm goin' on ain't no child's play, and there may be hell to pay before I get back.''

Well, the poor young fellow was almost in tears. I put my arm on his shoulder and told him that I loved horses, too, and his horse would get the best care that I could give him. I knew how to take care of horses and I'd look out for him as best I could.

He nodded, kinda grim faced, and I asked, "What's his name?"

"Jupiter."

"That's a good name for a big horse. Jupiter, you and I are gonna put on a ride that's gonna make your master proud. Son, how is he as a swimmer?"

"What do you mean, sir?" said the lieutenant.

"I mean crossing rivers."

"Oh, sir, he is about as good a swimming horse as there is in the state of Tennessee. I rode him from my family's horse farm at Coopertown, near Clarksville, the one hundred sixty miles to board the troopship at Memphis. On the way we swam the Cumberland and Tennessee without the slightest trouble. I think that you will like him, sir."

I patted the young fellow on the back and said, "I know I will, son. Now, you just take that good saddle off of him. I've got one of my own, much rougher than that. You don't have to lose a saddle along with the horse. I'm gonna keep the bridle, 'cause he's used to that."

With that he got a knowing, relieved look in his eye. He saw that I knew something about horses. They don't like a new or different bridle bit any more than you like changing a pair of shoes. I quickly pulled the saddle and held it out to the young lad, who gathered it up.

Then I done something that showed them I really did know how to ride a horse. I just bunched that horse's mane at the fore part of his withers in one hand and crouched down and jumped clear up and on that seventeen-hands horse without anybody helping me. Them boys was bug eyed: Occasionally they had seen some real good rider be able to hop up and stick his foot in the stirrup and swing over, but they never did see somebody get onto a seventeen-hands stallion from on the ground and holding nothing but the horse's mane in his hand.

One of the young officers said, "My God, he's like a cat."

I couldn't help but feel pretty good about that. Kinda give me a smile.

I started out in the direction Cosgrove had gone with Wesha, figuring that I had to get my saddle and blanket and some other things I'd need.

I had saddled Jupiter, put my rifle in the scabbard, tied on a bedroll, and gathered up a few biscuits by the time Wesha come riding up in his war paint, his lance in one hand and that 1873 Winchester snug in an antelope-hide scabbard. He was wearing his war feathers, and he looked beautiful! I'm telling you, when you see a Shoshone with high cheekbones, piercing eyes, and that wonderful frame of broad shoulders and magnificent waist and athletic legs, stripped down for action, you know that you're looking at somebody that is going to count.

I opened up my buckskin jacket and showed him that I had some dispatches wrapped up in an oilskin to keep dry. I said, "I have to take this talking paper to two white chiefs with many pony soldiers same as General Crook. Follow me, Blood Brother, we go for the Sioux."

He nodded and we mounted our horses. Even though it was night we rode down to Goose Creek in the starlight at a good lope. We rode until we come near to the junction of Goose Creek and the Tongue River and started up the Tongue. I was headed for the Bear Tooth Pass and the basin of the Big Horn River. Well, we rode all that night, loping, trotting, and then walking, all at different times to get the most out of our horses and to save them. When dawn broke, we was looking out on the Big Horn Basin.

We could see the Absaroka Range in the northwest, maybe sixty miles off, but halfway between was the Big Horn River, which we was gonna have to cross.

Me and Wesha found ourselves looking out at that big open stretch of the basin itself and couldn't help but wonder whether we was gonna be damn foolish and cross that in midday, knowing that the country just north of us would likely be holding at least a smattering of Sioux. We had been traveling all night with little chance that any hostiles had seen us, but now, going out into the open country and kicking up trail dust, we'd be visible for miles around.

Of course, there was some ravines in the country and a little bit of scattered timber, but there was gonna be times when we would have to travel in the open. I talked with Wesha about it for a minute while we sat on our horses. We knew that there should be a lot of Sioux up north of us. We could damn well bet that after the Battle of the Rosebud them warriors was goin' back to their village in the canyon where we almost got trapped. They was gonna take down their village and skedaddle out of there and get their women and children as far away from the cavalry troops as they could.

That would mean the whole Indian camp going down the Rosebud, maybe thirty or forty miles, and then heading out in some other direction.

Our thought was that they would cross the ridge between Rosebud and the Little Big Horn and would probably settle down by the Big Horn River. But we was just guessing. They could easily double back and head for the Big Horn Mountains or somewhere else.

We mulled it over for a little while and then I told Wesha what I thought was the obvious. What the hell, we was on a desperate mission between the commands—if we was gonna be so damn fearful that we had to travel only at night, we was gonna be slower than hell in getting Crook's message through and maybe miss the whole point of it. We didn't have no choice: we could travel twice as fast in daylight and we had to take advantage of it.

We sat there a little longer scanning the basin for any signs of hostiles. It was a mighty damn big basin, so there would always be the chance of seeing the smoke of a campfire, or maybe some dust, or maybe some dark figures moving along a ridge in the light of the rising sun.

I had a pair of field glasses that General Crook give me when I left, telling me they might help keep my ass out of trouble. Well, my God, with them glasses I scanned that basin for nigh on to fifteen minutes, checking it back and forth and looking at every little thing that seemed to be important. Nothing was moving except a few antelope and some deer feeding in the distance. No buffalo, no elk, and no Indians.

I told Wesha the best way to sneak across that basin was by traveling in the ravines and wherever there happened to be a little timber. We'd take advantage of every hiding place we could, but even then there'd be parts of it we'd have to travel in the open.

Well, that's what we done. We started right around sunrise, so I expect it was about ten in the morning when we come up a couple hundred yards from the banks of the Big Horn. We'd been as careful as we could, following our plan of keeping hid, and I thought that we done right well.

When we got close to the ridge, we didn't see no signs of nothing. As a matter of fact, we just come out of a small bunch of timber maybe a couple of hundred yards from the river. Before exposing ourselves both Wesha and me scanned the far banks up and down as far as we could see, me with the field glasses and Wesha with just his open eyes. I reckoned that Indian could see as well with his eyesight as I could with them field glasses, and I never did consider myself no slouch when it come to seeing things in the distance.

Well, we looked and looked until I guess it got plumb embarrassing, kinda like we were cowardly. There was no use doing anything but push on, not so fast that we'd kick up any dust, but we sure as hell couldn't help being seen between where we were and the banks of the Big Horn.

We hit a slow trot, just enough so we wasn't kicking up dust but still moving at a good pace, and we come up on the riverbank just as nice as you please. We looked down the bluffs on our side and didn't see nothing. We dropped down quick onto the riverbed itself and for a minute or two looked at that roaring stream in spring flood knowing that we was gonna have a time crossing it.

We seen that downstream from us, maybe fifty or sixty yards, was an island about halfway across the river. I reckoned that the island was about fifty yards long and covered with some timber, and I wondered whether it would be a good idea to use that island as a stopping place. Then I decided against it.

On our side of the island there was a steep bank and I could see it would be hell to get the horses up that. The island kinda tapered off downstream and you might be able to cross that end, but the current going by the island would be faster than it was out in the open river, so I decided that the best thing to do was to just start crossing where we was.

I nodded to Wesha and we started out. Our horses soon was in clear up to their chests and was beginning to have trouble keeping from floating. We held their heads up and helped work along, holding our rifles over our heads to keep them dry.

We was about a third of the way across that river when we got the Goddamnedest scare you can ever imagine. On the other side there was a gentle bank, where I'd picked to land. That bank went back maybe fifty or sixty yards over open grass and then there was some timber.

Out of that timber, as if they were magic, come stepping about fifteen Sioux horsemen with bright feathers, painted ponies, and all. I could instantly see they was well armed with magazine rifles, for only a few of them carried bows or lances. I don't know about Wesha, but it plumb scared the shit out of me.

Wesha seen them at the same instant, and looked quick at me. I must have been the most white-faced white man he ever seen. I took one quick look downstream at that island, motioned to Wesha. He seen what I meant and both of us slid off our horses into the water and at the same time jerked our horses' heads downstream. That way we was hiding behind the horses, protecting ourselves some from the shooting.

It didn't take the Sioux but a few seconds to see what we was doing and that we was no longer good targets. But I knew if they killed my big black stallion, Crook's message weren't going through. Maybe I was gonna get killed in the process anyway. All and all it weren't a pleasant feeling.

Sure enough the Sioux started following us downstream a little bit, and begun yelling and whooping and shooting. There weren't nothing except the heads of our horses as targets and those dumb sons of bitches was mounted and that ain't the way to do any accurate shooting. It would start getting tough for us only if they slid off and really took aim.

We was going downstream fast with the current and, like I said, had only a few yards to go before we would get to the safety of the island. When their shooting started we could hear them bullets singing by and splashing water all around us. Why in hell neither us nor them horses ever got hit, I don't know. I sure drew a healthy breath when we slid in along the eastern bank of that island and out of sight. Christ, I was scared!

There weren't nothing to do but keep drifting down back of the island and in a few seconds we was at the downstream end, a low place where we could get out and head into the timber. As we clawed out way up the bank, I yelled at Wesha and give him my horse's reins, as I slid off with my rifle. He got the idea quick and headed for the deep timber to protect the ponies.

I struggled ashore and quickly got in a crouched position. Hell, it was a little island only fifteen yards across. I peered out through the alder bushes and seen what I expected to see— them damn fool Sioux had come downstream opposite us, and was starting to wade out to meet us. They could cross that open water in the matter of a little more than a minute.

They must have knowed that somebody would shoot at them when they come across there, but they probably expected two frightened men who'd be shooting wild and not hittin' much good. What they didn't count on was the rifle of Cat Brules.

I knelt down, took careful aim, and started to do some terrible execution. In times like that a minute's a hell of a long time. I started working the Sioux warriors that were still on the bank, fixing to kill them while they was still good targets. I knowed that those crossing the river couldn't come at no gallop, so I had plenty of time to kill them when they got up close.

I reckoned that I shot six times, and killed as many warriors on the bank, by the time the river crossers got in close. The remaining warriors that was on the far bank got sick of the situation and whirled around and headed for the timber. The dumb bastards crossing the river probably could not even hear the shots above the roar of the water and if they did, they didn't look behind them to see what was going on. I reckoned all they figured was that whoever was shooting was doing some damn poor aiming and was missing them.

The first rank of them was only about twenty yards from the bank when I began to kill 'em. I am proud to say that though there was seven or eight of 'em in that bunch, there weren't one of 'em that ever lived to reach dry land.

I run into the thick undergrowth where Wesha was holding the horses. He'd heard the shooting, and although he couldn't see nothing that happened, there was a smile on his face. He heard the number of shots I got off and knew that there was a dead Indian for each shot.

Wesha said a few words in Shoshone as to what our action should be. We couldn't be sure if there was other warriors around, or if them that was driven back into the timber on the far side wouldn't wait until we come out. It seemed almost sure they would. They had seen a lot of their kin killed, and they sure would be reluctant to leave the bodies and run off like scared sheep.

I had a high regard for the fighting qualities of the Sioux after Rosebud, so I didn't expect 'em to do any damn fool runnin'. Consequently, what it amounted to was that we was pinned down on that island. Whatever number of warriors was left that had beat it for the timber would be laying for us and there wouldn't be any way for us to get out over that open water, climb up the far bank, and not get shot at. What's more, if we started downstream they'd follow us and nail us as we come out. Time was a-wastin' and we needed to be on our way, but we sure as hell couldn't show ourselves out in the open with a bunch of real mad Indians waiting to get back at us.

It looked like we'd have to stay there clear to nightfall, which in that time of year would be around nine o'clock and a long wait. All kinds of things might happen, and we had at least seventy miles to go.

We sat there together and thought about it a little bit. Finally, Wesha turned and looked straight at me—we was squatting down in the grass chewing on some stems, and I knew by his look that he had an idea I'd better pay attention to.

He made the sign real quick for me to stay where I was and cover the far bank with a rifle. He knowed that I could do it as well as any man living. He showed me his war club tied to his belt, his own rifle, and then made the motion of going downstream. Low and unseen, by himself, on foot, he was goin' to stalk them Indians in Indian fashion. Meanwhile, I was to keep watching like hell and do what I could to keep care of the horses. It seemed like one hell of a good plan to me.

In fact, I didn't see no other way. I held out my cut hand and took his again in mine, squeezed it, and nodded. Both of us understood real clear what was going to happen.

It took Wesha about ten seconds to peel off the blanket and anything else that he had on him that was useless. He'd stripped down to the breechcloth, which was a warrior's way of getting ready to fight. He had his rifle in his hand and his war club tied around the other wrist. He crept over to the east side of the island where we had come up with the horses, where he couldn't be seen, and slipped off into the water real quiet.

I thought that he was plenty smart, and it was with a thrill that I watched that beautiful athletic body of his ease out into the deep water, and seen him take a deep breath and then completely sink out of sight. He done it so well that I never seen him again until later that afternoon. He just plumb disappeared, but I knew what he was doing—he was floating downstream as fast as the current would take him and maybe rolling over onto his back once in a while and sticking his mouth above the water for a little air. He'd do it so there would be no splashing, no sight or nothing, and from two hundred yards away the Sioux would never see him.

Well, it was a long wait. I didn't know what to expect: maybe there would be some other hostiles who would come up and join what was left of these, or maybe these had run off and we hadn't seen them. Maybe Wesha would get himself in trouble when he got across the river downstream, and I might never see him again. I put that thought out of my mind quick. He weren't no child, he was the top warrior of the Shoshone nation, and if I was gonna bet on anybody, it would be him.

It had been close to a two-hour wait, and anxious as I was to get going, that was plumb hell. I got to fidgeting around, wondering what I ought to do, maybe get up and try to get those horses out of there, or try to cross the stream myself— and then I decided I would do nothing and just let Wesha have his way.

About ten minutes after I had made that decision, I heard a Goddamned war whoop from the other side. Two or three of them, as a matter of fact. Then I heard a shot, and from out of the woods two Sioux appeared on a dead run going upstream. I guess another one was down in the tall grass.

And I knew then just exactly what had happened. I didn't try to explain it to myself right then, 'cause in a flash I killed them two bucks. Then I waited for a few minutes to see what would happen. My guess was that when I'd heard the war whoop it meant that old Wesha had crossed the river successful, and stalked them damn fool Sioux. He killed a couple of 'em with his war club, and then when the others run out into the open, he shot one of 'em and I had killed the other two.

I waited awhile to see if there was anything going on, and Wesha took his time about coming out into the open hisself. I tell you it was a grand sight seeing that Indian blood brother of mine walking out from the woods with his rifle in one hand and war club in the other and two Sioux scalps hanging from his breechcloth belt. I just stood there and watched that magnificent sight for a whole damn minute, as he casually walked over to that buck in the tall grass and took his scalp.

Gathering up the horses, I climbed on Jupiter and started across the river, making a sign for Wesha to be ready to mount. He wouldn't be out in the open if things wasn't cleared.

I rode up to him and stopped for a minute. I was sitting on my big black horse, leading his, and he was standing there motionless. Then a big grin come across his face and I couldn't help breaking out laughing, and damned if he didn't do the same thing. I'm telling you I never seen an Indian laugh like that fellow did, and me too. Oh, hell, I guess, except for my long-dead pal, Pedro, there wouldn't be no other man in the world that I'd trust like my blood brother.

We traveled hard the rest of that afternoon and crossed the Shoshone Branch of the Yellowstone with an hour of daylight left. We pushed on and struck the Stillwater about midnight and what I reckoned to be maybe fifteen miles upstream from Absarokee.

I had been testing that big stallion all night long and sure had a lot of respect for him. He kinda reminded me of my old horse Spotted Tail.

Wesha's horse done good too. It was one of them beautiful painted stallions that the Shoshone are so famous for. Looking at him I could see a likeness to some of the horses that my wife, Wild Rose, had brought with her when we come on our trip to make our new home in the southern Rockies.

That memory kinda twisted my heart, so I quickly veered away from it, and began thinking what I was doing right at the moment. After all, I had gotten into this campaign at Wesha's suggestion. Like he'd said, I needed a good war, and now I had one and it was a dandy and exciting. If there ever was a branding iron that would burn the sorrow and endless mourning out of my heart, it would be the flash of war.

We headed out again on the hurry and got to the Shoshone River before sundown, crossing it without any trouble. When we hit the Stillwater it seemed like a good place to stop and rest our horses. It was along a roaring stream with nice clear water, so we were able to fill our bellies with a little pemmican. We ate and rested for what I judged to be about forty minutes.

I noticed that Wesha used the Indian technique of warriors on the warpath. When he rested, he didn't sit down or lay down on his side. He laid down on his back with his arms and his legs extended. He stared up at the sky and took some long, deep breaths while relaxing every muscle in his body. Like most Indians he knew how to rest as well as run, and it was a wonderful sight to see.

As we started out again, the big warrior rolled right out of that position and into a run for his horse. He untied him and sailed right up on his back just as clean as anything you ever see. Just to show off to him I done the same thing, only my horse was one and a half hands higher than his. In the starlight I could see his teeth shining in a smile at friendly competition like that.

When we reached the trading post of the Crow Agency at Absarokee at dawn, we was feelin' kinda fidgety. We'd come out of the darkness, one Indian and one white man with rifles, into a place loaded with Crows. But we was soon recognized for what we was, and made our way to the agency stores.

There was a man standing under a lamp, which had pretty well faded out by the coming of the dawn. I rode up and asked this fellow if he knew the whereabouts of Agent Clapp, who, the Crook's adjutant had informed me, was the Indian agent of the Crows.

The fellow was kinda slow to give out any information until he figured out who we was. I hastened to get him into action by telling him I was a courier carrying one important dispatch for Colonel Gibbon and General Terry. Right away he come alive and said, "Yeah, the agent's home is over yonder in those pine trees, but he don't get up this early. He's usually at the agency around seven o'clock in the morning."

That seemed reasonable enough. But, it now being about four o'clock in the morning, I told him that we had to see the agent right away. I suggested he come with us. This fellow seen I meant business, so he was right obliging. We trotted over to where the agent's little house was standing in a nice location in a grove of pines.

I got off my horse and banged at the door. After a little time I heard a voice calling, "What in the hell do you want?" I told him right quick, "I'm a courier from General Crook. I need to arrange for some transportation and if you're Agent Clapp, I'm calling on you to be of some help."

With that the old boy opened his door and stuck his head

out and said, "Okay, wait a minute and I'll get dressed and be right with you." In a few minutes he was dressed and was carrying a rifle. He stepped in front of the door and said, "Well, now, what in the hell is it you want to know and what am I supposed to do for you?"

I'd heard something about Agent Clapp not being too fond of the military, feelin' they made a lot of commotion among the Indians that was unnecessary. He knew the country and had things going pretty well with the Crows. Since they had been behaving themselves up to that time, he didn't want things riled up.

That didn't make no difference to me. I had a mission to carry out, so I come to the point real quick. I said, "Do you know the whereabouts of Colonel Gibbon or General Terry or General Custer?"

"No, I don't know anything about Custer and Terry. All I know is they are supposed to be coming up the Yellowstone to meet Gibbon. Gibbon was here in April, but he ain't been back here since."

"Can you give me some idea where you think they might be? Would they be along the Yellowstone?" I asked.

"As far as I know some Crow scouts went out of here a few days ago to join them, and I think that is where they went, down the Yellowstone. Whether they have gone in any of them rivers like the Tongue, the Rosebud, or the Big Horn, hell, I don't know. Nobody knows that in this big country. Hell, man, it is eight hundred miles between here and Fort Abraham Lincoln on the Missouri, and in that distance there ain't one single white man's dwelling. This is still wild country, just like it's always been since Lewis and Clark come through here."

"Yeah, I know that," I said. "What I'm looking for now is the best information I can get to their whereabouts. I'm a courier and got important information for them, I gotta get it to them quick, and need your help. General Crook give me a requisition for anything I need for this mission."

"So," he says, "stranger, you're a courier for General Crook's command? Where is General Crook right now?"

"Mister, that ain't none of your business. I been instructed not to give out any information other than what's needed. I'm headed for Gibbon and Terry, and I need some kind of transportation to get there. I'm guessing that they are meeting somewhere down on the Yellowstone. Have you got any ideas?"

Well, the old boy kinda bristled a little bit, then shook his head and said, "Hell, no. I told you I don't know where they is, but it's most likely they'd be down the river someplace. That's the way to go to find out."

"Yeah," I said, "but if I start riding down along the bank of the Yellowstone and have a long ways to go, it's going to take me a long time. What's more, maybe the mouth of the Big Horn is too deep and strong to cross. Maybe the Rosebud too. I ain't sure about any of them rivers, never having been in this country. I think that the best thing for me to do is to arrange to go down the river in some kind of a raft or something. Can you give me any help on that?"

Clapp scratched his head a minute and said, "Let's see, there is a Frenchie named Beauvoir, an old trapper—he's got a skiff and keeps it down at the mouth of the Stillwater on the Yellowstone. I believe that's the best way for you to go. You're right. Riding them horses down, you'd be a long time making it. Now, you know if you cross the river here, you could get across the Yellowstone and could hit Gibbon's military road."

"Gibbon's military road? What are you talking about?" I asked.

"Well, when Gibbon come down here he had several troops of infantry and some of cavalry and a lot of wagons and stuff. He had to have him a road, so the road builders went right along with him, but they was on the north side of the Yellowstone and to get to it you've got to cross over. I understand the road ain't nothing to dream about. I think, mister, if you are anxious to find them folks, you'd better go down the Yellowstone in a boat. The current is about five mile an hour now at flood time, and if you got a skiff and two men working it, you could make ten to twelve mile an hour. Hell, in ten hours you could be a hundred twenty miles down. You can't do that on a old horse."

That seemed real simple. I said, "Well, let's get to it. Let's find this Frenchie and get the skiff."

Clapp nodded. "He lives about five miles below here and I reckon I'd better saddle my horse and take you down there because he's kinda hard to find. He lives off the trail and if you didn't know how to get there, you'll have difficulty. First of all, I want to see your requisition form. After all, somebody has got to get paid for this, including me. Before I go to all that trouble and put Frenchie to work, I want to make sure you're who you say you are."

That kinda ruffled me a little bit, but when I got to thinking about it, what the hell, I knew he was right as rain. Nothing wrong in showing him the requisition, anyway. So I opened my shirt and took out my military papers, but not the dispatch.

He studied the requisition order over, and said, "That's genuine enough. Be glad to help you, mister. Just don't get so annoyed every time things don't go exactly like you want."

Well, I had to laugh and agree. I realized, maybe all the riding and shooting I'd done had made me a little bit gnarly. After all, Clapp was a damn good man. He went and got him a horse, saddled up, and we started down the trail.

The trail went down alongside of the Stillwater. While we was riding I pumped him for all the information I could get. "Did you say that Gibbon was here in April?" I asked.

"Yeah, he come down here with his troops, building his military road as he went, and camped right opposite the mouth of the Stillwater, across the north side of the Yellowstone. He forded across one time. I think that the water was a little lower then, 'cause the snow in the mountains wasn't melting that fast in April. Anyway, he come in here and was on a military mission, same as you."

"He was? What the hell was he doing?"

"Well, he was looking for some Crow warriors to go with him. I guess they're the blood enemy of the Sioux, and he knowed that their chief could raise eight hundred mounted warriors," Clapp explained.

"Yeah," I said, "I heard that the Crows had been fighting the Sioux for hundreds of years."

"Ain't no love lost between 'em. Seemed to me like a hell of a good opportunity for them Crows to go along."

"That would be good for Gibbon, too, wouldn't it?" I commented. "Eight hundred mounted warriors ain't no handicap when you've got them for allies. That is, if you can keep them from buffalo hunting on the side all the time."

Clapp laughed at that. I told him a little bit about what had happened when I was with Crook's command, without giving him any information as to the exact location of Crook's doings. Well, we got right more friendly then and he said, "You know, it was the damnedest thing. Old Chief Blackfoot had this big powwow and Gibbon got up and give him a long speech, round the campfire. He said that for ages the Sioux had done nothing but devastate the Crow hunting grounds, burn his villages, and carry away captives. They had done all kinds of bad things and now here come the pony soldiers, from the great father, who was going to help the Crow eliminate them Sioux.

"I couldn't understand why old Blackfoot didn't want to go! I thought maybe the Crow people had lost their guts or something. Course, it's true that all the other tribes are terrified of the Sioux. The Sioux are a big, big nation, all tough fighters as Indians go."

After hearin' that I thought to myself, that makes sense. The Crow are much fewer, and that's why the Sioux have kept backing people up—the Shoshone, Crow, and Blackfoot—all the way to the Rocky Mountains, pushed them clear into the interior, where the going is not so good. You and I know that all the game is out on the plains where the feed is easy, it ain't up in the mountains where the snow gets twenty feet deep in the wintertime. But even though the Sioux were so powerful, I still didn't understand why old Blackfoot didn't want to throw his eight hundred warriors into the white camp to fight their blood enemy, now that he had the big chance. And Gibbon didn't understand it either.

"Once more Gibbon started doing a little cussing and calling the Indian chief a coward and shamed him. Asking him what kind of a man was he? Gibbon really done everything he

knew how to do to get that damn chief to go along with them.
The chief just shook his head, but finally, you know, he kinda
give in a little bit, and he said he would give Gibbon some
scouts.

"Gibbon said that he could use them, all right, but he
already had the best scout in the country signed up and said,
'Who's that?'

"Well," he told me, "he signed up Mitch Bouyer."

"Mitch Bouyer. Hell, that guy is famous!"

Clapp agreed. "You know that, too, don't you? Next to
Jim Bridger he's probably the best man ever to come through
this country. He started out scouting for old Sir George Gore,
the Scotsman that come here about twenty-odd years ago.
You've heard of him, haven't you?"

I nodded. "Yes, I sure as hell have. I guess that Bouyer
was a real young man then."

"Oh, yeah, he was only eighteen or nineteen years old
when he guided a geological expedition through here surveying for what's gonna be the railroad, sometime. He done a lot
of other stuff too. Anyway, there ain't no doubt about his
scouting ability. He's real handy to have around, 'cause he
speaks Crow, Sioux, French, and English. His mother was a
Sioux, and his dad a Frenchie, a trapper. Got a Crow wife
too."

"Well, I understand he's quite a fellow, great fellow."

"He sure as hell is. You know he speaks pretty damn
good English too. Now, I suppose that he got that down in St.
Louis, but, you know, he's a real obliging guy and a hell of a
good-looking man. He looks like an Indian, with strong Indian
features, built like an Indian, but he's got a pleasant face. He's
real athletic, but always wears white man's clothes and doesn't
have any trouble getting along with the white man. He doesn't
speak broken English or anything like that. He speaks just like
you and me."

"You mean like you," I said. "My English ain't too damn
good."

Clapp laughed and looked over at me. "Well, I reckon
both of us have had some difficulty with being in the wilder-

ness all the time. You get a little out of practice speaking any kind of parlor-room stuff.''

"That's exactly right. Seems like to me there was a long period that I didn't speak nothing but Shoshone.''

"Shoshone?'' he asked.

"Yeah, I had a wonderful Shoshone wife.'' When I said it he looked down at the ground and he didn't say nothing. I guess that he was a sensitive enough man that he wasn't going to dig into an old wound, so he let it drop right there.

"Well,'' he said, "in order for you to catch up with old Mitch Bouyer and his reputation, now, you just got two more languages to learn. You gotta learn French and Sioux or Crow, or something. You just speak English and Shoshone.''

"Yeah, I reckon that I do, and it will be a cold day in hell when I pick up the rest of those languages.''

We got along good, you know. This guy Clapp was a good man and was just trying to do an honest job. He was one of the few agents I seen that was real honest. That had something to do with the way the Crow acted toward the white folks, because if you have a good agent living up to what he says he's gonna do and keeps the faith of these guys, then the Indians are all right. It's when you start griping and hooking them that you have trouble, and there are plenty of agents who was doing that.

We had ridden about five miles down the Stillwater on the west side and were coming to a little creek running alongside a kinda obscure trail that went back into the timber a ways. We followed that trail to a clearing where there was a wickiup. Sure enough, Beauvoir was sitting in front of a fire. By God, if he wasn't a French trapper from beginning to end. His Indian moccasins, capote, coonskin cap with a tail on it hanging down the back of his neck, and of course, a beard that was a mile long. I also noticed an old Hawkins rifle there, and that did kinda date him.

I seen right away that he was on good terms with Agent Clapp. I couldn't speak French, so Clapp done the talking.

Anyhow, after a lot of palaver with the old boy, Clapp translating to me what the objections was, the old boy was kinda still hard to pull off the rock. He said, hell, if we go downstream, it would be all right, but at this time of year it was high water and moving so fast, you couldn't paddle or pole the skiff back up here. He would either have to haul it by himself or get a horse to do it. I agreed with him about all that stuff, as there were no doubt about it. He was just building up the price, but, hell, I didn't have any counterargument. All I wanted to do was to get the hell down there.

Finally Beauvoir said that he would loan the skiff to the government for the sum of two hundred dollars for the purposes of the traveling down the Yellowstone, but no farther than the mouth of the Tongue River. Boy, that seemed like a hell of a lot of money to me, but then I'd never fooled around with government stuff before and realized that I wasn't spending my own money.

We sat down and old Clapp, who had a lot of experience writing out government requisitions and all, filled out all of the papers I give him. I agreed to everything and we finally signed the Goddamn requisition and give it to the Frenchie. We went on down about twelve miles to the mouth of the Stillwater, where it run into the Yellowstone.

Meanwhile, all the time we was riding down this trail, old Wesha was following along behind, very patient-like and saying nothing, as usual, in true Indian style. He had great dignity and though he couldn't understand what we was talking about, he knew that I was figuring something.

When we come up on Frenchie's pirogue, he untied the boat and dragged it over to the edge of the embankment. I took what stuff I needed off my saddle along with my bedroll, my rifle, and all the ammunition I had. With the bandolier belt I had I could carry damn near sixty rounds.

When we'd gotten the pirogue loaded and were ready to start, I explained to Wesha, "I'll just go along with this fellow, and we'll meet again. If you come down the river to the mouth of the Big Horn, I'll make my way back up somehow after delivering this message and meet you there. Leave some sign there, and let me know what direction you're going in. I should be back in four or five days, I reckon." I told him this in

Shoshone and he agreed. Then we just put our palms together and that was all there was to it. He didn't say nothing else, he just climbed on his painted horse, taking the lead rope of the big black stallion I'd been riding, and started off down the river.

I waved good-bye to Clapp. Wesha had disappeared into the timber on his own way.

There's nothing like traveling on a river when you are going downstream. Boy, we made such terrific time, I couldn't believe how easy it was. When you are on land, you're plugging along, riding on a horse, swaying in the saddle with each step. But when you get on a river, it is real smooth and you move right along. The current was moving about five miles an hour at least, and we was probably paddling another four or five miles an hour, so we was making about ten miles an hour going down the Yellowstone. That's pretty good going. We must have pushed off near nine in the morning and five hours later, at about two in the afternoon, we come up on the mouth of the Little Big Horn.

I can tell you, the smartest thing I ever done was to take that pirogue, 'cause by the time we got to the mouth of the Big Horn we found it was in full flood, and, hell, you could never ride a horse across there.

As a matter of fact, on the way down, we seen where Gibbon had built that military road, and forded the Yellowstone two or three times, but that was back in April. Now the river was going like hell, this being June and the real runoff. I was damn glad I wasn't trying to ford it now.

We were lucky and didn't see nothing all through the afternoon, and everything was going just fine. I figured that if we had to go clear to the Tongue, we could get there sometime around ten or eleven o'clock at night, maybe midnight if we had to go a little slower. I was bound and determined that we wasn't gonna get off that damn river until we found the troops.

It was just before sunset, and I figured that maybe we had fifteen miles to go to the Rosebud, when we come up on another set of rapids. We had been hitting rapids, not big ones, not any real tough stuff, just places where the river either narrowed down a little bit or got a little rocky underneath, and set the water churning a little bit. There seemed to be enough water to keep from hitting any rocks, and I was plumb sure that the kinda boatman that Frenchie was, why, hell, we wouldn't have no trouble.

That's right where I made a mistake. We was coming around a gentle turn, and it seemed like the water was foaming a little bit, but I didn't pay attention until all of a sudden we hit, with the damnedest bang you ever heard, some big boulder right underneath us. We didn't see it until it was too late and that pirogue just jumped through the air. It was like we'd been hit with a hammer, and it knocked out about half the bottom and we didn't take very damn long to settle.

Of course, we couldn't keep any balance and as we rolled over I reached back quick and grabbed ahold of the bedroll and the rifle the best I could. I went into the water and turned over a couple of times, and I'll tell you it was a running stream. Trying to swim and hold that stuff up, a couple of times I thought I'd have to let go of the bedroll, but I managed to stay with it. We wasn't too far from shore and Frenchie was a good swimmer, but he was hanging tight to his pirogue. He wanted to save what was left of it.

He floated with that pirogue better than I did and he went about a hundred yards down, pushin' that sunken hull. Finally he managed to get it angled over so that he could get close to the bank and beached it.

If it had just been me swimming, I'd have been okay, but with rifle and bedroll I didn't make near the time he did. When I got to the edge of the bank, which was only about a thirty- or forty-yard swim, I was sure worn out. I made a grab at some alder bushes there and I lost the bedroll. That damn bear-hide sleeping bag started down the river. I let go of the bushes and tried to follow it a little ways, and then I thought, hell, I better save myself. Well, Frenchie seen what was happening and I'll be damned if he didn't wade out and grab that bedroll. I was grateful as hell to him.

I got on the shore there where it was shallow and plopped out of the water, me, my rifle, and all my clothes soaking. I walked on down to where he was, and we had a laugh about it. It wasn't funny, though; the whole damn bottom side of the pirogue was knocked in and was no use to us. We was gonna have to do something, but for us to do the carpenter's job the boat needed, well, that was out of the question.

We would have to leave it there and come back and get it, or Frenchie would. Right then he started breaking up some bushes to make a fire. When I shook my head, he kept nodding and saying, *"Oui, Oui."* He talked a lot of French, and I figured what he meant was that we'd get a fire going and dry out our clothes in a hurry.

"Listen, we aren't about to start a fire down here," I told him. "This country is crawling with Sioux. We'll get dry enough, if we just keep a-plugging, that's all. We gotta walk."

I worked the lever on my rifle until I got all sixteen shells out of the magazine and done my best to wipe them off, and then I blew through the barrel to get rid of as much water as I could. That's about all I could do. I figured it wouldn't rust for a day or two, and by that time I'd be someplace where I could clean it out.

Meanwhile, I had to hope to hell that I didn't have no sand or anything else that would stop the action in it. Seemed like it was in pretty good shape. So I reloaded and put a shell in the chamber with the hammer on safety, and reached down my belt and pulled out another shell. Putting it in the magazine made sixteen there, in case things got desperate. Anyway, I kinda laughed at my precaution because it really didn't make too much difference what I was doing. We had one hell of a long walk and I didn't know how big the Rosebud was at its mouth or whether we could get across it and we wasn't making any ten mile an hour now. We was making about two mile an hour, in the dark. We kept that up until around midnight, and then I was beginning to drag. Come to think of it, I'd been up something like sixty-three or sixty-four hours without sleep and had been on the move all the time. Rode some horses for nigh on to a hundred miles, stopped to fight some aggravating Sioux, and rode the boat for another hundred. That was almost three days, and I was getting near the end of my rope.

Frenchie hadn't done nothing like that, but you could tell he was pulling pretty hard, too, so I motioned that we'd better crawl into some bushes and go to sleep.

It was quite a bit past dawn when we come to again and there was nothing to do but to keep plugging. We went down to the shore and got us a little water to drink and had a little pemmican, so we both had some food in our bellies to start out again. Man, it's surprising what a difference that'll make. Just the water alone puts a man back in some kind of shape, so we couldn't kick none. I had pretty well made up my mind that we was gonna have to swim a little to make it across the Big Horn.

We were gonna have to be careful. I reckoned we was about ten miles short of the Rosebud, and it would be another sixty miles from there to the Tongue. At the rate we was traveling it was gonna be tough. In the daytime we could do a little bit better. We could make us about three miles an hour, maybe. I sure did long to have Frenchie's skiff again.

Come to think about it, the old boy didn't make much profit on this deal. It was gonna cost a lot to get that skiff back up the creek and fixed.

Moving along as fast as we could on a stretch that was kinda level, alongside the river, we was just passing through some tall grass and some reeds, when I heard the greatest sound ever in my life. I knew it from all the times I'd heard it on the Mississippi. It was the whistle of a steamboat.

The whistle was faint, so I knew that it was quite a ways away, and I was just praying that it wasn't gonna head downstream before I got there. I decided that we better kick up to a jog. Frenchie complained all the time about how fast we was trying to go, but I made me no mind.

Well, it was only about another fifteen or twenty minutes when I begun to see some stuff on the other side of the river. I seen some workmen and figured that they were working on Gibbon's military road. That meant that they was coming back up, and maybe somebody would be helping us. At least it was possible.

I tried to yell across the river at them guys, but the sound of the current was too strong. I never did raise them, as they was back a little bit from the river. I kept on and after about ten minutes I begun to see all kinds of tents and stuff.

It was Gibbon's camp. He had been there for some time, I found out later, but had gone down the Tongue to meet with Terry.

I heard that steamboat whistle again, and, by God, this time it sounded pretty near. I waded in a little so I could see. I saw two things that looked awful good to me. One was the opening maybe a mile or so below where the Rosebud was flowing out into the Yellowstone, then about two miles below that, pushed up against the shore, was that steamboat, the *Far West,* next to a big encampment.

We made as good time as we could, and it wasn't too long before we come up on the west shore of the Rosebud. I looked at that stream and thanked God it was nothing like the Big Horn, nothing near as big. I could see we was gonna get across pretty easy. Might have to swim a little section there, but it wasn't too bad. We got in about chest-deep water and lost our footing a little, in the current, but swam and made it to the other shore.

Well, there was all kinds of goings-on. We could see horses moving, and maybe two miles away the steamer and the encampment. We done plugged along and got there just before noon.

5

Conference on
the *Far West*

Coming up on the camp, I seen there was a lot of troops lined up and the Indian allies was going around and around in circles. They were singing songs and dancing, and was pretty damn lively.

The steamboat was against the bank with a gangplank where you could get aboard easy. I figured that's where the headquarters was, so I went up to the sentries standing there and told them, "I'm a dispatch rider and I got a message for General Terry."

The guard called the corporal and he come down to check me over. I opened my shirt to show him that I had all this stuff, and I guess that he was pretty well convinced. I told him that we had come down in a pirogue, from up above the Stillwater, and wrecked the damn thing about twenty miles up the river. We'd had to come the rest of the way on foot through the night.

"Well," he said, "come aboard. We'll report to Terry's office."

I had to wait there at the gangplank a few minutes, which seemed like a long Goddamn age when I had something important and had come all this way. Finally, the guard comes out and says, "Okay, you can come in now."

I went in expecting to see General Terry, but, hell no, I just seen Major Edward Smith, his adjutant. Smith was standing stiff-like, looking real formal. I said, "I got to see General Terry to deliver this message."

"General Terry is not here right now. He is out on temporary parade ground, reviewing Custer's Seventh Cavalry before they go up the Rosebud."

"Oh, are they going up the Rosebud? Well, maybe he ought to have this message. I don't know just exactly what's in it, but it's important."

"Well," he asked, "who's it from?"

"It's from General Crook."

"You came from General Crook! My God, how did you get here?"

"I crossed way up there," I said, pointing northwest.

"Where's General Crook?"

"Sir, I was told to give out no military information. I wasn't to give our position or nothing. I was just supposed to give this message to General Terry and nobody else."

"Well," he said, "General Terry is not here. Now, what are you gonna do about that?"

"I don't know. But I'm gonna figure something out."

"If you want, you can stay here and wait until he comes, but that's kinda senseless. You better give me the message. I am his adjutant and I will see that he gets it."

"I don't know what to do about that. I was told by General Crook—that I was to give it to General Terry in person."

Smith shrugged. "Suit yourself. That's the dumbest thing I ever heard."

Then, outside there was a big commotion and we all stepped out of the cabin and stood on the deck to watch the Seventh Cavalry marching up from their encampment. They had been brought up from the Tongue, and camped two miles downstream from the mouth of the Rosebud. Custer's orders was to ride up the Rosebud and try to find those Indians.

A week before Major Reno, in command of a long scouting trip, had crossed a huge Indian trail forty miles up the Rosebud and, heading west, had seen the trail of a big Sioux village. That big village had to be in either the valley of the Rosebud or the valley of the Little Big Horn.

Hell, I could tell them where they was on the Rosebud. They was just north of Dead Man's Canyon, least that's where they'd been last, but then, of course, with an Indian village you can't tell a damn thing about it, as it was liable to move the next day.

I stood there and watched the whole show. I must say it was quite something. Their Indian scouts was all there, and they had a bunch of Arikarees, some Crows, and three or four Dakotas. How the hell they ever got Sioux to go against Sioux, I don't know, but they'd done it. Anyway, the Arikarees, who we always called Rees, was apparently urged by Custer into singing their death songs. They was going around in circles, singing to beat hell.

After all that was over, here come the cavalry. It was a snappy-looking outfit. Considering how far them boys had come—seven hundred miles up from Fort Abraham Lincoln, riding and marching all the way, by God—they looked pretty good.

People was cheering and Indians raising hell, war-whooping and dancing around. I could see that up on a hill overlooking the whole thing was three officers: Custer and General Terry and a third that I thought was probably General Gibbon.

When the order for march was called, Custer mounted his horse, galloped down to the front of the whole column and give the signal, and they started out. It looked like it was gonna be the beginning or the end of the world, I don't know which. It sure was some celebration. They was all out like they was gonna lick the hell out of the Sioux, straighten things up, and from then on everything would be okay.

As Custer rode up where the steamboat was he halted the column and got off his horse. I had been talking with the adjutant Major Smith and noticed there was a man with Smith who didn't say much while all the ceremonies was going on. He'd eased over next to me. A fine-looking fellow, looked part Indian, wore white man's clothes, and spoke good English. He asked me in a kinda soft voice if I had really come from Crook. Was that true?

"Hell, yes," I said.

"Well," he said, "we're sure glad to see you. I want to shake hands with you. My name is Mitch Bouyer."

"My name is Cat Brules, and I'm glad to meet you, too, sir. You're one of the scouts, then?" I remembered Bragg said Bouyer was here.

"Yes, I'm in charge of the scouts, but report to Lieutenant Varnum."

"What scouts are you talking about?" I asked him.

"I've got some Crows and some Rees."

"How many?"

He told me, "About eight or nine Rees and four Crows. Any one of them Crows are worth about a hundred of them Rees. Them Rees come all the way from the Missouri, and don't know nothing about this country, and they're also scrubby fighters."

"I suppose you know plenty about this country?"

"Yeah, I do. Been around this country for many years. I'm not bragging at all, just know it."

I liked the way he talked. He wasn't all Indian, 'cause he had blue eyes, but he sure had the dark complexion and the high cheekbones. Of course, when he told me he was Mitch Bouyer, why, I plumb near swallowed my gullet, because next to Jim Bridger he was the best-known man in the country.

He kept questioning me a little bit about where I had left Crook. I told him that I wasn't supposed to say nothing, but that I was just carrying some dispatches from Crook.

"Has Crook done any fighting at all?" he asked.

"Yeah, he done a little. He run into a bunch of the Sioux not so long ago and he took a pretty good hammering."

"Did he lose a lot of men?"

"Sure lost a few, wasn't no child's play. Had some wounded that he had to send back down the Bozeman Trail to Fort Laramie in the wagons."

"Well," he said, "so, he was somewhere near the Bozeman?"

I kinda stuck my foot in my mouth on that one. I said, "Well, yeah, kinda along the Bozeman there for a hundred or so miles."

"Were there any Indians with you?"

"Yeah, we had some Crows and a troop of Shoshone," I told him.

Surprised, he said, "I'll be damned. The Shoshone are out too."

"There weren't very many of them, only about eighty."

"How did the Indians do? How did they fight for you?"

I didn't realize that he was digging away at some real sensitive stuff, and I was trying to be pleasant and obligin'. "The Shoshone fought real good, but them Crows hung back a little bit. They sure are a good-looking bunch of men, but, by God, they got too much fear of the Sioux for some reason. I can tell that."

Bouyer grinned and said, "Yes, they do. The Crows are good fighters, good warriors. You said that they didn't fight so good?"

"No, they kinda hooted around, and when they come up against the Sioux they come running back yelling, 'Heap Sioux, heap Sioux.' "

"Maybe they was just showing the better part of valor, that's all. I mean, if they were badly outnumbered."

"Yeah, they probably was. But the Shoshone dug right in, and I'd have to say this for the Crows, when they finally got cornered they fought pretty good. You know how Indians are, they fight when they feel like it and don't fight when they don't."

Bouyer just nodded. "How long ago did you leave Crook?"

"A few days ago."

"How did you come through all this country swarming with Sioux and get by with it?"

"I shot my way through in a couple of places, but it worked out all right."

"That's real interesting, stranger. I see that you have some Comanche moccasins on."

"Yes, sir."

"Did you ever fight Comanches?" he asked me.

"No, I never did fight no Comanches. I used to hunt 'em."

He bust out laughing real hard, and said, "I see what you mean. Say, I know that old Bapt Pourier real well, do you know him?"

"Yeah, I sure as hell do. He's my friend, he got me in this scouting."

"By God, I wonder if you're the fellow he was talking about. He was telling me about a fellow he knew who was a hell of a scout, hell of a gunman. He was an absolute dead shot. He said his name was Cat Brules. He had eyes like a cat, he said—by God, that son of a bitch never missed shot."

Bouyer looked at me again, straight in the eye, and said, "You wouldn't be that Cat Brules old Bapt was talking about, would you?"

"Well, I don't know what he said, but he and I done some shooting, and he used to be reasonable proud of what I done."

"I wish you'd do something. I wish you would come with us. What are your orders?" he asked.

"I don't have any except to get these messages through."

"Well," he said, "I'll tell you what—in the military, if you are under orders to report to another commander and your orders don't carry any further specific instructions, then you're attached to the unit of the commander who receives the message. I think it's maybe the best damn thing ever happen to this command."

"That's all fine and dandy, but I'm supposed to go back to General Crook," I argued.

"You said you don't have any *instructions* to go back to General Crook."

"No, I don't, but I can't go with you, 'cause I don't have no horse."

"What happened to your horse?" he asked.

"I had a beautiful big black stallion, but left it with a Shoshone friend of mine up there at the Stillwater. I told him to ride down to the mouth of the Big Horn and I'd meet him there."

"What's his name?"

"Wesha," I told him.

"Wesha, Wesha. Boy, that's a familiar name. Hey, isn't he the son of Chief Washakie of the Shoshone?"

"Yep, that be he, and he's my blood brother." I showed him my hand.

"Well, he's a damn good man. We better pick him up too. He's got your horse, has he?"

"I hope so. He's still got it unless the Sioux killed him and stole it." I kinda shuddered when I said that. I hoped that Wesha didn't get into any kind of trouble, but knowing him as I did, I was pretty sure he could take care of hisself.

"By God, that's good news. I'll tell you what—Gibbon is going on up the Yellowstone and up to the Little Big Horn. Custer and Gibbon are supposed to meet someplace in that country and squeeze the Sioux together up there."

"Well?" I said.

Bouyer went on, "Gibbon's party can take a message telling Wesha to follow them, and you can meet him later. Is Wesha one of the scouts?"

I nodded. "He's under Crook with the Shoshone outfit there. I guess he's under orders, as much as any of these Indians are."

Mitch laughed a little and said, "Yeah, I know what you mean. But anyway, Wesha will be persuaded to come if he knows that his blood brother is down here and he can join the command. That way he's got a good chance to go into the Sioux country without getting hurt. Otherwise, I don't think he could make it."

"Maybe not, but I wasn't figuring on that. I was going to hotfoot it back up the river and meet him there."

"Well," Bouyer said, "I think you're attached to this command now, and you'll be coming with us. Let me tell you, Custer needs every scout that he can get. He doesn't know nothing about this country, just between you and me, and he's awful eager—too eager. I understand in the Civil War he jumped from something like second lieutenant up to a general because he was such a hell-for-leather cavalry leader, always charging. But sometimes in Indian country that isn't the best way.

"I was down here three weeks ago with Lieutenant Bradley, Gibbon's chief of scouts. I had my Crows out and we come up on a hell of a big village. Saw the smoke in the distance, and was trying to get a count on it, but the Crows didn't want to go any nearer to it. I came back and told Gibbon two days later but he didn't believe me. These generals just don't believe us! Reno came down the Rosebud the other day and said he seen a big trail up there. That could be two or three villages, one come through and then two—three weeks later another one, and then later on, another one—still they think it's just one damn single village trail, constantly moving its campsite. But there could be two or three villages leapfroggin' each other. Which means there's three times as many warriors as they were thinking. If all them villages get together, there's gonna be one hell of a lot of hostiles up there. Custer's gotta know about it, and then he's gotta believe it. I think that between the two of us we could do some scouting with these Crows. They're good men and they know what the hell they're doing, but they gotta get the right kind of direction."

"Yeah, aren't they under Lieutenant Varnum?" I asked again.

"Yeah. Varnum, he's a West Pointer. He's brave and he's fair, but he doesn't know Indian fighting. I tell you, it was the funniest damn thing I ever saw when he got the notion he ought to be drilling them Crows like soldiers.

"Hell, he takes a bunch of these damn scouts and tries to line them up, make them stand at attention, do shoulder arms, march in cadence, column right, and all that stuff. They didn't know what it all meant. They'd all stand there with real comical faces, and the minute he turned his back, they'd giggle and point at him. As soon as he turned around they were all standing stiff again.

"But those West Pointers are still darn good officers, and that's why we gotta help them. That's why I want you to come with us. Now, you're already enlisted in the scouts, and I'm just gonna take you to Lieutenant Varnum and have you join the bunch.''

Well, I sure liked Mitch Bouyer, and when he said he was a damn good friend of old Bapt, that did it for me. To be real honest I didn't see how in the hell I was gonna get back to find Wesha except to walk. As a scout, if I could get a horse, and go somewhere on the Big Horn, I had a pretty good chance of meeting Wesha again.

"I'm gonna need a horse, till I see Wesha again."

"Yeah, I know. I'll get you a horse, by God," he replied.

"Now, wait a minute. I've had some officers tell me that they would get me a horse. But a lot of them cavalry horses ain't nothing but plugs. I've had some damn good horseflesh under me—my black stallion was seventeen hands and a damn racehorse.''

Bouyer laughed and said, "Hell, I can't get you something like that, but I'll bet you get a good horse. You just let me talk to the remount boys—I may have some influence around this outfit.''

I didn't say anything. I was standing there watching Custer, who was walking up the gangplank of the steamer.

By God, here was the great Custer, the golden-haired boy of the West, walking past me. The Indians called him "Son of the Morning Star"—"Yellow Hair," or "Long Hair." Everybody heard he always wore his hair long, in golden locks. But they was cut off short this time.

Later on, I was told he had it done just to please his wife, who was always afraid his beautiful head of hair would be a prize scalp for some Sioux. She had dreams about it and told him how frightened she was. The story goes that he had old Varnum cut his hair with some horse clippers back at Fort Abraham Lincoln before the campaign got under way.

Custer was an athletic-looking fellow in his mid-thirties, about Bouyer's age, I would say. I think both was ten years older than me. Custer didn't look for anybody but Mitch Bouyer. He walked up to him, took him by the arm, and turned around. They started down the gangplank together and the whole ranks of the Seventh Cavalry began to cheer.

Everybody knew Mitch Bouyer, and if Custer was taking him as a scout, they knew damn well they was gonna be headed in the right direction for sure. There's nothing worse than the cavalry column getting misled by scouts. It happened lots of times on the frontier and when it did, the morale went to hell. When they saw the best scout in the West with Custer, they was mighty pleased.

Well, Bouyer went over and got on his horse. I seen he had a damn nice horse, and figured if he was gonna get me one, I could count on it being a good one. I didn't know how he was gonna do that, 'cause he was so occupied. Custer mounted, too, and then led Bouyer right up in front to ride with the column. He started a few yards away from where the other officers were standing—Gibbon ("Old Gray Beard" is what the Indians called him) and Terry (they called him "No Hipbone"). They were waiting to review Custer's troops.

Of course, all them fellows had a sense of the dramatic. They was trying to put life and snap into their Indian allies by doing this. The Indians had been doing all the dancing, singing, and putting on all this powwow, so that everybody would know what a hell of a bunch of fellows they was. The troops and the Indians was kinda selling themselves to each other, which was pretty amusing. Meanwhile, Custer rode past Gibbon and Terry, who were standing at a salute just a few yards upstream. Custer gave them a nice snap of a salute and the whole regiment passed by in review.

I heard Terry say to Custer, "All right, General, you've got your command now. Just don't forget to wait for us." I know now he meant for Custer to wait for Gibbon, who was going to the mouth of the Big Horn and then up the Big Horn River and then to the Little Horn. They was all to get there at the same time.

The answer that Custer give them might be a clue to what happened, but I couldn't hear what he said. Some people said he said, "I will," and some people said he said, "Don't worry, I won't." Everybody knew Custer had been in bad fettle with President Grant and others in Washington for talking about some of the Indian agents and how crooked they was. A few of them agents was related to the President. Custer was supposed to command this whole operation, but the President relieved him of his command. It was only the begging of Sheridan and Tecumseh Sherman, who had faith in Custer as a cavalry leader, that got him reinstated as commander of the Seventh Cavalry. They put General Terry in as overall commander. And I guessed that mighta made for bad feelings.

Custer was mighty glad to be with the Seventh Cavalry. It was pretty evident to everybody he was out to make a name for himself again and get to be the hero boy. He sure did all right during the Civil War. What's more, he did pretty good in the Indian campaigns, down on the Washita, when he busted the southern Cheyennes. That was back in 1868—he was a big hero out of that deal. He got in some trouble down there, too, by disobeying orders. I didn't really know much about it, except that it got pretty sticky for him.

Anyway, it was a grand sight seeing the cavalry outfit riding by. I guess I could understand a little bit about all that military pride, but I kept thinking nobody with that big of a gang was gonna get anywhere near them Indians.

That day Custer continued his two-mile march up to the mouth of the Rosebud and turned left upstream, then marched ten more miles. That was a total of twelve miles before he pitched camp that evening and finally let his command settle down a little bit.

Meanwhile, I heard that Gibbon and Terry was going up the river in the steamer to the Big Horn, then up to the Little Horn as far as they could go to meet Custer. They figured that it was gonna take them about three or four days to make the trip. I thought that was real nice, and I would just stay on the steamer with them.

First of all I had to get the message to General Terry. I could see he was busy as hell with a bunch of officers out there and so I just stood around waiting for him to come back. Pretty soon his adjutant, Major Smith, came up the gangplank and said, "You have a message for General Terry?"

I said, "That I do, sir."

"Well, you can give the message to me. I will see that he gets it."

"No, sir, I ain't gonna do that. I was told to give the message to no one except General Terry."

"Goddammit, you can see that he is busy. Right now he is seeing that this Seventh Cavalry gets off," he snapped. At that time the Cavalry was still marching by. "I'm his adjutant and it's just the same as giving it to him. Any military person knows that."

"Yes, sir, but I don't know that. I'm following the orders I was told."

Smith become real exasperated then and said, "Look here, Brules, let's get right down to the facts. You're a scout, enlisted in the forces of the Army of the United States, and are subject to the rules and regulations of the Army. I might remind you also that you are subject to the penalties of disobeying such rules. Right at the moment we are engaged in a military operation, we are in a combat area and about to enter into action with the enemy. I want to make you aware that disobeying the orders of a superior officer in a situation like this brings a very severe penalty."

I studied him a minute. "You know, Major, I'm plumb confused. As I see it, I'm obeying them to the letter, orders that I've been given by my superior officer, General Crook. What's more, he's superior to you and I don't see how you can countermand such orders, combat zone or not."

With that the major said, "You damn fool. I can put you under arrest right now and take those orders away from you. Don't you see that? Now, why don't you hand them to me?"

"Major, you can call in a squad to arrest me, but don't try it. I'm a dead shot and the fastest gun you've ever seen. I'm here to deliver this message to General Terry and no one else. That's by orders of my superior officer, General Crook, and I might remind you, by God, that he's also your superior."

Smith stood there just getting red in the face, boiling mad, sputtering, but he didn't see no way out. He was facing a dead gun and he knew it! It wouldn't do him no good to get himself killed. It was hard for him to bring himself under control, but he was just about there, when in the cabin door Bouyer came. He said, "Come on, Brules, Custer wants you and Lieutenant Varnum. He sent me back to get you. Come on, we've got you a good horse, come on right now."

"I can't do that, Mitch," I explained. "I gotta stay here and give General Terry the message from General Crook, and I ain't giving it to someone else."

"Oh, come on, Brules," Mitch said, "you don't know the way of the Army. Giving a message to the officer's adjutant is the same as giving it to Terry. That's technical—them's the rules. The adjutant is just trying to get you to do the right thing."

"The man's a damn fool," yelled the adjutant.

Mitch Bouyer turned to him and held his hand up. "Now, just a minute, let me handle this. Brules is a hell of a fine scout and an absolute dead shot. If anything, he is probably the best shot in the whole West. He doesn't understand about Army regulations and is only trying to do what's right. Why don't you let me talk to him for a minute?"

"Mitch, I'll do almost anything you say, but I don't understand this. I was told to deliver the message to General Terry in person, and I don't see how anyone else constitutes General Terry."

Mitch took me by the arm and said, "Now, listen, son, just take it easy. I'll tell you again, if you present a message from another officer to a senior officer's adjutant, it is, in fact, delivering it to him. You've accomplished your mission, you've done damn well. Now, why don't you just hand over the papers and quit all this fussing? I've been scouting for these people for years, and I know what seems impossible to outsiders and doesn't make much sense is all right with the Army. This is the Army way. Now, you do it, and come along with me."

The advice coming from a man of Mitch Bouyer's fame and standing, boy, it was hard for me to argue. He seemed to be talking sense, so I finally said, "Well, Mitch, probably no man in the world could talk me out of this except you. I've got such respect for you and I don't think that you'd run me the wrong way—I guess I can do that."

I turned to the adjutant. "It seems like I'm disobeying General Crook's orders, but if Mitch Bouyer says that I ought to give this to you, by God, I'm gonna do it." I undid my buckskin shirt so I could get at the oilcloth strapped around my waist. I took the message out and handed it to Smith.

He didn't open it up at that time, but said to Bouyer, "Thank you, Mitch, for putting some sense in this scout's head. Let's just let the whole thing go. Don't get yourself in trouble again, Brules. The Army doesn't work very well that way."

Well, I was mad enough to chop his head off right there, but I just swallowed it and said, "Well, if it wasn't for Mitch Bouyer you wouldn't a had a chance of getting this. You got it now. You better damn well see that the general gets it."

All the adjutant did was to go "Hump."

Mitch said, "Where is General Terry right now?"

"He's standing right over there on that knoll, reviewing all the troops that are passing by, and talking with Gibbon about some business," Smith answered.

We stood there for a while watching and waiting for the conference group to break up. Finally Mitch said to me, "Goddammit, come on. He'll give the message to Terry later on. Let's get you a good horse."

Well, I was real interested in a good horse, so we done just that and went down to where they had a bunch of ponies corralled near the pack train. Mostly they was a pretty sorry bunch of animals, I thought. Finally I found a gray stallion that looked like he might be all right. He was powerful as hell, with a nose like a Goddamn gallows tree, but he looked like a big, strong animal, and I thought he was probably about the best I was gonna get.

I led him off with a lead rope and halter, just put my hand up on his withers, took ahold of his mane, vaulted up on top of him, and rode him around bareback for a minute. He seemed all right and I slid off him, and checked his teeth and feet. I run my hands over the muscles in his legs, which were pretty impressive.

"You'll need a saddle. I'll get you a McClellan." Mitch called to one of his packers, who come running over with it and a blanket. He threw that on the horse, cinched him up, got a bridle and bit, and adjusted it to get a smile on his lips just right so it wouldn't pull him too hard. I was ready to go. I led the gray over to where I'd piled my stuff, tied my Winchester and scabbard on, and my bedroll. Hell, I was set.

I begun to feel pretty good and I figured that if I stuck by this Mitch Bouyer, he'd guide me through all the Goddamn red tape and the funny orders and stuff that them pony boys had and we'd be all right.

Then Mitch said, "Come on, Brules, we gotta catch on up with Custer. I know that he's gonna camp about ten miles up the Rosebud, so we better move right along." We kicked on up to a lope and just kept steady on it and followed the trail.

I didn't say nothing. Didn't even look the adjutant's way when I left as I hoped I would never see the son of a bitch again, but I thought about it a little bit and it wasn't no use in letting guys like that bother me none. I'd done the best I could and I'd had the best advice from the best guide in the West and I reckoned I was all right.

6

The Rosebud
and the Crow's Nest

On the way to Custer's camp Mitch told me a little more about Lieutenant Varnum, Custer's chief of scouts. He was a different breed of cat. He was a man that brought his West Point training into the Old West. I told Bouyer I didn't think I could hold still for much of that drilling or marching stuff.

Bouyer just laughed. "Well, if you handle yourself right, you won't have to do any, because he's gonna see you're a white man and a scout," he said. "He knows that the scouts got brains of their own and know as much as the officers, and maybe a damn sight more, about the West. He won't try to push you on that, but he always thinks them Indians need to kinda toe the mark and straighten up a little. It's pretty hard work for these West Pointers to look at the Indians, naked jaybirds as they is, and believe that they really could make any kind of soldier. To be real honest with you, if they do get kinda fidgety and decide that it's every man for himself, they're gonna take off like they've done all their lives. That starts a stampede, and once men get to running, white men or Indians, they scare the shit out of themselves. They just keep going, and then the attacker gets more fierce.

"Anyway, just take Varnum at his face value," Bouyer went on, "give him room. I won't let him push you around any."

When I met Varnum, it was better than I thought it would

be. He was mostly pleasant—took a look at me and seemed to give an eye of approval. Mitch helped a little bit by saying, "Lieutenant, you might know big Bapt Pourier."

"Indeed I do. A fine man, and a fine scout." Varnum nodded.

"Well, he's a good friend of Brules here and told me something about him," Bouyer said. "Pourier claimed that Brules was the best shot in the West. Said he never saw such shooting in his life."

"Best shot in the West?" Varnum said, kinda mocking-like. "Well, I'm glad to hear it, and hope it's true. Brules, we welcome you aboard. Obviously, you're a good man, and I need good men. I want you to stick close to me. You look out after me and I'll look out after you."

You know, I kinda liked that. I thought, that fellow has got some sense. Just as long as he doesn't start pulling any of that West Point stuff on me, I'll be all right with this man.

That night Mitch and I set our bedrolls beside the fire and went over to the chuck wagons to get our grub. On the way back he started talking to me again.

"I want to tell you, this is gonna be a tough damn campaign."

"Well, why's that?" I asked. "Rough country or something?"

"No," he said. "The country is not rough, not near as tough as some of the Lolo Trail stuff in the Bitterroots. No, this is good open country, and there's a lot of good defensive positions in it. What these officers don't seem to understand is that there is a damn sight more Indians out here than they think there is. Just 'cause they haven't seen them and counted them exactly, doesn't mean that they aren't here.

"Their experience with Indians is that the Indians is always gonna run. You know, that's just about true, 'cause in no time in the history of Indian warfare, that I know of, have the Indians ever stood up to a cavalry charge. They always break and run, and that's what these fellows count on.

"These troops can go up against an Indian cavalry and infantry force as big as they are and whip them easy—maybe with a few casualties. They can go up against a force maybe even twice as big, and beat them after a hard fight. Spook some of them and get them running, and the rest of them will go. But, by God, the Army can't fight four or five times their number.

"Just to show you how plumb difficult this situation gets, let me tell you a little about what's been happening. You know, there is supposed to be a three-prong attack in this campaign— Gibbon had come down from Fort Ellis, near Bozeman, Custer and Terry had come across the open prairie into this river country. They're supposed to keep the Indians from going north. They don't want them going up to Canada where they can't follow them.

"Crook's coming up from the south, as you know, with a bunch of troops, and they are supposed to meet somewhere up here at the headwaters of the Powder or the Tongue or the Big Horn or something. The plan is they are gonna squeeze these Indians all in here. That's a fine idea, only damn trouble is they don't know where the hell the Indians are."

"Yes," I said, "Crook told me something like that."

"Well, then, you know that much," Bouyer said, "but let me give you an example how damn far off we've been. When this expedition first struck the Yellowstone and started up that country on the left bank, still a ways to come to the Powder, old Terry had to make a decision right there. Was he going on past the mouth of that river or look for Indians up the Powder? He was pretty damn well convinced that there'd been Indians at the Powder or the Tongue. He thought the Rosebud was a bad bet. He sent a party out with Major Reno to see if they were up the Powder or the Tongue. I was just supposed to guide 'em.

"Anyway, I knew Goddamn well that concentration of Sioux was not in either of those valleys but in the Valley of the Rosebud, a bit to the west, 'cause I'd seen the smoke from the villages. Now, I didn't expect for one damn minute that those villages would still be there. That ain't the way of the Sioux. Them nomad people keep moving all the time, and there wasn't any way they would keep on being at that place, but at least I'd have a chance to show Reno what the hell it was about. If I could show him some traces of them big villages, at least these guys would be on the track and understand where the Sioux had been and maybe where they went. That is, on up the valley of the Rosebud or across the height of land and down into the Little Big Horn Basin.

"I kept pushing Reno to go up and take a look at the Rosebud, cross over to it—it was only about thirty miles more than what we'd covered, but he kept worrying. Maybe he thought it was a violation of his orders, but on the other hand if he come in with the information about those villages, why, then, maybe they wouldn't chew his ass so bad, see?

"Finally he decided to break orders and cross over to the Rosebud. Almost all military campaigns, as far as I can see, are a reconciliation about what's practical and what's been ordered, and I think the real heroes are the guys that work both those things together to the best advantage.

"We started off and climbed the height of land between the Rosebud and the Tongue. Reno knew that one of the reasons he was ordered not to go into the valley of the Rosebud was because Terry didn't want to flush the covey. If there was a bunch of Indians in there, they wanted to surprise-attack them, not let them know we was in the area.

"Reno realized if he spooked the camp and they got the hell out of the country, why, then he would be up for court-martial for sure, 'cause he disobeyed orders. But if he found the camp, or found traces of it, and didn't spook nothing he'd probably be forgiven, maybe get a medal or something.

"Anyway, he got up his guts and did it. We crossed over with the troops, and when we hit the Rosebud, we turned west and rode ten miles up the river to one of these big campsites and counted the tepee rings.

"Well, I kinda helped him on that. I found three places where there was a big trail and traces of three villages, but he thought it was all the same village, of course. He was sure they was the same bunch of Indians that had just moved a short distance and camped again.

"Then Reno decided he better get on back. His grub was

getting short, the horses and mules was getting footsore, and the men were pretty wore out. We had traveled damn near two hundred and sixty miles all told.

"Well, Terry was real furious at first, about Reno disobeying orders. But I reckoned that Terry's anger at Reno was somewhat tempered when he learned the important information about the Sioux headin' up the Rosebud. That saved him from making a damn fool mistake and wasting the whole summer going up the wrong rivers. Hell, we could have told him the same thing a month before—if anyone would have listened.

"I'm telling you, Brules, there's two things that they still didn't understand. We usually figured two warriors to the tepee, so if they found five hundred tepees, they was up against a thousand men, which they could handle easy. That isn't exactly what the case was, and as we go on up the Rosebud now I'm gonna show you what was evident, but what Reno didn't see the whole time."

Then I done asked Bouyer, "Why in hell didn't you tell them?"

"I don't tell them anything until they ask me," Bouyer said. "That's the military way. It stuck out a mile that the Sioux knew all about this expedition coming up the Yellowstone. How in the hell could you hide it? You got twelve hundred men coming up the river, you got six hundred men coming down the river with Gibbon, you got a damn steamship honking and blowing and puffing up the river. Jesus, the Indians knew what the hell was going on. Yet they weren't spooked, they weren't running away, and why weren't they? Well, because there was a damn sight more Indians than these people understood, and they felt safe in their strength and wouldn't run.

"What Reno didn't notice was old trails covered over with new ones, and the one village site that seemed to be moved a short distance, every few days, was really several villages leapfroggin' one another. That means that there is two or three times the number of tepees and the number of Indians in the whole thing than they figured on. I reckon that there is anywhere from twelve to fifteen thousand Indians all gathering around Sitting Bull. That means anywhere from twenty-five to thirty-five hundred warriors. Maybe the tribal circles are separated now by five or six miles each, but he can call them all together and they know their own strength, or they'd be disturbed as hell about an outfit like this cavalry expedition coming into the country.''

Bouyer didn't say nothing more for a while. He was plumb worried that the commanding officers of this whole campaign had no notion of how many Indians they was up against. I was the fellow that could back that up, because that's the thing that surprised the hell out of Crook. But it was hard to credit that many Indians.

Later that evening Bouyer began to talk again. ''This fellow Sitting Bull is a great medicine man. He's not a fighting Indian, not a warrior, but he's a damn good medicine man, and they believe in him. He's like a prophet and he's told them that now is the real time to fight—that *now* is their last time to fight. He's got some allies—as well as a good many of the tribal circles of the Sioux.''

''What circles has he got here, do you think?'' I asked Bouyer.

''He's got Hunkpapa, Oglala, Miniconjou, Santee, Sans Arc, Teton, and two to three others, plus the fact that he's got damn near the whole kit and caboodle of the tribal circles of the Cheyennes—the northern Cheyenne, that is. Them southern Cheyennes are way down in Oklahoma in Indian Territory now. They aren't any part of this fighting-Indian stuff anymore. The northern Cheyenne are tough people and able. On top of that he's got the Arapahoes.''

''What's the Arapahoes like?''

''Well, they're a different tribe from any others, not a big tribe, but they're fighters and they've thrown their hat in the ring with the Sioux.''

''Then what you mean is, this whole league of Indians is all gathered together to make a last stand and give the white man a bad time.''

''That's exactly what I mean.'' He nodded. ''The problem is, our commanders think they're chasing a small bunch of

Indians that are going to skedaddle the minute they get close to them. They're afraid that when they come up on them, they'll run off and there won't be a battle and nobody will have the glory. That's not gonna be the case.

"These Sioux are not gonna budge. They are in very great strength. There's whole bunches of them coming from the agencies. Where the ones that have wintered out here was maybe in small numbers of four or five thousand and wandering around, living off the buffalo, the rest of them was back on the reservation drawing their rations.

"Now, Sitting Bull's got so big that, by God, they're starting to pay attention to him. He's had real good success in getting everybody together and he's kinda a dreamer. These tribes have been pouring out of the agencies, the Chimney Rock, the Red Cloud, and all the others."

"Well, Chief Red Cloud ain't here, is he?" I asked.

He said, "No, no, he's an old man now and he hit his glory about twenty years ago when he knocked hell out of all the whites coming across the Overland Trail, but his son is one of them that's here. There ain't nobody that's really got command of these savages, but the Sioux are under Sitting Bull's influence and he's giving them the go-ahead. Of course, those Indian agents down on those reservations don't know how many Indians are there or how many are gone. It's a hell of a big reservation and they can't count 'em. The warriors get together and slip off during the night and nobody says anything. It's an old Indian deal, just like them Comanches. You know how that works, Brules."

"You're Goddamn right I know, Mitch. Those sons of bitches would go in to the agency all the time and play good—real good Indians and all that—so they could draw the rations and get straightened out. Three weeks later they'd be out murdering the immigrants, burning the wagon trains, and carrying off the women. Man, you ain't telling me nothing."

Mitch just smiled. "That is just exactly what these redskins been doing. *This* time, though, they're not only doing that kind of thing, but gathering way back in the wild country.

You know, this is the last real wild country in the United States.''

"Yeah, I know that.''

"For seven or eight hundred miles along here, a lot of this country isn't known very well.''

"Well,'' I said, "it's been pretty well known since the Lewis and Clark expedition, I guess.''

"No,'' he said, "Lewis and Clark went up and down the Missouri, and on the way back Clark made a side trip down the Yellowstone, but he didn't stop off much. He didn't explore this backcountry and there is thousands of miles of it nobody really knows—I mean the lay of it. For instance, Clark never knew the first thing about the country south of the Yellowstone. It's a damn cinch that all they saw was some mountains in the distance, and they never did see the Absarokas or any of them.

"The maps our officers have now are the ones that were drawn up by the railroad survey group that I helped guide through this country. They aren't accurate. Lots of times they're just mostly guesswork. The survey team can't do everything. They can't travel through everything, so they've got to just estimate where a lot of this stuff goes, and that, by God, is what they done.

"All this is big country and wild country and the Indians know it well. They know where to hide. You got to admit they're pretty damn sharp when they can hide a gathering of some fifteen thousand of them, which I reckon there are.''

"I agree!'' I said.

"Yeah, I reckon there's at least that. The white man has a hell of a time even deciding where they are. While he's chugging up and down the rivers and blowing bugles, these Sioux are just laying back and waiting. As a matter of fact, they're not trying to attack the army at all. I'll guarantee you that they will hit the lonely wagon train or a bunch of trappers. Hell, they killed three hunters or trappers right off Gibbon's camp about a month ago. They'll pick on those guys, but they won't fight a bunch of troops, they're not here to fight. They just want to be left alone, but they'll damn well fight if they're pushed.

"These troops are going in there thinking they're gonna smash the hell out of them. That's what they think they're gonna do. My personal opinion is that they're biting off more than they can chew."

"Mitch, your mother was a Sioux, wasn't she?"

"Yes, she was, still is." He said that with a kinda grin.

And I grinned back at him, and said, "You speak Sioux, then?"

"Well, I certainly do, it was my childhood language."

"Now, your father was French, wasn't he? Do you speak that too?"

"Yeah, my father was a trapper. I don't speak French as fluently as I do Sioux, but I speak it well enough to get along with any of those Hudson Bay guys."

"And you're married to a Crow woman?" I asked.

"Yes, I am." He bristled a little. "She's a damn fine woman in anyone's book."

"Yeah, I bet she is. She wouldn't be married to you if she weren't."

He looked up and grinned. "Uh, what the hell do you want? Here you are being complimentary as hell. It has to be for something. Now, just what do you want to know?"

I laughed and reassured him. "No, it's just curiosity, but how long did it take you to learn the Crow language?"

"I'm not real fluent in it, but I can get along. My wife and I understand one another, which is the most important thing."

"That's sure as hell right," I agreed. "If you're married to a Crow and your mother was Sioux, you must know these Indian ways pretty damn well."

"I'll tell you, Brules, I know them well enough to know that there is a damn big force of Indians out there, and these generals are just kidding themselves if they think that they can handle it with the men they've got. Tell me a little bit more about General Crook. What sort of a fellow is he?"

"Well," I said, "I think he understands more about Indians than these other generals I've seen, which ain't many."

Mitch laughed a little and said, "Well, I think you're about right. At least he has enough sense to be cautious and not get himself sucked into a trap."

Well, we rode up the Rosebud for three more days, seeing heavy trail signs and several village sites that Custer still insisted was one village constantly moving short distances.

On the night of the twenty-fourth of June 1876, about eight o'clock, Lieutenant Varnum rode into camp mad as a wet hen. He'd been sent out on a pointless mission by Custer, and had rode about seventy miles, and that's a hell of a ride.

When he reported in that night, Custer told him that he knew he was too damn tired to do anything else, but he said, "The Crows tell me there is a place about seven miles due south of here that they call the 'Crow's Nest.' It's a high point and from it, they say, you can see all the way down the Rosebud, and at the same time, a long way down the Little Big Horn. This is important. I want a reliable officer to go with the Crows up to the Crow's Nest, and report back to me by courier on what the hell you see. I can't trust these Crow scouts to tell me the truth."

Varnum said, "Well, the officer you are talking about is me. I may be dead tired, but, by God, I'm in charge of the Crow scouts, and I'd be insulted if you decide that you want to use some other officer for this."

I guess Custer kinda liked a guy with that much guts. Anyway, he said, "Well, then, you're in charge. You go ahead and take them, Varnum."

Varnum called the Crows together and some Rees and, of course, Mitch Bouyer and me, and we headed out at nine o'clock for the Crow's Nest.

We had about seven miles to go, and it was kinda hard riding in pitch dark through the trees. We had long since left the Rosebud at Busby Bend where it turned south down to Dead Man's Canyon. Goin' on up a little stream called Sand Creek, we just kept trying to stay out of sight. One thing that Varnum did right was let these guys do some smoking once in a while. He would get down into a hollow where there was a lot of timber around and he would let these fellows go ahead and light up. I think that it was probably all right, 'cause the hills was so steep around there, and the timber so thick, that nobody could see very much.

Well, it was at one of these stops that all of a sudden old Bouyer just took off by himself. Said he was gonna do a little scouting on his own. This seemed kinda strange to me, 'cause what in the hell would he be doing that for in the middle of the night?

After he'd been gone for a little while, I heard a wolf call and then some others answering and calling back and forth like they do. That sure is a beautiful sound. I like it much better than coyotes. Them coyotes yip too much, but a wolf just bays and you can hear it go from the side of one hill to another. They sure sound good. I got to thinking, boy, it was a long time since I'd heard a pack of wolves howling. Then I wondered, where the hell did them wolves come from, 'cause I didn't see no wolf tracks all the way up the Rosebud. I'd been looking at everything, as I naturally would. I was always readin' sign. I'd seen plenty of deer tracks, coon stuff. Didn't see no bear, but I'd seen some antelope and one thing and another. But, hell, now comes a Goddamn pack of wolves, calling out loud and no tracks anywhere. Still, I reckoned that they come from the other direction or something, I couldn't tell.

Well, we got up and lurched on to the camp at the Crow's Nest. That was a little hollow down in a nice place with timber all around, and just back of it to the south was a grassy knoll, raised about three hundred feet. From there you could see over the tops of the trees and anywhere you wanted to look.

Of course, it was pitch black, and we all was ready for some sleep. I was just about to lie down when in come Mitch Bouyer. Goddamn if he wasn't a shock to see, 'cause he was wearing a vest. He hadn't been wearing no vest when he left, and this one was a beautiful Sioux vest, all beaded. God, it was a good-looking thing.

"Well," I asked him, "where in the hell did you get that?"

"Oh, I found it down in the bottom of the hollow there,

and thought it was too good of a thing to leave. Hoped it might bring me good luck. So I slipped it on and come on up here.''

Two of them Crow scouts said that they was going on up beyond the grassy knoll, which was just back of us, to some peaks about a mile away where it was even higher so they maybe could see better. Anyway, come the break of dawn, we clawed our way up on the knoll and started looking around. It hadn't been five minutes after daylight when them Crows come running in.

Them peaks of the Wolf Mountains was about a mile to the south of us and I reckon about five hundred feet higher. So they coulda given the Crows a little better view, but actually they couldn't see much more than we could. As they'd come down they was jabbering away, saying they'd seen a campfire and some white horses on the hills, on the other side of the Little Big Horn.

After Varnum, who had sore eyes from his long, dusty ride of the day before, said he couldn't see them, Lonesome Charley Reynolds, who had been with us all along, took one look in the distance and then got out his field glasses and looked and nodded. That's all you're gonna get out of Lonesome Charley. He never says a word. Strangest man you ever seen. I don't know if anybody ever heard him say anything. They said it was on account of some damn woman down in Santa Fe or south of the border, I don't know, he sure was a strange duck. But he was one hell of a scout, and when he nodded—that was it.

I took another look, and I could just make out a very faint blue cloud that the Crows was looking at. They kept telling Varnum when they was looking at the hills where the horse herd was, there wasn't no way to see the wigwams, the lodges of the Sioux, there, 'cause they was behind the bluff. But you could sure as hell see the pony herd, and it was big.

It was awful hard to see individual horses at that distance, maybe twelve mile away. By God, what you could see was the white specks. The Crows kept telling Varnum, "Look for worms, look for worms," 'cause a bunch of horses moving kinda looked like worms on the side of the hill. Varnum had been watching Charley Reynolds close, and he'd been watching the other scouts, Hairy Moccasins, White Man Runs Him, and them fellows, and there was no doubt in his mind. Then he asked Mitch Bouyer and Mitch nodded, and he turned to me and I said, "Hell, I can see the horse herd on the hills, the west side of the Big Horn."

With that Varnum decided he had better notify Custer. He told Charley Reynolds to write out a message to Custer, which Crooked Horn and a couple of the other Ree scouts were to take back to him.

From the Crow's Nest the Ree scouts could see Custer's own camp position about seven miles away, and they knew they had to ride them miles in a hurry. They was off in a cloud of dust.

Standing there I couldn't help comparing them Rees with the Crows. The Crows was big handsome fellows and had plenty of guts and was jovial kinda guys, but them Rees was funny little squirts that was a much darker color, dirty and scroungy, looking half starved. They was all for battle and bravery until they got anywhere near the Sioux. Now that we'd found the Sioux camp, they began to get all upset and scared plumb to death. Jesus, they started singing their death songs. Boy, Varnum stopped them from doing that in a hurry. He said, "You sons of bitches shut up and stop weeping and wailing. You're a long ways from getting in a fight with the Sioux. Wait till you're dead, then you can bawl all you want."

Crooked Horn's Rees party left our Crow's Nest about five in the morning, when it was plenty light. Meanwhile all of our scouts had been up on the grassy knoll watching for the signs of the village and waiting for Custer. They looked over just to the north and saw, on the other side of Walker Creek up on the ridge, two different groups of horsemen, about half an hour apart. One of them was a man leading a pony and a boy riding behind him—Indians, looking like Sioux. The other was several horsemen above the column that was coming up Davis Creek. They started riding over in the direction of the Sioux village, and both Bouyer and the Crows decided they ought to ride over and cut them off.

The Crows, Mitch, and I started down off the knoll through the hollow and run into the roughest country I think I'd seen. We were floundering along and got off our horses and started climbing on foot to get around. It was obvious that we weren't getting anywhere. It was tough country and by the time we got into a position where we could see anything, let alone cut off any of those Sioux, they had disappeared. Varnum had the Crow scouts spread out on this crazy kind of side trip just to get the coverage.

The damnedest thing happened when we were down in the bottom of one of these ravines. The Crows started making noises like crows—like the birds call—"caw, caw." Mitch Bouyer sat there and listened very quiet. I don't remember if he called back or not. Finally Varnum asks, "What in the hell are they talking about?"

"I don't know," Bouyer said. "I just don't know."

It seemed funny that they would be doing those crow calls then. Anyway, we all got back to the Crow's Nest in time to meet Custer as he come in.

When Custer arrived, he went right away up to where he could get a good look at the Little Big Horn, but by that time the warmth and haze had come up—it being close to ten o'clock in the morning. The haze obscured whatever view there was, so Custer couldn't see nothing. After he studied it with field glasses, he said, "Well, hell, I've got as good a pair of eyes as any of you and I don't see a Sioux camp at all."

None of the rest of us could see it by then either. It wouldn't do any good to try to tell him anything, because he was dead set on the idea that there wasn't a village there at all. Or if there was, it was a small one, maybe three to four hundred tepees, and might contain five to seven hundred warriors, which would be no problem to him.

Custer had the habit of trusting only certain people, and one of the men he trusted and was fond of was the Ree scout Bloody Knife. Course, Bloody Knife hadn't been up there looking in the early-morning hours when the air was clear.

There was a wealth of knowledge available from the Crows. They were all familiar with these Wolf Mountains and with the layout of the Rosebud and Little Big Horn. Since Custer couldn't speak Crow, he used Bouyer as his interpreter.

Bouyer was not only the most educated man on the whole expedition, speaking Crow, French, Sioux, and English, but he was also the most informed. He'd been the first one to spot camps in the Rosebud Valley. What's more, he could read sign better than most people, and he knew this country quite well. Custer thought of himself as quite a sign reader, but even he had the sense to know that he couldn't analyze a trail like the Indians nor a half-breed like Mitch Bouyer.

Anyway, some reason, and I couldn't fathom why, Custer had taken a dislike to Mitch, though everybody else liked him to beat hell. Bouyer seemed to have his reservations about Custer too. It would have been a hell of a big help to Custer, if Custer had listened to Bouyer, but recently when those two got together it was like striking flint on steel. The sparks really flew.

I could see Custer, Bouyer, and some of the scouts standing around talking. I was too far away to hear what was said, but I could tell that some tempers were flaring. It was obvious that those two men were arguing to beat hell. At one point there they both stomped and looked at each other and, by God, I thought they was gonna draw their guns.

Later, I questioned some of the Crow scouts who could speak a little English. There was two of them and they each had different versions. One of them said that Bouyer told Custer, "There are more Indians in that village than you have ammunition, General."

The other one heard Bouyer say, "General, if you don't see more Indians in that village than you ever saw in your life, well, then, you can hang me."

Custer was reported to have said, "Well, that would be a damn good thing to hang you, wouldn't it?"

Somebody else told us, in pretty broken language, that it sounded like Custer said to Bouyer, "You're talking like a Goddamn Sioux."

"Well, I am a Sioux," Bouyer reminded him.

Then Custer said something like "Well, if you're a Sioux, what the hell are you doing in this area? Get the hell out."

"I don't need to get out of here any more than you," Bouyer snapped. "In the first place, this is our land—Sioux and Crow land—and I'm part of each tribe. I have more right to be here than you have, General."

Whether those things were true or not, I don't know, but I could see Custer was frustrated. He just turned and walked away. Then he vaulted up on Vic, his favorite horse, and rode off in a huff. But, by God, Mitch Bouyer mounted up and rode off after him—and so did the rest of us scouts.

Custer give the orders for us to move down and join the column. On the way, damn if we didn't run into his kid brother, Tom Custer, and Lieutenant Calhoun, coming out to meet us. It turned out that Captain Yates of Company F had lost a box of hardtack that fell off a mule on the trail from Busby Bend. Yates had ordered his Sergeant Curtis to take the squad and go back down the trail to recover the load. When Curtis got back there with his squad, he found Indians working on the hardtack box. Curtis fired on the Indians and drove them off, but now the Indians knew from the tracks on the trail that Custer's whole cavalry detachment was on the way to hit the village.

Later, we learned that this bunch of Indians was Cheyennes under Chief Little Wolf, who had left the Red Cloud Agency to join the hostile camp. They'd come on the trail of the Seventh Cavalry and followed it up to this point. After being shot at they scattered, circled to the north, and proceeded on to the big village of Sitting Bull. The truth of the matter is that they didn't get there in time to alert the village. However, we had been discovered. These Cheyennes were for sure the second bunch of Indians we'd seen who could warn the Sioux camp.

Custer was sore as hell that Calhoun and Tom Custer would leave the column to come and tell him. He chewed them out bad and sent them back in a hurry. I sorta wondered whether he was really as mad at them as all that or whether he was mad at the news that his approach was known. Anyhow, it was right there that Custer set forth on a whole line of plans and activities that led to the disaster.

7

High Noon and
the Height of Land

When we got to the column, the first thing Custer done was signal for Officers' Call, and the bugles began blowing and the officers gathered. He told them they had been discovered by the enemy, and no more precautions should be taken to hide the command. His original plan had been to remain behind the ridge all that day and rest up, then make the attack the following morning, June twenty-sixth. That way the men wouldn't be so tired, and Terry and Gibbon would be in position to attack from the north. Now that they had been discovered there was only one thing to do, and that was to ride as fast as they could and hit the village before it separated and all the Indians run off. That's what Custer feared most. What never seemed to get through his head was what Mitch had been telling him all along—this was one hell of a big camp of Indians, probably the biggest that had ever come together. All along them Indians had known about the expedition coming up the Yellowstone. They knew where Crook was, they already fought him at the Battle of the Rosebud. They knew the total force against them, and they didn't think there was any reason to be upset, because they had a lot more warriors than the whites had. They weren't in a running mood. They had come to the last country of the buffalo—the last place where all the Indians could live the way they had in the past, roaming the plains and working the buffalo for a living.

Sitting Bull had given them the idea that this was where the white man must be stopped. To stop him this camp of Sitting Bull, with some thousand lodges and at least three thousand warriors, had to stand their ground. They was in a fighting mood and there wasn't no running away. So it was that Custer, misreading his information that day, give the fatal command that set the wheels of tragedy in motion. At high noon he led the whole expedition across the height of land from the basin of the Rosebud to the basin of the Little Big Horn, and that sealed his fate. The God of War, I guess, had closed the iron gate behind him.

From that height of land Custer went just one mile before he called a halt. At that time Custer split his command. He still had fourteen miles to go to the river. That was a pretty good ride—even at a trot it's two hours away. But on a hot June day when the men and horses hadn't had water since six o'clock the night before, that wasn't good.

Custer was afraid that some of the Indians would escape to the south, and as a matter of fact Terry had cautioned him about that. So, he gave orders to Captain Benteen, the third officer in command, to take three troops, D, H, and K, a force of one hundred thirty-six men and five officers, and hit out in a southwesterly direction. They were to continue until they struck the Little Big Horn River, making certain there weren't no Indians running away to the south. Benteen was instructed that when he had completed this mission, he was to turn north and pick up the trail of the command and rejoin Custer.

The next thing Custer done was put Major Reno, who was second in command, in charge of three more units, A, G, and M, plus Lieutenant Varnum and his nineteen Indian scouts, a total of one hundred and twelve. He ordered Reno to proceed down the little creek that flowed west and follow it to the Little Big Horn. Then he was to cross the river and attack the Indian village from the south. Meanwhile Custer told the officers he personally would take the remaining five troops, C, E, F, I, and L, a force of two hundred and fourteen men, to back Reno's attack. Just exactly how he was going to do this he didn't make clear, but I kinda think I know what his plan was.

There was still a separate unit of eighty-four men in the pack train, which was ordered to follow Custer's main command. It consisted of all of Troop B under command of Captain MacDougal, plus one other officer, an NCO, and six civilian packers. The pack train carried forty thousand rounds of extra ammunition plus supplies. It was an important element, but with all them mules, it was slower than the second coming of Christ and was always laggin' way behind. If the Indians had only knowed, they could have cut off the whole train, destroyed Custer's supplies, and captured his ammunition.

Well, Benteen headed off, reluctantly, in the southwest direction a few miles toward the Little Big Horn. Then he stopped and sent a lieutenant forward another two or three miles to see what he could find and report back. He did this very wisely to save his command from crawling all around such tough country. Custer and Reno rode on down the small creek that fed into the Little Big Horn River.

Both Reno and Custer's columns came into a marshy stretch of land on the north side of the creek. To me it looked like a good place to water the horses, and I was kinda surprised when neither Custer nor Reno stopped, but they both had plans to water their horses farther on down the line.

After we left the marsh, we come to a flat plain along the creek bottom. It had widened out considerable and there was evidence that a Sioux village of some kind had been there in the recent past. The most surprising thing, by God, was a Sioux lodge, sitting right in the middle of the flat open space and another one nearby that had been wrecked. The first lodge sure was a beautiful thing to see. It was all made of buckskin and had them tepee poles crossed at the top and the wings opened to keep the smoke from any fire made inside going just the right way. It had beautiful paintings on the outside, and I could imagine the Sioux artist that had done all that drawing in such careful ways. I never saw nothing like that in a Comanche camp.

Anyway, as we rode up to it, the scouts opened up the flap wider and there inside, layin' on a scaffold, was the body of a warrior. It looked like he had been shot up. He musta been a casualty at the battle of the Rosebud. That meant all them Sioux raising hell with Crook on the Rosebud had now come down here and joined Sitting Bull.

Now I felt, deep inside, what Mitch Bouyer had been telling all of us—there was one hell of a big village ahead and there was gonna be a terrible battle. I kinda had a different feeling about the Sioux after seeing that. I couldn't help but recall my wife Wild Rose's body that I had hoisted up near the roof of the cabin, so she'd be safe way up there on Lone Cone Peak. The thought of it kinda stabbed me to the heart. Somehow I knew that this Sioux family had been through the same thing, and they'd buried their warrior the best way they could.

They must have broken down all the other tepees and taken them along, leaving that one standing in memory of their loved one. I doubt if they ever thought that the pony soldiers would come on, and a good thing that they didn't.

We hadn't gone more than a hundred fifty to two hundred yards beyond the tepee when I looked back and seen that some son of a bitch had set fire to it. I don't know if it was one of the soldiers or one of the Crows, but it sure seemed kinda useless. The whole thing went up in flames and I reckoned that the warrior's corpse was cremated, maybe just like it had to be in order to free his spirit.

It sure made me think that white man or Indian don't have a hell of a lot of regard for the other fellow's feelings.

We continued on down until we hit a creek that was coming in from the north. When we got there Custer turned and started due north, with his command following him. Major Reno kept on; I guess he figured that he was gonna have to cross the Little Big Horn River, which was not very far away, and he could water his horses then.

When Custer headed north, Mitch Bouyer and me turned to go with him. One of the Crows went with Reno. I believe it was White Swan. All of the Rees went along, too, as did Lonesome Charley Reynolds and Custer's favorite Ree scout, Bloody Knife. They all stuck right close to Reno.

Some of the Crow scouts went with us were Hairy Moccasins, Goes Ahead, and a young Crow named Curly.

Custer rode along the small creek north a ways, stringing his command out properly, and watered their horses. Seemed to me a pretty good move, and give me some confidence Custer might know what the hell he was doing after all.

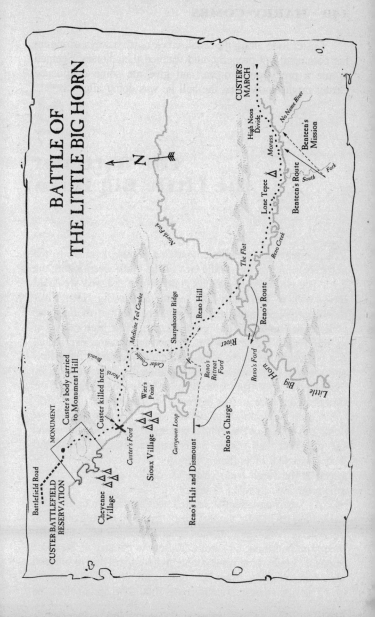

BATTLE OF
THE LITTLE BIG HORN

N

CUSTER'S MARCH

High Noon Divide

No-Name River

Benteen's Mission

Morass

Benteen's Route

Lone Tepee

South Fork

The Flat

Reno Creek

Reno Route

North Fork

Medicine Tail Coulee

Sharpshooter Ridge

Reno Hill

Cedar Coulee

Custer's body carried to Monument Hill

Branch

North

Custer killed here

Wier's Point

Custer's Ford

Garryowen Loop

Sioux Village

Reno's Retreat Ford

River

Reno's Ford

Reno's Route

Little Big Horn

Reno's Charge

Reno's Halt and Dismount

MONUMENT

CUSTER BATTLEFIELD RESERVATION

Battlefield Road

Cheyenne Village

8

The Battle of
the Little Big Horn

After the horses had been watered, Custer kept on to the north, working up the saddle east of the bluffs overlooking the Little Big Horn. When we had gone a short distance, we could look down to the south and see the Little Big Horn River meandering less than half a mile away. At that moment we couldn't see no tepees of the village, 'cause the bluffs ahead of us interfered. The tepees was pitched around the river bend, just outta sight. But sure as hell, we could see across the valley, and see that there was a damn big horse herd on the hills, by the dust that was rising from them. It looked like them Indians was bringing their horses in, maybe to mount up.

Custer kept on climbing for about ten minutes till we come out on top of the saddle, where we could look down and see the south end of the Sioux village. It sure looked big! There was lots of milling going on. We knew Reno was engaged at the south end, 'cause we could hear the firin' right where he was expected to be.

As we progressed, it started to come clear to me that something was really wrong. Like I say, I'm no military man, but when a commander comes up on an enemy force to attack them, the first thing he's gotta find out is the size of the force opposing him, where it's located, and compare that to his own forces and position. Then he's gotta cook up a plan of action.

The first steps, reconnaissance, should be done before the

action plan is made. Because maybe it's not going to be an attack at all. Maybe the plan of action may call for a retreat. If not, you can set up your attack according to the plan that meets the situation. The trouble was, Custer, being in such a damn big hurry, afraid the Sioux was gonna run away, he done the reconnaissance at the same time as the attack, and it sure as hell didn't work.

With Reno heavily engaged already, Custer knew he had to find someplace to hit the village. Maybe the north end, but someplace, and quick, so there would be pressure at both ends of the village. Even then, Custer had no idea how big the village was, and didn't know enough about the terrain to find a place to get down off them big bluffs and attack now!

I think that he was plenty surprised when he found out how far he had to go before he could ford the river. The east side of the river was high bluffs, better than a hundred feet, maybe two hundred feet in some places. There wasn't any way to get troops of cavalry across, so he kept working to the north, downstream, moving as fast as he could without exhausting his horses, until he come to the Medicine Tail Coulee.

The Medicine Tail Coulee is a big ravine that run about a mile and a quarter down to the Little Big Horn. It met the river in the flat area and looked like a good place to ford. Hell, we'd already come three miles down the river from where Reno had crossed. Custer must have seen at this point, if he went clear on down to the north end of the village, it would take too long to get to Reno. He had to cross the river now at this point, which was just in front of him, even if it was only the middle of the village.

Custer still had no idea of what he was getting into, what position he had put Reno in, or what he was going to put his own troops up against within the next few minutes.

Cutting into the Medicine Tail Coulee was a small draw called the Cedar Coulee, that intercepted the Medicine Tail. Custer started down this little draw, but drew his horse to a stop, turned, and said something to Bouyer. Custer let his troop stop and have a breather, but he himself turned west, with Bouyer, the three Crow scouts, and me tagging along. We rode up the steep ridge that led to the bluffs, where we could look north through the gap of the Medicine Tail Coulee and see a stretch of the river a couple of miles off.

It must have been one hell of a shock to Custer, 'cause I know it was to me, when we all looked down that draw and seen the village of the Sioux. It stretched way up to the north—with hundreds of tepees—maybe a mile or better beyond where the Medicine Tail Coulee ran into the Little Big Horn. It was a real shocker! And it was plumb evident we was only looking at a small part of the village. There had been more than three miles of village hidden from our sight by the bluffs!

We could hear Reno's firing, and knew he was in heavy combat. By God, he was still two and a half miles back of us. We had a mile and a quarter to go down the Medicine Tail Coulee and another mile to the end of the villages. It meant that there was four miles of that damn village. It staggered the imagination.

Custer didn't say nothing, but I remember thinking where in the hell did all these goddamn Indians come from? Jesus, I didn't know there was that many on all the Sioux and Cheyenne reservations. They sure must have slipped out without them agents knowing a damn thing about it. And now all we got is a hundred troops under Reno down at the south end trying to get at them. Custer was about to ride down this Medicine Tail Coulee with only two hundred and fourteen men to attack and destroy the whole village.

Custer turned and started back down the hill, kinda grim faced, toward the waiting column. He looked at all of them troopers, dressed in blue, sitting on their horses, looking up anxiously, seeing the commander coming back. They knew that he would be giving them the plan of battle now and that whatever he said was a key to what was gonna happen in the next hour or two. They knew that their lives was gonna be in danger, and whatever decision he made would be a big one. I'm sure Custer knew he was in a lot of trouble, but there weren't no way that he could back out of it now.

Whether he liked it or not he was gonna have to go down

the Medicine Tail Coulee and attack the hostile camp somewhere at about its middle. That wasn't good, but it was better
than nothing. When he got within about fifty yards from where
the troops was all waiting, Custer turned to Bouyer and the
scouts and said something that made me think he was a pretty
decent fellow.

Custer said, "Mitch, you dismiss your scouts, tell them to
go on home. They were hired to find the enemy, which they've
done. They were not hired to fight or to get killed in this battle
that's coming up. That's soldiers' duty, and we're about to go
do it."

Gatherin' himself together he kinda put on his old
Custer's assurance and bravado, an attitude that had carried his
cavalry charges all through the Civil War, each time to a success, and a way of bolstering his troops that never failed. He
pulled his horse up and touched his spurs, just a little to put
him into a prance, and as he jogged along the side of the
column he began to call to the troops, "Custer's luck, boys.
Custer's luck. We caught them sleeping, they're all asleep
down there. Nobody there now. Nobody ready for us. We're
gonna give them hell."

Well, the troops let out a wild cheer, and Custer broke into
a gallop to reach the front end of the column about four hundred yards below. He signaled to advance and the whole outfit
moved out in a quick trot. We watched them go for a while.

Then Bouyer spoke to the Crows, and they all turned and
began riding back up the hill on a kinda angle so they was
looking down on Custer the whole time that he was weaving
down the Medicine Tail Coulee.

Of course, I followed, staying as near Mitch as I could,
which was my custom. Couldn't help thinking that Custer had
to be a pretty fine guy to think that much of his scouts. Lots of
people hated Custer's guts, especially some of his officers,
Benteen and some others. But most of the men thought highly
of him. They always loved a good commander who had a lot of
guts, willing to fight, and willing to lead in the fighting.

Pushing along about as fast as our horses would take us,
we come up on the edge of the bluff, looking straight down on

the Little Big Horn. We could see for miles up and down the river.

I took a deep breath and said, "My God!" Bouyer looked at me quickly and shook his head. The Crows was bug-eyed. Laying out there below us, from way upstream to the south to way down to the Cheyenne villages in the north, there was over a thousand tepees!

God almighty, I'd never seen anything like it. Some folks later called it the "metropolis of the prairies," and damn if it wasn't. There were hundreds and hundreds and hundreds of lodges. The Miniconjou and Oglala to the south. The Santa, Teton, Hunkpapa, northern Cheyenne, and Sans Arc to the north—even a few Arapaho lodges. One tribal circle after another. Incredible, plumb dizzy making.

You know, that medicine man, Sitting Bull, must have had a hell of a lot of spirit power over them Indians, because they was sure answering in great quantities when they heard his call. I don't reckon any Indian leader in the history of the country had ever put a force together like that. It wasn't no wonder that they didn't give a damn where Gibbon, Terry, Custer, Crook, and the rest of them guys were coming up to get them. There was enough of them to just plumb choke them to death. I was so stunned that I couldn't speak.

At that moment the three of the Crows did something that I couldn't believe. They started shooting at the village with those .45-70's they had. Just three or four shots, kinda as if they was firing in defiance at an enemy camp that they couldn't do nothing about. Strangely enough, Mitch Bouyer joined them. He fired a couple of shots and then took off his hat and waved and waved, as if he was swearing at them and telling them to get the hell out of there.

I wondered if them fellows was trying to scare off the Sioux. That seemed plumb impossible, yet I couldn't figure out what in hell they was doing. It didn't seem right to me. Those cavalry carbines wouldn't carry that far. It was useless shooting. For a minute or two after that there was a kinda silence, except for the soft murmur of the river three or four hundred feet below us.

Then we heard a voice calling. Some voice out of the Sioux camp. It was the voice of a warrior, with heavy lungs, and he kept repeating something all the time. Kept repeating, "Wica-nonpa," again and again, and I seen that the Crows didn't understand what the Sioux was saying. They was asking Bouyer what that fellow was talking about. When I asked Bouyer, he turned to me and explained in English, "That's someone calling to tell me to go back."

"Telling you to go back? What the hell does he mean?"

"Well, he's just telling me, he's calling me by my Sioux name."

I said, "Your Sioux name, what's that?"

He said, "It's Wica-nonpa! Two Mans."

And of course, right away quick I could see what it meant. That he was half white and half Indian. Maybe that was another way of saying "half-breed"—and that he was two kinds of men.

I said, "Well, are they trying to ask you to make a retreat here?"

He said, "No, they are not asking me to retreat. They're not asking me to make the troops retreat. They know that I can't do that, but they are telling me to get out before I get hurt."

I thought about it and reckoned that them Sioux had it in for Mitch. It would go hard for him if they ever caught him alive. There he was, born of a Sioux mother, and now he come leading all these damn pony soldiers in to shoot up the village and kill their women and children. Hell, yes, they'd be ticked off with him and tell him to get the hell out of there. Mitch spoke to the Crows. I didn't understand what he said exactly because I couldn't speak Crow, but when I asked him a few minutes later he said, "I told them to go on home. To turn and go back to their village on Pryor Creek."

"Yeah," I said, "what did they say?"

"Oh, they said a lot of stuff."

"What do you mean, a lot of stuff?"

"Well, they just said that they ain't goin' 'less I go with

'em. They tried to make me go, they tried to get me sentimental and all.''

"What do you mean sentimental?''

He paused a minute and said, "They say Magpie Outside is waiting for me in my tepee on the Stillwater, and it is safe in the Crow villages.''

"Magpie Outside? What the hell are you talking about?'' I asked.

"That is the name of my woman. That is the name of my Crow squaw.''

I wasn't too sure if what I was looking at was right or not, but it seemed like maybe his eyes were getting a little watery, misty, maybe.

Anyway he turned and talked to the Crows for a few minutes, and it was a pretty heated argument. They kept taking ahold of his arm and pulling on him and doing all kinds of talking and jabbering and all. He said, "Brules, I'm mighty glad to have met you, you are a fine man. Someday I hope that we'll get together again and we'll do some hunting.''

"Mitch, what the hell, these guys are right,'' I said. "If they want to get you to go back, why don't you go back with them? What's the matter?''

He shook his head, and sighed. "I can't. I just can't.''

And then, I'll be damned if he didn't mount and turn his horse around, and start down the hill as fast as he could, making a kinda diagonal run off the hill to try to catch up with Custer. I stood there plumb amazed and so did the Crows. As we watched him go, them Crows was the saddest-looking men I ever saw. I don't know if they was bawling, but they was doing the next thing to it. I guess they sure loved old Mitch. Any man in his right mind had to know that it was gonna take a lot of luck to get through a battle with a village as big as this and come out with your whole hide.

As we stood there on that ledge and watched, I saw and I heard something awful. Way down at the south end of the village where Reno had been fighting, we could see that Reno's line had long since gone. I could hear some roaring that appeared to be about due south of us and out of sight, around some lower bluffs that was between us and the ford where Reno had crossed. But the roar increased, and it got louder and I couldn't figure out what in hell was happening. Then we heard a lot of firing along the south end of this ridge up close to the water. I guessed that's where Reno must have retreated to, somewhere toward the river, upstream about two miles to the south. The firing had died down now and all that I could hear was a roar. Out of it come howls, yells, and screams, and Indian battle cries.

I thought, God, they're making mincemeat out of Reno. He only had one hundred and twelve men, plus them Ree scouts that were useless as tits on a boar. By God, the howling that was going on plumb scared me to death—I realized that it was getting closer all the time, and I didn't quite understand.

As it developed into a steady roar, I began to see what it was. Through the open patches in the timber I could make out flashes of galloping Sioux, coming downstream as fast as they could ride, headed for the Medicine Tail Coulee. It appeared like they'd ended their fight with Reno, 'cause he was nowhere in sight, and I reckoned that he'd been driven back across the river. But anybody could see that the Sioux had got the message that a bunch of cavalry was coming down the Medicine Tail Coulee, and the Indians was coming along the river to meet them.

When I realized this, I jumped up on my horse and cut out northeast, going down the hill real fast to where I could see what was going on.

First thing I seen was Custer's column was halted, still in the long line. Bouyer had caught up with him and was riding on his left side. It looked like the front of the column had reached the ford, the rear of it being maybe about four hundred yards back, and had stopped to wait for orders. Looking way downstream toward the Cheyenne camp I saw no warriors of any kind. I didn't see no activity. I figured that maybe after Reno attacked, word had gone down fast through the camp and all the squaws had left, but I didn't see no warriors so I reckoned that they was all at the south end.

That's what Custer seen and thought the camp was asleep.

I reckon that he paused down at the bottom of Medicine Tail Coulee just before he crossed the ford because he didn't want to walk into a Sioux trap. Them Sioux was real good at that kind of stuff and I know Custer didn't want another Fetterman massacre.

I started using my field glasses on the Cheyenne camp and the Sans Arc camp, which was right next to them, and I seen maybe three or four warriors, that was all. Three of them was on foot running and one was on a horse. Seemed like one was old. I couldn't tell, but he wasn't moving very fast and they were coming toward the Medicine Tail Coulee. Suddenly, they reached a low ridge about one hundred yards from the ford, threw themselves behind it, raised their rifles, and began shooting. I was pretty sure they weren't gonna keep doing that, 'cause there was only five of them, and no five men is gonna stand up to two hundred and twenty soldiers.

I figured that Custer maybe had stopped at the edge to make sure that it was a good place to cross. After all, there was gonna be over two hundred men and horses following him. Then all of a sudden I seen them front riders start to move, and I knew that Custer was starting to cross the creek. They disappeared from sight around the shoulder of the north end of the bluff. I moved real quick to the east, high up on the hill, to see what was going on.

When I got high enough, I saw a sight that just plumb made me sick to my stomach. Right out in the middle of the river was a group of horses without riders, and I could see the riders standin' in the water. Couldn't tell if Custer was one of the ones that was down off his horse. I just couldn't see his horse, but I couldn't see him, either, so I suspected that maybe he was part of it.

Then I seen three or four troopers was leaning down in the water, picking something up. They raised an officer who had been hit, and I seen them trying to load him on a horse as if he was wounded. Then it struck me. My God, that wounded or killed man had to be Custer.

If there was that many troopers gathered around a fallen comrade, it had to be the commander. A single trooper of ordinary rank would not get that much attention. The commander was surrounded by his staff, and his staff was digging him out of the problem.

They put him over the back of his horse with troopers holding him on each side and brought him up on the bank again. They gathered together. There must have been some kind of shouting and orders given, but I could hear nothing about that. They was at least five hundred yards from me.

Then I seen that the attempted crossing was over, and the military initiative of a charge was lost. The staff, with Custer thrown over his horse, started down the river a little bit. A shouted command had come up along the columns, and I saw them all turn by the right flank. That put them in a long line abreast, working up the hill toward the northeast. It was an order that had to end in a defense position—with 'em all strung out in a line when they reached the top of the ridge to the east.

My heart sank because I realized there wouldn't be no charge into that village. Only Custer would have done that, and undoubtedly them fellows down there, even above the rush of the water, could hear with horror the roaring of them coming Sioux.

With their leader gone there was nobody to give the troops the spirit. They probably didn't know who was now in command of the cavalry. The officers next in command were Reno or Benteen, but they was miles away. Who was gonna be leading? Whoever it was, he was too far back up the line of troopers, back up the Medicine Tail Coulee train, to see what was happening and to know what to do. The only guys near Custer was his adjutant and some staff types. How in the hell were they gonna command a charge? What they was thinking about was to get Custer, the great hero, the great wonder, leader of everything, onto his horse and get him the hell out of there. The whole fire and light of the campaign had gone out—right there.

As I said, the whole column of two hundred men turned on their right flank and started up the hill toward the northeast, crossing to the north of the Medicine Tail Coulee, trying to reach the ridge maybe half a mile away.

The group carrying Custer was moving up the hill toward what looked like the highest point of land on the north end of that ridge. A couple of times they'd get out of sight, disappearing for a minute or two, and afterward I seen that they'd been down in a deep ravine they had to cross. I jumped back on my horse and started south up the hill a little bit so I could see better.

I stayed there and watched the whole ragged line wandering, hopeless-like without a leader, going up that hill, as the roar of thousands of warriors, coming to defend the village, was getting closer. It was like some great big beast yelling.

Right away quick I seen a bunch of them Sioux warriors crossing the river at the Medicine Tail Coulee from the west to the east—the same crossing that Custer was gonna make the other way, but didn't quite do it.

The troops was two or three hundred yards from the river when the Sioux arrived. Riding at the head of the Indians, with a complete war bonnet, was Gall, chief of the Oglalas. He rode splashing hard across the ford and up that hill. There must have been two thousand savages following him. That broken line of troopers, only about two hundred men, looked awful ridiculous. They couldn't keep on retreating and there wasn't no way they could gather themselves for a charge, so somebody gave the order to dismount. From what I could see of the command, it was a headless monster. There was no order or system to it at all—just panic.

I never heard such a sound as the roaring of them two thousand Indians coming up that hill. I thought that I better start withdrawing now—in the excitement they didn't see me back here, but they'd spot me after a while and it didn't make no difference how good a shot I was, there was too damn many of 'em. I felt kinda like Bouyer when he done told Custer, "There's more damn Indians down there than you got ammunition."

Standing there with nothing but a lever-action Winchester and a .38 revolver, I'd have to be plumb stupid to get involved.

So I wasn't a damn bit ashamed about retreating. I knew that it was what you had to do sometimes, and also knew that I had plenty of guts when it come to any kind of a decent combat, even when the odds was stacked against me. But in this case it wouldn't be practical.

I kinda watched the battle over my left shoulder as I trotted back across the ridge where the Crow scouts had gone. From that height, when I finally got about a mile and a half away, I heard the troops trying to fire volleys, the roaring, shouting, and the Indians riding all around them. It seemed like some of them fellows had taken Custer up to the highest point—which, incidentally, got named Custer's Stand. Those troopers was all gathered around there doing their damnedest. They finally settled down and done some steady, controlled firing and stopped the charge.

I'll say this, they'd done some pretty good fighting. For a few minutes there it looked like they might just, by luck and the grace of God, hold them Indians in a kinda siege which was gonna last as long as them boys had ammunition.

Unfortunately, right in the middle of all that fighting, I seen a terrible thing happen. The horse holders was a little bit back of the troops in front of a ravine, and damn if some of them Indians didn't circle around, charge in there, and spook those horses. Must have killed the horse holders, but the worst part about it was the ammunition packs was in the saddlebags on them horses. Of course, Indians always go for horses anyway, and the cavalry horses was usually a lot better than their ponies, so there was a bunch that went after them, figuring they would be a big prize, which indeed they was.

The fighting was getting more and more sporadic with the loss of ammunition, while the cavalry was slowly falling back toward the top of the hill where them boys had dragged Custer. The circle was closing in, and then, by God, there was a hell of a lot of whooping and hollering. From the north side, clear around back of the troops, there come three or four hundred warriors. The one that was leading them was stark-ass naked, it looked to me.

I learned later that it was Crazy Horse, and, my God, he

rode right over the top of Custer's men and that was the end. It just seemed all the Indians was doing was riding around shooting at guys on the ground, the wounded, and the fellows trying to crawl away.

One or two troopers had started off, riding like hell, but they had a whole bunch of Indians riding after them, trailing them by only thirty or forty yards. Well, they didn't have a chance. The Indians shot them right out of the saddle. I saw one trooper get clear down to the Medicine Tail Coulee again and cross, despite a whole bunch of Indians shooting at him, but he was nailed before he got too far. He died out there alone on the prairie. He was a brave man, but he couldn't handle them kinda odds. When I saw that happen I thought, God, that could have been Brules, sure as hell.

Bouyer had said again and again that we was going into a terrible battle, and he even told Curly, one of the scouts, when he dismissed him. He said, "This man is crazy, he's gonna take us into the middle of a massacre, and every one of us will get killed."

There was one thing that I kept thinking about Bouyer. I asked myself time and again, what did the damn fool go back with Custer for? Custer had dismissed him—he wasn't a soldier under any kind of orders. He was a scout and he had been dismissed. Besides, Custer had told him once before, I think up at the Crow's Nest, to get the hell out of the country. Bouyer obviously hated Custer, but he followed after Custer like a faithful dog, like he loved him. Now, I knew that couldn't be the case, because too much bitterness had built up between them two guys. But what in the hell *did* Bouyer go back for? I figured the poor fellow was surely dead with the rest, and could never tell us.

9

Weir Point and Reno Hill

When the fighting died down, I decided to drop out of sight and make a run for it up the trail that Custer had come down. I'd try to maybe get across over to the Rosebud and go down to the Yellowstone. If I didn't get spotted somewhere, maybe I'd save my hide and get out all right. It was sure a hell of a feeling, but I didn't see that there was anything else to do. I'd stood up against a lot of Comanches, and some Sioux, ten or twelve or twenty of them, but not three thousand. Not by a damn sight.

Working my way down toward the trail, I was surprised as hell to see a whole troop of pony soldiers coming toward me, all in their blue uniforms and riding pretty fast. There was only about thirty or forty of them. I wondered, what in the hell are those dumb bastards doing, trying to get down here to rescue two hundred men that have already gone down under several thousand Indians?

As I come riding up to them, an officer with a pair of field glasses was looking at what was left of the fight. I seen that the men around him was kinda nervous and pointed their guns at me. I called out, "Wait a minute, boys. I ain't no Indian."

I heard some of the boys talking in the troop and kinda speculating on what the hell was going on, but there wasn't any of them that realized Custer'd been wiped out with his whole command. They was saying that it must have been some kind of rearguard action, and that Custer had probably gone on down the river to hook up with Gibbon and Terry.

When I got up close an officer or fellow asked me, "Scout, who in the hell are you?"

I told them who I was and that I had been with Custer and his Crow scouts. He nodded, saying, "Yeah, we seen the Crows just come back. They're back up there with Reno."

"Back with Reno, what do you mean?"

"Well, he's back here on a hill. Goddamn, it's been hell! The Indians run him right back up the hill, and he's half out of his mind, but we're coming to help Custer. Reno don't seem to have the guts to want to do that."

"Well, you're too late to do any good for Custer. No help you can give him now," I told 'em.

That information seemed to stop them right there. We had a pretty good view of things, and they could see across the battlefield and what was going on. The firing was dying away, but no one could make out what really happened. The commander of this small troop was Lieutenant Weir, and when he realized what I meant was going on down in the valley, he was plenty distressed. "All right, scout, stay here with us, and we'll decide what we're gonna do."

Just about that time the Indians in the distance stopped all their firing and whirled around to see what was going on. Of course, they spotted us and let out a yell and started riding in our direction.

"Holy shit, Lieutenant, you better get the hell out of here and get back with the other troops," I shouted. "How far is it?"

"About three quarters of a mile."

"Well, my advice would be for you to start now." I could see that Weir was a brave and intense soldier, and a young fellow who was kinda true to tradition.

"No," he said, "we're gonna stay here and meet them."

"Well, Christ almighty!" I said, and turned away—there weren't no use arguing with a military man—and I started up the hill.

Weir yelled at me. "Hey, scout, you're gonna stay here."

"No, sir, I'm not. I've been dismissed by Custer. I was told that my job was through, and lookin' at the way he done his and what you're doing, I kinda think that's right. I believe I'll leave."

For a minute I thought that he was gonna pull a gun on me to stop me. He was so Goddamn mad that he started to reach for his revolver, but the sergeant said, "Take it easy, Lieutenant, take it easy, sir. That's Cat Brules, one of the new scouts that joined us down at the Rosebud. He's been with Bouyer all the time. Folks say he's an absolute dead gun. I don't believe that you'd get your gun out before he'd kill you."

Of course, what the sergeant said was true, but I also knew that if I killed Weir I'd have a dozen guns on me, and I'd never make it. It would have been a tense deal. After a moment I thought maybe I should swallow my pride and go along with these guys. Maybe this damn fool lieutenant would change his mind after I talked to him a little bit.

I stopped for just a second, and watched him real careful to see if he'd draw that gun. When he didn't, I opened my mouth to say, "Well, I see that you're in desperate shape, Lieutenant, and I'll join you." But I didn't get to say it, 'cause coming right over the hill was a whole bunch of other troops. I thought, what in the hell—guess maybe we're gonna make a stand here.

Well, it turned out to be Benteen, and he only had about three troops with him. A captain, Benteen took a good look around, and said, "Lieutenant, you must see that it's impossible for us to do anything but begin an organized retreat at this point. I know what you're thinking, and I'm not going to bring charges against you for what you just did to Major Reno. I almost believe what you said was true. But that does not give you the right to disobey a commanding officer and take a troop of men out into the face of the enemy, where the only possible result is a complete loss of your entire command."

I couldn't understand for a minute what the hell Benteen was talking about, but later I heard why Weir was so upset at Reno. The reason was, Reno had turned coward and shown the white feather. He took his troops out of that mess, running at the head of them, scared plumb to death.

That is no way for any commander to handle things. Troops look at their commanders to stay cool. If you don't do that, you're gonna get the shit kicked out of you. Troops hate a coward for a leader, 'cause he's liable to leave them in the lurch.

Weir had heard the heavy firing that was going on around Custer, and kept yelling at Reno, "Goddammit, let's go up and help Custer! Let's help Custer!"

Well, the kid didn't know how bad a jam Custer was in—that there weren't no way they could help him. When Reno wouldn't give the orders to advance, and told him to sit on his ass and stay right where he was, why, this kid said, "I'm going alone." He started out, and his troop had enough confidence in him so that they began following him without orders.

In a few minutes I seen Major Reno coming along, and he sure looked like shit. He'd lost his hat, had a kind of a handkerchief tied around his head, and, boy, his eyes were rolling and seemed like he was almost frothing at the mouth. He didn't have a bit of courage left.

The guy who was running things was Benteen, although he was only a captain. Benteen called for an orderly retreat, and Reno moved about two hundred yards, back up the slope toward what was the best position, which was later called Reno Hill. We were working up to that position when the Indians began closin' in on us. The boys were steady and some of them was pretty good shots. I lay down there and went to work with them, busting Sioux just as fast as I could work the lever.

The Sioux stopped and began to circle and see what they could do to get at us. Meanwhile, the orderly retreat continued. Slowly, one line of men would pick up their weapons and go back between the others and get behind them and get set up and start to cover their retreat. Then the order would be given for the next line to back up. They did a pretty good job.

In about fifteen to twenty minutes we was back up on top the hill. That's where I found out what Reno had done. It was a sad story. Even Weir got the message.

When Reno first seen the south end of the Indian camp down in the valley, he didn't see how big it was. His horses was tired, his troopers was tired, but he lined all them guys up and started his charge, maybe a mile away.

Well, them horses was plumb blown by the time they got within three hundred yards of the village, and Reno began to see what the hell he was getting into. Thousands of warriors were running around grabbing horses, riding around, yelling and shouting in a big cloud of dust. He looked to the left of him and he saw that there was a canyon, kind of a draw. It was called Beaver Creek. He thought that there might be a whole bunch of armed Sioux all sitting up there waiting, and prudently, he pulled up and stopped.

Now, you can't blame him for that. It wasn't a Custer move, but still it was probably pretty good military judgment. Well, there was a lot of timber along the river on his right-hand side. The left was open and run up the hills.

The western end of Reno's line was made up of about sixteen or seventeen Ree scouts, and that's asking for trouble because them Rees wasn't very good fighters.

He give the order to stop the charge and dismount. One trooper out of four became a horse holder and started taking the horses to the rear, getting them out of the way. Now, Reno's line ran all the way from the timber along the creek to out on the prairie, with the Rees at the west end.

Of course, when the Sioux seen that the charge wasn't coming, they began to get organized themselves and they come out and started shooting at Reno. They seen that the western end of his line was Indians, and knew they wasn't near as tough to fight in a running battle as the troopers. They began to put the pressure on 'em, and them Rees started giving way. Reno could see that his line was crumbling. He gave another order and it wasn't a bad one—to fall back around and form at the end of the timber—which they done. Up to that time losses wasn't but just occasional, things was going all right. Under a cool commander it might have been a good move.

There was another thing that he could have done. At that point Reno could have retreated into the woods. That's what mountain men would have done. They would have all gone into the woods where they could do their firing from underneath logs, instead of over the top of them where they could get picked off. They could have stayed in there and done just as good a job keeping the Indians away as the Indians would have done, and what's more, they would have had water for the troops!

But U.S. Army troopers didn't fight the way mountain men would fight. They'd been taught different tactics; the woods would have confused them, and they would have been plumb terrified as the Sioux began working through the woods and picking them off.

Reno had moved his line back so it was kinda laying parallel with the woods, and he was still out in front of them. Bloody Knife, who was Custer's favorite scout, was standing next to Reno.

Bloody Knife had been with Custer on several campaigns, and Custer had given him to Reno kinda to bolster the command up and give him some advice in fighting Indians. Well, it was unfortunate, but old Custer's plan didn't work there either. Poor old Bloody Knife took a bullet right in the head. It just busted his skull wide open. The worst thing about it was that Bloody Knife's brains spilled all over Reno's coat. That spooked Reno.

Reno lost his guts right there, and panicked. The sight had terrified him so, that he give an order to the boys to mount up again. Then he give them another order to dismount. Oh, God, they dismounted and the order went up and down the line, and finally old Reno gave them another order to mount again. He himself mounted and, by God, went off at a dead gallop, deserting his own troops, yelling, "Follow me."

The whole damn command had been given different orders and the fellows way down at the end of the line didn't get the last command. They didn't know what the hell to do and so panic broke out. Some of them lieutenants in the command tried to stop the panic and kept yelling, "Hell, no, let's don't run. Let's not run from Indians. We've never run from Indians. Let's settle down and do an orderly retreat."

But the commander had gone nuts. They said old Reno was wide-eyed as hell, plumb terrified, and he plunged across the Little Big Horn at the first place he came to. Of course, he had stumbled on a hell of a poor place to cross because of the steep bank on the other side. The horses was falling back, clawing, and then the bank got wet and the wetter it got the more slippery it got. Meanwhile, the Sioux with Winchesters was just pumping bullets into them poor devils.

Reno finally made it to the top of a hill overlooking the river, where he thought he could at least make some sort of a stand. The troops started pouring into a kind of low swell at the top of the hill, but Reno's surgeon, Doctor DeWolf, was killed and so were a lot of the other fellows. Only about half of his command made it to the top of the hill.

Some of the men, led by Herendeen, hid out in the woods and had some hair-raising experiences, but every one of them made it up to the command position later, during the night, showing what an organized fight in the timber could have accomplished. Actually, the pell-mell retreat that Reno led was not a complete massacre—but it sure was an unnecessary and costly rout.

That's what Benteen come up on, when he followed Custer's trail as ordered. Benteen hated Custer's guts. There had been bad blood between them for a long time, and Benteen was enraged at being ordered on a useless mission southwest, going through country that he knew Goddamn good and well the Indians wasn't in, and where he would be completely out of the action. For a while I guess Benteen figured that Custer didn't want him to have any part in the glory of routing the village. Course, Benteen still didn't know how big the village was.

In fact, no one had known except Bouyer, and it always seemed strange to me how in the hell he knew that. He told the Crows and the Crows believed him and they kept spreading the word, but still nobody else would believe it.

When Benteen saw no Indians on his wild-goose chase, he half followed orders and turned north until he came to Custer's trail. Again, as ordered, he set out to find Reno but only after an inexcusable delay. I guess Benteen knew nothing about the north fork of the creek. So when he come to where the creek was running through all these marshes, he thought it was a good place to water his horses, and he took his time. Custer's bugler caught up with Benteen, and gave him the famous message from Custer. *Come on. Bring packs. Big village.—Come quick.*

Well, Benteen got this order, but of course the packs were on the ammunition train. The ammunition train was on slow mules, which was way behind, and he waited for a while for the train to come along but it didn't. He wasn't in any hurry since he thought, well, Custer's an excitable fellow and does all this stuff crazy-like.

There were some troops that were devoted to Custer, like I said. Benteen sure as hell wasn't one of them. As a matter of fact, when the disaster that struck Custer was eventually unraveled, Benteen didn't look very good. He'd been told by a superior officer to "be quick" and he didn't make a real effort.

The young officers of his troops was beginning to get fidgety over the delay while they was watering their horses. They was almost a half hour there and that would have given Benteen plenty of time to reach Custer. Course, all that would have happened would have been Benteen and all his men would have also been destroyed, so maybe it worked out for the best. Still, it was really a lack of military discipline for him to have taken it easy coming to the rescue of his commander. No subordinate officer has any excuse to do that.

Anyway, Benteen finally rambled off—the pack train hadn't arrived yet—and he kept going along Custer's trail. He crossed the creek and kept on. It wasn't over twenty minutes from that time when he seen Major Reno up on top of a hill surrounded by what was left of his command—wounded, exhausted, beaten troopers. It was a sight that would make you sick. Reno had lost his hat and, God, his jacket was a mess from Bloody Knife's brains spread all over it. He was scared out of his wits and blown off his judgment.

Reno rode out to meet Benteen, thinking it was the greatest thing in the world, 'cause here come another bunch of troops. It was obvious that Reno had had a couple of shots of whiskey to kinda bolster his courage a little bit.

Benteen followed Reno back and saw this big mess around the top of the hill. All these guys wounded, shot up and all that kinda thing, everybody spooked, and the horses in bad shape. When he got there he just naturally took command.

At that time they began to hear the heavy firing that I was watching a mile and a half north of them. When they heard it, Weir said, "Goddammit, Reno, you're the most cowardly son of a bitch in the world. Let's go to Custer's help! Let's go."

"Don't you dare move from that place," Reno commanded.

But Weir went out anyway and his troops after him, like I done told you.

Well, it was lucky for Benteen, and lucky for Reno, that Custer had gone down that Medicine Tail Coulee and sucked all those savages away. The Sioux would've pressed Reno pretty hard on the top of that hill, and he might have been obliterated before Benteen got there.

Benteen went ahead and took his men and joined Weir. A lucky damn thing he did 'cause that's where I was when Benteen come up. I'll tell you, it was pretty evident that the Sioux had cleaned Custer out. There wasn't hardly anybody left, we didn't see any fighting from that hill after that. From what we could see in the distance, the Indians was all shooting at the ground, which meant that they was dispatching the wounded, but there wasn't anybody fighting them.

Now the whole damn force, bloodthirsty as hell, was coming our way. Benteen saw that and Weir saw it. Of course, when Reno saw it he said, "Oh, hell, let's get out of here. Let's go back to where we can defend ourselves."

Benteen said, "That's the only sensible thing to do, but let's not go back in a rout. Let's start moving our men according to the proper military procedure for covering a retreat," which they immediately done.

Well, they had some pretty sporty action but they got back up the hill, which was the best possible place they could be. It was the highest place around, you could see down the Little

Big Horn Valley, and you could see all around. It had a big hollow in it that was a kinda bowl—they could fort up in that. The trouble with it was these fellows knew if they were trapped there, it was gonna settle down to a siege.

Digging in is quite a chore when you haven't got any shovels. All they had were spoons out of their kits and stuff like that. They realized they was in a bad way, but they kept digging with their hands, and tried to make as much of a barricade as they could with some of the horses that was dead.

They had to put their wounded in what they called the hospital area, and then put more dead horses around the wounded so that any shots that come in would hit the horses first. Of course, anytime a man is wounded and starts losing blood, he is struck with an awful thirst. But there was no water.

There's the difference between being stuck down in the timber, like old mountain men would have done, and being up on this lonely hill. If you'd been down in the timber, you'd have the river at your back. Up there on that hill, how were you gonna get water? I mean, Christ, it was four hundred yards down to the river and there was Indian snipers all around.

About that point Reno said, ''Well, God almighty, where's the damn pack train? Where are they?''

I could hardly blame him for yelling like that about the pack train. I sure would have gone back there and told those guys to get those mules going, beat them up to a trot, and see if they could get to the battle before everyone was dead.

Thanks to the careful withdrawal, which Benteen had set up, the Indians was pretty well in check. If an Indian got up too close, he met heavy fire. Them Indians stayed hidden in the brush as much as they could, cautious about attacking.

Now that the troops had Benteen there, who was cool and knew what he was doing, it put a little backbone in the outfit. In any case, a few minutes later here come the pack train. The boys put up one hell of a cheer at that—forty thousand rounds of ammunition and another eighty men, plus a bunch of mules that they could use as a barricade if they had to. Also the pack train had some shovels and picks. There weren't very many of them, I guess only three or four, but, boy, the men could pass the shovels from one guy to another, and they started digging. They dug to beat hell and they made themselves some trenches, if that's what you want to call them. At least, they were out of sniper fire of the Indians.

The Indians, rather than taking the chance of a charge when they weren't ready to do it, occupied a ridge to the northeast. It was about four hundred yards away, maybe five hundred. Some of them Indians had old Buffalo Sharps rifles, which was long-range guns, and even the Winchester would carry that far, if you knew how to use it. So they started going to work on the besieged troops, raising hell. You get some bullets going into a herd of horses, and get them stampeding around with wounded laying on the ground, and the damn horses was liable to trample all over them. Guys were yelling and trying to hang on to the horses, but nobody wanted to show himself because of sniper fire.

Later, Reno decided to call for volunteers to go down for water. That wasn't any fun because even though the sniping had died down, there was enough to make life kinda wild for anybody that had to go down off the hill, through the open area, with no cover at all till they got to a ravine where they would have some protection. That is, if they could keep the Indians out of the ravine. Then they still had a dash of about fifty yards in the open, and had to stay there until they filled their canteens and stuff, and then make a dash back. Of course, they could only do that if they had covering sniper fire from our side.

The first bunch that went down, I'll have to say this for him, was led by Reno. He started down looking for this Doctor DeWolf who he had seen killed down there just after they crossed the river. DeWolf was a good friend of Reno's and I guess that made Reno feel like hell. He said he wanted to bury him. Seemed to me like he was kinda making up for what he'd done wrong, because going out there risking his life to bury a man, at this point, didn't seem the thing to do. I thought, wait till after the battle and if there was a little peace and calm and if we survive, that's the time to bury him.

Varnum knew that I was a hell of a shot, and he asked if I

was willing to go partway down, too, and hole up back of a ridge there to shoot any Indian snipers that was working on the water party.

"Brules," he said, "I'm not going to order you to do this. That's damn near a suicide mission. But somebody has to cover these poor devils who've volunteered to go down there."

"Hell, yes, I'm a better shot than anyone around here, I'll go."

So, as the rest ran down to the ravine, I and three sharp-shooters that come with me went down the ridge, staying out of sight and waiting. When the firing started, I laid down on the ridge there and got a good bead on where the shooting was coming from. I couldn't tell exactly because the Indians was hidden, but I could tell about where the shots came from. The thing was, after I'd shoot there wouldn't be any more firing from that place, so I must have been doing some damage. We kept on like that, and kept getting more enthusiastic and farther down the hill and closer and closer to the river. What I wanted to cover was the last forty yards that our boys had to rush like hell over. We kept the fire up on that part, and we was able to keep it so some of the soldiers could get the canteens full, and start back up the hill to them wounded men.

Well, we kept that going until sundown, when we was all about parched and pretty well wore out. It had been a long day and a bad one.

That night things begun to get a little tighter. Course, not all the Indians that had been down there beating up on Custer came to attack us. If they had, they would have cleaned us out, but still there was a thousand of them around us and it weren't healthy. Some of them come up the south end, close enough so they were actually throwing rocks into the camp at night.

That was pretty spooky, 'cause a lot of these boys had been bad shot up during the day, their morale was low, and they knew that something terrible had happened. One of the things they blamed Custer for was not coming back and getting rid of them Indians. Little did they know that Custer was lay-ing there dead as hell.

It didn't do no good to talk to the fellows about it. I didn't say anything about what I had seen. It wasn't necessary. What was obvious was nobody was coming to our rescue, and we was gonna have to fight this out. We was surrounded by a hell of a lot of Indians and if they spent four, five, or six days working on us, well, there weren't gonna be any of us left. We knew that we just had to stay right there and hope help would come before that.

I'll say this for Benteen: When those damn Indians was throwing rocks at us, he went to Reno and said, "I'm asking, sir, for permission to charge where they're attacking." Well, Reno didn't want to do nothing like that. Finally, Benteen said, "It has to be done. It simply has to be done, otherwise they will be right in the middle of us here."

Finally Reno gave in, and Benteen went down to the south end and gathered some boys together. He told them that they could not put up with this; they were gonna have to charge the bastards.

He ordered a few of the guys to line up, and when he gave them the signal, they all charged over the hill and shot the shit out of everything in sight. The Indians got up and run like hell. The fellows that was sharpshooters was picking them off as they run down the hill. It was pretty dark, but they could see enough to do some damage.

Well, Benteen came back and went up the north side, and they did the same damn thing there. It was by doing that kind of stuff that he kept the Indians away from where we was, so they couldn't gather and press us, which would have been fatal.

I'm telling you that even though the sun didn't go down till around half past nine at that time of June, and it got light again about three-thirty in the morning, that was the longest damn night I ever spent in my life. I reckon every man in the command felt the same way.

It was terrible listening to those poor boys that was wounded too. You'd hear them groaning and once in a while, when something hurt real bad, they'd give out a scream. Or you'd hear somebody working with some fellows and two or three of 'em say, "Oh, hell, he's gone." They'd move the body out of there and make room for the next one to be treated.

We had one doctor and he was the busiest bastard in the world. He just went from one end to the other. But what can you do in a deal like that? The most important thing was to get these poor wounded fellows some water. Time and again the boys went down the hill, risking their lives for water. And I tried my damnedest to cover them. I think I did a fair job of it too—although I must say it wasn't a one-man job. There was a lot of other riflemen workin' with me.

They was brave men that went down for water. I take my hat off to them. I'll tell you this, you can bet all them wounded fellows would sure take their hats off to 'em any damn time of day or night. A lot of them got the Congressional Medal of Honor and damn well deserved it. Wounded fellows that survived remembered them water carriers till the day they died.

Dawn come early and the place was a mess, but by that time we had dug in pretty good. There had been a lot of horses shot, and they begun to stink like hell and the dead men stunk too. We spent the whole damn day fighting off them Sioux and it wasn't a happy day. There was the moaning of the wounded, and the crack of rifle fire occasionally from various places where them Indians was hidin' out. The Indians didn't want to get hurt and weren't taking any chances. They must have figured all they needed to do was hold us there and keep popping at us and killing our horses.

All the night before, we'd heard the damn tomtoms going down in the valley and the wild yells that went with their dancing. Those sons-of-bitching Sioux were just celebrating the great victory over the paleface. But no one in our camp really knew how Custer had made out, so they didn't know the Indians were celebrating their victory over him.

Varnum was pretty well upset with them Crows—Hairy Moccasins, White Man Runs Him, and Goes Ahead. They all went and got canteens during the night and said that they was gonna go down and get some water for the wounded boys. Finally, Varnum took the bait and told 'em to go ahead. Of course, he never saw them again.

I asked Varnum what he thought had happened to old Bouyer and how he'd made out. I thought maybe he'd been smart enough to get through all this. Varnum just shrugged— no answer!

I kept trying to tell myself that maybe I hadn't seen Custer shot and maybe he didn't go down, and maybe he'd made it to the top of the hill. Still, it had looked to me like every man in that command was gone, because of them Indians roaming around over there, yelling and hollering without incident. They couldn't be riding around like that, right out in the open, if there was still troops in there.

We had plenty of ammunition, that was one thing. We had forty thousand rounds and we wasn't gonna run out. They was gonna have to rush us, but we couldn't stay there forever.

We had to get something to eat, but most important we had to get water. If they shut us off from water for twenty-four hours and guarded the hell out of the river, we couldn't make it. That's all there was to it. Somebody'd have to make the rush, and in making the rush we'd all be killed. So there we were.

Well, the next morning at dawn, the sharpshooting started up again and it kept up most of the day and things got plumb unbearable. The stench of dead horses and the stench of dead men was worse and all around us. There was no sanitation or nothing like that in the camp. Everybody had to do the best they could and I'm tellin' you, in close quarters like that it was terrible.

Firing from a long ways off, the Indians kept popping at us all the time, killing our horses, and it became pretty damn discouraging. By the middle of the day the wounded were suffering worse from lack of water, and it had got even tougher to get down to the river because there were more Indians around.

I know, 'cause I'd done some covering, shooting from the ridge, and it was a thousand yards down there to the water. That was a long thousand yards, I can tell you. Part of the way you could keep covered, but you couldn't all the way.

Then toward late afternoon we began to get something

else to fear. We saw that there was a lot of fires going in the valley. We thought that maybe they was gonna try to burn us out. Well, that didn't make much sense up there where we was—we weren't down in the timber. So how was they gonna get it done?

The smoke kept getting thicker and thicker and then, kinda strangely, the firing around us slowed up and finally trickled down to almost nothing. It was like that for an hour or so, and we was wondering what them red devils was up to. Then we seen a long column of Indians moving along with their travois and squaws, headed up toward the Big Horn Mountains. We realized that, even though they could have stayed there and laid siege to us and wiped us out, they was moving out.

We began to think, by God, maybe Gibbon and Terry were coming up the Little Big Horn from the Yellowstone, and maybe the Sioux had decided that they'd had enough of fighting. As it turned out, that's just about the way it was. We went through another night laying there not knowing what was happening. We was pretty used to the horrors of what was going on around us, but then the next morning we seen a lot of dust coming at us from the north.

At first our instinct was to think maybe them damn Indians had worked around and was getting up another attack. But soon you could tell through field glasses that it was a cavalry outfit. By God! it was Terry and Gibbon and close to a thousand troops and plenty of armament. So that's why them Indians moved out. I'm telling you that we was the gladdest men you ever saw when we spotted them troops coming.

10

Like White Antelope
on a Hill

We was able to walk around that morning, and the firing had completely disappeared. It seemed like all the Indians had left. It took several hours before the command got up to us and we didn't dare leave our position, but when they finally got there, General Terry sure had some bad news.

He told us everything that I kinda saw and expected—that the whole command of Custer's troops, with commanders like Keogh, Yates, and Calhoun, were all wiped out. There wasn't a single man left. Lieutenant Bradley, who'd been chief of scouts with Gibbon, was now with Terry—he'd gone around and inspected a few things.

Bradley said it was the damnedest fight. He was ahead of everybody as they was coming up the Little Big Horn. Of course, they had been too far away to have heard any of the firing the day before. When he was about five miles away from Custer's Hill, he saw what he thought was a hill full of antelope. He thought that he was looking at a herd with their white rumps showin' as if they had their heads down feedin'. He got closer and closer, and kept putting his field glasses to it. Those white specks didn't seem like anything you could explain till he got within a few hundred yards, and was horror-struck to see the whiteness was no herd of antelope—it was the corpses of dead troopers! They had all been stripped naked of their uniforms and most of them had been horrible mutilated.

I guess if either a Sioux or a Comanche went to work on a white man's body, there wasn't a hell of a lot to put together afterward. Of course, they wanted the white man's clothes— boots, britches, and shirts and all that. They stole them, along with the horses, saddles, and everything they could get their hands on, and they wanted to take those carbines, even if they weren't as good as a Winchester. A lot of those Indians didn't have nothing but bows and arrows, and were glad to get them single-shots and the ammunition that went with 'em.

Some of the cavalry horses was real nice because they was thoroughbred stock and a far, far superior horse to those Indian ponies except for one thing: You had to take oats along for them to feed on, 'cause they couldn't survive on the prairie grass. There wasn't enough nourishment in it. The Indian pony, he got along on anything. You could almost feed him on a sandbag. Surprising how well them Indian ponies did compared to the white man's horses.

Anyway, when Bradley got up to the slaughter place, he said it was a horrible sight, and he couldn't believe that there wasn't a living thing around there. He counted something like two hundred dead men. Of course, by the time they got there those bodies had been two days in the hot sun and two nights and they was beginning to stink like hell. It was a pretty terrible business, so he wanted some men to volunteer for grave duty to bury those fellows.

Well, I wasn't keen on burying anybody, but I sure as hell wanted to find Mitch Bouyer. I felt like he was a newfound friend of mine. Now, I still entertained the hope that he'd slipped off down the river somehow and maybe he was gonna be all right, but I damn well wanted to go down and make sure. So I told them I'd volunteer.

It was the damnedest mess you ever saw. Piles of horses and all kinds of stuff that the Indians hadn't picked up. Blankets was all gone and all that. I began looking and looking and looking for Mitch, and couldn't find him. So my hopes was rising all the time.

At that point Bradley asks me, "Well, Brules, where are the Crow, where are the Crow scouts?"

"Except for Half Yellow Face and White Swan, who was with Reno—one of them is wounded so the other one stayed here—the rest of them are gone, vamoosed," I told him. "Got the hell out of here. They had a bellyful of white officers' mistakes."

I don't suppose that made Bradley feel good, but I was just telling him the Goddamn truth. It was exactly what all them Crow fellows had told me. Jesus, they had never seen anything like it. They didn't think a bunch of Sioux could whip a bunch of white men as easy as that and clean them out. I guess that the whole rest of the world didn't understand that one either.

I followed Lieutenant Bradley around the battlefield with the burial crew. He did not go back to the top of the hill, so I didn't see the remains of Custer, Boston Custer, Tom Custer, the newspaper guy, Kellogg, or any of them fellows. But Bradley said it was a funny thing. He said that Custer was kinda propped up between a couple of other guys, almost in a sitting position. A burial party had been left at the battlefield, while Terry came on up to where we was all jammed in there on the hill. They had been given instructions to box or bag up Custer right away and take him down to the *Far West*.

Bradley didn't want to talk about it too much, but he did tell me that Custer had two wounds. One was on the left side in the region of the heart, that looked like small-caliber stuff, and then another shot on the left temple, where he had powder burns. He also told me that Custer wasn't scalped. Now, I find that Goddamn hard to believe. Custer had some pretty fancy blond locks, and although cut short would have made a good scalp for any Indian.

All the Indians later on told everybody that they didn't know they were fighting Custer at the time. They knew a lot about Custer. The Sioux called him "Yellow Hair," and the Crows called him the "Son of the Morning Star." Anyway, it wasn't till after the battle was over that they recognized him and realized who they had been fighting.

The story was give out that Custer was killed up there on top of what they call Monument or Custer Hill, and that he was probably the last man or next to the last man to go down, and he was standing there firing away while everybody else around him was shot up. One newspaper fellow said, "They were falling around him like sheaves of corn." Well, them's fancy words, but if what I saw was correct, Custer was killed very early in the battle or even before it really began. It took the punch out of the troops, otherwise there might not have been the rout it was.

Of course, when he got knocked off his horse, there weren't no way to tell whether Custer was dead or mortally wounded, but I could sure see all those guys getting off around him, slingin' him back over his saddle, and then carrying him along. The whole staff then started trying to get back up to high ground. By that time none of those fellows had any desire to go charging into the Sioux village. They heard the roar of them three thousand Indians that was out after their blood, and I guess that kinda panicked 'em and they moved up the hill as fast as they could go.

I'd seen Chief Gall lead the Indians across the Medicine Tail Coulee in the charge up the hill against Custer's troopers. I guess Gall had got the message that somebody was attacking at the north end of the village, so he'd rallied all his warriors and gone racin' downstream. When those Oglalas rushed up that hill, I thought it was the damnedest, most horrid sight in the world. Those troopers in blue didn't look like much, just like tiny little specks in the terrible sea of howling warriors.

Anyway, Bradley and I kept looking around and trying to figure out where Calhoun and Keogh was. First I thought they must have dismounted at that point and kinda withdrew to protect Custer, but I don't think that's the case. I think they all arrived up at the top of the ridge about the same time. They was all strung out along the hill and moving to the right flank when I saw them. There wasn't anybody following anybody. Then when Gall hit them, and he hit them hard, they settled down at the topmost place and did the best fighting that they could. Of course, I didn't see it all because by that time, I'd hightailed it out of there. There was an overflow of Indians and some of them was coming around mighty close to me.

I continued lookin' over the battlefield, trying to find Bouyer. I looked across along the hillside of bodies of them troopers—troopers that I seen a week before come out with the band playing, flags flying, marching by Terry, Gibbon, and Custer in review, marching away to a fine tune, marching to their death. It was a horrible thought. There they lay on the hillside. I didn't see one single body that hadn't been stripped absolutely naked by the Indians.

The squaws had come out and cut all the clothes, boots, and everything off them bodies—the material of their uniforms and leather from them boots being better than anything the Indians had. A lot of them had never seen a white man, let alone the clothes he'd be wearing, fancy buttons, belts, and stuff like that.

Something that really bothered me was how white all them dead bodies was. I said to Lieutenant Bradley, "God, ain't that a terrible sight? They all look so white."

He said, "Yes, yes, indeed they do look very white." Then he started to tell me what had happened when he first seen the battlefield. He was riding with his scouts ahead of Gibbon's column. Being ahead of all the rest of them, he started riding through the battlefield and looking at the carnage, the dead horses and dead men, and had to stop a couple of times to vomit. He said that even the horses didn't like to be amidst all that death. The stench of it made them awful spooky, and they acted like they wanted to get the hell out of there.

Then, there was one more terrible thing that was beyond the comprehension of any civilized man. Them bodies had been terrible mutilated. There was gashes along the thighs from the hip clear down to the knee and wide open, intestines had been cut out and allowed to ooze out all over the ground. All of them corpses was scalped, of course, but some heads had been taken off, or hands or feet. On almost every corpse I seen, the private parts had been removed.

Most of this work, of course, must have been done by the squaws. Them that is handy with knives all the time from skinning game, dressing it out, and butchering everything that come their way. The only difference was, no Indians that I know of was cannibals, so they weren't gonna eat anything that was before them, but they sure did slice it up.

What they took the men's private parts for was beyond me. Later one of the Crows told me they done that for a sort of fertility charm to hang in the tepee, and the whole tribe would have more children and grow to greater strength. Even if I don't know nothing about history, I reckon that the Indians wasn't the first ones to have them kinds of practices. But they sure didn't sit well with the white man in the West back in 1876.

When you come right down to it, no troops act very damn good when they get in a struggle. There was some bad things done by our boys at the Sand Creek massacre back in 1864 in Colorado. Them troopers paraded around afterward with a lot of trophies that were not the kind of thing that so-called civilized troops would show off.

Another thing that was hard to take was them hundreds of dead horses. Some of them was beginning to spoil pretty bad and in a lot of cases their heads were shriveled and their eyelids were closed. They was closed in a way that didn't look like they was a-sleeping, but like them horses was crying for the real sorrowful things that man had done, not only to them, but to himself. The more I looked and my imagination run, the sadder and more disgusted I become. Why is it, I asked myself, that men can be such damn fools and so cruel? The horse don't want to go into combat, but what can he do? A man puts a steel bit in the horse's mouth and a saddle on his back. They're just slaves sacrificed at their master's will.

I remember seeing one horse laying there on the ground with most of his lower jaw shot away. He looked like his teeth was sticking out in a rage, like he was gonna bite the first man come around. He was like some kinda monster with that expression. Then I seen another one whose mouth was wide open and the teeth was all there, like he was laughing. I thought, what a hideous laugh that is. He's laughing at the stupidity of these dumb bastards that was all dressed up in their uniforms and marching to the tune of drums, and the flags flying and all that. Now here they are, laying deader than doornails on account of the stupid idea of trying to force other people to do something that they don't want to do.

11

Bouyer and
the Deep Ravine

I was ordered to ride out and check for the enemy, and pick up any information I could. So, I very happily rode off to get away from the stench—out where there wasn't any more dead bodies laying around, naked and chopped up, where the grass seemed green and clean again, and the wind was blowing and the wildflowers growing. To go where things was natural and unspoiled by man.

I kept on working around the bowl-shaped hollow of the north and south Medicine Tail Coulee till I got over to a place where there was a real steep ravine. It was the one that I saw Custer's troops going down into after he was shot, and they was carrying him on his horse to get to the top of the hill.

Well, I came to that part of it, and, boy, there was lots of dead guys around there. Historians later figured that there must have been a charge there to try to get to the river and maybe break loose toward the end of the battle. As far as I know that might have been so. All I can say is there was a lot of dead troops inside the ravine, but I certainly didn't see a fight going on between the Indians and any troopers at that place when I watched everybody moving up the hill at the beginning of the battle. Hell, no, there weren't that many killed yet. They were working their way up toward the top.

That deep ravine fightin' musta come later. It might have been after Custer was dead and there wasn't anything but chaos. Maybe some of them fellows thought, well, Christ, the thing for us to do is run and get down near the water and timber and hide. A lot of them troops that was with Reno's, at the south end of the valley, did just that. A whole bunch of his men come out of that timber a day or two later, unharmed.

Anyway, when I come up on that deep ravine, I saw a whole bunch of bodies down in there and I begun to ride down and try to look around and, God almighty, I found him! I recognized Bouyer down there even though his head was bad smashed in and his face pretty disfigured. It was hard to tell him from the others, but there was no doubt in my mind from his boots and some other things.

When I seen it I'd called for Bradley. So he come over and said, "Yeah, hell, yes, that's Mitch Bouyer, you can see that. He's bad beat up and everything, but there's no doubt in my mind that that's Mitch." Even though the top of his boots was took off, pieces of the heel was there.

Another thing that surprised me, as I was looking around, was these pieces of white paper that was all torn up, bloody as hell and muddy. I picked up the papers and looked at some of them. They said something about Cloud Peak Camp and something else. Of course, I can't read very well, but I could see enough to make out something in the beginning about the Sioux Expedition Commander Crook, Cloud Peak Camp, and Goose Creek.

My God, I kept looking at that thing and my mouth was wide open! Holy Christ, it was the message I'd carried from Crook to Terry that Bouyer had persuaded me to leave with the son-of-a-bitch adjutant. How come the damn thing was in what appeared to be part of Bouyer's boot?

You know, when the Indians would take a boot off a fellow, they didn't care about the shoe part like the moccasin, but they liked the outsides of the boot to make a legging of sorts because it would save a lot of chafing if you rode long distances. I couldn't figure out about the dispatch, though. Had it been in Bouyer's boot tops?

Lieutenant Bradley was making some notes and taking some measurements and one thing and another. He wasn't bothering with me, so I figured that I'd start riding down the Little Big Horn and look for the rest of Gibbon's troops. He told me they was only four or five miles behind. Sure enough I seen them in the distance coming up and they'd probably run into the same surprise as Bradley.

I seen that there was some Indian scouts, riding in a bunch with the main body, and then I checked a couple of times and looked hard again, and, by God, I'll tell you, among all them ponies, there was my Jupiter. Old Jupiter was there.

I spotted that big, beautiful stallion being led by an Indian on a painted horse, and that splendid-looking Indian couldn't be no one else but my blood brother, Wesha. He was still a long ways off, but I was awful glad to see them and I rode out toward him. I was on a strange horse and I probably looked like the rest of the scouts, and he didn't spot me right away, but it wasn't long before he did. He kicked up to a lope and come my way in a hurry.

Well, you know when a white man's old friend would come up he would leap down, shake hands, maybe throw his arms around you, punch you in the chest, then tell you how great it was to see you. No Indian would do a thing like that. It was a sacred moment and my blood brother knew it well. It had been almost two weeks since I'd seen him, and he knew that a lot of fighting had been going on, and he didn't know if I'd made it through or not. So it was no time to be making any jokes or anything, not with an Indian. He rode up, and as he got real close, as if it was a ceremony, he stopped his horse, slid off, holding him by the reins, and raised his right hand, the blood brother hand. I stopped and done the same. We stood there for a moment looking at each other, and then walked slowly together. When we come face to face, he held his hand up again, but this time in front of him and I held my hand up and we held them together. This is the greeting of a blood brother.

He stood back and said, "My blood brother, the Great Spirit has been with you. Your medicine is good. My heart has been heavy, but now it is light, for you are alive though there has been much fighting." He looked up at the hill, more than a mile and a half away, and pointed to where those white bodies were shining in the sun, laying scattered about. "I have seen the fierce work of the Sioux. Many of your pony soldiers lie dead. There must be much weeping in the lodges of their women. Many were young, strong, and rode out in their blue coats with shining buttons. Now, they lie naked on the hillside.

"Where is the great leader of these pony soldiers who lie so dead on that hill? The one they call Yellow Hair? The one who killed so many Cheyenne on the banks of the Washita many, many winters ago? The Sioux and the northern Cheyenne who were with them must have remembered this battle or they would not have killed so many of Yellow Hair's pony soldiers. How is it, my brother, that you are still alive while so many lie dead?"

I could understand the Shoshone language, but I didn't speak it with the same grace. I had to explain in slow stumbling words, "Yellow Hair, the great leader, lays dead among his men at the top of that hill. I have not seen him, but Lieutenant Bradley came and told me. We are here to bury Custer's troops.

"The soldiers of No Hipbone came to us where we had been pinned down by the Sioux fire, and told us that all was well now, that the Sioux had left. Indeed, we saw them yesterday afternoon marching away in big numbers. We saw their lodges packed on their ponies and travois. There were many, many of them. As many as leaves on the trees. I have never seen so many red men."

I added, "But you and I are meeting once again because of the blessing of the Great Spirit, and being able to live together is indeed good medicine."

Wesha nodded in agreement. I went on, "Now, my bother Wesha, I must tell you a sad thing."

Wesha looked me in the eye and said, "My brother, is there anything more sad than what we see upon that hill?"

"Yes, those were men that died with a strong sense of faith in what they were doing. They died according to the laws of all their people. They died with good faith, but here I found my friend, the scout Bouyer, with pieces of paper that took away my heart.'' Wesha looked up at me and waited. ''There were pieces of paper, Wesha, my blood brother, laying all around—pieces of white paper. They had come out of the scout's boots when the squaws cut them up. The papers had blown all around and I went to look at them and, my blood brother, I hang my head in shame to tell you what they were.

''Wesha, my brother, how can I tell you this? All the long ride we took, all the fighting and killing of those many Sioux warriors, when we crossed the Big Horn far upstream, and all those things that happened at the mouth of the Stillwater. Giving you, my blood brother, my horse to follow me, not knowing where you could find me. My going down the stream in the Frenchman's pirogue. All this was for nothing—to bring the talking paper from the great general Gray Fox, who was still at Cloud Peak at the foot of the Big Horns, to No Hipbone, chief of all this expedition. That message Gray Fox told me was so important, that you and I risked our lives to carry, never reached No Hipbone, although I was within a few yards of him. I was forced to give the message to his adjutant. How that message ended up in the boot of Mitch Bouyer, the scout, I cannot say, but there is no mistaking it, for the words were there. All that ride and all that fighting that you and I did, my blood brother, I am ashamed to tell you—it was for nothing. For the message lay with the scout Bouyer and not in the hands of the general.''

Wesha made a sound, but said nothing more.

''I would have sworn on my life that the scout Bouyer was a good and faithful man. I'm sick at heart, my blood brother. There is nothing worse than holding a man to be your friend, one who vows to be your friend, but in truth is your enemy.''

Wesha simply made a noise of assent and disgust, but he said nothing more. Well, I understood that; he was in deep thought.

Finally, Wesha said to me then, ''My blood brother, at a distance I did not recognize you because you were only a scout on a strange horse.''

''Yes, I guess that's right.'' In English I said, ''He ain't much, but he's still a-walking.'' I don't know how much English Wesha knew, but he laughed and it was good to see him laugh.

"Wesha, you are the greatest friend in the world," I said. "Thank you for bringing me that beautiful black stallion. Damn lucky you kept him, because he would have been killed here. I guess that this pony I got from the remounts was one that stayed back. I didn't see no place where he was hit except just a crease across the chest from some bullet going close. I rode him down here, but I sure as hell don't want to ride him back, not when I'm looking at that beautiful black stallion, Jupiter."

Wesha understood enough, I guess, because he laughed again. I liked to see that Indian laugh. He'd be stern and dignified, but in the presence of his blood brother, it was as if he was a boy again. It was the same with me. We'd laugh back and forth at any little simple joke.

Wesha told me he come up on No Hipbone's troops at the mouth of the Big Horn and seen the steamer going upstream and the men marching on the east side of the river.

He went up a ways where he could swim across and joined them. Of course, them army officers immediately tried to make a big order out of everything and sent him up to join Lieutenant Bradley. Well, when Wesha got up there leading this black horse, Bradley didn't know what the hell to do with him. Nobody there could speak Shoshone, certainly Bradley couldn't, and neither could the Crows.

By sign language Wesha made it known that he was leading a horse that he wasn't gonna give up for nothing. It belonged to his blood brother who had joined No Hipbone somewhere down the Yellowstone, and he wasn't giving it up until he found his brother again. Wesha was the kind of warrior that none of them Crows wanted to argue with, and for that matter neither did most pony soldiers. Lieutenant Bradley, being a smart man, let it go at that, although he done cast envious eyes on the black stallion.

We mounted up and started on a big circle, me riding Jupiter and leading the army nag.

After we'd circled the hill of the dead men, we went on

back south with Lieutenant Bradley to see what was going on at Reno Hill. That's the name we give right away to the place where Reno had fortified. We done that as a kinda checkup before we headed back north to the mouth of the Little Big Horn. We wanted to see what was being done there, and it seemed to be the most likely meeting place for everybody.

To be right honest I didn't know which commander to report to. I'd never met General Terry, I'd only met his adjutant. General Custer was gone, and it was a long ways back to General Crook at Cloud Peak Camp at the foot of the Big Horns, if he was still there. I reckoned that he was, 'cause, knowing him, I didn't think he'd move until he got the Fifth Cavalry from Fort Hays to join his command.

I didn't know how long it was gonna take him to get the news, but it seemed to me that somebody would get to a telegraph station at Bozeman, being the closest place, wire Cheyenne, and have a courier come up the Bozeman Trail to Cloud Peak Camp and give the news to Crook. No other way but what it had to be a couple of weeks before he'd hear, at least!

I didn't know then that Crook was a member of one of the Crows' secret societies and understood the Indians. Within two hours of the time of the battle one of the Crows told Crook that Custer and all of his troops had been destroyed. How in hell they got that information there that quick, damned if I know. No horseman could make it in that time and I didn't see no smoke signals. There was some mysterious way the Indians passed along news, but I don't know how.

Of course, Crook didn't believe it, either, and it wasn't till a couple of weeks later before he got any true confirmation. Musta been a hell of a shock to him to learn what the Crows told him was right.

Anyhow, that's what happened there, but me and Wesha went along to Reno Hill, to think about what the hell we'd do next.

12

A Sad Journey

The wounded had to be taken eighteen miles from Reno's Fort down to where the *Far West* lay at the mouth of the Little Big Horn River. The only way they could be carried was on travois, which was painful as hell for them poor devils. They was dragged, bouncing and bumping, down in back of mules, but it was the only way it could be done. There weren't no wagon wheels around. No man could carry another man on his back that distance, and to pack them on the back of a horse, unless they was only lightly wounded, would be an agony for 'em. With the dust from the travois and the horses' hooves, and the mules braying, and the drivers from the pack train doing their best to pull together what was left, them weary troops, with their heads down and carrying their guns in a down position, sure was a sorrowful sight. The commanders rode off to the side and I could see that they was in a dark mood. Why the hell wouldn't they be? They'd seen the biggest disaster in the history of the American Indian warfare from the standpoint of the whites.

Me and Wesha kinda looked at each other, trying to figure what to do.

I knew the wounded would be taken back to Fort Abraham Lincoln, clear down on the Missouri, but Gibbon and Terry were going either to Gibbon's camp on the Rosebud or to Terry's supply depot on the Mizpah. So I was trying to figure out how I could get back to General Crook. I discussed it a little bit with Wesha. He was real keen on joining his Shoshone bunch at Cloud Peak Camp. He knew that his brother warriors had been laying in there for nigh on to three weeks, which don't sit very well with the Indian nature. They want to fight or go home, and there hadn't been any fighting for them since the Battle of the Rosebud, clear back on the seventeenth of June.

No matter how he went, it would take Wesha another week to get there, and he was afraid that unless Crook started some action, all his friends would pack up and go back to the Wind River.

Anyway, the important thing was, we had to figure out a better route than the way we come. All the time we was discussing this, it turned out that a big scouting party of pony soldiers had left Crook's detachment and gone north into the Big Horns for hunting and scouting. The party was known as the Sibley scout, after the lieutenant who was commanding it.

That was about the toughest scout ever pulled by the cavalry, and it lasted almost two weeks. Sibley run smack dab into all the thousands of Sioux that was leaving the Big Horn battlefield. They was spread over a lot of country, and every which way he turned there was more Sioux than he ever wanted to see. It's a long story on how he got his command out of there, but they lost all their horses, and some of their men, and had to walk home clear to Cloud Peak Camp.

Well, the Sibley scout done gone down in the annals of United States Cavalry as one of the toughest deals that the U.S. Army ever encountered, and the fact that any of them got out was just a miracle. Miracle and the caginess of the scout Frank Girard, but that's another story. Only reason I mention it is that when we found out about it, we decided we knew what we was doing when we said we didn't want to go back the way we come.

Yet we still had the problem. Wesha told me in real simple language that he wanted to get back to his people as best he could and then he wanted to go home. He put it pretty plain-like. It was them two beautiful wives he wanted to see again and damned if I blamed him. He said, "My heart aches for them and when I think of them my loins turn to fire. I know that their thighs ache for me." Well, that's putting it pretty straight. I didn't blame him a damn bit. Hell, if I had two beautiful girls like that waiting for me, all hell couldn't have stopped me from going home. I'd swim any river, climb any mountain, I'd sneak by any force of Sioux warriors to get there. That's the way Wesha felt, but he just wanted to have me say it was okay for us to separate and for him to go his way. I sure as hell wasn't gonna tell him anything else. The right thing for him to do was go back to them wives.

The next morning we started out for the mouth of the Big Horn and traveled down the east bank. The steamer didn't leave with the wounded until one-thirty in the morning, but we knew that they was gonna make a fast run and would pass us, and we wouldn't get no chance to be ferried across the Yellowstone River to hit Gibbon's camp and military road on the north bank. As we was riding along in the dark on the east bank of the Big Horn the steamer come a-sailing by us about two-thirty in the morning, with the wounded and the generals aboard, moving downstream awful fast. The captain give us a whistle as he went by and it wasn't too long before they was gone out of sight and round the bend.

I must say that Wesha was mighty impressed at that steamer. He had lots of respect for that puffing and blowing and all them paddlewheels churning. Man, you could tell that he kinda read things straight. He realized real quick the men who built those kind of machines and who could build railroads like he'd heard of was more than a match for the Indians. He knew the Indian couldn't fight the white man very long, and the best thing to do was make friends and pick up their way of life and come out with something a lot better than what they originally had. Yet to try to tell that to the average warrior was out of the question, and Wesha knew it.

Anyway, me and Wesha, along with a bunch of Crows, rode down and come to the mouth of the Big Horn early that next morning. We looked down the river and there about a mile below us and across the river was the steamer anchored to a landing at Pease Bottom. We rode like hell until we was opposite them and waved and made enough hullabaloo that the crew cast loose and come over and ferried us across the river. With us on that ferry trip was the young scout, Curly, who Bouyer had sent away before the battle to save his life. He became a great messenger hero when everyone heard he was the only survivor. He was a modest kid and always said he was never in the fighting, but the newspapers would not believe that.

The Crow scouts didn't waste any time asking Gibbon for leave to go back to their village on Pryor Creek to see their families again. Gibbon give them permission to do so, and had a scout named Tom LaForge go with them. LaForge's mission was to reenlist the Crows that had left Reno's command or had given up on the bad turn of the campaign. Them Crow scouts was good scouts and they was bad needed. Maybe a little leniency and giving the boys a little time off, like that, would be all right, and Tom LaForge was the kind of man that could get them turned around.

Well, I figured the best thing to do was to stick with Tom LaForge. He had been a good friend of Mitch Bouyer, so he had to be a pretty good man himself. I'm sure he didn't know nothing about the shady side of Bouyer, and I reckoned that he'd know his way around. As I saw it, I was under General Crook's command, and sure as hell from what I'd seen of Gibbon and Terry, I didn't want to get mixed up with them.

Not too long before Tom LaForge had fallen in love with a girl named Cherry, a real pretty Crow according to everyone who had seen her. What's more, she was a real close friend of Mitch Bouyer's wife, Magpie Outside. In fact, I understand that the two couples shared one house, not a lodge or tepee, but a house built on the agency. They got to be such fast friends that they agreed that if anything happened to either one of them, the survivor would take care of the other one's family. Well, now Tom LaForge was going back to the Crow village, and gonna have to tell Magpie Outside that Mitch was dead. That was gonna be tough enough, but then he was gonna have to take care of her and her children right along with two of his own.

Taking care of four children and two wives was a full-time job for any man, 'cause, according to Indian custom, he was gonna have to treat Bouyer's widow just like a full wife—same as Cherry. That was gonna be tough, but I reckoned that Tom LaForge was up to it if anyone was. Plus, he was about as knowledgeable a scout as any you could find in the country.

I finally decided that if I stayed with Tom LaForge and went with them Crows back up to the Crow country, I could wait to hear when Crook made his way to the Yellowstone and then join him at someplace along the river. I explained that to Wesha, and he seen the reasoning was for the best and agreed to stay with me. As LaForge said, "there weren't much use us standing around." We was gonna have to do one thing or another.

We started up the military road, moving right along. After a day and a half of good hard travel, we come on Pryor Creek, and much to our delight found the Crow village. They'd moved from the Stillwater over to Pryor Creek, coming downstream two weeks earlier.

There was lots of joyous greetings going around, because a lot of them squaws and relatives thought that the scouts had been lost with Custer in the battle. When they found out they was alive, everything was fine again except, of course, for poor Magpie Outside. Tom LaForge was trying his best to keep her from being too upset. He told her about the pact he had with Mitch—that either man would take care of the other's wife and children if they got in bad shape, and that, by God, from now on she was part of his family. He was afraid she was gonna start doing the kind of grieving that most Indian squaws done when their braves was knocked out of action. That is, to start wailing, and cutting herself up some so she would bleed. Tom got her stopped from that early enough, and after that all she did was just bawl.

From what I could see of Magpie Outside, she was a pretty fine woman. She wasn't no beauty, but she had a lot of character. She carried herself real proud, and she finally raised them two boys of Mitch's to be fine young men.

Guess it was only two or three years after that, that Tom

LaForge's wife, Cherry, died of some disease, probably tuberculosis or something that the Indians didn't have no immunity from. When she died, then old LaForge married Magpie Outside in a formal ceremony.

Anyway, we got to the Crow village sometime in early July, I guess, and it was kinda nice duty, to hang around that Crow camp. The Crows saw to it that Wesha and me was well taken care of, but I could see Wesha really getting concerned about his Shoshones that was with Crook, and about his wives back there at the Wind River Reservation. When I thought about how beautiful them wives was, I couldn't blame him. Of course, he was also the protector and caretaker of both them girls, and he also saw that things went right for them.

I noticed a difference in things at the Crow camp, compared to how they was in the Shoshone village. With the exception of the agent house and perhaps one or two outbuildings, the village was all the regular lodge or tepee setup. There's a men's side of the tepee and a women's side. There was a very careful etiquette about the things you was supposed to do in order not to offend anybody. You sure had to know your manners or you'd soon find you wasn't welcome. Well, Tom LaForge's home was run like any white man's, where you had more freedom, mixed with guests, same as any white family. Sure made it easier on everybody, and certainly bore out the idea that any Indian girl lucky enough to get a white man for a husband was a hell of a lot better off than her sisters. She was pretty apt to get a decent house to live in, with a stove instead of just a fire that ran the smoke out through the top of the tepee. A damn sight warmer in the wintertime, maybe cooler in the summer. It certainly stood up to the wind and snow better than any Goddamn Indian lodge. On the other hand, of course, a house couldn't be moved and the lodge could, easily and quickly. They was a nomadic people, following game herds, so they had to have that type of structure to be able to get going when the herds moved.

While I was there, I met White Antelope, who was a real looker. I swear that I had never seen a girl any more beautiful. Like most Crows she was tall and well formed, had real nice eyes and a smooth complexion. She was polite, had a cheery laugh, and spoke a few words of English.

Of course, I spoke no Crow, but when Tom introduced me to her, I thought it might have been the doing of either Magpie Outside or Cherry. Seldom does anyone, white man or Indian, put a man and a woman together that haven't met without being aware of the potential consequences.

It didn't take White Antelope very long to have me understand that she thought I was just the kind of man that would be right for her. She was well aware that an Indian woman was better off if she could marry a white man. Not only would she have all the stuff that I just explained, but also she would have better clothes and would be better treated. No doubt she wouldn't get whipped as much, if at all. She sure as hell would have lighter work than an Indian squaw.

I admit, I ain't exactly opposed to the charms of a beautiful woman, and just seeing her stirred me a little. But, of course, it come to a shuddering halt when I began to think of Wild Rose. I kept thinking that my wife wouldn't like me to be with another woman so soon after her death. So I sure as hell didn't propose to be. No matter how pretty some gal was, she could never equal my Wild Rose, and my heart just wasn't in it.

I was quite a different man than the young fellow who come up the Chisholm Trail hopin' to find a good-looking whore. That kind of thing was no good for me now. I'd had the sweet loving of a beautiful woman that cared for me more than she did for life itself, and to think of mixing those feelings I had about her with another woman, no matter how nice she might be, was, at that time, a plumb impossibility.

Of course, it was kinda hard on White Antelope, 'cause she sure was good looking, and must have had a lot of bucks admiring her and all, but what she wanted was a white man, and I looked like a good one to her. She had her eye out for me and I could tell. I think it was with some despair she finally come to the conclusion that it weren't no use spending much time on me. I was sorry about that, 'cause I liked to see her around and hear her cheery laugh, but that was all. Indeed, she come back several times during my visit, even though she knowed she was out of consideration.

Well, as this was going on and I was resting in the Crow camp, getting back some of my strength that had been pretty well shook up during the campaign, I got to thinkin' about Mitch Bouyer.

It shook me to the roots finding that message to General Terry had been sidetracked and throwed to the winds—the winds that swept over the battlefield of the Little Big Horn. I was truly shocked by finding those papers, and I wished that I'd never seen 'em. It made me sick to my stomach. I felt that I'd been betrayed by my good friend. Yet I couldn't fit the circumstances together right. How in the hell did that message come to be in Bouyer's boot? It wouldn't have been there unless he'd put it there. How in the hell could he have gotten it? And why would Bouyer want the message? What good would it do him? I remembered the stiff conversation I had with the adjutant, when he told me that delivering the message to him was the same as delivering it to the general and that I'd followed my orders. Major Smith must have put the message on his desk when Mitch and I went out to get my horse. Before we rode out of the camp, Bouyer suddenly went back into the office 'cause he said he'd forgotten something. That had to be when he picked up the message and took it. He knew that letter lay on the adjutant's desk and was real important, and he wanted to see it bad.

God, how I hoped that what I had done was the right thing. I didn't know what General Crook would say when I saw him. My mind kept turning things over, and I looked back and began to question what had happened all along the way. I wondered now what Mitch Bouyer's real feelings had been.

I talked about Bouyer with Tom LaForge, and he listened very intently and thought a lot. He came back to me and said, "You know, Brules, Bouyer was a very complicated man. I've known him for years, but nobody really knew him. The Sioux were right in calling him Two Mans, because he had two distinct sides to him. There was something he was trying to do that we don't any of us know. I've noticed from time to time that he was a mysterious fellow and there was a whole side of him I didn't know. I, too, kinda wonder what the hell he was up to.

"Now, Brules, I'll be going back down with the scouts about the middle of the month, but you better stay here—why don't you go over to the Stillwater and talk to Clapp of the Crow Agency over there? You met him. There were some doings over there in the Crow Reservation in the middle of May or earlier, maybe April. They changed things a lot, and I could never find out exactly what happened. Clapp knows something that I don't know, and maybe he can put you onto some of the Crows that could tell you more. Bouyer's actions sound crazy as hell, yet I never knew Mitch to be crazy. He always had a good reason for doing whatever he did."

Well, I didn't want to push the subject no farther. It just seemed to me that it would make everybody upset and nobody seemed to know the answer.

I couldn't help admiring the way Tom LaForge went about his work. His mission was to round up a bunch of Crow scouts, and I don't know how in the hell he did it, 'cause Curly, Hairy Moccasins, White Man Runs Him, Goes Ahead, and all them fellows—they knew what scoutin' for the army was like, and was fed up with it. Tom not only talked them back into it, but also a whole other bunch. So when he left he had a good group of scouts, maybe thirty or forty. I sure hated to see Tom leave, 'cause I felt real comfortable with him. Anyway, he headed on down the Yellowstone, about the middle of July, I reckon, with them scouts to join Gibbon and Terry, wherever they was.

I hung around for a few more days. The presence of White Antelope didn't make hanging around too tough. But somehow I just couldn't get serious.

It had only been three months since I'd lost my beautiful Wild Rose, and I knew that it was gonna be many a long year before I ever looked at another woman in a serious way. Now, that didn't mean that I didn't watch White Antelope walk around a little bit, and seen how nice and graceful she was, how long her dark hair was. She had snapping eyes, a real creamy-like complexion, a nice butt, and I thought that she was a real beauty, but that's as far as it went. She couldn't figure out what was the matter.

After I'd been there for a week or so, I got to thinking about the advice that Tom had given me. Maybe I would try to find out a little bit more about Mitch Bouyer by going over to the Crow Reservation and seeing Agent Clapp again.

I'd tried to talk with Magpie Outside, but since she'd lost Mitch, she was plumb forlorn and grieving, and I wasn't gonna get no information out of her. Besides that, I don't think she spoke a word of English, and I sure didn't speak a word of Crow.

The thing that made my mind up was the way my blood brother, Wesha, was feeling. He wanted to get back and meet up with his own people. He felt pretty damn sure they'd still be with Crook.

Here it was the middle of July, and the battle of the Rosebud had taken place on the seventeenth of June. I thought maybe Crook woulda pulled out of there and done something, but, no, he was waiting for reinforcements. He knew damn well he didn't have enough men to whip Sitting Bull's warriors.

13

The Medicine Man

When I told Wesha why I wanted to go visit Agent Clapp, I thought old Wesha wouldn't care that much about it. I was wrong. He was pretty keen to do it, and said that he thought it was one damn good idea.

Anyway, one day toward the third week in July or later—I kinda lost track of time after a while 'cause there weren't no big special event—we saddled up our horses to head off. I still rode Jupiter, my big black stallion, and that paint of Wesha's was no slouch. Wesha looked like seven million dollars traveling along on that horse.

We went on up the military road till we come to a place opposite the mouth of the Stillwater on the other side of the river, and guess how we crossed that river? By God, you're right, we swam again! This time the big melt had gone off, but it was still running pretty swift, so we had to really swim the horses good. Still, it was easier than the way we crossed before. When we crawled out on the Stillwater side, we figured we'd take off our clothes and let them dry in the sun, put them on some rock or something. What bothered me more than anything else was gettin' my rifle wet. I knew Goddamn good and well it didn't do a rifle no good to be underwater.

One of the things that Indians didn't do was take good care of their rifles. They just didn't appreciate them mechanical instruments the way the white man does. I knew if my rifle's breech-block action rusted up, one fine day it might not work just when the enemy was charging down on me. That's plumb embarrassing! Could be fatal. I wanted mine to work perfect when I most needed it.

So what I done was to get the rifle out of the scabbard, and use a soft strip of deerskin hide I'd had around my neck like a bandanna, and I wiped it off as best I could. Then I got a real straight willow limb and shaped it down until it made a good ramrod, took a piece of that skin and put it in the muzzle, and poked it down through the barrel and all the way out the breech. I didn't have no oil. I knew that the mechanism of that gun was getting mighty dry in this climate, and mighta picked up a little sand or something underwater, and I sure didn't want that to happen. I done the best cleaning job I could possibly do. I figured that when I got up to Agent Clapp he might have firearm-cleaning equipment I could use to get my rifle back in slick order again.

Well, Wesha watched me for a few minutes, then nodded and went about doing the same thing to his gun. I'd taught him to do that back when we'd gone hunting in the Wind River Range. Wesha caught on quick to white man's ways. I got to laughing sometimes, thinking, by God, if you could just send Wesha to West Point he'd end up a general—damned if he wouldn't.

We hit up along the trail of the Stillwater and come to the Absarokee Agency there. Clapp was there, and we talked to him awhile and told him what had been happening. We asked him how things was with him and he said pretty good, but he sure wished to hell he could get off enough time to go hunting. I kept that in mind, and two days later Wesha and I set out to a little creek nearby and killed us a nice buck. I dressed it all out, skinned it, dried out the hide, and took everything back to Clapp along with the meat. We kept just enough for us to eat. Boy, was he ever pleased.

After that he got real chummy. I figured that if I could just sit there and talk with him a little bit, well, maybe I'd get something from him. I gradually worked around to the question of Mitch Bouyer, and how well did he know Mitch? The minute I mentioned Mitch, he just kinda shook his head and clammed up, and didn't say nothing. Trying to pump information out of him seemed like trying to get water out of a dry hole. I kept at it, hinting around this way and that, trying to brag on Mitch for a while, and then ask about things that I didn't understand. I had to go out and kill another deer or two and give 'em to old Clapp real casual-like, before he finally asked me what the hell I was hanging around there so much for. I asked him, "Am I bothering you?"

"Hell, no," he said. "I like your company, Brules. You're a hell of a guy. I know you have been all around and I sure do like your stories of the Comanches and all that. I was just wondering what you're doing."

"Well, I'll tell you what I'm hangin' around for. I want to get back to General Crook, but I'm Goddamn if I want to go up through country that's loaded with Sioux. I seen how many damn Indians there was in that village on the Little Big Horn, and the country is liable to be full of them. They've got scattered out now, which makes it worse, 'cause about anywhere you go you're liable to run into some. It only takes two to be more than me."

"Yeah, I understand." He nodded. "Maybe you ought to lay low for a while." He said he figured after they'd had all this military pressure, probably Sitting Bull would get the hell out of there. "Of course, just between you and me and the gatepost, Sitting Bull is about three times as smart as those cavalry generals. They ain't gonna catch him. He's gonna zig-zag around and give them a hell of a time, but the bands are sure as hell gonna have to break up around wintertime. There may be some of them other chiefs that aren't quite that wily and the cavalry will come up on them, but Sitting Bull's too damn smart. When he gets ready, I think he'll go to Grandma's Land."

"You mean up in Canada?" I asked.

"Just that, you got it. It's good for him. The only problem with it up there is that it hasn't got enough buffalo."

"I didn't know that."

"It's a funny thing, same kind of country and everything else," he said.

"Maybe they can't stand the cold weather up there."

"Oh, hell, the buffalo can stand any kind of cold weather, you know that. With that coat on the front of him so he doesn't drift like cattle do and get smothered, he faces into a storm and stays with it. That's not the reason, it's something else, something about the soil up there just isn't the buffalo habitat. Those Sioux gotta have buffalo, so they can't stay up there too long. But Sitting Bull's not gonna get caught by any of these present cavalry leaders that Uncle Sam has sent out here."

After a few days I found out that Clapp liked to fish, and I talked to him about going on a little fishing trip. He told me there was one stream that he really liked to fish.

He did take a day off at last, and of course, Wesha went with us. He wasn't gonna let me out of his sight. In fact, I wasn't gonna let him out of my sight either.

Clapp said to me one time, "That Indian is damn fond of you, ain't he? He sure as hell don't want to take his eyes off you, and he don't let nobody get too near."

"That's exactly right. I'm damn fond of him, if you really want to know. He's the best friend I've got. And we're blood brothers."

Anyway, we fished on a small stream that came into the Yellowstone, just maybe four or five miles further upstream than the Stillwater. We had good luck—by God, the trout were just a-biting and we had some fun. We cooked the fish over a fire, and that's when I got a chance to question him a little bit. I said, "What is it about Mitch that made him so different from everybody else?"

"Well," he said, "you know the Indians, and not just the Sioux, called him Two Mans because he was a different kinda guy."

"There's lots of guys that is half-breed," I pointed out.

"Yeah, I don't only mean that, I mean he was just different. He had something going on all the time. One of the things that he had going was his relationship with the Sioux."

"Well, there are several Sioux scouts around that are going against their own people."

"Yeah, they don't want to get caught at it either. Goddamn, boy, if there is anything makes the Sioux mad is their own people coming against them, and showing the white man how to fight them. When one of them gets captured doin' that, he's in for one hell of a torture, don't think he ain't.''

"Yeah, I imagine that's the case. I'd sure feel that way, too, but since Bouyer was half Sioux, why did he go against them?'' I asked.

Clapp looked at me real sharp and said, "I don't believe he was against them.''

"What the hell do you mean? He did fight them.''

"No,'' he said, "I don't believe he did. And I think there is a lot more to it than that. Maybe something personal in his life.''

Well, here we was sitting by the banks of the stream after making a good catch. The trout had been hitting pretty well. Clapp turned to me after mullin' it awhile and said, "You know, Brules, I been thinking this thing over real careful, and I'm not too sure that you haven't got onto something. I think you better talk to Running Wolf. He's a medicine man and commands considerable respect. He's pretty old, and he don't get mixed up in the politics, and never in the fighting. He's way past warrior age, but he knows a lot. He seems like he knows about everything that goes on in the Crow nation at one time or another. Maybe you should talk to him, if you can find the son of a bitch.''

"Well,'' I said, "where do you suppose he'd be?''

"No idea, but I'll make some inquiries around. Chances are he's not very far away. I'll check tomorrow or the next day and let you know.''

That was all I had to go on. We went back to the agency that evening and I told Wesha about it, the best I could. We could make ourselves easy understood about things that was real simple, like any kind of fighting or military tactics or talk about women. When it came to talking about something real tricky, I didn't know just how to get the idea over to him.

I explained the best I could that I didn't understand why the Crows hadn't done as good a job as they ought to. He nodded at that, and I said, "They didn't have no warriors in

Gibbon's bunch, just scouts, but remember, there was some Crows up with Crook—two or three hundred of them. They run like hell when they seen the Sioux, and it was your Shoshones that straightened them up and turned 'em around again.''

That got Wesha's attention. His eyes gleamed and he agreed. He knew what the hell I was talking about. Then I told him what Clapp had told me about the medicine man Running Wolf. Wesha's eyes brightened, he nodded vigorously, looked me straight in the eye, and said, ''You see medicine man, see quick. See medicine man. If anybody know, he know.''

Two days later we heard Running Wolf was living at a tributary fork of the Stillwater, only about seven or eight miles upstream. Clapp told me, ''You're gonna need an interpreter, 'cause neither you nor that Shoshone warrior of yours speaks Crow.''

''Well, what are we gonna do about that?'' I asked.

''We'll get one of these Frenchies around here—we'll find one,'' he offered. ''If they're in from trapping or if they're trying to fix a boat, we'll find them around.''

Sure enough, the next day we got ahold of a fellow that was somehow related, I never found out just how, to the Frenchie that took me downstream on the Yellowstone in the pirogue.

I still had quite a bit of money that Crook's adjutant had given me when I carried the message to Terry, and figured that I could use some of that to keep the man interested in getting something out of Running Wolf.

The next day Wesha and I hit off on our horses to go up the Stillwater, Frenchie on a mule. It wasn't very long before we come up on the tributary, and there at his lodge was the old medicine man sitting out front by a small fire, smoking his pipe.

Well, we done some introductions, and said nothing about anything except the game situation, the weather, and a few unimportant things for three or four hours. I had a real good knife that I hated to part with, but I thought that if we could get the information, it would be worth it. So, after a long while, I took this knife out of its sheath and put it down, sorta halfway between me and the old medicine man, and I could see the old boy's eyes just gleam.

I had Frenchie explain that we was gonna ask some questions, and if we could get the answers that we was sure was the truth, we would be glad to give him that knife.

That old medicine man was pretty cagey. He told Frenchie that he *could* tell us a lot of things that other people didn't know, but some of the things he was unwilling to tell, and there wasn't no knife nor nothing else that was gonna make him do it. On the other hand, if we was gonna ask reasonable questions and he wasn't violating nobody's confidence, he would go ahead and tell us. Well, that seemed fair enough. I thought that maybe the old duck might be a square shooter.

I decided I ought to give Frenchie a little talking-to ahead of time, so he wouldn't get off the track. I told him, "Now, when you're translating, it's real important to ask him questions that ain't gonna get him upset. Otherwise he'll quit talking, and that ain't no good. When I ask him something, I want to be sure that we're saying the right words to him, 'cause sometimes things get mixed up and people get the wrong idea."

Frenchie nodded and said he understood. He seemed real sharp.

So with that I begun to ask Running Wolf some questions. First thing I said was "Do you think that the Indian's ever gonna beat the white man?"

He shook his head for quite a long time. "No, never win, Indian never win. If Indian keeps on like always, someday he be no more."

I asked him, "Is there anything that the Indian could do that would make it so that he wouldn't be completely defeated?"

The old boy thought for a while and replied, "Indian must stop fighting Indian. Indian must all together fight white man, even then maybe Indian never win."

Well, I thought, the old boy's on the right track when you stop to think what the white man's got to work with. He makes the ammunition, he makes the rifles, he's got a military machine that is bigger than anything the Indians can put together. On top of that he's got railroads and everything else to move stuff around, and when the railroads come into this country it's gonna be a different story. An Indian can't stand combat for very long, 'cause he's got to stop and look for something to eat. The white man has got his supplies provided, and there ain't no way that the Indian can fight that. The Indian's numbers is held down by what he can get to eat. If he's got to depend on game, he can't have a very big population. By farming the white man can support a hundred families, where the Indian, by hunting, can only support one. Pretty soon the Indian is gonna find that he's got a hundred to one against him. Them's bad odds.

I still needed a hell of a lot more information, so I started pumping away. I asked whether he remembered when Old Gray Whiskers—Colonel Gibbon—come in to the agency at Absarokee in April trying to get Chief Blackfoot and eight hundred of his warriors to help him fight the Sioux?

Running Wolf nodded and said, yes, he remembered that.

"How come the chief of the Blackfoot wouldn't give Gray Beard no warriors? It didn't make sense. After all, them Crows and Sioux were blood enemies for a thousand years, and there the Crows had a chance to join up with white folks and really clean up on the Sioux, and damned if they didn't back off. What's the cause of that? Are the Crows poor warriors and not fighters? Are they cowards?"

Well, with that the old boy kinda bristled, and said, "No, Crow fine warrior. Good fighter, smaller nation than the Sioux, but hold own all the time. Crow very good fighter."

I kinda had the same idea myself, but I still couldn't understand why they wouldn't join up with Gibbon. Gibbon got only scouts out of it. I asked, "How come Blackfoot let him have scouts?"

The old man just kinda shrugged his shoulders and didn't say anything.

Then I asked him outright if he knew anything about a fellow named Mitch Bouyer. When I said that, that old medicine man really clammed up. Well, I was afraid for a minute I'd doomed the conference and our conversation. Quick-like, I begun to ask him some other things.

Running Wolf began talking and Frenchie was shaking his head. He started giving me bits and pieces, something about Two Mans and Two Bodies, and something about Powder River and the Tongue River.

Then there were something about a powwow and more about Two Mans. I thought maybe Frenchie didn't know how to translate better.

Finally the Frenchie began to get impatient, and I hoped that I wouldn't lose my translator here, 'cause then I wouldn't have nothing. I figured I better back off. The old boy was still the problem, and, damn his hide, he knew something and I had to find out what the hell it was.

So, I said to Frenchie, "Let's ask him if there was a powwow."

With that the old boy looked around, looked at me a couple of times, mumbled something, and nodded his head. I said, "All right, ask him about the Tongue River. Was it on the Tongue River?"

"He said he didn't know whether it was the Tongue or the Powder, but it was near the headwaters of one of them."

"Well," I said, "can you find out *when* the hell was this damn meeting?"

Frenchie was having trouble with that too, 'cause the old man would say something about the month of green grass. I said, "What the hell month is that?"

"I think it's about March or early April. That's about the way of the moon, the moon of fresh grass," Frenchie guessed.

"That stands to reason," I said. "Let's get this straight. There was a powwow up on the headwaters of the Tongue or the Powder and it happened sometime in late March or early April. I want to find out more about this powwow."

He asked the old boy, using the name for the whole Sioux nation, which was different from the tribal circle names. The old medicine man looked at him straight in the face and said

Sioux, and then he also said the name for the Crows, Absarokee. He said, "Absarokee there too."

"Now, wait a minute, this sounds like bullshit to me. You're talking about a meeting between the Crows and the Sioux—deadly enemies? They had a meeting in the month of green grass at the headwaters?" And then I looked back at him.

The old man started getting mad, and Frenchie said, "Yeah, yeah, that's what he said."

Then the old man started talking again, without being questioned, and I could hear the same word coming up all the time about Two Mans, Two Mans. I jumped in. "Wait a cotton-picking minute here. I know something about this." I told Frenchie, "Ask him again if he knows anything about the scout named Mitch Bouyer, that we mentioned before."

Well, he asked him, and with that the old boy drew himself up, folded his arms in his blanket, and looked at me as if I was the scum of the earth. He didn't answer for a minute or two, and then he turned to the Frenchman and said, "This white man is ignorant, everybody knows Two Mans."

I thought, now we're getting somewhere. "Was Two Mans at this meeting?"

The answer came back, "Only a stupid coyote would not know that Two Mans was the only one that could bring about this meeting."

Well, that made sense, 'cause he spoke both Sioux and Crow and was related to both. I guess he was about the only man in the country that could put the two nations together.

At my proddin' Frenchie asked him if all the Sioux and Crow were there. The old man shook his head hard. "No, no, not all of them. There were several Sioux circles—the Miniconjou, Hunkpapa, Oglala, and maybe Sans Arc—but there were a lot of Sioux circles that weren't there. It was just the chiefs and their leading warriors in the tribe."

If Bouyer didn't get all the Sioux and Crow, that might account for some other things that went on.

Frenchie had mentioned the chief saying something about *pointe d'un couteau*. And I asked about that again.

But old medicine man just shook his head and lapsed into silence.

We sat there a good half hour. I knew we was getting close to something real important, so I tried to go at the problem from another side.

Then, Goddammit, I suddenly remembered that, just as the white man swears on the Bible, the Indian swears on the "point of a knife." If you swear on the point of a knife, it means that if you tell a lie anyone may pick up the knife and drive it through your heart. That's the Indian way of saying, I tell the truth so help me—I ain't bearing no false witness.

Well, what was Bouyer swearing to? I had Frenchie ask, "Did this swearing have anything to do with fighting the white man?"

The old medicine man nodded vigorously and said, "If Indian going to win, Indian not fight Indian, Indian fight white man."

This old boy was telling us the Indians had got together for an alliance between the Crow and Sioux. It sounds like Mitch Bouyer set up the whole damn thing. When I first met Bouyer I knew he was a complicated man, but I never dreamed he could be a traitor.

"Ask if he knows anything about Yellow Hair." The old boy shook his head. "Wait a minute, ask him if he knows anything about Son of the Morning Star." That was the Crow name for Custer.

Now, the minute that we asked that the old boy said, "Yes, yes, he knew about Son of the Morning Star."

"Ask him if this powwow had anything to do with Son of the Morning Star."

The old man nodded.

I asked if he knew anything about No Hipbone. Again, the old boy nodded plumb vigorous. No Hipbone was the name for Terry and Gray Fox was General Crook's name among the Crow.

"Now, ask him if Gray Fox, No Hipbone, and Son of the Morning Star was what Bouyer was discussin' at this conference."

He asked him and the old man nodded yes, and muttered something faintly. I asked Frenchie to pick that up. Frenchie came back with "Indian agree must not fight Indian. Indian must fight white man."

"Well," I said, "here we go, we've got something now. Let's see if they made a treaty." Frenchie asked the medicine man, and slowly the medicine man nodded.

I could see what the plan was. If the Indian was gonna win, he was gonna have to have a treaty between longtime enemies and they was gonna go against the white man together.

"Was anything writ down about it? Was there anything like that?"

The medicine man nodded yes, there was something writ down.

Of course, the only man there that could write must have been Mitch Bouyer. "Ask him if Mitch Bouyer wrote this treaty," I said.

The Indian nodded. "Yes, that's right."

"How did he write it? Ask him what did he use to write the treaty."

The medicine man replied very straight that he had a piece of paper and he wrote with the lead point of a bullet!

"Can you find out what the hell the terms was? What did they have to do, give up territory?"

The medicine man shook his head. "No! Treaty simple! Both tribes give back stolen horses, and swear to never fight again from the time sun goes down."

I got a real bad feeling about all this. I thought, I've got something here that I wouldn't give to Terry or Gibbon, but I might give it to General Crook, 'cause he understood the Indian ways. In fact, he was a member of some of the Indian secret societies and he knew a lot.

"Ask him what about this swearing on the point of the knife? What did Bouyer have to swear to?"

I began to see things were really kinda complicated. I thought this meeting had plenty to do with Bouyer's action before and during the battle. Especially when he disappeared and come back again with a beautiful Sioux vest, and especially when the Crow scouts went up to the bluffs of the Little Big Horn and fired warning shots into the big village!

Frenchie listened to the old man, who did a lot of jabbering, and one name kept coming though all the time—"Son of the Morning Star."

Pretty soon Frenchie turned to me, shook his head, and said, "It is hard to believe. It is hard to believe."

"What the hell is hard to believe? What do you mean?"

"Bouyer swear for something bad."

"What did he swear to?"

"He swear to kill Son of the Morning Star."

You could have blown me over. Bouyer swore that he would kill Custer? Why would he want to kill him? Frenchie must have translated it wrong or something. Shit—he was Custer's scout.

So I ask Frenchie to keep asking. The old medicine man was sitting there shaking his head, and Frenchie said, "You can't shake him from that. That's what he said."

"Now, what in hell was Bouyer gonna gain by killing Custer?"

With that the old medicine man drew himself up, as if we was the stupidest couple of bastards that he had ever seen in his life, and said, "Again, Indian fight Indian—no win. Indian stop fighting and join together. Fight white man only way to win, only way."

"Well, God almighty, what the hell does killing Custer have to do with this?" I stopped and thought to myself, Jesus, if Mitch Bouyer swore to kill Custer himself, in order to get this treaty put together, that might account for a hell of a lot of things that was going on.

On the other hand, I just couldn't believe it. So I done a kinda dumb thing, I guess. I told Frenchie to say that I had known Two Mans, he was a good friend. I cannot believe what the medicine man has said. He must explain more.

That old medicine man stood up, wrapped his blanket around himself, looked at us with eyes that was burning, and said, "White man crooked, no want to give knife. Trying to

say medicine man liar. Medicine man not liar, white man liar.''
He turned, walked away, leaving the knife on the ground. That
sure cooled me down fast, and I realized I'd overstepped the
bounds. I picked the knife up, and ran after him and held it out
in front of him, to show that it wasn't the knife, I just couldn't
believe the story. The old boy, with dignity, kept waving me
away and marched on back toward his tepee and went inside.

I figured I had messed up the whole thing. I hadn't got the
information I wanted to have, only bits and pieces, and I'd
made Running Wolf sore as hell, just 'cause I had made a
stupid remark. I didn't really mean I didn't believe the old boy,
just that what he was telling me was so weird, I didn't see how
it could be true.

Anyway, I left the knife in front of the tepee, and Wesha,
me, and Frenchie rode back on down the Stillwater toward
Absarokee.

I recalled what I knew, and tried to figure where Bouyer
fit into this and what the hell he was doing.

When Custer was shot, and all them boys had to dismount
and get him back up on his horse, he was either dying or dead.
Once that happened there was no further thought of carrying
on any charge into the village. Who in the hell was gonna lead
it?

What leaders they had was back up the column, and the
shock of it all was that nobody really realized what had just
happened.

I could see that plain as hell. I'd watched it. Crazy Horse
and the rest of them Sioux bucks had been upstream fightin'
and drivin' Reno up the hill. When the Indians got the message
that another cavalry outfit was comin' down the Medicine Tail
Coulee to attack at the middle of the village, boy, they come
a-runnin', and you could hear the roar of them.

Now, what the hell was it that suddenly give the alarm to
Gall, Crazy Horse, Rain in the Face, and some of them other
chiefs who was all down there pounding Reno? Then, by God,
I remembered when Bouyer and them Crows was on top of the
bluff firing them old muskets into the camp—that was the
signal!

Folks who heard about that afterward said it was done 'cause they were firing in defiance. Well, in the first place, Custer would have had a fit if he had known they was firing in defiance, because he was trying to keep his whole approach secret, and he done pretty good until them guys fired from on top of the ridge.

Damn it—that's what Bouyer was doing. He was warning the Sioux they was being attacked from another direction! At Bouyer's signal them bucks that had been chasing Reno up the hill turned around and started riding like hell for the other end of the village!

Lots of people argue that there was no fighting at the river, and that Custer never went down to the river, 'cause they didn't find no shells. Up on the battlefield, where there was some pretty hot engagements, they would find six or seven hundred shells, at different locations, proving there had been a lot of firing in those areas.

That's right—there was no shells found at the Coulee Ford because there was no mass firing at the bottom of the Medicine Tail Coulee. There was only one Oglala warrior and four Cheyennes, trying to hold two hundred and twenty men from crossing the river. They must have been mighty good shots or mighty lucky, but there was no more firing because the Oglala and the Cheyennes cut and run after they fired.

I also remembered that night that Bouyer went out on a scouting expedition of his own when we was clawing our way up to the Crow's Nest. Well, scouts did that sorta thing from time to time, but it sure was a crazy thing to do in the middle of the night. How in the hell was he gonna see anything? Then he comes back with a brand-new beautiful beaded Sioux vest. Where did the son of a bitch get that? Damn him, he said he found it on the ground! Well, that's Goddamn unlikely!

In the Indian world that was a precious vest. It was like possessing some beautiful jewels or something that you'd hang tight to. Somebody give him that! And what were them wolf calls, when there weren't no wolf sign the next day? He must have had a secret meeting with them Sioux down there. They gave him that vest as a reward for what he was doing! Or they might have given it to him in hopes of being able to identify him in the fight that was coming up, so that he wouldn't get killed.

Well, that might be some kind of protection, but, Jesus, in the thick of combat, you couldn't be too sure of it. I just didn't know how to work it all out. I did recall that when Bouyer and Custer parted at the Crow's Nest, both of them was mad as hell. They was still arguing about how many Sioux there was. Then much later that morning Custer dismissed all us scouts. I rode out with Bouyer and them four Crows, Curly, White Swan, Goes Ahead, and Hairy Moccasins. That was real vivid in my memory. Then we got up on top of that big bluff, and they fired into the camp. While we was still up there on that ridge, we heard some calling from down below, using the name "Wica-nonpa." They was yelling in Sioux. The Crows there asked Bouyer what they were yelling about. He translated, "They're yelling, 'Two Mans, you get back, go away, go away or you will be killed.' " I thought then that they was trying to scare him out. Now I seen that they weren't doing that, they was telling him that he had finished his job and to get out before it was too late. But he hadn't finished his job—not in his own mind.

When one of the Crows said to Bouyer, "You must come back with us. You must come to the Crow village. Magpie Outside is waiting for you," Bouyer shook his head and said, "I can't do that, I can't. I cannot go back with you."

So, what the hell was going on there? He told all of us to leave while we had a chance, but he himself turned and rode down the hill toward Custer's column. I could see him riding along the bluffs before he pitched down into Medicine Tail Coulee and caught up to ride beside Custer.

That was kinda crazy, wasn't it? Why in hell would he feel a loyalty to a man who had been insultin' him, calling him a coward—even a liar—and tellin' him to get the hell out of the way?

At the time I kept thinking if Custer said all that kind of stuff, why was Bouyer so damn loyal to Custer?

Now I could see it. No, he didn't go back down on that

trail for any loyalty to Custer, for any love of being a scout, or for any loyalty to the dying point. He went back down that trail to kill Custer and to keep his word to the Sioux and the Crow.

I could see it now clear as hell. Yes, sir, that's exactly what happened. That's what the old medicine man was trying to tell me. Bouyer had sworn on the point of the knife that if the Sioux and the Crow would join forces, stop fighting, and sign a treaty, he himself would kill Long Hair, the big enemy of the Sioux.

But why? Then I remembered something I'd heard about Custer and one of Bouyer's relatives, maybe his half sister. Something happened to her, down on the Washita, in 1868, when Custer had his great victory. He took a lot of Indian women and children prisoners. It was said that Custer and some of his young officers, considering the squaws spoils of war, forced themselves on the women.

I don't know nothing about that, but there was a rumor going around later—back in 1870 or so—that a squaw in the Sioux camp had a young boy that weren't all Indian. He had blond hair and was called Yellow Bird.

When I got back to Absarokee, I got ahold of Clapp and told him what I had discovered. He was very interested, saying, "Well, I wasn't sure of this, but I knew something was going on."

I also asked Clapp about the story of the squaws who were taken captive, and whether they were molested by the officers. He said there was rumors going up and down the frontier about it, and Custer did get into some trouble one other time 'cause he didn't protect 'em. But Clapp didn't know the details.

Most of it could have been just rumor. I had no idea, 'cause I didn't know any of the people or talk to any of them, but Mitch Bouyer had some damn good reason for hating Custer. Course, on the other hand, it might well have been because Custer treated him as if he was kinda stupid. Custer would criticize Bouyer and run him down in front of his officers and men. I don't know if that would be enough for Bouyer to swear to kill him.

This is all speculation and I can't say one way or another, but there was some deep reason why Mitch Bouyer was mad at Custer, and was out to get him. In my opinion he didn't swear he would kill him just so he could bring the Sioux and Crow together. I think it was more than that. Maybe he used it as an excuse, but it certainly cast a different light on the whole situation.

I ain't never gonna forget that afternoon of June twenty-fifth, when I stood there with the Crow scouts and watched Bouyer wave good-bye to us, and gallop on down the slope to join Custer at the bottom of the Medicine Tail Coulee. Indeed, I recall seeing him, in the distance, ride up on Custer's left side. But, as I done told ya, the head of the column disappeared around the shoulder of the bluff to the north and I didn't see what happened.

I ran east, along the ridge, so I could get a better angle. When I got there I could see the head of the column again. That must have been an awful sight for the troops who stopped and saw men dismounting in the middle of the Little Big Horn to lift someone up from the water. I knew that it had to be Custer, bad hurt or dead. My heart sank because I knew that the force of the charge had been lost. After that, everything began falling up on the hill in the confusion, and the roar of the Oglala charge, coming from the south, was drowning everything else out, even the noise of the river.

Ten years later, when they had all them gatherings in 1886, and I was with General Crook when he came back to the battlefield, I had a chance to talk to some of them Sioux. They all said that the village at the north had emptied out, that there was only four warriors down there, three northern Cheyenne and one Oglala. The Oglala, named Bob Tail Horse, had the job of keeping a sacred buffalo head or something in one of the tepees, and that's why he hadn't joined up with the rest of the warriors at the south end of the village. As to the Cheyenne, they lived right there in that village and had been just loafing around. When Custer's cavalry troops came down the Medicine Tail Coulee, there was nothing left for these fellows to do but defend themselves. Now, you know and I know that there ain't no four Indians that are gonna stand up against two hundred twenty cavalrymen, but it is true that they did take some potshots, and perhaps one was lucky!

Bob Tail Horse told the story of how he stepped out from his tepee and looked over the upper side of it and saw a big bunch of blue-coated pony soldiers coming down the Medicine Tail Coulee. Of course, at that time he didn't know it was Custer, nor did any of the Indians. He just said that the man who was leading the column was riding a sorrel horse with four white socks that was quite a prancer. Well, that had to be Custer, 'cause that was the description of Custer's favorite horse, Vic.

He said that when he saw the string of pony soldiers coming, he let out a yell, and he and the three Cheyennes ran to a ridge just a bit south and west of the ford. They got down behind it and started shooting. They had three old rifles. I don't know what they were, but they was small caliber and kinda antique. One of the braves had a bow and arrow, 'cause he'd been out fishing before the battle started, and that was what he was carrying.

The Indians knowed that they didn't have much of a defense. They did take a few shots, for luck, and beat it. Their shooting performance didn't need to be any better, 'cause they dealt the fatal shot of the whole battle.

Then I wonder about another possibility. Did Bouyer come up alongside Custer as they was crossing the stream, and shoot him? I don't think so. Maybe he had the intention of doing that, but I reckon it wasn't necessary. When Custer's body was found it had two wounds. One was in the left breast and the other was on his left temple, both fatal. The wound on his head was caused by a shot real close, 'cause powder burns was on his left temple. Was it possible for Mitch Bouyer to ride up, come right alongside him, pull out his six-shooter, and blow a hole in Custer's head that close, and ride away? Hardly!

I really don't think that Bouyer killed Custer. 'Cause if he had, he would have been shot to pieces by the rest of the men right as they stood there. Nobody could have gotten away with that. Bouyer didn't need to kill him, he saw he was already fatally hit. Remember, I found Bouyer's body about a mile away from there in the deep ravine. He'd never have made it there if he had shot Custer in the presence of the staff.

As far as the small bullet in his left breast is concerned, I think that was the lucky Oglala shot with a light-caliber rifle, and that's what killed him. Custer hesitated just before starting across the creek, which made him a good target, and all four of them Indians shot and ran. One of them made a lucky hit, and I bet that's the bullet that hit Custer in the left breast.

Then who in the hell shot him in the temple?—'cause Custer didn't commit suicide. He was shot in the left temple but he was right handed, and besides, it weren't in Custer's nature. He'd fight to the last.

As far as the temple wound, I think it come from the Sioux squaws that went over the battlefield after the fight was over and shot everybody in the head to make sure they was dead. Lots of those dead troopers had that same wound.

When I found Mitch's body up in the deep ravine along with a bunch of other dead guys, he'd been fighting all the way. He was a long ways from where Custer went down. That damn vest didn't do him no good. On top of that, some Sioux had stripped it off his body after he was dead. Christ, there'd been thousands of Sioux riding around, everybody madder than hell, a pitched battle, smoke and shouting, dust flying, and the troops going every which way. Bouyer didn't have a chance, and got killed right along with the rest of the cavalrymen.

Well, them are all the thoughts and wonderings that I had about what had happened to Mitch Bouyer, but it was sure a strange story. I reckoned I'd tell it to Crook someday and he could solve it, that was if I ever seen Crook again.

I returned to Pryor Creek and the Crow village. My friend, White Antelope, greeted me like I was her man, although she and me was the only ones that knowed I wasn't. In any case, I stayed for a few days there just kinda wondering what to do next, when a mail courier come up to the agency and stopped by the Crow village. He was full of news. Crook had finally come down the Rosebud and joined Terry and Gibbon at the military encampment on the Yellowstone. They was having a big powwow there, and the courier figured that the next action would be against the Sioux.

Crook had been delayed because he'd been waiting at Cloud Peak Camp for reinforcements from the Fifth Cavalry, out of Fort Hays, Kansas, under Major Merritt. But the Fifth Cavalry had been delayed by an engagement at War Bonnet Creek with several thousand northern Cheyenne who'd come out of the Standing Rock Reservation fixing to join Sitting Bull. Merritt had been marching up the Bozeman Trail to join Crook, and got the message that the Cheyenne had left the reservation and was headed to join the other hostiles. There was nothing for Merritt to do but turn aside and make a dash to intercept them Cheyenne, and stop them from joining up.

He did a three-day march all in one steady ride, and got himself in a position at the big bend of War Bonnet Creek. Meanwhile, the supply wagons that was coming across country were way behind them. The wagon train was coming down one side of a ridge runnin' north and south, and down the other side come thousands of these Cheyenne. They was gonna meet right where the ridge stopped, and Merritt could see the whole thing.

The Cheyenne was aware of only the wagon train. They had no idea that there was twelve hundred troops laying back of another ridge, facing them as they was coming down. It was a perfect trap, and I suppose well worth that hellish triple march.

There was another thing about that particular engagement that was right smart, which was in the story Jack Finerty wrote later in his magazine article. He was riding with Merritt that day, and he wrote all about what happened there.

It seems Buffalo Bill was scouting for Merritt. Lots of folks who saw how he dressed up with his blond hair, cowboy hat, and pearl-handled pistols thought that Cody was just a showman and couldn't perform. Finerty told me later that nothing could be further from the truth.

"By God," he said, "those Indians came riding down War Bonnet Creek, often sneaking a look over at the wagon train and fixing to murder it. At the head was Yellow Hand, chief of the northern Cheyennes, and Bill Cody saw him coming from a long ways away. When Yellow Hand got in close, Cody came straight for him, and damn if that Yellow Hand didn't see it and run like hell toward Cody. Both of them was firing pistols at each other as they rode.''

Finerty said it was just like watching two knights on horseback challenging each other in one of them jousts. Bill Cody got in close enough to be accurate with his pistol, and he just shot Yellow Hand through the head. Old Yellow Hand peeled off his horse. Cody jumped off, took Yellow Hand's scalp, and yelled, ''The first scalp for Custer.''

Finerty was real certain and definite about how well Cody did. He said that Bill Cody sure as hell lived up to every word of his reputation on that day, and it was a proud time.

Anyway, after this hand-to-hand combat them troops just marched over the top of the ridge and the Cheyenne seen them, which plumb stopped them in their tracks. They began to mill around, trying to figure out what to do. Merritt made up them Indians' mind for 'em by giving the command for the Gatling guns to open up. The destruction was pretty bad. Them Cheyenne turned around and headed like hell back toward the reservation, with Merritt's troops shagging them all the way.

On account of all this it took damn near two weeks before Merritt got back on the trail, but it was worthwhile. God knows what would have happened if a thousand more of them Cheyennes had been able to hook up with Sitting Bull's forces. But by that time Crook was really gnawing at the leather, wanting to know where in hell his reinforcements was.

Funny thing, it was only two or three years later that telegraph lines was all through that country, and there wasn't no need to work in that vacuum of ignorance. You had instant information and you knew where to be and how to be there in a matter of hours.

It was still a real wilderness then, though. God knows there wasn't no telegraph wires in there. Telegraphs had to come to Bozeman around by Salt Lake and across the transcontinental railroad route.

Anyway, when Crook met with Gibbon and Terry, and all them troops was finally united, there must have been better than two thousand of them.

Once the courier passed along the news, Wesha and I didn't waste no time. He saddled up that fine painted stallion, and I saddled Jupiter. I rubbed noses with White Antelope, and we was mounted and off. Both our horses were in damn good condition, having rested all that time on good pasture, and it didn't take us two days to make it down the new military road on the north side of the Yellowstone to the Rosebud.

We seen there was two encampments, one on the north side of the river and the other on the south, where the general headquarters was located.

We didn't have no trouble crossing that river, with plenty of transport barges around, and it wasn't long before I checked in with General Crook's headquarters. First I talked to his adjutant, Captain Bourke. He told me that the general had been wondering where I was all that time, and if I was dead or alive.

I told him what had happened, and he seemed to understand, nodded with a kinda grunt, and said, "Well, the general will be anxious to see you."

I didn't get to see General Crook for a couple of days, but kept reporting back to the adjutant just to let him know I was still there.

I got to thinking a lot about what I was gonna tell General Crook, and decided that I ought to take it easy on how much information I should part with. I could see no reason to tell him about the medicine man, or about Mitch Bouyer—not right now. All them soldiers was dead, and until we really got it sorted out, we might just have a useless ruckus.

When I was allowed to go into Crook's tent, he arose with a kinda smile on his face, and reached out with that paw of his and said, "Hello, Brules, glad to see you back. A terrific ride, I hear. But neither Gibbon or his adjutant, nor Terry or his adjutant, knows anything about the dispatch I sent. Now, sir, kindly tell me just what the hell happened."

"I didn't give it to Terry," I confessed. "I give it to his adjutant, Smith, sir, but only after he done twisted my arm a lot. Everybody was backing him up by saying that if you delivered a message to the adjutant, it was the same as delivering it to the general. Now, I don't know nothing about military procedures, sir, and I did keep holding out to see General Terry, but they said he was too busy and I wasn't gonna get a chance to talk to him. Give it to his adjutant, they said, that's regular military protocol. So that's what I done, sir.''

"Yes, that's right, son, and you did the right thing. I guess Custer must have got the message from Terry's adjutant when he was on his way. I didn't think to check that with Terry, but I wondered why he didn't have it.''

I didn't offer any explanation, though I knew damn well why Custer never got that message. That dispatch was tucked away in Mitch Bouyer's boots. Anyway, Crook seemed satisfied with as much as I told him. I had to wonder if he really was, but I was glad I held my tongue, because the information that I had would just upset the hell out of him, and at that point he couldn't do nothing about it.

"Well, Brules, you rode like hell. Probably by the time you got the message to Custer it wouldn't have changed his plans anyway. I couldn't have got there for a whole month, as it turned out, so it wouldn't have made any difference.

"Come and sit here, and tell me a little bit about the ride,'' he said.

I told him quickly what had happened to us on the way. When I got through, he clapped his hands and said, "By Jove, that Shoshone warrior of yours, your blood brother, is some man, isn't he?''

"Yes, sir. He sure as hell is,'' I agreed.

"Both of you are good men, and we're glad to have you back. Now, you're not quitting here now, we've got a long way to go, and we're going to give them hell from now on. We're dividing up. I'm not in favor of the way Terry insists on using his wagons all the way. All of my men have been equipped with only a blanket, and not even an extra set of clothes. We are supposed to rough it through, and that's what we're going to do. We've got to drag these savages out of this area some way or another, and we're going to do it!

"Persistence is the thing. The Indians can't feed themselves, they got to keep moving and they will never be able to form again in a big group the way they did on the Little Big Horn. We must press them hard, even in the winter. We've got to give them no peace. No peace for the wicked, that's our motto.

"We're going on with this campaign if it takes us five years, and we will clean them out. It's the only way it can be done. Meanwhile, we have to chip away at the buffalo herds, shut off the commissary in that manner. Without the buffalo the Indian can't live. Once we see that the herds are pretty well exterminated, we'll be in good shape. It's a damned shame to have to destroy those beautiful buffalo, just to round up a few thousand savages, but I'm afraid that's the way it's going to have to be done."

Well, that was a shock for me to listen to, but he knowed his business and the more you thought of it, of course, it was exactly the idea. Those Indians was gonna have to come in. It was gonna be damn tough during the winter when they didn't have no food. That's what was gonna make them bend. It was a damn sight easier to handle a band of Sioux on an Indian reservation by passing out beef, than it was trying to kill them in the wilderness.

14

A Dismal March

When Crook finished explaining the plan, he said, "Glad to have you back, Brules, and your good friend Wesha. I want to congratulate both of you. You did a fine job, you're good military men. Very soon now we're going to head south down toward the Little Missouri and see what we can find down there. We may even go as far as the Black Hills, but we're traveling light and fast and that ought to be your style."

He stood up and shook hands with me. I did feel kinda bad about not telling him the whole Bouyer story, but I thought I ought to let it wait.

Me and Wesha waited in that camp for four or five days while them fellows made up their minds. Finally the command was split, Terry went off with his men, wagons and all, and Crook started southeast to the Little Missouri. We had short supplies even when we started, but Crook was desperate to make contact with some of the Sioux from the Battle of the Little Big Horn.

It made those military fellows plumb wild with anticipation when they knew that there had been maybe fifteen thousand Sioux in that camp and, by God, they hadn't been able to catch up with any of them when the battle was over. How the hell could that many Indians hide themselves, even in that vast country? Of course, they come across their camp signs and all that sort of stuff, but the Indians were just too smart for them and moved too fast. That's why Crook didn't fool with wagons and insisted on every man carrying his blanket. One day's rations and a couple of utensils was all they got to feed themselves.

When Crook moved out it was sometime in the later part of August. I'll never forget the day. It was raining to beat hell, and the trails was muddy. We just worked our way on down a little ways to the Big Horn and hit out cross country for the Little Missouri. We kept going, day after day without any contact with the hostiles. Supplies started to get short.

Crook was absolutely opposed to doing anything but fighting the Indians as straight as he could. He figured on getting to the Black Hills before our rations ran out. So we moved right along despite the weather, and all that mud that would cling to our feet and the feet of our horses and mules. It rained the whole time. Cold and miserable, we slept with just a damn little woolen blanket on the ground every night, and we was soaking wet from dawn to dusk and all through the night.

When we got to the Little Missouri, it was a real disappointment. There hadn't been anybody around there for a while, trails were all at least thirty days old, and no sign of Sioux whatsoever.

Even the regular troops was getting cussing mad and disappointed, and was losing their confidence in the campaign. The general couldn't find no enemy, and kept the troops slogging along in the rain and mud, half starving. About that time they began eating their horses, and that made me feel like bloody hell. I'll tell you, the idea of eating a horse was so bad, I couldn't stand it, but every now and then we'd see a carcass of one that had either died and been eaten, or had been butchered, because the fellows was so short of food.

I kept a real close eye on Jupiter. He was doing right well, better than I ever expected, wasn't thinned down, nothing like them cavalry horses. I sure as hell didn't want to see him get ate by the troops. I guarded him close, and I could see that Wesha did the same thing with his mount. As a matter of fact, when they started eating horses, Wesha got real disgusted. I couldn't help thinking about why the Lewis and Clark expedition bought some horses from the Shoshones over in the valley of the Columbia, 'cause they were starving, and butchered them to eat, and how disgusted the Shoshone was at that time. Shoshones never killed horses, horses was too valuable, and, by God, that's the way I felt about it too. I figured that I'd starve to death before I'd eat my horse or let anybody else have a taste of him.

Anyway, what with the bad weather and the bad planning and no Sioux, finally them Shoshone got sick of it and decided to go home.

Wesha come to tell me one night when I was laying in my bedroll. "Tomorrow, blood brother, we leave for our homes in the Wind River Range. It is with a sad heart that I leave you, but these are my people and they wish me to go. They were worried about me all the time that I was with you, often thinking me dead, and now they wonder if I have deserted them or if I think more of you than I do of them.

"My heart is sad because of this, divided between you and my people, but I am a chief of the Shoshone and it is for them I live. I have to leave. As I told you before, my brother, these men long for their wives and I, too, have to see my women again. You know how I feel about them and how I ache for them. Now I must go."

I want to tell you, when he told me he was leaving, I had terrible mixed feelings. I knew I might never see my blood brother again. We had been so close that I didn't see how I could manage without him, or fight without him. But he was leaving because he loved his people. I had to understand that, and I had to know that's what made him a chief and a great man. Then, too, I couldn't help but smile at what he said about his two wives, and I had to wonder why he hadn't left earlier. By God, in his place I'd be back with them, and not in any white man's command listening to a bunch of generals calling orders.

It was a real dreary day, cold and kinda bitter, bitter like real parting was always bitter. The Shoshone warriors was wrapped up in their blankets, with their heads hung low, sitting on their bedraggled ponies, that had taken a lot of punishment from lack of rations and hard riding.

At their head there was Wesha. Even in the rain and cold he was a magnificent figure, sitting on his painted stallion. I was standing there holding Jupiter, and it was a hard moment. The rain was coming down the back of my neck, through my collar, and was plenty uncomfortable. I was soaked to the skin and half starved.

Of course, me and Wesha had been a little better off than the rest of them troopers, 'cause every now and then we'd pull off and do a little hunting. We kinda had our private commissary, and when we killed something, we'd eat our share and then pack the rest of it into camp for the rest of the scouts. We wasn't suffering so bad as them poor troopers, but it still weren't no fun.

Wesha looked at me for a long time before he gave the order to move. Finally he reached down with his right hand, and I came closer and held mine up to his. We clasped them together, them hands with the scars of the blood brothers' ceremony. It was like part of me was going away. Then Wesha leaned back into the saddle, made a motion to the rest of his band, and they started off, moving quiet like ghostly figures in the morning rain and fog. I watched them pass by with the strangest feelings. I could still see Wesha at the head with his war bonnet, and I watched until he was too far away to distinguish.

As I watched Wesha's column pass over a ridge and move out of sight, I thought to myself, there goes the shining Shoshones. If any people on this earth ever shone, they did. Maybe that's why they were named like that.

For the next dreary days we plugged on, and on the fifth day out from the Little Missouri the whole outfit was down and out. The troops was just exhausted and food supply was about gone, even though they was eating horses.

In any case, I figured that we had about three more days of plugging along. There was some guys that just gave out, and sickness moved in and they had to be transported. Crook seen this was a real tough job, and got Colonel Mills to take a hundred picked men and the best horses that was left and make a dash for the Black Hills for some supplies and more horses.

Mills had only been gone for about ten hours when a courier come in to say that Mills had found a Sioux village of forty-eight tepees. He'd already attacked them, driven them off, captured all kinds of pony herds and a big supply of food and buffalo robes. But the Indians were forming again, and most of them had come back fightin', and Mills was in a bad way.

When Crook got that word, he give the order to move and, by God, we moved. We caught up with Mills at noon, and found him located in a big open bowl in the side of a mountain.

Mills had done a good job destroying the camp, capturing the pony herd, and gathering the food supplies, but the Indians had come back and were circling around the rim of the volcanolike buttes, pouring heavy fire into us with their Winchesters.

Well, it was a battle, but the only real consequence of it was that we trapped a bunch of warriors in a ravine. They had their squaws with them, and Crook and his men was pouring heavy fire on them. Crook was pretty brave. He'd walk back and forth with the troopers being killed all around and he didn't seem to pay any attention. He must have led a charmed life, 'cause not many others would take that kind of chance.

Anyway, he was bound to get those damn Indians out of this ravine, so the fighting was hot. When he heard the screams and cries of women and babies, he finally called for a ceasefire. He had his Sioux interpreter, Frank Girard, tell them that under the flag of truce they would let the women come out and they wouldn't be harmed. By God, they did come out, and they told us what the story was.

The chief, American Horse, was there in the ravine. He had been shot in the guts, and his squaw wouldn't leave him. We resumed firing and kept on pouring it heavy into the position. Most of our soldiers was for giving no quarter, they was for killing them Sioux just the way the Sioux killed Custer and his men. Crook had a different idea. He figured a few more Indians wouldn't make that much difference.

Under the white flag he had the interpreter call again and

say that if the warriors stepped out of the ravine and gave up their guns, they would not be shot, but would be well treated. The Indians finally agreed to do it, and it was some sight when American Horse come out of there, holding his belly 'cause his guts was all shot away. His squaw was helping him keep everything together.

It was a hideous sight, but old American Horse didn't make no sound, even though he must have been in terrible pain. He acted like a chief of the Sioux and walked with dignity right out of the ravine. We took him over and laid him down. The surgeons went to work on him, but they said it was no use fooling with it—he was a goner.

Then his children and wives got around him, acting very affectionate, which was a heart-rending thing to see. The old boy breathed his last during the night, and Crook seen that the women and children was taken care of and nothing happened to them.

We hadn't any more than disposed of American Horse and his family when the rims of Twin Buttes broke out again with Indian fire. Them gray-white Twin Buttes was a strange formation, looking in some ways like the old castles in Europe with stone towers, but all natural and not man-made.

They was maybe three quarters of a mile around in a half circle facing east, and made up of strange tall rocks. They was covered with stubby pine, with some spruce and juniper. I was startled to see that looking down on us, from the rims of these buttes, was a tremendous number of Indians. They had suddenly come up from somewhere, maybe the rolling Badlands to the west. They had got the message or heard the firing and come to the aid of American Horse's people.

One big chief, riding a white horse, was taking a lot of chances, and he seemed to be running the show. Later we heard it was probably Crazy Horse, trying once again to deal a fatal blow to the whites. This time there weren't no George Custer riding down a ravine with two hundred troopers to attack three thousand warriors.

This time it was General Crook with about two thousand trained troops: they was soaked from the rains, and damn near starving and weary from the march, but they was good troops ready to obey commands. The officers was yelling orders. The whole mass of troops formed themselves in a long skirmish line from one end of them buttes to the other. They took advantage of the terrain—humps of earth and rocks—and begun pouring a heavy fire into the Indians up on the cliffs.

It started with the occasional pop, pop of the infantry's Springfields, and then began to increase when the cavalry carbines come in and there was rapid shooting. There weren't none of our soldiers that had repeating rifles. They was all single shots, but there was so many of them that if they could load and fire fairly fast, it sounded like repeaters.

It was nice to see the way they handled things. They stayed in line and kept moving toward the cliffs in orderly fashion; no Reno panic this time. As they began working up against the walls of the cliffs and doing some real good firing, keeping themselves under cover most of the time, losses were few and nobody panicked. A few soldiers gettin' shot didn't make it a defeat, and sure as hell didn't make a rout. Them boys showed that this time they meant it, and they would stay with it. It was beautiful to see.

The commands of the officers and the orderly manner they was executed by the troops made me plumb proud, and changed my mind a little bit about the U.S. Army. The battle was prolonged, but not very bloody.

With evening drawing on, the Indians began to see that going up against a steady formation of maybe two thousand pony soldiers was a different proposition. They weren't causing the panicky rout of Reno, or the disorder of two hundred leaderless men whose ammunition train hadn't got there. Finally Crazy Horse drew off his warriors. The firing died away, and quiet settled over the battlefield.

You know, it is a strange enough sight when a fellow can look at a battlefield and think it beautiful—something has to have happened to make it look that way. Most battlefields is horrible sights, covered with bodies of men and horses, but when a streak of sunlight come out in the west between them dark clouds, it lit up the whole bowl of Twin Buttes, and them cathedrallike rocks all around stood out bright red. What had been a battlefield that afternoon, covered with cavalry troops and wild Indians firing away trying to blow the guts out of each other, was now a beautiful green basin with a clear creek running through it. This same basin that had been covered with a roar of gunfire and shouting was now a peaceful place.

The light of the sunset didn't last long. The clouds formed and the rain started in again. Another cold and miserable night. We tried to get a good night's sleep, because we knowed we had at least a two-day hard ride to the Black Hills, and was still real short of rations.

Next to me when we was restin' was a Lieutenant Lawson, and beside him was the reporter from the *Chicago Times,* Jack Finerty. It was only a short time before exhaustion carried us away in sleep. The only thing that we heard was the sound of the rain and moans of the wounded. Dawn broke, if you could call it that, all gray clouds with rain. We started to break camp and done it in fast order, and first Major Powell and Major Munson's infantry moved out and then Captain Philo Clark's Second Cavalry. The artillery pieces that was available all passed as the rearguard of the Fifth Cavalry dismounted and was standing by their horses. After they passed, the rearguard had no more than mounted and started off to follow us when they were suddenly attacked by some of Crazy Horse's warriors who had come down through the ravines. They hit the column with great force.

However, these troops were hardened campaigners, cool in a crisis, and did not scare easily. As the column marched off, the rearguard showed itself to be competent to handle the situation alone. They kept up a steady fire, which drew farther away as we rode on down the trail. Handicapped though they was with their single-shot carbines, discipline prevailed, and our boys just done fine.

We rode away and it weren't too long before the rearguard drove the Indians back. Crazy Horse, riding his white stallion up on the rim of the bowl, gave the signal for the retreat. He must have realized he wasn't facing no George Armstrong Custer this time.

We continued two more days of march under pitiful conditions through the Badlands, slipping and sliding on the muddy clay. The poor wounded was dragged in the travois back of some mule, for a wet long ways. Several times the mule driver would call a halt, and some men would get together and remove part of the travois from its frame with the bodies, carry it to the side, and lay it down in the soaking earth. Then two men would take shovels from the pack mules and go about the dismal business of digging a shallow grave.

In the middle of the second day we crossed the Belle Fourche. Once the weather improved, we could plainly see the Black Hills in the distance. That night we reached a mining camp in a gulch, where we were received with a tempestuous welcome. Them miners knowed they would never be able to carry on their operations unless the U.S. Cavalry and Infantry was out there guarding them against them red devils who claimed the land.

We stayed in the camptown that night. Some of the fellows slept in a hotel and said it was sheer hell. It was infested with bedbugs. I'd been through that before, so I climbed up the side of the gulch a little ways from town and found me a place where I could roll up in my buffalo robe and keep my horse picketed.

The next day when we went into Deadwood, the folks went absolutely crazy over General Crook. He was cheered again and again, and was invited everywhere in the town. I didn't see much of it, but we could sure hear the crowds cheering wherever he went.

Jack Finerty told me Crook had got orders from General Sheridan, who was the commander of the entire Army in the west, to meet him at Camp Robinson down on the Rosebud Reservation, better than a hundred miles away, and that he was to be there by the next night. Finerty was going with him.

They rode off on some damn fine horses that had been brought in by Captain Teddy Egan's beautiful Grays Horse Troop and made available to the general and his party. Them horses sure looked beautiful, nothing like the old broke-down plugs we'd been stumbling along with. For the first time in the campaign Finnerty found himself mounted on real good horse-flesh.

I met Finerty some years later and he done told me that this was the greatest ride of his life, on a marvelous horse, full of energy and spirit, that had been well fed and cared for. In fact, Finerty hadn't started the campaign with a very good horse and he'd found hisself walking most of the time, 'cause that piece of horseflesh that he was dragging along wasn't worth a damn. Now he was mounted on a fine horse and General Crook, who was a strong rider, took off at a gallop and they rode to Robinson, a hundred and four miles, with only one stop of two hours during the night.

It was there, Finerty told me, that General Sheridan planned the campaign that was gonna destroy the scattered groups of Sioux and Cheyenne that had spread all over the place after the Little Big Horn.

As for me, I wasn't feeling very good right then. Seemed like the old wound in my left arm was actin' up. Maybe it had been the long marches and the bad weather, I didn't know what the hell it was, but I knew that I just wasn't well. They stuck me in a hospital tent for a while. I kept fretting about my horse, but an orderly come told me that he was taking good care of him.

Soon, with the rest and decent grub, I was back on my feet, feeling pretty good, but a little resentful that I hadn't been chosen by General Crook to accompany him to Phil Sheridan's headquarters.

I set around Deadwood for a few days, taking in the sights and having a little fun. I seen Lieutenant Bradley again and had a fine talk with him. He had been made chief of all the scouts, not just Gibbon's. I done told Bradley how it was with me, that I had come a long ways with the Shoshone, and now that they was back on the reservation, I would like to go back there for a while until something developed with the campaign. During that winter or spring I'd be glad to come back, but I done told him I had a little daughter at the Shoshone Reservation, and that she was real important to me.

Course, Bradley told me that he thought I ought to have a

little time off, as I'd done damn good service. He said, "I understand, Brules, but I don't see how in the hell you can travel from here in the Black Hills straight over to the Shoshone Reservation. The country is full of Sioux that we didn't defeat. Crazy Horse's band is still out there, so is Dull Knife of the Cheyennes and others. They are all fierce chieftains with strong followings of braves, and I don't think that you should travel across that country alone."

"I don't intend to do that, Lieutenant," I explained. "I intend to go back up to the Yellowstone, and then work my way up to Pryor Creek and join up with them Crows. I'll figure a way then, so maybe by the early winter I'll get back to the Shoshone people, after the Sioux have got the hell out of the mountains and gone back to the plains to do their hunting and hiding."

"Yes," he agreed, "that makes sense. Two Crow scouts, White Swan and Hairy Moccasins, have been given leave to go on back to the Crow village on Pryor Creek and wait for further orders. Maybe you'd better go with them."

15

Patrol on the Yellowstone

I knowed them two Crow scouts, White Swan and Hairy Moccasins, was good, and I figured if they didn't go the way I wanted to, I could just say adios and go my own way. So I traveled with them and had no problem at all. We went down the Little Missouri until we struck the Yellowstone. We crossed to the north side of it, and traveled along the military road until we come to the village on Pryor Creek.

When I first arrived at the Crow camp, the Crows greeted me like a long-lost son and friend. I sure was glad to see White Antelope too. She was all over me like a tent, acting like I was her long-lost hero. She was plenty disturbed at my condition, and she collected some herbs, and made it plain that she was gonna start taking care of me until I got real well again.

It sure was nice to have a woman thinking about me. Course, there wasn't any damn way I was gonna marry her or even bed her, 'cause I was still mourning the loss of my wife. Wild Rose was still in my heart. On the other hand, even a lonely son of a bitch like me needs company, and it was real comfortable to be with her for a little while. Only thing was, I was having one hell of a hard time telling her that we ought to be friends and not get nothing mixed up.

That was real difficult for me, because there was a few times on dark moonlit nights when I was in her company and we ended up rubbing noses and clasping arms. Things went no further than that, but it was hard to explain to her just what the trouble was.

She knew about Wild Rose, but Indians faced such troubles with an even spirit. She couldn't understand why, if my squaw had been dead almost six months, I wasn't consorting with a woman again. She just figured that she'd be the woman I'd take up with. Like I say, sometimes it was a temptation, but when things got right down to it, I didn't have no desire for any other woman. Wild Rose was still too strong in my feelings.

I reckon that stay from October to November up in the Crow camp on the Pryor was a good thing for me. My arm was still giving me trouble, and I was just plumb run down and wore out from all the marching in the cold and rain. Maybe it got to my arm a little bit, making the old wound the grizzly give me start acting up.

White Antelope was a good nurse, and like I said before, she had a real great figure. Sometimes, when I was lying half asleep, she'd come and bend over me, and I could look halfway down her shirt and see her breasts. I was thinking that was some gal. I'd get a lot of funny ideas, and then I'd come to my senses and fight them all back.

Still, just being in White Antelope's company was good medicine in itself. It weren't long before I was feeling first rate again.

I'd done a lot of thinking about what had gone on in the battle of the Little Big Horn and the strange things Mitch Bouyer had done, the way them Crow scouts had acted. I had pretty well figured out, in my mind, what had happened. I couldn't help wondering about that whole campaign. It seemed to me like a clumsy operation, when you come right down to it.

Crook was the smart one, when he hit on the idea to keep them Indians on the move, but I have to say that at that time I didn't see how the U.S. Army was gonna get anything done. Hell, Custer got within fifteen miles of the biggest Indian village there ever was before he discovered it was there.

However, I didn't take account of the toughness of some

of these generals, when they really got pushed around. In the early winter of 1877 Crook put together a pretty strong outfit of several units and gave a cavalry commander, MacKenzie, the right to go looking for hostiles, especially around the Tongue and the upper part of the Rosebud again.

By God, if MacKenzie didn't bust into Dull Knife's camp in a surprise move right in the middle of a snowstorm. The village was about a hundred and eighty tepees and a hell of a big herd of horses. MacKenzie did terrible damage to Dull Knife and drove his people off half naked, without any food and without any horses. The troops brought them horses back from the Indian camp to their camp and shot them all, 'cause they couldn't use them and they didn't want them to get back into the hands of the Indians. Well, that setback, and the fact that the white man had attacked them in the winter, was something that kinda put the spook in them.

Then it happened. Along come General Miles, who was a hell of a good officer and had been a good friend of Custer's. Coming up the Yellowstone with Terry, he was put in charge of setting up the details, which he didn't cotton to very much. What he done was move up and down the Yellowstone and fortify it pretty good to keep the hostiles from escaping.

He also came up with something that none of the other commanders had thought of. He dressed all his troops in bear-skin clothing—big warm fur hats, coats, and boots, so they would be plenty warm no matter how arcticlike that Montana weather got. He also done another thing: he didn't use any cavalry.

He was an infantry officer, and he believed that was the way to get the Indians. He pounded them until they found out that there was no rest for the wicked. By God, it didn't make a damn bit of difference how cold it was, what storms there were, Miles's men was plowing through the snow headed for any damn Indian village that they ever heard of, going from one place to another raising hell.

What's more, he took artillery with him, and I don't need to tell you that artillery was hell on tepees. When they'd find a village or a few lodges, he'd surround the place and start firing his artillery, blowing things all to hell. There weren't no defense them Indians had against artillery, and all they could do was run like hell. They was scared shitless.

Well, you know it got damn tiresome for them savages, always being pushed out, leaving their food and horses behind them. And Miles was relentless as hell.

Meanwhile Crook, who didn't believe he could fight in that kind of weather, had pulled back to the Black Hills to winter it out. Not old Miles.

Of the two generals I liked Crook the best, because he was more of a gentleman, and I think that he understood Indians better. On the other hand, Miles was a tough son of a bitch and kept hanging in there tight. His greatest success was in the Wolf Mountains in January of that year, 1877. He fought Crazy Horse, who had some five hundred Sioux and Cheyenne warriors with him, in a raging snowstorm, and it ended with the Indians being swept from the field by artillery and infantry. This taught the destroyers of Custer that the U.S.–trained troops, when properly commanded, could whip them.

Miles put on so much pressure that in late January, Sitting Bull and the Hunkpapas crossed over into Canada where they couldn't be attacked. Grandmother's Land was a haven—the great mother, Queen Victoria, spread her arms a long ways.

The spring of 1877 a big bunch of the Cheyennes surrendered to Miles, whom they called Bear Coat, on the Yellowstone River. The ironic part was that, only a few months later, Crook sent emissaries to the Sioux who pretty well persuaded them to give up. A huge number of them wild and hostile Sioux who had busted Custer all to hell come marching in to surrender at the Red Cloud Agency.

From then on small parties of hostiles kept on coming, and on the sixth of May, 1877, a procession of more than a thousand people and about twenty-five hundred ponies approached Camp Robinson, and offered to surrender.

I found that damn hard to believe. I thought the war with the Sioux was going to go on for years. I didn't see how the clumsy cavalry and some of them boneheaded generals was ever gonna get the Sioux to surrender.

As a matter of fact, the main thing that beat the Sioux was hunger. Them buffalo herds had been cut down something terrible, and they hardly existed at all up in Canada. Sitting Bull and his gang was really starving to death. The rest of them knew they would be well fed on the reservation. They'd been chased from place to place by Miles and MacKenzie all through the winter, with no rest, no food, no clothes, to amount to anything, and had lost a lot of their ponies. They got to thinking, maybe life wasn't so damn bad back on the reservation.

What surprised me most of all in this was hearing that when them thousand warriors come in to Camp Robinson, riding at the head was none other than that big bastard, the bravest of all the Sioux fighters, old Crazy Horse. He had his principal chiefs with him, and they rode in almost defiant-like, breaking into their war songs as they surrendered, throwing their Winchester rifles to the ground.

One would think things was almost over at that point because the back of the Sioux nation seemed to be busted, but others, who knew better, knew that across the line in Grandmother's Land there was a much bigger bunch of Sioux that hadn't given in yet.

Once Crazy Horse surrendered, he was more of a problem on the reservation than he had been out in the wild. He was belligerent and difficult, and the Army viewed him as a big thug who was in the center of all troubles. He wasn't used to being confined, and began raising hell wherever he went on the reservation. The other chiefs started to feel he was a real troublemaker and might get them into trouble if he acted too damn smart.

Crook heard about that and planned to imprison Crazy Horse, which didn't set well with him. When the Indian police went to arrest the old war chieftain, he resisted mightily and there was a hell of a scuffle, and he was stabbed to death.

It seemed like when them big war chiefs of any of the Indian tribes was killed, it took the punch out of the most of the rest of 'em. There weren't no more real troubles with the

Sioux for many years. The next time it happened was in 1890 at Wounded Knee, but that was a different story.

All this time I was still at the Crow Reservation, enjoying myself no end and all recovered. I lived the quiet, peaceful life, doing some fishing, hunting, and making friends with a few of them Crows. I got to where I could speak a smattering of the Crow language, and some of them knew a little Shoshone, so we got along all right. I never did have any trouble with peaceful Indians. If you treated them decent, they was fine. They would laugh at your jokes and all. I was real polite with them, too, never crossing tracks with them in any way that I could help.

It was getting along in the summer of 1877 and things was just beautiful in that part of the country, and I got to feeling pretty good about life again. Then I got a call from Crook. The message I got from the general's courier arrived around the second week in September, ordering me to join the campaign against the Nez Perce.

My first reaction was that I didn't want to disturb what I was doing and I didn't have nothing against the Nez Perce, so it didn't seem like I should get mixed up in things. On the other hand, I thought that I kinda owed something to General Crook. He sure had a magnetic personality, if that's what you call it. It made most men want to do their best, and I guess I was no different. It seemed like an honor when he called on me to come, saying fine words on how I was one of the greatest scouts and General Miles would need me bad.

So, I picked up my rifle, gave White Antelope a long squeezing hug, and started down the military road along the north side of the Yellowstone to report to Miles at Fort Keogh.

16

The Nez Perce

During the middle of June many battles had been fought around a terrific march that Chief Joseph of the Nez Perce had led from the Lapwai Indian Reservation on the Clearwater River in Idaho. The march had covered some seventeen hundred miles of the toughest country, probably the toughest in the whole United States. In fact, most of the Nez Perce were on the trail that the Lewis and Clark expedition had took some seventy-five years before, going the other way. It was one hell of a march, and I'd been hearing reports of it all during the summer as I was loafing around with the Crows.

I heard a hell of a lot more about the march as the summer progressed. I finally got into some of the action. In the first place, them Nez Perce Indians were, I reckoned, about the finest Indians in all the whole United States. I think in some ways they was even better than my beloved Shoshone. Chief Joseph and his kid brother, Ollokot, were about the best-looking Indians you ever laid eyes on. You could take Chief Joseph and his brother and put them in top hats and tailed coats, and if you stuck them into the House of Lords of the British Parliament, you wouldn't know them from any of the other lords there, except maybe they'd be better lookin'. They was such fine-looking men and they possessed plenty of brainpower.

I remember hearing of some of the debates Chief Joseph had with the whites, regarding the whites stealing the land, and was about as eloquent as anything you would want to hear. He would have given Daniel Webster a damn good going-over.

One thing about the Nez Perce was they never tortured nobody and never mutilated the dead. They had also done good things for the whites for a number of years. I'm not sure whether they did any scalping or not, but I kinda think that they didn't. I'll tell you one thing, when I finally saw Chief Joseph, I couldn't help comparing him with his fine looks and his upright bearing with that son of a bitch Chief Satanta of the Kiowa Comanches.

By God, if you was to look at Satanta—that terrible face, bowlegged body, and long arms—you knew you were looking at a fierce son of a bitch that was a real primitive man. When you looked at Chief Joseph you were seeing the best of the human race.

I rode down that old military road on Jupiter, making good time. We made the ride from Fort Pryor to Fort Keogh on the Tongue River in a little over a day and a half.

All that time I just kept wondering what the hell was really going on. Why was I leaving a nice Crow camp in beautiful country, with a lot of good friends, good hunting, good fishing, and the warm arms of a friendly girl? Maybe she wasn't my girl, in that sense, but she was sure a good friend.

Here I was riding down to join General Miles at Fort Keogh and getting back into the Indian fighting again. Two or three times I told myself, Brules, you're the dumbest son of a bitch. What's more, maybe you're crazy. Until this day I don't doubt it, considering all the things I went through, but a man keeps moving and that's the kinda man I was. I had to keep a-rolling.

Well, the old military road was a pretty good way to go. There'd been so much traffic back and forth that by September of '77 it was like a boulevard, being traveled over so much. I knew most of it backward and forward, so as I was riding along I got to thinking about them Nez Perce. I already told you what kind of people they was, but now here we was with a hell of a fight on our hands. I got to wondering, was it another one of them Indian uprisings or was them Indians trying to take something away from the whites? Maybe it had something to do with the whites wanting the land and trying to get it away from the Indians. Of course, that is just exactly what it was.

This time it was the valley of the Wallowa, which had belonged to the Nez Perce for many generations, longer than anybody could count back. Now here come a lot of immigrants thinking it was damn fine farmland and they'd like to have some ranches in there. They was working against the Bureau of Indian Affairs and everything else to try to open up the area for settlements.

One of these young men of the Nez Perce was named Joseph. He had the same name as his father. His father had gotten along fine with the whites for a number of years after they moved in. As a matter of fact, old Joseph had been converted by the missionaries and had taken up Christianity. For a long time, until close to the time of his death, the old man claimed fidelity to their religion, but it didn't do him no good. His relations with the whites always went downhill whenever there was a quarrel. He was never treated decent by the whites, so he eventually rejected Christianity and went back to his own mountain gods.

Young Chief Joseph was brought up in that atmosphere and he didn't believe much of what the whites said. He was very eloquent in his defense of the Nez Perce's ownership of the valley. On the whites' side there was a General Oliver Howard, a commander with a pretty good reputation for dealing with Indians like Cochise in Arizona, and was supposed to be a human kind of a fellow. He was a real Bible thumper, so much so that he was called the "Christian general." He was all for the Indians, backed the Indians on the idea that the white people had no right to take the land. He was gonna find a solution. His idea of the solution was to have the Indians sell the land to the whites at a good price. The Nez Perce chiefs didn't want to sell the land at any price.

In the end it turned out the Christian general wasn't as Christian as he was made out to be. With a couple of meetings, I think one in '76 and the other around May '77, he was real persuasive about everything that he had to say about holding on to the land. What really got things riled up was when one of the chiefs, old Too-Hool-Hool-Zute, spoke out with such clarity and force that he got Howard's temper up. Howard got mad, had him arrested and thrown in the jug at Fort Lapwai. That was Howard's solution—real simple. The general had broken the deadlock by showing the rifle.

Well, Howard started getting real tough, telling the Nez Perce they had thirty days to move to a reservation that had been provided for them or he would send in the soldiers—in other words, get the hell out of the Wallowa Valley and leave it to the whites.

That made the chief bitter as hell, but he had sense enough to see that war against the whites was suicidal. While they was moving out, one of the young warriors got drunk and in his fury killed four whites. Some other warriors followed the example and killed still more, and of course, that brought out the cavalry.

One hundred cavalry from Fort Lapwai rushed over to where the trouble was, and plowed into the Nez Perce in the battle of the White Bird Canyon. They got the surprise of their lives—most Indians ain't necessarily good marksmen, but that was not the case with the Nez Perce. They were excellent fighters and pretty near dead shots. When they got though messing around, the cavalry had been cut to pieces and driven back, leaving one officer and thirty-three troopers slain and many others wounded.

Of course, as soon as that happened, the whole damn Northwest Command mobilized and took out after the Indians, with General Howard in command of at least four hundred infantry and cavalry. At that time the Nez Perce band amounted to about eight hundred, three hundred of them being warriors.

Except for some skirmishes that happened in the chase, the Indians easily evaded the Army units for almost three weeks. Finally, Howard caught up to them and attacked their village on the south fork of the Clearwater River. Well, the battle lasted for two days, ending in the rout of the Indians, although they had given the Army some tough punishment.

If Howard had followed up real quick, he might have ended the Nez Perce war right there, but he didn't. He stopped and regrouped when he found out how tough the fighting was and allowed the Indians to escape. That set the stage for one of the greatest episodes in Indian warfare in the United States.

Following their defeat the Indians called a council in the Weippe Prairie about the middle of July and, after plenty of powwow, resolved to move the hell out of the country. They were gonna do a trek across the Bitterroot Mountains to the plains of Montana. For generations the Nez Perce had made that journey to hunt buffalo on the plains, and they hoped, this time, to reach safety with the Crows or even join Sitting Bull in Canada.

Everybody figured that it was Chief Joseph who had made the decision, but it wasn't that way. All the chiefs joined in and decided what they ought to do. At that time Chief Joseph was not the big war leader—it was his kid brother, Ollokot, who was a hell of a fighter, kinda the Crazy Horse of the Nez Perce.

Howard continued to delay, and that gave the Indians a chance to get organized. They started up the winding Lolo Trail, a tough trail that nearly defeated the Lewis and Clark expedition.

By the middle of August those damn Nez Perce had crossed over the pass of the Bitterroot Mountains, dropped into the Bitterroot Valley, crossed the Continental Divide and the Big Hole River. There one of the chiefs, called Looking Glass, talked the others into pausing to rest.

That was too damn bad, because the delay allowed Colonel John Gibbon and a column of two hundred infantrymen from Fort Shaw to catch up with them. That was the same Gibbon that had just missed being in the battle of the Little Big Horn.

The second week in August, Gibbon attacked at daybreak, driving the Nez Perce from their lodges and killing at least eighty-nine of them in the first sweep. But them Nez Perce were tough fighters and they rallied, counterattacked, retook their village, and pinned down the troops for two days, while the women and children made good their escape.

That left Gibbon with seventy-one dead and wounded and he done went back to his station at Fort Shaw. The Indians was in full retreat, led by Joseph. They crossed Yellowstone Park, which had just been established, hurrying like hell, plumb terrorizing the visitors that was there, and barely missing the Chief of Staff of the Army, General Sherman, who was on a pleasure trip through the park. I don't know how close they come to him, but he must have been awful glad when he heard about them going on by, because he didn't have no military unit along.

Meanwhile General Howard kept a-followin' them Nez, but could never quite overtake 'em.

By now the telegraph was active, with more lines everywhere than there had been the year before.

Lieutenant Colonel Sturgis, with some of the Seventh Cavalry, was on down the Yellowstone, and moved to block the eastern edges of the park, but the Nez Perce was too smart for him. They feinted one way—and Sturgis followed their direction—then doubled back, through the intended route, slipping out of the mountains and onto the Montana plains.

As soon as the Seventh Cavalry found that out, they raced after them and caught them at Canyon Creek on September thirteenth. The Nez Perce had come into the land of the Crows—a place where the chiefs thought they'd found a haven. So they were plumb surprised and their hopes collapsed when they found the Crows were scouting for the whites against them. This left the Nez Perce with only one alternative, and that was to dash two hundred miles to the north. It was the last hope that they could have to rejoin Sitting Bull, who would welcome them.

It was unfortunate for the Nez Perce, but again Looking Glass made the mistake of urging them to rest up, as they was plumb worn out from their trip. He figured that the soldiers had been left far behind, and he counseled that the pace should be slow and daily marches cut short.

The Bible-reading Howard, who had been following them closely, figured that they would do just that kind of thing. So, rather than push them hard again, he slowed up and gave them a chance to settle in a little bit.

17

Tragedy at Bear Paw

Then General Miles arrived on the scene at Fort Keogh at the mouth of the Tongue. "Bear Coat" Miles had been a commander of a garrison, and was a pretty tough veteran of Sioux warfare, having given them hell the winter of '76–'77.

He'd made himself almost an independent commander, controlling the whole of the Yellowstone with the idea of stopping these tribes. Course, quite a few Indians had passed him in one way or another, on their way to Canada, because he didn't have but five hundred troops.

Suddenly, Miles was called away from the patrol of the Yellowstone to do the job of intercepting Chief Joseph before that leader reached Canada. Miles knew from the telegraph system there was no stopping Joseph at the Yellowstone, 'cause he had already crossed that river up near where they'd had the battle of Canyon Creek.

One of the things Miles needed was scouts and plenty of them, including Crows. Miles got hold of me by sending a courier up the Yellowstone. He went on and got some more Crow scouts, but I didn't wait for them.

When I got his orders, I covered about fifty miles, riding to the mouth of the Big Horn River, and found one of the garrisons that Miles had established along the Yellowstone. In addition to the garrisons Miles had established a courier system that rode back and forth every day, up and down the river, to keep them in touch with one another. He knew that before the battle of the Little Big Horn there hadn't been no communications among Gibbon, Terry, and Crook, and decided he wasn't gonna have anything like that happen again. So he had the couriers riding pretty hard.

When I stopped at the garrison, the lieutenant in charge said he could see I had been riding like hell and where was I headed?

I told him I was on my way to Fort Keogh to meet General Miles, as General Crook had ordered me to do so. He said I was lucky, 'cause a courier had just come in that morning saying Miles had left Fort Keogh yesterday around noon. Now, by God, it was two in the afternoon, so he must have made at least thirty miles.

The lieutenant told me, "He's headed for the Bear Paw Mountains. They think that's where Chief Joseph is going with the Nez Perce if he's going to Canada."

"Yeah, that's where Joseph's going, all right," I said, "but I got to intercept Miles someway. How the hell am I gonna know where to go?"

"I have an old map here of the Yellowstone region, if you want to take a look at it," he offered.

"I sure as hell do." I dismounted, tied my horse, and went into his headquarters that was made out of a tent arrangement. He looked around and dug up the field map.

I saw what the situation was. Miles was headed for the Bear Paw Mountains, and was gonna strike the Missouri River where the Musselshell come into it. Now, if he had four or five hundred soldiers, I sure as hell could overtake 'em if I could get within twenty miles of them. I could see their dust.

Looking at the map it was plain that if I cut out at the mouth of the Big Horn and went straight across country almost due north, I'd strike the Musselshell at its big bend. The Musselshell flowed east until it got opposite to the bend, and then it turned north and struck the Missouri just about where Squaw Creek come in.

I thought that Miles was smart enough to go down the valley of Squaw Creek so he could keep watering his stock. If I'd cross over and hit that bend of Musselshell and follow it down, I'd come out just right, providing I didn't run into any Sioux along the way. Most of them Sioux had gone back to the reservation and things was quiet. There was only your odd man out someplace, and if it was only two or three of them I could handle that.

I thanked the lieutenant. He asked if I didn't want a little grub to take along, and I said I could use it. He saw that I got some jerky and hardtack, and I filled my canteen again, watered Jupiter in the Yellowstone, and then headed straight for the Musselshell.

I figured it was about a forty-mile ride, and if I kept a-rolling I'd be in water country before me or my horse got too thirsty. It wasn't like being down in the Canadian River area where you'd go a long, long ways between waterholes. Montana was much better that way, 'cause there was a lot more moisture up there.

Well, I rode Jupiter at a steady pace and by sundown I had made it to the Musselshell, where I watered my old friend, and then kept a-going. Jupiter seemed to be in good shape and knew it was gonna be a hell of a ride. I rode all through the night, and in the morning I seen a creek coming in on the right. I figured it was Squaw Creek, and I was on the right track.

Crossing the Missouri with that bunch of troops would be a hell of an operation, and that's where I thought I'd catch up with them. Sure enough, about nine in the morning I come up on the whole works trying to cross the river. Miles was traveling light—all he had was a cavalry outfit and mounted infantry—and he wasn't wasting no time, but getting six hundred men to swim the Missouri is quite a job. Some of the men went across in pirogues and some leading their horses, letting the horses swim free of them while they rode in the boat. There is always some horses raising hell, and some of them don't want to go in the water, and it can be a messy situation. You got to watch out for your gear—your saddlebags and all get soaking wet, which ain't fun, and then you gotta get dried out over the other side.

Anyway, I reported to Miles's headquarters, 'cause he was

still on the south side of the Missouri, watching the crossing to make sure that he got all of his men over there before he went across. Now, Miles was a different kind of guy from General Crook. Crook had a lot of charm and was very much the splendid gentleman, but Old Miles was a tough son of a gun.

When I reported to Miles, he was very military-like but pleasant enough. He shook hands with me and said he'd heard from General Crook that I was a hell of a fine scout and was glad to have me on board. He wanted me to get to work right away looking for them Nez Perce. He told me that there was no question about it, he had to intercept them before they got to the Canadian border, 'cause we couldn't touch them once they did. At least not without starting a war with England, and none of these Indians was worth that.

I said that I understood and I would do the very best I could.

Miles said, "There is one thing I want to tell you, Brules, just find the Nez Perce. By God, they've run the hell out of the cavalry all over the place. General Howard's been tracking them all this way, and Gibbon even tried to cut them off at the Yellowstone and got outplayed. Gibbon finally did catch them at Canyon Creek, but they're such good fighters and crack shots, they did better than any other Indians we've been up against.

"You've got to admire them, Brules. For three months those eight hundred Indians made a trek of seventeen hundred miles. Their chiefs outwitted and outgeneraled, and their people had to outmarch and outfight, a considerable portion of the United States Army. That's a hell of a note. It's up to us to stop them now, before they get away, otherwise we are going to be the laughingstock of the nation."

He figured Howard was pushing them pretty hard, and we'd have a chance to intercept them, but we'd have to get moving, so he was forcing his men across the damn river just as fast as he could. We was probably gonna march all through the night.

Miles said, "Now, I don't know where they are, probably up around Bear Paw Mountains somewhere. I don't really know whether they've crossed the Missouri yet, but I rather suspect that's the way they are traveling. Just as soon as we get across here we're going to get on the move. We have about seventy miles to go, and we've got to go fast.

"You probably need another horse, Brules. You've ridden nigh on to a hundred miles, haven't you? You have a lot more riding to do and that horse of yours must be all done in."

Right quick I seen a danger sign. "No, sir, he isn't all done in. I take real good care of him. He and I are good friends and we get along fine on the trail. He is one of the best horses I have ever had." I wasn't gonna leave Jupiter at no army post just to get a fresh horse. I'd probably never see him again.

"Well, that's fine, then." Miles nodded. "There are some pretty good horses here, but we've been pushing them pretty hard. If you think you can do it, you go ahead. I'll tell you one thing, though, I don't think that you ought to swim that horse across the Missouri. It's too hard on him if you're going to use him for night scouting here. You need to get somewhere up near the Bear Paws by morning.

"My staff and I here will be crossing the river in about an hour in one of these little steamers that we've been using. Get your horse on board and you can come with me.

"Then, I don't want you wasting time, I want you to get the hell off that steamer, try to find what you can, and talk to the other scouts, get them to spread out.

"I understand you used to scout with the Crows, and must know a whole lot of what they want. I have a few Crows here, so I would like you to get with it and take charge.

"It will be an hour or so before we cross, and I see they've got the mess tent down, but you can go over there and tell the cooks to give you something to eat. By God, you're on a special mission for me."

I said, "Yes, sir." I went over and got some oats for old Jupiter first, and seen to it that he had plenty to eat. I felt him over and felt his legs. They was a little bit tight. I pulled the saddle off him so he could kinda rest up. I give him a back rub and all that kinda thing, checked his feet, seen that he didn't have no stones. That Montana country that we'd been travelin' over was pretty much grassland without much rock. By God, he seemed in real good shape, he didn't act like he was wore out or nothing.

I knew that it was good medicine not to swim the Missouri, 'cause it would take something out of Jupiter and that little extra might be just what I needed when we got up around the Bear Paw Mountains. I talked to him a little bit and told him that he and I had a hell of a ride to make. He looked at me with those beautiful eyes of his kinda as if to say, "Say, boss, what are you doing, bullshitting me like that? We already come on one hell of a ride." I laughed and he nudged up against me. I think maybe he understood that I needed him bad, but he went right on munching his oats.

At the cook tent, or what was left of it, I told the cook that General Miles had sent me over there to get something to eat.

The cook looked at me and said, "Well, Goddamn, I've had more son of a bitches coming in here trying to get something to eat the last minute. We're all packing up 'cause we've gotta cross that river, and we've gotta be sure that this food doesn't get all wet when we're doing that. Now, we're supposed to have a barge to do that. Goddamn, I don't see no barge, I don't see none of that."

"I understand your problem, but I got one too," I said. "Now, ain't you got a piece of bread, for Christ's sake, or maybe some meat and potatoes?"

He said, "Yes, of course I do. That's just what I have time to feed some horse's ass like you. Just what I have time to do!"

Well, I didn't get mad at him. I kinda was amused, you know. A fellow who'd said that to me, most of the time I'd take him on, but I hardly lifted my eye. He was a fat old boy and I kinda liked him. I knew that he was bullshitting away and just venting his problems. Jesus, if he was a cook for an outfit like that, he had one hell of a job. I had a good dirty story I told him, and he got to laughing to beat hell and done a pretty good job of fixin' me up with something to eat.

Then the time came to get back over to where Miles was, and I got Jupiter all saddled up, and went on board this little boat. It was a steam launch, one of several that they used up and down the river for the campaign.

Anyway, we got across there about dusk and Miles had his troop camp there that night. He said they were gonna get going about three o'clock in the morning, but I couldn't wait. I had to move on. It was a good starry night and I just moved along kinda figuring if I kept riding, I'd make it to the so-called Little Rocky Mountains. They was just a bunch of hills that was named that way out of humor. I figured that I'd pass right around them and try to hit the Milk River somewhere along in there and ride up and down and see where them Nez Perce crossed.

When dawn broke them hills was just a bunch of sharp peaks in the distance. After riding all night I stopped to water Jupiter and fill my canteen again. Then I thought, I'll go to one of these hills and climb a ways. I tied him up and walked over to where I figured I'd get the best view of the area.

By then it was about seven in the morning and I was mighty tired of riding all night, and could see that the old horse was too. I looked all around but couldn't see a Goddamn thing. I knew that Miles was headed this way and I thought I hadn't better get out too far ahead of them. I should be able to see them coming with the dust they would kick up.

So I done what I'd always done. I went back to the willow trees where I'd tied Jupiter—they got more willow trees in Montana than they do cottonwoods. I laid down by the horse and went to sleep. I passed out cold and must have slept two hours when the horse begun scratching around and—woke me up. Christ, I thought, there was something going on, and reached for my rifle right away. Jupiter was looking off to the southeast. Sure enough, in the distance I seen dust from the troops coming. I figured they'd be there in another hour.

I felt pretty rested, so I thought I'd just go. I kept sashaying, going a little to the east, then cutting over and going a little bit to the west. Stopping once in a while to see whether I could get any kinda idea of an Indian travois trail. Didn't see a damn thing.

When I got within sight of the Milk River, I tried to figure out what best to do, whether to try to go down the river a ways and see if the crossing was there. I didn't see no tracks or anything on the east side of the Little Rockies.

I knowed that Miles had gotten word when he was crossing the Missouri that the Indians had crossed at Cow's Landing. It was a supply camp of the Army and there was a steamboat landing there. There had been a small guard of about thirteen soldiers left there to take care of things, and when several hundred Nez Perce showed up, them thirteen boys decided they weren't gonna take them on and just barricaded themselves in a log setup.

The Nez Perce went down and raided the warehouses at Cow's Landing, taking all kinds of stuff and resupplying themselves. The Indians was hungry: the women and children had been gathering any roots and food they could find, and the hunters had been hunting alongside the moving tribe, but they still didn't have food enough. When they hit those warehouses, they took every damn thing they could. They didn't kill no soldiers, just raided the warehouses. It looked something like what the Comanches done at the Linville raid on the coast of Texas. The difference was that the Nez Perce was busy making it to the Canadian border and didn't bother to parade around like the Comanches had done.

I traveled about ten miles till I seen some smoke in the distance. I approached cautiously and with my field glasses I seen that it was a big Indian camp, a beautiful place. The broad, grassy plain was threaded with mountain streams flowing into Snake Creek, and flanked by timbered buttes.

They tell me that in former days thousands of deer, antelope, and buffalo had ranged on this land. It was a favorite hunting ground, and I later learned that the Nez Perce had camped there, only forty miles from the Canadian border, just because of their love for this land.

They was still way ahead of the Christian General Howard's troops. The Indian squaws and children were exhausted with the travel, and the warriors was looking to do some hunting for meat. So they hadn't paid no attention to defenses.

The place was called Alikos Pah, a beautiful place to

camp. When I seen it I thought, my God, them Nez Perce have come some seventeen hundred miles through the mountains, and are now only some forty miles from the Canadian border. They ain't got the slightest idea that there's a big cavalry and mounted infantry outfit, not thirty miles away, coming fast and gonna hit that camp hard.

You could see the Bear Paw Mountains in the distance flanking the camp to the west. I went up a slight mound and had a good look at all the country. When I was sure of what I was looking at, I turned around and headed fast for Miles. I knew he was coming up the east side of the Little Rockies the same way I'd done, but he might head for the Milk River and miss the Indian camp.

I rode as hard as Jupiter could go. In about an hour I come within sight of the dust of the column and perhaps twenty minutes later, hell-bent for election, I pulled up beside Miles and his staff.

"Well, Brules, what have you got to tell us?" Miles asked.

"General, the Nez Perce camp is about twenty miles due west of us, and if you just head for them Bear Paw Mountains you'll come up on them. They're camped in a big grassy place, a creek runs though it, and it goes into Snake Creek. They don't look like they're fixing to travel or anything. I think you can make it up there pretty good and be in a position to hammer them."

Now, why in the hell I was the first scout to report the location of the camp to Miles I don't know. He had several Crow scouts out there, but maybe they was more interested in getting hold of the Nez Perce horse herd than reporting their position. Whatever it was, it was plain that Miles hadn't had any word on the location of the camp until I rode in and told him.

"Good work, Brules," Miles said, and turned to his adjutant. "Give the order, we're moving out fast."

I could keep up with the column without working my horse too hard. Miles had put them on a steady march, not in a trot or gallop. We wouldn't do that until we got in close to the camp. He was too good a soldier to make the same mistakes as Custer. He was gonna make a reconnaissance before he attacked.

We covered them twenty miles in about four hours, but three hours out Miles was in a good enough position to see the camp with field glasses, and tell just about what he was up against.

Something I couldn't figure out was how in hell the Nez Perce hadn't seen our column. If they'd had any scouts out at all, they would have picked it up. We'd moved within about three miles of the camp and there was no sign of the Nez Perce being aware that there was a cavalry outfit coming hard for them.

They must have thought they were so far ahead of the Christian general and Sturgis, who had been following on their trail, that there wouldn't be an attack anytime soon. Course, they had no idea about the telegraph message delivered to Miles at Fort Keogh, or that he'd made this dash with his troops to head them off.

It was almost a sad thing. As I was going along with the column I kept thinking, why, you damn fools, you Nez Perce, wake up! You're gonna have a hell of an attack here! But they seemed to be just enjoying a pleasant afternoon.

We was about a mile out from getting them by surprise, just by sheer good luck. We formed a line of attack and the cavalry was ordered into a trot. When they got in closer we opened up into a gallop. The Nez Perce was just packing up to make a leisurely departure.

I learned later, they had no idea that they was being attacked until four young warriors seen some dust in the distance. At first they thought it was a buffalo herd. Then all of a sudden they seen that it was a cavalry unit that was attacking. It seemed like the camp was mesmerized for a few seconds by the thunder of them hundreds of charging horses, but them Nez Perce were terrific fighters and they rallied quick.

Two of their chiefs, Ollokot, who was Chief Joseph's brother, and another chief called Too-Hool-Hool-Zute, came quick to their senses, and set up a line of defense back of a ridge. They lined up about a hundred twenty warriors, all damn good sharpshooters, and waited for the charge of six hundred cavalrymen.

Twenty warriors, the very best shots, was to do the shooting first, and the others was to save their ammunition till called upon. The twenty warriors waited until the troopers got within two hundred yards and started going to work. It was the damnedest thing you ever saw. Troopers was falling like leaves.

I couldn't believe such shooting. It was so tough that it plumb stopped the charge. Them Nez Perce were smarter than hell, 'cause they was pickin' off the officers. The death rate of officers and sergeants was unbelievable. Next, the other hundred warriors cut in with their fire—it was a carnage. The thunder of the charging horses was replaced by the roar of rifle fire and the screams of the wounded.

The Nez Perce wasn't taking any losses at all. The soldiers backed off about seventy-five yards from the ridge, dismounted, and barricaded themselves. It was remarkable to see how them Nez Perce fighters could bring themselves into action with so little notice.

There weren't any more charges that day and both lines held. Nez Perce from all around, who had heard the firing, come running up to help the first hundred and twenty warriors. Miles, seeing his charge wasn't gonna work, began a new strategy. The infantry entrenched themselves and kept the warriors busy. Meanwhile the Crow scouts of the command circled around the Nez Perce camp to steal the horses, and round up the few warriors and women and children that had fled the camp at the first sound of the fighting.

Miles tried to encircle the camp and cut them off from water, but each time small groups of sharpshooters done damage to the soldiers and held them down.

Some groups of Nez Perce raiders had been cut off from the main body, and without realizing what they was doing in the smoke of battle, they fired on their own people, killing a bunch of warriors under Chief Husishusis Kute.

When dark came, both sides began to dig in. Most of the

night everyone was digging trenches. The Nez Perce found themselves working in damp earth, making deep ones for the children and elderly, and waist-high ones for the warriors. The elders did most of the digging with knives, but had constructed an amazing web of trenches and tunnels.

On top of this the chiefs was able to dispatch a small group of warriors who got through past the pony soldiers. They made a dead run to the Canadian border to get help from Sitting Bull.

The trenches and pits was damp, 'cause the Indians had not had a chance to get the blankets and stuff that they had in the camp. Children was crying and the women was huddled in the deep pits trying to keep them warm and stop them from howling.

Women came out of the trenches that night, crawling around, look for small bunches of dried grass and what sticks they could find. They started small fires with buffalo chips and the grass.

Some young bucks made it down to the creek, by staying on the safe side of their horses, and picked up water, which they brought back in buffalo horns for the women and children.

The Nez Perce lost between twenty and twenty-five warriors, including Ollokot, who was their main war chief even though he was Chief Joseph's kid brother. He must have been a hell of a warrior, because he was the nearest one to the soldiers and held a whole piece of the line by himself, firing from behind a small rock. Ollokot was a handsome fellow who had a hell of a lot of guts. I seen the rock afterward that he hid behind, and it wasn't no bigger than a small table. I don't know what stray bullet got him—maybe he put his head up just at the wrong moment. They say that Chief Joseph, when he heard of the death of Ollokot, was plumb grief stricken. I heard he almost went crazy trying to go out there and get the body, but the fire was too deadly.

I'll say this for Miles's troops, they weren't like Custer's bunch of raw recruits. They was tough veterans that had been through a lot of fighting and had certainly had lots of target practice and knew damn well how to handle rifles, which was mostly them Springfields. They was a lot better than the cavalry carbine.

By now things was really bad. Like I said, when darkness fell, the Indians got to digging them trenches and it was a pretty good job that they did too. Our troops had formed a ring around them, and the sentries was listening to them all during the night. They heard them strange chants for the dead, and the crying, cold, and hungry children, and the moans of wounded braves.

The warriors that had survived was so crazed by all the hell that they had gone through that they was a-talking to themselves and imagining they was in their beautiful Wallowa Valley, the land of the Guardian Spirits. Some of them even tried to climb out of the trenches, shouting hysterically for vengeance against the soldiers, but was pulled back by them who still had their senses.

Many of them didn't know if they had lost part of their families when they split up.

Chief Joseph didn't know if his wife and daughter was alive or dead. He knew they was being pursued by the soldiers while making their way to Canada under the protection of a few warriors. I ain't even too sure if he ever heard of them again.

When morning come, a wet, heavy snow was falling. There was little shooting that morning, but by midday the clouds lifted some. The snow stopped and Alikos Pah was an eerie, silent expanse of white, with gray, low-hanging clouds. It didn't appear there had been any fighting at all.

Miles pulled up all the equipment he had. His attack had been plenty tough on the Indians already, but now he brought in the artillery, which consisted of Gatling guns and a Napoleon gun, and started a steady bombardment of the Nez Perce positions.

You can imagine what it must have been like for them Indians, laying in shallow trenches and taking shellfire. Miles had been real effective, all through the winter and spring of '77, shelling Indian encampments, artillery being harder than hell on tepees. It weren't no better for them poor Nez Perce who was lying huddled in them wet trenches with snow all around.

But I guess Miles must have found himself in kind of a fix too. He couldn't keep on charging them Nez Perce: they was too good of riflemen, and he had already lost a third of his men to their fire. If he waited too long he was gonna give Sitting Bull a chance to come down and help them Nez Perce. Miles wasn't no dummy and he knew the Sioux had been crossing the border with hunting parties after buffalo. And some Canadian tribes, that wasn't real happy to have the thousands of Sioux parked on them, were pushing.

I guess that old Miles, being a pretty proud man himself and all, figured victory was close to his grasp and didn't want to share it with anybody. He knew that old Howard, the Christian general, that psalm-singing son of a bitch, would be showing up pretty soon, as he'd been pushing these Nez Perce for the better part of the summer. So, being no fool, Miles decided to send a white flag to Joseph, hoping to arrange terms for surrender. He knew them Indians had to give up, but the question was, would they give up in time? About midmorning Miles sent two Nez Perce scouts he had with him, the Christianized ones from Lapwai, to approach the Nez Perce line. Speaking their own language, they yelled to their kinsmen that they ought to surrender. They called them brothers and told them they fought well, but now was the time of peace and rest. They promised them that if the whole tribe surrendered they would be treated well.

The Nez Perce warriors respected the white flag and didn't fire on them. The scouts arranged for a meeting between Miles and Chief Joseph. Miles, like a lot of other whites, knew that Joseph, although he might not be the war chief, was a wise man, and he'd have enough power to arrange a surrender if the terms was right.

Miles, with a small staff of officers, and Chief Joseph, with his warriors, met under the white flag between the two lines of the fighting camps. Miles had with him a white scout,

named Tom Hill, who spoke fluent Nez Perce, to do the translating.

Miles asked Chief Joseph to surrender and stack his guns.
Joseph, being smart, answered, "In return for what?"

All Miles could say was, good treatment.

Then Joseph asked him, as I understood it, if the Nez
Perce would be returned to their home in Wallowa Valley.

Miles said maybe, but he couldn't make any promises.

Joseph knew damn well that Miles wasn't the final commander of the whites by any manner of means. That request
might have to go all the way to Washington, and Chief Joseph
knew it. He was a smart trader and he held out. He said to
Miles, "We want a promise first and then we will surrender,
but we will only surrender half our guns. We need the others to
hunt the buffalo. We have no food."

Miles couldn't make no such promises. He had strict orders never to deal with the Indians except on the basis of
unconditional surrender. So Chief Joseph turned sadly away
and started back under a white flag to his own lines. Then
Miles did a thing I never forgave him for, a thing I know
Crook would never have done, and that damn few generals in
the U.S. Army would have even thought of. He immediately
gave orders to have Chief Joseph surrounded by troops and put
under arrest. That was nothing but a violation of the white flag,
and Miles's reputation went way down with the Indians.

Chief Joseph was wrapped up in blankets, tied, and put
away in a tent under guard. Why Miles done that I don't know,
but there was a couple of things that must have been preying
on his mind.

One of them was that if Sitting Bull decided to come
across the border in answer to the pleas of the warriors that had
been sent to find him, he was only one day's ride away. Com-
bining Sitting Bull's warriors with all Chief Joseph's, they
could have made Miles another Custer. Also, Miles knew that
General Howard was coming up pretty quick.

Right about that time I guess the Great Spirit, seeing that
his Nez Perce children was being mightily abused, decided to
give them a hand. Anyway, a damn fool lieutenant named Je-

rome got so fascinated with them Nez Perce that the stupid bastard rode into their camp, and the Nez Perce warriors took him hostage.

Miles was Goddamn mad that the stupid lieutenant would tear way up ahead of the front column like that and get his ass captured. Some say Miles was cussing and saying that if Jerome was as stupid as that, he ought to pay the penalty. But there weren't no way that Miles could do anything but trade back Chief Joseph for Jerome. If he hadn't done that, he would have been damned to hell by the U.S. Army *and* the American public, and he knew it. He arranged the trade, reluctantly, and when Jerome got back to Miles's command he chewed him out good and proper.

As soon as the peace conference was over, the firing began again. Again Miles was using his Napoleon gun and a couple of Gatling guns, and he was shelling the hell out of the Nez Perce positions. It must have been a hell of a day and night for them Nez Perce with half of their people gone, their position getting worse, running out of food, freezing, being shelled, and all the good warriors dead.

In the middle of the next morning along came General Howard with his six hundred men. So there was more than a thousand troops surrounding the Nez Perce, in the cruel, freezing weather. The Nez Perce situation was very bad.

All this time I was watching the proceedings with a hell of a lot of interest. Of course, I had taken part in the pursuit and was responsible for being an outlying scout and picking up the location of the Nez Perce camp, but this was something real different. In all of the times I fought the Comanches, Sioux, Blackfoot, Utes, and Apaches, I'd never quite had the same feeling I had about Miles and his troops cornering the Nez Perce.

It seemed to me that the whole Nez Perce campaign was a sad one. It was started by error and kept on being full of errors. There was lots of human sacrifice, lots of hurt, and lots of suffering, all for no cause.

True, the Nez Perce was called the Land Treaty Indians. Some had been baptized and made Christians and they kinda accepted things pretty strong. Joseph's father had been a hell of a good Indian, learning the Christian ways, learning to speak English and to read and write, from the missionaries at Lapwai. Old Chief Joseph kept telling his sons and all the others in the Nez Perce nation that if they learned about the white man's ways, the white man would be willing to do things for them.

But after old Chief Joseph had been cheated a number of times, the treaties and promises broken, and one dirty trick after another played on him, he gave up. Before he died, he denounced the white man's ways, the Christian religion, the English language, and anything else he could think of that he'd been so devoted to for over thirty years. I suspect that young Chief Joseph must have felt the same way. He had always listened to his father and wanted to learn more about the white people and how they could do them so much good. But he'd seen how bad things were, and so he'd helped to lead his people into a war that was against hopeless odds.

When them Nez Perce was making their seventeen-hundred-mile retreat, occasionally they would come upon a wagon train or a lone ranch, and a few of the young bucks would cause some death and destruction. It was only natural that the word spread through the white frontier that somebody had to get these Nez Perce bastards. That was the way it went when one bad deed brought another.

The problem with the Nez Perce was that they didn't listen to their chief for long. They would elect a chief and follow him for a while, as long as things was going well. But when things got nice and peaceful, and they thought they was way ahead of General Howard, they'd loaf around and wouldn't put out sentries. They just took it easy, no matter how much their chiefs kept yelling at them to keep moving toward Canada if they was gonna be safe. In the end it was a damn shame that they stopped in those meadows only forty miles from the Canadian border. From the top of one of them hills they could see Grandmother's Land, just straight to the north. They had waited just a little too long.

It was a strange thing about the Nez Perce, but they never

did anything without meeting together and deciding as a group. That might have been some of their strength, but like all people they had their differences of opinion. Now that things was looking hopeless, with them facing a combined force of Miles and Howard, and they was running out of food, freezing, and getting low on ammunition, they knew they was at the end of their rope.

In the council there was three different proposals as to what they should do. Chief White Bird proposed to make a dash to Canada with all those who could and would following him. Chief Looking Glass preferred to hold on with the hope that maybe Sitting Bull might yet come to their aid. Chief Joseph proposed surrender. He pointed out that the Sioux was only a day's ride away, and it had been four days since the messengers had gone to Sitting Bull.

The warriors, women, and children begun crawling out of their pits and lines and started to separate. Many families broke up when relatives decided to go in different directions. Well, with all the decency that's involved in the Nez Perce character, those that were gonna stay gave the best of the horses to White Bird, who was gonna have a long ride. White Bird took with him one hundred and forty men and boys, and ninety-three women and young girls.

Only the fittest followed White Bird, because they all knew the hardships they would endure on the ride. They knew, too, the soldiers would pursue them, and there would be more fighting. Some were on horseback, but many more were on foot. They pushed forward, left in the middle of the night under the cover of a snowstorm, on the long, cold ride to the Canadian border.

Although Chief Joseph was for surrender, knowing that the case was hopeless, Chief Looking Glass felt they should hang tight in hope of help from Sitting Bull. He kept telling the Nez Perce, you'll be sorry if you surrender. All you're gonna get out of a surrender is the deception of white men. They'll promise you one thing and cut you off when they have you disarmed. You'll wish you were dead.

When dawn broke there was an Indian coming from the

northeast, riding toward them in the distance. Looking Glass was so excited that he climbed out of his fighting pit and pointed toward the Indian, exclaiming to all those who surrounded him that here was the sign of help. It was a cruel thing that happened then, for the Indian he was pointing at wasn't one of Sitting Bull's Sioux coming to help them, but a Cheyenne scout, working for Howard and Miles.

Looking Glass stood there, completely exposed, a smile on his face, certain that at last rescue was coming. The Cheyenne scout dismounted from his horse, knelt down to get a good rest for his rifle, and put a bullet straight through Looking Glass's chest. It killed him instantly.

Chief Joseph knew that the only course was surrender. He was the last of the remaining chiefs and his decision was final. He made an address to his people in the final war council, and then taking two braves with him rode out to a small butte that lay between the two forces. The two braves each carried a pole with a white flag attached.

Miles and Howard approached while the interpreter, Tom Hill, stood by. I can't never forget that scene. It was one of desolation and destruction. It seemed a symbol of the lost hope of the human race. All around was dead horses, Indians, and troopers.

We seen two corpses of braves stripped to the waist, lying on their backs, their arms spread out, looking at the sky with dead eyes. The bodies of a couple of troopers was laying where they fell, face down, their hats popped away from their heads, their coats muddy from the fight, and their heavy boots turned in.

I can still remember the way Chief Joseph looked. Them two braves with him was wearing blankets that showed the suffering of their retreat. Joseph himself wore a black shirt made of some kind of cloth that I didn't know, with beads and designs on it standing out real clear. The bear claw necklace around his neck laying out on his chest seemed like the only dignity he had left. The blanket he wore around his waist reached to his feet and was held up by a rope belt.

Chief Joseph stepped in front of the two warriors with his

rifle in his right hand and he held up his left hand in the sign of peace. Then, with Tom Hill, the interpreter, translating in a quivering voice, he gave the surrender speech. I understand it was the same speech as he had given his war council an hour before.

I'll never forget that moment for as long as I live. It struck me clear to the heart. My eyes was kinda swimming in tears as I seen that I was looking at no mean Comanche, no fierce teeth-gashing Sioux, but the finest of American Indians, the very top of their race. A man full of courage, dignity, and a broken heart.

At that moment, seeing for myself the vast difference there was between tribes and how really decent and magnificent some Indians could be, I realized it was the same with all races, there was good and bad in all.

I couldn't repeat the great Chief Joseph's surrender speech exactly as he give it, but this is about what he said.

"I'm tired of fighting. Our chiefs have been killed. Looking Glass is dead. Too-Hool-Hool-Zute is dead. The old men of the tribe, they who have made decisions, are dead. My brother, Ollokot, who loved the young men, he, too, is now dead. It is cold, we have no blankets, the little children are freezing to death. My people, some of them have run away, they have gone to the hills, but they have no blankets, no food. No one knows where they are. Perhaps they are freezing to death. I must have time to look for my children. I must have time to see how many of them I can find. Maybe I shall only find them among the dead. Hear me, my chiefs, I am tired, my heart is sick and sad."

Then Joseph pointed to the sky with his left hand and said, "From where the sun now stands, I will fight no more forever."

I want to tell you that talk brought tears to many of the strong men who watched it. It sure as hell tore me up, and I watched with a heavy heart as them three Indians rode to the line of waiting officers and Joseph quickly dismounted. He walked where General Howard and General Miles was standing to receive the surrender.

He wanted to surrender to Howard, the Christian general, who he knew, despite being nuts about converting everybody to Christianity, was still a man of good heart. He sure as hell had no trust in Miles. Miles had violated the white flag, seized him and bound him and thrown him into a tepee. So he offered his Winchester to General Howard.

Howard, however, although a superior officer, motioned for Joseph to surrender his rifle to the hated Miles. It was a military tribute to the man who had brought about the surrender. It was real generous on Howard's part—he'd followed the Nez Perce for seventeen hundred miles of grim pursuit and fighting.

So Chief Joseph handed his rifle to Miles and then stepped aside, took his blanket, and covered his head in shame. I'm sure that he wanted to hide his weeping from the hard gaze of his enemies.

Slowly, what was left of the Nez Perce—eighty-seven men, a hundred eighty-four women, and a hundred forty-seven children—all followed in silence, under the guns and gaze of the white troopers. All that remained in that wide plain, which had once been the rich hunting grounds for herds of game, was debris and the carnage of battle.

The Nez Perce was marched slowly back the long distance to Fort Keogh, a new military installation named after one of Custer's captains at the Little Big Horn. The fort stood at the junction of the Tongue and the Yellowstone, and was headquarters of Miles's command.

The plan was that the Nez Perce would be taken care of there through the winter, and then sent back to the Wallowa Valley.

I got to say that both Miles and Howard had been pursued, beaten, and frustrated by these brave warriors, these magnificent riflemen. Yet they had nothing but respect for the Nez Perce and wanted to see the promises they'd made to Joseph carried out.

Only thing was, back in Washington the Bureau of Indian Affairs, other politicians, and men of high positions cared not a damn for the promises that had been made. They saw no purpose in keeping this trust, and in violation of the agreements they sent this poor surrendered remnant of the Nez Perce six hundred miles away to Fort Abraham Lincoln, where they could be maintained most cheaply.

It was a horrible sight. Any of us who had anything to do with the campaign and had seen the bravery, the capacity, and the honesty of the Nez Perce was ashamed of our government's action. Not only was our prisoners taken to Fort Abraham Lincoln, but in the spring Chief Joseph and others were sent down to Fort Leavenworth. There virtually imprisoned, they suffered the white man's diseases, malaria, smallpox, and so forth, and died in great numbers.

Eventually, they become accustomed to the climate. They began working the soil, and gathering grapes, and began to survive and accumulate some herds of horses, cattle, and sheep. They were an industrious people and their character was not destroyed by their contact with the whites as had been the case with so many other tribes.

General Howard wrote a book about the whole campaign. Women's groups took up their cause. All of this had a big effect on the American people, and in 1885 the stupid government was pressured into moving the Nez Perce back to their beloved land in the Wallowa Valley.

Looking back on it, even though I didn't have much sympathy for Howard and his fanatical religious ideas, I have to say he was a very decent man and he'd done his best to see them Indians was treated right. As I said before, some called Howard a psalm-singing son of a bitch, but he had a hell of a lot of good in him too.

I'll say only one thing about that Nez Perce campaign, and this may sound funny to you. Sure, I did some scouting and was the first to spot traces of the Indian camp on the meadows, but me, Brules, the Comanche killer, the dead gun, the Indian scout, panther of the mountain—as Wild Rose used to say—I am proud to say that I never fired a shot in the Nez Perce War. That may sound funny, but it's the truth.

I never had the feeling that I had to draw a bead on the Nez Perce. I wasn't hired to do the fighting, only the scouting.

Nobody noticed it and nobody called me to task. It wouldn't have made no difference if they had, 'cause there wasn't any way I could see killing people from that tribe.

I've done a lot of mean and contemptible things in my life, I guess, but one thing that I can say—I never killed a Nez Perce. When the Nez Perce War was over I kinda lost interest in scouting and campaigning, so I traveled back to Fort Keogh with them Nez Perce captives, which was a dreary deal. Getting across the Missouri weren't no joke, and marching them back all the way to Fort Keogh and the Yellowstone was a tough job.

I stuck around Fort Keogh for a while, but it didn't seem like anything was going on, so in late October I went over to headquarters to see if I couldn't get mustered out. Well, when Miles heard that I was thinking of quitting, he sent for me and give me a kinda lecture. He told me I was one hell of a scout and so forth, and he sure appreciated my finding that Nez Perce village. He also heard I was one hell of a shot, but never did see me shoot.

Well, I kept winking out of the other eye when he said that because, like I done told you, I didn't do no shooting in the Nez Perce campaign. Of course, Miles didn't know that, nor did any of the others, and I never bothered to change any impressions.

Anyway, he praised me high and said he would like me to stick around for a while, 'cause what he was gonna do was set up a bunch of fortifications all up and down the Yellowstone. He said the Yellowstone was the way to open up the West, but people was afraid of coming up there on account of all the troubles with the Sioux. If he could put a chain of forts in there and protect the travelers, he thought that the region would start filling up, and that's what you needed to keep the Indians out.

He said he thought, for all intents and purposes, the Indian troubles was over as far as the United States was concerned. Only trouble was that ''old son of a bitch Sitting Bull'' (that's just the way he put it) had moved on up to Canada and was under the protection of Queen Victoria. The British made no attempt to fight the Sioux and was very friendly with them, give them a place to stay and all that.

Intelligence information told Miles that Sitting Bull's main camp was on Mushroom Creek in the Woody Mountains' northwest territory. There was a Major Walsh there in the Royal Northwest Mounted Police, one of them red-coated fellows, that was in charge. He was awful high on Sitting Bull and thought he was a fine man. He kinda winked every time the Sioux would cross the boundary and come back into the States to do some hunting.

When you come right down to it, those damn Sioux was crossing the boundary all the time, hunting in the United States. It wasn't only hunting, they'd bust a wagon train or tear up a ranch or something. They was just keeping the settlers out of there.

It was apparent that them Sioux was getting bolder and bolder, and Sitting Bull was gonna have to do something to keep his hold on them. They longed to come back into the States, to their old hunting grounds. In fact, most of the ones who hadn't gone to Canada had already started coming into the different agencies. So it sure as hell was gonna be that way with the Canadian group if Sitting Bull didn't do something. Guess he figured that it was kinda like slowly bleeding to death.

So we was gonna have to patrol that line. We would have a visit with Major Walsh one of these days and ask him to tell them Sioux that if they was gonna be Canadians to be Canadians, but they wasn't crossing the line. Well, in them days the line didn't amount to nothing, it was just a bunch of little pyramids that surveyors put along there.

I remember many years before that, there was a big ruckus about selling most of that northern country and we was gonna go to war with the British. Our motto was "Fifty-four forty or fight," which had something to do with the latitude. Well, Jesus, that would have put us another four or five hundred miles up into British Columbia, and from what I seen of them blizzards that come down, Montana was bad enough. Let the damn British have that country. The game weren't so good up there, nothing like it was in the States, and we better hang on to our own.

Well, whatever I thought didn't make much difference, but old Miles was telling me that I ought to stay in the service and do what I could to make things work. I agreed to stick along for a while and help patrol the Yellowstone route. With the military road on the north side of the Yellowstone a fellow could ride up and down there pretty good now. There was boats traveling back and forth, and already Miles had put in three or four forts and he had patrols going too. I figured after a while he'd make it so that people could come there without losing their scalp. It looked like it might work, so I was willing to give it a shot.

He asked his adjutant to come in, introduced him, and asked about some letter or something that had come from Crook's adjutant. Crook by this time had been moved down to Omaha and was made general for the military division of what was known as the "Territory of the Platte." That's where Phil Sheridan had been, but he'd got promoted from there to Chicago.

While Crook was at North Platte, his adjutant wrote a letter to Miles at Fort Keogh to be forwarded on to me, 'cause Crook knew I'd joined up with Miles on the Nez Perce campaign. He had information for me he thought I'd be interested in.

The letter was addressed to me, but of course I had to get Miles's adjutant to read it. What it said was something like this: "that he, Crook's adjutant, Captain Bourke, had written to the folks of Lieutenant Wilson, who had been killed in the Sibley scout. He told them that I had brought the horse, Jupiter, back to the command and he was in real good shape thanks to the 'excellent care' that I had given the horse in the campaign under very difficult circumstances."

It was kinda flattering, but, hell, any damn fool who had as good a horse was gonna take care of him. It didn't take no special brains or nothing great on my part, just plain common horse sense. Now, he inquired, what did the parents wish to have done with this horse? The horse could be sent back to

Tennessee, if they so wished. Then old Captain Bourke, being a prudent military man, said, of course, this would be at the expense of Wilson's family. If they wished it returned, it would be shipped properly on one of the steamers that went down the Yellowstone to the Missouri, on down to the Mississippi, and would stop somewhere along about Memphis. They could go there and pick up the horse.

Well, of course, the kid's folks had been, naturally, all broke up when they heard about the death of their boy, and when they got this letter concerning the horse, it brought back sad memories. They wrote back and said they knew Jupiter would be serving the best scout in the Army, and that Brules would take good care of Jupiter because Brules had told their son that and it had proved that way. Considering all expenses involved, the fact that the horse was a very fine animal, but not up to their stud stock, they thought the best thing to do was to make a present of the horse to scout Brules in memory of young Lieutenant Wilson.

Well, Captain Bourke read that letter to me, and I damn near broke down. To think that kid would have said so many nice things to his family, who must have been plumb devastated with his death, and to think they would have the decency to do something nice like that and give me that horse. I tell you, I didn't know what to make of it. It seemed to me that maybe this whole Sioux campaign, the Nez Perce, that Sibley scout, and everything else, had been plumb ill fated, but everything was somehow made worthwhile by the decent people in the world.

I told Bourke that I loved that horse and was glad to have him. I sure didn't want to see him go into the regular remuda of the command, get beat up and shoved around like I'd seen happen to them other horses. I'd take that horse, and in the name of that boy I'd take the best care of him I could. Then I thought, that's a hell of a note to have a scout, cowpuncher, and mountain man riding around on a fancy horse like that and have even a fancier name like Jupiter. I normally would have called him Blackie, but the boy had said Jupiter was the name and, by God, from that time on Brules was gonna ride a horse called Jupiter. If anybody wanted to make fun of it, they better be damn careful what they said.

Bourke kinda laughed and said, ''Well, Brules, I can see you're the right man for the horse, there is no doubt about it, and we will so enter it into the register of the command. Best of luck.'' Then he got up and we shook hands.

All that winter I worked out of Fort Keogh under orders to ride the military road back and forth from the different posts that had been set up. Sometimes I acted as a courier and took mail, but most of the time I just kept an eye on what was going on and reported what I'd seen to General Miles. This was pretty good duty, because lots of times I'd extend the scouting and go up to Pryor Creek and visit White Antelope, whom I was still real fond of. She was some gal, and put up with all my funny ideas about my devotion to Wild Rose.

Things was pretty calm then for quite a while, and there wasn't no fussing going on. In the spring of '78 I took a notion to go buffalo hunting along with three or four of them Crow warriors that was kinda anxious to hunt. We all knowed that there was gonna be an end to the buffalo herds. There wasn't the millions around there that had been, just a few scattered herds of a hundred or two hundred animals. If a fellow was gonna do some hunting, he'd better get at it. As a matter of fact, five years later, in 1883, the buffalo was all gone, so it turned out to be the right thing for us to do. I went off with these three Crows, and we hunted up north between the Yellowstone and the Missouri. During that time we only run into two small bunches, but we killed a few animals, and the meat, hides, and tongues was worth a lot to us.

One thing I noticed at that time—them bucks weren't no fools when they went hunting. It was different when they was on the warpath, but when they went hunting, they took their squaws along. That made for a happy time and they had somebody to do the skinning, cutting, and packing of the meat. We had taken some mules to carry the packs out.

I took only one hide for myself, as a reward. The rest of the time I just enjoyed hunting with them braves. They was real pleased that I give them most of my share of the hunt, and them Crows seemed to like me, my ways, my hunting ability, and especially my shooting. I didn't waste no ammunition and never failed to kill an animal when I shot. On the other hand there weren't no bravery about that, 'cause lots of times we done just what the old-timers used to do, we rode right up alongside of them in a dead gallop. I was never very strong on the idea of shooting from a moving horse, but, God almighty, if you got a target as big as a buffalo and you ride alongside of him, you can damn near shove the muzzle of your gun into his shoulder and let go.

Anyway, we packed home with them hides, which were still winter hides, they hadn't begun to shed none for the spring, and, boy, were they great. There is one thing about hunting in that Montana country, in the wintertime in those big open plains: when the wind come up, the cold got something fierce. I was glad to be equipped with General Miles's bearskin coat and cap and them heavy boots. It's surprising how warm you could stay even in the worst weather. Them Crows just kinda pulled their blankets around them, and they must have suffered, but they never did complain about nothing, which was typical Indian style.

When we come back to the Crow village, all the relatives of them hunters was just as glad as could be. It was like the old times when warriors would come in from a successful hunt with plenty to eat and nice big buffalo hides. It was kinda sad to think it wasn't gonna be for long. I would get to wondering what the hell the Indian was gonna do when he didn't have nothing to hunt. Them Indians didn't cotton to any farming, didn't understand it and didn't want no part of it. It didn't seem risky enough, didn't seem exciting enough, and what's more, it just wasn't their way.

Well, things went on like that all through the winter, and when the ice broke out of the Yellowstone that spring, my thoughts began stirring. Even though it was only mid-March, I got that feeling of wanting to wander again and do a little hunting. I sure longed to spend some time tracking grizzlies down there in the La Sal Mountains, a long ways away. I'd dream about it at night, and it got to be quite a notion with me, stronger and stronger all the time. I kept thinking that I would maybe get a chance on the way to see my little girl at the Shoshone Reservation on the Wind River. Maybe I'd check on Wesha again so we could sit around the fire, laugh, and tell some lies.

I was looking forward to it, but all that was not to be. One day a courier come in from Fort Keogh while I was staying with White Antelope on Pryor Creek. He had a letter for me from General Crook. I was real proud to get a letter from the general. I knew that everybody thought well of him all through them Indian Wars, from Montana to Mexico, so I felt real good about it being personally addressed by him. On the other hand, I had a funny feeling, wondering, what the hell does the old buzzard want me to do now?

I got the post trader there to read me the letter, and it told me that I was to report right away, quick as possible, to General Crook's quarters. Well, come to find out from the letter, his quarters was way down on the Platte River at the junction of the North and South Platte, right by where old Buffalo Bill had his ranch called Scout's Rest. Crook had settled there on the railroad because now he was in charge of the Military District of the Platte, meaning most of Montana, Wyoming, Colorado, Utah, and the country to the west.

Of course, I figured he wouldn't be writing me if he didn't need me for something, and usually when he give me a task to do, it was a good one. I packed up, give White Antelope a good hug and nose rubbing, and set off down the Yellowstone for Fort Keogh.

As I was making my way down the Yellowstone, I stopped at the military encampment across from the mouth of the Rosebud. I bought a mule from a surveying party that was trying to fix a way for the railroad to come up through the Northwest. They had a pack train of mules, and, boy, one mule in that bunch was the biggest animal I ever seen in my life, and so homely! He was as big as a moose and damned if he didn't look like one. He had him an old Roman nose, big ears, sad eyes, and plumb ugly lips. But his ugliness made him almost beautiful.

I sure cottoned to that mule, bargained, and got him for a good price. If he'd been army property, I wouldn't have had no luck. The government never did sell their stock out in the field unless a campaign was over, and then they'd run them animals into someplace like Omaha and have a big sale.

But a sergeant told me that all these mules belonged to the railroad surveying group, most of them young engineers who was looking forward to going out to the Northwest where things was wild and rugged. Them surveyors had a little trouble—some of them had caught some kind of fever. It seemed to act like malaria, but it wasn't malaria, 'cause it had something to do with the cold weather. I don't know what it was, but there was one young fellow who was so sick that they was fixing to send him down the river on the next steamer that come by. Only trouble was, he'd been told he could take only personal belongings, but not his mule. Damn if his mule wasn't that big old son of a bitch that I'd looked at and liked so much.

When I found that out, I knew I had the natural solution—why, I'd buy that damn animal if the fellow would sell him to me. Right quick I went to see him in the hospital tent, and he sure wasn't feeling good. He just didn't want to be bothered with much of anything, but one thing he kept worrying about was what was gonna happen to his mule. When I asked him if he wanted to sell the mule he said, "Oh, hell, yes! That'll take care of what I was gonna do with him. Sure is a fine animal."

Of course, as soon as he thought he had a buyer, he perked up and I could see the price of that old ugly going up and up. I said, "Gee, he sure is homely."

"Well, he may be homely," he says, "but, by God, he's a hell of an animal. He can draw a big load like you wouldn't believe. I've seen him haul logs when other mules just plumb gave out."

"Yeah," I said, "you don't need to keep telling me how good he is, I know he's good. Otherwise I wouldn't want to buy him."

"Well," he says, "what do you want to pay for him?"

I said, "As little as I have to, but I don't want to gyp you none." I was saying to myself, like hell I don't. Then I said, "He's kinda old, ain't he?"

He said, "Old? No, he isn't that old. He's about seven or eight, just in his prime."

"Well," I said, "he's sure ugly, and I don't know what I'd give for him. What do you want for him?"

"Well, hell, he'd ought a bring four hundred dollars."

I said, "Jesus, four hundred dollars! Where do you think you are—back in Missouri? This is up in the frontier country, nobody's got that kind of money around here."

Of course, what I really should have been saying was, he's worth twice as much up here in the frontier as he would be down there where there's lots of mules around. But anyway, we kept a-bargaining around, him talking big money and everything, but we finally shook hands on three hundred and fifty bucks.

That was a deal that I never regretted. That mule was the best son of a bitch I ever saw in my life.

After I give the fellow the money, I went out to get that old ugly. Right there at the company base was a settler who had a store with food, supplies, and everything you'd ever need. He had all kinds of different things you couldn't get up there in Montana, and, by God, he had some apples. How the hell he'd kept them all winter, I don't know—maybe they'd froze up or something, but he had several bushels.

I hadn't had a apple for so damn long that I bought a few from him. I didn't give no money, but traded him some jerky I had left over from the buffalo meat that I got. That's about the way I handled that one, but when I bit into that first apple it seemed like the best damn thing I'd ever tasted in my life. I left the store munching away and went on down to see my mule.

When I got down where all the horses and mules was staked out, I found him and told the horse guard, a big black trooper with a wide white grin, a "buffalo soldier," that I had bought him and sure wanted to take him away.

He said, "He's da biggest Goddamn mule, but, Jesus, mister, he's ugly! Ain't he?"

I said, "I don't give a damn how ugly he is. You know what he can haul!" I went over and looked at him. His ugliness kinda made me think. He had big old sorrowful eyes, tears a-flowing all the time, his ears was drooping, and he was just right then a regular clown. Man, he was lots of mule and I knew I loved him.

I sat there and thought it was interesting that this guard would think so—I asked the guard, "Where in the hell are you from?"

He said, "I's from Mississippi, suh."

I said, "Well, you kinda have a lot of mules down in that country, don't you?"

"Oh, yes, suh. Mule the best damn animal—twice as good as a hoss. They can do anything. Hell, a mule da best friend a man has, especially a farmer. I've been taking special care of this here one. Suh, you say that you bought this mule, but are you gonna finish eating that apple?"

I said, "Hell, yeah, I'm gonna finish it, why? Do you want some of it?"

"No, suh, I don't want nothing, but when you get through eating dat apple would you give de mule de core?"

I kinda laughed and said, "Well, hell, yeah, I'll give him the core!"

"Well," he said, "I've kinda got a-hankering to him and I bet that he'd like that."

I took another bite out of the apple, stepped up to the old ugly, and I held out my hand real flat with the core on it. Boy, he sniffed at that core and, whiff! That core plumb disappeared. He had some kind of vacuum on that big mouth and the core just went out of sight.

Finally a white stableman come up and ask me, "What the hell is the name of this mule?"

I said, "Jesus, I didn't ask him. I don't know what it is."

"Well," he said, "he sure is king of the mules."

"By God, that's his name."

"What, King?"

I said, "Hell, no. Not King—Alfred's his name. Alfred is that guy—ever heard of Finerty?"

He said, ''Hell, no. I never did.''

I said, ''Well, he was that newspaper reporter that come on the campaigns with us. Real educated fellow, knew all about everything. Knew about them Napoleon wars and all that. All about the fighting over there somewhere in Russia or something, where the British fought the Cossacks and they had some kind of a charge called the Charge of the Light Brigade or something. He knew all about that stuff. He was always talking about the Greeks and their warriors fighting at Thermopylae.''

''Thermopolis—you mean that new cow town starting on the Big Horn, up at the headwaters?''

I said, ''Not Thermopolis, Wyoming—I ain't talking about that. Some Thermopylae or something over there where there's a narrow pass and all them Greek soldiers, years and years ago, done held the Persians off. Anyway, he told me all about it. I couldn't understand what he was talking about half the time, but he said that there was a king of England real long ago named Alfred, one of them early warrior kings. You call this animal the king of the mules—by God, then his name is gonna be Alfred. I'll tell you why. I'm riding a horse called Jupiter.''

The white guy said, ''Jupiter? Jesus Christ, you're getting real fancy—you've got a horse named Jupiter and now you've got a mule named Alfred.''

I said, ''That's right. That's exactly right, and I'm traveling in style, so you nor any other man better not make any Goddamn snotty remarks about it. I've had lots of horses, and I would have probably called that mule 'Old Moose Head' and Jupiter 'Old Blackie,' but the boy that I got Jupiter off of, well, that was the name he give him, and just so he ain't lonesome or in the wrong kind of company and just so that mule don't feel downtrodden and having somebody high-hat him a little bit, he's gonna be a king. So his name is Alfred. King Alfred, that's the mule, by God. Jupiter and King Alfred.''

That was the best Goddamn combination I ever had. Of course, that mighty Jupiter was out of the fine bloodlines of Kentucky and Tennessee racing thoroughbred and, Jesus, you couldn't beat him. I knew I was real safe when I was riding him, because if I ever got stopped by a band of Sioux or anything like that and they wanted to give me a bad time, I could just outrun them. As far as the mule was concerned, he was a packing fool. He could pack a load like you never seen, never get tired, always had a good disposition. The only thing I had against him was that he liked apples too much.

Well, I got to thinking about it and why in hell did I go buy a mule? Well, I thought, I'm gonna make a long ride and pack a long ways and that will be nice. I got a good horse now and a damn good mule and, Brules, you're about a free man again. You're out moving around. Now the only thing you've got to do is go get your discharge.

Then I thought, that's crazy as hell. How am I gonna get discharged? I just got a letter from General Crook telling me to get my ass down to North Platte, that he's got something for me. Well, at least we're going in the right direction, 'cause I'm heading south to pass the winter. I've had a bellyful of winter in Montana. I'll play ball with Crook and if he's got a mission that I'd like to do, I'll go along with it. If it ain't, I'll figure some way to get out of it.

I pulled out of that encampment the next morning and made good time. Went past Fort Keogh and kept right a-going, having my orders. When I passed the mouth of the Tongue, I headed up toward Mizpah Creek and cut over to the Little Missouri. Three weeks later, with the Black Hills behind me, I was coming up on Fort Robinson. In another few days I made it to North Platte and reported in to General Crook at Fort McPherson.

When I finally made it to Fort McPherson, I went in to see the general and he greeted me like I was his favorite scout—which maybe I was. I told him where I'd spent the winter, and he winked and said, "I hear that you've got a real beautiful Crow girlfriend up there, is that right?"

"Yes, sir, she's a beauty. Her name is White Antelope and she's a good woman, but, General, I was aiming to go do something else. I thought I'd go grizzly hunting and was thinking that just maybe, sir, you might go with me."

Old Crook looked at me, smiled, and said, "I'd love to be going with you, Brules. Nothing I'd like better than a good hunt like that. Matter of fact, I want to send you over into some country that's a bit like that and maybe you'll enjoy it.

"You told me about how when you were a young fellow you went hunting grizzlies over there in the La Sal Mountains? I'm going to send you right near there, and when you get through with your mission, you can go over to the La Sals and have yourself a good time."

"Boy," I said, "what's the mission, sir? I'll start today!"

"I'll tell you what I want you to do, Brules. I want you to go down to Denver—"

"Denver?"

"Well, you are just going through Denver, on the railroad."

"Hell," I said, "can't I just ride my horse down?"

"No, you're not going to ride down there at all. You know, we've got railroads running through the country now, Brules, and you're going to take the railroad. You're going to put your horse in a boxcar—"

I said, "My horse's name is Jupiter."

"That was young Lieutenant Wilson's horse, wasn't it?"

"But, sir, I got a mule too."

The general roared with laughter. He said, "That's right, you do—what's *his* name?"

"King Alfred."

"So you've got Jupiter and King Alfred."

"Well, I'm not gonna call him King Alfred, I'll just call him Alfred. Jupiter and Alfred—now, ain't those good names?"

Well, I thought General Crook would never stop laughing, but he said, "That's the greatest thing, Brules. You call them both just that way, Jupiter and Alfred, and if anybody gives you a bad time about it, you're the man to set them straight. I can see that by just looking in your eyes, and anybody else is going to see the same thing and they'll back off. Son, you won't have any trouble at all."

"Well, I ain't aiming to, General. I don't mind being ragged a little bit, but just as soon as I get used to not being so highfalutin with riding Jupiter and having King Alfred around, I'll do what you say, General. What do you want me to do? Where are you gonna send me?''

"All right," he said, "I want you and your animals to take the train from North Platte to Cheyenne, and Cheyenne to Denver. Then I want you to go on to Colorado Springs. They've got a narrow-gauge railroad that runs down to Walsenburg and then over La Veta Pass to Alamosa and goes as far up as—Adjutant, am I right?—I think it's to Del Norte."

"Yes, sir, that's as far up as the railroad goes."

"Then I want you to ride over the top of Cochetopa Pass. You know where that is?''

"Know it?" I said. "It was at the Cochetopa Pass that I learned I was gonna be a daddy."

"Well, Brules, you've been everywhere and I'm glad to hear it. You know the country, and you'll go on down the Gunnison to the Ute Agency at Los Piños. I want you to check in at the Ute Agency, and see Chief Ouray and take a message to him, which is real important.

"Now, here is the trouble. The northern Utes are giving us a bad time. The agent there has written that he has had great difficulty getting the northern Utes to start any farming activities, and the Indians are becoming rougher and more insulting all the time. He is hinting that he may need some troops. I wouldn't be surprised but that he's right, and I'm quite sure he'll need them eventually, but I can tell you if we have to go fight the northern Utes, I don't want the southern Utes in the middle of it.

"Ouray of the southern Utes is a very wise man. He was born in Taos, and I don't know if he's full-blooded Ute or not, but he has a little education and is smart enough to see that he can't beat the white man. The way the Ute Reservation stands now, it's the whole western half of Colorado. It's obvious that it is a complete impossibility to leave a few hundred Indians all that territory to live, while thousands and thousands of white farmers need land to work on. We're going to have trouble, but when we have it we want to have those southern Utes and Chief Ouray on our side.

"I know Chief Ouray. I had some powwows with him in Taos when I was there last. So, I want you to take this letter to him. It's very congratulatory, telling him I'm sending some things he wants to have, mostly powder and minié ball, but nevertheless, things that he likes. Then I'm going to make some slight complaints about what the northern Utes are doing.

"I'm going to hint that he's too smart to do the same thing, that those stupid tribesmen of the White River Agency in northern Colorado are eventually going to lose all that big reservation. Ouray is smart enough to see that. I don't want to send him a letter through the mail, I'm not even sure that the mail goes in there. I want this carried by special courier, and you're going to be that courier."

And, guess what I said? "Yes, sir!!"

He shook hands with me, saying, "I'll see you again, Brules. You're too good a man to stay out of my sight for long. Behave yourself." The last thing he done was wink at me. "Have a good grizzly hunt, son. Maybe you'll bring me back a hide."

I said, "General, I'd be proud to do that. Let's just see what happens."

Crook's adjutant wrote me out a requisition so I could get train tickets and a boxcar with a stall for my horse and mule. He wanted to know if I wanted to ride up in the day coaches.

"Hell, no, I'll ride back in the boxcar with my stock—my family. I ain't never been on a train, and I'm kinda nervous about it."

He laughed and said, "Well, there is a lot of noise. But it moves right along, goes day and night. Beats hell out of riding a horse."

"Sir, nothing beats hell out of riding a horse," I insisted. "A horse is the best damn transportation ever made, but I'm willing to try a train, 'cause the General orders me to do it."

Me and my stock—my family—we was a little nervous with all the noise, but we got to Denver all right. There we boarded the narrow gauge. There's some difference between that and the standard railroads. Them cars are about half the size, and them boxcar accommodations ain't near as good for the stock.

As we went up through Colorado Springs, I spent most of the time staying back in the caboose with some of the fellows. They was telling me all about the way Colorado Springs was a-growing and how there was gold strikes near Denver, up in Black Hawk and Central City. Somebody was saying there might be some gold found around Cripple Creek, but I don't think they had any strike then to amount to anything—it was about twenty years later for Cripple Creek.

Anyway, we chugged along, and damn if that little old locomotive of the narrow gauge railway wasn't a wood burner. They didn't have no coal or anything, just piles of wood the fireman kept pouring to it.

We went up through Walsenburg in the shadow of them Spanish Peaks, and on over La Veta Pass into the San Luis Valley, and I kept thinking, my God, here I am in this train when I used to ride across all this. I remembered how long those rides was. Nearly two days to ride across that San Luis Valley and the mountains stood out in front of you all the time—you never seemed to be getting anywhere. With the train it was different, it wasn't too long before we was at Del Norte.

It was a real good feeling to off-load them animals. I left them in a corral for the night, seeing they was well watered and provided with oats and otherwise cared for. I went to the pitch house, right near the railroad station there, and slept like a log.

The next morning I packed up my saddlebags, and put a pack on that mule. Man, could he carry a load. I'd had bought a lot of ammunition and some other things, on the way through Denver, so's I'd have plenty of what I needed. Even had some things I figure I'd trade to the Indians.

18

Hard Ride
at Hatch Gulch

I traveled on up the Rio Grande and crossed over Slumgullion Pass, moving steady until I came to the Los Piños Agency of the Utes. Didn't have no trouble getting ahold of Chief Ouray—he lived down on the banks of the Uncompahgre River about ten miles below the agency. I was surprised when I seen him, 'cause he was different from most other Indians I'd been used to seeing.

It wasn't like seeing old Chief Washakie or Sitting Bull or Chief Joseph. I never did see any of them but what they was in Indian clothes. But old Ouray was wearing white man's stuff—he wore a regular shirt, trousers, and hat. He did have a bear claw necklace around his neck, which give him a lot of credit in my book, having one myself. I think he seen my necklace and liked me too.

Chief Ouray praised me for the long trail I had taken to get there. He could speak good English, and when I said I'd brought him a letter from his brother, General Crook, he was real pleased. He didn't read it right then—matter of fact, I'm not sure that he could read, but he didn't want to let me know that.

The Utes treated me real good, having me put my horse and mule in a pasture nearby. I rested up for a couple of days, seen what I could trade at that Los Piños Trading Post for ammunition and beans and bacon and other supplies, and then

I hit out, riding Jupiter and leading Alfred. I soon found out I didn't need no lead rope for that mule. Alfred just kept following along like a dog. He was so damn fond of that thoroughbred Jupiter that you could never separate them. I think he liked travelin' in the company of aristocracy—kinda proud-like.

I worked my way down the Uncompahgre, my intention being to cross up into the La Sals. I hit the La Sals just about the same place I'd hit them when I'd gone on my first grizzly hunt. But as I climbed on up through those mountains, I began to have a bad time with myself.

I got to thinking of Wild Rose, and it seemed like her presence was everywhere. I couldn't get her off my mind, didn't want to, really, but I sure was getting gloomy and sad. I made a big effort not to go anywhere near the creek that flowed down around the southeast side of the La Sals, 'cause I knew if I came around the campsite where Wild Rose and I had spent them happy months, I'd probably shoot myself rather than go on.

It didn't take me long to locate where the grizzlies was. I was real pleased and surprised that there wasn't no trails into their roaming ground as far as I could see. There was a lot of good grizzly sign, and after a day or two of scouting I come within sight of what I was looking for and started to go to work.

I must have been up there on that mountain for the better part of six weeks all through April and early May of '79, just as them grizzlies was coming out of hibernation. Their coats was in fine shape, and being an old grizzly hunter who'd paid his price, I knew a little bit more about how to go about it. Before long I had me some good full-grown grizzly hides; some of them boars, some of them sows, and a three-year-old. Figuring I'd done pretty good I decided to head down, maybe go into the town of Moab and see if I couldn't sell off them hides.

When I quit hunting I was on the south side of the La Sals, and remembering how steep it was around there just southeast of Moab, I decided to keep a-going straight and drop down the easy part of the mountain to a stream around the base of Mount Peale.

That campground me and Wild Rose had was way back upstream, maybe five miles. I was careful not to go near it. But that was a mistake, because the mountain got a lot steeper than I figured on, and to make matters worse I came up suddenly on some slick rock. Nobody but a damn fool would try to take the animals over that stuff. They'd slip and break their necks and yours along with it. I checked Jupiter immediately. I didn't think I could turn him around on the narrow trail we had, without him gettin' one foot onto that slick rock, and that would be the end of all of us. I worked with him, talked to him slow, and managed to slip off quiet-like and back him up a little, although he done some considerable snortin', trying to tell me he didn't like the situation worth a damn either. You get a thoroughbred hot-blooded horse that is as big as Jupiter, and try to get him turned around in a narrow space on the steep side of a mountain in the middle of an outcrop of slick rock, and you've got your hands full.

I sure demonstrated that to perfection, 'cause I got the horse turned around all right, but scrambling around to lead him off, I put my right foot down on some of that slick rock. I lost my footing and slid down maybe thirty feet, and off a ledge onto a rock pile. I wound up with a hell of a pain in my left shoulder. We was at about the twelve-thousand-feet level on the mountain. When you've been beat up by a bad fall at that altitude, you don't want to have to chase a horse that's been spooked.

Fortunately, old Jupiter, bless his heart, just stood there and looked at me. Gradually I got myself together and worked around the side of the rock plate. I found a place with a little grass where I could climb up. My arm was killing me all the time, but old Jupiter just waited and when I come up close to him, he kinda nuzzled me a little bit, like he always done. He put his head against the middle of my back, trying to say, "I know it's a tough one, boss. It's a tough one."

I had to figure some way to get on him, so I got above him on the hill and climbed on, with my arm hanging there, dead-like. Damn, it was painful! That kinda took the life out of things a little bit and made me feel like my afternoon wasn't gonna be so good. I knowed that I had to get down into Moab to get my arm fixed. There wasn't no doubt about it. As much as I hated going into civilization, and having folks gaping at the six or seven grizzly hides loaded onto Alfred, I knew I had to do it. Alfred watched the whole scene, looking at me as if to say, "Boss, what the hell are you doing now? You're always gettin' yourself in a jam." Alfred didn't have to talk: he just looked at you and you knew Goddamn well what he was thinking.

Well, I kinda apologized to both of them. "We're going on down the hill here, guys, and let's just get it done nice and easy. I'm real proud of you, Alfred—the way you don't mind getting packed with them stinkin' hides, you know?" I had fleshed the hides as good as I could so there wasn't no blood on them, but you know they still stank like hell. Most mules won't stand for it.

After losing a lot of height I come upon a sheer cliff about four hundred feet high, all smooth red rocks, and when I got close enough to the edge to look down, I seen a surprising and beautiful sight.

There was a ranch down there with green hay meadows, buildings in particular good shape, and a river meandering through it all. From up that high I could see there was good fences, and lots of cattle and horses in the pastures. I decided to go on down and see what's what.

I started to look for some way to get down off them high cliffs, but didn't have much success. They was sheer straight and in some places an overhang, with no place to get down. It looked like a fellow would have to get his horse to grow wings. Strange thing about it, as I was working along the edge I realized that there was no wind blowing, that everything in that canyon below was real quiet. In fact, so damn quiet, you could hear the voices of the cowhands and others above the soft murmur of the stream. I could hear them so clear, it seemed like they was only about thirty yards away instead of more than four hundred.

Well, I kept going along them cliffs for quite a ways, looking down with awe at that spread that lay out across the bottom of the canyon. I couldn't remember ever seeing any place as beautiful, except for maybe the sights and wonders of the Broken Arrow.

A cleft in the rock, with steep walls maybe a hundred and fifty feet high and a narrow passage about fifty feet wide, opened up. It was as dark as twilight in that cleft, and the trail real steep. The goin' was tough and kinda spooky, and it was cold in there, too, but at the bottom end the sun shone bright against the darkness of the canyon, and a fellow could see the blue water of the creek. Once you broke out into the sunlight again, it was like being reborn.

Old homely Alfred was plodding along behind Jupiter. Alfred looked like some huge wild creature, with all them bear hides packed on him. Them bear hides must have weighed sixty pounds apiece, and besides that he was packing a whole lot of other stuff, but that five-hundred-pound load didn't seem to bother him none. He just followed me and Jupiter wherever we was heading.

As I was moving toward the corrals with "my family," the biggest man I ever seen stepped out of the corral gate and stood there with his hands on his hips, his feet wide apart, and a big grin on his face.

He was sizing me up as we come on him, and I could tell he liked what he saw!—a grizzled mountain man with a coonskin cap covering his ears, riding a fine stallion, rifle slung in a scabbard on his left, followed up by the biggest and ugliest mule in the territory, loaded down with bear hides. He couldn't help liking what he saw if he was any kind of a man.

There weren't nobody else around, but I could hear some women's voices coming from the main house, the kitchen most likely. There was some noises back of the barn—it sounded like somebody was shoeing horses or something. Looking out at the field I could see the first hay crop had been stacked, and it weren't too far off from the time of the second cutting. Mount Peale, the south peak of the La Sals, towered above the ranch, way up there in the blue sky, and even though it was nearing summer there was still a lot of snow on gray rock up near the peak. You could see clear up to the timberline, and above it them great open slopes of the mountain grass where I'd had all my fun with the grizzlies.

I looked down at this big fellow as I pulled Jupiter to a halt. He wore a plain cotton shirt, brown pants, and a set of heavy black boots that come almost to his knees. He come straight over to me. When he got close I realized he was mighty tall, maybe six foot six inches, with shoulders like an ox. His sleeves was rolled up, and I could see that he had hairy forearms and hands almost as big as a bear paw.

Now, most usual, when a stranger come near me, it made me real shy and fidgety, but I didn't mind this man walking up to me at all. He had a big flaming red mustache and blue eyes that was mostly smiling.

He stopped in front of me and said, "Welcome stranger, looks like you've been doing some hunting."

I hadn't talked to no human being in more than two months, and I didn't feel much like talking yet, so I looked at him and just nodded. He told me his name was Ezra Slade.

He started talking about unsaddling my horse, unpacking the hides, and turning Jupiter and Alfred out into the pasture.

Finally, he fixed to talk about grizzlies. "Yes, sir, when I seen them hides, I knowed there was a real hunter come to visit us. Ain't many men in these parts that come out of the mountains packing such a bunch of grizzly hides. I reckon you're a fair hand with the rifle, judging by your hides, and seeing the way your gun stock's scratched. Ain't that right?"

I still hadn't said nothing, but I nodded.

"That's a mighty fine rifle, the '73 Winchester. It's a heavy-hitting gun. I happened to see one that come down on a freighter from Salt Lake about four months ago. Understand it has better balance than the old '66?"

Not knowing what to say—it seemed a long time since I'd been with humans—all I done was nod my head, again.

He kinda laughed and said, "All right, son, there ain't no use of talking about it all now. We'll talk some more after you get settled in, 'cause I'm hoping you'll stay awhile. Now here comes Hannah telling us grub's ready.''

A thin, bony, gray-haired woman was coming from the kitchen of the main house. Hannah, it turned out, was the first wife of Ezra Slade. She must have been about forty-five years old, but she was a real old-looking woman—hard used. It showed in the pinched-up set of her face and the coarseness of her hands. Her thinning gray hair hung down kinda stringy, and her voice crackled and croaked when she talked. Yet, when she got near Ezra Slade, her eyes lit up and she looked up at him like he was lord of the earth.

Ezra hisself looked to be nigh unto fifty. His thick red hair and beard was streaked with gray, but he hadn't lost any of his vigor, or if he had, he must have been an uncommon man when he was young. Hannah was kindly, but she was sharp and sorta brittle. I could tell she hadn't decided whether I was worth bothering with. She said, ''Mr. Slade, your meal is on the table.''

''Thank you.'' He turned toward me and said, ''This gentleman is going to join us.'' Hannah looked at me kinda sharplike and snorted a little. Then she walked away.

Ezra stepped up beside her, put his arm around her, and started walking with her back toward the house. It sure were a sight. That scrawny woman, who might have been a real good-looker when she was young, and that big, powerful man with his arm tender around her. Couldn't help noticing as he walked away the strength in his legs and the broadness of his back. God, as big as an ox. I made up my mind that he was one fellow I sure weren't gonna get into no argument with.

At that point Slade called, ''You come just in time for grub, son. Why don't you slip off that horse and tie him over there by the corral? I see that mule is kinda well behaved and don't need no rope, I guess.''

''No, sir, he don't. He's real fond of traveling with the aristocracy of a thoroughbred.''

Ezra Slade laughed at that, and said, ''Well, he's one hell of a mule too.''

''Yes, sir, he's king of the mules.''

"What's his name?"

"He is King Alfred. I call him Alfred for short. I named him after one of them English kings I'd heard tales about."

The booming laugh of Ezra Slade, which I was to hear many times with great pleasure, burst over me.

I didn't want to ask for no favors or anything, but when I swung around my horse and started to get off, it was evident that my left arm was useless. Ezra seen me damn near take a spill gettin' off and he stepped over quick to help me down.

"What's the matter, stranger? Are you hurt some?" he asked.

I nodded. "I don't know how bad, but I done me a little sliding on the slick rock and fell off into a pile of boulders. I think my left shoulder is broke."

"Say, you've got to be taken care of right now. Come on, let's get your stock over here in the corral. I'll have one of the boys take care of everything." He whistled to one of the cowboys, who came runnin' over, and told him, "Joe, take this stuff in—and those grizzly hides, we'll handle them in a little bit, just as soon as we unpack that mule. But right now we got to do something for this man. I think he's pretty bad hurt. Let's go in here to the shed here and take a look at his shoulder. Stranger, do you mind taking your shirt off?" He led me into the shack.

When I took my shirt off he could see that, my God, my shoulder was pretty near around to my chest. I had what they called a dislocation or something. Slade said, "I declare, that's something else now. Listen, there's a fellow here on the ranch that studied medicine in Salt Lake City, and he may know something. Looks to me like your shoulder's just plumb wrenched around in front of your chest and we've got to reset that somehow. We gotta do something."

He told the cowboy, "Run over and get Elmer." He turned to me. "He ain't a doctor yet, but he can fix you up, I think."

Pretty soon a young man came trotting over—nice-looking fellow—and I told him what had happened.

"Is this the only place you're hurt?" he asked. "You're kinda banged up aside your head a little bit here."

"My head and the rock are about the same hardness, so it didn't do no harm there. Everything is all right, but my arm's really hurtin'."

"Yeah, I bet it is. This is gonna hurt, but I'm gonna reset it. Now, I'm gonna lift it up here, and I want you to just kinda relax."

He took my left wrist and held it tight in his right hand, then he shoved his left arm in my armpit and just kinda give a whirl, like he was tearing off a branch or something. He made a big circle and there was a pop. My God, you know, I just felt like screamin'. I didn't say nothing but I sure was chewing my tongue so much, a little blood come out. God, that hurt! I could feel my shoulder snap back in and it was back in place again, but, hell, I could hardly use it. My arm was hangin' there useless.

"Well, we've gotta make a sling for that, but you're not as bad hurt as you might be," he explained, then started checking the rest of me. "Now, let me look at your back here a little bit. You're bruised all around. Here's a place where you took a hell of a beating, but I don't see anything but a few cuts in the skin, and I can treat those. I don't see anything broken. The way you hit, you're lucky as hell you didn't break your neck. You just dislocated that shoulder, and you're gonna have to take it easy for a few days. I'll make you a sling right now."

He took the bandanna from a cowboy standing there, and put it around my arm, tying it in back of my neck. "There, stranger, you're all set now, but you lie down somewhere. That's as bad a wrench as I ever saw, and you took a heavy beating on the back of your shoulders and neck."

Ezra quickly agreed. He told me, "You can go right over to that shed right there and lay down. There's some hay in there and one of the girls will bring you something to eat. You just take your time. Never mind about the mule and that good-looking racehorse you've got. We'll put them all away. You just take it easy. I'll see that one of my daughters comes out and takes care of you."

Well, I'll tell you I was in no condition to argue, and so I just kinda slowly wandered over toward the shed and lay down there. Of course, it was in the shade and I lay down on the hay, my eyes was goin' around and around, and I kinda passed out there for a while.

I want to tell you here and now that Ezra Slade was one of the best men I ever knowed. Ezra was a Mormon, and I ain't saying that to give you no ideas about Mormons. Most folks may think they're a terrible lot, what with their different ways. Of course, what gets people upset is their having so many wives. Then, too, there was lots of talk in the early days that the Mormons was killing some of the other immigrants. Well, that may not or may be so, and I ain't saying, 'cause I ain't got no firsthand knowledge about such things.

Ezra Slade had him a big, beautiful ranch eighteen miles southeast of Moab up Hatch Gulch. That distance sticks in my mind for many reasons, and so does Ezra Slade and them folks that was living there. Yes, sir, I ain't too sure that them that hates the Mormons, and goes to running them down all the time, isn't just jealous. Them Mormon fellows had some of the right ideas. I hear tell that there's always good pay on a Mormon spread. They almost never gets into debt, and them that does always pays off quick. I know for sure they're hard workers. Ezra Slade sure was—never seen a man work so hard in all my life.

I don't know nothing about their religion, but I know they believe in it real strong, and that ought to stand for something. There's lots of folks that claims to be Catholics or Protestants or something, and me and you both know they ain't nothing. They're just going through a kinda form. But that sure weren't the way of the Mormons that I knowed. They believed in everything about the Mormon faith, and they believed hard.

Mormon women was expected to do their share of work, but it seemed to me that them Mormon men that had three wives worked three times as hard as a man that had one. They had to see that each wife was took care of proper and all got equal shares. If the wives lived in different houses, the husband had to cut the wood for each one, see she got plenty of supplies, had a good dry roof over her head, and had the clothes she needed, a horse or buggy, and whatever else she wanted. About the only thing he didn't haul for her was her water. All them Mormon wives went to the well and got their own water for cooking, drinking, bathing, and such.

Damned if I know how Brigham Young done it. They say he had over twenty wives. I don't know much about how Mormons' wives got along with one another. From what I seen, there was plenty of bickering, but there's always lots of bickering among women, so what the hell? One thing I do know, each one of Ezra Slade's wives thought he was a good man, and they seemed to be right happy with him.

Later, I come to like Hannah, even though she acted sharp and cranky. I reckon if she'd had an easier life, she wouldn't have looked quite so old. Seemed like she wasn't getting out of life all it ought to give her, yet she was mighty proud of Ezra. I learned more about their children as time went on, but I seen there was quite a few of them, and they was most all red-headed like Ezra Slade.

The ranch sure was a real nice place. It was set down at the bottom of one of them red cliff canyons that is so frequent around them parts. The canyon was a third of a mile wide, and the red sandstone cliffs that run on both sides of it was any-where from three to five hundred feet high. The cliffs was like guardian walls that run the whole length of the meadows, as far as the eye could see. They was crowned on top with scrubby oak brush.

The nicest little stream run through the main part of the property. It skirted from one wall of the canyon over to the other, running through the hay meadows, murmuring and rippling across the rocks just as pretty and clear as you please. Later on, when I got up close and looked into them shady pools alongside the cliffs, there was the biggest, nicest trout a man would ever want to lay eyes on.

There was a well, even though you could get water out of the creek. I reckon anywhere you dug in that canyon you could pick up the water level about ten feet belowground.

Sure was a relaxing place. When I come to, I sat up and

looked around. The main ranch house was built of logs with a wood shingle roof, and there was a real big barn built from good lumber that must have been shipped in. The barn was painted bright red, the only red on the place. Ezra done that for Hannah, I heard. She liked red barns on account of being brought up around them in Indiana, before she come out here with them early Mormons.

Beyond the main ranch house was three little houses set right up against the cliff. From what I could see, they was built of right good lumber too. All was neat and painted white with green roofs and stood about sixty yards apart. Each one of them had a flower garden around it, and a vegetable patch, and a good solid pole fence to keep the stock out. A path run from the main house over to them three little houses, and partway along it branched off to the well.

I found out that Ezra dug that well hisself, the first spring after he'd homesteaded the ranch. The water running down the creek in the spring got mighty high and roily from the melting snows, so you couldn't drink it. In the fall it was different, but just as bad, 'cause then there was two or three thousand head of beef wading in the stream.

The well had a steep roof and a real old turning handle on a spindle with a chain for the oak bucket. It looked just like them wells I seen on nice farms back in Kentucky when I was a kid. Course, we didn't have no fancy well, and my mama mostly used the river water.

Their houses, including the ranch house, faced the south, so it got the warm sun in the winter and was sheltered from the north wind. The big old red barn faced north. It had a real good roof and swinging doors for the hayloft, and below was what looked like stalls and a couple of wagons sat inside.

On the far side of the barn was some mighty fine corrals, a calving shed with two branding chutes, and a rig alongside the barn to feed the stock in the corrals. Them corrals was laid out real good, with part of the stream coming through them so there was plenty of fresh water. I could see right away that Ezra weren't no slouch when it come to ranching. It seemed to me that he had a little bit of paradise stuck away here, far out on the edge of the wilderness. I hadn't ever envied any man in my life before, but I couldn't help thinking that Ezra Slade had maybe found the best way of living. I wondered whether me and Wild Rose could have made the same at the Broken Bow, if we could have just stayed there long enough.

I sat out there all that afternoon, just soaking up the sun and dreaming. Along come the sunset and some of the children walked over my way from the ranch house. There was a little barefoot girl, about eleven years old, skinny and freckled with red hair, leading the bunch. From the looks of her I reckoned she was Hannah's child. She was wearing a calico dress and acted real shy when she walked by. She seemed kinda pleased that I was sitting there, but was too shy to say anything. Right after she took a good look at me, she and them others lit off lickety-split back to the ranch house.

I watched the sun go down and the shadow of the canyons creep over the valley. Up to the north the snowy peaks of the La Sals was still sticking up in the sunshine. I sat there watching till all the light faded and them peaks was just shadows against the night sky. I began to get sort of cold, so I walked over to the half cabin by the woodshed, that the cowboys used, and lay down on my mat to get some sleep. It had been a long time since I'd lived inside four walls, but I guessed I'd get used to it if it didn't last too long. One of the little girls knocked at the door with a tray of food. After I took it and thanked her, she run off real quick. Having the tray delivered showed I wasn't going to eat with the family in the main house.

The next couple of days went on like that, but every day I'd stand around the corrals and watch all the things going on, learning more and more about the people and their activities.

Ezra had him three good cowhands that was handy with the rope and knowed how to ride. They lived in the bunkhouse. I reckon that at one time he'd had more help than that, but now he had a couple full-growed boys of his own out tending cattle, and others that was old enough to help him with the light work. The sons still at the ranch was from twelve to fifteen years of age, all likely lads, strong and growing like weeds, and every one of them as redheaded as Ezra. The rest of Ezra's children—and there was lots of them—was a mixture of boys and girls, from big kids on down to two-year-olds. All of them was barefoot and bright eyed, running around, having a grand time, enjoying life on the ranch.

Ezra was a kindly man, no doubt, judging from the way he treated me and everyone else, but he sure was the boss of that ranch. When he said jump, they all jumped, and as far as I could see there weren't no arguments put up by no one when he give orders, from the oldest hand to the toddlers.

I'd been there for about two days when I first seen Ezra's third wife, Sarah, and I didn't cotton to her. She was just the opposite of Hannah—a stout, wall-eyed woman with a snout like a pig. She had a strange way of waddling along when she went to the well for water or from the main ranch house to her place. It give you the idea she weren't all fat but had lots of muscle. I seen her go down to the icehouse once and dig out a big block of ice from the sawdust. She carried it on her shoulder clear up to the ranch house, and it didn't seem to take much effort for her.

Sarah would stand with her hands on her hips and her feet apart, yelling at the kids. Kinda reminded me of the bellowing of a sour old buffalo cow. About half the time she walked around with a switch in her hand and give them kids a lick here and there, to make them move and do what she was saying. I never could figure out why Ezra ever took her on, her being as ugly as she was and having all them bad ways, but I reckoned he had his own reasons. I guess the Mormons out there on the frontier didn't worry so much what a woman looked like, but what she could do. She was expected to carry her load, and that Sarah could do it. Funny, though, her kids was different than Hannah's, all of them was surly-like and built stocky like her. Her oldest boy—a lad of about twelve— looked like he was growing to be as big or bigger than his daddy, and a heap sight meaner.

After a while I got things concerning Ezra's wives better sorted out. I couldn't help but notice that one of these three houses, the one that was the farthest away, didn't have no kids running in and out of it like the other two. Either from my weakness or just 'cause I was slow getting onto the ways of living around people, it took a while before I learned that it was the house of the grown daughter of Ezra's second wife, Naomi. Naomi had died years ago, and her daughter was named Melisande.

I won't forget the first time I set eyes on Melisande. One real fine morning I had got up early, and I seen her come out of her little house, holding a shawl around her head and carrying a water bucket. As she come down the steps I seen she was barefoot, and when she got out into the sunshine, she let the shawl slip down from her head to her shoulders, showing her long, beautiful auburn hair. She moved with an easy grace as she walked, almost like she was dancing.

In a quick minute I knowed she was another one of the kids, maybe Hannah's oldest daughter, but as she drawed closer to the well I could see she didn't look like Hannah, and she didn't move like her. Hannah walked kinda like she was on stilts. Studying this girl, I could see that she weren't no child. She had a swell to her bosom and a way of moving her hips that showed she was a woman, and ready for things that no child would think of.

Just watching her, my heart got to quickening. I seen how graceful she was turning the handle of the well spindle, and I got a real thrill as she picked up the well bucket. She bent way over from the waist, and a slight breeze made her dress wrap tight around her thighs and hips. I breathed plenty hard, all the time she carried her bucket back to the house, marveling at her grace and ease as she moved along. Her shoulders and her head hardly moved from the level, yet her legs and hips swayed with every step.

Although she carried the bucket in her right hand, it wouldn't have surprised me none to see her lift it up and put it on her head like them Mexican women did going back and forth with their water jugs. She sailed up the steps as if that big bucket was a child's pail, and slipped into the door of her house, like a vision disappearing into thin air. I reckon seeing that lovely girl just then was the best kind of cure for a man as sad as I'd been. Long after she was gone, the blood kept pounding through my veins and throbbing at my temples, and my heart banged away like an Indian drum.

As I walked away from the corrals and stretched, I realized I was starting to have trouble with myself. After all, I thought, it's been three years since I've needed a woman. True, White Antelope was a friend, but I never took her. Now maybe this girl's ready to take me.

I spent the rest of that day watching for her to show herself again. About noontime she come out to pin some laundry on a line that was strung by the side of her house. She went back indoors for a while, and then my heart jumped when I seen her come out again and walk on past the well, straight to the main ranch house. After she went inside, I just shut my eyes and basked in the sunshine, dreaming about the way she swayed when she walked, wishing I could touch my hand to that long, shining mane of auburn hair.

I watched her every day after that. Around noon she went to the main ranch house and stayed there till after dark. I'd watch careful to see whether she come out; if she did, it was only to go quick to the outhouse, to the well, the icehouse, or the big vegetable garden by the main gate. I could tell how things were going by the snatches of conversation I'd hear coming out of the windows of the main house. When Hannah and Sarah got in there in the afternoons, they would give Melisande trouble for one thing or another. This seemed to be like their favorite thing to do.

It was maybe a week after I'd first seen Melisande, and I heard the voices of Hannah and Sarah scolding away like mad. Sounded like poor Melisande couldn't do nothing right. I caught a murmur of her soft voice making a protest, and that was followed by the sound of a sharp slap, then silence. I guess them two old harpies didn't like her, or maybe they was more than kinda jealous on account of her being the daughter of Ezra's favorite wife. It made me feel uncomfortable, but it was Ezra Slade's problem, not mine.

I walked down to the creek for the first time and knelt down and got ready to wash my face. The pool I was looking into give me a good reflection of myself, and I couldn't hardly believe it was me. My hair hung down near to my shoulders and my beard was so matted and hairy, it looked like there was just a couple of eyes peeking out of a bird's nest. I washed up good and that made me feel a whole sight better. I walked out through one of the gates into the west pasture, and then on down about a quarter of a mile, where I seen the real steep trail that come down the ravine. I decided I'd take the trail on foot and look around a little at everything. I done just that, waded across the creek and made my way up the natural staircase, inside that gloomy passage of clefts, until I came out in the sunshine on top. From that eagle's view I got another look at Ezra Slade's spread where it lay clear up and down the valley. It sure was an inspirin' sight.

Every day I kept a watch for Melisande, and always tried to be where I could get a good look at her, without letting on that I was paying any attention. It weren't too easy to do, 'cause I knowed by instinct that I wouldn't be welcome over by the main ranch house or down anywhere near them little houses.

I made it a regular habit to walk to the well to get a drink. Hannah had left me a big tin cup hanging on a nail over by the door, and I began going to the well about every hour or two, pouring me two or three cupfuls and sitting there in the shade drinking them. I made quite a point of doing this, 'cause I wanted to be there at the right time.

Funny part of it was that drinking that extra water was probably the best thing I could have done for myself. I kept on pouring it through me, and in a few days I noticed a big difference in the way I felt. The well water was real sweet and cold, and it weren't no disagreeable thing to go sip on it every now and then.

I hadn't seen much of Ezra Slade, 'cause he'd gone down to Moab and then up the mountain to the high cow camp. When he come riding in off the trail that wound down the ravine from the north, I made sure he seen me go to the well and get me a cup of that cool, sweet water. I stayed right there by the well while he rode in.

Slade tied up his horse and walked over to me. When I smiled and raised my hand in greeting, he grinned and said, "Say, young man, looks like you're doing all right. I reckon there ain't no way to keep a good man down. I figured you was such when I first seen you. It ain't every man that can kill and skin out seven grizzlies, then pack them hides down the mountain by hisself. No, sir, I reckon there's a lot of hunter in you, and I aim to make you a proposition. Are you in the mood for listening?"

I just nodded and fixed my eyes on his. He gazed back, real fascinated, and said, "Yeah, you're just what I need to clean out them grizzlies that's been raiding my cattle. Before we get down to business, tell me what to call you."

"My name's Brules, Mr. Slade. Cat Brules. You can call me Brules."

"To be real honest, I been having a time with grizzlies getting into my cattle. Last year they cleaned me out of better than three hundred head, about half of them full-grown stock.

"The whole time we been on this ranch, nigh unto fifteen years now, we ain't killed but four grizzlies. I killed two of them myself. I can't seem to hire any hands that are good hunters, and none of us has done any good trapping them. I sent for some bear traps from Salt Lake and I have a few of them strewed all over these mountains. I guess the grizzlies are too smart or else we don't know how to lay traps, 'cause they sure ain't done us no good."

Slade sat down on a chopping block, picked up a wood splinter to chew on, and kept talking. "I reckon you may have some other plans, but I've got a need for a grizzly hunter, 'cause I'm gonna have to clean them bears outta these hills or go broke in the cattle business. The bishop up in Moab tells me that there's more grizzlies now than there was when he first come here twenty years ago. I reckon that's so, 'cause their feeding is better with all the cattle around. It's easier for a grizzly to kill a beef critter than it is to knock down an elk. They've been having easy feeding lately, and that's why they're on the increase.

"Tell you what I'll do, Brules, I'll make you a proposition

right now. I'll give you a dollar a day and keep, same as the cowhands. I'll furnish ammunition, horses, and pack outfit— anything you want, and I'll pay you seventy-five dollars a hide for every one of them grizzlies you pull down. How's that for a good deal?''

I didn't say nothing, just kept looking at him and sipping water.

He kinda got uneasy after a minute or two and said, ''Well, you don't wanta say right now? Why don't you think it over? I got to go back up to the cow camp in a couple of days and I'll talk to you when I get back next week. By that time you ought to have made up your mind—you're welcome to stay as long as you like. I hope you decide to work for me, but even if you don't, I hope you hang around here long enough to talk it over again. Of course, I can't blame a man for being spooked about grizzlies, if he's had some near escapes, and I'll understand if you don't have the stomach to go back and try them again.''

Now, that was the wrong thing to say to me, or the right thing, depending on how you look at it. I reckon I turned bright red, and I could feel my cheeks getting hot and flushed under my beard. I weren't no coward! I tossed that water from the cup halfway across the yard and said, ''Mr. Slade, you got yourself a grizzly hunter.''

Then I turned on my heel and walked off toward the lean-to. As I ducked under the low door, I seen that he was still standing there by the well with a big old grin on his face. Taking his hat off he wiped his brow with his sleeve and shook his head, then he put on his hat and went on toward them houses where all the redheaded kids was coming out to greet him. They did lots of shouting and yelling, so I knowed they was glad to see him.

19

Melisande

I stayed in the lean-to for the next day while Slade was around. I was still fuming a little over what he'd said. I knowed that he hadn't meant nothing wrong by it. He just mistook my natural way of not liking to talk for being spooked and not wanting to hunt again. If only Slade had known how much I loved to hunt, especially grizzlies and Comanches, he would have knowed I weren't taking the position just for the money. That didn't mean too much to me, although I thought it was damn good pay.

What really counted was the chance to go back and do some hunting. I got to thinking about how rich I'd be if somebody had paid me them kind of wages to kill Comanches. I would have made somewhere between fifteen and twenty thousand dollars, and that would have been nice, almost as nice as the satisfaction of getting revenge on them varmints.

So that day, I stayed inside the lean-to and didn't come out—even when I seen Melisande going to the well. Next day Ezra Slade pulled out again, taking a pack train up to his camp in the high country. I reckon he felt he'd spent enough time with his wives and was ready for the quiet life of the trail again. I couldn't help thinking he wasn't living a half-bad life, even if he did have them two crow-bait wives to contend with.

That morning he left fairly early, and as soon as he was out of sight, I went down to the creek to clean up. About ten o'clock in the morning Melisande come out of her house with a bucket in her hand, looking as bright as the morning sunshine. As I watched her floating down them steps, heading toward the well with that beautiful easy grace of hers, my heart started pounding again. I wanted to go toward the well to meet her, but I was stuck in my tracks.

Here was old Brules—the grizzly hunter, the Comanche killer, the hard-eyed gunman who weren't afraid of hell or high water—froze right there in his tracks, made plumb helpless by the beauty of a young gal walking to a well with a pail in her hand. It sure was ridiculous, but it was God's truth. I couldn't move for the life of me. I watched her every step till she finally reached the well, put down the pail, and hung the well bucket by its chain.

By the time she started turning the crank of the spindle, my breath was coming so quick, and my heart pounding so hard, that I had to turn away for a minute to get hold of myself. My brain was racing, as I told myself, damn it all, Brules, now is your chance. Ain't you got the guts to get going?

With that I took my tin cup and started for the well, just like I'd been doing, only I reckon I was moving a little faster than I meant to. I was about halfway there when she stopped turning the well crank and leaned over to look into the well. Her back was to me, so she didn't see me coming, and when I was about twenty yards away, she leaned over the well edge to grab the bucket chain and hoist it up. Her thin skirt clung to her legs, and I seen the real tight curves of her bottom.

I just caught on fire. I couldn't have said nothing to her if I'd wanted to. All I did was just keep walking slow, my eyes on every curve of her body, my arms aching to reach out to her, turn her around, and hold her close to me. I watched as she lifted the bucket out and leaned over to start pouring it into her own. I made kinda awkward shuffling noises with my feet on the gravel, and she looked up real quick and seen me for the first time.

She almost dropped the well bucket and clasped one hand to her breast. "Oh, hello! I didn't see you coming," she said in a soft, silvery voice with a little throb.

I stopped dead in my tracks, and just stood staring at her

bosom and that pretty V that went down into her dress. Then I run my eyes up over the ivory of her neck and past her pretty chin to cheeks that was the color of red apples against the ivory.

I never seen such beautiful skin on any woman in my life—clean and perfect and softly glowing. She had red lips and perfect teeth, a pert nose, and blue-green eyes. The whole breathtaking picture was made complete by her shining mass of auburn hair, falling in gentle curves below her shoulders.

She took a good long look at me, too, stopping to meet me dead in the eyes. Her pupils widened and she blushed real bright. She didn't say nothing, just quick put her shawl around her, grabbed her water bucket, and glided off in a flurry of skirts and hair, leaving me standing there, helpless and tongue tied, watching her every move.

I knowed I had it bad. I'd heard it told many times that when a man saw the right woman, he'd know it and nothing need be said, nor could there be any wishing away of the facts. He'd just know, no power on earth could change it none. That's just the way I felt.

I watched her skim over the ground toward her house and up them steps to disappear behind the door in a flash. It was like seeing a graceful antelope sail over the horizon and disappear from sight, leaving nothing behind but a thin wisp of dust that its running had kicked. Or like the bright color of a sunset, clear when you first see it and, a few minutes later when the sun is down, gone forever.

I must have stayed there nearly five minutes, without making a motion, till I become aware of a few other things. The sun was hot on my neck and there was a hum of bees about. There was also a face at the window of the kitchen in the main ranch house—the face of the old sow, Sarah—looking at me not forty yards away. The door of Hannah's house was slightly cracked open, and somebody stood watching from in there too.

That shook me back into the world and I went over quick-like to the well and drew up a fresh bucket of water. I dipped in my tin cup and started pouring that sweet water down my throat like it was hot whiskey. I made a big show of scraping around with my feet, and then throwed the last part of water out of the cup and started on back to the lean-to. I noticed I was walking much faster than I had before, and realized that I was giving my feelings away to anybody that was watching.

I went into the lean-to quick. My red capote was hanging there and I put it on along with my dandy Navajo belt. I untied my lariat, shoving the .38 in my belt, grabbed my old hat, and come outta that woodshed like I'd been shot from a cannon. I run across the yard and vaulted the pole fence to the horse pasture, heading off at a dead run for where all them horses was banded together in the shade of the cottonwoods down by the stream.

After I'd run halfway across the pasture, I stopped and let out a whistle. I seen Jupiter put his head up, so I whistled at him two or three times again, and then started calling him, cussing to him kindly-like all the while. As I began to move real slow toward him, I could see he was thinking it over. Then he made up his mind to come my way. He'd been roaming in the pasture with some loose mares, and I wasn't absolutely sure if I could cut him away from the mares and the geldings in that pasture. I guess old Ezra had seen his quality and hoped to get a few good mares with foal while we was there.

At first Jupiter come along real easy and I thought I was gonna be able to walk right up to him. Then he stopped, come a little closer, and stopped again, while I kept coaxing and cussing him all the time. The rest of the horses followed along behind him, but every time he'd stop, they'd stop with him and wouldn't go no farther. I guess he had showed them early on that he was lord and master.

He closed the distance to about forty yards when something changed his mind. Damned if I knowed what it was. Maybe he seen the lariat dragging behind me, even though I was holding most of it coiled up behind my back. Anyway, suddenly he whirled and started out at one helluva run, the whole herd following him. I started to run, too, knowing it was doing no good.

He tore around the meadow and went on down to the creek, splashed across, then wheeled through the cottonwoods just going like bloody hell till he come up against the fence on the far side. Although I was cussing mad at him, 'cause I hated to chase a horse in open pasture, I couldn't help admiring the way his tail streamed out behind and how his proud neck was held. Every now and then he'd kick and buck a little to show them mares what a real sport he was.

I kept working him over toward the northwest corner of the pasture, and finally got him and the others bunched up there. He stood still, looking at me as I come in real slow and steady. I kept at a good angle to let me get a rope throwed at him before he could take off to the right or left of me. He pawed the ground and then made a pass to the right, so I moved over that way a little bit. Then he went around ducking in and out among the mares, and started to run to the left. I dashed over there and he come back to the right again.

I reckon it was a mighty good show for any of them back at the ranch that was caring to look, but right then I was aiming to get my rope around that stallion's neck if it was the last thing I done. Finally I worked in real close, and like I expected, he made a dash for it, but I was too quick for him. I had my rope whirling and when I let drive, the noose settled over his neck just as nice as pie. I was real surprised, not having been roping for a long time, but then the fun really started.

I sat right down on that rope, checking it against my butt when I seen he was gonna draw back real tight on it. As it come taut, he lifted me clear off the ground, and I had to dig in with my heels and fight him all the way. I was bound and determined to wrestle him down, and that's just what I done. He finally got quiet and I worked my way up the rope. I kept talking to him all the time and that seemed to help.

We musta stood there fifteen minutes, making friends again, and then I led him off just as nice as you please toward the corral. I tied him to the hitching post and then got my saddle, bridle, and blankets. But I sure had one helluva time saddling him up. A couple of times he reared back and near snapped the lariat. He probably would have, if it hadn't been made out of rawhide.

When I finally got the job done, I become aware of what

was going on. Most of Ezra's kids had come up to sit on the top rail to watch the rodeo. Ezra's cowhands was standing there, too, probably just come in from irrigating the hay meadows. They was carrying them Mormon Winchesters—shovels, or what most cowboys called idiot sticks—and had on them Russian rubber boots they wore when they worked in water. Also I seen the womenfolks watching there by their houses.

I figured the way Jupiter was acting, I was in for a wild ride when I got on him, so I worked him around to where I was on a high piece of ground and he was still on the level. He was a hell of a tall horse and I had to take every advantage.

When I landed in the saddle he stood there for a minute, holding his ears flat and fighting the bit. I tried to get him to ease off, and he went to dancing around stiff-legged. So I knowed then the action was gonna start, and it sure did. He put his head down with a jerk that liked to tore off my left arm, and took off bucking, bellowing, rearing, and naturally raising hell. I was just as mad as him, and maybe a little madder, and was determined to stay right with him.

After he banged hisself up against the corral fence a few times and the dust settled down, he kinda stood there blowing and puffing, me still sitting on him. A big cheer went up from them kids sitting on the top rail of the corral, all clapping and yelling things like "Attaway, Brules, you rode him to a standstill! You sure showed him who's boss, Mister Brules. You sure can ride." Well, I guess watching a big beautiful racehorse like Jupiter go to buckin' like a bronco must have been a sight. They'd seen plenty of buckin' horses actin' crazy, but they'd never seen a Thoroughbred stallion act like that before.

It made me feel real good, but the shouting kinda stirred Jupiter up. He begun racing around the corral and I had a time checking him. I worked him over for about ten minutes, and then yelled at one of the older boys to open the gate of the corral and let us out. There was a dirt wagon road that went from the ranch house right on down to Moab. I figured there weren't no gates on it for a long ways, the pasture being on the other side, and if that big horse really felt like working off some steam, that was one place we could do it.

When Jupiter saw he was clear, he went out of that place like a tornado. I just let him stretch out and gallop full speed, and every time he showed signs of slowing up, I put it to him again and just kept him going. I knew deep down he was a good horse, just acting sporty.

Anyway, he took me down the road on a good hard swinging run. I let him slow down to a trot and then to a walk, and that's when I done some real hard personal cussing right up in his ear. I told him I was plumb ashamed of him acting up like that. I told him I knew he'd gotten all excited about them mares, but that didn't give him no excuse to forget his fine breeding. When a great fifteen-hundred-pound horse as big as Jupiter goes berserk, boy, you got a handful. To be real honest I was kinda proud of him.

About eight miles out I finally turned Jupiter around and headed back toward the ranch at an easy lope. When I got near the horse pasture, I seen the gate to the trail that crossed the road and wound up the ravine into them red cliffs. Not wanting to go back to the ranch right then, I turned Jupiter and crossed the creek and put him to climb up to the top. It was a real steep, rocky grind up through that narrow gorge, but he kept churning and we busted out on top in a few minutes. I rode him back along the edge of the north cliff where I could look right down on the ranch.

That's when I found out how good sound traveled clear up outta the canyon. I could hear voices echoing off them canyon walls and snatches of conversation drifting up real plain. I drawed Jupiter right by the cliff and sat there listening for a few minutes. I could look out over the whole ranch and see all that was going on. I could hear the chattering of the little kids as they went running back and forth, and I could eavesdrop on the cowpunchers coming outta the bunkhouse and making their way over toward the main house for dinner. It was a sunny noon in early summer and there was a few pleasant white clouds floating by, high up in the blue.

It sure was a peaceful scene and it was plumb surprising how clear the sound of voices traveled back and forth between them canyon walls. All of a sudden I recognized the sour, hoarse voice of Sarah talking to Hannah, saying, "Yessiree, there's a certain young woman around here that thinks she's so high and mighty, she don't have to work. Here it is noon with them field hands coming in for something to eat, and there's just you and me to do the fixing. Land sakes, when I was a girl her age, my mama kept my nose to the stove all day long. It's bad enough now, and it's gonna be a sight worse when we start the second cutting with the hay crews coming in every day. I reckon you'd better say something to her."

Hannah's shrill, scratchy voice carried real good. She answered, "She's gonna have to do her part. Ezra Slade's a just man, but he's hard—mighty hard—when it comes to somebody shirking."

Sarah said with a grunt, "Did you see how she looked at that young hunter that's living out there in the lean-to? Did you see the way she acted when he come up to her at the well? Land sakes, she's a flirt if I ever seen one."

Hannah's sharp voice said, "She'd better stop that nonsense. If I know Ezra Slade, he's liable to take a strap to her backsides. He's fair and slow to anger, but he's awful heavy handed. Most of the kids know that."

Then the wind come up, and the snatches of conversation was so scattered, I couldn't make out nothing much else.

I reined Jupiter away from the canyon rim and rode out through the oak brush and back up into the foothills. On the slope up ahead I could see bunches of quaking aspen, and my heart got to longing to be back there in the tall timber country where my soul was free and not so crowded. I could kinda think better there, and I needed to work over some of the ideas that was buzzing around in my head.

I couldn't help thinking how strange it was that old Ezra Slade had him them two older wives and then that beautiful young daughter Melisande. I wondered why he hadn't taken another wife. I'd only heard the sound of Melisande's voice a few times, but I couldn't forget the melody of it. I knowed I was deep gone over a woman, and, damn it, if that woman weren't just a child. Turned out she was just short of eighteen, a real marriageable age on the frontier where some got married at fifteen or sixteen, but to me, who was twenty-nine years old, she seemed plenty young and I was plumb embarrassed about my feelings. I didn't know too much about women, but I sure could tell that this one was a real high-class gal. And it was real plain that she got shook up when she looked at me too.

Then Jupiter scraped his shins and stumbled on one of the deadfalls laying there in the deep grass just as we was entering the quaking aspen, and I come to my senses a little and had to laugh at myself. I was thinking along that way when there was a sudden crashing in the quakies off to my left, and damned if I hadn't flushed the biggest buck I ever seen in my lifetime. He went thumping his way out of the aspen groves and off around the side of the hill, sporting a rack that looked near like an elk and running with that heavy stomping motion that comes with the biggest of them mule deer. He had the deep red of summer and I could see that his neck hadn't thickened and he weren't in the rut yet. I reckon he'd just been resting hisself in the shade of them quakies and was kinda put out by having someone come along and stir him up.

As I went on up the mountain a ways, I felt a little more free in spirit, but troubled just the same. By the time we made it into the blue spruce, the sun was getting low in the afternoon sky and long shafts of light was working through the branches, shining on the west side of all them beautiful tall stately trees. Riding along relaxed, I let Jupiter go plugging easy-like up the hill, crisscrossing now and then so he wouldn't take the grade too hard.

After about an hour it got chilly, as we was working our way up into the high altitudes. I'd stopped to let Jupiter get his breath, when I heard something important and real familiar—the squeaking and chirping of a bunch of little elk calves and along with it, every now and then, the sharp barklike sound of a cow elk calling to her young calves. I stopped there, waiting for what I hoped was coming—that high-pitched whistling call that always sends shivers down your back—the bugle of the bull elk. I told Jupiter in a whisper, "Hold it, boy, I'm waiting for the call of the granddaddy of them all—the herd bull."

Then I woke up—why, Brules, you damn fool; this is

barely July. The rut ain't gonna come on until September, and what's more the bulls' horns is still in velvet. They ain't growed their full length yet. After a minute we started climbing again for maybe two or three hundred yards, then broke out into a big park. There they was—a whole herd of elk. Must have been two hundred of them all in a band, grazing on the side of the hill. I pulled up and started looking around. There was a few small spike bulls and such standing around the side of the herd, but nothing else. Then I seen him standing over there on the hill above them—the old harem bull—beautiful, and king of them all.

For a while I watched the brown-and-white rumps of all them cows feeding way up there and that old bull with the dark shag like a lion's mane on his neck and shoulders. Finally, having seen enough, I nudged old Jupiter in the ribs and we trotted on out into the park. The whole herd turned and looked at us. They seemed plumb shocked with curiosity at first and stood there almost motionless.

Then they started out of there like they was hauling the mail, the old bull leading the herd up the mountain. They looked like a brown river that flowed in and out of the tall grass and then poured in a long stream deep into the forest. I could hear them crashing through the timbers. They was getting out of there and they wasn't making no bones about putting some miles between them and me.

I drawed up again and sat there till they disappeared, thinking about how wonderful the world was, how all them cow elk seemed to be doing just fine under that big old bull, and kind of wondering if maybe them wives of Ezra Slade's might be doing just as well. That was a thought that weren't too pleasant, and I shook it out of my mind.

I sure was confused. First of all, I felt happy again up there in the forest, moving around free on the mountain. For sure the only reason I'd stayed down there on that ranch, sleeping in the lean-to that shut me away from the sky, was on account of Melisande. Maybe the reason I didn't want to leave just yet was a kind of sickness. I reckon it was a sickness for which there ain't no remedy. I was plumb heartsick for Melisande. That's the truth of it.

I had to face it. I was being pulled in two different directions. There was something telling me to go back to Ezra Slade's ranch, and something else saying I ought to stay up on the mountain where I was free. I got to thinking about that. I didn't have my rifle with me, and I didn't have no blanket or nothing to keep off the rain. I hadn't figured on coming up the mountain at all, but I decided to find a good spot to hole up for the night under the stars. Maybe a night of breathing pure mountain air would clear my head.

By that time I'd worked Jupiter back down to the quakies. Next to a quakie patch I seen where there was a little open park for feed. I tethered Jupiter there using the lariat. Then I went about and gathered me a big pile of last year's leaves. They was dry and hadn't been rained on. I found me a good log and packed them leaves alongside up to where they was three feet deep and then, not having nothing else to do—nothing to eat and no easy way to start a fire—I just set down on the log awhile and watched the light fading away in the west while the earth turned bright gold and yellow, then red with the shadowy blues.

I knowed I was happy and didn't need the things that maybe other men needed to make it so for them. Oh, sure, I liked Ezra Slade's ranch, and I would have liked to have had all them horses and cattle and them beautiful buildings and corrals and barns and hay meadows, all them things. Sure, I'd like to be rich like that, but I don't reckon I'd like to work as hard as he did to come by such a place. I preferred to be way up there in the big timber country, wandering around, gazing at nature and enriching myself with what I seen. No, I would have been plenty content if only I hadn't kept thinking about that auburn-haired girl with the gray eyes—Melisande, and the curves of her body that set me afire.

Real soon I noticed a chill wind sliding down off the mountaintop and I begun to shiver a little, sitting there in my shirtsleeves pondering on all that was plaguing my life. So I piled the leaves up on the south side of that big log and rolled up in them and packed them around me. That's a way to stay warm if you ain't got a blanket roll—stay out of the wind and keep them leaves packed around you. You'd be surprised—you can stand lots more cold that way than you'd think.

The next thing I knowed, the bright morning sun was filtering down through my leaf blanket. It was one of them startling bright mornings that you have up in the high country, where everything's so clear it seems like you're living twice. I'd worried that when I rolled out of the leaves I'd be stiff and weak from all the workout with Jupiter, but it weren't so. I felt great, and even though I hadn't ate since yesterday morning, my heart was light and it seemed like my body was tingling all over with fresh energy.

I looked out over the red of the canyon country, straight down below where I could see the green meadows of Ezra's ranch a long ways off and its pretty stream flashing and shining in the sunlight as it wound through the meadows. From where I was, high up on the mountain, them red canyon walls that hemmed in the ranch seemed right small. Didn't look like they was much more than big fences, even though I knowed how high they was. I could see just a little bit of them corrals and buildings that wasn't hid by the canyon and they looked like playhouses down there.

I grabbed my saddle and bridle and walked to the grassy place where I'd tethered Jupiter. I knowed I was gonna have a little rodeo this morning, but it weren't too hard getting him saddled up, though he done some crow-hopping and kind of looked at me with fire-eyes, despite the cussing I give him. When I thought things was all ready, I worked myself around on the uphill side where I could get on easy and put a little weight on the stirrup. I felt him hunch his back a little bit, so I stepped down and kicked him in the belly and then vaulted into the saddle.

This startled him and give him a couple of things to think about real quick, the kick in the guts and me landing on his back. Before he'd had time to make up his mind what happened, I twirled his head uphill and smacked him across the rump with the reins. Although he pranced around stiff-legged,

I kept him headed upgrade so he didn't have a chance to cut loose. I had a bad minute thinking about what would happen if he managed to turn his head downhill and start bucking, but he didn't get that smart. He just crow-hopped a little more and then started churning and charging up that hill.

I knowed it was a hell of a way to treat a fine thoroughbred horse like that. Should be able to pet them and talk to them and quiet them down, but on the other hand if the son of a bitch is gonna forget his fine breeding and all, and go to acting like a bronco, well, then, hell, you've got to treat him like a bronc. One thing about them: If ever you get a thoroughbred horse to bucking, you'd be surprised how all the muscles and bones can get to you. A bucking thoroughbred is something to be damn careful about. You get fifteen hundred pounds bucking you around, it feels tough.

I let him climb about five minutes till he was blowing real good, then eased him around on a contour and patted him on the head and talked to him, scratching him between the ears and cussing him swell-like. He settled right down, and so I swung him around and begun to work down the slope toward the ranch. Me and him had a grizzly-hunting contract and I'd decided we was gonna honor it.

I spent a great part of the morning coming off the hill, keeping mostly out of sight. Guess I was plenty reluctant to go back down there and face folks again, the wilderness and shyness coming back in me strong. I knowed I had to do it, and it was kinda like a real bad chore that you keep putting off, but you know it's coming up and you might as well get it over with.

When I got close to where the trail started down the ravine into the valley, I caught a movement out of the corner of my eye. I jerked Jupiter up quick, just from instinct. I seen that there was somebody standing right by the mouth of the ravine along the trail. The figure was holding an arm up, like it was shading its eyes to look up along the mountain.

First I thought maybe it was one of them kids, 'cause it was too small for a man. Then I decided to get a better look and eased out from behind one of the oak bushes. Jupiter whinnied and the figure turned slightly, looking in my direction, and then whirled around and went down the steep ravine trail out of sight. My heart pounded, 'cause I'd plainly seen the twirl of a skirt and some flying auburn hair. I dug my heels in the stallion and made it down to the top of the trail in a mighty short time, making no mind as I crashed through the oak brush and out into the open. Instead of taking the trail down the ravine, I run Jupiter right near the cliff and looked down into the valley.

Sure enough, after I watched for a spell, out of the walls of the ravine and onto the road by the pasture come Melisande. She was barefoot and she run like an antelope. She was wearing a light-colored blouse with a dark skirt that fell near almost to her heels, but it sure weren't slowing her up none. Her long auburn hair was streaming out behind and her white legs was showing up plain as she run. Even from way up there on the canyon rim watching her small figure far below, I could tell she was all grace.

My heart kept pounding in my ribs. I sat there and followed her as she run past the corrals and the well and on over to her own house, where she just darted in and disappeared. I wondered at her actions as I started down the dark trail. I let Jupiter have his head as he picked his way down through the ravine, his hoofs banging and blasting against the rocks.

Coming down that trail was strange—all in shadows, narrow and steep—and then breaking out at the bottom onto the soft earth of the fertile valley that was all hay meadows, murmuring stream, and swaying cottonwoods, a kind of paradise all walled in by them tall red cliffs.

Jupiter pranced real fancy crossing the creek as I come riding down the road, and I seen there was lots going on by the corral. There was horses and mules that hadn't been there when I left, and I recognized the handsome gelding that was Slade's favorite mount. Parked over by the storehouse was a supply wagon the cowhands was unloading. The noise of kids playing around and wives shouting was mixed with the general commotion, and above it all Ezra Slade's voice booming out the orders for all to hear.

There's always excitement a-plenty when the supply wagon comes in. All the things that everybody has been waiting and looking for is there, along with the regular supplies. Watching the unloading is an excuse for a social gathering. Everybody seemed to be enjoying theirselves, including the dogs that was barking and yipping around the place. In some ways it reminded me of a Comanche camp, only it didn't have so much color, and sure didn't have the stink. If it had been a Comanche gathering, there would be them young bucks galloping their horses around and yipping and howling and stirring about, just to attract attention.

It was quieter here. The kids sat on the corral rails or darted around, playing and watching the goings on. The women had gathered around the supply wagon, to see what was coming off that would be for them, but Melisande was nowhere to be seen.

One of the cowhands, a fellow I didn't cotton to named Torker, seen me riding up and called out, "Damned if it ain't that stinking old mountain man, Brules, coming back."

All of a sudden everyone was looking in my direction except old Ezra Slade, who had his head down looking into the wagon. In a minute Slade raised up and took a hard look at me. He stood there by the wagon tongue, a giant figure, wearing a big floppy old black hat that would have been oversized on anybody else. He shoved it to the back of his head to get a better look as I kept right on riding toward him.

When I got about sixty yards away, damned if that voice of his didn't come thundering out, "Well, hello, Brules, we're glad to see you. We weren't sure what happened to you. Welcome back."

I was kind of embarrassed at everybody looking at me and confused by what he said. But the way he said it showed he was true and genuine-like glad to see me, and I couldn't help but feel happy that I'd decided to keep my side of the bargain.

I guess Slade's kindly words made that Torker jealous, 'cause he let out a yip and said real loud, "Look at Brules. Dirty as a hog. Boy, if we ain't got us a real mountain man.

Been up on the mountain, wallowing around in bear dung, trying to get his natural stink back.''

A few cowhands and kids all busted out laughing. It was kind of like a gale of laughter, sweeping around the whole doings as I rode closer, and then it died out sudden-like. When I reined up near enough to look at all of them, I done it slow and steady, moving my eyes from one to another. The laughing stopped and them cowhands got a little embarrassed, turned their eyes away, and set on about their work.

Ezra Slade, looking like a red-haired giant from a kid's fairy tale, stood there with his hands on his hips, and that big black hat of his shoved back. I seen that he weren't afraid of nothing, and always wanted to get the best out of everything. So he just stood there and looked at me with a grin on his face. I could tell that he liked me, and to be real truthful, he was one of a few men that I could say the same thing for.

He was a man I could respect and like, and there wasn't very many of them. Seeing him stand there grinning made me feel better—kind of like a drink of whiskey that run through you like fire and made you feel like maybe things was all right again. In Ezra's eyes there was plenty of understanding. I could tell I didn't have to explain nothing I'd done.

I just broke out in a wide grin and Ezra grinned right back. There was a sort of a hush when everybody seen us two men looking at each other, and then I turned Jupiter around and walked him real slow through the gates of the corral and up to the hitching rail.

20

A Celebration

I didn't eat no breakfast the next morning. I had me a mission, a plan I was gonna carry out in first-class shape. I took out my hunting knife and my whetstone, and went to work sharpening it real fine. Then I walked over to the tack room of the barn, where all of them mule harnesses was hanging on a rail, and found a can of lard that was used for softening up the harness leather.

I took me a fistful of lard, along with a colored shirt I'd bought in Denver, a flamin' red bandanna, and my fancy pair of buckskin britches, and went on down into the pasture where the creek meandered around in some deep pools. I found a place where the pools was real clear and calm, and by wading down through the tall grass and willows, I got to a low bank where I could lean out over the edge and see my reflection in the water.

I got to admit that when I took a good look, I kinda scared myself—my hair was long and hanging in tangles clear down to my shoulders, and my beard stuck out in big matted twists. I leaned over and ducked my whole head underwater, working with my free hand to loose up the worst of the tangles. Then I sat up and smeared the lard all over my beard to soften it up.

It was a danged long, hard job that I was tackling there, but I was bound and determined that I was gonna do it. I took out my hunting knife that was now sharp as any razor and went to work slow and steady, taking my time, but shaving off that beard for sure. I reckon I must have worked near an hour and a half on it, nicking myself every now and then, but not too bad. When I got through, I bathed my face good in the cool water and wiped all the grease off. Then I took my knife and cut off my hair till it come down to just below my ears.

Next I laid out my fancy duds that had been given to me years ago by old Valdez when I said good-bye to him and his family down in the San Luis Valley. That was the time I had to tell him and his folks of Pedro's death, and the thought spread over me like a dark cloud. But I put it out of my mind quick and took up the business at hand. I ripped off that old dirty buckskin shirt and pants and slipped into the creek water, washing myself all over with sand and gravel and rolling around in the water, in a way that I hadn't did in a long time.

Boy, that water was sure cold, coming right off the snows of the mountain, but I reckon it done me lots of good. When I crawled back out of the creek, I didn't feel only clean but all glowing and healthy too. I slipped into them other duds careful and slow-like, surprised that they was in such good shape after all that traveling. Now, I reckon by the standards in St. Louis they wasn't much in style, but right there on that Mormon ranch in Utah Territory, they was all that a man could ask for when he needed to fancy up.

I walked over to the stream to take a look. What I seen reflected there made me plumb joyful. Damned if I didn't look like some important young cowman. Yes, sir, like a gentleman rancher or something else high and mighty. In any case, a heap changed from the mountain man that had been there before.

About an hour before noon I walked back to the woodshed. I timed it that way 'cause I knowed there wouldn't be no one around the corrals, all the hands being out around the ranch doing work and the women being busy in the houses. Also, in the morning, the kids was kept inside doing chores or getting some learning. I made it to the woodshed without no one seeing me, got my saddle and bridle, and went out to the pasture again. I laid the saddle down in the tall grass at the edge of the west pasture fence, untied the lariat, and took off toward Jupiter.

I could see his black hide shining in the sunlight clear across the pasture. I whistled and he come close enough to let me spin a loop over his neck. I checked him close and we done some seesawing, but he settled right down. Then I patted his neck and talked to him for a couple of minutes. After that he led real easy right over to the fence, and I didn't have no trouble saddling him up.

Before I mounted him I saw him hunch up his back a little, so I led him around the pasture a ways and then vaulted into the saddle when he weren't expecting it. I jerked his head up and reined him in a tight circle to let him get his snorting over with. Then we just ambled off toward the corner of the pasture, where the cottonwoods was the thickest around the creek, and I got off and we both rested in the shade till the early hours of the afternoon.

I was planning something special, and it was the perfect day for it. I knew that the day after the supply wagon come back from Moab—which I guess was maybe three times between April and September—there'd be some kind of celebration at Ezra Slade's ranch. It usually started off about three in the afternoon with maybe some horse races and a little bronc riding, a few tries at calf roping, and some steer wrestling. These stunts was mostly done by cowhands on the ranch and Ezra's biggest sons, but once in a while they was joined by Mormon visitors who stopped by on their way through the country, or by a couple of neighbor families.

Whatever kind of contests or show-offs that went on would usually get through around five or six o'clock, and then everybody that had been watching—the women and children, Ezra, and the rest—would all go down to a special spot in the meadow where they'd have a picnic. There was a place for a campfire, and they'd fixed up some rough log tables and benches out of half-cut logs where folks could sit down. Toward dark, after everybody had ate their fill and was sitting around the fire, there'd be lots of singing and dancing. The old boy who lived on a ranch twelve miles down the canyon always came with his fiddle, and I heard he sure was some fiddler.

Them Mormons really knowed how to have a good time,

all careful and proper-like. There weren't no drinking, 'cause Ezra didn't allow "spirits" on the ranch. Maybe some of the cowboys that wasn't Mormons would once in a while have something hid away of their own. I weren't even too sure of that, 'cause it would be easy enough to spot by the smell, and I reckon that Ezra would run them off real quick.

In spite of nobody drinkin', it seemed like almost every time at one of them parties, fights broke out. I reckon it's the nature of young bucks—red or white—when they're around womenfolks and having a high time, to start showing off by knocking the lights out of some fellow they'd been harboring a grudge against. Of course, Ezra would break up them fights right away, but not always before somebody got a black eye or a bloody nose. I knowed all this and planned accordingly.

Late in the afternoon I heard voices. When I stood up and looked over by the corrals, I could see a crowd gathering. There was about thirty-five people on the ranch, and, with what visitors might stop by or come for the occasion, I knowed there'd be quite a bit more than that before long—maybe fifty.

I stood up and dusted off my fancy duds, and swung into the saddle of my prancing black stallion. I started riding real slow toward the corrals, keeping along the edge of the cotton-woods and the side of the hay meadow. I figured I probably wouldn't be seen at that distance right away, everybody being interested in what was going on at the corrals. I sure didn't want to show up till my time was right.

There was a helluva lot of yelling and shouting coming from around the corrals. It sounded like some boy was riding a bucking horse to a fare-thee-well. Then I heard timbers crashing and some loud screams, and I'll be damned if a big old roan stallion didn't bust through the side of the corral and come tearing out across the pasture. His hackamore rope was waving in the breeze and his saddle was empty.

It was plain to tell what had happened. The cowboy had done a good job of riding till the horse hit the sides of the corral with such force that he busted down the logs. It would be pretty unusual for anybody to stay on board through that.

I didn't give no thought at that moment whether the rider

had been hurt. What I seen in front of me was stirring my blood—an unbroke horse running away heaving and bucking and jumping. Something just snapped in me and I started acting by instinct. I put the spurs to Jupiter and he took off like he was shot out of a cannon. I caught up with that roan bucker like General Jackson overhauling the Yanks, I reached down and grabbed his lead rope, and it weren't long before I had him snubbed up and tucking alongside.

Jupiter weren't used to having no horse snubbed up close to his flanks, and he took the trouble to kick the hell outta that roan a few times, which done some good, 'cause it kinda quieted that horse down. I turned and headed toward the corral. I knowed by this time that everyone had seen me, them all having their eyes on that runaway horse. I intended to be just as casual as you please when I come up on them folks, and not let them know that I was rattled by there being so many of them.

Once I looked down at my belt to make sure my Smith & Wesson was where it ought to be. When I seen that black hand grip showing up real plain, I sorta took comfort. But the nervous way I felt, you've thought I was some young Texas Ranger riding up on a bunch of Comanches instead of nice Mormon folks enjoying theirselves at a picnic. As we got up close I noticed there was a loud, busy hum coming from the crowd, which I reckon had something to do with everybody trying to figure out who was in that fancy getup and riding a black stallion.

Sure, some of them knowed I rode a black stallion, but they wouldn't expect me to look like no rich young rancher dressed up all fancy, riding along just as casual as you please. The last time anybody around the ranch had seen me on that stallion, they'd seen a filthy old mountain man in buckskins with a dirty, matted beard and his hair all tied back like a half-Indian. Now here come the same black stallion, but the man that was sitting on top of him was clean shaved and trimmed, wearing a first-class Western outfit.

It was sort of amusing to me as I rode closer. I knowed the surprise weren't gonna last long, but I couldn't help thinking how funny it was. I guess I begun to grin, and when I did I felt more relaxed. To be real honest I was right surprised that none of them folks recognized me till I got within a couple of yards of them. Then of course it was that same cowhand who tried to rile me before, old loudmouthed Torker, who had to go shooting his mouth off in a voice that I'd begun to hate.

He let out a yip and hollered, "Hey, everybody! Look what we got here! Old Brules. All dressed up in some fancy cowboy duds. Where you suppose he stole them? Same place as the horse, I'll bet."

Then he slapped his leg and acted like it was all in fun. I kept the grin right on my face, but it got a steely look to it, and my eyes bored holes right through the son of a bitch as I rode up. He kept on laughing for a minute till I got close enough to where he could get a good look at my eyes. Then he floundered around a little and shut up.

I rode right on past him and the rest of them, right into the corral with that roan bucker cinched up tight beside me.

There was a kinda murmur in the group, and I heard Hannah's voice say, "Now that he's cleaned up, ain't he handsome?"

I seen a look pass among some of the younger girls that made me feel ten feet tall, like maybe I weren't such a hateful character after all. I looked for Melisande, but she must have been off in the ranch house or somewhere.

Finally, I seen Ezra Slade standing by the corral gate, them black boots of his spread wide apart and his hands on his belt, with a smile on his face, and he was looking square at me. I rode right up to him and handed over the halter rope of the roan. Then, without saying a word, I turned right away.

Ezra's booming laugh burst out, and he said, "Thank ye, thank ye, Brules. I don't care much about the bucking horse, but I was afeared that saddle might have got tore up in the brush."

Then he turned to everybody with a wave. "Well, folks, the corral's busted and I reckon that ends the rodeo. We'd better go down to the picnic grounds. By the way, Brules, wait a minute, please."

I drawed up my horse and turned to face him. He walked

right up easy and stopped close to the stallion's head, and I was kind of surprised that Jupiter didn't toss away from him. It seemed that Slade had a good way with animals, and he was able to put his hand on Jupiter's forehead without no trouble.

He looked up at me with a real congenial smile. "Now, son, just because you look better than any of the rest of us"— and he winked at me as he said it—"ain't no use you feeling that you can't mingle with us common folk. Why don't you slide down off that horse and come join us at the picnic? You'll have lots of fun. We got games you can join in, and besides that, I'll be plumb disappointed if you don't."

"Okay, thanks," I agreed, and in one easy motion I swung down off Jupiter.

Ezra Slade throwed his arm over my shoulders, saying in the same easy voice, "Attaboy, Brules, come on down here now. We want you to join us, and we're all gonna have some fun."

The way he said it was so hospitable and infectious-like that I couldn't help but feel good. I didn't say nothing, but I was sure grinning. I walked along, leading the stallion, and Ezra kept his arm over my shoulder. The whole crowd moved out behind us toward the picnic grounds that was maybe a hundred yards away. Not knowing what else to do I kept a-going, leading Jupiter and walking stride for stride with Ezra, my big silver spurs a-jingling at every step.

At the picnic ground I broke off and tied my horse to a nearby spruce tree that was growing in among the cottonwoods. Then, with my hands on my hips, I walked slowly over to where everybody was gathered. The women was busy scurrying around, laying out the food on the tables, and some of the boys was working hard to get a fire going, while a few other folks was setting up horseshoe pitching and other games. There still weren't no sign of Melisande.

A bunch of smaller kids was sweeping up an area that I reckoned was gonna be used for the dancing. Just then someone rode in on a gig with a keg on the back, and I thought maybe there was gonna be some hard liquor flowing or at least some beer. I should have knowed better. I found out that it was a cider keg, and that was as close as they was gonna get to any real two-fisted drinking.

Then I seen something that touched a nerve of mine. There was four punchers standing over by a big old cottonwood that had a round blaze cut in it. They was all lining up to throw a knife at that blaze. It kind of put my mind back on them times with Pedro, and I couldn't help easing over to watch.

It didn't take long to see that none of them was decent knife throwers. I don't mean just that they wasn't as good as Pedro, 'cause I never seen any man even come close to being as good as he was with a knife, but I mean they couldn't throw their knives worth spitting. They was only standing about ten feet away from the tree most of the time, and only once in a while would one of them stick a knife in. I knowed I weren't no great knife thrower, but I could sure do better than that.

I still had a fancy ivory-handled knife that Pedro had given me when we was in Albuquerque. I never got rid of it, being a real keepsake for me in memory of him, but right then I weren't thinking about the fact that it was hanging on my right hip. I stood watching for a few minutes and then turned, without saying nothing, and started to walk away.

Behind my back, but plenty loud so I could hear, one of them cowpunchers said, "Well, there he goes in his fancy clothes. Did you get a load of that ivory-handled knife? Don't reckon he wants to get them clothes spoiled by mixing with us."

"Hell, that ain't no throwing knife. He can't do nothing with that knife. That's just for show," another one said.

I reckon I was about twenty feet from the target when they said that, and it really rawhided me. I turned around real slow-like and stared at them all—each one in turn. They all had them wide-mouthed grins from the jokes they was making at me when I turned, but when I looked at them real hard, them grins kinda slid off their faces.

I don't know what made me do it, but I reached down with my right hand and real slow-like drawed out that knife. I raised my arm till the knife was pointing at the blaze on the tree and then, with the quick snap motion that Pedro had taught me, I flicked it off. It done four turns, which is what it should have done, and stuck just as clean as a whistle right in the center of the blaze.

It was my first throw in a long time, and I was twice the distance where them clowns had been when they was trying to hit the tree. I weren't no knife expert, but I sure could do that much. Thanks to Pedro I knowed before I let go that I weren't gonna miss. The only thought that went through me at all was, well, Pedro, I reckon you'd be proud of me with that one.

I walked over real slow, pulled my knife out, slipped it back into its sheath on my belt, and walked away. Over the back of my shoulder I could feel them cowpokes' glances like fires burning in the back of my shoulder. There was amazement. There was envy. There was hate. But there was some friendly admiring and wanting to get to know me too.

All them things go into making the difference between men, but that weren't no concern of mine. I weren't trying to impress them fellows or make them look bad. I didn't care what they thought of me. It was what I thought of myself. I knowed that I weren't no expert knife-thrower, but I sure could throw better than them clumsy oxes, and I wanted to prove it to myself.

When I wandered on back to the picnic grounds, a bunch of kids begun to cluster around me. At first some of the young boys come up to me saying, "Mister Brules. You gonna ride that bucking horse again? How about that pistol you got there? Can you shoot as good as you can ride?"

Right away, here come the young girls too. Oh, they was only kids—all the way from six or seven years up to fifteen. A couple of them grabbed at my arms and pulled me along, saying, "Come on, Mister Brules. Come over here. We want to show you where we're gonna dance. We got it all cleaned up. You ever do any square dancing, Mister Brules?"

It didn't take long to find out that I was already a favorite with them kids. Most things didn't make much difference with me—not killing Comanches, nor sleeping with whores, nor gambling, nor being in battles with the Sioux—but there was something that made some difference to me, and that was kids. Kids is kind of tender, forming beings. They ain't real folks yet. They're just beginning to find out what it's all about, beginning to take measure of things.

So when the Mormon boys and girls begun to cling to me, it kinda made me feel good. I reached out and grabbed about four or five of them kids, and I just throwed my arms around them and kept walking along and kidding with them. They was laughing and joking and clapping me on the back. I didn't know what for, except they thought I was some kind of hero or something. Whether it was my bronc riding, or my knife throwing, or the stories they heard of my grizzly hunt, or just me—I couldn't tell. Anyway, we was all getting along good, and that made joy come to my heart.

I liked them kids. They was all bright eyed and freckle faced, and had one shade or another of red hair, except for some that come from neighboring ranches. As we walked out into the open field, I started asking them little questions about the things I knowed—like how to follow the trail of a game animal, or how to make jerky, or walk without making no noise—and none of them knowed. They got all excited and begged me to show them.

It was funny. I thought them Mormon kids would have had lots of learning, and I reckon they did, about books and them things. But about nature—well, it seemed like maybe that had been neglected. I could understand why—all their learning had been done indoors at their mothers' knees, none of it outside.

After it got dark, I asked them if they could tell at night whether they was going north or south or east or west.

A couple of them likely lads said, "Sure I can tell you."

"Well, which way is east?" And they pointed. I asked, "How do you know?"

One of them answered, " 'Cause this canyon runs east and west, and the river, it's flowing west. It's going down to the Colorado."

"Yeah, but supposing you wasn't here at this river? Supposing you was up in them mountains somewhere? How do you know which way was east and west?''

Then they all giggled and churned around as if they didn't know, and the girls didn't know, either, and they thought it was kind of funny.

You know, as amazing as it was to me, there weren't one of them kids that even knowed the stars. Now, when I was a river rat, living with my daddy on rafts on the Mississippi, all of us kids knowed how to tell where the north was—we knowed the Big Dipper, and so we knowed how to find the North Star. I pointed out the Big Dipper to them kids, and you should have heard how excited they got. I guess none of them had ever been out at night with anybody older than theirselves, and looked up into the sky and asked something about it.

I showed them how the Dipper pointed to the North Star, so if it weren't clouded over, they could always find north. Then I showed the Three Sisters, the Great Bear, the Sword and the Belt, and all them stars that I learned when I was a kid, laying on my back looking up at the sky, floating down the Mississippi.

When I finished, one of them little girls hooked her arms around in mine, and said, ''Oh, Mister Brules, we sure like you. Let's go back over by the fire, where my mama's got some cooking and things. Aren't you hungry? Don't you want something to eat?''

I looked down on her little short form and grinned. She was a cute, freckle-faced kid, and even in the starlight I could see that all her heart was in her eyes. So we went over by the campfire, where they was all gathered around.

And then finally, I seen Melisande. She was busy helping Sarah and didn't look in my direction, and I was sure flustered myself. The women was serving up the food, and I gotta admit, it was mighty good grub. We all moved over to the tables and ate till we couldn't eat no more. Somebody started playing a guitar and singing, and the rest joined in.

Their songs brought tears to my eyes. Some of them was about the lonely country of the West and about the sadness of trying to find some promised land and never really getting there. Many's a time I've thought about it afterward during the long years that have been mine since that time. I ain't too sure but what that ain't the story of my life—always looking for something that you ain't really gonna find, always the promise, always something over the next range of hills, always something beautiful and pure, way out yonder, just beyond your reach—you know if you could only get there you'd find happiness. Sometimes I think that the Great Spirit fixed it that way so that we'd keep going. He didn't want us to pause none in the trail of life, 'cause if we done that, the whole story of all the life on this earth would be over.

The singing went on for a couple of hours, and then somebody said, "Come on—let's get the dancing going. Where's that Jeb, the caller?"

An old grizzled cowhand stood up and waved to the bunch. All of them waved back and shouted at him, "Come on, Jeb, let's get the dancing going."

The fellow with a guitar hit up a high-stepping tune, the fiddle joined in, and the old boy started calling. Pretty soon the folks come out into the circle of firelight and lantern light—the men and the women hopping and twirling around and keeping time with the stomping and calling.

All of it was a mystery to me, but I sat there on the edge of the firelight and I watched all the swirling—the men in their boots and neat-fitting pants, wearing real bright shirts, and the women in them long, ruffled skirts. I heard things like "allemande left" and "allemande right" and "do-si-do." It didn't mean nothing to me, but I liked sitting there by the fire with my eyelids drooping more and more, seeing the fire kind of dancing along with the music.

As I watched the flashing of the skirts in the firelight, I seen Melisande. She was dancing and whirling with such grace that it seemed like she had the lightness of a deer, while all the rest of them was stomping around like a bunch of wallowed buffalo.

All of a sudden the light growed real clean and bright in front of me. I rose from my squat position near the fire and stood looking at her with my hands on my hips and my heart and lungs trying to burst theirselves. She would disappear among the dancers and then back she would come with a whirl and a lightness that was like a wisp of smoke.

I stepped up close to the dancers, close to one of them oil lanterns, watching, feeling something so strong inside of me that I could hardly keep my mind. One part of me wanted to turn and run like a wild man up into the forests again, back to the safe things I knowed in nature. The other part told me to wade right in among all them dancers, grab that girl, and hold her close to my heart.

I didn't do neither one. I just stood there shaking and watching. The dancing got to going at a faster and faster pace, and the dancers was weaving in and out. Out of it all come Melisande with her skirts whirling and her hair tossing, and then it happened. I don't know what it was. Maybe she hadn't seen me there before, or maybe she had knowed where I was all afternoon and evening. But suddenly, there in the firelight she looked straight at me.

It was just for an instant, but her eyes went wide. They shone, and I knowed it was only for me. It was like she was trying to tell me something. The look she give me was so bright and burning, her eyes could have set fire to the prairie. Then she faded in amongst the dancers and didn't look at me again. Pretty soon the music stopped. The fellow with the fiddle had run up a little thirst, I reckon, as did the rest of the dancers. So the crowd eased off to the cider barrel and to a punch bowl that the women had fixed on one of the picnic tables.

Now, while there weren't no hard liquor served, some of the boys had some hid away, and they was partaking of it on the sly.

It might have seemed to some outsider that the dancing was all over now and everybody would take off to bed, but that sure weren't the case. When they put on a dance in them parts, it lasted all night. Everybody was expected to keep going till daybreak, and then there would be some breakfast fixing and people would go about their work. Maybe they'd take a nap sometime the next afternoon, but folks in them days was real hardy and had lots of stored-up energy. Besides, there weren't much time to have fun, so when it come, they didn't shut it off easy.

I eased off in the dark and walked out into the meadow to look up at the stars. I could hear lots of noise back by the cottonwoods and could see folks moving around where the light of the fire and the lanterns was flickering. There was laughing and singing and some whooping and hollering, but out there in the pasture it was peaceful.

I was thinking about the quiet beauty of the night, when I heard a different sound behind me. I don't expect it was much of a noise, maybe just a soft step in the grass, but my ears was so tuned to them things from years of Comanche hunting, and my nerves was so taut, that I couldn't do nothing but obey my instinct. I don't expect it took more than a flash, but I leapt sideways and whirled around. I ended in a half crouch, balanced on the tips of my toes with my gun drawed. My actions might have been following my instincts, but the results sure made me pause.

A tinkle of laughter broke out in a familiar voice that sounded like music but give me a thousand different feelings. There stood Melisande in the darkness with her hand pressed tight to her throat, looking kinda amused. As pretty as you please she said, "Oh, excuse me, Mr. Brules. I'm afraid I startled you. My, you certainly are a formidable-looking person."

I plumb choked up, not knowing what to say, feeling like a fool. My heart had started pounding at the sound of her voice. She waited for me to answer, but my tongue stuck tight to the roof of my mouth and I couldn't say nothing.

There I was, crouched down in my gunning position with that Smith & Wesson—which had come instinctive-like out of my belt—loaded, cocked, and pointed right at her breast. Only a light pressure on the trigger and the most beautiful thing I'd ever seen would have been completely destroyed—by me, the fool.

For a second I froze with horror. And then, shaking a little, I moved the pistol barrel down, hardly daring to think about what could have happened. I ain't never been nervous or touchy with a handgun before or since—I can slip shells in and out of chambers and magazines, cock, load, unload, point a gun here and there and everywhere you please, and never point it where I don't want it, always with a steady hand and never miss a shot—but right then I was so shook up, I was almost out of control.

When I got that gun tucked away in my belt, I tried to stand up like a man meeting a lady, instead of a wild animal waiting to be attacked. It was another minute before I could quit shaking and clear the cotton out of my mouth so I could talk sensible.

"Ma'am, you ought not to have did that. I ain't used to having people sneak up behind me. Reckon I overacted some."

She answered without meeting my eyes. "I wasn't sneaking up on you. I was walking over to my house for a few minutes. It was so dark, I didn't see you till it was too late. I didn't know you frightened so easily, Mr. Brules. I'm sorry. You certainly are a strange man, aren't you?"

She made a graceful little curtsy and smiled, and with a swish of her skirts she swept on by me. Following her outline as she made her way across the pasture, I just stood there with my heart still jammed in my throat, choked with rage and embarrassment. I'd finally got me a chance to talk to her, and instead of making a good impression, I'd acted wild, then got tongue tied and made a fool of myself.

I reckon you been in the mountains too long, I thought. You don't know how to act polite with nobody, let alone a lady. About the only women you're good for anymore is whores, and you ain't even gone near *them* since Wild Rose died. Right then I done some good cussing at myself, but it didn't seem to help none.

I walked around a little bit, looked up at the stars, got to thinking about things back and forth, and figured I'd better get hold of myself. I was sure acting like a goon, and what's more, I already had a good head start on not knowing how to get along with folks.

One thing I kept remembering. She said she was going over to her house for a little bit. That meant she must be coming back. I figured she'd walk back the same way, unless she wanted to avoid me. If she wanted to do that, there weren't nothing I could do about it, and there wouldn't be no use of my wasting my time dreaming after her no more. If a woman don't want any part of you, you'd better be seeing the signs early and quit following the trail.

On the other hand, if she was interested—and that look in the firelight during the dance sure must have meant something—she'd probably come back the same way looking for me. I'd be ready this time and maybe able to speak.

I must have stayed there the most part of an hour, walking around in a small circle, picking up hay stems and chewing on them, and gazing up at the stars. Every once in a while I looked over to see if there was still a light in the window of her house, wondering when she was coming back.

I told myself, Brules, you're in a hell of a fix. That woman has plumb got to you. You're hard hit.

I started thinking of what things I was gonna say and do when she come back—smart ways of acting—humble ways of acting—polite ways of acting. I decided I'd step up and say, "I want to offer my apologies, Miss Slade."

The word *Miss* hit me like a sledgehammer. This young girl that I was so took with was Ezra Slade's favorite daughter. She might even be promised to one of her friends or neighbors. Thinking that made me feel kind of sick, and I decided to go get my horse and belongings and leave the place before I made a worse fool of myself. But there was something in me that just couldn't leave without seeing her again. So I waited till, through the darkness, my eyes picked her out coming across the pasture.

I had plenty of time to get my speech ready and I was bound and determined to do it, but when she come up close, again I couldn't say nothing. I just kind of stared at her. Finally, half fumbling, I took off my hat. I couldn't say "Miss Slade" nor "Melisande" or nothing like that. I just spoke to her straight and said, "I sure didn't mean it the way I sounded."

I stood there holding the brim of my hat, turning it in my hands, and feeling like the damnedest fool that ever come around.

She stepped up to me real close and slipped her hand in mind and said, "I know, I know. You don't have to say anything."

Feeling her little hand touch mine was like being struck by lightning—a shock went through me from one end to the other, just as if I'd been plowed open by the slug of a Buffalo Sharps. To say my heart was pounding—hell, it was plumb bucking. It seemed to me that if I'd wanted to do it, I could have took off and flew. All I had to do was spread my arms and I'd sail away.

The way Melisande set me afire was something I ain't never been able to figure out. That's just the way it was. Out there in the pasture of Ezra Slade's ranch in the red canyons of Utah, I got a look at heaven. Right then and there I lost myself. I took her in my arms and give her a long, long kiss—the kiss a man gives when he's searched all over the world and at last found the dream that he's been hunting for. I reckon I held her so tight that I nearly crushed the breath out of her.

Oh, she was the sweetest, softest, stirringest thing I'd ever touched before or since. Her lips was sweet and her breath was like the scent of honeysuckle. I don't know how long I held her and kissed her, but time stood still. The light of the stars quit winking and the sound of the wind died and the murmur of the stream hushed, all waiting for us two. The way she clung to me, and the hotness of her lips moving against mine, told me I weren't alone in the way I felt. There was two of us in that kiss, and we was dancing in the stars.

Then, like the swift shadows of wild game passing in the forest, or the flickering of geese wings on the sheen of the water, she spun out of my arms, whispering, "On the mountain trail—wait a few minutes, and come meet me!" And she dashed away in the darkness.

What a damn, stupid fool I was that night! I could have

run after her and caught her, and took her away with me right then and there—but I didn't. I should have, but I didn't. I was so dumbfounded and dizzy from whirling in the stars that there weren't no sense in me. I watched her go, helpless to follow after the next best thing that ever come into my life, a vision that was moving off like it was going away to a wide, dark ocean.

I stood froze there for a long, long time, before I began to notice that things came alive again—the murmur of the stream, the sound of the soft chill wind slipping down from the peaks, and the stars twinkling. They was all moving again. Yes! The world had stood still, but now things was moving, and they told me in a way that only a mountain man knows that they was witness to my confusion, and they was telling me to let her go. But I was all tore apart and couldn't move one way or another. I needed that girl. I burned for her. I'd go to hell for her.

I don't know how long I stood out there alone in the field with these thoughts whirling, but it was quite a spell. As a matter of fact, there begun to be a streak of light in the east by the time I figured I'd settled my confusion.

I eased up toward the bonfire. All this time the music and the dancing had been going on, and I had heard the sounds of men's and women's voices and some singing and laughing and clapping, but it had all been like in a dream. The only reality for me was that slip of a girl had come into my arms in the starlight and passed on again, leaving me alone in the darkness.

Something inside me was saying, "Step forward, Brules, step forward if you're a man. Reach for her, Brules. Reach for what you want. If you don't, she'll be gone forever."

This was the strongest of my thoughts when I got back into the firelight. I stood there watching all them dancers milling around, and all them cowpunchers and other folks standing around, every now and then yipping and hollering and making no sense at all. Right in the middle of them, making the most noise, was that snake Torker, carrying on like he was the center of everything. He acted like he was getting liquored up.

I glanced past Torker and saw Ezra Slade standing by one of the wagons that was parked on the rim of the firelight, with that good-natured smile of his shining in the light and a gleam of pleasure in his eye. I reckon he was one of the few men that I ever knowed who never had no evil thoughts, and his face sure showed it right then. I don't know nothing about religion, or what makes men the way they are, but that night I seen the noble spirit coming through his face. I thought to myself, Maybe he stands close to God. I ain't seen nobody else look like his soul was so clean.

I was shook out of my daydreams by loudmouthed Torker calling out, "Well, I'll be damned. There he is again, our greasy prince, standing there in all his splendor. Ain't he a brute for clothes, though? There's Señor Brules, that dirty-smelling mountain man. He's all fixed up fit to kill, only this time, boys, he ain't out to kill grizzlies nor nothing like that. He's just killing them gals."

There was a burst of laughter. "Yes, sir, there's a real man for you fellows! Ain't you got no manners? Bow to the guest of honor who thinks he's a special gift to the womenfolk."

The music had eased up just then, and the sound of Torker's voice rose above the crackling of the fire. It was strong enough so I knowed everybody heard, and was turning my direction, and I felt plumb naked. Seemed like there was a hundred eyes looking at me, and it made me feel right squirmy. Some of them eyes was curious, but lots of them didn't hold no love, and it was easy to see that. I ain't sure but what it ain't more pleasant to face a pack of wolves or wild Comanches than some of them civilized folks when they're down on you.

I wanted to turn and run—go back up to my mountains, to my forests, to my sky with all the stars—but I was as stuck there as if I was bound and shackled. I couldn't turn away on account of, right then and there, the lovely girl come swaying out from among the dancers when the music stopped. I guess Melisande had got tired and give up waiting for me up on that trail, or maybe she hadn't gone at all. Leastwise I hadn't seen her come back, but there she stood again. A flush colored her

face when she seen me standing there out on the edge of the
firelight, and when she looked me full in the eyes, I knowed I
didn't want to leave.

I hoped that someday I'd have an excuse to kill Torker,
but now didn't seem like the time. I walked right past him and
his bunch toward the fire, and then he stepped out and started
jigging along by me, acting kinda comical and making fun of
the way I was moving.

Guess I do have a stride that's different from most men,
'cause I walk on the balls of my feet like a cat. He was mim-
icking away there and getting a big laugh from the people. I
didn't pay no attention, just kept going toward the fire and on
past it to a point about sixty yards out at the edge of the light,
away from the crowd—not sure what the hell I was gonna do
when I got there.

Torker answered that question for me. He'd been boozing
it up, all right, 'cause he danced around in front of me, his
breath stinking of cheap whiskey. He yelled in my face, "Say,
Brules, you think you're too good for any of the rest of us,
don't you? Well, you ain't, see? And this is what we think of
you!"

With that he reached out and grabbed my fancy shirt and
give it a yank that ripped it clear open. When he tore my shirt,
something exploded inside my brain and I ducked into a slight
crouch. My right arm—my good arm—come up with the fist
clenched. I put all the strength of my back and shoulders and
legs into that punch, and it caught Torker right on the tip of the
jaw. It would have cold-cocked a lesser man, but at least it
caught Torker off balance. He went over backward and started
to roll to his feet. Now, Torker was a big man, I reckon nigh
unto two hundred thirty pounds. He outweighed me by fifty or
fifty-five pounds for sure. He was a mean, hard son of a bitch
with high cheekbones and a jutting jaw, like some of them
river fighters I used to see. I knowed that even if he was loudmouthed and a comic, it didn't necessarily mean that he was
just a bag of wind that didn't have no guts or strength.

I'd been in enough scrapes before to see he was a stout,
tough fighter, and I knowed in a flash that I was facing some-

thing that would keep my interest. Even as tough and well placed a punch as I could deal out, it weren't near enough for a hard man like him. I didn't expect it to be. While he was rolling, I followed, and as he come up on his hands and knees, I kicked him in the jaw hard enough to knock out half of his bottom teeth. It was the kind of kick that had a sort of a pop to it instead of a smack.

I could see by the way he rolled that he was hard hit. I guess it made him mad and he lost his head. I seen him start to reach for his gun. All I saw was my white hate, and the ugly look he had on his face.

At that time there weren't no man in the West that could draw to me—sure as hell not some slob like Torker who'd just been kicked in the jaw.

While he was still clutching for his gun, I leapt six feet sideways and landed in a crouch, holding my revolver about three feet from his brain. I got to say it was almost comical to see the look that come over his face. He thought sure as hell he was going to die, and I would have liked nothing better to happen. Just a squeeze would have scattered his brains all over the grass.

Right then something cooled quick in me, like a red hot iron being dipped in cold water by a blacksmith. I growed icy cold and didn't move. I just kept looking at him with eyes that burned through him. I could see by the way his face was twitching with fear that he knowed somehow he'd run into something lots rougher than he ever figured on.

I said real slow, "Torker, you got to be a real fool to draw against me. Now, drop that gun."

He had his gun drawed out of the holster, but it was pointing down at the ground and not at me. He was froze there like a statue, like he was plumb fixed in bronze.

When I seen what it was like, I eased my weight onto my right foot, still holding my gun dead on his head, and with a quick jab of my left foot I kicked the gun right out of his hand. It went off with a roar and back at the fire a couple of women screamed, but the gun itself flopped down on the ground about eight feet away in the plain sight. The look of stupid amazement on Torker's face would have made me laugh under other conditions. Right then I weren't laughing.

Somebody a ways behind me said, "Wait a minute, boys."

I started to back away slow and easy, looking Torker right in the eye and keeping my gun on him. I moved back maybe ten feet, and then I said, "Stand up, Torker."

Real clumsy-like he worked that big carcass of his up to a standing position. Not knowing what to do with his hands— whether to hold them out to his sides, or up—he let 'em dangle. I seen a stream of blood rolling out of his lower jaw and the glint of two white teeth laying on the ground. That give me great satisfaction.

From where I stood, I could see his gun, and that there weren't nothing but the pasture out beyond. The circle of folks was all to the left and behind us, so right then I decided on teaching him a lesson. I looked at his gun glinting in the firelight, and seen it was one of them .44's that all them two-gun boys liked so much.

"All right, Torker," I said. "Go pick up your gun."

He just stood there and started to whimper like the big baby he was. "No, you're gonna kill me. I reach for my gun and you're gonna kill me."

"If you don't reach for it I'll kill you for sure, but I ain't gonna kill you, you scum-sucking pig. I'm just gonna teach you a lesson."

He kept blubbering. "Please don't make me do it. I know if I reach for my gun, you'll kill me. You'll say I drawed."

"You've already done that." I said, "Get over there, you yellow-bellied polecat, and pick up that gun. Go on. Get!"

He started moving forward real slow and easy, watching me on the one side and looking toward the gun on the other. I heard a murmur in the crowd, and somebody started to say something. I told them, "Shut up or I'll kill him."

Fearfully, looking over his shoulder at me and then down at the gun, he kneeled down and stretched out his hand to reach for the butt. I waited till his hand was about two inches away from it and then my .38 exploded.

There was a scream in the crowd, and Torker jumped back, wailing, "I knowed it. I told you so. He's going kill me."

I laughed. "I ain't going to kill you. I ain't going to do nothing to you. All you got is a little dirt in your eyes. Now go after your gun."

He looked down at where his gun was, and I seen surprise on his face again, 'cause that .44 was sitting about a foot and a half away—blowed around by my shot. From where I stood, I could see that I'd scored a mighty good hit just back of the trigger guard and busted the handgrip itself.

He reached for it again and I let drive. There was more screams, and this time he jerked back and looked at me with the eyes of a whipped dog. His gun had bounced another two feet and its chamber case was smashed. One thing for sure, that was a gun that would never be used again. I had no intention of firing all my six shots, leaving me unarmed. Two was enough to teach him a lesson. Torker was just standing there looking helpless and foolish. The rest of the crowd was stunned. I could feel they wasn't all in sympathy with me—some of them getting annoyed at the way I was doing—but that didn't make no difference to me.

I knowed I'd made an enemy out of Torker, and he'd likely try and bushwhack me sometime, but I wanted him to know that he'd better be good at it, 'cause he was up against a gunman like he hadn't never seen before. Besides that, the only reason I weren't killing him now was on account of my respect for Ezra Slade and it being his ranch and his party. Out of the corner of my eye I spotted Torker's hat laying in the dirt back by where I first kicked him. It was one of them round tops like I seen the Crow Indians wear once in a while, and an idea hit me. I took three quick steps over and picked it up.

"Torker," I said, "I don't like you. I don't like anything about you, and it sure wouldn't hurt my feelings to kill you, but this time I'm going to let you go. Just don't cross my trail again, you stinking polecat. If you do, it'll be the last crossing you ever make."

I threw his hat out in the darkness and it went sailing

way out beyond the firelight. As I done so, I twisted and fired at it. Danged if that didn't 'cause lots of commotion. I didn't know there was still a bunch of kids up and around, enjoying the festivities, but there must have been ten or twelve boys that run like hell out into the darkness looking for that hat. Pretty soon one of them let out a yell and they all come running back. One was holding the hat up for everyone to see—and I looked at it with satisfaction too—'cause damned if there weren't a bullet hole right through the center of it.

I took a leather clip of shells out of my pocket and reloaded my .38, so easy and fast, most people didn't see it. Then I slipped it back into my belt, and turned and walked out of the firelight. I went over to where Jupiter had been tied so long, untied him, and started leading him across the pasture. Seemed like I didn't have to worry no more about deciding what to do. It didn't take no wise man to see that I'd just now wore out my time at Ezra Slade's ranch. Since I was feeling in full strength, there weren't no good reason to stay. Let that Torker do the grizzly hunting—maybe one of them bears would take revenge on him for me.

Yes, sir, there was a lot of trouble brewing on account of me, and although I kind of thrived on trouble, this had some flavor about it that weren't to my taste. No, it was time I moved on out where I belonged. It was still early summer, there was still lots of time to live free out in the mountains before I'd have to find a place to hole up for the winter. I was thinking, I might head south, maybe down Arizona Territory.

I walked across the pasture leading my stallion, heading away from the firelight and all the partying doings, with them thoughts running through my mind. There was a wide streak of the dawn coming from the east, and when I got back to the woodshed, I tied Jupiter outside and went right to work fixing my pack. I crawled out of them fancy duds and rolled them up in my blanket roll. It felt real good, slipping back into my buckskins. I liked them, even though they looked dirty and greasy on the outside.

I put together all the rest of my outfit—loaded the bear hides onto Alfred again, and by sunup I had Jupiter pretty well set up. I took one last look around at all the nice buildings and corrals, and one little house in particular. As I swung up into the saddle, I reckon I felt about as heartsick as a man could feel, thinking how another beautiful dream had been tore out of my hands. Jupiter hisself acted kind of quiet for once—maybe he knowed what was happening—but anyway he didn't try bucking, just give a couple crow hops and we was off. I turned and started up past the barn and corrals to the road that led west.

I'd just made it past the angle of the barn, when Ezra Slade stepped out as big as a mountain, wearing a smile on his face. He held up his hand and reached for the bridle rein of the stallion. I knowed Jupiter would never go for that, and might raise a little bit of a ruckus, and I checked the stallion. After all, I owed Slade a lot for his hospitality, and it did seem real impolite for me to be leaving without at least bidding him good-bye.

He spoke up before I had a chance to say anything. "Now, Brules, I know why you're fixing to leave, and I'm not saying I blame you. There's some folks that just don't know when to leave a man alone, and if a man don't happen to fit into their way of thinking, then he's going to be teased and abused. Although I ain't a man of violence, it kind of pleased my heart to see you kick the turkey out of that Torker. He didn't have no business rawhiding you like that.

"He got what was coming to him, son, and I know it and you know it, but I'm afraid it isn't going to be long before he starts on you again and someday you might have a real gunfight. There ain't any doubt in my mind if it comes to that, you'll kill him. But killing is something that I don't want no part of at my ranch."

He stopped to think a minute and then went on. "But that's not all. I know what kind of man you are and I know your heart's in the mountains. I also know that you're as good a hunter as ever I saw in my time, and, Brules, I need your help. These grizzlies have been raising Cain with my cattle for years, as I told you, and I don't have anybody that's a good enough gun to handle them. Just this past two weeks the foreman up at the summer camp counted sixty-three dead critters when he was riding on the roundup, and all of them was grizzly kills. That's no good. That'll break a man in the cattle business real fast. I reckon when the count is made for the summer, I'll have lost better than three hundred head, and I can't stand it anymore.''

He looked at me with real pleading on his face. ''I'm asking your help. Them grizzlies will be a little lower down than they was when you was hunting back in May. If that's the case, they ought to be easy meat for you. Stay on awhile, and if you don't feel like coming to the ranch, we can get supplies up to you on the mountain, but I sure would be grateful if you'd help me clean out them grizzlies, and I done made you a good paying proposition.''

I liked Ezra Slade and I knowed there was things I ought to be grateful to him for. It really didn't seem like hunting out a few grizzlies, which I liked doing anyway, would be too tough a price. Then, too, he'd really gotten to me, asking me to help like that.

I could see nothing but trouble with Torker and the others, but then there was Melisande. My feelings for her was burning me inside and out. I was being tore up in about three different directions. I knowed I had to make a decision fast, and there was a lot of facts to be took into consideration.

Looking back, I got to admit that the most important thing was my longing to stick around on account of that wisp of a girl.

Everything kind of added all up, and I said to him, ''All right, sir. Let me see what I can do. I'll let you know about the supplies.''

Then I started off down the road. The sun was just coming up and I could feel the warmth of it as I rode west. In less than a mile I had to leave the bright light of the sun and turn north into the shadows, where the steep staircase trail worked its way up through the narrow gorge. Jupiter's hooves clattered and echoed as he clambered his way up over the rocks, then suddenly, he shied quick-like and moved up against one of the canyon walls. I done a little cussing till I seen a figure standing up ahead. When I got a good look at it, my heart leapt up in my mouth.

There was Melisande, standing in the trail. Damned if she weren't wearing the same pretty dress that she had at the dance, except that instead of having shoes now, she was barefoot. There was still deep shadows in the canyon and her face weren't blessed with the rays of the warm sun. Even so, the beauty and the grace of her couldn't be missed. She shone with her own light. I loved her and hated her for what she done to me, but every time I run up against her it was the same.

I checked my stallion, while he snorted and stamped a little, and then settled down with his ears up and looking straight at her. Melisande was only twenty feet away, standing there with her hand to her throat and looking at me in a strange way. For a long time we held still and stared at each other, trying to keep from saying things yet having to make each other understand.

Finally, I done something that weren't much like me. I busted the silence by saying, "Now, tell me, lady, what are you doing here on this trail?"

She flushed—I could see it even in the gray shadows of the canyon—and spoke. "Mr. Brules, I couldn't let you leave without seeing you again. Not without saying good-bye. Why didn't you meet me here last night? This morning when I saw you packing up to leave, I hurried back up here to try to catch you. Oh, please, don't go off like this!"

She looked like she was gonna cry, then them bright, shining eyes met mine and she added, "Can't we at least talk for a minute?"

When she got through saying that, I felt like the fire inside of me was going right out the top. There just weren't no way that a lonely Comanche hunter and scout like me could handle this kind of talk. Not from her. No, I knowed that I'd go under if I kept trying to match wits or sayings with such as her.

I sat there staring at her from my horse, who was stepping on one foot and then the other and pawing the rocks. Then I done the only thing my heart wanted to do. I slipped out of the saddle, took a quick turn with them reins around a cedar root, walked over and took her in my arms. The soft feel of her and the way her body bent against mine was like stirring the thunder of a volcano.

There ain't no describing it. Inside of me, all hell was ready to break loose. I kissed her then with so many strong feelings it was like I was pouring my soul into hers and she was answering back. In that kiss I heard the scream of the eagle, the bugle of the bull elk, and the long howl of the timber wolf, all mixed together with the sweet sound of the wind in the pines. When I finally let her go, I was shaking like a leaf, and from the looks of her she felt the same.

She took my hand in both of hers and said, "Oh, Brules, Brules, my love, I suppose I should call you Mr. Brules—but, dear God, what can I call you? Do you know what you are to me? What is it? What is it between us? Please don't go away forever! Come see me again! Promise me you will!"

Well, I didn't have no balance to answer her. Course, what I should have done was get back on my horse and say, "Girl, you must be plumb crazy to run away from your father and all you got back at the ranch just to come up to be with me. You've lost your head. You're the damnedest willful girl I ever seen. What you need is a good switching."

That would have stopped it all, right then and there. But I didn't say that. I couldn't say that, 'cause I knowed why she was there. She was there 'cause she had to see me. And somehow, I had to see her. All I done was turn away, mount Jupiter again, and sit there staring at her. Finally, I said, "The few folks I've ever cared about have called me 'Cat.' "

She give a little sob and started toward me, but I motioned for her to stand back. "I just made a deal with your father to do some grizzly hunting to clear his summer range, so I'll likely be back to collect my pay."

She looked at me and let her eyes burn deep into mine. "Then you'll be back! And I'll be waiting for you, the first night of the full moon, up where the forest trail starts down into this canyon."

With that she gathered her skirts, slipped past my horse, and run on down the trail. I was amazed at the way her tiny bare feet went jumping and skipping over that rocky trail without the slightest hesitation. I watched her as she went down, growing smaller and smaller, and then disappearing around the mouth of the canyon.

21

Duty

I kicked up the stallion, and Alfred followed, clanging and clattering through the shadows of the trail, till we broke out on top in the bright morning sunshine. It was oak-brush country and I headed on up, my heart singing but my mind sad. I couldn't reconcile neither the one nor the other. All I knowed was that there was a woman down that canyon that stirred me so much, I couldn't bear it no longer. She was the daughter of one of the best men I ever knowed. Me and her had no claim on each other and yet here we was, caught in a trap with no way out.

The other side of it was here. I was riding up the slope of my beloved mountains, toward them high peaks with the snow-caps on them, up through the quakies to the blue spruce and on to timberline—up where the grizzlies was roaming. I had a job to do, a chance to help out a man who'd helped me, a chance for me to feel like I was doing something for somebody. The hunting lust was still there too. I loved the hunting and the killing of big game, and grizzlies was sure that.

So it was, singing on one side and sad on the other, as I made my way up through the quakies, wondering all the time what this world was all about.

Early in the afternoon we broke out above timberline and worked east. I weren't real sure just where I was going, or how I was going to go about hunting them grizzlies.

Without making no big effort or paying special attention,

it weren't very long before I come upon what I was looking for—big bear tracks. I seen it was a big boar, and the tracks was fresh. I picketed Jupiter and Alfred and followed the trail on foot. Around late afternoon I come up on the bear throwing granite rocks aside, looking for marmots. There ain't nothing so exciting as seeing a grizzly heaving table-sized rocks around as if they was pebbles when he's looking for them whistle pigs.

No, sir, there's nothing that's stronger than a grizzly. You sure get that impression fast when you see one at work. I done some ducking and crawling for maybe an hour to get up above the old boy. When he was a hundred and sixty yards away downhill I dropped him with one shot through the brain. I skinned him out that night and was on my way again at daybreak, packing that wet hide back down the mountain on Alfred, who was damned unhappy about the whole deal.

It must have been near lunch when I pulled up in front of the ranch house, 'cause I could hear the hired hands talking, and seen Sarah poking her face out the window to find out who was coming. I called out, "Is Mr. Slade at home? I got to talk to him."

Sarah went off and right away here come that redheaded man—I later heard that folks around Moab who wasn't Mormons called him Mormon Red—and he had his usual big smile on his face.

"Brules, my boy," Slade said. "Looks like you got a big one there. By the Lord, that was quick work. You ain't been gone forty-eight hours. What can I do for you?"

"Mr. Slade, I'm showing you I was serious. Now, if you'll give me some supplies, I'll go back up there and clear out them grizzlies for you."

That idea sure pleased him, and he was all for having me come in and take a meal there, but I allowed as how I'd just as soon eat in the woodshed and headed in that direction. I throwed the bear hide and saddle up on the corral fence, and rode old Jupiter bareback out to the stream in the pasture. I turned both Jupiter and Alfred loose and cleaned myself up good.

When I got back to the woodshed, Hannah come out with

a big plate of hot fixings—fried chicken and biscuits and gravy and some fresh yellow corn. She didn't say nothing to me, even when I told her, "Thank you." I kind of wondered if she was sore at me for the way I done Torker. That food sure tasted plenty good, and when I finished I walked back out to the pasture and had me a nice nap in the cottonwoods.

I caught Jupiter and Alfred again before they got to feeling too free and sporty, and turned them loose in the holding corral where there was a feeder of hay and fresh water from the stream. One of Ezra's older sons come out of the barn carrying a pack saddle, and another son brought over a double pannier full of food supplies for me. So I was ready to go grizzly hunting in fine style.

All the rest of that afternoon and evening I kept a sharp watch out for Melisande, and I got to feeling kind of empty when I didn't see no sign of her. Just at dusk Ezra Slade come out to where I was relaxing in my old place on the chopping block. He asked if I had everything I needed, then grinned. "Good hunting, Brules. We'll see you in a few weeks." He went back to the ranch house, and I waited a little while longer in case Melisande come out to the well. I seen a light come on in her cabin, and when it went out about an hour later, I give up and went into the woodshed, where I spent a misery night thinking about her. By the time the sun come up the next morning, I was well on my way back up the mountain, figuring how many grizzly hides I could collect before the first night of the next full moon come around in about three weeks.

In that time I killed nine more grizzlies, including an old sow and her two cubs. Now, that may not sound like much, but I can tell you that hunting around and fixing to find grizzlies when you need them wasn't the easiest thing, even in them days when they was plentiful and you could scout them out with field glasses.

There's something strange about them old bears. When you least want to see them, you see them all the time, and when you really get to hunting for them, it's hard finding them. Seems like they have a sixth sense. I ain't got no doubt but what they wind you a long ways away sometimes—maybe when you're clear around the other side of the mountain—and then they just ease off across the valley or down another hill. They're mighty clever, too, about the way they walk when they want to hide their tracks. I sure saw lots of grizzly sign, but nine bears was all I actually come to see when it got right down to it, and that was what I killed.

I'd salted out them hides, and one afternoon I figured it was time I done a good job of loading them onto Alfred and started on down the mountain. It was after a storm, so there was some snow on the ground, but it thinned out as I went down through the blue spruce and was just a few patches in the quakies. At dark when I broke out of the oak brush there weren't no snow at all.

By the time I got close to the ranch, the moon was well up in the sky, and I could see everywhere. I got to wondering if maybe I was a little bit mistook about full-moon time. Maybe it was yesterday—or maybe it would be tomorrow. Then I got to worrying that Melisande might not be there to meet me. But I wouldn't let my thoughts rest on such a thing, 'cause I knowed I couldn't have really stood it. Still, my fears was mounting as I got closer and closer to that dark canyon ravine and there weren't no sign of her.

I'd already begun to feel my heart sink and a boiling rage was coming up in me, when her graceful form moved out of the shadows with the swiftness of a deer. The stallion shied a little, and I swung off of him in a flash and wrapped her in my arms. She was wearing a heavy cape and her cheeks was like ice, but the warmth of her lips told me that her heart was in her kiss. All I could think of was, Oh, hell, every time I hold this woman it seems like nothing else amounts to a damn!

I felt I was drifting down a swift stream with no place to climb out—like being headed toward the falls with no way to hold back. I don't know how many times I kissed her, nor how long I stood and held her, but I could tell by the pounding of her heart that she felt the same as me, and slow-like we sank down to the ground. I moved my hand from her waist down the beautiful curve of her hips and past her thighs, and then up and back again many times while I kissed her with a rising passion.

It seemed like there was no end to the pounding of the blood in my temples, and the man in me was really seeking her.

I run my hands over her legs again, and then reached up and lifted her skirt to touch the woman of her. Like a frightened wild thing she twisted out of my arms and rolled away from me. She rose quickly, and I stood up with her, surprised. She eased farther away slowly, and I could see she was distressed.

Then Melisande said them words I ain't never gonna forget till the day I die. "No, Cat, no—no—I can't. I just can't. I can't be your woman. Oh, my heart tells me I am, but the Mormon law says I'm not."

When I heard that, I thought I was gonna sink through the ground. Slowly, I realized that I was talking to a woman of character, and she was saying exactly what she meant. She was closing the gates of paradise when she said it, and I could almost hear the clang of them as they crashed shut.

If I was any judge of her, she was as hot as fire when it come to the passion of her heart, but she was as cold as steel when it come to keeping her word. She was that kind of woman and there weren't gonna be no shaking of her will, even by me, even though I knowed at that minute that I was the love of her life.

Them words she spoke was enough to send a man to hell, 'cause I was sure right then and there that I'd lost her forever. If only I'd followed her up the mountain that first night like she asked me to, I could have carried her off before she had time to think things over, and both our lives would have been mighty different.

Then I stepped forward and grabbed her by the shoulders. I started shaking her, and I saw her eyes go wide and her mouth go firm. "You gotta be crazy to lead me on, and then tell me something like that!"

I shook her hard again and I felt her stiffening in my arms. She broke away, crying a little, and said, "Look at me, Cat. Look at me and listen. I'm telling you the truth. I love you, but I can never be yours."

With that she started crying so hard, she couldn't talk no

more. I never seen such a flood to wring out the heart of a man. Her whole body shook as she stumbled over to me and held me tight. It seemed like her sobs was coming from the depths of her soul. Nothing ever hurt me anything like hearing her sobs, nothing except maybe when I lost Wild Rose. Listening to her crying that was so full of pain, and knowing there weren't nothing I could do to ease it, near drove me crazy.

I held her there in my arms a long time, and finally her sobbing slowed some, and I eased her down to sit beside me on the ground. Things all around was lit up by the cold full moon. I reckon I was still shook clear to my boots by what she'd told me, and for some long awful minutes I didn't know what to say. Then, kind of feeling a growing warmth or maybe seeing a new light in the far distance, I begun to think about her in another way. I begun to ask her some questions—simple little things—and slowly, between her easing sobs, she started answering me and quieting down some more. I hugged her close and petted her hair, and got her to talking about herself.

She told me that when she was twelve years old her mother, Naomi, died. Naomi was Ezra's second wife, between Hannah and Sarah, and his favorite. Things changed after her death because the other two wives took after Melisande. Hannah, the old scarecrow, and Sarah, with a snout like a pig and a nature just as sour, was jealous, and had hated her from the time she was born.

I reckon Ezra Slade seen this, too, for she told me he was extra nice to her. When she was fifteen he built her that new little house, so she could have her own place and wouldn't be underfoot all the time. He seen that she had plenty of firewood and all them things that was necessary, and he had her belongings brought over and placed where she liked them best.

She begun to weep again, only this time not with them deep sobs that was coming from way inside of her, but rather the bitter weeping of a woman that's knowed a hurt that she can't understand or change.

Then she sat up, wiped her cheeks on her cloak, and looked at me. Her pale face was shining in the moonlight. She swallowed hard and said real quick, "I'm going to be married next month!"

I looked at her, feeling like I'd been hit with a club. "You can't be telling me the truth, girl?"

Staring down into her lap, she nodded, and burst out weeping again.

I lifted her chin and kissed away her tears and held her in a passionate embrace, for now I could see some light. Here was my chance. Feeling them familiar stirrings mounting again, like the old Brules hot on the track, I knowed I was stalking down something that would be more worthwhile than any hunting I'd did before. Slow and careful-like I told her, "Well, you ain't really his wife, so you can come and be mine. That ain't no marriage. I'll sure take better care of you in that way. Melisande, you come with me. You're my woman. It's meant to be. I can tell it when I hold you, and even more when I kiss you. You ain't gonna belong to no other man but me. You'd better come with me."

I could feel her heart pounding. She looked at me with the eyes of a suffering creature that was being slowly torn apart.

Then she pushed me away, saying, "No, Cat, no. In my dreams of you, and in your arms, I've been following the fancy of my heart, but it can't be. It just can't be. That's the law of God, even though my heart is aching. I don't have a choice, Cat. I must follow it."

"Now, you just stop thinking them silly things, and come away with me. Then everything will be all right."

"No, Brules. No, I can't. I just can't."

"What the hell you mean, you can't? I thought you loved me."

"I do, Brules . . . I do . . . I do . . . I love you more than life itself."

"Then what the hell are you talking about? Why can't you come with me? I'm asking you to marry me—I'm not giving you some kind of a deal without marrying you."

"Oh, Brules. That's not it, you don't understand."

"No, that's for damn sure, I don't understand. What do you mean?"

"Brules, I'm seventeen now, but I'll be eighteen next month."

"Well, what the hell has that got to do with it?"

"Well, it has a lot to do with it, because when I'm eighteen, I'm betrothed to be married."

"To be married? What the hell are you talking about? To one of them damn cowboys down there? One of them young squirts that's going around here thinking he's hot stuff? Hope it isn't that guy Torker, that would be awful."

"No, no, it's not Torker. Believe me, I agree with you about him. I am not marrying a young man. I am marrying a very prominent, well-established rancher who lives north of Moab. As a matter of fact, he's a bishop in the Mormon Church."

"Oh, for Christ sake. Melisande, you got to be kidding. Who is this guy? Some fellow who inherited the place or something? Why is he so well established? Come on, tell me."

"Well, he's been in this Mormon country and an important person in the church for many years, and my father thinks that he will make a fine husband for me. I suppose that's so."

She cringed a little bit and seemed uncomfortable. I was in a state of horror, but I kept pushing her on it.

"Who is this guy? Do you love him?"

"No, I hardly know him."

"Well, if you don't know him, don't love him, what the hell are you doing marrying him?"

Then she looked me in the eye and said, "Brules, in the Mormon Church the father almost always chooses the right bridegroom for his daughter. My father has chosen this man to be my husband because he knows that I will be well taken care of, and that I will be able to raise his children in security, and in good standing with the church and in the eyes of God. Although I don't know this man now, except to have met him once, I know that I will learn to love him later on, and be happy that I can raise his children."

"Oh, for Christ sake!" I said. "What are you talking about? What *are* you talking about? How old is this guy?"

"Well," she said, "he's, I don't know exactly, but I think he's about fifty-five or sixty."

"Sixty! Has he got any wives now?"

"Oh, yes. He has four wives, but they are all older, and they all have children, and they say that I will fit in very well. I am looking forward to taking the vows." She paused for a moment, and sort of took in her breath again. "I know that I will like taking care of their children, and it will be fun—there'll be lots of them around. They tell me that some of the girls are almost my age. I know I will love them and will be a real comfort to them."

"Holy Christ! You mean you're going to be wife number five to this old guy? Good God, and you are walking away from me!"

She broke down and started to cry again. "Yes, I know. I know, Cat. Oh, if I could only go with you."

"Well, what in hell is stopping you? Christ, all we got to do is get up on this horse right now and get out of here."

"Oh, no. I can't, I can't. I am betrothed and I will be sealed to Moses Hopkins for the rest of my life and to Joseph Smith for eternity. That is the faith of our Mormon Church and that is the will of God. I was brought up in this Church, and have been taught my faith since I was a child. It is what I must do."

"Oh, God, Melisande. There must be some way out of this. I mean, it just doesn't seem right to me—this fellow, is he a big, strong, handsome fellow like your father? Your father is a very fine man and a leader from every point of view. I can understand why women would like him."

"No, he's nothing like that." She laughed, as if the idea were ridiculous. "Hopkins has a great big beard and he isn't nearly as tall as father. Daddy is about six foot five. Moses Hopkins is, I would guess, about five foot six. He's got a big round stomach that sticks way out in front of him. He drools on his beard sometimes, and his nose runs, and he sweats."

"Oh, God almighty. Damn it to hell! That's the worst thing that I've ever heard. You've got to be kidding! He probably stinks too? You're standing here, you beautiful girl, telling me you love me, but you're gonna marry this sorry son of a bitch?''

"Cat, I love you more than life itself,'' she repeated.

"Well, then, Goddammit, come on, Melisande. That is ridiculous. I'm only twenty-nine and—'' With that I begun to lose my bearings. A terrible conflict was beginnin' to rage in my mind as I thought, oh, God, Wild Rose is dead three years now. And now at last I've found a girl that I'm crazy about. There is nothing wrong with this. . . . Then my attention came back to Melisande. She was just the most beautiful thing I ever saw. She was standing there looking at me, with the saddest eyes, and I thought, well, Wild Rose don't have to worry none—Melisande isn't going to be my bride. There is nothing I can do about it. Nothing makes any damn sense. This girl is going to marry a fat old bishop of the Mormon Church even though she tells me she loves me—and, by God, she's going to do it because her religion tells her that's the thing to do.

"Melisande, I'm going to say to you right now the things that need to be said, and I'm hoping that it will bring you to your senses. Here you tell me that you love me better than life itself. You know I'm cut out for you, and like you know, our love comes from way out yonder someplace and it's much stronger than either one of us. Now, I may not be a Mormon bishop, but I'm a worshiper of the Great Spirit. In fact, I'm one of his priests. Yes, nobody every made me a priest, I didn't go through no ceremony, but the Great Spirit don't put much on ceremonies. The Great Spirit, he doesn't care about that, he just runs everything—that's all. You can throw the religions of Christianity, Mormonism, Mohammedanism, and all others together—it don't make no difference. The Great Spirit runs them all and he's the one I'm looking to.

"He was never on this earth, he created it and all that's in it. I know it when I'm in the forest or in the mountains, when I hear the rivers run, when I hear the thunder rumblin' or the wild winds blowin', when I see the snow falling or watch the sun settin'. The Great Spirit is doing that. No man could ever come close to doing such things.

"I don't care what religion or what priests, the Great Spirit was here before they ever came and he's going to be here long after they're gone. What I'm saying to you is, come with me, girl, 'cause the Great Spirit done put us together, and you know that. You know it come from way out of someplace, and I'm telling you that it come from the Great Spirit. He's the one that we should be worrying about, and not some religion that somebody who's been living on this earth has concocted up.

"I ask you again, Melisande. I love you with all my heart, I burn for you, when I touch you I can hardly stand it. You seen that. You got to believe me, girl, you got to go with me. I am the one that you should be with the rest of your life, and not some old man who has four wives that come before you."

While I was talking to her like that, her eyes begun to get wide, and she begun to stare at me as if I was talking about something that come from the earth itself, I guess. I don't know, but she seemed plenty impressed. I thought that maybe I was gaining ground so I said, "Come with me, Melisande. We will worship the Great Spirit together—that's the real God. Come with me. We'll hear the song of the stars, and the sigh of the wind in the trees will be telling us something, telling us that we should make love together, and that we should always be together.

"I'll take you everywhere. You have no idea of what wonderful things we'll see together. It's going to be a great life, you've got to come with me. I'm sure of it. Listen to me, girl."

I could see her breathing heavily, and she was holding her hand next to her throat like she done when she had great feelings about something. I could see her eyes, wide and shining, and her breast was heaving with the short gasps she was takin'. Suddenly she threw herself at me, put both arms around my neck, and kissed me like I'd never been kissed before by any white woman. As I put my arms around her waist and lifted her off the ground and held her, I thought for one damn fool minute that I had won.

Our lips were still sealed together, until gradually I put her feet back down on the ground. I started to put my arm around her waist and to lead her toward my horse, with my heart beating like a triumphant drum.

My flash of happiness was short-lived. For in an instant she whirled from my grasp and started to run away from me. I leapt after her, and took hold of her by the shoulders, lifted her off the ground, and shook her like a rag doll. I was screaming at her all the time, "Damn it all, damn it all. You listen to me. Get some sense into your head."

I was losing her again, but I weren't ready to give up. Lifting her chin, I made her look at me. "Woman, you can't go and live with a man that has never loved you and never will. Look me in the eye and say you'll come with me."

I seen, with an ache, that she was afraid to meet my eye. She started crying, and I was close to bawling myself. I told her, "You can't never love him. You couldn't kiss me like you do and still go love him."

When she looked up, I seen the glistening of tears on her cheeks in the moonlight. "No, Brules, it's true, I can't. With you it's a passion of my heart. It's a feeling so strong that it *must* have been created somewhere far outside of both of us, like you say. It's something we know nothing about. Why, O God, why is it here to test us? I only know that I cannot disobey my father. I love him in a certain way. He is a great man, so kind and so strong and such a protector, I must do his will."

Right then I knowed how a drowning man feels. My feet had turned to lead. My heart had sunk to where it never would rise again. I knowed I was going down for the last time and that there was no hope for me. In this slip of a girl was more strength than in a hundred men. I seen that the love of my life was slipping away as quiet and as easy as wild game fades into the shadows of the forest.

Yet I still wondered if I could do something to keep her. Maybe grab her and throw her on my horse, and go up the mountain and off to the north somewhere, or maybe down to Arizona Territory. No, that never would work. She would hate me the whole time, and she would leave the first chance she got.

I figured, well, I've killed lots of men and maybe the thing for me to do is to kill Ezra Slade or maybe Moses Hopkins. Oh, I could've killed them, all right, but it wouldn't have did no good, 'cause she would hate me for sure, and I still wouldn't have her.

I don't know how long we sat there side by side without saying a word. There weren't nothing to say. She didn't make no move to go and I weren't hastening her. As sad as I was, just feeling her presence made a difference.

Finally, maybe it was an hour or two hours later, I don't know, but the moon was high in the heavens when she put her hand on mine, and said, "Cat, the night is getting on, and I must go."

With that she rose slowly, gathered that heavy cloak around her, and started walking toward the canyon. She'd took about three steps before I grabbed hold of her arm and whirled her around. I took her in my arms and give her one more long kiss, a kind of good-bye that had to last a lifetime. She hung on to me and kissed me back. Then, quick, like the deer she was, she slipped away down into the black.

I picked up the lead rein of Jupiter and was glad that both he and Alfred was still so tired that they didn't spook and I could walk up to them easy. I led them back up the mountain a ways, where I found a good place to bed down, and rolled up in the leaves. My mind was all messed up and I had no place to go. I couldn't think about nothing. It was kind of like I was in a daze, plumb stunned, and not knowing how big the loss was that I'd just received. Ever so slow, wrapped in them dry, sweet-smelling aspen leaves, life and warmness come back to my body, and I closed my eyes in sleep.

The sun was in the midmorning range when I rolled out and stretched around. It had been a fitful sleep, and I reckon my sluggishness was part fear of facing the day. It was one of them times when you wish you had been dreaming, but you wake up and remember that the worst is true and there ain't no getting around it.

I sat there for a while wondering what to do—whether to go down and try to see her again, which I knowed would do no good, or maybe kill old Ezra, or go on up north and try to get over my misery. I didn't know nothing. I just didn't know what to do, so I sat there soaking up the sun. After a while I figured I might as well deliver them grizzly hides. I led the horses down off the hill, walking just to stretch my legs and make the time pass slower.

I ambled out of the canyon mouth and turned left on the familiar road that run past the pasture gate and up to the wood-shed where I'd spent so much time. I was about halfway to the corrals when a dog started barking, and some of the kids come running out and seen me leading the black stallion and the pack mule loaded with grizzly hides.

Well, you would have thought the place was a volcano that had just blowed. The kids begun yelling and hollering and their mothers come bursting out of their houses. The men left the corrals and blacksmith shop, the barn and the hay bins and other places, and come trotting over to see what I'd brought in. Then I heard old Ezra Slade's voice callin' from the ranch house. He was waving me a welcome, and I could see he was mighty pleased over the big grizzly haul.

I let them grizzly hides slide to the ground. Then, picking them up one by one, I throwed them so they was hanging over the corral fence with their fur side up. The fur was good and I was real proud of them—nine grizzlies. There was three old boars, three sows, and a three-year-old, and then the old sow and her two cubs. That was a lot of grizzlies for a three-week hunt, although I heard tell of hide hunters in the olden times doing better than that in some other parts of the country.

I looked around for Melisande, but she weren't there. Then old Ezra walked up and slapped me on the shoulder. "Brules, I'm proud of you. The others ain't killed nine grizzlies in as many years. Always knowed you were a hunter just to look at you. From the looks of the hides, you did some fancy shooting too. I don't see but one hole in each of them."

I didn't say nothing, 'cause there weren't nothing to say. He'd seen it all. I weren't one to go wasting ammunition when

I was ambushing anything—Comanches or grizzlies. None of them grizzlies even knowed I was nigh unto them, though one old sow must have got a whiff of me when the wind shifted, 'cause I remember her standing up on her hind legs and looking around. I shot her in the throat and she rolled fifty feet down the hill till she come up agin some rock. She was dead all the way.

That didn't make no difference now. Weren't no use in my hanging around. All I wanted was to get my money and head for a distant country. Where I was going, I didn't know yet, but I sure knowed I had to get out of there. There weren't no reason for me to stick around and suffer a lot more heartaches.

Ezra Slade went on, "I want you to hunt for me again. One whole season of working like this, and you'll clean all the grizzlies out of this country. Then we can run our cattle with some hope that we're gonna gather most of the stock we've turned out."

I still didn't say nothing, just leaned against the corral near them hides, and began picking my teeth with a piece of straw. Several times Ezra tried to get me to talk, but I didn't see nothing to talk about.

Finally Ezra Slade said, "So, Brules, when do you think you might go out again?"

I just shook my head, and said, "Mr. Slade, I'd be thanking you for paying me now."

"Now, wait just a minute. You're gonna stay around, aren't you?"

"Sorry, Mr. Slade, I'm leaving, and I'll take my pay now." Then I walked over toward the lean-to. In ten minutes I'd packed up what belongings I'd left behind and tied them on Alfred, along with my bag of other stuff and my extra ammunition and the seven hides I'd come in with in the first place. I led my stallion over to Ezra Slade's headquarters and waited outside for him to come out and pay me.

Meanwhile, there was still kin crowding around, but the women had left and most of the cowpokes had gone back to their chores. A couple of the kids kept asking, "Brules, are you going away? Ain't you coming back? Boy, we sure hate to see you go, Brules. You could kill more than them nine grizzlies, couldn't you, Brules?''

I didn't answer none. I just kept staring off at the canyon. In a few minutes Ezra come out onto the porch and down the steps to the ground where I was standing. He had some greenbacks in his hand that he started counting out.

''Well, let's see,'' he said, kind of slow and none too friendly. ''There's nine of them bears, but two of them is only cubs. My deal with you was seventy-five dollars a bear. Seems to me them cubs would count as one whole growed bear. That makes eight at seventy-five dollars apiece, which is six hundred dollars. Ain't that right?'' And he held out the money.

I stood there with my hands on my hips, feeling a mite put out with him. ''Mr. Slade, there was nine grizzlies, and the one I shot earlier for you. That's seven hundred and fifty dollars, and we'll forget the dollar a day you promised me.''

For a minute Slade flushed a little and I seen his eyes go hard, then the kindly light come back in them, and he boomed out laughing. ''Well, I reckon you're just as good a trader as you are a hunter. All right, sir, I said seventy-five dollars a bear, and we didn't make no mention of cubs, so here's another seventy-five dollars. And seventy-five more for the earlier one. Now, you're coming back in the spring, aren't you?''

I took the money and slipped it into my shirt pocket, without saying nothing. Then I just eased up and vaulted onto my horse.

Ezra Slade walked up close and reached out. ''Here's my hand, Brules. You're a great hunter and the best shot I ever saw. Hope you come back to these parts. We enjoyed having you.''

I put out my hand and we shook. While he was holding it, he asked, ''Say, Brules, did you come all the way down the mountain this morning? Was you anywhere hereabout last night?''

I don't think I changed a wink. I just didn't say nothing, which is my habit. That's the best way to answer most questions.

He looked at me real keen, and then shrugged his shoulders. Slapping my thigh he said, "Well, good luck. We hope to see you in the spring."

With that I headed up the road. It being midafternoon by that time, the trail was in the shadow again, and we clanked up over there till we come near the top.

All of a sudden Jupiter put up his ears and jumped sideways in one of the toughest sashays I seen him pull in a long time. And, God Almighty, there in the middle of the trail sat Melisande, barefoot, wearing a shawl around her head and shoulders. I could see by her eyes and the swelling under them that she'd been crying. I couldn't help thinking how different she looked from when I seen her in that same place three weeks before.

I was sure surprised and, I guess, just a little shook up— having got used to the idea that I weren't never gonna see her again.

I said to her kind of cross, "What're you doing? If Ezra finds you up here, he ain't gonna like it."

"I know," she answered. "I couldn't face you with all that crowd hanging around when you were loading off the grizzly hides, so I sneaked away in all the excitement and came up the canyon to say good-bye."

For just a fraction of a second before she said that, I hoped maybe she'd changed her mind, but I should have knowed better. She was only showing me, in spite of everything, how strong she felt for me. I got a mite irritated about her constantly being there to tempt me when there was no way I could have her.

So kinda disgusted-like I said, "Melisande, I'll thank you for stepping aside and letting me and my horse pass. Seems like we talked this all out last night."

Then she stood up quick and said, "Don't go for just a minute. I want you to know one thing, Cat. Wherever you go in this world, I'll be thinking of you, and I'll be praying for you all the days of my life."

Well, that kind of touched my heart, but I didn't want to let her see that she had an effect on me, so I told her real casual, "That's mighty nice of you. I reckon I do need someone to pray for me. I ain't got a special God, like I told you, just the Great Spirit and the world of nature. They're good enough for me. Seems as long as I don't get mixed up with people, especially women, I'm all right. Now, you'd better be getting back there before old Ezra Slade comes looking for you. I'll bet he ain't no man to cross, especially when it comes to his womenfolks.''

"That's another thing I want to tell you," she said. "He came to my house last night while I was with you. I know he did, 'cause I noticed his boot tracks out front when I got back. I saw him this morning, but he didn't speak to me like he usually does. I'm a little worried, and I wonder if he suspects anything. I must go, Cat, but remember, I'll pray for you. And I'll always love you. God bless you. Good-bye!''

With that she stepped over and put her hand on my knee and tilted her poor tearstained face to look up at me. I leaned down and, against my better judgment, put my arm around the back of her head and give her a long kiss.

She pulled away, crying again, and whispered, "Please, dear God, give me strength. And, Cat, please go now."

I touched my heel to Jupiter and churned on up the hill. When I turned to look behind, she was running with that swift gait of hers, down through the narrows almost back to the creek. I topped out on the ridge where I wouldn't be outlined against the sky, and stopped to watch.

Down below she come out onto the road and stood in the sunlight, gazing back up the canyon, just a tiny figure there below. It was plain as could be that she was looking up the canyon, hunting for me in the shadows. While I waited there, she took one last look and then turned and slowly, with her head down, started walking back toward the ranch.

It would have been better if I'd just gone on up the mountain then, like I intended to do, minding my own business, but I reckon that weren't the way it was wrote in the stars. For the life of me I couldn't help myself and I turned east, working over toward the rim of the cliff to where I could look down on the whole ranch and watch Melisande walking home. I stayed well back from the rim, so I wouldn't be spotted by them that was at the ranch house, nor by her down below. Then I got out them field glasses and looked down.

What I seen made my heart sad. There was the great valley of the ranch with the meadows still green. It was a warm Indian summer afternoon with the stream shining like a silver ribbon winding through the meadow.

Real plain I could hear the sounds of dogs barking and children laughing and the general work of the ranch going on. Out in the pastures them herds of cattle was scattered, and in the horse pasture a fine band of Ezra's cow ponies was grazing peaceful in the afternoon sunshine, flicking their tails at the flies.

It was a scene to warm a man's heart—a paradise—and it seemed like every living creature in the valley should be happy. I knowed it weren't so, for there, walking slow along the dirt road, was a young girl with her head down and her face in her hands, weeping. I sat there on Jupiter watching her awhile. I couldn't take my eyes off the whole scene. And then, 'cause something was burning powerful in my heart, I kicked Jupiter up and cantered about a mile, till I was opposite where the ranch houses would be below.

I dismounted and tied Jupiter to the nearest oak brush, knowing Alfred would stay with him, and worked my way along, lying real low just like I was hunting Comanches, till I got to the canyon rim and could look down. The wives' houses was direct beneath me. There weren't no wind that afternoon and all the sounds was traveling real clear. I could hear someone chopping wood, the kids playing over by the corrals, and somebody working in the blacksmith shop. I could even hear the voices of Hannah and Sarah in the kitchen. It was so still that even though they was at least four hundred feet below, I could hear every word.

Using them field glasses I could see, way off by the woodshed, one of them cowhands was over in the blacksmith shop holding a pair of tongs and pounding away, straightening out some horseshoes.

On the laundry line that run beside the ranch house, I could see the clothes of the kids and the women, and I reckon some of the stuff that Mormon women wasn't too anxious to show—them pantaloons and underthings—everything hanging straight down 'cause there weren't no breeze. Then I looked down the road and seen that Melisande, walking along real sad-like, was drawing closer to the ranch buildings.

She was weaving back and forth on the road. I knowed she was turned inside out 'cause every now and then she'd kick the dust with her bare feet. My eyes just feasted on her, the curve of her hips, the length and grace of her legs, the round swell of her bosom, and that long stream of auburn hair that fell down her back. She was a sight to see through them strong field glasses, and I could have kept my eyes on her forever.

Just then I heard something from the ranch-house kitchen that turned my attention there. It was the shrill voice of old Hannah. She was berating someone, and once in a while I could hear the voice of Sarah laughing, but it sounded more like snorting than laughing. First I weren't paying no mind to what was said, and had no idea who they was talking to, but 'cause they was so loud, I guess I started listening more careful. Then I heard something that got my attention right quick.

Hannah's voice shrilled out, "Now, Ezra, I mean Mr. Slade, you know better than that. She weren't there most of the night. You seen that for yourself. After I told you she was gone, you walked over there and took a look. I seen you do it in the light of the moon. I seen you going over to knock at her door, and there weren't no answer, and you just walked away. She weren't there and you know it, and we know it. I ask you now, where was she? Where is she now? What has she been doing? I tell you, she's been trifling! She's been making a fool of you, Ezra Slade. You've got to know. I ain't aiming to see no young slip of a girl making a fool out of my husband."

Then Sarah grunted. "That's right. Hannah speaks the truth. That Melisande is heading for trouble. She ain't behaving herself, Mr. Slade. She's gonna disgrace you, and the bishop she's betrothed to ain't gonna like any of this. Fact, if he hears about it, he's liable to throw her over—"

Then the deep voice of Ezra Slade cut in. "Sarah, if you

was a man you'd have the sense to keep that mouth of yours shut once in a while.''

Hannah shrilled back. "Ezra Slade, Sarah speaks the truth. She's telling you just what everyone here knows. That girl—that little hussy—may be your daughter, but right now she is making a fool out of you. It seems like you're plumb afraid of her. You ain't been correcting her nohow. She don't do her share of the work. Even with no kids of her own she still ain't no good at helping with ours. When it comes time to do the heavy chores, she's always out in the field picking flowers or something.''

She paused and then went on. "That is all right, but when it comes to her fooling with that young mountain man, who has the eyes of a killer, when it comes to her making eyes at him, swishing up to him for everyone to see, and heading off up the mountain to sin with him, then I've got to say, Mr. Slade, you ain't the man I once thought you were. If you was, you wouldn't let that go on.''

The deep voice of Slade boomed out in slow, measured tones. "Women, that'll be enough. You hold your tongues. I want to hear no more of this from either of you. I'll tend to this in my own way when it needs doing.''

When Ezra Slade spoke, that was the end. Everyone knowed it, and his wives knowed it, so the shrill talking stopped.

For a little while after that I lay up on the rim of the canyon, watching that sweet gal coming along the road, closer and closer to the pasture gates, with a slowness in her walk that told me her heart was sad.

No more talk come from the kitchen, but I hadn't seen Ezra come out, nor the women, and I didn't know quite what to make of it. It seemed like they was staying there in silence, all of them boiling mad, and no one daring to say anything for fear of what might come of it. Funny, though, it didn't disturb no peace in the valley, where everything was shining, still and quiet in the sun. It seemed like the clocks stood still and the only moving thing was the figure of a girl coming on up the road. She was almost to the pasture gate.

At that minute the stillness of the valley was plumb shattered by the door of the kitchen house bursting open. Old Hannah come out with a tub of dishwater in her hands, which she sloshed onto the dirt in front of the porch. She dumped it, and then stopped a minute and looked around till her gaze rested on Melisande coming up to the gate. She acted like lightning had struck her. She straightened up real quick and dashed back into the kitchen.

Hannah's voice was almost screaming. "Mr. Slade, if you ain't believing me, take a look at her out there right now. She's coming through the gate from the road. Where's she been, I ask you? Where's she been? I'll tell you where she's been. Didn't you just see Brules ride out about two hours ago? That's where she's been—out trifling with him. Now you know what's going on. If you're any kind of a man, Ezra Slade, you'll straighten her out right quick."

I heard some crashing of furniture, as if old Ezra had brushed something aside in a hurry, and the door of the kitchen burst open. He come barreling through that door like a bull out of a loading chute. He was a slow man to boil, but he boiled hot when he come to it. His charge carried him across the porch, down the wood steps, and out to the corral yard.

Then he stood there, watching Melisande as she turned from fastening the gate. She was, I reckon, eighty yards away when she stopped and looked at him kind of like a frightened deer. There was as deep a scowl showed on his face as ever I seen on any man. His chest was heaving like he was having a hard time getting his breath. I watched him through the field glasses, and seen that his hands was clasping and unclasping as if he was trying to get control of hisself.

Melisande was awful pale. Holding one hand to her heart she looked at him with wide-open, frightened eyes, as if she was froze with terror. Suddenly, she throwed herself around and started running across the yard toward her little house. She hadn't gone ten steps when Ezra's voice snapped out like the crack of a bullwhip.

He hollered, "Stop!"

Melisande stopped in her tracks, and turned slowly to face him, her hand clasped against her throat.

Looking straight at her, he asked, "Girl, where have you been?"

She licked her dry lips, her hand still clutching her throat, standing there like some animal that was too frightened to move.

"I said, girl, where you been? Tell me! Where have you been?" Ezra boomed out. With that he moved toward her, like a big old grizzly that seen some beautiful young doe standing there watching him.

My field glasses were focused on Melisande's face, and I seen her eyes get wider and wider from sheer fright. I knowed Slade's every move carried the ferocity of some powerful animal whose wild anger had finally been aroused. Out of the corner of my eye, I seen the kitchen door open slightly, and Hannah and Sarah looking out on the whole thing kind of wide-eyed.

Ezra, for all his bigness, could move at surprising speed. He covered the length of that ranch yard as if it weren't no way at all. When he got over to Melisande, his actions was the closest thing I ever seen to a grizzly on the kill. Them big paws of his reached down and grabbed her by the arms and lifted her clear off her feet, shaking her hard enough to rattle the teeth out of her head. He looked clear out of control.

Then he stopped shaking her and pushed her down so that she was almost on her knees. He was holding her hard, and I could see the muscles of his jaws tightening. His face was jammed within an inch of hers, and I knowed that here was the most dangerous of all the animals that ever walked on earth—the violent man.

I realized, all the sassiness of Melisande had bothered old Ezra Slade just like it had me. Now that the circumstances was such as to drive him clear out of his mind, I feared he was gonna kill her, right then and there.

She didn't say nothing. She just kept looking at him with them wide eyes, her bosom heaving. I could see that the way his strong hands was closed around her soft skin must have been hurting her plenty.

Leaning over her he yelled, "Melisande, where have you been, girl? Have you been with that man Brules?" Then he shook her again. "Speak! Have you? Have you?"

She gasped out, "Yes, but, but—"

With that he pushed her to where she sprawled flat on the ground and said, "There ain't no *but*'s to that. Get up! I'm gonna teach you a lesson."

He reached down and grabbed her by one arm, jerking her to her feet. Carrying her half off the ground with his hand under her arm, he started walking with great strides toward the barn. It must have been about a hundred and fifty yards to the barn, out of sight of the ranch house, but in plain sight from where I was.

Old Ezra didn't waste no time getting there. Sarah and Hannah run out on the porch and down the steps to watch them. They got frightened then—them old crows—and I was filled with disgust when I heard them calling, "Mind you, Mr. Slade, you be careful. She's just a young thing and you're a heavy-handed man. You better know what you're doing."

I could see them watching, both of them real scared of what they'd done. Sarah turned to Hannah and said, "God Almighty, she's gonna get a whipping like you never heard of."

Ezra made short work of getting around the cottonwoods and into the barn. If I'd had any doubt in my mind of what was gonna happen, he cleared it up fast.

In two quick strides he stepped over and jerked the whip off the buckboard. The stock was about four feet long with a short, narrow lash at the end—a good stiff whip that would make anything or anybody jump if they was to get a slice of it. There was a middle-sized empty water barrel standing by the door that must have been taken from one of them wagons. Ezra kicked it over, and it rolled end to end in front of him.

With one quick motion he spun Melisande around. He moved so fast, I could hardly seen how he done it, but he reached down and peeled that girl's dress up over her head just

like you'd skin a rabbit, and twisted it in his left hand. While
he held her over the barrel with one hand, he reached down
with the other and just jerked the pantaloons clear off of her in
one swipe. He didn't pull them off, he ripped them off.

I ain't never forgetting that sight as long as I live. There
was that girl's pretty bare bottom laid out there in the sunshine,
just as white as could be. The sight of it plumb took my breath
away. She sure had the longest, most beautiful legs I ever seen,
and the roundest, barest, best-looking bottom that any female
ever sported. In some ways I was real twisted up at what I
seen. I was astonished, kinda shocked, excited, mad, and sure
wondering what to do.

Standing there, holding her hard with his left hand and
raising the horsewhip with his right, was the towering figure of
Ezra Slade. I was struck with what looked like the sheer un-
fairness, the one-sidedness, of it all—a big strong man with a
horsewhip in his hand and that pretty little girl laid as bare in
the afternoon sunshine as the day she was borned.

There weren't but a second to wait, for Ezra set to with a
will. He laid it on just as hard as he could. I started shaking all
over. With them field glasses every bit of it was just as clear as
if I was thirty feet away. I could hear the hiss of the horsewhip
and see the fiery red welts that each blow was raising. They
was increasing at a rapid rate and all her skin was changing
from that pale white to a fiery red.

She began moaning and saying, "Oh, dear God! Dear
God!"

Then she was pleading, saying, "Please, Father, please,
oh, please stop! Oh, I beg you, please stop! I'll mind you, I
promise, I promise! Please!"

And then I guess it got too much for her, or else she just
plain panicked with the rising fury of the whipping. Anyhow,
she started to scream, and her screams echoed through them
canyon walls for everyone to hear. Each time it pierced my
heart like a knife.

A whole minute I just stayed there watching, glued to
them field glasses with my heart pounding and my hands shaking. Then, something snapped in me, and I jumped up and run

back to my horse. I jerked the Winchester out of the saddle scabbard and made it back to the edge of the cliff in about two jumps. I worked the lever to slam a shell into the chamber and knelt down, sighting in the rifle.

As I laid the bead right down on the back of Ezra's neck, the strangest kind of thoughts was running through my mind. I was asking myself what I was going to do. Was I going to kill him 'cause he was whipping Melisande? I thought if she'd been my daughter acting that way, maybe I would have done the same thing myself. Then I reckoned the reason I wanted to kill him was 'cause it was him whipping her instead of me, but finally I got real alarmed at the way he was keeping up that terrible vicious whipping.

Ezra Slade was never going to know how close he come to death that afternoon. The bead of my rifle was dead on the right side of his neck. I could see so sharp and clear the muscles working as his arm was rising and falling. Anger raged through me and I was going to kill him for sure.

The damnedest thing happened then. Sudden-like Ezra straightened up from that half-crouched position he was in. He looked down a minute, as if he was surveying the damage he'd done, or looking at the woman she was, I didn't know which. Anyway, all of a sudden he just throwed that horsewhip away, with such a mighty toss that it landed way out in the dust of the barnyard, and he turned and walked off.

I stood there sweating for a minute, not knowing what to do. There was poor Melisande still laid out bare over the barrel and sobbing her heart out. There, walking away high, haughty, and grim faced, was old Ezra Slade, looking like one of them old southern plantation owners, plumb satisfied after punishing a slave. "Correcting," that was what they'd called it, and Melisande sure had been corrected.

Everything began swimming in front of my eyes, and I was plumb sick at heart. I felt like pitching forward headfirst over the cliff and ending it, but somehow I got hold of myself. I staggered upright and stumbled over to where Jupiter was. I run the rifle back into the scabbard real easy, stepped up and swung into the saddle, and started riding away slow up the mountain with Alfred following. I was terrible sick, and my thoughts was full of hell. For a minute it crossed my mind again to turn back, step to the edge of the cliff, and put bullets through the whole bunch of them down there. Then somehow the urging of that went out of me just like water runs out of a dry desert draw.

God, I thought, God almighty, I damn near killed Ezra. That would have been a hell of a note, and it wouldn't have done no good. The whipping was about over, it wouldn't have relieved Melisande none, and I would have had the awful situation of having shot her father. All hell would have broken loose around the rest of the ranch, and although I could have took care of myself, defended myself, Melisande might have come away from there hating my guts for killing her father. If anything could have made her go on and marry that damn Mormon bishop, it would have been that.

I was real glad that I hadn't given in to my crazy rage and put another small ounce of pressure on the trigger. The thought of it made me shudder.

Still, it all kept riling me, and I kept thinking about her. I felt mighty sorry for her having got that whipping. You shouldn't beat up a woman like that to make her do what you wanted her to do. That was an uncommon whipping. It was plumb wild and mean, and that wasn't like Ezra. I don't know what got into him, except it was pretty clear that he sure was disturbed about what she'd been doing, and maybe his sense of possession kind of got a little stronger than it should be.

Well, anyway, I couldn't worry about that. I was on my way and I weren't never coming back, and I was going with a heavy heart. The afternoon sun was lighting all them canyons and mountains to the east of me, and I got to thinking about what the hell I was going to do.

I weren't in no hurry about nothing. Had some pemmican and feed for the animals, and I figured I'd just wander for a few days before making up my mind. Did I want to go back up to the village on the Pryor? Maybe I should do something else.

Finally, I come to a nice grassy place that was kind of a

little meadow in the quakies. I thought that it made a good place to camp. I could see just the tip of the San Juans showing up over the Uncompahgre ridge. It was a good time to sit and think, and let old Jupiter and Alfred have their way.

22

Escape

When the sun went down, the evening shadows spread out, and it began to get a little nippy. I just laid there listening to the fire crackling, and occasionally one of them animals stomping a little bit. I looked up at the stars and watched them slowly moving across the heavens, parading their stuff right across the old dome of the sky.

My family was right with me, munching around, and it was a good place to lay down and go to sleep. I didn't need no cover, 'cause it wasn't raining or nothing. All I done was take one of the bear hides and rolled up in it.

Hell, I was just as warm as toast then, though it got pretty cool up there around nine thousand feet. I got to thinking more about bear hunting. Yeah, hell, there is no use in worrying about it, you can't get no good hides now this time of the year.

I kept talking to myself and working up things. What I was really trying to do was to forget Melisande. I had to admit that there wasn't no forgetting that girl. I'd tried a dozen times to put her out of my mind, but I couldn't. I lay there thinking about her, and thinking how great it would have been if I could have had her by my side.

I kept saying to myself, "Brules, you're like a damn drowning man. You're so stirred with that girl that you can't honestly just walk away from her and not feel something bad. You know that somehow, in the back of your mind, is the idea that you're going to see her again."

How in the hell was I going to do that? She was going to be married to that damn Moses Hopkins. The idea of my beautiful girl in the arms of that old son of a bitch made me upset.

Then I got to thinking, bullshit, bullshit, she's worth too much for that. I've been hurt bad, and she's turned me off but, God, I've got to try once more. I've got to see her again. I wonder how bad she's hurtin'. I better go see her.

Once I got that idea in my head I couldn't get it out. When I got up, the horse and the mule looked at me like I'd lost my mind, which was correct. I started figuring, well, Jesus Christ, let's go back. Even if it's nighttime we'll make our way down there. It might be kind of tough, but it couldn't be past nine o'clock or nine-thirty—something like that. I figured that I could make it down in three hours.

I just moved off that mountain as fast as I could. I figured, what I'll do is tie the mule and the horse up on top of the cliff, and with them Comanche moccasins I've got, I can move damn silent-like. I'll go down that canyon with no light or nothing—I don't need nothing like that, 'cause I can see very well in the dark. If it's a moonlit night, the stars is always straight overhead somewhere, and, by God, I'll sneak over, tap on the window, and see if I can't get to talking once more with my love.

When I decided that, I was filled with energy. We went down through the night same way we come up, and sure enough, a little past midnight I could smell the piñon wood from the chimneys of those houses on the ranch. Then I tied old Jupiter to a tree, threw a noose over Alfred's head, drawed it tight, and tied him up too. I started on down toward the ranch on foot, fast as I could move.

I left my cartridge belt and a bandolier behind. If something happened, whatever damage I needed to do, I could do in the first few minutes, and then I better get to running. I had six shots in the .38, and I figured that if I couldn't defend myself with six shots, I ought to save the last one to blow my brains out.

Sure, I was shook up about a woman, but I sure as hell wasn't shook up so that I couldn't use that .38. I hoped that I would never be forced to do it. The idea of having to kill somebody like Ezra Slade or someone was just out of my thoughts, but then, when a man's got to defend himself, he may have to do something terrible.

When I came out of the canyon onto the meadow, I moved real slow across that grass, crawling like a panther. When I got up close to the edge of Melisande's cabin, I came up on my knees and slowly got to my feet. I could see just the outlines of the windowsill, and I reached up and tapped on the window. I held by breath as if my life depended on it, and in some ways I think it did.

There wasn't any noise at all, and I thought, oh, God. I was pretty sure Melisande wasn't going to sleep very good after that whipping she got. Then the thought came to me that maybe the other wives got to feeling real sorry for her, and had taken her over to the main house and maybe rubbed her backside with some ointment or something.

In the cabin there was nothing but silence, and I tried again. A tap, tapping on the window. Suddenly, I heard someone coming up to the window. I tapped once again, and in a low tone I said the best word in the language. "Melisande, Melisande." With that the window, which was hinged on top, flew open.

"Oh, my God, Cat, Cat!"

She started bawling. I whispered, "Make no noise, honey. Don't make no noise. For Christ's sake, I come here to visit with you."

She was so plumb excited, she had to stop and get control of herself. Then she said, "Oh, my God, my darling, you're the most, oh, God, it's just so wonderful that you're here. Father gave me a terrible whipping."

"Yes," I said, "I know."

"You know? How do you know? You were gone."

"No, honey, I was watching over the side of the cliff."

"You mean that you could see me from way up there?"

"No," I said, "I done had me some field glasses. I could see as if I was right there."

"Oh," she said, "what an awful thing. What an awful man you are. You saw me all bare and everything."

"I sure did, honey. I'll say that you sure did get a whipping. I never seen anything like it. I was suffering right with you."

"Oh, Cat," she said, "you have no idea how that hurt. It hurt so much, I wondered if I could stand it. It was terrifying. I've been licked before, but not like that."

"Man," I said, "he just lost control of hisself."

"I think so too. I never knew my father would do anything like that to me," she said. "But why did you come here?"

"Honey, you know damn well why I come here. I've come to see you again, and see if you can't get that fool notion about Moses Hopkins out of your head."

All this was said in whispers, and with that she replied, "Oh, God, oh, Cat, what a wonderful thing it is. I thought I'd never see you again, and here you are. Cat, Cat, for God's sake—take me away. Take me away with you. I can't be here any longer."

Boy, I want to tell you it was the best thing I ever heard.

"Man, Melisande, it's wonderful, wonderful! Of course I'm going to take you, gal! What the hell do you think I come back here for? But the way you was talking I thought you—"

"Yes, but that was before my beating," she said. "Yes, my father has the right to whip me when he wants to, and he has only done it once or twice before in my life, and not very hard. But this time he was terrible, he was like a mean animal."

"Yeah, I know. I damn near killed him."

"You did what?"

"I had the sight of my rifle on his neck and I got awful close to pulling the trigger," I told her, "but just when I got ready to do it, thank God, he stopped and threw that whip away."

She nodded. "I didn't know why he stopped, but it was a tremendous relief. What hurt me more than anything else, more than even the whipping—although that hurt terribly—was that I realized that my father was not whipping me because I was a naughty girl, for doing something like a kid would do. He wasn't whipping me for that. He was whipping me because he was wild with rage because I had spoiled his hopes.''

"What hopes are you talking about, honey?"

"He thought I was trifling with you, and that I'd been deflowered. I know that is what he thought, and I think if he'd seen you then, he would have shot you."

"He would have had to shoot damn quick."

"Yes, I know," she agreed. "I mean he was still so mad because he thought that he could never give me to Moses Hopkins. That I had been spoiled, not only in his eyes and in the customs of the people, but in the eyes of the Church! I was no one to be married to a famous Mormon bishop.

"I had to be pure as snow. The fact is, I was pure as snow, but he didn't think so, and so he took out his rage on me. Do you know what? I'm no longer the betrothed to Moses Hopkins. I've made up my mind. I'm no longer sealed to him in life and to Joseph Smith for eternity. I sure am not! Those chains have been broken, and now I'm not going to stand for any more treatment like this. I don't need to. My father was the one who broke the bond of betrothal and the seal with Joseph Smith, and I'm loose now and I want to go with you. You are my love, and I'm going with you wherever you go."

I said, "You sure are, honey." I was so excited, I tell you, I just reached up and took her face in my hands and gave her a long, wonderful kiss. "Now, listen, we've got to get the hell out of here. Don't make any sound—it will spoil everything if I have to shoot. You got stuff you want to take? Can we get some things together?"

"Well," she said, "I don't have very much. I have one other dress and a few other things."

"Do you have a bag or something that you can take them in?" I asked.

"I've got a kind of laundry bag I could use. I never go anywhere."

"Never mind, that's good enough. Now, honey, you get those things together. You got any shoes?"

"No," she admitted, "I've never used shoes. I've got strong feet and they are pretty tough. I walk everywhere, even on the hot rocks in the summertime. I'm used to a thorn or two."

"Don't you have anything?"

"No, just that little pair of moccasins I had at the dance the other night."

"Jesus Christ, put them on. I'll fix you up later. I'll make you a pair of moccasins out of buckskin that will be the best thing you'll ever have. You just come with me, now. All you have to do is come with me. I'll carry your bag to where I've got the horse and mule, up on the canyon."

"My God, I can't ride a horse," and she started to cry. "I'm so sore, I couldn't make it. Cat, what am I going to do?"

God Almighty! I'd never thought about that. I said, "Never mind, honey. Never mind about that. Are you stiff, is it hard for you to walk?"

"I don't know how well I can walk. My legs are sore and . . ." She asked, "Did you see me coming from the barn?"

"Yes, and you were just kinda walking real taut and stiff-legged."

"That's right, I walked like an old woman, didn't I?"

"Honey, no, you don't no more resemble an old woman than I do a Comanche," I assured her. "You just come with me. I'll tell you what—I'll throw you over one shoulder and carry the bag with the other hand."

"But you can't do that. I'm heavy!"

"Heavy, hell. Come on, girl, get your stuff quick, hurry up, don't talk. We'll handle it. The important thing is to get out of here. We're wasting too much time. Somebody will find us or the dogs will start barking."

I could hear her scrambling around there and trying to get together some things that women need. I was saying, "Hurry, hurry." Finally I said, "We'll make do no matter what. Hell, you can come without anything. Do you have any kind of a coat?"

"Yes, I have a very warm sheepskin shawl."

"Well, Jesus, bring it. Come on, kid, we have got to go. Now, do you want to come out the window or go around by the door?"

"Oh, I'd hurt too much pulling through that window," she said. "I'll just open the door very quiet and you come around there."

"Come on, and I'll meet you right around the corner."

I went around the corner of the cabin and told her to open that door real quiet-like, because anything could happen.

Well, she come out, and she could hardly walk. I said, "Come on, honey, I'm going to lean down and take you over my shoulder. Can you bend over any?"

"Bend over! Don't even talk about that!"

"Well," I said, "you'll be all right. Just hang over my shoulder."

"All right, but you aren't going to swat me or anything, are you?"

I knew that she was kidding.

"No, not if you're real good, but it sure would be an opportunity to impress you."

"You're a mean man, that's a cruel thing to say."

"Well, I ain't, really. You're going to be all right. Give me a kiss first. Come on, be real quiet."

I settled her over my shoulder and started as fast as I could go down that road toward the creek. I knew I couldn't go through the woods without scratching her up some, so I took a chance in the open and made it to the creek, waded across, and then started up the ravine. That little girl, I suppose she weighed a hundred and twenty pounds or so, but she was just light as a feather as far as I was concerned.

Anyway, I went up through the rock stairway like a panther would, moving silently from rock to rock.

She said to the small of my back, "I don't know how you can see anything in the dark."

"Never mind that, I can see. Just keep quiet, real quiet."

When we come out on the top of the cliff, I was blowing pretty hard, but I set that sweet girl on her feet and put my

arms around her, and I give her a kiss that she couldn't make
no mistake about what I meant or how I felt.

She clung to me just as hard as she could. I could feel her
crying; she just shook all over with sobs. She sure had been
under a terrible strain and all. Anyway, I hugged her and
kissed her, and tried to kiss the tears off her cheek. After a few
minutes she quieted down, and I told her, "Honey, you know I
made a hell of a mistake."

"Do you mean bringing me?"

"Hell, that was no mistake. No, the mistake I made was
when we was crossing that creek. I should have told you to pull
up your dress and sit down in that cold water."

"Oh, I wish I had."

"Never mind, there is a creek up here about mile or mile
and a half, and you'll have a chance again."

Suddenly she said, "My God, what is that big animal
there? It frightened me to death."

"That's old Alfred. He ain't going to hurt you, he kinda
likes girls. He's not going to bother you, he's just carrying the
rest of my stuff and a bear hide on top. I kept one of them bear
hides unrolled, just 'cause I thought I might want it. Maybe I'll
make a nice cozy coat for you."

"Oh," she said, "that will be wonderful, but what are we
going to do now? There's no chance that I can ride a horse."

"I know that, and there is no way that you can walk
behind us, not the fast pace we'll be going. Course, I could
take you over my lap and across the saddle, but you'd be
hanging like a sack of grain."

"You know what I can do? I can kneel up behind you on
the back of the horse, on his rump. I can kneel up there and
put my arms around you and hang tight. I'll just stay close to
you like that, and then I won't have to sit."

I said, "Well, hell, that's fine. Only thing is, Jupiter here is
a damn big horse, seventeen hands, maybe even more, and it
may be hard for you to get up on him. I'll tell you what: I'll go
get him over here by this log. Everything's packed and saddled
up, I just tied him up here so that he'd be ready when we got

here." I untied the mule and tied the rope around his neck so that it wouldn't be dragging.

"Aren't you going to lead him?" she asked, about the mule.

"No, he doesn't need no lead rope, not Alfred. Hell, you'll never separate him from Jupiter."

"Maybe he doesn't want to get separated from you."

"Oh," I said, "I guess if I was the only thing around he'd follow me, but what he's in love with is Jupiter. He don't know that Jupiter is a boy like him, 'cause being a mule he's kinda mixed up anyway. Now, if you'll stand on this log here, I'll get on Jupiter first, and then I'll lean down and pick you up and swing you around behind me."

"Good," she said. "I'll put my hands around your neck so that I can squeeze up and give you a kiss every now and then."

"Well, that's going to hurt my feelings to beat hell, but go ahead," I teased.

When we got her up there, she said, "I'm all right if I just keep kneeling forward. I don't know how long I can stay in this position, though."

"Well, honey," I said, "we've got one hell of a long ride, 'cause they'll be coming after us soon, and they'll track us— there's no mistaking a mule and stallion tracks like this. When we get over there in the mountains somewhere and start crossing some creeks, I may be able to throw them off, but not for too long.

"Mormons are bad trackers, you know, nothing like a Comanche, Sioux, or scouts, but we can do some good just moving along. If we keep riding till daylight, we'll get in a position where nobody can come up on us without having to cross my rifle. That's going to be a pretty strong barrier.

"Keep your arms around me, and I'll move Jupiter up into a kinda trot. He's got a nice single-foot and it's real smooth, no jouncing to it—let's see how it goes."

So we started off through the night lit by the moon and the stars. I was on a big black stallion the likes of which damn few people ever saw, and behind me, on her knees with her arms around my neck, was a gal that I loved more than anything else.

We started going along, moving pretty fast, going in and out of the timber, mostly quakies, and then into some open parks. Every time, old Alfred would crop some grass, and we would get a litle bit ahead of him. He done that two or three times and we got a little too far ahead of him. He started to bray, so we stopped a minute. When Alfred come up, I could see them big ugly teeth a-shining in the night. I said, "You son of a bitch, shut up. We're trying to be quiet and get out of here."

He was hee-hawing away. "You just stay with us," I said, and done some quiet cussing.

Melisande said, "Now, Cat, you're not to use language like that!"

"Oh, honey, I plumb forgot I had a lady with me," I apologized. "You're right, and you better tell me every time, 'cause I've been with men for a long time, and I get kinda loose mouthed. I'll try to stop it."

She leaned over and give me a kiss and hug and I said, "How are you doing, honey?"

"I'm doing all right, but my legs are getting a little tired."

"Well, I think we've gone about four miles but we've got at least—"

"How far are we going to go?"

I said, "Well, we got to go at least twenty."

"Twenty miles! I can't do this for twenty miles."

"Well, we'll have to figure out something else." I kinda reached around and gently touched her backside and said, "Is your bottom still sore?"

"Don't do that," she said. "Of course it's still sore, but you aren't supposed to touch me like that unless I say you can."

"Well, you're my girl, ain't you?"

"Sure I am, but you've got to ask. Besides, I'm too sore now, so stop talking about it."

Well, I could tell who was going to run things. She sure

had her own mind, and I realized that I shoulda had more sense—I didn't have no business being rude to her.

We went on for a while, and got up pretty close to where we was getting out of the quakies and into some pine. I was trying to figure all the time what I was going to do next. I knew that if I could cross over onto the Uncompahgre Ridge I could follow that right on down toward the canyon west of the Blues. When I got the chance, I'd cut across the west slope of Monticello in the night to avoid any farms or ranches, and duck down into the canyons. Nobody would find us down there—it was quite a long ways from where we was. It musta been damn near sixty miles.

It weren't too long before I begun to hear some running water, and sure enough we come up on one of them cold creeks that come down off the snows. It was really little, maybe only three foot wide, but big enough to serve the purpose.

"Well, here we are, Melisande. Here's the beginning of the cure. You're going to feel a lot better."

"I'm going to feel what?"

I said, "You're going to squat down for a minute, and put your bottom in the cold water of that stream."

"Oh," she said, "it's too cold."

"Well, if you don't want your butt to keep burning you, you're going to sit there. Does it still hurt?"

"Oh, God, yes. It still burns."

"Is it still hot?"

"Yes," she said, "and you don't have to put your hand on it to find out. It is still hot! I don't think it's getting much better."

"God, that's a long time—must be eight hours."

"Yes, I know, but it's been awful. I should know, it's *my* bottom."

I figured a minute, and then said to Melisande, "Old Alfred's gonna come to your rescue. What you really want to be able to do is not to sit or kneel, you want to be able to lie down on your stomach like you were doing in bed, but still keep on moving. I'm gonna sort of move these grizzly hides around on

Alfred, so the whole load is more flat on top, and then we'll set up a litter you can lie on just as comfortable as you could want.''

She said, ''But he's already carrying so much—can he manage me too?''

''Hell,'' I said, ''you think something as light and smells nice as you's gonna make any difference to the king of the mules? Anyhow, he'll be plumb delirious. I expect I'll get jealous! Now please go soak in that nice cold stream while I put it together.''

I made a kinda bag. Forming a square-covered frame from quakie saplings I tied together at the corners and adding cross-pieces, I set it up on Alfred's load of hides.

Melisande came out of the water after a few minutes, saying, ''Wow, what a tremendous relief!''

''Now,'' I said, lifting her up, ''I'll fasten you in with ropes so you don't fall off.''

Once she got comfortable, we pulled up out of Hatch Gulch and kept on veering kinda to the south. I got the horses across the Dolores River easy, 'cause by that time of year it was down pretty low, and we didn't have to do no swimming. I found a place in the juniper trees where I could hide our whole outfit. I had some oats for the horse and mule and, by putting them both on a picket line, kept them in real close.

Poor Melisande was plumb done in. I had to pick that little girl up off the litter and just lay her down on the ground. She didn't want to talk about nothing, do nothing, see nothing. All she wanted to do was to curl up and go to sleep. Every time she'd move, she'd kinda moan because she was hurting so bad. I thought she should go soak her behind again in the Dolores, but she was too damn tired to do anything like that, and I just let her sleep.

I was anxious to keep moving because I could just imagine what was going on at the ranch this morning. It might be almost noon before anybody noticed that Melisande was missing. For a while everybody would be thinking that she'd stayed in the cabin kinda moping and wouldn't come out.

But then there was always the chance that one of the

wives, feeling a little guilty, would go back there and take some porridge or something to her. Who knowed what would happen? Maybe old Ezra would have a terrible feeling about what he'd done, and would go back there. Well, by God, if they didn't find her anywhere, then I could guess what a hell of an uproar it would be.

I allowed us to take about two hours' rest, and figured that we better get moving. I was gonna try to cover our tracks. I found a good place where there was a lot of rock and I didn't think our tracks would show, and we got under way again. Poor Melisande was dying for sleep, so I put her back onto the litter, and I think that she went right off real easy.

I pulled out all the knowledge I ever had about covering my tracks. I did things that I'd done on the prairies years ago, and up in the Sioux county, and I counted on Ezra and them not being good at reading sign anyway.

It was my intention to circle toward the southwest and head for that maze of canyon country that stretched west of the Blues, all the way to the Colorado River. The country was a confusion of stand-up rock canyons that was like a labyrinth, and I figured, by God, nobody would find us in there.

We just kept a-traveling, and by late afternoon of the second day we come around a kinda curve in a canyon into an open bowl place. By God, it was the damnedest sight you ever saw. Right up on the red cliff about halfway up, facing the sun, was a little dead city. It had houses, windows, a tower, and things like that. It wasn't big, but it was sure a shocker. It looked like somebody had built a castle or something there a thousand years ago.

Course, everybody in that country had heard of cliff dwellings, but this was the summer of 1879, four years before the Wetherill brothers made the great discovery of Cliff Palace and all them other wonderful cliff dwellings in the Mesa Verde country.

These canyons had these little cliff dwellings, not as big but still quiet and mysterious, and you kinda wondered about the people that lived there.

When we come around the corner and seen it, Melisande

said, "Oh, look at that," and she held her hand to her mouth, she was so surprised.

It sure got a man to thinking. I wondered how them folks made a living in this canyon, and then right away quick I began thinking about water. I looked around but didn't see nothing right away. I did see a couple of side canyons where there was cliffs in the rocks where the water had come down. You could see the marking of where water had come down in the rain and run out into that flat sandy bottom.

There was kinda natural basins alongside the cliffs, and the funny thing was they was usually on the south sides of the canyon, looking north. That would mean that the snow, rain, and everything else would last longer on that side where the sun didn't get to it.

I thought, if there's any water in here, it's got to be in a place where it would be real handy for the cliff dwellers. They could come down off their ladders with a bowl to pick up water and go right to those basins. It looked natural as hell.

I went over and got the spade out of the back of the pack saddle and set to digging in that pool-shaped place in the sand. I made the hole kinda wide, and then deeper, and it wasn't long before I was starting to get to the brown sand, and then to my great joy, it started getting wet.

I dug a trench in the wall of the water hole so the horse and mule could come down and do their drinking. But first I got out and let it fill in and quiet down and get clear. Then I filled the canteen for us, and we drank our fill. It was the sweetest water you ever had in your life, and nice and cool.

Well, we filled the canteen a couple of times, and drank again, and then we let the hole fill up. I would say that when we got through, we had about a foot of water standing in a five-foot hole. It seemed plenty for the stock.

I didn't have to tell Jupiter about it none, nor Alfred. They hadn't had a drink since we left the Dolores, and they was really prancing up and down to get there. They went in and pulled that water hole down something fierce. It got to where they was sucking sand. I hauled them away and dug the hole out some more so it could fill up again, and then let them at it again.

I knew if we was gonna stay here for a while, I was gonna have to dig a hell of a lot bigger hole, but I had plenty of time.

23

Honeymoon

The next morning I was up early, and Melisande slept a little longer. I went to get the stock from where they was picketed and took the horse and mule down to let them drain the well again. I kept them there for another half hour until the well filled up and they drank it again. Then I took them over and picketed them where there was a little grass for them to feed on. I give them some oats that we had in the pack bag.

That day I done what I knew I had to do—I dug all day at that well. When I quit digging, it filled up and the water cleared pretty quick. I had beautiful water, about a foot and a half deep for the whole basin of it. There was enough to keep that horse and mule in as much water as they would ever want. I dug again a couple of alleyways at each end and at both sides so they could get down to the water easy.

Then I moved over about twenty yards away and dug us a small well. When that was done, I took an ax and cut me some cedar-tree limbs, cleaned them off, and made me a fence around it with a sort of gate to keep the stock away.

I done most of that by midafternoon. Then I asked Melisande if she was as hungry as I was. I didn't feel like eating no more pemmican, but wanted to do a little hunting to see if we couldn't get something better to eat.

She laughed kinda funny-like and said, "Well, I know that we had to have water, and I kept waiting for you. But did you realize that we didn't have breakfast?"

"Yeah, I realized it, honey, but I thought if I didn't say nothing, you might forget."

"Forget? I can feel my tummy against my backbone. I'm empty, I need something to go on. I don't see how a great big man like you can get along without food. I get all hungry early."

"Honey, I was hungry too. But during the times I spent with my blood brother, Wesha, hunting in the Wind River Ranges, and a-scouting and fighting in the open plains around the Big Horn and the Yellowstone, I learned not to complain when I didn't have nothing to eat."

"What is this business about your blood brother, Wesha? I didn't know that you had a blood brother. And what do you mean you didn't complain when you didn't have something to eat?"

"Wesha done told me, when we hunted together and I asked him why he never got hungry. He said he did but he learned to forget about it. That seemed to be the way of all Indian braves: they was taught to go a long time without water, without food, and not to do no complaining and keep their spirits up. The best way to do that was just not to think about it."

"When you're hungry as the devil, how can you not think about it?"

"Well, I'm real hungry now, now that you mention it, but before I'd forgotten it. Anyway, honey, let's not fiddle around, let's go get some buckskin. Hand me my rifle and we'll go up the canyon here. You be real quiet and don't chat none. We'll find something. I don't know what it will be, but I saw some deer tracks up there yesterday, and I'm going up where it's open."

It didn't take us long. We went up the canyon about half a mile. The sun was getting low and this should be about the time that the game would be coming out. When we eased around one of the curves in the canyon walls, sure enough we seen there was one of them side canyons in the rock where the deer could come down from up above. There was a lot of them down there. I seen several does feeding on the green grass right at the edge of the sand.

I picked the biggest one. She looked fat and fit, and I seen by the way she was carrying herself that she was a dry doe and didn't have no fawns. That's the kind I wanted, and the best of it was, it didn't rob no fawns of their food. I took careful aim and shot her through the head. She dropped just like somebody hit her with an ax. The rest of the herd dashed off.

The head is the place to shoot game if you're gonna eat it. A lot of hunters make a shoulder shot. Course, it's just as deadly—it goes in and smashes up a lot of bone, goes through the heart and lungs, and death is instantaneous—almost as fast as the head. Most hunters take that shot because it's easier, a lot bigger target, and just as fatal. The trouble with a shoulder shot is it spoils some of the meat, and if you're real hungry every bit of it counts.

Melisande came running up to the doe and looked at it for a minute and didn't seem to know what to do. I couldn't help but remember, years ago near Hatch Gulch, when I was getting over my bad arm. I used Wild Rose's shoulder for a rest and fired with one hand, and killed a buck on the side of the hill. Wild Rose let out a yip, drew her knife, and started up that hill as fast as any antelope. She had that buck half butchered before you could say Jack Robinson.

In Melisande's case she had the frontier woman's attitude toward game—she was glad to have it, but she didn't quite have the same approach as an Indian woman. Rather she was waiting for me to make the next move.

If we'd been in a hurry, like we were sometimes, I'd have just took the back straps by cutting the meat off both sides of the spine, at the head of the rib cage. That's the best meat there is on any animal, but we needed more. I figured to use the whole animal, so I went to work and dressed it out.

Dressing out a deer or any wild animal is easy enough, if you know how, and if you're good with a knife. Course, to somebody that's new to it, why, it seems like a messy job and something that they have to get used to.

I showed Melisande how to dress out that animal, how

we'd pack it back to camp with the mule and hang it up and skin it out, 'cause we'd be using all the hide for something, thongs to set rabbit traps, and some of the hide to make moccasins and other things when our others started wearing out. Deerskin makes good moccasins, but you gotta make the sole with elk hide, which is much tougher.

I made short work of dressing that animal out. I turned it on its back, and starting at the V of the rib cage and using both hands, my knife cut right through the rib cage to the throat, severing the windpipe. Next, by cutting around the pelvic structure and loosening the whole works, I pulled out the entire insides in one quick pull that left the good meat, carcass, and hide unspoiled.

I kinda watched Melisande when I was doing this, thinking that maybe she would squirm a little. To the Indian woman, of course, it was the work of every day, they wouldn't pay any attention, but a nice civilized Mormon girl like Melisande might be a little flinchy. She wasn't, though, and I was proud of her. She told me she'd seen cattle butchered and knew something about it, but she didn't know anything about game. Well, now she knew, and she said she felt sure she could do it if she had to.

"There will be plenty of times when you will have to, because that's what we got to live on in this country until all the turmoil kinda subsides a little. I bet you that all hell is breaking loose in Mormon land looking for the daughter of Ezra Slade."

Right away she said, "Oh, I wouldn't want to go back there. I want to be with you, I want to stay with you, Cat. I'm with you now, and I'm not going any other place."

"I have to agree with you. If I go back there, they will just string me up. They'll hang me for kidnapping," I said. "No, my life wouldn't be worth a damn with the Mormons. How it would fare with you, I don't know. I kinda think that your dad would be pretty mad all the way around. He's sure going to have to do a lot of accountin' to old Bishop Moses Hopkins for your disappearing. That's a unhappy kind of thing, telling him his betrothed run off with a no-good mountain man or is lost and they can't find her nowhere.''

She nodded and said, ''Well, both of us have got to stay away from that.''

''Yeah, that's why we're hiding out in this wilderness. It's gonna take pretty good scouts to come back here and track us out, and I don't think that they're gonna do it right away.''

We packed back to our little lean-to shelter, and I hung the doe up and started skinning her while Melisande got a fire going to heat some water. I talked with her a little bit about what we needed to live on, and she was real bright about what it took and what was going to be expected of both of us.

We begun discussing the things that we could do, where we might find some chokecherries, cerise berries, and a few other things that would be useful.

''You know, what we can do is to make some pemmican. That's easy and we can stay alive on that for a long time.''

''What do you mean, pemmican?''

''Well,'' I said, in kind of an expansive way, as if I was lecturing to a class of college folks, ''pemmican, little lady, is the greatest contribution the American Indian made to civilization. It was pemmican that made an Indian free, made him able to travel long distances, without having to stop for food.''

''How?'' she said. ''How could he carry enough food supply?''

''He could go for a month or two on the amount of pemmican he carried.''

She said, ''First of all, tell me what is pemmican?''

''You make pemmican by taking the meat, like backstrap—you can use other meat, but backstrap is the best thing to use—and string it out and dry it in the sun. That's what you call jerky. Then you take that dried meat and you grind it up with rocks. The Indians use some kind of rock gourd or rock plate has kinda a cradlelike look to it, and they take another stone, using it like a mortar and pestle.

''You grind this dried-up meat until it comes to nothing but powder, and then you take that and mix in it all kind of different things, like cerise berries, chokecherries, and juniper berries.

"You get that stuff all dried up and then you put it into a little pouch that you carry around your shoulder or hanging from your waist or someplace that's convenient. Of course, you can always pack a little on a horse. That stuff will last you for a long time. When you need a meal, maybe twice a day, take some of that powdered pemmican and make it into a kinda wad about twice the size of a bullet, and while you're holding it in your fingers you dip it in water, and it molds into a kinda ball, like putty. Better still, hold it into the cup of your hands and take water out of a stream, toss it into your other hand and let it mold. When you've got a nice little ball, you put that into your mouth and chew it, slow and steady, and swallow it, and drink a lot of water afterward.

"Well, that damn pemmican swells up inside your stomach and does away with your hunger pains. It makes you feel like you had a full meal. It's real powerful stuff. Now, first thing that you've got to know is that a man can go a long ways without anything to eat. He can live for five or six days, maybe ten days, without food if he can get water, but he's got to have lots of water. He will be weaker than hell at the end of that time, but he can still survive. But if he don't get water, he's gonna die within a few hours.

"Now, if he eats pemmican with the water twice a day, he's got food in him. With food in his system and the necessary water, he can go for a long time. He can go for three or four weeks, a month and a half maybe, eating that stuff. He will begin to get hungrier and hungrier, but he'd still get along all right. He'll live and keep his strength and during that time it means that he can travel great distances.

"If he can make himself go thirty or forty miles a day, which under good going he ought to be able to do easy, why, in ten days he's covered three or four hundred miles and in a month he's traveled twice that or better. That made it possible for tribes to travel as much as a thousand miles to find game when they were out of food. And the Indians done invented it. It was a great invention.

"When man is driven by hunger, you know, he'll do a lot of damn things. It's like Finerty told me."

"Who is Finerty?"

"Oh, I'm sorry I didn't explain that. Jack Finerty was a reporter for the *Chicago Times,* and he was on the campaign of the Rosebud and Little Big Horn. He was a real educated man, he was. I learned a lot from Finerty. I liked him, too, he had lots of guts."

"You have strange friends," she said. "You must tell me about them."

"I'll tell you all about it someday, but right now let's stick to the subject. I'm talking about how we survive when we've got a shortage of grub, my little lady. Something like that could easy happen to us, and we better know what to do about it.

"I'll tell you what the Apaches do sometimes when they run out of food. They cut the blood vessel of one of their ponies, around the neck, where if he bleeds it don't hurt him much, and they drink the blood that comes out of the horse. Then they take some mud and patch up the wound on the horse and let it go at that."

"Ugh," she said, "that's awful. I never thought of that. That's a terrible thing."

"Well, it is a terrible thing, and a white man probably couldn't do that except in extreme emergencies, but, you know, you can do a hell of a lot when you're starving to death. I don't want to be talking to you about that, because I don't think we're gonna get into anything as bad as that. Not with all the game around and with my rifle with me. We're gonna have plenty to eat, and you needn't worry. I was just talking about extremes."

"Well," she said, "let's not go to extremes. I just think you better take care of me, 'cause I'm gonna be depending on you."

"Well, I reckon if any man can take care of you, I can."

She looked at me with a kind of look that stirs a man up a little bit, and I got to thinking about it for a minute whether I wanted to take her in my arms. I decided against it, though, 'cause she hadn't given me no signals that her backside was in good enough condition for me to be hugging and squeezing her.

Anyway, after I done give her this lecture on pemmican and how tough it could get in the wilds and all, I thought I'd better lay off for a while before I scared the poor girl to death. There was really no need for such talk, because I knew, with my rifle, we'd get by.

While we was sitting around the firelight that night, I said to Melisande, "Well, little girl, looks to me like you're feeling a lot better."

"I'm not as sore as I was before, but I'm not in good shape yet." She looked straight at me and said, "Cat, I'll let you know when the time has come for you to make love to me."

I must say, my jaw just kinda fell open. I'd never been addressed quite that direct by a woman, but I seen that she didn't mean anything about it except the truth. I was longing to take her in my arms, I was longing to have her, but I knew that she wouldn't tolerate me until she was feeling right. This girl was dead honest and she knew that we was together out there in that beautiful wilderness, and that we was a man and a woman, both of us young and strong, and there wasn't any doubt what was gonna happen. She wasn't making no bones about it, she was just being real practical, and, once more, she was being real, real sweet.

I just leaned over and put my hand under her chin and lifted her beautiful face, even more beautiful in the moonlight, and give her a nice long kiss. I told her that I really loved her and that I longed for her, but she was gonna have to give the signals.

I wanted to move on down toward the Colorado, but before we could do that I had to make us some water bags out of deer hides. I had to kill several more deer before I had enough hides—I wanted four bags. Then it took us some time to get our gear together, and finally, a couple of days later, we headed out.

The first day was pretty discouraging, 'cause we did have

a lot of times when we had to get through some narrow places in the canyons and once we had to climb up on a ridge. The second day, though, it seemed like fortune kinda smiled on us. We'd come to a place where it looked like we wasn't gonna be able to get through. The rock got so narrow and the going was so rough that it didn't seem we could make a horse trail through there, but we saw where we could climb up over the ridge to the south, and maybe go down in another valley, and do just as well.

When we topped out on that ridge, we started down what looked like a pretty easy hill. Our water bags was getting low and the horse and mule was a fussing to get at them all the time, being awful thirsty. We had to sympathize with them, but we couldn't let go of our purpose.

I won't forget the moment when we come out on a little ledge of rock and looked down into this steep ravine. Down at the bottom we could hear the sound of running water. I let out a yip and said, "Melisande, sure as hell, we got a creek, it's flowing into the Colorado. All we got to do is follow it and with any luck we'll make out all right."

Melisande was riding behind me, and she reached around and give me a kiss on the back of my neck. She said, "I knew you'd do it, Cat."

"Well, you had a lot more confidence in me than I had in myself. I wasn't too damn sure that I wasn't leading us into hell. Now it looks like we're gonna make out all right," I told her.

We got to the creek after quite a struggle—the ravine was pretty steep in places, and the stock had a hell of a time turning to cut back and zigzag. When we got down near it, we finally come to a place where that horse and mule got plumb out of control trying to get to that water. They was so anxious! Of course, when they got there they went to work just a-sucking and blowing. We done the same, only we went upstream a little ways. That tiny little creek was all clear, clean, and beautiful, and we drunk to our heart's content.

We followed that creek down a ways until it widened out

into a nice little park between the cliffs, where there was grass for the stock. It was an ideal place to camp.

Years later Melisande and I would still remember that beautiful campsite. We called it Water Canyon.

It sure was ideal, and that night as we was sitting around the fire, the moon come up and shone between the canyon walls. We sat there with the stars and moon above, the rippling sounds of the little creek running through.

I remember thinking how quiet it all was, so quiet that you could almost hear our hearts beating. I didn't know about Melisande, but I could sure hear mine, when I studied her beautiful face in the moonlight, her lovely hair hanging down, that pert nose of hers and her full lips, her bright eyes that even shone in the moonlight.

She had her knees brought up under her chin, and her hands folded under it. Most of the time she was a-looking at me and, I think, feeling a little uncomfortable maybe. I wondered what she was thinking about me, sitting there in my old black hat and sharp, short beard. I didn't suppose I was any stage actor or nothing, but I knew enough to play up to the mood.

I thought, if I just give it time, things will take their natural course. Only problem was, when was I going to know? She'd probably let me know when the time come. But then, I couldn't hardly count on that. After all, she wasn't the kind of girl that was going to push herself on someone. She might be shy, too shy to make any move, and there I'd be standing, slack jawed and lop eared and doing nothing when I should have been making love to her.

So I asked her, "Honey, would you like to have a drink of water out of that stream? I've got this tin cup I've been packing, and I'm going down to get some."

"Oh, I'd love that," she said. "I keep getting thirsty, it would be wonderful if you'd get us some."

I went down to the little creek, about ten yards away, and dipped me a nice cup of water, drained it myself, so I could take her a full cup, and headed back to the fire. I knelt down beside her and handed her the cup, which she took in her dainty hands and lifted to her lips. I watched her turn her head up as she drank that cold, clear water.

"You know, water is the greatest drink in the world," she said when she finished.

"What do you know about that? You never have drunk no whiskey or anything, have you?"

"Oh, no," she said. "Certainly not, but I've had lemonade and jerryade and all those things that they do to fix up water so it has a different taste, but I just like pure water."

"Well, gal, you stick to that arrangement. I agree with you. Water is wonderful tasting."

We sat there in silence for a while looking at the fire and listening to its crackling, then I slowly eased over next to her. I took it real calm and quiet, until I was up against her side. If she hadn't wanted me, she could have eased off easy and given me the clue that she either wasn't ready for me or didn't want me anyway.

She didn't do that, she stood her ground, and when I leaned against her, she began leaning against me a little bit. I leaned over and put my arm around her shoulder and drew her to me. I kissed her on the cheek, and she turned her lips up to me, and I took her in both arms. When I put my lips against hers, I knew I was in paradise.

My heart was thumping like a war drum, and I began to kiss her all over her cheeks, and on her neck, and draw her closer to me and hugged her tight. I told her, in a kind of rasping voice, how hungry I'd been for her and how I'd longed for her. She put her hands back of my neck and drew me to her, saying, "Oh, Cat, you don't know how I've wanted you so. I love you more than anything in this world."

I'd been noticing that she was walking much better, and that she could sit on my horse, back of my saddle, without complaining about any soreness. I figured that she was probably feeling back to normal again after her awful experience. It seemed like that had been ages ago, but now that I counted up, it had only been about nine days. All that was over, and I had her in my arms and knew that if I wanted to love her, I could.

Like all them Mormon girls she was wearing what a good

girl wears, a kinda gingham dress and them big white pantaloons that come down over her knees. They wasn't made of silk, but kinda linen, and they was real smooth. I ran my hand back up and felt the curve of her bottom. Then I went up to her waist and put my hand inside the waistband and felt the bareness of her.

I went cautious, real cautious, with my hand again down to where I could feel the faint traces of them welts. I was a little surprised at how much they had subsided from the fire-red stripes I'd seen from the cliff. There was just a trace of them, but there was no mistaking what they was. Yet my hand didn't disturb her none, didn't give her any feeling of hurt or nothing, and I was real gentle and careful.

I said to her, "Oh, I'm so glad those welts aren't as bad as I thought they'd be."

"Well, they were bad enough then," she said. "You have no idea, Cat, how that hurt. A whipping hurts worse than anything you ever felt in your life."

"I know, I know well," I agreed.

"How do you know? What do you mean you know? You've never had a whipping."

So I undid my shirt, pulled it off my shoulders, and said, "Honey, just put your hands along my back there."

She put her little soft hand over my shoulder and down my back, holding me close to her chin, and then she let out a small gasp. "Oh, those are terrible welts. What are they from? What happened?"

"Them's from Comanche quirts you're feeling. I know what you mean when you say that something hurts so bad that you can't believe it. I think that you're probably right, gal," I hugged her and laughed with her a little bit.

Then I said, "Come on, now, let me see your bottom. I'll bet it's all right."

"No, sir. You're not going to see my bottom."

"I've already done seen it," I pointed out.

"Yes, but you weren't supposed to do that, and that's very embarrassing. I'm sorry that you didn't have the decency not to look."

"Well, I turned away right away. I didn't keep looking, but I just had to once, I couldn't help it—your pants was down!"

She was silent for a minute and said, "Cat, you know something? It feels good to have your hand there. I don't feel like those things hurt me anymore. Instead of having a whip I've got a nice warm hand being gentle with me, and I like that. You can put your hand back there if you like."

Well, it didn't take me very long to move on from that point. Ain't no use in spending the time telling you we was wrapped up in each other, and it wasn't long before we got married, right there in the bottom of that canyon, under the stars and moon. We was married as well as any man and woman could get married. We didn't need no preacher, we didn't need no witnesses, we had the witness of the Almighty, the Great Spirit.

We made strong promises to each other of how we'd never part to the end of our days. I was so much in love with Melisande, and I think that she was as much in love with me.

What a wonderful thing it was, I thought, that two people could meet so perfect and to each other's liking. That marriage wasn't arranged or nothing. Nobody said that you have to do this or that you have to do that or you should do this or do that—nobody but the Great Spirit, and the beauty of nature and all the things that was singing for us.

We didn't wake up till late the next morning, 'cause it took the sun that long to be high enough to shine down in the canyon. When we come awake, we hugged each other again and we made love once more. It was the most glorious thing that could be. When we went down to the creek to wash our faces, Melisande said to me, "You know, we've got to find a hole big enough in this creek to bathe in. I need a bath."

"If you need one, what do you think about me? Tell you what we'll do, honey, let's just walk down here a ways, downstream, and see if we can't find a place that would be big enough. Maybe I can take that shovel out of Alfred's pack and dig us a hole."

"Oh," she said, "that would be wonderful."

We found just such a place where the creek kinda made a sharp left turn and, in doing so, had dug half of a hole out that was almost big enough to get into, and water was running through it at a pretty good clip. I went back up, got a shovel out of the pack, and come down there to move the rocks and dirt around, until we had a big enough pool to get into. We left it for a while until it cleared up after all my fooling with it.

We sat on the edge of the stream. We hadn't had nothing to eat in the morning, but we didn't feel it. Just sat there in the sun, and when the water cleared, I said, "Ladies first."

"Will you turn your back and leave me alone?"

"Why?"

"I don't want you to be here," she said. "Tomorrow maybe you can see me, but not today."

I thought, women are funny like that. Heck, I know all about this girl—why should she be worrying about something like that? But it was her wish.

"Oh, all right, you go ahead, and when you're through bathing, you call. I'll go up and get a fire started and I'll lay the coffee out."

I always carried coffee. Every prospector, every cowpuncher, everybody else, carried coffee in his saddlebags. If you had a pot, that was all you needed, you didn't need to have no kettle or nothing, just a pot to boil it in, and it was a mighty good drink.

"I'll get the stuff started, and when you get through, I'm gonna take a bath. I need one worse than you do."

She just laughed, and I laughed, and I felt like turning back and looking. Then I thought, Brules, you don't have to be no Peeping Tom. This woman is yours, you can see her anytime you want to, but you've got to take it easy. Now, leave her alone, she wants to be alone, and you go on and mind your own business.

I got the fire going, and put some coffee on it, and pretty soon I heard this wonderful rippling laugh behind me. Here come Melisande, skipping along, her dress blowing in the breeze, feeling like a million dollars, I guess. She came up and just threw her arms around me and kissed me a dozen times and told me how happy she was.

Well, of course, I was as pleased as I could be. I'd been an awful sorrowful fellow for the last three years, and now I had me a lovely girl that I loved a whole hell of a lot.

So I went back myself to the water hole, took off my old clothes, and got in there. I didn't have any soap, but I could use the soft sand from the sandbar there to kinda scrub with, and I did a pretty fair job of getting clean.

Once I had a good look at myself in the reflection of the stream and seen that damn beard. I thought, well, the next thing I'm gonna do is shave. So that she can see me the way I was when we was having the dance at Ezra Slade's ranch. I think that she'd like to see me that way. I'll ask her and if she wants me to shave, I'll do it. At least I'll do it once!

It was a happy time. I had that horse that I loved, the mule that I loved, and I had a girl that not only did I love, but I was plumb crazy about. I had joy in my heart for the first time since I'd lost Wild Rose.

There weren't any use trying to compare things, because it wasn't even the same kind of situation, and loving Melisande didn't reduce none of my feelings for Wild Rose. They never would leave me for the rest of my life. Man has to have a woman and I couldn't have had a better one than Melisande. She was just a beautiful girl and full of laughter, fun, and good sense.

All during that summer the heavy heart that I'd had for the last three years was lifted up again, and I felt the way I had when I was a kid. Of course, I was thirty years old, and I didn't have the same kind of snap that I had when I was twenty, but I sure made up for it with experience. I reckon that right in them years, and for the next ten years, I was at my very best.

Anyways, when I come back, there was Melisande pouring coffee out of the pot into that little tin cup. She was saying, "You better have some of this coffee. It's the best thing I ever tasted."

"Course it is, who do you think made it?"

She stuck her tongue out at me. "You don't lack for confidence, do you?"

"Well, you can take everything that I say with a smile, can't you?"

"I always smile at what you say. Now, come on, we've got to get breakfast."

We had plenty of meat, we had backstraps we could roast over the fire, and a small sack of flour, so we could make some biscuits. We just plumb enjoyed ourselves.

For the next couple of months we lived like that, just getting along, making our way in the wilderness. We had plenty of meat, of course, and there were other things that we could eat. We found them little ears of corn that the old cliff dwellers had planted, on a number of occasions.

That first cliff dwelling was not the only one we saw in those canyons. We come across several of them and always at the foot of them, somewhere, was the traces of an ancient garden, which had long since gone to pot, but there were often cornstalks still growing. In addition to that the ancient people had planted the Anasazi bean, which was kinda like a black bean, but it seemed like it was more tasty.

I patterned out some buckskin britches for Melisande, which fitted her right well. First she thought they was kinda hot and they wore on her a little bit, but I told her, "Wear them pantaloons you got underneath and see if they don't feel better."

I made her a pair of moccasins too. I made them not clear up to the thigh like Comanche moccasins, but right below the knee, and they worked good. I didn't have any elk hide to make good soles with, so I put in three layers of buckskin, and it seemed to do about the same job. Course, it was easy enough to make the laces, and she was right proud of what she wore.

Then I made her a buckskin shirt and she was all equipped. One thing, she didn't have no hat. I could see she was beginning to get pretty burned from the blistering sun around the cheeks, the end of her nose, and so forth. If it was wintertime, I coulda made her a coonskin cap, but that wouldn't do her any good here in the hot country. I didn't know just what to do.

She solved it by getting some reeds down near the stream and weavin' a hat that looked like a damn tepee. At least it come down over her face and kinda gave her some shade.

All in all we got along fine, and the surprising thing to me was how much Melisande really enjoyed herself. There was no complaining about she didn't have a pump and a bucket, a sink and a stove, and all them things women seemed to have to have. She kinda enjoyed going wild, and you know she was pretty good at it. I tell you that in a year's time, she'd have been as good as any Indian squaw. She was just real bright and had lots of natural ability and plenty of energy, and that combination is tough to beat.

Sometimes I used to sit looking at her and thinking she was the most beautiful thing I'd ever seen. Just the idea of her company was so great, and I realized how lonely I'd been. Not only that, the sound of her rippling laugh was a great spirit booster.

All that time, during that summer, it was a paradise. Sometimes I'd tell her about some of the adventures I'd had, but I never said nothing about Wild Rose or the Broken Bow Ranch. She seemed to be having a wonderful time and I sure as hell was, and I never wanted it to end. Finally, I got to telling her that it would be nice if we could move up to the mountains and do a little elk hunting. We needed some elk hide and I was kinda anxious to see them big racks a-moving in the brush or through them blue spruce forests. I told her about elk meat being the very best, and also that we needed them hides to make lots of things out of.

"Well, whatever you want to do, I'm with you," she agreed. "I'll go where you go because I know it will be good."

It was mid-September, I reckoned. That would be the time that the elk would be bugling, and I sure had a longing to hear that. We kinda kicked the idea around for a while, and then one morning I heard a very strange sound, high in the sky. I looked up and seen V after V of them sandhill cranes all headed to the south. A day later I seen a V of Canadian geese, and them honkers was calling back and forth like the sandhill cranes but with a different cry.

That turned me inside out, and I said this is hunting time. That's where we're going, we're gonna get the hell out of these canyons and we're gonna go hunting! Besides that, the more I got to thinking about it, I had just about used up my ammunition. I had some left but not too damn much, and if we was gonna make our way through the winter we had to have more. I figured that I might be able to get some over at the Los Piños Agency. That was the place to go. That's where old Chief Ouray and them fellows was. The Indian agent there would probably have ammunition in the agency's store. Winchester ammunition by this time, in 1879, was pretty standard through all the West.

So that morning, when the second bunch of geese come over, I told Melisande to pack up, that we'd be going. When I told her, she jumped up and said, "All right, let's go. I'm anxious to see some other country too. But you know something?"

She came over and put her arms around me. "You know, Cat, this has been a wonderful time. This has been a honeymoon, the greatest thing. What a beautiful place we found to spend our time. I loved these canyons, I loved the old cliff dwellings, I loved the valleys and this little stream that runs through here. I'll remember it all the rest of my life."

I give her a big hug and kiss, telling her, "So will I, honey, but life moves on. Let's be on our way. We're gonna have some wonderful times ahead, and we oughta look forward to 'em, okay?"

By the time we'd made up our minds to go it was early October. We packed up one morning and worked our way out of Stream Canyon, carrying what water we could.

We hit the Uncompahgre a couple of evenings later, made a quick camp, just hobbled the horses, and didn't light a fire. I didn't want anybody coming around there yet. We'd just go along with the pemmican again. That was the only time I heard

Melisande complain at all. She said, "Have we got to eat this stuff again?"

"Yeah, unless you want to eat raw elk meat." I'd shot me an old elk cow on our way down.

She said, "Well, why don't we light a fire?"

"Honey, we're right in the middle of Indian reservation. We may not have any right to be here. I don't know, but we're downstream about ten miles from the Los Piños Agency, and I'd rather check in there with the Indian agent before we go making a camp at night that might be disturbing to somebody. We'll just have to get along.

"I know pemmican's no luxury, and you're getting more of a lesson than I wanted you to have, but I'll promise you that we'll get out of here at daybreak and be in Los Piños for breakfast. I reckon that we can do something there. Must be a post exchange, and white folks around, and there's got to be someplace where somebody's cooking so we can eat real food. I'm just sure on that.

"Besides, we can shop most of the day for stuff that we need, if we're going on from here. I think that we'll go up the Gunnison somewhere after that. Right now, we better lay low and just do this."

She took it in good spirits, but she was plumb tired. Both of us were so, and after we hobbled the stock and unloaded them, we just rolled up alongside the pile and went to sleep.

At daybreak we was up and on our way again. By another hour and a half we come on that trading post at the Los Piños Agency. There was a blacksmith shop, a couple of houses, barns, but mostly everything had to do with the Indian reservation. There was some white folks there, too, but it was an awful small place. Nothing but dirt roads, chickens, and cows around.

I went to what looked like the nearest thing to a livery stable, where a fellow had some horses tied to a hitching rail. Standing by it was a big strong fellow who had some of the main tools of a blacksmith shop. I asked him where the Ute Agency was and the agent's name.

"His name is Stanley, Bill Stanley," he said, pointing toward a building with a porch.

"All right," I said, "I'm gonna go over to speak to him, see what's going on."

As we walked over to the agency, I felt a little embarrassed. Everybody was kinda looking at us. Here was a guy with a good-looking woman with him, and he had a beard that was thicker than a tumbleweed bush, kinda dirty from riding all over, and carrying a 1873 Winchester. Also I never went anywhere without having a .38 in my belt.

They could tell that I'd been out in the timber, and wondered how such a good-looking girl would be with me. She wasn't no Indian squaw, they could see that. She sure was a looker, even in her buckskin outfit.

Together we walked up to the agency, and I asked Melisande to stand by with Jupiter and Alfred while I found out about things. Inside there was a long counter with a lot of different Indian stuff, hides, and skins they'd painted and other things around. There was a couple of people back of the counter when I stepped up, so I asked, "Is Mr. Stanley here, the agent?"

They said, "Yes, yes."

"Just wondering if I could see him for a minute?"

The man who I guess was a clerk put his pencil behind his ear and went on into the other room. Pretty soon the agent come out. He seemed like a nice fellow, except he had them spectacles on, them four eyes, and that was kinda strange out here on the frontier. I didn't say nothing about it, but they sure looked funny. Anyway, I told him that I was here to buy some ammunition and supplies. I asked him if he knew anything about hunting, 'cause winter was coming on, and I'd have to get a few things I'd need, and maybe he could direct me around.

Then I said, "By the way, I've got some grizzly hides for sale."

"Grizzly hides? I don't know what we'd be doing with them here."

I thought, well, man, you must be new to this part of the

country. Hell, grizzly hides were the passport to everything, but I reckoned he was one of them city boys, and didn't know much about it.

"Where did you get those grizzlies?" he asked.

"Oh, up in the La Sals where I always hunt, where I've been hunting since '74."

"I'll be damned," he said. "I don't believe that you'll want to be going back out hunting right now."

"I don't know why not."

"Well," he said, "things aren't disturbed right here in this part of the world, but they are up north—the northern Utes. We just got a dispatch from military headquarters at North Platte, Nebraska Territory, that the northern Utes up around Meeker is getting a little worrisome, and the agent's sending for troops or something."

"Well, I'll be damned. I didn't know anything about that." Of course, Crook had worried about that.

"Yeah, hell, they're trying to round up all the scouts around the country and everything. Jesus, we got a message in here just yesterday from a courier. They're looking for some scout they said was up hunting grizzlies in the Salt Mountains." He looked at me and asked, "Say, your name ain't Brules, is it?"

"I be he."

"Well," he said, "I'll be damned. Mr. Brules, we got a message for you."

"You got a message?"

"Yeah, the courier brought it in yesterday from General Crook, Fort McPherson at North Platte. Hell, he's calling you to active duty!"

24

Two German Knights

"**C**alled to active duty? What the hell do you mean?"

"I've got lots of correspondence right here in the office for you and about you, Brules. Step in here a minute and let me get it. Here we are," he said, walking into his office, and handing me a stack of papers.

"Here's a letter from Crook's command, addressed to me. Read it for yourself and see."

I took the paper from him and looked at it a minute, and said, "Hell, you read it."

He looked at me a little bit and kinda smiled. "Okay.

"To Agent Stanley,
Los Piños Agency,
Uncompahgre River, Colorado

"Office of the Commanding General,
Territory of Nebraska, Fort McPherson,
North Platte, Nebraska

"This command is desirous of locating and calling to active duty Scout Brules, presently on leave. Your assistance in locating this scout and informing him of his orders will be greatly appreciated.

"It is presumed that the Scout Brules is engaged in bear hunting in the area of the La Sals Mountains, specifically the southeastern and southern portion of Mount

Peale. The command would be grateful and will bear all expense for dispatch of some southern Ute scouts for the purpose of locating Brules. He can be identified easily, as he will be mounted on a seventeen-hand thoroughbred black stallion and will be followed by a large pack mule.

"Inform all scouts whom you may send to look for Brules to approach him with extreme caution, only one man at a time, and evidencing peace sign. Brules is very alert and an absolute dead shot. Any attempt to use unusual tactics may have serious consequences. If this scout is encountered and is approached in a friendly manner, you will find him cooperative in the extreme. He will return with the scouts to the Los Piños Agency and contact you. Any information concerning the progress of the search for Brules will be appreciated and may be forwarded by courier to the telegraph station at Del Norte, Colorado.

"Now, here's your active duty order. It's dated:

"September 28, 1879
Office of the Commanding General,
Territory of Nebraska, Fort McPherson,
North Platte, Nebraska

"Order #648.

"Attention of Scout Brules.

"You are hereby ordered to active duty, and will remain at the Los Piños Agency until you receive further orders. Prepare yourself for an extensive campaign in the area of the White River Agency, northern Colorado.

"A personal letter, from the general to you, came on the same date. By God, Brules, you must rate some with this general. He's a very powerful man in these parts. This is on his personal letterhead. It says:

"Dear Brules:

"I am calling you to active duty per Order #648 to the care of Agent Stanley at Los Piños Agency, Uncompahgre River, western Colorado. For your information, we have been receiving reports from the Indian agent Meeker at White River Agency that trouble is brewing among the northern Utes. The agent himself has been roughed up by one of the chiefs and is in a state of near panic. He has requested the War Department to furnish troops.

"In answer I have dispatched Major T. T. Thornburg, with a small command of three companies of cavalry and one of infantry, to proceed posthaste to Meeker agency, and to establish order and protection for the agent and personnel at the agency.

"We do not know whether further trouble will develop, but if it does and a general Indian war breaks out in that area, we are extremely anxious to be sure that the southern Utes, with whom you are acquainted, remain at peace. If we can keep them friendly, we will have the advantage of potential communication with the northern Utes and in addition will avoid a general Indian war of a bloody nature in western Colorado.

"Now, Brules, here comes the bad news. This is dated October 10, 1878. It's another order for you.

"From Military Department of Nebraska,
Fort McPherson, North Platte,
Office of the Commanding Officer

"You are hereby notified that hostilities have broken out at the White River Agency among the northern Utes. Agent Meeker and all other white male personnel at the agency have been killed. Mrs. Meeker, Josie Meeker, a maid, and child all have been taken captive and their whereabouts is unknown. Major Thornburgh and three companies of cavalry and one of infantry have been ambushed fifty miles north of the White River Agency. Part of

*the command has been destroyed and the remainder
pinned down. Major Thornburg and two other officers
have been killed and the command has suffered some fifty
casualties.*

*"This word comes from courier Rankin, who was able
to pass through the Ute lines, at night, and ride to the
railhead at Rawlins."*

"Jesus Christ," I said, "that's about two hundred forty
miles. That's a hell of a ride. They ought to give that boy
Rankin a medal."

Agent Stanley nodded and continued to read:

*"It is now imperative that you contact Chief Ouray,
and gather him and the other chiefs together at the Los
Piños Agency for the purpose of peace talks.*

*"From your descriptions of Chief Ouray he will serve
as an excellent ally, if we can win him to our cause. This
command is most anxious that every effort be exerted to
this end. Stand by for further orders."*

"Well," I said, "ain't that a hell of a mess. Where the
hell is Ouray now?"

"He's out hunting somewhere. Brules, I took the liberty
of sending some scouts out to locate him. He is a very cooperative fellow, and I'm sure that he'll be in here soon. He has
sense enough to know that the Indians really can't win in the
long run and that they'll only lose territory by causing distur-
bances. These quarrels, and some of them very legitimate Indian claims, have to be settled in a peaceful manner, by law.
Fighting only ends in the Indians' reservations being drasti-
cally reduced.

"Between you and me, that bunch of northern Utes are a
bad gang. They've got some mean chiefs up there stirring
them up. One of them goes by the white man's name of Johnson. Another chief up there is Colorow."

"Yeah, I guess Ouray is an Indian name, ain't it?" I
asked.

"Yes, it is. It is a Ute name, means 'the Owl.' In other words, he talks straight. You can count on him. He'll go right to the point, he does it every time.

"Ouray is pretty well educated, you know. He was brought up in Taos and speaks not only English and Ute, of course, but also Spanish. A very valuable man to have on our side, and we want to do everything we can to keep him that way."

I nodded and said, "Well, ain't no sense in my going running off here in every direction. I'd better stay right here and wait for further orders like the general says."

"Yes, Crook's a pretty good man, isn't he, Brules?"

"Well, I'll tell you. I ain't much on these military fellows, but this guy Crook is a real man. He understands what things are all about. You know, he understands the Indian's point of view as well as the military's. I've had a lesson or two from him on the military, and they was well worth listening to. Country's damn lucky to have a general like Crook. Some folks thinks he's overrated, but he ain't at all. He's a member of several Indian secret societies and they have a lot of trust in him. They think of him as a right kind of fellow. They call him Gray Fox.

"Is there more to that order?"

"Yeah, there is. Says here:

"For your information three cavalry troops of buffalo soldiers who have been located at Granby, Colorado, have been ordered in support of the Thornburg engagement."

"God Almighty," I said. "Them's black soldiers—buffalo soldiers."

"How good is them nigger boys doing in this stuff?"

"Well, I don't rightly know because I haven't worked with them very much, but I've knowed some scouts that have, and they say they're pretty damn good men if they just give 'em a chance. You keep downgrading fellows all the time and calling 'em niggers, and they won't have much use for you or themselves. But those boys fought in the Civil War, most often, and you give them a chance and they're as good as any man. I understand that some of them come from African tribes that was pretty warlike—least that's what Crook told me, and I go by what he says.

"Anyway, Jesus Christ, ain't that something," I said. "We've got us an Indian war in western Colorado!"

The agent nodded in agreement. "It looks damn serious."

"How do you feel about these southern Utes that you got here—like Ouray?"

"Oh, I think that we can hold them if we're careful and treat them right, and don't go telling them how they've got to live their lives all the time. Just tell them that we want to keep this from breaking out any further. Let them know we'll pay them well for being scouts and helping us locate them lost women," the agent explained.

"Boy, I'll bet the newspapers, the *Rocky Mountain News* and *The Denver Post,* are raising hell. You know, that is one thing that gets the white folks all wrought up, Indians running off with their women."

Right away quick I began to think about Melisande and what we was gonna do. Right now she was waiting for me with the horse and mule outside the agency.

"I reckon your plans have been kinda changed for you, ain't they?" the agent said.

"They sure as hell have."

He looked out the window and seen where Melisande was standing holding Jupiter by the reins. He asked, "Uh, well, I reckon your lady there—we're gonna have to make some arrangement for her, aren't we?"

"Yeah, she's my wife."

"Mighty fine-looking lady."

I didn't say nothing, but I sure as hell agreed with him. Looking at that lovely girl holding that beautiful, big black thoroughbred stallion, I tell you, I thought both of them was thoroughbreds.

There she stood, slim, with that auburn hair of hers laying along the back of her neck down over her buckskin shirt. Her clothes looked pretty darn good. We'd done real well when we were out there in the canyon country—man, she did look beautiful! It was gonna be tough to leave her.

It was the first time I had thought about that, but knew I had to go and she couldn't go on a war campaign. What the hell was I gonna do with her? She was gonna be upset when she heard the news, but I guess soldiers have to be soldiers, even scouts.

Now, Brules, I thought, real confused, what the hell has happened to you? What are you talking about? You're no soldier, you're just a damn scout. I guess that lecture that Crook give you about discipline has almost sunk in, hasn't it?

I told the agent, "I don't know what I'm gonna do, but . . . I'll—"

"I have an idea," he said. "Right back of the agency here, we got a little cabin, and my wife would be real glad to have your lady stay here with us. I believe that she'll be safe. I don't think we're looking for any real trouble with these southern Utes. You can make your own decision on that, but I think that it would be a good place."

I began to take a hard look at the situation. Where in the hell could Melisande go? Not back home, and not back in those canyons by herself. She sure couldn't come with me, so this seemed to be the ideal plan. Tonight I'd have to have a talk with her.

I told the agent, "I'll just wait for whatever Crook thinks he's gonna do. I suspect that he'll want us to take a bunch of these warriors from the southern Utes and go to White River and bargain with their kinsmen, and maybe I'll have to go along."

"That's probably what Crook has in mind," the agent agreed. "We'll have to wait and see. Things move pretty fast. Been a whole week passed, and I guess that by now there are reinforcements, and the Utes are out of there, but where in hell are those women? It's gonna be a big job to find that out."

"I suppose that's what they'll want me to do—see whether we can find 'em."

Then I turned to him and said, "Stanley, I'll tell you,

when Ouray comes in here, first thing we better do is find out if these southern Utes have had any connection with them northern Utes at all. If they have, maybe they can find out where in the hell those women are being kept. That's the first move, because you know what's gonna happen. You can bet those girls have all been raped, but they will be alive still. If them troops come up, or anybody goes in there real sudden-like, or if we go in there and rush them or something and do it the wrong way, them bastards will tomahawk their captives. We won't get a one of them out alive. All we will be doing is chasin' some corpses."

He nodded, and then suggested, "Why don't you go out there and talk to your little lady, and see whether she'd be interested in staying here?"

"I'll be doing that. I'll be back with you."

So I walked on out to Melisande. She had her little old grass bonnet on, and she tilted her head up and looked so pretty in the afternoon sun there. Man, I thought, that's a humdinger of a gal I got here. When I walked up to her, she was beaming. I put my arm around her, and she threw her arms around my neck and give me a good kiss.

"Honey, guess what?" I said.

"Now, tell me what. You found a gold mine or something."

"No, I didn't find no gold mine, damn it, but the northern Utes is broke out. We got a war, an Indian war."

"Oh," she said. "That's awful. Is it gonna spread down here?"

"I don't think so, honey. We're gonna keep these folks quiet. I think Ouray will be here sometime soon. Tonight he's up hunting by—I think he's up around Horse Thief Trail. But they'll find him all right. He should be in here tomorrow or the next day, and we'll get a chance to talk to him."

I decided I wouldn't say anything more to her at this time. By God, if things was gonna get bad, active duty or no active duty, I was gonna take her someplace that would be safe, like back to Del Norte. I didn't know just how I was gonna do that if Crook had some important mission for me, but I figured we could slip off and make it over there in a couple of days of hard riding and get her situated there. She'd be at the end of the rail line and would be all right.

Anyway, I said to her, "You know, maybe I'll have to go out on a campaign."

"Oh," she said, "you're not gonna leave me, are you? I'll go with you."

"Honey, you can't go on any campaign."

"Yes, I can go. I can go anywhere you go."

"Well, the agent there, he was sorta looking you over from the window, and he said you're a right smart-looking girl. I told him you were my wife. . . . You are, aren't you?"

"Of course I am. No woman could be any man's wife any more than I am yours. Where you're going, I'm going."

"Well," I said, "that's great, but it doesn't work that way in war. I mean, you just can't have a woman along on a campaign. The Indians don't even take their squaws because, Christ, it hampers them, slows them up some."

"Well, I don't slow you up a damn bit."

"I know that you don't, hon, but it isn't practical. Anyway, Stanley says that he and his wife live over in that house there, and right back of it is a cabin, and you could stay there."

"I don't want to stay here and be all alone. I don't want to be with those strange people," she said. "I don't know those people or anything."

"Well, we can meet them and become acquainted," I pointed out. "But first of all we've got to find a place to put these animals. There's the agency corral over there. They have to have someone acting as stableman, they got lots of horses around here and lots of riders. Let's see."

We went over, and sure enough the stable fellow, Sam, was just as nice as he could be. He sure was admiring old Jupiter. "God, what a horse! What a horse! You can sure run away from the Indians on that one, can't you?"

"Yeah, but the trouble is, I don't usually go running away from the Indians, I usually hunt them up."

Sam laughed and said, "Well, you got you a hell of a horse to get you out of a jam, if you get in one."

"That's what I count on him for."

"And that mule, what a beautiful animal that is," he went on about Alfred.

"Hell, he ain't beautiful, he's ugly, ain't he?"

Sam looked at me, and looked at the mule and said, "You know damn well that you feel the same way I do. He may be a big ugly mule, but, by God, he's beautiful. Look at the size of him, look at the hindquarters on that son of a gun. You can just tell that he's a bright animal. When you look into his eyes, he's thinking all the time."

I went back in and seen Agent Stanley again, who was back in the office of the agency. "Say, Stanley, you know I'm unpacking this mule now, and I got a load of grizzly hides on him. Is there someplace cool I can store 'em?"

"You can keep them in the icehouse," he said. "It's right next to our place, and we got a watchdog who raises hell before somebody could get in there. Course, we keep it locked up in the summertime, otherwise we'd have everybody stealing ice from us."

"Where do you get it?"

"Oh, there's a pond up here. We run some water on the Uncompahgre River into the pond, and when it freezes up we saw the ice out and pack it away in there with some sawdust. The usual way."

"That seems ideal," I agreed, and thought I'd better mention Melisande again. "You know, my wife, she's a little bit twitchy about staying with folks that, you know, she might be inconveniencin' and everything. Yet sure as hell, I'm gonna have to go on some kind of a scouting trip here, if I don't do nothing else. I can smell that from all them telegrams that's come through here."

"You're right about that," he said. "I'll tell you what, you just have your lady come over and both of you have supper with us tonight. I'll tell Mary. Don't worry about it. I'll bet you she and Mary get along just fine. After all, it's good if Mary has some kind of intelligent woman to talk to once in a while—there's nothing but Indian squaws around here."

Of course, for a minute I felt like saying, "Well, goddamn

you, I had a beautiful Indian girl once and she was intelligent as any white woman. Just 'cause she didn't shoot her mouth off all the time don't mean she hasn't got brains." Then I thought—back off, Brules, back off. This is a different deal, 'cause you know Melisande would love to have some conversation, and it'll be just fine.

I turned to him and said, "Stanley, that's a real nice offer, and we'll be happy to do that. Meanwhile, I'll just lead the pack mule over and load those grizzly hides into the icehouse, if you unlock it for me."

When I introduced Melisande to Stanley, he said, "Very pleased to meet you, ma'am. It's nice to have a beautiful lady here once in a while. This is a pretty lonely post."

I could tell Melisande was pleased, and she said, "How nice of you, sir. I appreciate your complimentary remarks. It seems to be a very fine place you have."

With that, Stanley just beamed away. I seen that my wife, Melisande, was gonna be real diplomatic. Boy, she went on telling him how great everything was, the way things was run so good, and what a strong, handsome fellow he was. I want to tell you, she had him prancing around there. When he left I said to her, "Aren't you ashamed of yourself, just making such a fuss over that fellow?"

"Well, you have to be polite. Manners are very important."

"Honey," I said, "I know that, but the kind of attention you're paying to this guy, I may have to spank you if you don't stop that."

She stuck her tongue out at me and said, "Oh, Cat, you're not gonna do anything like that."

"How do you know?"

"Well, I know a way to stop it." She took my arm, moving real close.

I didn't argue none about that, knowing she was right as rain, but I said, "We've been asked for supper tonight, and we're gonna meet Stanley's wife. We'll see what those folks are like, and I'll bet you his wife will be a wholesome woman. You may like her."

"I got along with everybody on our ranch. I never had any trouble doing that." Melisande shrugged.

"That's right. You was right popular there, and it'll be the same thing here. Anyway, number one, we're gonna put these bear hides in the icehouse, now. That's a hell of a good place to put them, isn't it? They'll keep fine."

While we off-loaded all them hides and packed them away, Stanley went to get his wife. Mary Stanley come over and she was just the nicest gal, kinda buxom. I could see that Melisande cottoned to her right away, and Mrs. Stanley was so happy to have a white girl around to talk to. She was just as nice! Why, she said, "Land sakes, you can just have that cabin, child, and it'll be just fine. You can have anything you want, you can help me in the kitchen if you want."

"I'd love to do that," Melisande said, polite-like.

So I saw that everything was just going great, and we had some new friends. There was only one trouble, and that was all my trouble. God, I had to sleep in that cabin. There was one big bed there and that suited me fine as long as I had Melisande with me, but I hadn't been inside any kind of a building for a long, long time.

I got real nervous when I was in a building. Had a hell of a time sleeping that first night. As we was laying there, I was tossing and kicking, and finally, I told Melisande, "Honey, I'm gonna get up and go outside. I'm gonna get my bedroll and get down under the stars."

"You think you're gonna get away with that? You want to go out there and sleep with the stars, and I understand why, 'cause you're an outdoorsman, but you aren't going out there alone in that bedroll. I'm coming right with you."

The next morning Mrs. Stanley seen that we was sleeping outside the cabin, and she thought that was the funniest thing in the world. I told her that I wasn't used to being indoors, so I had to sorta work up to it easy. Everybody was real good natured about it. It was a nice grassy place right there by the edge of the cabin, and we didn't bother nobody.

Of course, Melisande said, "Wait till it gets to raining cats and dogs, then we'll see if you're gonna stay out here."

"I've stayed out in a lot of rain," I reminded her.

"Yes," she said, "but that's just stupid. When it starts raining, you better come in the cabin and join me. I'll try to make you comfortable."

About the fifth day we was there the courier came from Del Norte, which was at the head of the telegraph line and railroad. All the mail was delivered to Stanley, and he told me, "Well, Brules, you got another order from General Crook."

"Oh, is that so? Let me see." I looked at it for a second and I said, "You read it."

He smiled again and said, "Okay.

"This is signed by an adjutant, Captain James A. Clark. It says:

> *"By order of the commanding general, Scout Brules is to put himself at the services of Senator Adams and Count von Donhoff, who should be arriving at the Los Piños Agency within the next few days.*
>
> *"Brules will assist the senator in arranging and accompanying any kind of effort the senator may require on his mission to search for the Meeker women. The object of the mission is to rescue the women by some means other than frontal attack. If and when the women are found, great caution should be used in approaching the hostile camp, lest the savages destroy their captives before they are taken away from them.*
>
> *"The commanding officer places high trust in your capability to conduct this mission with dispatch and expertise."*

"Well," I said, "ain't that the damnedest thing. Tell me, sir, what the hell do they mean by expertise?"

"Oh, that means you're an expert at something, and you do it right."

"Oh, okay, I get the idea. Now, who in hell is Senator Adams? Is he some United States senator out of Washington, or something?"

"Oh, no. He's a state senator only."

"Do you know anything about him?"

"Yes," he said, "I know him very well. I'll tell you. He was the agent here at Los Piños before I came. He speaks fluent Ute, and he's on very good terms with Chief Ouray. He's a tough woodsman and a good shot. He is also a general."

"Well," I said, "I'll be damned! That's good to know—we ain't taking no dude out there. 'Cause this is gonna be tough, by God. I mean, finding Utes and getting their captives away from them is no cinch."

Stanley said, "Yes, I know."

"Well, what are you gonna do to get Chief Ouray to give us some warriors?" I asked.

"The chief arrived last night, and I'm gonna have a visit with him. I think that we can get him to understand how much we need his help."

"Yeah, well, now tell me more about this fellow Adams."

"He lives in Colorado Springs and his name wasn't always Adams. He had a German name, like Schwanbeck something. I remember that before he married his wife, she told him she wasn't gonna marry anybody by that name. She wasn't gonna be no Mrs. Schwanbeck. She was of English decent, and she made him change his name to Adams."

"Oh, so this guy is a Fritz? We used to call them Fritzes in the infantry."

"Yes, he is, he's a Fritz, all right, and a pretty bright one. He's real respected around here."

"Who's this Count von Donhoff?"

"I'm not sure about that, but I'll find out, and give you all the information I learn. Meanwhile, you let me handle it."

"Don't think I'm not going to," I said. "Boy, all I'm gonna do is take them wherever they want to go. I kinda like the idea of sneaking up on a Ute camp like that. I used to do that with the Comanches and I'm pretty good at crawling on my belly and getting in close."

"Did you ever kill any Comanches?"

"Some." I thought it better to leave it be at that. Stanley shrugged; he would never know more about it. If I ever tried to tell him that I waged a one-man war against the Comanche nation for four years, why, he'd think I was the biggest liar. I figured I'd better shut up.

When I got that wire, I tried to figure out about when these guys would arrive at Los Piños, and how much time I had to get ready. It only made sense that von Donhoff and Adams had just gotten the word, too, a few hours ahead, less the time that it took the courier to get here from Lake City, which was maybe five hours. So I guessed they would be here in about four or five days, but I didn't have to wait that long.

Along about the middle of that afternoon here come four horsemen. They come from the direction of Alamosa, and they was moving right along. You could see from the condition of their horses that they'd been pushing the hell out of them.

I said to myself, "By God, here's Senator Adams and Count von Donhoff already." The other two guys was cow-punchers from the ranches that they had borrowed relief horses from.

When I first come across there in '74, there weren't no horses in this country at all, just a kinda foot trail from where the miners come in. Now, five years later, there was several ranches nearby, and that's where Adams's boys got his re-mounts. I reckon that them two cowboys had come to take them horses back, 'cause sure the horses weren't good for nothing else right now. They was all wore out, and Adams and von Donhoff would have to be given mounts by the Utes. Since there was plenty of horses at Los Piños, there wouldn't be any trouble about that.

Well, I'll tell you, when they come a-whipping in, they was plenty dust covered and you could tell they'd ridden a hell of a ways. They must have left Del Norte sometime yesterday afternoon, so they had been riding all night long and all this day.

I kinda eyed them two fellows and I thought, by God, there's no greenhorns here. They were tough men, good men. Just the way they got off the horses, you could tell that they was real horsemen. They was at ease, and the way they stepped around, you knew that they was a long ways from being wore out. That's something after a twenty-four-hour ride like that.

Old Stanley come out of the office and went right over to them. It was easy to see who was Adams, 'cause Stanley greeted him right away as an old friend.

I slowly started going over toward them. I'm not very good about shoving my face in among strangers, but if I was gonna have to do the guiding, I was gonna have to know them. So I kinda eased over, and Stanley quick-like introduced me. I want to tell you that when I looked at those two men, both of them Germans, their ruddy complexion, their bright blue eyes, their robust bodies and handshake, right away I liked them plenty. Course, I could tell even though they was educated, it was obvious that they was real men with a lot of balls.

When he greeted me, Adams spoke without an accent, just as American as anyone could be. He shook my hand and told me, "Yes, sir, Secretary Schurtz tells me that Crook says you are the finest scout in the West and that you could get the job done better than anyone else. I'm glad to meet you, sir. I understand you're a dead shot."

I didn't know what to say. I just kinda nodded and shook hands and turned to the other fellow. The count had a real strong German accent, but he did speak English—lot better than mine, I reckoned. He had a firm hand and bright eye, and I knew I was looking at one of the best.

I don't take to fellows very quick, but when I do it's usually a sure shot. One thing I noticed about them fellows: they was handsome as hell, well built, but both of them had bad scars on their faces, like they'd been in some kind of knife fight or something. At first I thought it was just a natural thing, but, no, they both had them, in different places, but along the cheeks and jaw. I figured that I was gonna have to ask Stanley what the hell was going on.

Stanley didn't waste any time taking them fellows into the agency and getting them something to eat and some coffee. They sat around the table and listened to what Adams had to say. Real quick he come to the point. Adams asked, "Do you have any information that could help me with the location of the Meeker women? Do the southern Utes know what the northern Utes did with them? Have they had any communication at all?"

Stanley said, "Yes, Charles, they do. Nearest Chief Ouray's men can make out, the women are located in a camp on Cottonwood Lake over on the other side of Grand Mesa about half a mile down from the top."

"Cottonwood Lake, yes, I think I remember. Well, there are three hundred lakes on that mesa up there. It's hard to know which one is which, isn't it?"

"Yes, I think so, but you wouldn't miss this," Stanley said. "We all know that is the spirit world of the Utes, and they go up there for worship. By God, when you're up there on that plateau you think you're hanging your feet over the end of the earth. Looking around up there, you can see why they thought that."

Adams nodded and said, "That's right."

"Anyway," Stanley went on, "you know Cottonwood. You can't miss it, 'cause it's 'cross the other side and down off the Cap Rock, and it lays down there, almost a dead straight angle north bearing for Rifle Creek, after you've crossed the Colorado. If you just lay a line straight across the mesa and start down the other side, right there is where you're gonna find Cottonwood Lake.

"Just where they are on the lakeshore is the question. There's a lot of timber around that lake and they'll be pretty well hid, I guess, but that's where they are."

Adams nodded and said, "What distance do you make it from here?"

"It's about eighty miles to Grand Junction and then you've gotta turn and go up the Colorado, so I'd say about a hundred and thirty-five miles."

Those fellows had come that far already from Del Norte, and Adams looked at von Donhoff and kinda raised his eyebrows a little bit. Von Donhoff just shook his head and nodded. It was gonna be another real ride, and Adams said, "What about horses?"

Stanley said, "We've got them for you, Charles. Don't

worry about it. Yes, we've got some good horses here. You'll have fresh mounts, and Chief Ouray says that he'll send thirteen of his scouts. The old man himself is feeling kind of bad."

"You mean Ouray is ill?"

"Yes, he's got something wrong with him. I don't know what it is, maybe just old age. He won't be able to go, but we'll get him here in a few minutes, and you can see what he has to say. He's sending you some good scouts, and you'll be in good shape.

"You fellows have to have something to eat here. Mary's got it pretty well stewed up. You better settle down—don't you want to take a few hours' rest?"

"I'll see," Adams said. "Just as soon as we've had something to eat, I would like to talk with Ouray to hear what he has to say."

"That can be arranged," Stanley agreed, saying, "I've got something else you fellows would like." He went over to the closet, pulled out a bottle of whiskey, poured two stiff drinks, and put them on the table. Them two reached out, their eyes gleaming, and tossed them drinks down right now. I could tell you they really appreciated that. That was a hell of a ride they'd had.

There was a kinda commotion outside, so I stepped out, 'cause I figured that it might be Chief Ouray coming in with his braves. It was him, all right, with his Navajo hat and beads on his jacket, and the rest all white man's clothes and boots.

None of them Utes wore real wild clothing like the Comanches done. Hell, they was long past that. They had white man britches, 'cause it was much better material, and they had them black hats and they cut their hair just below the hats. They wore miner's boots too. There weren't no Comanche moccasins or nothing. There was no doubt that they was Indians, but they sure looked like reservation Indians.

Old Ouray recognized me right away, and grunted. He said in English, "Brules, hello, Brules. Stanley say you have big bear now, good hunt! Good hunt?"

Stanley must have told him about the grizzlies, and I nodded, as I knew that would be close to his heart. The old boy shook my hand again and looked me in the eye. The Indians have a funny way of doing things, you know. They have a brotherhood going, or something, but he wasn't exactly that way with me. Still, I could tell he liked me, and I was a friend, and I sure liked the old boy.

Four of the Ute braves come in and stood by. Every now and then old Ouray would ask a question or two and the Utes would grunt the answers. Of course, I didn't know what the hell they was talking about, but Adams sure did. Finally, Adams spoke to Ouray in Ute and they carried on quite a conversation.

Christ, I wondered if I was the only son of a bitch around there that didn't speak Ute. It looked that way and it made me a little uncomfortable, but then I looked over at Count von Donhoff. That handsome fellow sorta tossed his head at me and give me a wink, as if to say, "Well, Brules, we don't know what's going on here, but we'll find out, and it will all come out all right."

After all that conversation in Ute, Adams turned to me and says, "I figure it's about a hundred and thirty-five miles around to Cottonwood Lake, going up the other side. They would see us if we go up the side of the mountain from here, north. They might scoot taking the women with them. Or kill the women, if they get too excited.

"That is the one thing that we've got to be awfully damned careful about. We don't want to get those bastards stirred up. They're just like wild wolves, you know, and if they get excited again they get savage as hell, and the first thing they do is tomahawk the prisoners."

He turned back a minute or two and talked to Ouray again in Ute, and then turned to speak to a couple of braves. There was one fellow that seemed to be making a point that was real important. Then Adams turned to me and said, "Brules, here's what he says. If we go right off the point where the North Fork of the Gunnison meets the Gunnison River as it comes out of the Black Canyon, we'll hit the mesa on a long spur that sticks out. There's a trail up that damned thing, but it's a horse killer and man killer. It's going to be a mean son of a bitch, but it saves just about thirty-five miles.''

"Well, hell," I said, "that's where we're going, then, Senator, because thirty-five miles takes a better part of a day to ride, and we ain't got that kinda time."

"I think you're right. I think we've got to do that. Not only the time element, but coming over the top of Cap Rock we'll be looking right down on Cottonwood Lake. We can see what's there and what's going on. We've got less chance of being spotted before we get there."

There was some more Ute talk, and I think that what they was saying was how long would it take to saddle up fresh mounts and be ready to go.

By this time it was damn near ten o'clock at night, and it had gotten real dark. Adams turned to me and said, "Brules, I want to be looking down on Cottonwood Lake from the top at about daybreak, day after tomorrow. That means we've got to get going here, if we're going to make that sixty miles before we start climbing. We better get out of here before dawn."

"I figure the same way, Senator. What kind of a party are we gonna have?"

"We're going to have thirteen warriors."

"Yeah, but what kind of armament have they got?" I asked him.

He asked Ouray about that, and then Ouray talked to the Indians, and Adams came back to me. "They'll all have some kind of firearm. A lot of them will have that cavalry .45, '70 Springfield, single shot, but there's about four or five that's got Henrys, and one or two of them have 73's."

"Well, that sounds pretty good to me—better than you could expect, to have them all armed like that," I said.

That ended the powwow. Adams and von Donhoff went in a side room there and laid down on the floor and went to sleep right away. Ouray had him a shot of whiskey and sat around talking for a little while before he got up and left. It was now just Stanley and me sitting there with that oil lamp burning. He poured me another one, and I said, "Tell me about these fellows. I like the looks of them, but I kinda wonder. What the hell do they have those cuts on their faces for?''

"Brules, that's the scar of valor, shows you're a graduate of the university in Germany.''

"What the hell are you talking about?''

"I can only tell you what I know. Germany is a highly civilized nation, as you know, and they have got a lot of damn fine people. Sometimes they're bullheaded as hell, but the Germans are one of the strong peoples of the earth, and they're damn good mechanical people too. When you hear them speak it properly, German is actually a beautiful language. They've got a tremendous quality and class in their literature, poets like Goethe, wrote beautiful stuff. Wonderful musicians like Wagner and Schubert. They were just great.''

I sat there listening. Here's a guy, Stanley, read a lot, obviously. All the men here was educated, I was the only dummy in the bunch, but I absorbed it all 'cause it was what I wanted to know about.

I said, "What did you call that writer fella, Gehkre?''

"No, Goethe, Goethe.''

"You say he wrote poems?''

"Yeah, you'd like some of the stuff he wrote. God, I remember one line I learned, when I had to do a lot of reading in school. He was talking about a young prince—I guess it was a Westphalian prince. He said his father had a big castle with a lot of men at arms. He also had an old adviser, kind of the old fellow who held things together—the chancellor, you might say. He was talking to the young prince and he said, 'When the wild wars raged around thy father's house and spears were raised against us like a sea.' In other words, telling the boy, things were tough when his father was a young man, and the grandfather had to fight everybody. That was a pretty good way of saying it, wasn't it?''

"Yeah, I like that.''

"You know, the German mythology is really something,'' he went on. "They're always talking about in the old days, a thousand years ago or more. Maybe two thousand years ago. They had these stories about Valhalla.''

"What's that?" I asked.

"That was the home of the gods. If a warrior had done real well in battle, but was killed by overwhelming odds, he was picked up by a Valkyrie."

"What the hell is *that*?"

"That's a beautiful woman on a winged horse," he answered.

"Oh, that ain't *bad,* a beautiful woman on a horse picking you up, but you gotta get killed first?"

He laughed and said, "Well, it's how the myth goes. The horses had wings and the Valkyries would carry a long spear, wore helmets, and they rode with the warrior up to Valhalla, the home of the gods. The warrior was brought back to life again, and then things were wonderful. In Valhalla all the warriors did was have a big feast every night in the great hall with music, songs, and lots of drinking. Then at daybreak they'd form their ranks, march out, and do battle all day. They'd come back in and repeat the whole thing. Of course, they didn't die because they were immortal."

"Well, that don't sound like a bad heaven. What'd you call them—them beautiful women?"

"Valkyries, they came back all the time," he explained.

"Well, that appeals to me!"

"Then they have the story," he went on, "about the dragon's teeth."

"Dragon's teeth?"

"Yeah, they had some big dragon and, I forget how the whole story went, but I remember, when they wanted more warriors, all they'd do was plant these dragon's teeth, and they'd spring up full-armed warriors. It didn't make any difference how many was killed, they always had more to spare."

I said, "That ran the dragon a little short on teeth, didn't it?"

Stanley laughed like hell. Then he got serious and said, "Let's get back to the job you have ahead. Now, that trail up the mountain, I've taken it before. It's a son of a bitch, and you're going to have to ride a lot of it in the dark.

"You'd better get started on the first part of it just as soon as you can. If you can get there by about eight at night, when you can still see just a little bit, it won't be so bad, and then it's an easy ride across the top. But there are a couple of places where, if a horse slips, you're going to fall a thousand feet.''

''I don't plan on lettin' that happen,'' I said. ''Now, tell me something about them northern Utes.''

''Well,'' he said, ''they're not like these fellows, they're a bunch of mean bastards mostly, and a lot of them have strange names. Not like Ouray, which in Ute means 'the Owl.' Many northern Utes have American names like Johnson, Douglas, and Captain Jack. Other chiefs have Indian names of Colorow, Capote, Piah, Sarap, and Sah-patch. The situation got bad because the White River agent was going at things all wrong. He wouldn't let the Indians go hunting, give them their rations, or have anything that they'd bargained for until they did some planting. That's pretty hard to do to an Indian.

''You can't put an Indian behind a mule and a plow and just *say,* go out there and plant. He's a hunter. Now, it's different with a smart guy like Ouray. I don't think Ouray has any white blood in him, but he had white upbringing in Taos. He saw what all the Taos Indians planted, and that it made a lot of difference. If you have to hunt for game as your main source of food, that's a big problem, especially if it's scarce. You might starve. That's what is happening all over the West.

''The Indians are hunters and gatherers, as a rule, and don't do much planting. Let's say it takes about, maybe, a hundred square miles for one hunting family to survive. That's ten miles by ten miles. Jesus, if it's any kind of good land, that will support a hundred farmers. So it ain't fair, with all the movement West, for these bastards to keep holding out wanting to keep hunting all the time, when that same land will support a hundred fellows that will farm. That's the whole problem. That makes the odds a hundred to one against the Indian—the nomad, the hunter!

''You can make all the treaties you want to in Congress, and I know they've made a lot and busted them, but the pressure is too great. That's why Ouray is smart. He's got a whole bunch of farms here. They're called Ouray Farms, and he's got a lot of irrigated land. He's doing just great and he and Chipeta are raising crops. He realizes that, if the white man is whipping the Indians all the time—and it's obvious that he is, 'cause he keeps moving in on them—he'd better get more like the white man. These other dumb bastards are going to be hunters and fool around with stone tools for another thousand years, if they have their own way."

I looked at him and said, "Well, by God, it makes sense when you explain it that way. But finish tellin' me about how these guys got those scars."

"Oh, yes," Stanley said. "It seems at the great universities of Germany, where all the principal sons of the nobility go, they teach them all kinds of endurance, educate them very well in all the sciences, and on top of the literature and all that, they toughen those fellows up. One of their customs is to fight a duel with sabers."

"Jesus Christ, that's a good way to get killed."

"Well, they don't go that far. They wear some kind of vest to give them protection and so forth. Maybe they have something over their eyes and throats, but their faces are clear, and they go after it hard. It is an honorable thing, and if you've been much of a saber duelist, you can't get away without getting cut up a little bit. That's great standing, when you have those scars."

"Jesus, that sounds like a tough game to me," I said. "I wouldn't care too much about what the other fellow thought about me, if I was gonna get me all cut up with a saber—to hell with that."

Stanley laughed and said, "Well, that's right, but it's their tradition. The thing is, these fellows were classmates."

"You mean the count and Adams?"

"Yes, I guess I mentioned Adams's name was Schwanbeck. They was both in the same class, and so was Secretary Schurtz, Secretary of the Interior. Around the middle of September, Schurtz came through the Rockies on the Union Pacific from California where he'd been looking into matters for the Department.

"He wired Adams that he wanted to see him and get

together, being old classmates. Well, of course, Adams wires him back and says, hell yes, come, and guess who I got here? I got Count von Donhoff, who was in our class too.

"With that old Schurtz was real pleased. He arrived in Colorado Springs sometime in September, and he, Adams, and von Donhoff had them a hell of a reunion there. Adams told me that they sang stein songs, cheered, and drank beer until hell wouldn't have it. Told old jokes and lies about all the times at college and about what they did, the girls they was chasing and such.

"They just had a marvelous time, and then Schurtz got on the train and three or four days later he was back in Washington. Now, that just shows you what these damn railroads did for this country. Christ, it used to be months crossing the damn land, but, no, sir, Schurtz was back there at his desk in Washington, and guess what? Them Utes blowed the hell out of things just about that time. Of course, as soon as the Military Department of Nebraska got word of it, why Crook gets the word to Sheridan, Sheridan to Sherman, and Sherman notifies the Secretary of the Interior. 'You are in charge of the Indians. What the hell are you going to do about this? We're sending some troops in there, but you better be aware of what's going on, and you'd better do something.' I guess that's what they done.

"Meanwhile, Adams had gone back to Denver with von Donhoff, and they was staying in a place Adams had there, 'cause he'd been in the state legislature for some time. Adams told me that he got this telegram from Schurtz that said, you speak Ute, you know all about that backcountry. By God, you've got to go in and help get those women out of there.

"Adams showed von Donhoff the wire and von Donhoff said, 'Well, you know something? My ancestors, many hundreds of years ago, established a coat of arms. It had a knight in shining armor, rescuing a beautiful maiden from a terrible dragon. That's my coat of arms! I'm going in and help rescue the Meeker women with you.'

"Adams later said he couldn't help laughing, but said, 'Well, hell, I can't think of anybody that I'd rather have go along with me. It's going to be tough and dangerous.' Von Donhoff just said, 'Let's go.'

"Adams and von Donhoff, being in Denver, caught the next train to Colorado Springs, going on through Pueblo to Walsenburg and Alamosa. Adams had wired his wife to meet him at the railroad station in Colorado Springs with his Winchester and saddle. His wife was there just as nice as pie—I think he calls her Elizabeth. Of course, she was all upset and in tears that he was going into that terrible country, looking for savages. Why did he have to go after the Meeker women?

"He didn't have time to argue with her, the whistle blew and the train was starting to pull out. He threw the saddle and Winchester aboard, gave her a kiss, and jumped aboard again. Von Donhoff was watching the whole show and laughing like hell.

"They went down through Pueblo to Walsenburg and crossed through La Veta Pass. They continued on to Alamosa following the Rio Grande to Del Norte, which was the end of the rail line. They picked up horses without any trouble, and came right on across.

"They didn't get into Del Norte until something like noon yesterday. Since they didn't get under way with the horses until around five o'clock, they rode through the whole damn night and most of this day. Now they're going out tomorrow for another good ride."

Them fellows needed a little rest, and it was agreed that we wouldn't leave until three o'clock in the morning, so I went back over to the cabin. Melisande was in kind of a funny mood. I hadn't seen her like this before. She started by saying, "Well, you certainly have been gone a long time, Brules."

"Yeah, I have." Then I started telling her about those Germans and so forth, and she was real interested, and we kept talking about things.

Then she asked, "You have made a plan, haven't you, to go away on the warpath. You're going to try to do something with the northern Utes."

"Yes, that's right," I said. "I'm gonna take Count von Donhoff and Senator Adams that way."

"Is he really a senator? Is that German fellow really a count? He looks awful red faced to me. Is he really a count?"

"Yes, he is. I reckon that he's got a castle and all."

"Oh," she said, "isn't that wonderful? A regular count with a castle."

"Well, I haven't heard him talk about castles or nothing, but Stanley thinks he's got one and I'll find out for you."

"That's interesting enough, but there is something else. In the first place, I don't know whether or not I want to go on the warpath."

"Of course you're not going on the warpath, honey. What the hell—a woman going out here and trying to do some fighting and everything?"

"Just 'cause I'm a woman doesn't mean I can't fight."

"Wait a minute, Melisande. A warpath is no place for a woman. Even the Indian squaws, who are probably pretty good fighters around their own tepee villages, they don't go on any warpath, because it's too tough. A fellow has to travel all day and all night, maybe sleep out in the rain. You can't do that."

"I think that I can do what any man can do."

"Well, honey, that isn't the argument. I can't have the responsibility of having you along—I'd be scared to death. I'd be afraid that you'd get hurt or something. What if you was captured by some of those warriors? What do you think would happen to you?"

"I don't know. Would they burn me at the stake?" she asked.

"That's possible, yeah, but more than likely they would make a wife out of you."

"Oh, God, they couldn't do that."

"The hell they couldn't. They do it all the time with the captives. What the hell do you think that they try to catch the women for? Why didn't they kill the women right away? They take them away, they want to use them."

"Oh," she said, "that's terrible. I never knew that."

"I reckon it is terrible too. That isn't all that they do to you. I'm just telling you that you better—"

"I don't know, Cat. The thing is, I don't want to be separated from you. I want to be with you wherever you go."

"I understand that, honey, but going on the warpath is one place where we've got to part. I would never forgive myself if something happened to you—if you fell in with those terrible savages"—and then I thought I'd scare her to death—"and they made a wife out of you and got you with Indian babies and everything. Not only that, if you didn't agree with them, they'd burn you at the stake. Come on, what are you asking me to do?"

She didn't say anything.

"It is out of the question, you can't go. We're gonna do one hell of a ride tomorrow, maybe over a hundred miles, and it's gonna be in some damn rough country. We don't have enough ammunition for me to have you practice shooting. Before we get through, that's part of your education and you're gonna be a damn good shot with a rifle. You're gonna know how to load and unload it, take it apart, put it together, and see if the whole damn thing works. You're gonna know the difference between calibers, and we'll get you handy with a pistol and a rifle, and I'll take you lots of places I go. But I'm not gonna do it now, honey. There's no time."

Then she burst into tears and said, "This is awful. I didn't think that we were ever gonna have to be apart like this."

"Well, it's gonna have to be for now." I give her a kiss and a hug, and got her kinda quieted down. "I've got to be up around one o'clock in the morning to get everything ready for these fellows, to make sure that everything is right."

"What am I supposed to do in the meantime?"

"You like Mary, Mary Stanley. She's a nice gal, and you're gonna stay right here and will be well taken care of. I won't be worried about you, 'cause I'll know where you are all the time."

"I just don't like it," she said again. "I want to be with you."

"Honey, I'll try to quit going on these trips as much as possible. I'll take you hunting and we can be together all the time."

"Oh," she said, "that's going to be wonderful. But I don't know if I want to hunt grizzly bears."

"No, I don't want you to hunt no grizzly bears. Any grizzly, we're gonna give a wide berth to. We'll just hunt elk, deer, and antelope. You won't have any trouble that way."

To make a long story short I had to get some sleep, and knew that the best way to get this girl quieted down and to stop her fears was to take her to bed. That seemed to me to be a pretty good solution all the way around. I still didn't like sleeping inside in that cabin, so I pulled out the bedroll and laid it on the grass outside. We both stripped down and slipped into the bedroll, and it weren't long before we weren't worried about anything else. We was just plenty interested in what was going on between us. We made real mad love there that night, and she was soon telling me how much she loved me and there wasn't nobody else in the world. By God, I was telling her the same thing, and it was wonderful. It was like my cup was full again. The stars was a-shining overhead, the soft wind was blowing, and we both went off to sleep real quick.

25

The Meeker Women

I woke and got myself and Jupiter ready around three o'clock or a little bit before. There was torchlights burning in the yard to give everybody enough light to see what they was doing.

The thirteen Utes that was going with us was already saddled. I recognized several who had been standing at attention around Ouray's table the night before. Now I seen, from what they was wearing, that they was chiefs.

At the Los Piños Agency the Tabeguaches was one branch of the Ute tribe, and the other was the Uncompahgres. The two Uncompahgre chiefs who had been around the night before was Shavano, meaning Blue Flower, and Guero, meaning Light Hair. The third Indian chief, called Captain Billy, was a Tabeguache. The Uncompahgre chiefs was Uncom-mute—that meant Good—and Sapavanri.

Of course, Ouray was out there watching us leave, but he wasn't going. This was young man's stuff. Young men got the strength the older fellows don't have—they also got better nerves and more foolish guts. They move faster and are generally more aware of what's going on, but, by God, some of them is also dumber than hell. They don't know what the hell they're getting into.

The old boys have been through it, and they think, well, you know, this may not turn out quite as fancy as you think it's going to. You go to young men for action and old men for counsel. I liked to think that I was still young enough. I was only thirty, which is pretty old for tough scouting. At least that's what I was told, but, you know, I never did slow down, not to notice any difference, until I got around forty-five or fifty years old. Then I really did slow up, but before that I was cooking right along.

Well, I was standing there in the yard watching. I had Jupiter's reins tied around the saddle horn, 'cause I knew he'd follow me about wherever I went. Meanwhile I heard a hell of a lot of braying going on over at the corrals and knew it was Alfred. By God, Alfred wanted to go.

I'd thought about whether to take a pack mule along, but decided no—if we really had to run somewhere, I wanted a fast horse. If I get all by myself in some situation with a dozen northern Utes after me, I want a horse that gets out, gets going. I can't do that with a pack mule, and it was kinda sad, but this time Alfred just couldn't go along. That old mule was a-braying away, like he was saying, "Where are you guys going, you forgot me, how about me, damn it, come on and get me out of here." His braying sounded like "Aw, hell, aw, hell, aw, hell," and I had to laugh.

The interpreter fellow that was going along with us finally mounted, and it seemed like I was the last one to do so. I reckoned I better step over and say a word or two to Adams. I wasn't heading up the expedition or nothing, but it was my job to take care of him and the count. As I walked toward them, to see how they was getting on, damn if that beautiful stallion didn't come a-walking behind. I got over next to Senator Adams first and asked, "Are you okay? Is your equipment all right? How is everything checking out here?"

"Ah, Brules. Just fine, and we're sure glad to have you."

"Senator, it's my honor to be with you, and I'm going to do the very best I can."

"By God, Brules, that's a beautiful horse. Where did you get him? He must be seventeen hands."

"Well," I said, "he's a little better than that. He's pretty near seventeen and a half, something like that. I don't know. I haven't measured him in a long time, maybe he's growed some.''

The senator laughed.

''Yeah, I got him up there when I was working with Crook, and had to take a special message between two of the commands. They give me the best horse in the camp. I've always been very grateful for him.''

When I went over to check Count von Donhoff, he said, ''Yes, yes, everything good.''

''Well, that's fine, Count. We just want you to be well took care of here.''

All this time I was thinking, Jesus, if Melisande ever wakes up and finds that I ain't in that sack, and she comes running out, it will be real embarrassing. Maybe I should go over and give her a squeeze good-bye. But, hell, no, I ain't got the time now and I'm glad she's still sleeping. I was comfortable in that thought, and checking everything and everybody that was going, who they was and how it looked, when I heard Melisande's voice.

Here she come a-runnin', and she had her coat around her, but I knew that she didn't have another Goddamn thing on under that coat. She was barefoot and she yelled, ''Cat Brules! You've got to say good-bye.'' In three strides I grabbed her up in my arms and squeezed her good and give her a kiss. God, she was a beautiful girl. I mean it—the firelight made her long, beautiful hair and her lips and eyes look so great.

There was a kinda dead pause, and I knowed everybody was watchin'. Thirteen Goddamn Ute scouts, five Ute chiefs, a count, and a Goddamn senator, all looking at Brules having his love affair run off before them. They all had a real understanding look, though. I kissed her hard and said, ''Okay, now go on, get on back. Hurry up or you'll catch cold, get back in the sack. I'll be back here soon.''

With that somebody gives a yell and says, ''We're on our way,'' and I recognized that it was one of them wagon masters. God Almighty, I forgot that we were taking a supply wagon with us. Not only that, we had a buggy that some of the cowboys from the agency was driving, so that they would have something to take the Meeker women back. I thought, well, that's the silliest thing I've heard of in my life, taking them two wagons. They're not going to be able to bring them wagons everywhere we're going.

The whole column started moving out, and Jupiter kept looking back at me wondering where the hell I was. So I gave Melisande another good kiss and a big hug, and I run like hell and jumped. I took about six or seven strides getting over there to old Jupiter, then I hit the ground, just right, and made me a high jump, kept my knees up, and landed right in the saddle. That ain't easy to do with a big horse.

Count von Donhoff said, *"Mein Gott,* he's like a cat!"

"That's what they call him—Cat Brules. Now we see why," Adams told him.

Well, we kept pushing on for an hour or so before dawn broke, then it got light and we could see pretty much what was going on. We was headed down the Uncompahgre River in that kinda open sandy valley. It wasn't cultivated in them days. It just had sagebrush prairie on one side and sand dunes on the other, with the river flowing through the cottonwoods.

I found myself riding alongside Senator Adams and Count von Donhoff. I got to talking to the senator. I figured that any chance I had to talk to these gentlemen would be worthwhile. They was quite some boys, both of them. Like I done said before, when a guy looks like he is worthwhile, I want to know something about him. So I asked, "Senator, I understand from Stanley at the agency that you and Secretary Schurtz and Count von Donhoff—all you fellows went to college together. Is that right?"

He said, "That's right, Brules. We went to the University of Bonn."

"That's where you learned fighting with them swords or sabers?"

"Yes, sir, that's right."

"Well, I gather that's where you got them nicks on your face, Senator."

He said, *"Ja,* that is right."

Sometimes he still had a little German accent, you know,

but it was very faint. I could just picture Adams and I'll tell you, a two-hundred-and-fifty-pound man with one of them sabers would be something to be lookin' out for. You better be ready to fight.

"I had a Mexican friend once, a fellow named Pedro. Best friend I ever had except for Wesha, a Shoshone that I was real fond of. But, by God, that damn Mexican could throw a knife, and it was amazing how accurate he could be. He tried to teach me how to do it, and I can do it a little bit. But, boy, swishin' those sabers around, that's really something."

"Yes," he said, "you get used to it. You really have to do it, you know. It's the sort of thing to do at college."

"I reckon that's beautiful country there in Germany," I said.

"*Ja,* along the Rhine is wonderful. There are some marvelous castles and old ruins, like Drachenfels."

"Drachenfels?"

"Yes, Drachenfels—that means 'Dragon's Lair.' "

"Boy, I would like to see that sometime," I said.

"Ah, I have many relatives there, Brules. If you want to go to Germany sometime, you must let me know and I'll give you an introduction to them. You'll have a good time, I promise you."

No more was said about it, but I kept lookin' at them two fellows and seein' them scars of honor. They wasn't very bad, it wasn't nothing too disfiguring, but they was still there. I realized that maybe the German nation sure as hell was a bunch of fighters, and if the rest of them was anything like these two men, why, they was a power to be reckoned with.

After a noon stop we crossed the river. It was real low that time of year, so we didn't have any difficulty at all. Even got the wagon across, and the buggy, which was kinda jumpy, but we did it. We kept going down the river, and we stopped there at Whitewater, which was just an old trading post and not much left of it. We decided to take a spell of resting, 'cause we'd already ridden more than sixty miles and we was gonna have another thirty-five to ride that night.

We'd been there about an hour, resting in the shade of the

trees, and trying to get as much snooze as we could, when we was jolted out of our slumbering ways by a couple of Indian riders. They was northern Utes—sent by Colorow and Johnson—and, boy, they was in an agitated state of mind, and so was the Uncompahgre Utes when they got the message.

There was a big problem that I seen right away. The southern Utes were at peace, it was only the northern Utes that was having any problems.

Old Ouray had been doing his Goddamnedest to hold things together; he knew it was absolute suicide to fight the whites, and if they started a war, all they'd do was lose their reservation lands. They had a damn good reservation—almost half of Colorado—and he knew the pressure was gonna be hell from whites to get in there. Any excuse they could make about Ute atrocities or something like that, boy, that would be it. That's why he was so damn anxious to get those Meeker women out of the hands of the Utes, because if anything happened to them—if they was raped and killed—the whole damn place would go crazy.

By this time there was probably a couple hundred thousand whites in Colorado, and I don't suppose altogether there was twenty-five thousand Indians. Two or three times, Ouray told me later, he was right on the edge of going the other way and declaring for the Utes having a holy war against the white nation. Then we would've had one hell of a time. It would have been another one of them Sioux deals, and even if the Utes were never as powerful as the Sioux, it would have been bad. That was the first problem we had, to keep our own Ute warriors happy. The second problem was to keep the northern Utes from going crazy. When they'd get cornered, them Indians would act like wolves—they didn't act straight at all. If they thought we was coming in to fight, first thing they'd do was tomahawk their captives.

Now, here's what was happening, according to them riders. When Major Thornburg was killed at Yellow Jacket Pass, the second in command was a Major Merritt. Course, he took over the whole detachment, and when the buffalo soldiers from

Granby showed up, the troops was able to hold their own with the Utes. And the Utes backed off and left them.

Major Merritt started pursuing. He went on into White River Agency with the troops, 'cause he was strong enough not to fear counterattack, and he seen nothing but destruction there. Everything was burned up, the machinery and everything tore up and busted to hell, bodies all around. One fellow used the words *indescribable desolation*. Them is two big words, but I guess gives you some idea of what it was like. Course, everybody was sore as hell, so they began following the Utes.

The Utes kept moving their camp, but the infantry detachment that was following them kept a-plugging at them. Same old story. When you are fighting Indians, you just don't give 'em no rest, you just keep going and keep going. Eventually they've got to winter somewhere, and when they do, you bring up the artillery.

That's the type campaign that Crook and Miles had waged against the Sioux and the Nez Perce—just keep harassing them to where they can't find hunting, can't keep up, can't sustain a defense, let alone an offense. That's just what Merritt was gonna do, and he was on the right track. Of course, the Utes knew that they was sorta committing suicide to start this damn thing, and that they was gonna lose everything. In their trapped rage the only thing they could do was take it out on innocent prisoners.

So these riders come in to tell us that Merritt was pushing down Rifle Creek and had to be stopped before we could have any peace at all. Chief Ouray could still show them a way out, but somebody'd better stop Merritt if they didn't want things to blow all to hell. Senator Adams, of course, immediately saw the problem. He thought, Jesus, we have to get to the camp where the women are being held as quick as possible and see if we can't save them from some crazy tragedy.

We moved out of there right away, didn't finish our rest, but started up that terrible trail, going sort of northeast from Whitewater. It was every bit as tough as predicted, and there were some places where a misstep would send you and your animal a thousand feet down. It was real spooky, and even the animals were nervous, 'cause they knew what it meant to make a misstep or slip. They didn't like it any more than we did. In some places we got off and led our horses.

It started to get dark when we was only about three quarters of the way up, but I remember, just before the sun went down behind the La Sal Mountains, looking out at the great view. It took our attention off the nightmare of twisting defiles and sandy shelves, which we used to climb the towering cliffs above us.

After it got dark, the moon come up and made the trail seem half real. It was a struggle all the way and about as nerve-racking as anyone could want. We busted out on top of the mesa when the moon was partway up the night sky. It seemed like we was for sure entering into the spirit land of the Utes. The land they called "Thigunawat." Whether you was there in the daylight or the dark, it seemed like a world that was separate from everything else.

I ain't forgetting that moonlight ride across the mesa through the small park, and the tall blue spruce pines that darkened out the moon. Sometimes we'd pass a lake with rocks and weeds growin' around the edge. Wildfowl would spook up with the frightening thunder of wings. Occasionally we'd see a deer move across the flat country in front of us and dash away. We rode past alive and dead pine alike, and it was eerie as hell as we rode in the moonlight. We felt well spooked.

We didn't think there was much chance of being ambushed along the way, but you never could tell. Some Utes might have been on top when we started, and seen us begin the long trek upward—but we couldn't do anything about it, we just had to keep going.

I seen what kind of guts both Senator Adams and Count von Donhoff had, when they insisted on riding right up in front. Once we got into the lakes country, which was broken up by flat meadows of wild grass and ponderosa pine forests, then they didn't know what direction was right. So in the end the little Ute, Shavano, had to do the guiding.

He rode up forward and I rode right behind him. After me

come Senator Adams riding a roan horse, strong enough to carry his full two hundred and fifty pounds. After that, Count von Donhoff, and then the Utes, all in single file, everybody moving as quiet as we could.

Under the sliver of the moon it was like we was riding through a ghost land. Toward dawn we began to sense that there was a slight decline in the flat top of the mesa as we approached the north rim. It just was cracking enough daylight to see, when we finally got to where we could look down on Cottonwood Lake. I'll never forget that moment, hidin' in the trees and lookin' out over the edge of the cliff, across that vast basin, toward the valley of the Grand River.

Down below us, in the timber, was a great sight. There was Cottonwood Lake, a beautiful gem of clear blue water, like many of them lakes on Grand Mesa, but this one now had a special meaning, because as we looked down, we saw an open meadow with a whole bunch of tepees. The lodges of the northern Utes—a sight that made our hearts beat a thousand miles an hour. That had to be the place where the Meeker women was being held!

I thought about them. I knew there was the old lady—old Arvilla Meeker. She must have been fifty-some, but that wouldn't make no difference to savages if they was gonna violate her. Then there was young Josie, her daughter. I guess that she was a good-looker and would be a prize for some buck. Then there was Mrs. Price, she was a kinda helper. She'd been working as a maid or cook or something like that in the Meeker house. She and her little girl was taken right along with the rest of them.

Of course we knew that there was some real tough warriors in that bunch below. They was murderous bastards—it was their reputation among the Utes themselves. Johnson was the meanest of the bunch, I guess. We didn't know which chiefs were there, whether there was a lot of chiefs or warriors, or whether they was out across the Grand River and up Rifle Creek, fighting the troops. There weren't no way for us to know except to sit and watch.

I crawled out on a ledge of rock where I could get a good

look at the whole village. Using the field glasses General Crook had given me, I started scanning every one of them tepees, watching who was coming in and out. As usual, there was a bunch of naked skinny Indian boys running around. Some of them was doing chores and some of them just playing. There was some girls that looked like they had been picking berries.

The camp was situated on the other side of the little stream that run down from the top of the mesa and across that meadow. There was squaws all about, but I didn't see no white women.

After watching for fifteen or twenty minutes, which was hard, hard watching, 'cause we was really eager to get down there, I seen that there couldn't have been more than one or two warriors in the whole camp. The warriors, and probably all the chiefs, was the hell and gone out of there. They knew that the troops coming after them had been reinforced. One thing that the Indians had found out ever since Crook's campaign in '76, there was no such thing as rest for Indians that had gone hostile.

These Utes had committed an outrage. Maybe it had been stimulated by the whites, maybe it weren't quite their fault, but, by God, they'd done it and killed some white people, and the whites wasn't gonna relent. They was gonna get those bastards and they was gonna finish them off. These braves and chiefs knew it, and was just crazy as hell, liable to commit any kind of act.

When we couldn't spot the white women, it was decided that we would move down real quiet and surround the village. Then Adams would ride in, with maybe Shavano and some of the Utes—ride real peaceful-like—not make no charge or nothing like that, but just keep a-moving. We could have rushed the place, but if we'd done that and spooked somebody into firing a shot, then the whole Goddamn works would blow up, and we'd find our prisoners dead.

After studying the layout Adams said, ''You know, looking at that camp, I'd say the tepee that is to the north, the farthest one downstream, should be Johnson's. He probably isn't there, but I'll bet the Meeker women are in there. We'd better move on that one first.''

I couldn't see anything wrong with that logic, so we started down off the hill, with Shavano riding in front, and three or four warriors going ahead. Count von Donhoff, Adams, and me were riding abreast behind the Utes, just coming in without any hostile action, in a slow walk. Our plan was that we would just walk in easy and pass down the line to the last lodge, the big one that looked like Johnson's lodge.

What few squaws and children were there stood there just dumb-like. Adams had made a damn good guess, because just beyond the biggest tepee was another small tepee we hadn't seen before. Standing in front of it was a couple of Ute squaws holding up a blanket so you couldn't see inside. Of course, we knew right away, and I said to von Donhoff and Adams, ''They be there.''

I had no more than said that when the blanket was pushed aside and a white woman stepped out, holding a little child by her hand. No doubt who she was: a young woman, blond haired, blue eyed, fine looking, wearing a dress that had obviously been made out of a damn blanket, but looked pretty good. She was tall, stately, and narrow waisted and you could see that she was a real lady, despite the conditions around her.

Adams slipped off his horse real quick, dropped the reins, and started walking toward her with a quick step. When he got within about ten yards of her, Josie Meeker drew herself up like a queen and said, ''Indeed, Mr. Adams, I am very glad to see you.'' Considering all she'd been through, it was one hell of an understatement. Kinda made you proud of the white women. She wasn't married or nothing, just a young girl. I don't expect she was over nineteen years of age, a damn brave American girl. She'd been twenty-six days with them savages and she'd been through hell, but she didn't let on or moan none or weep. He asked her, ''How are you?'' and she said, ''Very well, thank you, sir, considering.''

Well, considering what? Twenty-six days with them Utes, you knew damn well that she'd been raped—everything had happened to her. There couldn't have been any question about it: it always happened to the white women. Then he asked, "Well, Miss Meeker, can you tell me who murdered your father?"

She didn't know, she said, because too much had been going on, and the women had been running around inside that house. They told later how they started to hide under the beds and saw that was no good. Then thought they could make a break for the woods and saw that wouldn't work. It all went to hell then, and it was at that time that Meeker was killed. Just who shot him, she didn't know.

The other question he asked her was "Now, ma'am, I have to ask you, have you had any violation of your person or anything of that nature?"

Of course she said, "Oh, no, sir. No, no, Senator Adams, nothing like that. Nothing like that."

Well, she was lying, because to women in them days, the idea of being violated, of being raped, was so awful and it had such a bad effect on everybody else, as if a woman was spoiled or ruined or no good after that, they wouldn't admit it. It was like a living death for them. So it was natural for her to say no because of normal modesty. They didn't talk about anything like that—white women didn't.

Now, you may ask me how I know that, and I'll just say that later on when they had the inquiry, when they got her back to Denver and they got talking about it, then she confessed what had happened to her. She was lucky because one of the braves, who was named Persune, plumb fell in love with her. Johnson wanted to rape her, but Persune ran him off. Johnson might have been a chief, but young Persune was a powerful enough warrior so that if it really came to a showdown in combat, he would kill Johnson and Johnson knew it. Trying to use his authority didn't work because this fellow had given his heart to Josie, and he tried to treat her like a lady. Course, he did rape her.

This discussion was in a confidential sort of conference, during the legal trial, but I know that to be the case. The young warrior Persune fell so damn much in love with her that he just begged and begged her not to go back to the white people, to stay with him and be his wife. Well, she had no intention of doing something like that. Later she went to Washington and became quite a lady. There wasn't any way she was gonna stay out there in a tepee with some warlike Ute, though she was grateful for his protection. Without it the whole bunch of them would have raped her, and that would have been a much worse deal.

Them women had a bad time of it—all of them, including the old lady, old Mrs. Meeker. They was all molested, and they got a good picture of what happened to the squaws. They told how Johnson had got real mad once at one of his squaws up there by Cottonwood Lake, and took a Goddamn rawhide quirt to her. They said that her screaming was something terrible. Now, that's the kind of bastard he was. He was just a no-good son of a bitch, like I done told you. We should have shot him when we saw him, but we didn't get that done.

Mrs. Price was there, too, of course. She'd made it through all right, and so had the little girl. But it didn't mean a damn thing yet, because, by God, we still had to get them out of there. We had to get permission from the Utes to leave peaceful or a lot of people was gonna die. That's what we were there to do, but then, how was we going to do it? There was three of us, and thirteen of Ouray's Tabeguache warriors, to fight the northern Utes. Right at the moment there weren't very many warriors around, but it sure would have been a matter of war if we just started to walk away with them gals.

God, we hadn't been there five minutes when out of the bushes comes Johnson and some of his warriors. He'd heard that we was coming somehow. Boy, he was roaring mad, and so were some of the other Utes. The only one that didn't come was Douglas, he was down watching Rifle Creek, holding an ambush to prevent Merritt's troops from coming through there.

It was a real tense situation, and while we was there, of course, they all crowded around—the women was kinda in the center of it—and our Utes was pushing up to get close. The southern Utes hadn't talked much during the trip coming up there. I'd only heard them talking the night before at that conference, and then only quickly. The funny thing was, I'd thought some of them words sounded familiar. I'd thought, hell, it's a different language, until I picked out one or two words that, by God, was Shoshone words.

I wasn't no good with other languages, and I couldn't do much good in Shoshone as far as really speaking the language was concerned, but I could understand a lot of things. I'd pick up a lot of words, and of course, when Wild Rose would talk to me, she would talk to me slow and then I understood almost everything she said. If I didn't understand, she would start over in English. So I kept listening the best I could, and I'd pick up various words from time to time. Now, they was all talking, gathered around, and there was quite a lot of hoopla going on. I sensed that of our own Utes, half of them was in sympathy with Johnson and them other northerners, and things was tricky there. As it turned out, the northern Utes was mad as hell that the Tabeguache Utes had come in there to help the white man.

Of course, what Ouray had been saying all the time was that if this Goddamn war went bad, the Ute nation would lose everything. Now, if they could help settle this fighting, they could preserve part of their reservation holdings. If they could just calm things down, they wouldn't lose everything as a result of this madness. Course, at one point Ouray had been thinking about maybe the whole Ute nation joining in one hell of a war to just kill all the white troops that were there—kill them all, kill every white person, kill the agents, and just kill everybody. Then reason got the best of him, and he seen that, Jesus Christ, there was two hundred thousand whites in Colorado at that time and, hell, they'd really form up and there wouldn't be no Utes left.

Up there on that mesa at Cottonwood Lake they was getting all excited. Everything Johnson's Utes had done was now gonna be declared wrong, and all the captives they got was gonna be taken away. No, sir, they weren't gonna give in that easy, and some of those of our own party of thirteen Utes was kinda swinging over to their way of thinkin'. You could hear the words going fast.

I moved over close to Adams and said, "General, it don't

sound as good as it might, does it? I heard the word *kill* several times and I've heard some other things, like some names. I don't follow it altogether. The only language I know is some words in Shoshone.''

He said quickly, ''Yes, Brules, the language of the Uintah Utes and the Shoshone are relatively the same. They are the Uintah Aztecan group.''

Now, I remembered that Stanley at the agency had said something like that, but when you talk words like *Uintah Aztecan,* I don't know what the hell you're talking about. They say that those tribes were related, not physically or anything like that, but somehow in the whole language system. I don't know quite how that works, but that's what they said.

I knew that the senator was also a general in the reserve, that's what Stanley had told me. So the first time I seen him get anywhere near combat, I started calling him ''General'' instead of ''Senator.'' I said, ''General, if I hear correctly, we could be in tight trouble, isn't that right?''

''Yes, it is a very difficult situation.''

''Well, I'll tell you, General,'' I kinda whispered to him, ''I'm in too close to do any good in action. I'm gonna ease off about thirty or forty feet away, where that tree is over there—that big ponderosa—and I'm gonna be standing by that and listening.''

''Yes, that will be a good thing for you to do, Brules. In case of any quick action you would have a chance of surviving.''

That made me kinda sore, and looking him straight in the eye, I said, ''That ain't what I mean, General. What I mean is that I've only got six shots in my revolver, and the revolver is all I can use up close. If you give me a little distance so I can swing the barrel of that Winchester of mine around, I've got seventeen shots. If we can work out a signal, you yell or something, then you and the count pitch yourself on the ground, so that you don't get hit, I'll clean out most of these Utes. They'll be running, but I'll bust 'em before they get to the timber. There's more of 'em than I've got bullets for, but we've got to figure that some of the Tabeguaches will hang with us.''

"I certainly hope that's the case, and your idea is a good one—at least we've got some military backup now. That makes me feel a lot better."

I said, "You could say *now,* for the signal."

"No," he said, "I'll say *wow* and you'll hear that."

"That's fine, that's just fine, and then you and the count hit the ground."

"Yes, I'll talk to the count about it right away."

So I just slowly eased back. Jesus, those fellows was arguing and shooting off their mouths, and I must say Adams was as cool as hell, and so was that count. They wasn't taking any shit off these Indians and it was wonderful to see the way they handled themselves. I thought, boy, I'm with the right gang this time. I slowly moved back of that big tree, kept watching, holding my breath, and gradually, without being too conspicuous about it, raised the barrel of my rifle, inch by inch, to almost a level angle where I knew that it wasn't gonna take me but a fraction of a second to get off the first shot. Then I was gonna be shooting as fast as I could work the lever, and, boy, there was gonna be a lot of dead Ute bucks around there. We were all going down, maybe, but we would be going down fighting.

Well, the wonderful part of it was, it never come to that. What with the diplomacy Adams used, and that old German count just standing there, absolutely still, with them blue, blue eyes a-looking at every Ute—one after another, just steady as a rock—the Indians gave in. There wasn't any doubt that them German boys was gonna give a good account of themselves when they come to anything. Fear was something that they didn't know nothing about.

It was a hell of a place to be, and the average guy would have lost his nerve and been scared shitless, but not these two gentlemen. Even the Utes on our side were getting excited.

We were there for five tense hours. Each time we would get down to the nut cutting, Johnson and Colorow would say, "We are not going to release those Meeker women, until you stop the cavalry coming down Rifle Creek."

We were saying, "Well, hell, we aren't going up there and

stop the cavalry coming down Rifle Creek, until you release the women.''

Five hours of this struggling, and none of us had had any sleep. We'd ridden all the day and night before, and Adams and von Donhoff had ridden two days before that, and they were plumb exhausted. They were gray with fatigue, but them saber-scarred veterans never blinked an eye.

Finally, Johnson asked Adams, "How sure are you that you can stop Merritt's column from coming down here?"

Old Adams says, "I'm Goddamn confident about it. I can do it, if you just let me get going, but we're gonna waste the whole day sitting here arguing."

It was about two or three in the afternoon. Adams told Johnson, "That's a pretty good ride from here, and I've got to get going."

Well, it finally come to that. The Ute chiefs agreed to release the women, and a lot of tension was suddenly eased off, and there weren't gonna be no fight.

I want to tell you that there was plenty of quiet rejoicing among most of us, because if the situation had exploded, the women would have got killed right away. Old Adams, you gotta hand it to him, never losing his temper, taking it easy, getting insulted every now and then, but he didn't lose his guts. He was a fine example of diplomacy under threat of death, and when he ended up, he had it all pretty well cased. The women were brought together, Mrs. Meeker, Mrs. Price, Josie, and the girl, and they all started down the trail. Not the tough way we come up, but another way that they figured would be real easy, though it was a little farther way to go. It was down off the middle of the Grand Mesa, somewhere down near the towns along the North Fork.

Count von Donhoff, that tall, elegant-looking German fellow, was to take the women back to where the buggies was waiting at White River, and then on to the Los Piños Agency. Of course, most of our Ute warriors went with them, and I don't really know how they made out, except that sooner or later them women got to Denver. That's where the big hearing was, and where everybody heard about how bad they had been treated.

Meanwhile, the important work for Adams was to cross the Colorado River, go up Rifle Creek, and stop Major Merritt from coming down and fighting the Utes.

The way General Adams had handled things was the smart way to do it. The women was safe, they was on their way: the Ute chiefs had decided to surrender and join Ouray. The only thing that we had to do was stop the cavalry from blundering ahead and screwing up the whole deal.

We made our way down and across the Colorado, which was not too bad that time of year. As we headed up Rifle Creek and come on Merritt's camp, we damn near got our asses shot off. All them soldier boys was just as tense as they could be, sentries and everybody else—here they see a bunch of Indians coming, a couple of white men with them, and they didn't know what the hell to make of it. It was after dark, and at the sentries' challenge, we advanced to be recognized, hoping that we wouldn't get shot to hell before we got in close enough to make ourselves understood. After Adams explained the whole thing, the sentries got the captain of the guard, and he come over and listened to the whole story again. Then he said, "Well, that's all fine, but whether we advance or not is up to Major Merritt."

"Take me to Major Merritt immediately," Adams said.

The captain of the guard shrugged. "He can't be disturbed, he's sleeping in his tent."

"Well, by God, I'm a general, and I'm ordering you to do this."

"Sorry, sir, you don't look like no general to us."

Adams sure as hell wasn't dressed like no general. Christ, I would have had the same attitude as the captain of the guard. Adams didn't have any identification, he just looked like a damn scout or something.

By this time we all was just done in and exhausted. Christ Almighty, we had ridden all the night before, been in five hours of tough conference there where the balance of everything, our lives included, was just hung by a thread. Then we'd had to ride another forty miles, cross a river, and come up on these bastards, and that wasn't no good.

Anyway, Adams turned to me and quietly said, "Well, Brules, what do you propose we do?"

"General, I'll get to Merritt's tent, and I'll get his attention, if you want to see him."

"Frankly, I could stand a couple of hours' sleep. Can you get him up in that time?"

"Yes, sir," I promised.

"They aren't going to move anywhere for three hours, but they might start early in the morning, so we'd better get to them."

"General, you just tell me when you want to see him. I'll get to his tent and I'll wake him up."

"I'm sure he's got his guards all around there," Adams pointed out.

"I'm just telling you, General, that when you want to see him, I'll have him here."

Adams laughed a little and said, "I expect that maybe you will. But what do you say that we take a nap, right now."

That's what he done, he just laid down and went to sleep, after he gave the captain of the guard a good cussin'. While they was all talking, I just slipped away in the dark. I left my rifle with my knapsack, and eased off into the camp real quiet. Everybody was looking at Adams and nobody was paying any attention to me.

I slid down through the camp and come to where I seen some soldiers standing guard, and I knew Goddamn well that was Merritt's tent. I didn't have anything on me that would make any noise or anything. I had my trousers tied on with a rope, and the ammunition belt was covered with a flap to take care of any scraping noise. I went on my hands and knees like a panther for a few minutes, and then slid right down on my belly, and started moving like I was coming up on a Comanche camp. You know something: I had a lot of fun doing that, 'cause there wasn't no Comanches out there. They'd be real tough to come up on like this, but them dumb pony soldiers didn't hear nothing nor see nothing. I went right past the lines in the pitch dark and come up to the tent and felt around, seeing if I could lift a corner. I had to cut one of the tent ropes to do it, and I done that real sly and slow.

I crawled in real slow, and there was old Major Merritt sleeping on his cot. Seeing all that damn equipment that had to be carried for him, all the blankets and his tent, his own cot and everything to sleep on, I thought he was traveling in royal style. I moved across the floor of the tent real easy, got up beside his cot, and kneeling, I took him by the neck just below his throat.

I put the pistol barrel up against his head and started tapping real gentle like. Boy, he woke up in a hurry. "Hold still," I told him, keeping my right hand on his throat and choking, so he couldn't yell or nothing.

"Major Merritt," I said, "I know that you're getting your beauty sleep, but Goddammit, you got an important mission here to take care of. You've got General Adams here to give you a military message. We just come from rescuing the Meeker women—they're on their way back to Los Piños—and you've gotta stop your march, right here."

He twisted and turned, but I went on, "Let me tell you something. I'm gonna ease off your throat, and I'm gonna let you talk, but don't make a lot of noise or I'll kill you. Don't sound any alarms, just keep it down to a whisper."

I eased off him a little bit, and he said, "Who are you? Who are you, anyway?"

"Just take it easy. I'm one of your friends, I'm a scout for General Adams, and we've come through by order of the Secretary of the Interior. Made contact with the Meeker women and got them headed back to the railroad. The promise was that we wouldn't rush the Utes. You can get up and meet with General Adams. He'll tell you all about it. I ain't gonna explain nothing. The only thing I'm telling you is you ain't going to give any alarm."

"Well, you Goddamn—"

"Now, I don't like to hear that kind of stuff from an old military man. Just stand up real easy. I know it's a surprise to you and all that, but I'll kill you if you move. I'm not gonna walk out of this tent holding a gun on you, 'cause you got some guards. I'm putting my gun away now that you're calmed down and you ain't breathing so hard."

"Why," he spat, "I'll have you put in irons, by God, before we get through here."

"Yes, sir, you can do anything you want about that, but right now I'm escorting you out to talk with General Adams."

"Ah, shit. What's going on here?" He shoved open the tent, and when the guard snapped to attention, he asked what was going on.

By this time Adams had woke up. He was standing right outside the tent a-fumin' and cussin', and so he was surprised and pleased to see me.

The guards said, "Major Merritt, there is a man here that needs to speak to you, sir."

He said, "Who is it?"

With that Adams said, "I'm General Adams, attention."

The colonel come to attention and said, "Yes, sir." He couldn't see Adams, and I guess that he figured that the big man was in uniform and everything. Adams started talking to him, straight and hard. He told him who he was and that he had ridden four hundred and fifty miles to stop the troops. We had the Meeker women, he explained, and had made a promise to Colorow, Johnson, and Douglas that the troops wouldn't move. He wanted to be damn sure that the major got that order and got it solid.

Dawn was beginning to break, and the colonel finally saw who he was talking to. At first he almost didn't believe it— Adams not being dressed like a general. After a while it all sunk in, though. Adams talked with such authority and knew so damn many people to mention, that pretty soon the colonel began to see that it was really all right. He cooled down and said, "Please, General, step into my tent. Won't you have some breakfast?"

"You're Goddamn right I'll have some breakfast, if you can get it."

So they went in to set on a couple of camp chairs around a small table and finish discussing everything. Before he went into the tent, Adams said, ''You better send somebody to the cook tent right away and bring this man some food''—pointing to me. ''He is just as hungry as I am, and he's ridden a hell of a distance. We're all tired and hungry.''

The colonel said, ''Yes, sir. I'll see that's done.''

Two of the men were sent over to the cook tent, and pretty soon they came back with some grub and some coffee. I must say that I was glad to have it. Meanwhile, Adams was in the tent with the colonel, and I could hear their voices talking about different things. After daybreak the colonel and general stepped out, and the colonel was all smiles, saluting and all that.

The colonel knew about Adams, of course, had heard about him. Everybody on the frontier had heard of Senator Adams, even the sentries who were standing around agape and everything and couldn't believe what they was hearing.

Of course, everyone was all smiles, and there wasn't enough that the colonel could do to accommodate General Adams, him being a kinda legend in his own right.

Merritt told him, ''I already had orders to stop here.''

''Well, Christ Almighty, you mean that we have ridden all this Goddamn way to stop you, and you were going to stop anyway?'' Adams asked.

''Yes, sir,'' the major said, ''I believe that is the case, but—''

''Well, I'm glad that Brules knocked your ass out of the sack then. I can turn around and go back now. Christ, you might have slept until ten o'clock in the morning and delayed me that much!!''

''Oh, no, sir, I would have been up by six.''

''Right now we need some fresh horses, and we're gonna get the hell out of here,'' Adams told him. ''You're going to stay right here, Major, and you aren't to move until you get new orders.''

''Yes, sir, I understand that,'' Merritt replied.

Well, we got the hell out of there, quick. We got some supplies from the cook tent, and, by Jesus, we really stocked up this time. Damn if we was gonna starve to death on this route.

Adams was feeling pretty high and happy about everything. He'd kept his word to Johnson, and he'd stopped the soldiers from going in and knocking hell out of them Utes. As a matter of fact, it was a damn good thing that Douglas and Johnson didn't know beforehand that Merritt had received orders to stop, because Adams wouldn't have had that bargaining point.

It all ended up good. It was an easy way out. You know, if you can solve something without fighting, you're a hell of a lot better off, but still you've got to be prepared to fight. That goes for nations just as damn well as it goes for men. If you're prepared to fight, prepared to stand up, lots of time folks will back off, 'cause basically it don't make no sense to fight if you don't have to. Now that I'd said that, it occurred to me I was still looking for a fight. Just what the hell was I going to do?

We got off real early and it wasn't much past six-thirty or so. There had been about an hour of daylight, we had fresh horses, and we was moving right along. Adams never spared nothing when he was riding. He just kept us moving. Hell, by four o'clock in the afternoon we was back at Los Piños. Our horses was wore out, but we was there.

When we got there we found out that the Meeker women had been received, and old Ouray was just plumb delighted. He was real nice to them and a-bowing and a-scraping like he could, an old gentleman.

Ouray was immensely relieved, when them women come through, to see they was all right. The women was packed in the gig, fresh horses brought up, and they started off to the railway at Alamosa. I imagine with relays of horses and all that, they probably made it in two days. It was a long damn ride, but by keeping those horses moving, and putting on fresh horses, they would make it.

I had been there, of course, for I'd come down the Gunnison last time in '75 from Cochetopa Pass with Wild Rose. At that time she done told me I was going to be a daddy. That was five years ago. Hell, lots of things had happened in the

West during that time. I learned that the telegraph station run clear into Lake City. So it wasn't too much of a job for a courier to make the distance in a day from the telegraph station at Lake City to the Los Piños Agency.

On the other hand, it was a hell of a lot different situation up there at the White River Agency, because the nearest telegraph station was Rawlins. You had to ride a hundred and twenty miles to Baggs and a hundred and twenty miles from Baggs to Meeker. If you wanted to go the other way, it would be much longer. You had to go down the Colorado and clear over to Ouray and back up to Lake City. Either way Meeker was a remote damn place.

Now, when we come into Los Piños, we told them at the agency that we'd had a talk with Major Merritt and that he'd been stopped in his tracks, not only by General Adams's orders, but, by God, by orders from the Department of the Interior. Well, you could just see the relief when old Chief Ouray got that information. Hell, he relaxed and was all smiles, and damn if he didn't want to pour some whiskey. Hell, we all had a drink. I sure felt a lot better, and it was kinda a joyous time there for a while.

Then Adams said, ''Well, as soon as we get something to eat and get rested up here, we're gonna start again.''

''Well, General, what's the big rush?'' I asked.

''Let me tell you something, son.'' Taking me aside he said, ''I'm not at all sure, just from the way the ladies were hesitant about saying anything, what went on. But when they begin taking evidence, somebody will find out. Newspaper reporters have a way of getting to things, and there is gonna be a military investigation. Now, I agree it's a fine mess, if those Utes can kill our soldiers—and you know they killed Meeker and ten employees of the agency—and get away with it! We can't have that kind of thing happening. We have got to have a fair trial and get it straightened out. But I want to make sure that when the women are questioned, the information doesn't get into the hands of the reporters like the *Rocky Mountain News* or *The Denver Post*.

''Jesus Christ, white women raped by the Utes! There are

many people that want to take over that whole Ute territory, run the Utes clear out of Colorado. They don't give a damn if they drown the Indians in the ocean. They don't care what they do with them, as long as they get rid of them—just like the Texans wanted to get rid of the Comanches. These Utes aren't all bad, and it's hardly fair. They had a hell of a big reservation and they're going to lose most of it right now, but we can't have this thing get out of control, so I must go to Denver.

"Now, Brules, you're one of the finest scouts I have ever known, and I want you to come with me. I need you, and I have a job for you. I'll take good care of you. I'll have you stay with me in my house in Manitou."

"General, I sure think that you're one of the finest guys I've ever worked with too. I've got nothing but admiration for you, but, sir, I've got a wife I just married, and I can't go off and leave her again. She don't understand this military stuff."

"Ah, yes. I remember her farewell when we left the other morning."

"Matter of fact, she is coming right now—she's coming on the run. She must have heard I'm here."

"Good God, she's a beauty," he said. "I don't blame you, Brules."

26

Winter Plans

Well, here come Melisande running. She just jumped and threw her arms around me and started kissing me and hugging me. She was crying to beat hell too. At first the officers laughed and enjoyed it, but when she kept a-crying, they kinda got embarrassed and moved off.

I was awful glad to see her. When she put her arms around me, and I felt that beautiful soft face of hers up against that grizzly old beard of mine, which she didn't seem to mind, I almost cried too. She kept a-kissing me on my lips and hugging me and putting her body right up next to me. I was getting the message all right, and I decided that the military could rest for a while. I'd given them all I had. I was taking my wife and going somewhere else. I didn't know where, except right then I was going back to the cabin we'd been given at the agency.

I had a thing or two I wanted to tell her, and I wanted to be with her for a little while. I weren't gonna be just talking. She wasn't acting like that's all she was interested in either.

Well, arm-and-arm we went off together and nobody bothered us none. Of course, when we got to the cabin, she broke down again and said, "I've been so terrified, I've been so worried. I heard all the terrible things that's been happening. I know what Indians do to people when they catch them, and I heard nothing from you, and then finally the Meeker women came in and they were all right. I thought you'd be with them.

Then I found out that you went on way up Rifle Creek or wherever it is, where you could still get shot, maybe.

"I can't stand this. There's no way, Brules. You mean everything in the world to me. You are all I have. I'm with you body and soul, I'm yours, I'm absolutely yours. You've got to be mine, because I can't live this way without you." She was sobbing as if her heart would break.

When I finally got her quieted down, I said, "I understand."

"I don't know if I can stand this scouting business of yours," she said.

"Well, hell, it don't look like I'm gonna do much more scouting. There isn't anything more to do. The Utes is the last that has blowed up, and there sure as hell isn't nothing in Wyoming. All them Sioux are on the reservations, and I don't like that military life anyway. Ranks don't mean nothing to me, nor the pay they give me—pay me one hundred and fifty bucks a month or some damn thing. Course, that is a lot of money, but, Jesus Christ, I can make more than that hunting grizzly or doing something else, like tradin' cattle."

"Well, let's just not part anymore," she said. "I have something very special to tell you and I'm very concerned about it."

"Sweetheart," I said holding her hands and looking at her in the eyes and kissing her every now and then. Boy, she was a beautiful girl. I was so happy to be back with her, my heart was overflowing. "How did you get along with Mrs. Stanley?" I asked.

"Oh, fine, fine, but, you know, she looked at me and said, 'Oh, you must have lost your wedding ring somewhere along the way.' "

"Oh, Jesus Christ. Both of us plumb forgot about that! That's my fault. I'll go right over to the store and buy you one, you betcha. The best damn ring we can find."

"I know you will, but we have to have a ceremony too," she insisted. "When we were out there in the desert and alone, in the canyon country, we were fine, but now we're with people, Brules, and we have to abide with their customs, and we—"

"Marrying don't mean nothing, I mean—"

"Yes, it does, yes, it does. It means a lot to a woman," she said. "It should mean a lot to a man too. And, I can tell you, it means a lot to everybody around us. So if we want to get along with people, we're gonna have to do it."

I started to rebel again, and pointed out, "That is the damnedest fool thing, ain't nobody married more than we are."

"I know that, but we've got to show the rest of the people that this is the case, and that we respect their customs and traditions." Putting her hands on the side of my face she held it close to hers, and said, "Please, you understand, we have to go through a regular ceremony."

"Honey, if you want to do that, you don't have to talk to me twice. If that's what you got on your mind, you are gonna have it right away. How do we do that around here?"

"There's a missionary at the agency. He's a man of God and he can marry us."

"Well, hell, let's get the son of bitch here right away."

"No, we have to do a little bit of arranging things, and we have to . . . let me talk to Mrs. Stanley and see what we can do. We have got to have a regular ceremony."

"Regular ceremony, shit—excuse me. Yes, ma'am, we'll have that, but let's get it going."

She laughed. "Gee whiz, most men are kind of spooky about getting married and don't want to hurry things up. Here you are just pushing for it."

"Hell, them guys ain't got a beautiful wife like I do. Of course I'm ready. You're mine, honey. I'm taking you wherever we go."

Well, to make a long story short, we went right up to the agency store there, where they had all kinds of stuff for the Indians and trinkets and one thing and another. We found something pretty damn respectable in a wedding ring, and I bought it. It cost twenty-eight bucks, and I give it to her.

"No, you can't give it to me now, you have to give it to me during the ceremony," she told me, pushing it away.

"Well, come on, let's get going."

"I want to talk to Mary and—"

"About what?" I asked, a little put out.

"You have got to get dressed up, you know. After all, you've been traveling quite a bit recently, and those clothes are not exactly—"

"Oh," I said, "I forgot about that, honey. Goddamn right. I'll get out my fancy—I got to find—where the hell did we put the pack off Alfred?"

"Alfred, you should hear Alfred," she said. "He's just singsongin' all the time, his heart is broken. You and the stallion went off without him and he's been complaining about it ever since you left. He felt as bad as I did."

"Let's get right over and see him, by God."

I took old Jupiter, who was tied up outside, by the lead rope, and Melisande by the hand. The three of us walked to within a couple of hundred yards of the corral. Boy, old Alfred seen Jupiter and us, too, and you should have heard that son of a bitch put on the damnedest symphony. He was a hee-hawing and going on something fierce.

A funny thing happened. Jupiter kinda raised his head, as a gentlemen and thoroughbred, an aristocrat. Yes, he kinda raised up his head, arched his neck, and sorta twisted his head around a little bit, as if he was saying, "Well, now, don't be crude, Alfred. I love you just like everybody else does, but if you're traveling in our company, you can't be crude."

By God, we got within about fifty yards of the corral and old Alfred, seeing that his manners weren't good, stopped. He just stopped and stood there looking at us. I want to tell you, them big old eyes of that mule, seemed like the tears was coming down. When I went in there, he come up to me and Jupiter, and he made such a fuss over all of us that Melisande said, "Isn't he a wonderful, wonderful animal? He knows all about this. He's so glad to see you're back."

"Damn, it's too bad we don't have an apple for him."

"I have been over in the agency store taking care of things

like that, Cat Brules.'' With that she reaches in the big bag she's carrying on her shoulder and here come a couple of apples. She gives one to old Alfred and it went *wang,* right up into his throat. As soon as she fed it to him, it was gone. Then she gave the other to Jupiter. Jupiter being a thoroughbred and a gentlemen, he curled his lips back from his teeth and gently bit the apple, in the most refined manner.

Melisande and me, we just got to laughing about it. Sometimes you see horses get together and stand with their necks around each other, kinda crossed over, but you don't see a horse and a mule do that. By God, old Jupiter, he didn't bother none on dignity or nothing, he just went up and got face to face with that mule and begun rubbing his head against the mule, and the mule was rubbing back and didn't make any noise. It was just as if Jupiter was saying, ''Now, Alfred, if you shut up and quit that awful braying of yours, I'll stay right here with you and we'll get along just fine.''

It was a sight to see. From there me and Melisande went over to the cabin, and I asked, ''Why don't you go see what you can do about making arrangements for the wedding? I'm going over where there's a kinda bathhouse rigged up—you pull a rope and a bucket of water slops on you and everything.''

''What are you going to do about this?'' She put her hand all around that big beard of mine.

''Oh, by God, honey, I plumb forgot about that. I've got to go down and get to the water, where I can get a reflection.''

''No, no,'' she said, ''you don't have to do that. I have a mirror.''

''A mirror?'' I said. ''Hell, I ain't looked in a mirror since I was a kid.''

She brings out this nifty little hand mirror, and I'm looking at it and thinking, holy Christ, how can she love a man like me? I look like a damn gorilla.

Well, anyway, real quick I thought I better get along with it, and I went over to the bathhouse, and, man, I cleaned up. I needed it. It's a wonder that I didn't chock up the whole system with the dirt that come off me from that trip. Anyway, I got all shaved, and put on a new shirt and an extra pair of britches and my best pair of Comanche moccasins, turned down to below the knee.

I thought that this was one time that I should wear a belt and not a rope around my waist. I took my concho from down Taos way, and I put that on. I looked kinda spiffed up. I picked up some torn cloth that I had in my possessions—was a piece of a flag that I'd found, all shot to pieces, at the battle of the Little Big Horn. I cut it like a bandanna, tied it around my neck, and stuck it down in my shirt. By God, I found an old comb, and even got my hair all combed out.

Melisande come back, all excited, and said, "Oh, they're gonna fix it all up. Mrs. Stanley is gonna arrange it. They'll have a wedding party and everybody will come, and the missionary will marry us. We're going to have a ceremony. Guess who's going to give me away?"

"Who?"

"General Adams. When he heard about it, he came right to me and asked me if he could give me away. He said that he'd never seen a finer man in his life than you. You miserable old bum! And he said he'd never seen a more beautiful woman than me, and of course, he was right there! So he's going to give me away and you'd better act nice, because he might not, at the last minute, decide he wants to give me away to you."

"Well, the son of a bitch better make up his mind now, because if he ever gets a notion like that, there'll be all hell to pay."

Melisande laughed and threw her arms around me. "Come on, hurry up. You look so wonderful. Gosh, you know what you look like?—like when you were at that barn dance that Daddy had for the cowboys. When you came in you almost knocked my eyes out you looked so handsome, and that's why I went up and hid, waiting for you. You broke my heart when you didn't come."

"Never mind all that stuff, honey," I said. "Look at how wonderful things is right now. Now, how does this look?" I strutted around showing off.

She began to straighten up a few things on me, and she

patted me on the chest. She made me turn around and said, "Oh, you look so swell." She hooked her arm in mine. "Now we're going. We're going to get married."

We was married there the next day in the missionary chapel of Los Piños Agency on the Ute Reservation. There was a few white people at the agency, and some Indians that was hanging around, but also there was Chief Ouray. By God, he done brought Chipeta, his wife. That was the first time I met her. What a great gal she was. Boy, she was a kinda queen. She knew where she stood about everything, and I don't know whether she could read or write, but she sure acted like it. It was easy to see that she was one hell of a lot of help to Ouray. She arranged things and was right in the middle of stuff.

Stanley, the agent, and his wife, Mary, were there encouraging us. Just before the ceremony they all got to laughing when I told them about being through a lot of Comanche wars and fighting Sioux, and being plenty scared at times, but never near as scared as I was now. Melisande rocked her head back and forth, and said, "He's just a big boy. He's not quite sure of himself yet, but he's a wonderful fellow and I'm certainly glad I'm marrying him." She said that all in a kinda meaningful way and some people got teary.

Well, damn if old Adams didn't insist on giving away the bride. He'd had a good night's sleep at the agency, but I knew he was itching to get going again, because all the arrangements about the release of the women and the capture of the Ute warriors was gonna be tough to handle and would need a lot of doing.

It was truly a joyous occasion, and Mrs. Stanley fixed up some eats after the ceremony. During the wedding I kept saying the wrong thing. Every time the minister would start to say something, I just didn't want to make any mistakes so I kept saying, "I do, I do, I do." It didn't make no difference if they was asking me a question or not. I just wanted to be damn sure that we was married and this woman was mine.

She'd keep poking me a little bit every time I made a mistake—telling me to shut up—but I didn't care. There was giggles in the crowd of whites when I'd pull a boner. The Indians didn't understand; they didn't know the ceremony any better than I did, so they didn't know when to cut in or cut out. The missionary asked me, and he asked her, "Do you take this man to be your lawful wedded husband?" and I kept saying, "I do," to be sure everything was covered.

So, that's how I come to get married. It was some kind of swell having a general give the bride away, you know. Even if I couldn't figure out what the hell was he doing giving her to me when I already had her? Civilized folks have strange customs. No wonder the Indians was confused. I decided I wouldn't get confused about it, I'd just go along with the whole show. It was all right with me as long as I had Melisande with me.

After the wedding von Donhoff and Adams hit the trail to the San Luis Valley. Instead of going across Cochetopa Pass, which seemed to me to be a wild and beautiful way, they took another trail. Otto Mears, who was gonna be the big railroad boy in Colorado history later on, had done built a toll road from Los Piños Agency to the Continental Divide and down into the valley of the Rio Grande.

Anyhow, von Donhoff and Adams took out with a couple of packers and some extra horses. They figured to ride it all the way through, because they was gonna have to have a damn Indian commission meeting in Denver soon about the whole Ute uprising. Meanwhile, the northern Utes was supposed to bring Colorow, Douglas, and Johnson and them other Ute Chiefs into Los Piños, and keep them there until there could be a commission meeting at the Indian agency in a couple of months.

It was a joyous time for a while around the agency there, and me and Melisande was kinda the center of attention. She kept working on me to sleep inside the cabin instead of outside. I realized she weren't no Indian squaw, she was a white girl, and although we may have camped out all summer, by God, her natural instincts were to be inside of a house. If I was gonna be with her, I was gonna have to do that. Well, I agreed to do it, but only if she would just spend time with me once in a while, out under the stars. She being a congenial and loving gal, she agreed.

Meanwhile, I didn't know what was gonna happen to us on this military thing. I didn't mind doing the job for General Crook. He was a real fine man and I was proud to serve with him, although most other military action I would just as soon avoid. What I figured was, I would just kinda wait there to see what was gonna happen. Then I thought, that's crazy, Brules, first thing you know they will ship you off to some other place. Right now you have a damn good gal, and you better take her along with you and get out from under this military deal right now.

I had Melisande write a letter addressed to General Crook, and had it put in the next courier dispatch. In addition to that I done sent a telegram to General Crook, by the Lake City telegraph, telling him that I wanted to go on extended leave again as I still had some hunting to do. I knew that he would understand. I told him I felt like I'd done my job as far as the Utes was concerned, and didn't see how he'd do anything that would need me from now on. After all, it wasn't time of war, so a military man, including a scout, could resign when he damn well pleased. So I told him I sure enjoyed serving under him and all that, but it was time I moved on. Besides, I was just married.

Well, move we did. I got to talking it over with Melisande. Winter was coming on, and we didn't want to go back to living in the canyons, and we sure as hell didn't want to go back into a civilized place like Denver. We'd be damn fools to go up to the forts at North Platte or anywhere along the Yellowstone. That wasn't no life to live, especially in the wintertime. The winters up there was real horrible.

First, we talked of going to Arizona, but I got to thinking about it. With our stock and all, I knew that we'd have to go across the Navajo country. Kit Carson had argued back around 1868 that the Navajos should be returned to their home country after the time of their imprisonment at Bosque Redondo. So a year later they was back and all supposed to be peaceful, but it was one hell of a big reservation, and riding through there with a white woman could start some trouble.

Then I hit on a thought. Goddamn, them old mountain men had the right idea! Each year when they got through trapping up around Jackson Hole and Green River, back in the thirties and early forties, they'd head for a nice place to spend the winter. That was Taos.

I had happy memories of Taos. The more I got to thinking about it, the more I realized Melisande would sure like that pretty country. That Taos pueblo was really something now, and them Indians was all quieted down. They'd had the hell kicked out of them by Kit Carson a long time ago. It was a beautiful kind of place and still had a lot of that old Spanish atmosphere. She'd been raised in a stiff Mormon family, and it would be kinda nice for her to see how different the Spanish was. I knew that she'd like the singing and the dancing, and it would be a hell of a time and place to spend a honeymoon.

So I told her, "Pretty quick now we're gonna pack out of here and go south for the winter."

"Where are we going?" she asked me.

"Honey, we're going to Taos."

"Taos, Taos. Where have I heard about that before?"

"Well, that was a place that belonged to the Spanish before the Mexican War, and now it's a nice place for us to go. There's a pretty mountain there, and there are lots of nice Spanish buildings," I explained.

"But," she said, "I don't speak Spanish."

"I know you don't, honey, but you'll pick it up fast, and they speak English too. God knows, I don't speak too awful good Spanish. We'll get along and it's a beautiful place." I told her all about the Indian customs and the dances and all that. How pretty all that country was, and I knew that she'd have some fun in seeing it. I reminded her how we'd seen them cliff dwellings down in the canyons, and sometimes we'd seen setups where the pueblo was built away from the cliff.

"Oh, yes, I remember that."

"Well," I said, "you're gonna see a real Indian pueblo and the way they live. The buildings are about four stories high, and I want to tell you, they're beautiful-looking places. You better consider going there with me.''

"Cat, you know that wherever you go, that's where I'm going.''

"Okay, but I want to take you to a good place. I don't want to ride you into the mouth of hell somewhere, and that's easy enough to do. There are still some awful bad places,'' I warned her.

"Oh, stop talking like that. Come on, Taos sounds wonderful, and we could go down to Santa Fe, too, couldn't we?''

"We sure could, and you'd enjoy it. You could see the Governor's Palace.''

"Palace?'' she said.

"Yeah, the Governor's Palace is down there. They have a lot of good things.'' I told her how pretty all that country was, and soon she could hardly wait.

We stayed at Los Piños for a few more days, until I got ammunition again and we got our supplies.

With Alfred, that big old two-thousand-pound mule, we could pack a hell of a load. Melisande could take some dresses that she'd bought at the agency store, and all kinds of things that she wanted—flour, bacon, coffee, and some pots and pans and dishes—all that kind of stuff that she hadn't had since she left home. After all, she'd left Ezra Slade's farm barefoot, as I remember, and almost bare assed. She didn't have nothing, so we had to get equipped again.

I want to tell you that it did her a lot of good to have all them officers and the Indian agent paying so much attention, and the ladies realizing that she was a lady. But after a while I began getting some kind of a funny feeling about, Jesus, maybe I'm traveling in high company with her, and here I am nothing but a damn scout. If I was gonna keep this girl, seeing the way she was handling things, I was gonna have to spruce up too. It kinda irritated me a little bit to think about that, but then, the more I thought about it, the better I thought it was. I did know that if I was gonna keep Melisande, I couldn't take her into a civilized place like Taos or Santa Fe or Denver without looking decent.

Well, the more I got to pondering on it, I realized what I could do about it. One thing, I could shave maybe twice a month and try to look like something that she'd be proud of, but I was damned if I was gonna give up my inside character. Brules was still a man of the plains and mountains. He knew how to shoot and hunt and fight and ride, and those little capabilities he wasn't gonna throw away.

About a week later we got a message back from General Crook, a kinda commendation for Scout Brules. It read something like

> *This command has been advised of your superb services in connection with rescuing of the Meeker women, and your great assistance to Senator Adams. You have been recommended for a decoration, and your request for leave has now been approved. You will be on extended leave. Good luck and good hunting.* Then he added, personally, *Adams tells me that you married a beautiful white girl. Boy, that is something, Brules. You'd better bring her around, I'll bet she's a sight to see. I hope that you're very happy with her.*

You know, I hadn't had nothing said about any women I'd had before, but I got to thinking, my God, this girl could get along most anywhere. I bet she'd get along at them officers' dances or something like that. She'd know just how to act, 'cause after all she was basically a lady. She wasn't no fancy lady from St. Louis or Chicago or nothing, but she was a good, sound gal, and women would take to her too. Goddamn, Brules, you have some social problems, ain't you? But, hell, as long as we loved each other, it was gonna be all right.

Melisande had to have a good horse and a riding outfit of some kind. I finally woke up to the fact that she wasn't gonna be riding behind me on Jupiter all the time and she wasn't gonna ride no mule. I talked to Agent Stanley and he said, "Aw, hell, we've got lots of horses around here. I'll sell you a horse."

"Yeah, but I don't want no broke-down Indian pony."

"No," he said, "we've got some pretty damn good horses. Chief Ouray, he's got some out at his farm there, and he knows a good horse when he sees one. He's spent plenty of time on them."

"I reckon he has. I'll go see if he'd sell me one for Melisande, and then I got to get a saddle."

"There's all kinds of saddles here. Christ, you can find anything around here. Somebody would sell you an old saddle."

"No, she's got to have a brand-new saddle, and a good one."

He laughed. "They got some in the agency store."

Well, I picked out a hell of a nice little saddle for her. She was so pleased when I showed her, she was a-kissing me and everything, so that it was almost embarrassing-like.

We rode north ten miles to Ouray Farms. That old boy wasn't feeling very good, but he come out and smiled. I guess he kinda liked us. He was moving kinda slow-like and looking around. It was his struggle to try to hold the Utes together that finally had got him down. He knew that no matter how bad or tough things were, the tribe had to keep from losing their temper. The idea of killing whites was crazy: all it was gonna do was cause the whites to ship them out to some hopeless desert place, and he didn't want that. He loved his mountains.

Well, I told old Ouray what I wanted. He spoke pretty good English, and maybe better than mine. When I told him that I was in need of a horse, had to have a horse for my wife and all that, he nodded plenty. We went out into the pasture, where he'd point to the different horses with his cane. Finally we saw one real pretty sorrel mare. Boy, she was a pretty thing, with a blaze and four white feet. He said, "This horse for you. Your squaw like this horse."

Melisande said later that she bit her lip when he called her a squaw.

Anyway, I bought the mare for one hundred thirty bucks, and she was well worth it. She was a good horse and served Melisande well.

Melisande was so pleased and so excited about that little

sorrel that she kept hugging and kissing me, and hugging the horse. After a while I said, "You love that horse more than you do me."

"No, I don't, my darling, but I'm really crazy about her. She's beautiful, just beautiful. I know that she's going to be fine—you picked her out for me and I will name her Tina."

"Yes, and you're gonna find out that she's a prancer," I explained. "And she's gonna have a single-foot gait, which is gonna be real sweet. You won't go bouncing up and down or anything. That animal will make real time going across country too. It's gonna be a great pleasure to you, just wait and see. Now, one other thing about it is that, normally, I don't like to have mares around other horses."

"Well, why is that? What's wrong with mares, just 'cause they're girls?"

"Yeah, just 'cause they're girls. In the first place when they come in heat, especially with stallions, you got all hell breaking loose. A gelding sometimes thinks that he's a stallion and gets to romping around acting funny so he's hard to control. But when a *mare* isn't behaving herself and really wants to raise hell, she can get your whole remuda going the wrong way, and it's quite a problem. That's why they aren't very popular among a lot of mountain men or trappers and hunters, or a lot of cavalry outfits."

"I don't understand that. I think that's nonsense."

"Well, you are gonna find out whether it's nonsense when this big seventeen-hand stallion starts getting himself all worried about the horse you're riding," I said. "My advice to you is you'd better get off her quick."

She laughed. "Yes, I think I'd better. My, that stallion is a big fellow. But I don't know why male horses—stallions—have to act so silly."

"Well, I don't know either, dear. I tell you, women just drive men crazy."

Changing my theme, I started worrying about where I ought to sell those grizzly hides.

"I don't see why you have to go away to sell them. Why can't you supply them to agents?" Melisande asked.

"What? Have them steal me blind?"

"Every man isn't a crook. There must be some men who are pretty decent, who would be straight," she said. "It is just a matter of trying to find out who the reliable people are. You take a bank. Some bankers, I suppose, are crooked, but there are bound to be good banks. There was a good bank in Moab."

"Yeah, I guess so," I agreed, "but to tell you the truth, I've never been to a bank."

She looked at me wide eyed and asked, "You haven't?"

"No, I just figured I'd rob one, one time."

She gasped, and I laughed and explained. "Oh, that was with Pedro Gonzales, and I done told you all about him. That's when he and I was gonna rob that bank in Taos. Course, the best thing we ever did was forget it, because we probably wouldn't have got much out of it and we might have wrecked our lives. I found this out: It's too easy making a living going straight. It would be a real big mistake for a man or boy to start cutting the corners."

Another thing that was bothering me a little bit was I begun to realize I was gonna have to give Melisande a decent break as far as living was concerned. I couldn't always have her packing along like an Indian woman. I knew that she'd been ranch-raised. She knew how to ride and milk a cow; she knew how to plant and hoe and wash clothes and cook and do all kinds of damn things. It wouldn't be so easy if she were some rich gal who had been raised in a big city. On the other hand, there was a big difference between Melisande and an Indian squaw.

Squaws are built for the wilderness and their very nature was kinda wild. They could stand all kinds of misfortune, and they didn't look for anything except a good lodge or tepee and some good horses to haul things around. A good hunter to keep them happy, feed them, and go with them to a rendezvous once in a while, and that's about all.

Things was gonna be different with Melisande. I knew that she had to have a house, but how in the hell was I gonna sleep inside a house?

I had a beautiful ranch in the Broken Bow. Me and Wild Rose had been real happy with it, and we seen how easy we could keep cattle in that area. The grasses were high and there was plenty of water and feed, and the snow weren't too heavy on the south side of old Lone Cone. Many's the time it passed my mind, should I acquaint this girl with that ranch? Then, somehow I decided that I couldn't do it, because the death of Wild Rose was still only three years in the past. Sure, I could have another woman, but I didn't think I could take that woman to a place where my Wild Rose and I had lived so happily. At least not for a long, long time. Maybe the best thing to do was just to say nothing about it now.

Then I got to thinking about kids. Supposing we had some kids, I said to myself—hell, what do you do then! We can't keep doing what we're doing all the time and not have any kids, unless something was real wrong, and I didn't hardly see how that could be. Can you imagine getting children to school from the ranch? God, that would be impossible. And then if they got sick, how are you gonna get them to a doctor? I thought I better put that Broken Bow Ranch out of my mind for a while.

Yes, that's what I better do—I'll take my beautiful girl to Taos, she'll love it there.

Besides the horse and saddle that I bought for Melisande, I thought that it might be a damn good idea to get her a nice little rifle and teach her to shoot. I couldn't think of any gun that would be better than that Winchester '73, but with just a thirty-inch barrel and chambered for a .32-20, which wouldn't give her no trouble to shoot. That little saddle gun was short barreled. It was light, it was small caliber, and it carried, I would say, maybe ten shots in the magazine. I don't remember rightly, 'cause I never used it very much—it was too light a gun for me to fool with. I don't reckon that you could kill an elk with it, unless you hit him in the head, which is pretty hard to do. It didn't have no real power for a shoulder shot or anything—that took a much bigger gun.

Incidentally, while we're talking about it, best thing to use on an elk was that Buffalo Sharps that you seen on my wall that Crook gave me after I worked with him down in Arizona on the Geronimo campaign. Them .50-caliber Buffalo Sharpses would lay a buffalo or an elk down real easy, but otherwise elk would carry a lot of lead. Boy, you use those light Springfield rifles, and if you didn't hit him just right he'd run off.

Anyway, I'd been telling Melisande all about that kind of stuff, and she was so excited that she couldn't see straight. I got some old newspapers to make targets out of, and we went over by some trees. I nailed the damn things to the trees and really worked with that girl to get her so she could handle a rifle. I showed her how to load and unload, how to put on the safety, how not to carry the thing with the hammer closed against the pin, but back against the safety—just about an eighth of an inch so that it would lock and not go off if you fell and dropped it—and how not to carry any shell in the chamber unless you really had to and was getting close to action. That was a good idea, 'cause you still have enough shots in your magazine to handle almost any game you come on.

We was going hunting, and I guessed that we could probably spend three weeks or so before snowfall. What I figured we'd do was just work them three forks of the Cimarron to see what kind of hunting we got. If it started snowing or anything like that, we'd get right down off that high country and move down to the creek bottoms.

I wanted to make sure that we didn't wait so long in the fall that we couldn't cross that damn Spring Creek Pass over there by Lake City on our way to Taos. So, one morning, we got all our belongings in the world onto Alfred, and we shook hands with everybody and got their blessings. Mary, the wife of Agent Stanley, was almost in tears as she seen Melisande going off, because she'd become real fond of her. Them two women had kinda the same backgrounds and they got along fine, and Stanley and I got to be pretty good friends too.

Anyhow, we pushed off one fine morning and followed the Uncompahgre up a ways and branched off and followed Cow Creek. We kept a-going until we hit that little stream that was coming off Owl Creek Pass and started up there. There was lots of game and most of the game was still way high up, because there wasn't any snow yet. Of course, we seen bands of elk, but funny thing, we didn't see no white-tail deer in that country, none at all—just mule deer.

It was beautiful, beautiful country. We did some hunting. The days went by pretty fast, and we was lucky, 'cause the weather held. We slowly climbed toward the pass leading into the West Fork of the Cimarron. We had to go across the foot of the north side of that enormous castlelike mountain called Courthouse Rock, squaring up against the sky at about twelve thousand feet. We swung around the base of that natural fortress and entered the basin of the West Fork of the Cimarron. It was grizzly country! I could see tracks and signs everywhere, but somehow we never seen a bear. I don't know why, but that's the way hunting goes.

We climbed out of the basin to that flatland that lays to the south. It then got to be easy traveling, and we circled around the headwaters of the Middle and East Fork of the Cimarron. Looking down toward the north it looked like pictures I'd seen of Yosemite.

We pushed on and made good time, passing Uncompahgre Peak to the south. By late afternoon we came around the mountain and looked down on Lake City. When we got above Lake City we made camp that night. I sure as hell didn't want to go into a mining town with my beautiful wife and have no place to stay, so we camped out. The next morning we pushed off about daybreak and made our way into town. It was just a good old mining town with a couple of whorehouses, a half-ass hotel, a store, and a bunch of corrals. It sure was a real shack town.

I was lucky to find a blacksmith's shop—I wanted to have one of Jupiter's hooves checked. I thought I'd detected a loose shoe, and I'd nailed it on best I could. It didn't take the blacksmith long. There wasn't nothing the matter with the shoe, just a loose nail that he pulled and reset. I'm telling you, he took one look at Jupiter and said, "Jesus Christ, where did you get this beautiful son of a bitch?"

I told him that General Crook had given him to me. I

could see he was thinking, you lying bastard, but he didn't say anything, just nodded and went on, figuring that maybe I'd stole it somewhere. When he come out and seen Alfred, he said, "By God, look at the size of that mule. Boy, ain't he something. That's a *beautiful* mule."

I said, "I think he's homely as hell, but he is plumb beautiful too." We both laughed.

By that time it was around ten in the morning, and I looked around to see if there was a Chinese joint. I knew that I didn't want to go into the hotel—they might have good eating and they might not. But if we could find a Chinaman's joint, the food would be all right. Well, I didn't find one, but I did find a general store and I bought some flour, coffee, and sweets that I thought maybe Melisande might like. She was standing outside holding the horses and, Jesus, I come out there and I was plumb shocked. Standing around, about halfway across the street, was a bunch of rough-looking miners. Them hard-rock sons of bitches were really tough looking, and they was all looking at my wife as if she was a fine horse or something. They was cracking jokes and seemed to be admiring every part of her.

Melisande was well aware that she was being admired. She was goin' to a lot of unnecessary effort checking the saddle blankets of the animals, walkin' around the horse and the mule, patting and straightening up harness. She was wearing tight blue jeans and boots—them Levi's that old man Levi introduced to the West twenty-five years ago. By God, she was swishing her backside to beat hell, and damned if I know why women get that way. Especially young women, it seems like they just gotta cause some attraction.

Well, by this time I was beginning to steam a little bit, and as I walked up she said, "Are we going to stay for lunch, Cat?"

"No, we ain't. We're on our way, baby. We're going to Taos. There ain't nothing in this damn place, just bad men and women."

"Well, some of those men are mighty handsome," she answered teasin'.

"Hey, cut it out. Get on your mare and let's get goin'."

She kinda laughed and swung on. I knew that she was kidding me just to get me wrought up, and it was workin'. As we headed out of the town, I could hear some remarks being made and a lot of laughter going on. I knew what those son of bitches was saying, and I just hoped that I could keep my temper and not have to kill any of them.

We got out of town and started up for Spring Creek Pass. We could pick up Otto Mears's toll road, but where we come on it wasn't any toll 'cause it was at the end. It was just a kinda wagon trail that went over the Continental Divide. When we crossed that, we'd drop down into the Rio Grande and be in good shape, with nothing to worry about. But we had to get across Spring Creek Pass before those heavy snows hit or we'd be in trouble.

I told Melisande that we'd better get over the Continental Divide. Once we crossed over there and dropped down into the Rio Grande, all the water that way went to the Atlantic and all the waters on this side to the Pacific. She got excited at the idea of crossing the Continental Divide, since she'd heard about it for some time. Spring Creek Pass was not high, only about ten thousand something feet.

We rode all the rest of the day and crossed about four o'clock in the afternoon. As we crossed, we looked down into the headwaters of the Rio Grande and it was mighty big country. To the west was all the drainage of them high mountains of the Uncompahgre. Looking at those peaks, we knew it was wild country and soon would be deep in snow. I sure was glad we had made it. Many times the difference of one day could mean that a damn blizzard come up that would last for a week, and you couldn't get over till it melted, and that would be next spring.

Now we was over and we was gonna winter in Taos. I looked forward to that. I kept telling Melisande she'd seen the dirty little mining town, but wait until she saw a beautiful town like Taos. That Taos pueblo has been there a thousand years, they have kept that place clean and decent, and it was real colorful and nice.

"Well," she said, "do they ever have any fun there?"

"Let me tell you, there is dancing and singing in the streets all the time. There are always festivals—they just have a wonderful time there. These adobe wall towns, you should see them. They're pretty as a picture. You've seen those Anasazi cliff dwellings at the bottom of the canyon, but now the Taos Indians live there. They've got a big sacred mountain back up there. You're gonna love it."

Well, she got more and more excited and said, "Yes, I'm looking forward to it. You say there is dancing."

"Oh, yes, there is gonna be a lot of dancing and music." I just built it up, but I didn't have to build it up that much, because that's the way Taos was in them days. It sure was a hell of a lot better place than a town like Lake City.

By this time I had Melisande excited enough that I didn't get no back talk. We dropped down and made fast time coming off the hill, which was the beautiful upper part of the Rio Grande watershed. We didn't make it all the way to the river before dark, but I wanted to camp a little early as I had a couple of things in mind.

I picked a nice spot on a little creek that was a tributary of the Rio Grande where there was plenty of feed. I moved off about a mile and a half from the trail so there would be real privacy. I got the animals picketed and we got our bedrolls all set up. I will say that Melisande was catching on fast. She knew how to make a shelter that would keep the rain off our heads, and she done real good with that.

She was working with some of the cooking utensils and I said, "Honey, come on with me, take my hand. I want to walk with you here and explain to you a couple of things."

"Okay," she said, taking my hand. "What is it?"

"You know, honey, when you're around a bunch of men like those miners in Lake City, you gotta be careful and not flirt, 'cause them guys are hungry. There's nothing but whores in a town like that and they haven't seen a decent woman for years, and here you are a plumb beautiful girl."

"Well," she said, "I like people, and I like men to admire

me. That makes me feel good, and some of them were strong-looking fellows."

"Yeah, they're strong all right, and hard up as hell. There just might have been some trouble, and I'd've hated to have to kill any of 'em."

"Kill them! I wouldn't want that! Why would you have to kill any of them?"

"Well, if one of 'em made a bad remark or bad pass, I'd probably paste him. If he reached for his gun, I'd have to kill him. If you don't want me to kill 'em, don't attract 'em around like flies."

She said, "Well, I wasn't doing that."

"Yes, you were."

"No, I wasn't!" With that she stomped her foot.

I looked at her and said, "You know what you need? You need a good spanking."

"Oh, what are you talking about?"

"Well"—I laughed—"I kinda got an idea that I ought to give you a spanking right now, by God. That's a good idea!"

Of course, she saw that I was half kidding and half serious. She started running and I chased after her and caught her. She was kicking around a little bit and was saying, "Oh, now, Cat, come on."

I said, "No, sir. This is as good a time as any!" There was an old log sitting there, and I sat down on the log and turned her over my knee.

"Now, you stop that, Cat!" She was kicking to beat hell, but me being about four times as strong as her, she wasn't gonna move.

Then she said, "Now what are you doing?"

"I'm taking down your pants! I'm gonna give you a good bare-bottom spanking."

"Cat, now, stop that! You are not going to do any such thing."

I was laughing, keeping it in a light vein. "Yeah, it's about time. Hell, yes." Natural as hell, I figured, a guy spankin' his new wife for actin' up. What's wrong with that? I kinda reached around in front and unbuttoned her blue jeans, and just pulled 'em down, by God!

She was wearing boots that come down around her knees and her jeans wouldn't pull down any farther, but there was her beautiful bare bottom. I want to tell you, that was a sight to see. Oh, God, she was a beautiful woman. She was kicking and twisting.

"Brules, I hate you. Stop this! What do you mean by doing this?"

I smacked her once good on the bottom and thought, boy, I really laid my brand on there, 'cause it's getting red with the sign of a right hand. This is *another* one of Brules's signs, I thought.

By this time she was saying, "Ouch! Now, stop this instant. Don't do this. You're acting crazy, Cat."

"Well, I don't really think I am," I answered, but then I stopped completely and said, "Goddamn, Melisande, you know something? You ain't got no whip marks on your bottom anymore."

"I haven't?"

"No, you ain't. There is one place over here where there's a little bitsy white line now, and there's another one over here, but that's all. All the rest of you is, Jesus, beautiful! It's just like it was before."

"How do you know what it was like before?" She kinda raised up on her elbows and twisted around as best she could to try to take a look at it herself, but she couldn't see very well from that angle.

"Well, I saw it a minute before the whipping started, and it sure was beautiful. We'll go someplace where there's a mirror and you can take a look for yourself, but I'm telling you, it's just as pretty as can be. There is nothing wrong."

She said, "Well, I don't want some clinical examination, Mr. Brules."

"I don't know what kind of an examination you're talking about, but whatever it is, I'm examining it and it sure looks good to me."

"You stop that," she said. "Let me up from here. I'm going to pull my pants up."

I said, "Just a minute, I got a whole new idea—much better than spanking." I put my hand back on her again and she relaxed completely when I said that. She wasn't kicking, she just laid absolutely still for a minute, and then she turned slightly and raised herself up and put her arm around my neck. She pulled me down to her and gave me one hell of a kiss. That was the kind of kiss that meant everything: you're my man and I'm your woman. You better take me when you can. I said, "Listen, I've got your pants halfway down, kick them boots off. I've got better plans than this."

She started to giggle and got rid of those boots in a hurry. I was so eager for her, I was trembling all over. She started fooling with my belt and it wasn't very long . . . I tell you, that was the greatest lovemaking I'd ever had. To this day I remember that it was real wild! You know, there is that moment when you're with a woman you love and you finally take her! There ain't no description for it. We was just wrestling for our lives. The sweat was running off both of us, and of course, when I gave her all the love I had, we reached a climax together. We curled up for a few minutes while I held her in my arms and we looked up at the blue sky all around us. There was nothing else in the world besides the two of us.

Suddenly Melisande started to laugh and pointed across the clearing. Jupiter and that damn Alfred was looking right at us with their ears sticking way up in the air. You could see 'em saying, "What in hell is going on?" We both burst out laughing and I said, "We had us an audience."

"We sure did, but I don't care. Look at Jupiter. What do you suppose he's saying?"

I said, "Well, with his nose in the air like an aristocrat, he's saying, 'Really, really, now, you know they shouldn't be carrying on like that right out here in the open.' "

We both laughed and looked at old Alfred. He was staring at us with those sad old eyes and them floppy ears. He just seemed to have the wisdom of the ages. He kept looking awhile, and seemed to be saying to hisself, "Well, I'll be damned. Ain't that wonderful? It's the way of the world. Now I'm going back and start eating again.'' Both of them put their heads down and started chewing in rhythm.

All I knew was that I had my gal. She was the most wonderful, exciting girl in the world. If I could just live this way it would be fine. I didn't want to do anything more. I just wanted to live with her the rest of my life, and it looked like that's what we was gonna do.

She hugged me and kissed me and told me what a real man I was, and how strong I was. She said she was so proud of me, and when she was in my arms she felt protected and I was the one to love her. I could have anything I wanted.

I said, "Well, now, you just kicked about my spanking!"

"Well," she said, "if you really want to spank me, Cat, that's okay too."

"Hell, I don't want to spank you, I want to kiss you, but if I ever get the idea I want to spank you again, I'll let you know."

"I'll bet you will," she answered.

Anyway, we spent the night there. We started off again next morning, and worked our way along, making pretty good time down to the Rio Grande River. We went on down through Wagon Wheel Gap and busted out into the San Luis Valley, still on the road running to Del Norte, and then on another twenty miles to Alamosa.

I'll never forget Melisande looking at that telegraph line stretched out, running across the open sagebrush stretches of that great big valley. The valley was damn near seventy-five miles long and fifty miles wide, and ranged by high mountains all around with snow on their peaks. I kept thinking, boy, you know, twenty miles down here and there's a railroad, and we can go anywhere we want from here at fifty miles an hour in ease and comfort, by just buyin' a ticket.

27

Taos

We kept riding hour after hour until we finally hit the trail that run from Fort Garland down to Taos. I thought of going along the road to Valdez's ranch. Then, I decided, no, I'd better leave things alone. It had been five years since I was there, and maybe the old boy was dead or something. Maybe the kids were around and wouldn't be too friendly to me, wondering who the hell the woman was I was bringing around. No, it's too complicated, I'll just go on into Taos. I can look up the Ruiz people later on, after we get settled. We're gonna make our own way.

So we made one more camp out in the valley of the San Luis, and that was a dry camp. We couldn't do nothing about that. I had a canteen and we had a little water. Since we'd watered the horses crossing the streams as we come, it wasn't bad. The next morning I kept pointing out Taos Mountain and how beautiful it was. We rode through the Arroyo Hondo, kinda funny Mexican farms, and we popped out on the plateau. Taos Mountain to the east of us, all covered with timber, was the sacred mountain of the Taos Indians and stood up there, looking just beautiful, as slowly we come up on the pueblo of Taos.

I want to tell you, Melisande's eyes just popped open. Boy, she couldn't believe it. Like Finerty used to say, the thing about these pueblo dwellers, they looked just like Arabs in the North African desert. They wear kind of a shawl over their head and their shoulders and they stand there looking out. They don't seem to say nothing, just stare at the view, taking in life.

I knew it would catch the imagination of that gal, stir her up, and it sure did. God, she was so happy. She turned to me, and said, "Oh, Cat, I'm so glad that you made me come here. What a difference. This is beautiful, a beautiful place. Moab isn't as good a place as this, and surely neither is Lake City. This is just wonderful."

"That's the only two towns you've ever seen, isn't that true?"

"Come to think of it, that's right."

"Well, no comparison. This is a wonderful place, these people have been living here for a thousand years."

"A thousand years!"

"Yeah, way back. Maybe as much as two thousand years. Nobody knows, but they have been living here because it's a great place to live."

"It certainly is. No wonder those mountain men used to come down out of Green River and stay here. You couldn't blame them for wanting to spend their winter in such a place."

As we was riding along real slow-like and looking around, we studied the people we passed on the street—some Indian gal with a jar on her head and a young Mexican woman in a shawl, and others. They was all pretty handsome, and I could see that Melisande was very interested. Especially in the colors of their garments and everything, because she'd never been used to anything like that. Americans dress pretty plain, and the Mormons in particular are that way, sort of not liking to put on a show, but the Indians and the Spanish people are considerably different. They love color everywhere. You see it in the paintings, their decorations, in the horses they ride, and in the way the women dress.

Of course, we took a long look at the pueblo, the two different pueblos, one on each side of the stream that run through there. In back Taos Mountain towered, and Melisande wanted to know all about it. I didn't get into it that much, because I didn't know nothing about the Taos Indian religion. I knew a little about the Sioux and a little about the Comanche, but I didn't know nothing about these folks.

Well, we moved on a little bit and come into the actual town of Taos—the white man's town. A lot of its buildings is built the same way—they're adobe houses, kinda borrowed from the pueblo dwellers because their stuff is so beautiful. The Americans and even the Spanish built things different, even though they used the same materials. It ain't quite as pretty as an Indian pueblo, but still it was a nice town, that Taos. A lot of big old cottonwood trees hanging around, and a marketplace and a plaza and all that. We was going along slowly, with the horses just kinda ambling and clip-clopping, looking for some livery stable or corral where we could bed down the stock.

We heard somebody singing in a beautiful Spanish high-pitched voice, full of melody, you know. There was faint notes of a guitar too. Sometimes when you was around an Indian pueblo, you'd hear a drum beating or maybe a flute playing, and the Indians singing with that sorta chant they had, but when we was in the Spanish town, it was a guitar and them beautiful voices we heard. I tell you, it was just plumb romantic. Melisande reached over and grabbed my hand and held it as we rode down through the streets.

I was a little away from the quarter where my friends, the Ruiz family, was when I last seen them, but we weren't gonna see them right away. We just wandered around and looked at things and finally found us a livery stable that seemed all right. It was run by a fellow about half Indian, but he sure as hell knew horses. You could tell that by just the way he acted. When we came in there, we caused quite a sensation. Some Indian cowboys, a couple of mule skinners and packers from the States, and some other white people was there. It wasn't like the old days, I guess, 'cause there wasn't any trappers there, the trapping business being all out of order.

Boy, when I rode into the corral with that beautiful stallion, you ought to heard them whistle. They took a liking to that horse right away, 'cause they could see what a hell of a horse he was. Then old Alfred, he just come along and stood there in his dignity, that two-thousand-pound mule, packing one hell of a load as if it was peanuts. He wasn't gonna take no guff off nobody.

Well, I bartered with the fellow that run the stables, and told him I wanted our stock took good care of, and asked if I could get a farrier to maybe reshoe them.

He had a saddle room there that was under lock and key, which looked good to me, and we put our saddles and pack outfit in there. We just laid down our packs in the place he kept a lot of stuff. When we lifted that pack off old Alfred, by God, we realized what that mule had been packing all this time.

To give you some idea what that mule could do all day long, up and down mountain trails: the load didn't bother him at all, but I couldn't lift it by myself. I had some help from the other fellows, and it took about four of us to get the pack off. I had the pack pretty well covered up with a tarp so you couldn't see what was in it, but them grizzly hides kinda worried me. They would be real easy for some son of a bitch to steal, and I knew that I was gonna have to get rid of them soon. I had to do something with them. Hell, this was clear down in November, but they was well salted and I took good care of them all the time, kept them from getting wet. I thought they'd be good: they wouldn't be slipping or anything, and they'd still be prime, but I couldn't hang on to them too damn much longer.

I got to thinking maybe I could sell them here in Taos, have them shipped out by one of them wagon boys, or take 'em down to Santa Fe. The railroad was about three quarters of the way out to Santa Fe, across the plains. It hadn't quite got there yet, but there would still be shippers at that point.

Right then I couldn't do anything until I got looking around town a little bit, just like I done before when I was with Pedro. I found out that there was a need for mule skinners and stuff like that. Maybe I'd have to work my way down to Albuquerque or something. I didn't know, but I knew one thing: I was gonna have to get them grizzly hides under consignment, and make some kind of a deal with a shipping company to move them. I figured that they would bring some good money in Denver, and that was the place to take them. Chicago was too far from the frontier to have folks appreciate grizzly hides, but Denver was hot for 'em, with them mining families there making a lot of money. I'd heard things was going real well, they was building what they called double-breasted mansions on the squares with all them red stones, towers, and all kind of stuff. Man, Denver was a going Jesse about that time.

Anyway, I told the stableman I was gonna leave my pack there, and I'd take good care of him if he take good care of me. I didn't want the pack opened or anything to come out of it. I didn't tell him it was grizzly hides. He probably thought it was cow hides. I said, "Ain't nothing but hides, but still they represent considerable work for me, and I don't want them messed up. I'm just looking around for a place to live."

"Well," he said, "there's a boardinghouse here. It's almost like a ranch house, you know."

"No, I don't think that's what we're looking for. We're looking for someplace we can stay for the winter, a small house or something."

"Oh," he said, "there's a lot of them around. Just go down in the plaza, and there is two or three stores where guys are selling or renting places like that. You may find one."

"Okay. That's what we'll do, and I'll be back here this afternoon. I don't expect to find anything wrong with this. I'll pay then for everything."

The old boy looked at me and saw that I meant business. He said, "You betcha, sir. It's gonna be just like you leave it."

I took Melisande by the hand and we started strolling around the plaza. Melisande just loved that plaza. Them Spanish towns have everything going in the plaza, all kinds of life, shops, marketplaces, and all kinds of people visiting and talking. Life is going on at a big rate, and it is real different from the main square in one of our towns in the Midwest or South. Them places got a big courthouse and kinda lawns around it, some cannons standing up on the front lawn that come out of the big war, but life in general is kinda formal, with people coming and going for business reasons. It don't quite have the same atmosphere and color that a Spanish town has got. Them Spanish make them plazas the center of all life, and that's where you meet people, and where all sorts of news travels. It's just different and real colorful. That suited Melisande just fine.

Before long we was able to talk to some folks and find out about some places we could rent. Sometimes we was having to talk in Spanish. Of course, Melisande had no Spanish at all and me, I just had that cathouse Spanish that I'd developed in places where I shouldn't have been. Between us, in broken English, with somebody to help out, we found two or three places.

In the end we located a place in the south part of town that was a little off the main beat from the road that run down to Santa Fe, but from it you had a pretty good view of Taos Mountain behind it. The house had two good rooms—one for a kitchen and one for a bedroom—and then a little place for a sitting room that would be okay. The thing that was real good was, outside there was a ladder that led to a roof like one of them pueblo roofs with a wall around it. The wall was about two and a half feet high, and that would keep you from rolling off, so I could sleep up there at night.

Right near where the house was, I found a pasture that would take our two horses and mule on a rent basis, so we had them fixed up.

Melisande got used to me sleeping up on the roof all the time, and would sleep up there with me. She not only got used to it, she liked it, looking up at the stars at night. Course, I must admit when a hailstorm come up, we both got right back into the house. For the first week there we just kinda settled in. We got all our stuff from the livery stable and moved in and had things spread out pretty good.

Then we'd just take the two horses and go for a ride around the town or out to the pueblo, looking everything over and just enjoying ourselves and taking it easy. Sometimes we'd walk around the square holding hands. I noticed that when I done that I got plenty of looks because of my beautiful girl.

They had seen a lot of guys like me, a buckskin son of a bitch with a beard, an old hat, a pistol in his belt, a knife, and a used-up outfit. I'd get the come-hither look from some of them

Mexican gals, but I was careful not to pay attention to that, 'cause I didn't want Melisande to get crossed up in any way about me. But, boy, I'm telling you, the men was looking at her all the time. The more I looked at her I thought, God, she is beautiful, with that auburn hair, her complexion was absolutely perfect. You know, just kinda that white-pink that was nice, and wonderful-looking blue-green eyes too.

One of the things that we got to thinking about was the financial situation. I figured that we were paying nine dollars a month for the house, a dollar for each critter in the pasture, and that added up to twelve dollars. Then, we'd have to eat, and could eat easy for a dollar a day. So altogether it would come to a rough forty-two dollars a month.

Well, I had some money left from the grizzly hides I'd sold to Slade, and still had the hides I'd packed with me. The main thing was to try to get them hides to someplace where I would get a decent price. Maybe the best thing for me to do was to go to one of them big shipping outfits.

I seen Hammond and Hammond Brothers and it looked like a pretty orderly place, and I understood that they done shipping. I made some inquiry around and everybody said, oh, yeah, they were a pretty reliable shipper. Somebody said, "Why don't you ask the bank?" Well, I kinda got flustered about that, because I remembered a time when I didn't quite have that same attitude about the bank.

Finally I got my hat into my hand and went in the bank, the Bank of Taos, with Melisande right behind me, looking as if she was gonna own the place. The cashier come up, and was just nice as hell and everything, bowing and scraping to her. I looked at him and thought, Jesus, you dumb shit, if you only knew that it wasn't too many years ago that I was fixing to rob this place.

Anyway, I inquired about Hammond and Hammond, and about bills of lading, and the bank clerk said that H & H had a shipping place in Kansas City where they could take the stuff, and they could have an agent sell it. He told me what their commissions would be and all that. They were reliable people;

if we got a bill of lading from them, then we could borrow against it, because it was good and they were good people.

Well, I finally went over and had a visit with a young guy in Hammond that looked pretty stout, a pretty good man. When I told him what I had, he got kinda excited. He said, "Jesus, that is worth some money. That's good. Where the hell did you get them?"

I told him that I got them over in the La Sals.

"Well, the hides haven't slipped or nothing, have they?" he asked.

"No, no. They was well took care of and, Goddamn, I hope they haven't slipped none, but I packed them and handled them good."

"Well, if they're in prime condition like you say they is and all that, they'll bring a bunch. Are they full-grown bear?"

"Yeah," I said, "yeah, I reckon that there's one four-year-old in there, and it's not that big, but the rest of them is. There's boars, big ones."

"Well, Jesus," he said. "That's worth some money. Now, a buffalo hide ain't worth very much anymore. Of course, now that they're running out of buffalo, maybe they're gonna come up again, but they've killed so many of them out here. Grizzly is rare. I think that maybe, well, you'd pay fifteen percent for selling them and then we'll take—"

"Well, what the hell is that gonna amount to?" I asked.

"Oh, hell, that's not gonna amount to too much."

"Well, that sounds good to me. Why don't I give you half the shipment, and you send it?" I agreed.

I had some grizzly hides left, and I shipped three with them fellows just to see how it was done. I have to say that a month later, I sold them for five hundred and fifty dollars apiece and that run to sixteen hundred and fifty dollars, and they subtracted a percentage, and then shipping costs. So we come out with about eleven hundred dollars plus the money I had gotten from Slade. Being satisfied with the deal, I had Hammond sell the other four. If that gal of mine didn't get extravagant, buying dresses and giving big parties and everything, we could be okay for a long time. I kinda thought that maybe she would, but I was gonna calm her down. She was still a young girl.

There was a spot of late-fall warm weather, and I told Melisande that I wanted to take her across the beautiful Eagle Nest Pass, and give her a view of that mesa country where I used to hunt Comanches. She knew about it from me talking it from time to time, and it fascinated her.

She jumped at the chance. "I want to see that, but what I really want to see is where you, alone with a rifle, took on half the Comanche nation."

"Well, let's pack up and get going. We'll just pack light supplies on Alfred, and with Tina and Jupiter we'll make good time. Alfred can keep up as long as he's got a decent load, and not lugging them grizzly hides around anymore."

So we started over Eagle Nest Pass, all that beautiful country that's in the Sangre de Cristos. In time we come to a point where we could look down over the valley of the Cimarron. I showed her them mesas in the distance, and told her how I'd traveled there sometimes by running and sometimes by riding a horse, and how I'd hunted Comanches all through that country. She was just wide-eyed about it. She had come to understand by that time what it meant, and how Goddamned dangerous it could be. I said I thought, looking back at it, that I was a damn fool to do some of that stuff, but here I was an old man of thirty.

She laughed and said, "If you're an old man, then I'm seventy-eight."

It was a great ride across that Eagle Nest and she appreciated it. When we come back, we looked down onto the valley of the Rio Grande and the Ranchos de Taos, down there at the end of the trail, and she was real excited about all we'd seen on our trip.

Anyway, we settled in at Taos for the winter, and it was a wonderful time. They've got all kinds of holidays, there's the Saint this and Saint that day and then, God Almighty, we had a general and his troops come through. I want to tell you that when them soldier boys seen Melisande, they thought that they'd died and gone to heaven. They sure looked at her. I then got to thinking that having such a beautiful girl ain't always an asset. I might have to worry about her a hell of a lot, and that weren't gonna be no fun.

We was living on pretty much what I'd got out of them grizzly hides, but I told her that we'd take a trip down to Santa Fe along toward spring. "We'll either pack our own horses or maybe I'll get a job mule-skinning."

"Well, I don't want you to do that. What will I do there?" she asked.

"You could ride the mule wagon with me."

"That would be fun for once, but I wouldn't want to get separated from our horses or anything."

"We don't have to get separated from our horses. We could take them along. But that would be kinda much on a deal like that."

I did some work in a rifle shop there, sighting in rifles and honing up stuff. That was work I could do real easy, and they paid me pretty good. It didn't amount to nothing, next to what we got on them grizzlies, but we was livin' pretty high on the hog.

We got along like that all through the winter, and into the spring, and couldn't have been happier. Things was going so good, I kept wondering about family. I said to Melisande one day, "Melisande, do you suppose that we're ever gonna have any kids?"

She stopped and said, "I don't know."

"Well, God, going the way we're going, we ought to have a whole bunch of kids by now."

"You're certainly right, but I don't know. I haven't had any problems and never missed a period. Maybe there is something wrong with me. I know that there is nothing wrong with you, I can sure tell you that."

"Well, how do you know?"

"Well, I just know!"

Well, that was all we ever discussed. I don't really know why, but Melisande and I never had any children together. We did have one hell of a wonderful life, though.

I went around and asked about the Ruiz family that I'd

known before, and I found out that somebody else was living in the house. The new people told me that the old lady and old man had died about three or four years ago, and that the estate sold the house and they'd bought it.

The next June, when I seen the snow on the Jemez Mountains toward the southwest was pretty well melted out, and the Sangre de Cristos on the southeast still showed some pretty good snow, I told Melisande that I had a wonderful trip in mind. That was the summer of 1880, and we rode down to Espanola. I was a little leery of going down to Santa Fe. I thought Taos was as big a place as we could handle right at that time in our lives, but I figured that I wanted to show her some country that I knew about. So instead we went on to San Ildefonso. Then we cut across the Rio Grande just upstream from the Black Mesa. She sure got a kick out of all of that, seeing another Indian pueblo. This one didn't have the traffic like the one at Taos. She got real interested in all the things the natives made, the way they worked with silver and their weaving and all that.

We also went up into the Jemez Mountains. There was a trail that run up to a little mission called Los Alamos, and there was a little church up there. Before we got up there I'd been told by some people around that we ought to look at the cliff dwellings in Frejolle Canyon and the caves in Tsankawi. So we did that, looking out from Tsankawi across the Rio Grande and back from where we come, and seeing the Chimayo Valley, and them beautiful Sangre de Cristos behind to the east took our breath away.

Melisande said, "I've never seen such gorgeous country in all my life. This is the place with absolute eternal peace, isn't it?"

"Well, I had never thought about it just that way, but it sure is beautiful and I get your idea."

"Maybe we could come back here and live here sometime," she said.

"That's possible." I still hadn't told her nothing about my ranch, and I didn't want to talk about that right then.

We took two weeks on that trip and come on back to Taos and had life as usual.

In midsummer of that year, 1880, we made another crossing of Eagle Nest Pass, and from the valley of the Cimarron into that big basin country south of Raton. That trip I got the damnedest surprise of my life.

I called to Melisande, "Honey, come here and take a look."

"Oh, my God, what's all that smoke coming up from?" she asked.

"That's from locomotives—that's the construction crew of the railroad. The Santa Fe Railroad. It's the end of the Santa Fe Trail that you're looking at right there, gal. There ain't gonna be no Santa Fe Trail no more."

Then I told her about the experience I'd had up there in Rawlins when I seen that transcontinental railroad going through there in 1876. God, that railroad had been in there for seven years, and it had sure changed that country. All of a sudden big loads of anything could be shipped—troops, horses, cannon ammunition, freight loads, all kinds of stuff—and folks could go back and forth across the country, in a few days instead of months. Only twenty-five years ago the same damn trip would take you six months, and you'd be all worn out and beat up. Yes, sir, when it come to opening the West, there wasn't nothing like the railroad. I was beginning to feel it, 'cause all the time it was around me.

Looking down at that railroad I was thinking that, the way they were laying track on that road, it was gonna reach Santa Fe by fall. Of course, that's just what it done. The way them engineers and railroad builders could lay track was amazing. They used to say that out on the open prairie, like it was around old Fort Hays, they could lay track as fast as ten miles a day when things was working right. That must have been one hell of a long day, but when you see how they done it, it made some sense.

Building a railroad could be a profitable business, and the more I got to thinking about it, I wondered where I'd been all this time riding horses. Then I kinda laughed at myself and started telling Melisande a few of the things I was thinking.

"You know, just in the last five years I've seen all kinds of things happening in the West. The Wild West is going fast. In fact, very little of it still remains, you know. Imagine them having a telegraph office clear in there at Lake City. I can remember up there in Yellowstone, we didn't have no communication at all. I had to make that ride from Cloud Peak Camp to the Yellowstone by way of the Big Horn Basin, and then get some kind of transportation down the river to meet Custer and Terry. Nobody had heard from anybody—where the hell they were or anything else.

"Well, by the time we left the Yellowstone, in 1878, there was a telegraph line up the Yellowstone quite a ways. I think it run clear, damn near to the mouth of the Big Horn River. Of course, it was a lot faster stringing telegraph lines than it was laying them railroad tracks. God Almighty, all you had to do was have a pole about every fifty yards or something and just run them right straight across the country.

"Of course, you'd get the Indians snipping them here and there. Even so, you could usually get them fixed pretty quick.

"Anyway, the way the railroads was coming in, it looked like they'd just be running all over the place. It was only a question of time, maybe another ten years, and there wouldn't be no place that you couldn't get to on the railroad."

Looking out over them plains, not far from where I'd sat in that rock slide when the Comanche tracking party was coming after me, figuring that with only eight shells and that single-shot Sharps, I was sure gonna be dead at the end of the day, I remembered how wild it had been with the buffalo roaming and all that. Now, the damn railroad was chugging across there and civilization was coming fast. Them railroad trains was getting to be fast and comfortable. I'd been told that now they'd got Pullman cars, that some guy named Pullman had invented a car where there was sleeping bunks in them. There were curtains, sheets, pillows, and toilets on the trains, and, by God, everything. They'd even got a dining car where you could eat. If you were a big man, like the president of the railroad, they told me that you could get a private car that you could ride around in all by yourself or with your party.

I said to Melisande, "You know, if that railroad is gonna to be down in Santa Fe by the end of this year or in the fall, the way they're going, it seems like it might pay us to amble on down there. I'd kinda like to go see that town of Santa Fe. I imagine that it's growed some. Christ, the last time I was there, it was with Pedro before we went buffalo hunting in '68. Good God, that's twelve years ago. Boy, I bet that town has changed."

Melisande hooked her arm in mine, put her cheek up against my shoulder, and happily agreed. "Gee, that sounds like lots of fun, Brules. Let's go. We'll just have a wonderful time. The Lord has given us a great time to live, we're young, full of strength and all that. Of course, you're an old man, Brules!"

"Well, hell, I'm only thirty!"

"But I'm just a girl bride, I'm only nineteen. You old man, you just took me away," she went on teasing me.

"Listen, honey, I'm young enough to handle you." With that I grabbed her by the waist, lifted her up, and held her off the ground.

"Put me down, put me down, now!"

"No, I ain't gonna put you down until I get a good kiss."

She threw her arms around me and kissed me, and I just let her down easy. Ah, that was a wonderful life with that girl, she brought great joy every day on this earth.

We hit back to Taos and decided that in another two or three weeks we'd head south again. We had made a lot of friends around Taos, and it was kinda too bad to leave, but we thought we'd just drift on down a little ways and see what was going on down the road. Man is never quite satisfied with everything he's got, he needs to get more, do something different. Sometimes I worried it might be a damn fool move, 'cause our days in Taos was pure heaven.

Late in October, when the colors was just so beautiful, and all the trees and everything had turned, the weather was the clear fall weather that you get out west. The sky blue, with the snow on the sharp peaks.

We got all our stuff collected, packed our mule again, and put some saddlebags on Melisande's mare, Tina. I don't know why we'd called her that. Maybe because she was kinda dainty and all. Of course, the big stallion, Jupiter, just looked things over as if *he* was planning the trip—not us. I thought, well, you high-bred son of a bitch, wonder which of the great stallions you got in your line. You can't be a thoroughbred and not have one of them. Either you gotta have the Byerly Turk or the Godolphin Arabian or the Darley Arabian. These are horses that date clear back to the 1600s, and that's what you gotta have in you or you can't run worth a damn. You wouldn't be a thoroughbred if you didn't have that in you, but meanwhile we can just kinda quit thinking like that, and wonder why you eat such expensive oats and special hay. You're a good-looking fellow, but you're an expensive S.O.B. You know that? I'd come up and nuzzle him and kinda put my arm around his neck, rub his ears and scratch his forehead, and he'd push up against me.

You know, a funny thing about it. When I would do that, sometimes old Alfred would be willing to take the backseat for a time, but, by God, I was gonna have to spend some time with him too. He was nudging me around—that big old ugly mule, with them beautiful eyes that looked so sad. Of course, when his mouth was open, he looked like he was laughing. When he'd hee-haw like that, he'd show you a set of teeth like a tiger. What a hell of a clown!

Anyway, we ambled down toward Santa Fe and had a real wonderful time. We camped out a couple of times. There was some traffic on the road there, and we'd pass occasional wagons coming and going. It was a fairly busy place, but when we wanted to get off to the side, there was plenty of places in little draws where we could go up and camp.

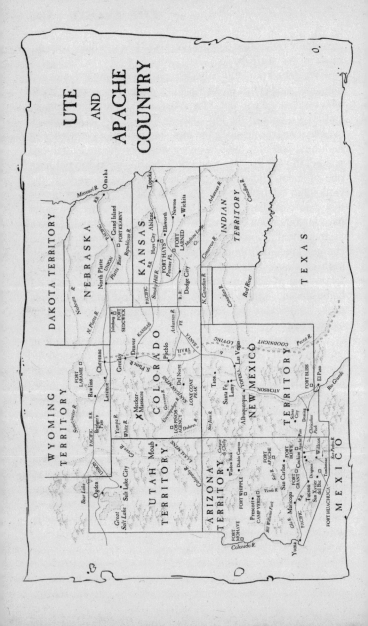

28

Santa Fe
and the Railroad

We arrived in Santa Fe sometime in the fall. I don't rightly remember when it was, but I can remember one thing—everybody knew the railroad was coming and, by God, it wouldn't be long. We made the same arrangements for staying in Santa Fe as we'd done in Taos. Of course, Melisande was all excited, 'cause Santa Fe was the biggest place she'd ever been in her life. She saw the Governor's Palace, the plaza, and them old churches that had been there since the 1600s, you know. God, she just couldn't believe it. Of course, she'd gone to school and she knew something about the Pilgrims, and about the war that George Washington fought, and all that kind of stuff. Still, it was hard for her to get the idea that the Spanish had been in this country since 1540. Santa Fe had been founded in 1609, some sixty years later.

Anyway, history wasn't what we was worrying about now. We was worrying about modern things like railroads. I'll never forget that big celebration for the railroad coming into Santa Fe. Actually, it didn't come to Santa Fe, but the little town of Lamy, just a few miles away. Apparently they was betting on going transcontinental, and that meant going on down to Albuquerque and out through Winslow and all that country out there. That would be a long ways. Santa Fe sure as hell wasn't gonna change its plaza to accommodate the railroad, and I guess the railroad wasn't gonna come up chugging all through that hill country to get right to Santa Fe. So they compromised on the little town of Lamy, about four or five miles from Santa Fe, and it served as a railroad setup.

We'd go out into the country and ride up toward Pecos or something like that and we'd see the train coming along. We could hear it whistling for miles away and, boy, Melisande would want to gallop over to the railroad track and watch it, and then we'd hear it chugging and chugging, coming down the track faster and faster, closer and closer. The old engineer would see us and blow the whistle, and Melisande would scream with delight as the train went roaring by with all the cars loaded with people, looking out the window. All them swells from way back east, New York or somewhere. I tell you, it just changed the world.

We'd sit there on our horses and think, God, even in a dead gallop we can't go as fast as that. I don't know, you'd have to shake your head and think about what was going to happen to the world when those big monsters was doing all that pulling and hauling.

It just meant that there was gonna be a big boom in the West, that's all. I thought that the Indian was gonna fade out with it, because now the Army could move troops around faster. It was the end of the Indian wars.

About that time that we heard, too, through newspapers and talk, about an Indian down there in the Southwest—down in Arizona somewhere. A fellow named Geronimo who'd busted loose.

I'd heard about the old chiefs like Cochise, and as a matter of fact Crook had mentioned to me a few times about his campaign in the Tonto Rim country hunting Cochise, and having real problems with those Chiricahua Apaches, but I didn't pay too much attention to him at the time.

It had all quieted down for a while until sometime last summer, when that damn Geronimo cut loose down there. He was run off into Mexico, after making some raids, burning wagons and farms. Just raising hell. But that was a long ways away and we didn't think much about it. It seemed like it wasn't any of our concern.

We had a nice place in Santa Fe that was up Canyon Road. It had a little garden, and Melisande liked to plant flowers and stuff. She loved the country there, she loved the view. She liked to look out southwest and see the Sandia Mountains down near Albuquerque. Of course, life was so much more active in Santa Fe than it had been in Taos. Taos was kind of a sleepy little town, but Santa Fe, when the damn train come in, the place blew up. They had to have hotels and everything, and we was doing pretty good there.

Well, we lived up there on Canyon Road for about six months and things was just fine, but Melisande was just kinda changed. She was so excited about the railroad and she wanted to know more about trains and what they did. She'd stand and watch them locomotives and be scared to death about how powerful they was, pulling those big loads, and the funny noises they'd made when they was in the station, puffing and blowing. One time we done rode quite a ways down the tracks to watch a train coming in, and she pointed to the tracks.

"It's funny when you look down these tracks," she said, "they all come together a long ways away."

"Yeah, but they're the same distance apart as they are right here. It just looks like that to the eye, but it's not so."

Now, the wonder of these railroads was just something that you couldn't believe in them days. Of course, the railroads had been all through the eastern part of the country long before the great War Between the States. They'd been there as much as fifty years ago, back in the 1830s. The engines had been getting bigger, and the trains faster, and the way they laid tracks better. Now the West was opening up awful fast compared to the eastern part of the country. In the eastern part it had took damn near two hundred and fifty years from the time the first settlers had hit on the coast until they got to the Mississippi River. The whole West was opening up in a matter of thirty or forty years, just with the telegraph lines going out and the railroads coming in.

It was evident that them railroads was like creeping steel claws that stretched themselves through the mountain passes and around over the plains and all the way to the coast.

Well, I guess it was sad, but it was kinda inevitable, it kinda just had to be, and sure, folks was living a little better without it being so savage and all that. With some law and order, towns growing up, and farms and ranches doing well, and all that. That was important, and the Indian way just wasn't good enough for the white people.

Something that come in with the railroad that was kinda interesting was the Harvey House, started by some Englishman of that name. He observed that there wasn't no place to get anything decent to eat along these railroads. At first there wasn't any dining cars, and everybody got hungrier than hell. They'd have to stop and go over to a hotel, but that might be quite a ways from the station and might not be much good.

So Harvey decided to start a bunch of restaurants right in the railroad stations, and called them Harvey Houses. He hired these waitresses who come out from the East. They'd come out on the train free, and he set them up living in dormitories with a supervisor. I mean, he wasn't running no whorehouse, he made that plain from the start. The trouble was that the girls was so scarce out there on the frontier that they was getting married as fast as they went to work in that Harvey House, so they began to look around for married women that was already settled there. Maybe they'd last longer, and the Harvey Houses wouldn't be losing them as fast as they was training them.

Melisande was looking around for places where she might go to work. She wanted to make some pin money, though we was getting along all right. If I got into mule skinning, that was gonna take me away from Melisande or she'd have to travel on wagons, and after she'd made one or two of them trips, she might get a little tired of it, you know. That wouldn't be any good. I had to figure out something to do to stick around. I went down to the stockyards, and after spending some time there, I decided, hell I could make a little money buying and selling cattle. That's what I done. I didn't have to work for nobody; I'd just pick up some good stuff in the stockyards, go to auctions, and put them together and make good shipments.

Melisande saw a chance for a good job and a good time. It wasn't more than four months after the railroad was in that the

Harvey House was set up, and she was down there and looking real perky and everything, and, by God, the manager gave her a job. She was to make twelve dollars a week, which was pretty good. I think she made two or three dollars a week besides that in tips. The only problem was that it was a long ways from our place on Canyon Road, but I was in favor of her having something to do for a while. Especially since we didn't have any children at home.

Of course, we wanted to be together, and I'd been doing a lot of stock trading at them corrals and stockyards, where the wagon train come into Lamy. So, if the railroad was gonna be there, maybe that's where we ought to move down to. There was sure some big shipping yards there, and I could do my cattle trading just as well.

We got us a nice little house in Lamy. There was a lot of houses been built by speculators, and we got one to rent right close to the station.

Melisande kinda liked the excitement of seeing the trains coming in. I liked it all right, even if the smoke from them trains annoyed me once in a while, and I was just as excited as she was about all the action that was going on.

Now I figured, by the fall of 1881, the railroad was going out across to Grants, Gallup, Winslow, and right on to maybe Flagstaff, Kingman, and California, but I sure figured it wrong. Those guys was lots smarter than I was. Instead of them plowing through all that mountain country, they just turned the road and went right straight down a couple of hundred miles to the valley of the Rio Grande, where laying track was real easy. Sure enough they hooked up down at Deming. They made a cutoff from the Rio Grande and left it at Deming, and swung over and struck the Southern Pacific, which was coming in from California. It was another company being financed another way, by a different group of railroad people, but it was enjoying the same system of all that free land.

The way they laid track, I don't think it was more than six or eight months before they was hooked up with the Southern Pacific. By God, there was another transcontinental railroad! Only, this time, instead of being up north along the Union

Pacific route, through Salt Lake and Promontory Point, it was down along the south border of the country.

I want to tell you, that was a big jump. Of course, there was the Texas Pacific coming in from Fort Worth too. It was just amazing what happened—instead of months to go to Kansas City from Santa Fe, why, it was two days and a night. If you wanted to go to Washington, maybe it was three or four days at the most and you was there. The whole nation could feel it—it was just a-throbbing with this thing going on. There wasn't any doubt that we was in the midst of a tremendous kind of explosion in the business and the doings of travel. A lot of wealth had to come out of this as lots more people come west, and they all had to have places to live and they had to have ways of making a living. Hell, America was on its way to one tremendous development and there was gonna be some big, big fortunes made out of all that moving.

Them old fellows like Blair and Gould, and John Jacob Astor of the fur trade, went into railroad development. It was the big deal in the West. The whole thing just changed right around us while we was there.

One day Melisande come in excited as could be and said, "You know what happened today? There were a bunch of the finest-looking men I ever saw that came in on the railroad on their way to California. Oh, they were all dressed up in those black suits, and they had kind of stiff collars and top hats, and some of them had cuff links made of precious stones. All of them had watch chains, and they were well shaved and some of them had mustaches. They were a handsome group of men. They came in and were very courtly and awfully nice to all the girls. They tipped so well. They were carrying on important conversations.

"You know we have a kind of private dining room at the Harvey House, and officers of the railroad and bankers from back east all meet there.

"And do you know what? All the waitresses try to get jobs in the private dining room. There are a lot of girls that transferred here from Harvey Houses in other parts of the country. They all have what they call seniority, and those girls all bid for that job of taking care of that private dining room, 'cause they say that the tips are just swell in there. They get lots of money if they're nice, and they take care of the gentlemen.

"One girl says that you've got to wait on them hand and foot, and when they cut their cigars, you'd better be there with a match and light them, and all that kind of thing. Make sure they've got coffee and everything. Always be fast about the service and you get to know them, the various ones, and know what they like, 'cause they come through back and forth all the time.

"One great thing about the Harvey House," she told me, "is that we girls get passes on the railroad and get to travel all over. We can go back all the way to Washington. If we're there long enough," she says, "we can take our families too."

Then she said, "I'm gonna take you to Washington, someday."

"Hell, I don't want to go to Washington. Maybe if some of them Apaches or Utes or something are going in and gonna have a delegation, it might be kinda interesting to go along. Right now, honey, I'm not anxious to see Washington or New York or none of them places. There too many people around and I wouldn't feel comfortable."

"Well, I know, my dear man, I understand. I'm a little that way, too, but it is exciting, isn't it?" She was just bubbling over.

"Yeah, it sure is, but what do you say we go for a horseback ride up the Sangre de Cristo Mountains, and get back to what is happening around in nature?" I reminded her.

"Oh," she said, "that would be fun, let's do that. I'm tired of wearing a dress, and a skirt and an apron and a blouse. I think I'll just get back in my riding clothes and we'll go."

That's what we did, we went up a ways and run onto a stream and done some fishing and had a good day. We was all by ourselves and nobody bothered us much. She kept being awful excited about this Harvey House thing, though.

Finally, one day she come in and said, "I've been made a waitress in the private dining room. Isn't that wonderful? I get a dollar a week more than I had before. Besides that, I know that I can make some money with tips, if I'm just nice to those gentlemen."

"Yeah, but, by God, don't be too damn nice."

She laughed and said, "Oh, you're just kind of jealous, aren't you?" She kinda pinched my cheeks.

I pretended that it didn't make no difference, but I got to thinking about it, and it was a thing that I didn't quite figure out and couldn't quite value, you know. I couldn't figure out how serious it was. I was fine with horses and rifles and stuff like that, but when it come to being in the business world— first place, you had to read and write and know what it was all about. You had to have some bank training, and I didn't know nothing about that. That wasn't my dish at all, and it even made me kinda nervous thinking about it.

Well, anyway, she kept telling me about all the people that would come through. One day, in the summer of 1881, a train full of real notables from California came in. Melisande was telling me about it, and said, "Oh, the nicest man came through, his name was Mr. Endicott. My, he was a handsome fellow and so well dressed and so polite. You know something, dear? He gave me a big tip."

"How much did he give you?"

"Why, he—he gave me a five-dollar gold piece!"

"You got to be kidding. When do you get a five-dollar gold piece for waiting on a table?" I said.

"I don't know, but he gave it to me."

"Well, I don't like that, I don't like somebody giving gold pieces to my wife."

"What would you have me do, darling? Would you have me give it back? I know that we need lots of new things. I thought it would be all right for me to take it."

I got to thinking about it, and I couldn't think of any reason why it wouldn't be, but it just made me uncomfortable, you know.

She told me another time, "Mr. Endicott came through again. He was going east to Washington and he remembered me."

"Well, did he give you another gold piece?"

"Certainly not. That was just a kind of present."

"Well, that's good," I said. "I'm glad that's the case."

"He's the nicest man, and I want you to meet him."

"Did you tell him about me?"

"Certainly I did. He saw the ring on my finger and he said, 'Mrs. Brules, I would certainly like to meet that fine husband of yours. I hear wonderful things about him, what a superb scout he is, and how capable a man. Those are the kind of men that opened up the West. You must be very proud that he's your husband.' Isn't that nice?" she said.

"Yeah, that's all right . . . I mean, I just don't know."

"You were always talking about us getting a cattle ranch or something like that, honey. A man like that could finance a ranch."

"Well," I said, "that's worth thinking about, yeah." They always irked me afterward, those talks with Melisande. I know that she was a sweet girl and straightforward, and I was never suspicious that she would have anything to do with another fellow. She was pretty damn straight, but I just felt a little confused about it. As far as I could see, it weren't doing no harm, and I was real proud that Melisande was being recognized for doing her job, still . . .

I asked, "Well, how old is this son of a bitch?"

"Don't talk about him that way. He's a very fine gentleman. I don't know how old he is, maybe forty or so. I don't know, I don't really have any idea. But he's in good shape—he doesn't have a potbelly."

"How do you know? What have you been looking at?"

"No, I didn't mean that! I mean that he is very tall and straight, with good bearing and broad shoulders and all that. He looks like he's in good physical condition. I don't know anything about it except that he's a charming man."

"Well," I said, "he sounds too Goddamn charming to me, you know."

"Don't be silly. A person like that doesn't mean anything to me. The only person that means anything to me is my wonderful husband. I just have to be nice to these people 'cause they're customers of the Harvey House, and they are very important railroad people. Someday we might want to borrow from a bank to get a ranch, and it doesn't hurt to know such people.''

I thought, that isn't bad, she's got the right idea. The girl has her head screwed on right. Anyway, I must say that when she made love to me at night, I figured, she can't have an interest in anybody else and be the way she is. Boy, it was a fantastic thing. I used to look forward to our lovemaking, and was just hungry to have her in my arms most of the time.

We got through the rest of that summer, and I didn't hear no more about Mr. Endicott. I didn't want to hear. In fact, it bored me plumb to death to listen to her when she talked about him. I guess that she kinda got the idea and even if he did go through, she didn't mention it to me.

29

A Train to Denver

While we was there at Lamy a strange thing happened. A train from the East had just pulled out, and me and some boys was weighing and counting cattle, when Melisande came running up. It was after the busy time at the Harvey House, and she come a-running from the telegraph office with this telegram she was all excited about. When I jumped down from the corral fence, she threw her arms around me, much to the laughter and amusement of them fellows doing the counting.

I took no notice of them, but give her a big hug and kiss. Bursting with her news she said, "We have a wonderful invitation."

"Invitation? What are you talking about, honey?"

"There's a telegram from General Crook. It was sent to all the stations up and down the railroad, but the operator knows us and knows who you are. The general's at North Platte, Nebraska. He wants us to come there for a reunion."

I said, "What the hell are you talking about, honey?"

"Let me read the telegram," she said, being real clever, and never embarrassing me about my trouble with reading.

She started out, " *'Addressed to Scout Brules from Headquarters, Third Cavalry, Military District of the Platte, North Platte, Nebraska. Friend Brules, this is not an order, this is just an invitation. Since matters have quieted down here in the Department of the Platte, and it appears that the Sioux and others are settled back on their reservations and not giving* trouble, it might be appropriate to have a gathering of our old Command, certainly as many officers and scouts as we can gather. A five-year reunion of the veterans of the Sioux wars. I have asked Baptiste, Girard, Herendeen, Hamilton, and old Joe Rankin, all good men, to join us in a reunion of the forces that opposed the Sioux five years ago in the basin of the Big Horn and the Yellowstone.

'' 'I was informed by the Ute agent at Los Piños that you had proceeded to Taos and perhaps from there on to Santa Fe. I have telegraphed both offices in the anticipation that this message will reach you.

'' 'In short, we would like you to join us and the rest of the scouts for a reunion and celebration here at Fort McPherson, North Platte, Nebraska, on September twenty-fifth, this year of 1881. There will be a number of festivities and gatherings. I am sure that you will enjoy seeing your old comrades of the Seventh and the Third. I know that they will be delighted to see you.

'' 'Phil Sheridan will be here, and it is my hope that Chief of the Armies General William Tecumseh Sherman will honor us with his presence. In addition there will be many frontiersmen and other people whom you have either met or of whom you have heard. I am arranging for a hunt or two, so be sure to bring your horses. As you know, the buffalo are mostly gone now, but there are still some elk and antelope, and we should have a glorious time.

'' 'Buffalo Bill has kindly set aside the facilities of his ranch Scout's Rest, here at North Platte, for some officers and ladies and for his friends among the scouts. It is everybody's choice, whether they wish to be on the fort or at his ranch.

'' 'It is my understanding that you have married a beautiful Mormon girl. By all means bring her along.

'' 'By separate dispatch I am forwarding your formal orders, which will entitle you to railroad transportation, as well as boxcar stalls for your horses. Plan to stay for a better part of a month. You will be extended the equivalent of officers' quarters at the post. We will be looking forward to meeting you *on the Union Pacific platform on the eastbound train at three o'clock in the afternoon of the twenty-fifth of September.*

" 'With all best wishes. Please acknowledge by return telegram.' "

Well, I want to tell you, when I heard that, I just about busted my gusset. It sounded like a hell of a lot of fun, and Melisande seemed to think the same thing. She was so damn excited that she could hardly speak, but she was sure jumping up and down.

Finally she said, "Just think, Brules, just think. We get to go to an army post, we get to go to a lot of parties, we get to see these wonderful generals, General Sheridan and General Sherman. Why, they are almost like gods. How lucky we are. What fun it's gonna be. I can see General Crook thinks a great deal of you, and I'll bet he's going to be very nice. Think if we get to go hunting, too, I can take my .32-20."

Well, you know, she went on about everything like that. I hugged her and kissed her, and said, "You betcha. Let's don't waste any time getting ready. We got to get our equipment and saddles."

"Yes. Of course, if there are going to be parties, and he did say there were going to be dances, I'll have to have something to wear."

"Something to wear?"

"Do you want me to go to the parties naked?"

I blushed clean through. "What are you talking about? That's not the thing to say. You mean you want some dresses."

"Certainly. I've got to have some clothes," she said, "and you ought to have a nice suit of some kind."

"A suit? What the hell is wrong with what I'm wearing?"

"Nothing wrong, my dear, except that old buckskin suit has buffalo blood on it. You need something new. You've got to be able to dress up a little bit. I'll tell you what, let's plan it so that we stop for two or three days in Denver, and then we'll get all the clothes and things that we need. But right now let's go back quick to the telegraph office and send General Crook an acceptance, telling him that we will be on that train. Oh, boy, isn't this wonderful?"

"Well," I said, "yeah, honey, it sure is and I'm excited. Them good guys like Girard, Baptiste, Herendeen, and old Hamilton, and all, will be there. Boy, it's gonna be great to see them again. I wonder how they're doing."

Right away quick we composed a telegram. I say *we* composed one—hell, Melisande composed it. She wrote how pleased we'd been to receive the invitation, and we would be on the train that arrived at three o'clock in the afternoon on the stated date.

"Where do you suppose we will stay? Will we stay at the fort there?" she wondered.

I said, "Sure, of course. Didn't he say that accommodations for both officers, scouts, and their spouses would be available at the post? But, wait a minute, can you get off work at the Harvey House? We'll be at least a month—that's a long time."

"I'll take a leave of absence. They wouldn't pay me for this."

"Yeah, but supposing they tell you that they don't want you to go?"

"If they did that, it would be just too bad," she announced. "It would be just a shame, because I would have to tell them that I was going to give up the job, and I would go anyway."

"Well, you better be careful what you say. You might not get another job again."

"I'm not worried about that. I'm about as good a waitress as they've got in there, and I'll bet you that I get my job back when I get through. The managers are real friendly to me, and I'm gonna tell them that my husband and I have a chance to be the guests of General Crook, the great General Crook, for whom my husband scouted in the Sioux Wars."

Melisande kept on bubbling. "Oh, how wonderful this is going to be. You know, all those generals, they travel in high company, and I'll bet that there will be a lot of notables there. There will be a lot of those swells from the East. Those fellows that own the railroads and the bankers that put up the money to build things. There will be some interesting people—I bet you there will be some foreigners there. I'm so excited, I can hardly wait. The only thing is, I'm a little bit afraid, Brules.''

"Why? What are you afraid for, honey?"

"Well, I'm gonna meet all those highfalutin ladies and men, and I'm just a ranch girl from Utah," she said, getting real serious.

"What do you mean? You're the prettiest thing that ever came around this country. In fact, you're not pretty, you're beautiful, and you will make all those Army gals jealous."

"Oh, no, I won't, because they'll have so much better manners, and they'll be so much fancier than I am."

"Now, wait a minute, honey. It ain't gonna be like that. You got an awful good education. You were taught very well in the Mormon schools you went to in Moab."

"Yes, indeed I was," she said. "I read quite a lot of literary works too. I not only had arithmetic, but I had some history and English composition. And a course on English poets."

"Poets," I said. "Well, what did you study them guys for?"

Melisande smiled and stroked my beard a little bit and said, "You of all people should know, because you have such a deep feeling for everything. Poets express deep feelings, and they say things that really make a great deal of difference to people."

"Well, I'm willing to take your word for it. Maybe one of these days you'll educate me," I told her.

She laughed and said, "There are so many things that you know about that I don't. I couldn't possibly educate you. You're so far ahead of me that there's no use to it . . . just because I happen to have a little schooling."

"Don't fool yourself, girl—that's important. That's where I'm a complete blank, and someday you have got to help me out."

"I certainly will. My ideal love, by the time I get through with you, you will be as polished as any gentleman from the East," she said.

"Well, that's kinda interesting. I don't know whether I want to be that slick." We both laughed at that.

When we received the invitation, it was the middle of August, and we done a lot of thinking and working out plans. We seen that we could take Jupiter and Tina, but we wouldn't be able to take old Alfred. We both was real sorrowful about that.

"Poor old Alfred, he's going to be all upset again when we go off without him," Melisande said.

"Yeah," I said, "I *would* like to take him—I'd like to take that mule and show him off."

"You can't do that, honey. You got this invitation and the orders for the transportation of horses, but taking him along would be overdoing it."

"Guess so, but you know what Alfred's gonna say when we pull out."

"Oh, yes. He's going to say what he said there at Los Piños. He's going to hee-haw, 'Aw, hell! Aw, hell! You guys are leaving me!' "

There was a good livery stable there at Lamy, right near the railroad, and I knew they could handle things all right. I reckoned that we wouldn't be gone a whole month anyway. We'd probably be gone only a couple of weeks, which I paid in advance, and I kinda talked myself around into not worrying.

I'll never forget when we climbed aboard that afternoon train and took a seat in one of the coaches, waiting for the train to start. Melisande was so excited. "Oh, Brules, this is my first train ride. I've never been on a train before, not even one of those narrow gauges, and this is a standard gauge."

"Yes, not only is it a standard gauge, but it's a transcontinental railroad."

"Isn't that wonderful?" She nodded.

Just then the whistle blew a couple of times.

"Oh, I guess that we're going."

The conductor was yelling, "All aboard, all aboard."

We could hear a couple of them trainmen down the line, and we had the window down, so we could see the old engineer up there leaning against the side of the cabin. He was waving and waving at the conductor, and the conductor was waving too. Then we were on our way, and there was a big kind of a puff and a lurching and the whole train started moving. Melisande held on to the seat in front of us.

"Well, it's so smooth, it's not like riding in a carriage or a stagecoach." She was amazed.

"That's right, honey. It's 'cause these steel rails are smooth, and they're laid clear across the country for thousands and thousands of miles."

"Look at the way the ground is going by us. Why, we're just sitting here, and the ground is sailing by."

"Yeah, that's the reaction that I had when I first rode a train from Denver to Alamosa. I remember it very well. But we are moving and the world is standing still. Believe it or not."

She got to laughing and said, "Maybe so, but they tell me that the world is turning, it's going around and around, and it starts in the morning and goes toward the sun and turns around. That's what makes the sun look like it's going down in the west."

"You've got it. Really the sun ain't moving at all, it's us who's rotating."

"Well," she said, "I've got to think about that a little bit, but right now, look out there. Look at the cows and the barns and the houses going by."

We was making pretty good speed by then, and the click-clacking on the rails was faster, and then we heard the whistle blow again a couple of times. The engineer was telling somebody to get the hell out of the way. All of a sudden we crossed one of them trestle bridges over a gorge, and you could hear the whole change of the rhythm of the beat of the clickie-clack stuff. All that suddenly stopped and there was kinda a roar as we passed over, and I guess that's 'cause the bridge was hollow.

"My God, what was that!" Melisande asked.

"Oh, we just passed over a bridge, honey. Didn't you see all them steel posts and everything going by? That's a railroad bridge. The railroad ain't gonna jump down in a hollow there and then jump back up. It's got to go smooth."

The train didn't go so fast winding out of the hills there, but when it got out on the flats it was chugging right along. I was looking out at that mesa country and thinking, my God, only eight years ago, in 1873, I was a-hunting Comanches in there. Boy, isn't this fantastic. Now we're just a-sailing along. Hell, I got to thinking how could them damn Indians ever attack a train? A great big locomotive like that, ten thousand times heavier than a horse, and the whole train going like the dickens. I decided, no, they wouldn't do it that way, they'd tear up the track and dump the whole train. Then they would attack it.

Then I thought, well, you silly so-and-so, there's nothing in this county now. The Comanches are done gone. Besides that, they'd be scared to death of this train, and the railroad's got people policing, and it's got telegraph lines too. Of course, I knew that the damn Indians cut them telegraph lines once in a while. Still, as long as the telegraph lines was working back and forth a little bit, everybody would know if Indians attacked, and there was forts all along and cavalry detachments. It's just old Brules scouting, and still worrying about them Goddamn Comanches, but this country is kinda what you'd call pacified now.

Well, the sun went down back of those beautiful Sangre de Cristos, and we watched it from the speeding train, seeing snowcapped peaks and all.

We slept the best we could, sitting side by side in the car, but we was moving along about as fast as a horse could gallop, you know. It was going all night long—that was the wonder of it.

About three o'clock the next afternoon we come into Denver, and we saw what a big town it really was. We was ten or fifteen minutes going by buildings, warehouses, stockyards, cement factories, and all kinds of different things. We finally come to the station and stopped, and we off-loaded our things out of the coach and put them on the platform. I run on down to the stock cars and got the horses off. Right there near the station they had a corral and livery stable. I took the horses in there and made a deal with the fellow, and he would keep them right there. He had me pay him in advance, of course.

I run on back and found Melisande, and she said, "You know, we've got to walk through the station—I just want to take a look at the Harvey House here. I bet it's a beauty."

"Okay, but we just got something to eat in Colorado Springs. We aren't gonna eat again, are we?"

"No, no we aren't going to stop for that. We've got to go to the hotel. Only thing is, I would like to know, sir, what hotel are we going to?"

"Well," I said, "I guess we'll just go to any hotel. What hotel do you think?"

"Didn't you make a reservation at a hotel? Didn't you wire ahead for a reservation?" she asked.

"A reservation? What's that?"

"Everybody that travels nowadays on these trains, they wire ahead to the station they're coming to and they get a room, and the hotel is already prepared for them. Now, land-sakes, we're liable to find we don't have anyplace to stay."

"Well, honey, I never did anything about a reservation. I always stayed in a boardinghouse."

"You're traveling in style now, Mr. Brules, and you've got to act like that. Come on, we've got to do things right."

She wasn't cross. She was kidding me most of the time, and I must say that everywhere I went, people looked at her as if she was the most beautiful thing that they ever saw. It used to make me a little bit nervous, you know. I'd look at some of those hotshots and think, beg your pardon, sir, but that's my wife and you just keep a-thinking about something else.

When we stepped into the Harvey House there and seen how nice it was, Melisande wanted to sit down and have a cup of coffee or something, which was fine with me.

We asked the waitress to come over and we gave her our order. A bit later Melisande asked her, "How do you like working in the Harvey House?"

"Oh," she said, "it's wonderful. We get to travel all over."

Melisande told her she worked in Santa Fe.

"Oh, I always wanted to go to Santa Fe. It's a beautiful city, isn't it?"

"Yes, it sure is," I agreed.

"Well, we're strangers here in town. What's a good hotel?" Melisande said. "Where do we go?"

"Well, if you want to go first class—"

"We certainly want to travel fine. After all, we're going to see General Crook up in—"

"Hush, don't say nothing about that," I jumped in.

The waitress raised her eyebrows. "Really, the famous General Crook?"

"Yes, we're going up to North Platte and see him. We've been invited to go up there."

"Oh," the waitress said, "isn't that wonderful? Well, then, you will want to stay at the best hotel, and the best hotel in town is the Windsor on Larimer Street. That's where Buffalo Bill stays when he comes here."

"Hell, that's where we're gonna stay. My old friend Buffalo Bill couldn't be wrong."

"Do you know Buffalo Bill?" she asked.

"Yeah, I know him. I used to hunt with him a little bit. I was on a campaign with him. I didn't see too much of him—just once in a while, when General Merritt come up and joined Crook's command at Cloud Peak Camp."

"Oh, I don't know anything about that. That's that military sort of thing, and I really wouldn't understand it. But then you would like the Windsor Hotel. You just go over there, and if they are full, I will give you a tip, sir."

"What's that?"

"Let them know that you know Buffalo Bill," she said.

"Well, thank you, madam, I appreciate that very much."

Melisande got that girl in conversation again to ask, "How much do they pay you here? They pay us twelve dollars a month down in Santa Fe."

"We only get nine dollars here. This is a big city and we get nine dollars."

"Well, what do you make in tips?" Melisande kept on at her.

"Last month I made almost six dollars in tips. Oh, that's one of the best parts of the business, and our boss encourages us to be really nice to the customers, telling us that's where we make our money."

As we picked up our stuff and started out, the waitress said, "You can hire a carriage to take you over there."

"Well, how far is it?" I asked.

"It's about six blocks from the station here. You go up to Larimer Street. . . . See now you're on Wynkoop. Then there's Wazee, Blake, Market, and then Larimer. When you get up there, turn right and go—"

"How much does a carriage cost?" I put in.

"Oh, I think that probably the fare would be a dollar."

"A dollar? Just to go around—we'll walk," I said.

With that Melisande gives me a kinda cross look. We said good-bye, and thanked the lady very much, and went out. When we got outside Melisande said, "Mr. Brules, if we're going to travel first class, let's travel first class. I don't see any sense in walking through a strange city dragging our luggage, trying to find a hotel."

So I stepped back, took off my dirty old coonskin hat, and bowed real graceful-like, sweeping my hat with one hand clear down pretty near to my feet and around in a circle and back up again. "Madam, ain't that just the thing. We're going first class."

She burst out laughing. "Now, come on, Brules, really. We've got to get into a carriage. Here's a nice little rig. Let's talk to this man."

I stepped up to him and asked, "Brother, you for hire?"

He said, "Well, what do you think I'm sitting here for, man?"

"Okay, we want to go to the Windsor Hotel," I told him.

"Okay," he said, and looked at us kinda funny. Of course, I was in my scouting outfit. I had blue jeans on, a leather shirt, and some Comanche moccasins that is the best footwear there is, and of course my coonskin hat. He looked at me as if I had come from out of the wilderness and I felt like, by God, I had.

As we was going along, Melisande studied everything. There were so many carriages coming and going, and crowds, people loading baggage, and all that kind of thing. The stores were all around, and there were guys standing on the corners selling newspapers. They had two newspapers in them days, the *Rocky Mountain News,* which was the morning paper, I guess, and *The Denver Post*. Well, the fellow standing there selling *The Denver Post* was just a kid.

Anyway, we went on down to that wonderful Windsor Hotel. You never saw such a splendid sight in your life as that Windsor. Man, that was a first-class place. When we got there, there was some of them lackeys in uniforms. Christ, when I first seen them, I thought it was some damn soldier boys, but I never seen any soldier boys dressed like that. They looked like they might be in the French infantry or something.

"No, no. I think those are porters, they are just going to help us," Melisande said.

Well, they sure helped us with the luggage. They acted like we owned the damn place. As I got out, I said to the driver, "Here's a buck," and handed it to him. Melisande poked at me, and I asked, "What's the matter, honey?"

"You're supposed to give him a tip. Give him ten cents."

"Ten cents, for Christ sakes? I haven't got ten cents."

"Just a minute, I've got something in my purse. Here, give him this ten-cent piece."

So I gave the guy the tip. He'd been sitting there waiting: he wasn't whipping up his horses to get out of there. Hell, I'd never heard of tips, and I didn't know what the hell she was talking about. Now, of course, I've been traveling around, and I know what it's all about, but in them days I didn't understand what the hell a tip was. It seemed to me like giving somebody something for nothing.

Inside I stepped up to the desk and said, "We want a room." The clerk was all dressed up in a black suit, white tie, real splendid-like. He was kinda looking down his nose at me 'cause I was in my scouting outfit. I guess I hadn't looked in a mirror for a long time. He said, "Oh, yes. I beg your pardon, sir, but do you have a reservation?"

"Hell, no."

He shrugged and said, "I'm sorry, sir—you know, we only have reservation guests now. We have no vacancies otherwise."

"Well, it ain't been so long ago that I come off a campaign with Buffalo Bill. He's one of my friends, and he said this is a pretty good place."

The guy looked and says, "You know Mr. Cody?"

I just nodded, and he said, "Well, sir. Excuse me, I didn't know that you were a friend of Mr. Cody's. Why, yes, what sort of a room would you like? We have a few rooms that we keep back for, shall we say, late arrivals or somebody whom Mr. Cody would be very interested in having stay here at the hotel."

Melisande signed us on for a real expensive room—nine dollars a night—and we started for the stairs. One of them fellows in the French infantry uniform picked up our bags and showed us up the stairs. We had a room that looked out toward the mountains, toward the railroad track. It seemed like it was good: it had two pull-up windows in it and curtains, and it had one brass bed that was going to be plenty big enough for us, and could have probably held Jupiter, too, and I thought that was just fine. There was a water pitcher and a basin in the corner, towels, and all that.

The porter helped us with our bags and got things set up, showing us, "Here's your closet back of this curtain. You can hang up there, and you know the men's bathroom is down the hall in this direction. On the other side of the corridor, but in the same direction, is the ladies' bathroom. Usually they're not crowded. There is a reservation pad on the side, and you can write your name down so that you take your turn when you wish to." He kinda lingered around the door and kept on talking and kept on wondering if there was anything more that he could do for us.

Finally Melisande whispers in my ear, "You've got to give him another tip."

"What?"

"Give him ten cents," she said, and handed me another coin.

Well, I went over and gave him the ten cents. Boy, that guy did bow and scrape, and everything was going great. So I said to him, "We want to do some shopping. We want to buy some clothes."

He sorta looked at us as if to say, "It wouldn't be a bad idea," but I didn't pay any attention to that. I asked, "Where should we go?"

"I recommend the Denver Dry Goods, sir," he said.

"Is that a good store?"

"Oh, they have most everything there. I would suggest that you go there, and there's another little store—it's kind of inconspicuous—around the corner from the Denver Dry Goods. It's called Daniels and Fisher."

"Well," I said, "that gives us a lead. We'll follow that out and if the tracks turn good, why, maybe we'll get a shot."

He looked at me as if I had lost my mind, talking about stuff like that. I always went around with my .38 in my belt and everybody eyed that, you know. Still, it wasn't out of the ordinary for men to carry guns in Denver in them days and a lot of 'em did it. You could tell the cowhands and the fellows that come from outside, hell, they had guns and they were gonna keep them handy. That was my attitude.

Anyway, Melisande and I left the hotel and went hand-in-hand down the street, looking around at stuff. We followed the directions and found the Denver Dry. By God, that was a big store. That was the biggest thing I'd ever seen. I'd seen some stores that I thought was pretty good in Missouri, but then, of course, I hadn't been in a store for maybe ten or twelve years, maybe longer than that.

We were showed around and Melisande started checking things. She didn't buy anything right away, but she looked at this and that. Finally she said, "I don't want to buy things right this minute. I want to look around and see the other stores. What was the name of that other place the porter said to go to?"

"Well, he said some store by the name of Daniels and Fisher might be good."

"I've looked and seen some of the things that I'd like to get, and now I think it's time that you took a look at things. Let's look at something for you," she said.

"What do I need? I don't need nothing."

"Yes, you do. You're going to feel awfully uncomfortable if you don't have something," she insisted. "You need a dress-up suit. Something to wear to a party or something like that. There are going to be lots of parties and receptions and we're gonna be there two or three weeks. You can't go around in those old smelly scouting clothes."

So we went around Sixteenth Street to Daniels and Fisher. They had lots of them things hung up in cabinets made of glass, and you could look and see what they had. Man, they had top hats too.

"I ain't gonna wear one of them Goddamn top hats. Christ, I'd have to duck every time I went through a door."

"You're supposed to take your hat off when you go into the house."

"Are you? I see. Well, anyway, I'm liable to sit on the damn thing."

"Brules, come on. We've got to figure this out."

We looked at things, and she said, "Now, here is a suit for you."

"Holy smokes! What's that?"

You know what it was? It was one of them coats that had a long tail on the back of it. You buttoned it around your waist and it hung down in back like a damn bird. Then it had a white collar and a white shirt and a fancy tie that was folded over a couple of times with a pin stuck in it.

"What the hell is that damn thing? Is that a wind scarf or something?"

"No, I think that they call it four-in-hand," Melisande explained.

"Four-in-hand? It sure looks foreign to me."

Melisande didn't even smile. "It is a nice-looking outfit,

and it would be just the thing for you to have. It would be just fine. Oh, there is a waistcoat for you."

"What do you mean, a waistcoat?"

"A vest. You put that on under your coat."

"You don't expect me to wear that *and* the Goddamn top hat, do you?"

"No, but I'll tell you how you'd look swell."

"How?"

"If you had a broad-brim Western hat like that." Then she pointed to one that had a kinda flat top to it.

I must say that I liked that better. I mean, it looked like it would do all right in real bright sunshine and all that. It would cover you good and it looked like heavy, good stuff.

"It's made by Stetson and it's a dress Stetson."

"Well, hell, Stetson. It's a damn good hat, everybody knows that. That ain't bad, really."

She had the clerk take out the hat that she'd picked, and I looked at it and put it on my head. Hell, it fit right well.

"Oh, you look wonderful," she said. "Look, Cat, stand up here to this mirror and take a look at yourself and just imagine yourself in that."

I looked in the mirror and thought, holy smokes, who is that guy? He's nobody I met.

"Imagine if you had a mustache and you just cut that big beard down—it looks like a brush pile. Honestly, you know, darling, you have the broadest shoulders and narrowest waist, and you're just as firm and strong and I'm so proud of you."

I was just a kinda beaming there, nodding to the salesman that was showing us the things. He was wide-eyed. He didn't know what the hell to make of us.

Well, that was enough. We said that we would come back tomorrow, and then we walked on back to the hotel. When we come in there, why, there was music playin' and a lot of swells sitting around. Some of them was having tea and some of them was having drinks and so forth. There was laughter in the bar. There weren't no women in the bar, but there was ladies sitting out in the lobby. I looked to where the music was coming from and there was a guy playing one of the old big grand pianos, and he was all dressed up in the same kind of suit that Melisande was talking about me having.

Another man with a big old bass fiddle was just a-strumming away, and a guy with a violin—they was playing this real smooth, sweet music.

"What kind of music is that?" I asked.

"I think that is chamber music," Melisande said.

"Chamber music? Hell, we got one of them chamber pots up in our room."

"No," she said, "it's not the same thing at all. Don't talk so loud. Everybody will think you're—"

"Well, everybody can think whatever they want to. I'm just a damn scout out of the mountains. I don't know nothing about this thing. You're the lady that got me into this. You had better take care of me."

She laughed. "I'm going to take care of you. Now, let's see. Look—have you seen these paintings? Aren't they beautiful?"

Some of them paintings were from Europe; there was horsemen all in red, jumping over fences and stuff—chasing dogs, and hounds; there was others that looked like old castles and stuff. Some of the Western pictures I recognized right away. One of the Hopi villages. There was another of Buffalo Bill. By God, it was a good one too. Everywhere there was pictures of him, on his horse, getting on his horse, riding in his show, and things like Buffalo Bill at the battle of so and so. Hell, we got the idea that he was well thought of, I want to tell you.

That music did sound good, but Melisande said, "Come on, we're a little late for our baths."

"Now, how do we do this?" I asked, when we got in our room.

"Well, you've got that coat, haven't you?

"I just got that duster that I used to ride in the wagon with."

"That's good. What you do is, you just walk down in your coat and moccasins. Leave your clothes here, and go into the bathroom. If it's busy, why, you sign up on the pad and come back. I'll be getting ready here. My reservation is for a quarter of six."

Well," I said, "all right, I'll go on down, but I feel as awkward as hell."

"You better take a towel with you."

So I done that, and put on my old duster. I said, "Oh, hell. I ain't gonna wear my old Comanche moccasins down there. I'll go down barefoot."

"You're supposed to have slippers."

"Slippers? What the hell are they?"

"Never mind, honey. We'll show you what that is tomorrow. Kind of like low moccasins."

When I go down, Jesus, the door is locked. Well, somebody's in there. I can hear some son of a bitch splashing around in there taking a bath. I look and there's a whole list of men. Hell, it goes clear through nine o'clock and I ain't got time. So I go back to her and say, "Honey, that thing is closed till nine o'clock."

"You're gonna have to have a bath," Melisande insisted. "You had better come with me."

"Jesus, I can't go into the ladies'."

"Yes, you can. You just do it like I say and nothing will be wrong with it. I'll run a bath and you can take a bath first and I'll take it second. Or, we can take it together. Come on, let's go." She said, "I'll go down the hall and if the coast is clear and the bath is open, I'll open the door and wave at you. You come and act like you're going to the men's bathroom, and then if there's nobody looking around, you just step inside and we'll lock the door real fast. Remember, you can't talk, 'cause they mustn't hear a man's voice in there."

So we did just that. They had big tanks of hot water that had been brought up, and you turned on a faucet and filled a bucket and put it in the bath, after you put a cork in the tub.

"Why don't you take your bath first, honey, and I'll take mine afterward," I said.

"There is not enough hot water left. Whoever gets through with this bath has got to get dressed and go downstairs and get one of those bellboys or something to bring up more hot water.''

''Well, hell. We ain't got time to do that.''

''That's right. It's a great big bathtub, and you and I are gonna take a bath together.''

''I would kinda like that,'' I admitted.

''Come on, let's get in there. Hurry up. I'll soap your back for you before I get in.''

Boy, I must say that I was trying to be real casual about it, but when she stood there and didn't have no clothes on at all, she was the most beautiful-looking thing I ever seen. I began, ''Melisande—''

''Stop playing around, now. We're not going to do anything.''

So I soaped her back, too, and we got in and got out of the tub together. Finally, as we were getting ready, I said, ''How the hell am I gonna get out of here? If people see me coming out of the ladies' bathroom, there's gonna be hell to pay.'' I was whispering all this stuff to her.

''Just a minute—let me look out and see if there is anybody in sight, and if there isn't, I'll tell you what you do. You go out, quickly, go to the men's bathroom, stay in there a minute or two, and then slam the door when you come out and make yourself real conspicuous, walk on down the hall, and go to our room.''

''Okay. Jesus, do you have the key? I don't want to be standing out in the hall.''

''Here's the key. You're all set. I will take my time and I will come later. Let me look out first.'' She took a quick look and nodded. ''Now is the time. Get out now, quickly, and I'll close the door.''

I stepped out, took three quick strides down to where the men's bathroom was, and tried the door. Christ, the son of a bitch was locked. I turned around and started down the hall, and I seen a woman that had her head out of the door was looking at me. I was dead sure that she'd seen me coming out of the women's bathroom, but I went on by as if I was the king of England. I didn't let on to nothing, and went into the room and started getting dressed again. In a few minutes Melisande came in.

"How did it go?" she asked.

"Honey, I got to tell you something. I went to go into the men's bathroom but it was full—some guy in there. There wasn't anything I could do; I couldn't go in. I quick turned around, and I saw this damn woman that was watching me all the time."

"Oh, my God. Did she see you come out of the ladies'?"

"I don't know whether she did or not."

"Well, let's hope she didn't. Then she would have figured you just went down to check the men's door."

"I doubt it like hell," I had to confess.

"I doubt it, too, because when I went by the door, she stuck her head out and said, 'Humpf!' I wondered what she was talking about."

"Well, now you know," I said. We both got to laughing about it, and decided, what difference did it make?

We kinda crawled into our clothes again, same old clothes that we'd been traveling in. We hadn't bought nothing yet. I began to feel a little fidgety then, because after seeing all them swell clothes in the store, I realized how dirty looking my stuff was, and Melisande's stuff wasn't too much better.

So I said to her, "You know, instead of us going down here and eating in this swell restaurant here at the hotel, where you are gonna have everybody bowing and scraping and everything, let's wait till we get our good clothes. Why don't we just go out and find a restaurant around town somewhere? Maybe we'll find a cowboy place or something and eat there, and we'll be comfortable."

She looked at me and smiled and said, "My, haven't you changed. I never thought I'd see a Brules who was conscious of what he was wearing."

"Well, it ain't entirely that way, but it's a lot different, you know, than coming up on wild game that don't notice what you're wearing. Coming up on these people—that's another story. I'm not too used to that."

"Sweetheart, I think that you have the right idea. Let's

just don't dress up tonight, but we'll dress up tomorrow," she agreed.

That's just what we done. As we walked out of the hotel, people was kinda staring at us and wondering what some old mountain man and his farm woman was doing there.

The best chance we had of getting something fit to eat, I thought, was if we could locate a Chinaman's place close by, so we went on out and found a pretty good Chinese place. It was good eating and was down near the railroad. Come to think of it, we could have gone to the Harvey House, but we didn't. It was all right—everybody else looked as bad as we did, so we didn't think nothing about it.

The next day, though, we really set out to get some clothes, and by that time I was interested, because I could see what Melisande was talking about. I thought that maybe it would be important for us to get the right stuff.

We went back to Daniels and Fisher, where we'd seen the hat. I settled on a coat that I figured was the right length and all. We bought everything that we needed. I had to have a pair of new boots and since I didn't have any black shoes, I bought black boots—snakeskin—that would do real good.

The stuff that we bought for Melisande was real outstanding. You know, she got two real pretty linen dresses. When she wore them, she looked just wonderful. She had to have some shoes for them, and they had these nice shoes that was maybe about an inch or an inch and a half on the heel and had a little bit forward tilt in there, and they was laced up. Nice white shoes that had black laces in them.

Something about them little higher heels—they weren't high heels like them Paris people wear, that I later learned about—but they was just normal high heels for good American girls. They kinda made her swish a little bit when she walked, and it looked real good. I was real proud of her. I thought she looked so wonderful, it was just unbelievable. Her natural beauty was so great that everybody was looking at her all the time.

Melisande got a beautiful gown, too, a ball gown. It was made of satin, a pink gown that was absolute gorgeous. It had some trimming on it. I don't rightly remember exactly what it was, but then she had some lovely shoes that went with it. She had to have two pairs of shoes, for Christ's sake.

The final things we bought was her traveling outfit, and that was the best stuff I ever saw. It was a neat black skirt and a white blouse. We bought a couple of them blouses, 'cause she said she had to have one to wear while she was washing the other. That made horse sense to me. The black skirt come down to just about her ankles. It was so smart looking, and then there was a jacket that went over her blouse, kinda like a coat, and it buttoned right at her tummy, kinda folded over the top of the skirt. It showed her figure to be just perfect. When she done up her hair good and all that, then she looked wonderful in it.

To top it all off we bought a beautiful big hat. It was a black hat, but it had some white tracing. Right now I don't remember what that tracing was, but it made the most beautiful outfit you ever saw. When she was dressed in that outfit, boy, she would knock the eye off an elephant.

She was real happy about it. She was skipping around there, turning and twisting in front of the mirror and looking at herself. Then she said, "I'll step up and say, 'How do you do, General Crook. How do you do, sir,' and I'll curtsy, and then when General Sheridan comes, I'll curtsy to him. If there are some of those English bigwigs—there's got to be a Lord somebody or another that's come for a hunting party—I'll say 'My Lord, I am so pleased—' "

I got to laughing at her, and I said, "Hell, you'll probably only meet a bunch of damn scouts, some army officers that ain't got nothing more than their pay. They'll all be wanting to crowd around you, that's for damn sure. I might have to do some shooting."

"You stop talking like that! What's more, Brules, you're going to have to leave your pistol in your room. You're not going to take that .38 around with you all the time as if you were afraid of your life."

"Well, when I'm taking you out, I am afraid of my life just judging by the way the menfolks is looking at you," I said.

"The thing for us to do now is to go get you a traveling suit. You have got to have something besides what you have. You have got that marvelous suit and the four-in-hand tie that goes over, but you are supposed to have a stickpin that goes in it."

"Yeah, I noticed that, but, hell, I don't want to get one."

"Well, if you don't get that stickpin in there, it is liable to come undone and you'd look mighty foolish, wouldn't you?" she pointed out.

"I'll feel foolish as hell in the whole thing anyway, but you're dead right about that. We'll go check at the jewelry counter downstairs and let's see what we can get."

Well, we went down there and they showed us these diamond stickpins and, hell, they had stuff for a thousand and five thousand dollars. Even the cheapest of them was three, four, or five hundred bucks. Well, I said, "Come on, honey, I'm not gonna get a Goddamn stickpin to wear just for a couple of nights. That's way out of my class."

She laughed and agreed. "Yes, I think they are. Do you have any ideas?"

"When we were coming up here, I noticed a kinda Indian curio shop that had some beautiful stuff in it, and I'd like to go by there and see what I can find."

So we made our purchases and they said that they was gonna wrap everything up and have it all nice for us when we got back. Then we went down the street to the curio shop. I want to tell you that it about blew my eyes off.

I've seen Indian things around trading posts, but when you get the effects of a big city like Denver, that must have had twenty-five or thirty thousand inhabitants and was a big market, why, they get the best from everywhere. There was a lot of Indian stuff that was just beautiful, and I saw some things that just turned me inside out. There was a Blackfoot shirt there. It was a beaded shirt that was done by some Blackfoot squaw and it had all kinds of colors in it and was gorgeous to look at it. Melisande got real excited about it and said, "That's just the thing for you, just the thing. I can see it on you."

When I put it on, she said, "Yes, now we've got to get

you some buckskin britches to go with it. Something that is real smart.''

"Hell, them buckskins don't handle so good. We found out about that, you know. If you get it wet when you swim in rivers—"

"Listen," she said, "this is a dress suit. You're not going to be swimming in rivers, you're going to be acting like a gentleman in it. It's your dress outfit, and you don't have to worry about it shrinking or getting it dirty while you're dressing out buffalo! Gee, come on, get civilized, Brules. Get civilized."

I laughed, and then we both did. It was just gorgeous.

"See this Navajo concho belt. It was made by one of those silversmiths who do beautiful work, and I want you to try that one."

By 1881 the silversmiths on the Navajo reservation had really got going. They'd been back on the reservation for twenty years then, and they was making a living any way they could think of, and the concho belts was just great. I found a thunderbird stickpin too.

I put that Blackfoot beaded jacket on and the pants, and then put that concho belt around and pulled it up tight.

"Oh, that is the most beautiful-looking thing. You, you rascal—now that you haven't got a beard but only a mustache, you're the handsomest man in the West. Why, Buffalo Bill hasn't a prayer looking like you," Melisande went on.

"Well, hell, he's got beautiful big blond curls and everything. I don't have that."

"Yeah," she said, "he can have the blond curls. But look at your magnificent face and, oh, everything about you. The shape of your head, mouth, and all that. Listen, don't tell me about any other men. My husband is the best-looking man in the West. You wear this outfit and I'm going to be having to fight off the women with a wagon spoke."

Well, sir, we bought that stuff and had them package it up, and went back over to Daniels and Fisher and paid for everything that they had packaged up, and the bill was something fierce. By God, you know, my stuff come up to eighty-nine dollars and fifty-seven cents. Melisande's come over a hundred and twenty-two, a hundred and twenty-three. Man, between the two of us, we blew two hundred bucks on clothes! Ain't that extravagant! That's awful, but they was the best-looking outfits.

Melisande and I got outside the store and hailed a carriage with all them packages, and he took us back to the hotel for a buck. Boy, I was spending money around there like a drunken sailor. Mountain man Brules handing out dollar bills like they was cigarette wrapping paper, you know. Acting like I was a millionaire or something.

I said, kinda sarcastic-like, while we was riding back in the carriage to the hotel, "By God, I believe I'll change my name to Endicott"—and then I saw I'd hit a soft spot, 'cause she didn't say a word.

She blushed pretty deep-like. Then she turned to me and put them beautiful eyes on me, and said, "Brules, that remark wasn't necessary." That's all she said and I never said nothing after that, but I realized that was some kind of territory I ought to keep out of.

Anyway, we come back to the hotel in good humor and all them French infantrymen took our boxes and stuff upstairs to our room. By that time it was late afternoon. So we decided we'd get straightened up and put on our new clothes and, by God, we'd eat in the hotel dining room this time. We was gonna be in style.

"What do you think we ought to wear tonight?" I asked.

"It's only about four-thirty, what are we going to do?"

"There's a damn good harness-and-saddle shop down on Larimer Street a ways here. I've been hearing tell about it and I'd kinda like to go see it."

"I'll tell you what, I'll wear my traveling outfit, and you wear your new buckskin setup with that beautiful black Stetson you got. We'll wander down the street together, arm-in-arm, down to that saddle shop. When it comes time for those musicians to start playing that chamber music, we'll casually come by, and we'll sit down at one of the tables in the lobby for tea."

"Jesus Christ, tea? What about some whiskey?" I said.

"Well," she said, "you order tea and"—she gave me a wink—"I'll fix something up for you. Don't worry. I know we'll get the waiter to go into the bar and get it."

"Hell, I'll go in the bar myself."

"No, you won't, either. You're not going into the bar and leave me sitting out there by myself. Somebody will get the wrong idea."

We went downstairs in our new outfits and walked through the lobby, and folks was a-staring at us and everything. We pretended that we didn't notice nothing, and went on down the block to the saddle shop. Man, they scrambled around there something fierce. We looked like Western aristocracy, and they were gonna get us the finest. But we didn't need new saddles, we was just testing out our new clothes.

So we went back to the hotel, and the chamber music was going. We sat down, and the waiters rushed around serving us, and people was looking back and forth. They would look at us and put their heads together. You could see that they was talking over, "Who's that handsome couple? Maybe that's Buffalo Bill's younger brother or something." Whatever the hell they was thinking, I don't know, but they sure was making a fuss.

We enjoyed ourselves plenty and people would go by and nod to us. Ladies would sort of nod and act like we really were somebody.

After we had our tea, Melisande told me, "In a little while we're going upstairs and I'm going to put on my ball gown, and you're going to put on your suit and we're coming down to have a fine dinner. We're going to act like we've just come out of the most marvelous party that you ever did see."

"Well, do you think that it's really fitting for a lady to be wearing a ball gown in just the hotel dining room?"

"No, it isn't, but I'm going to shock a few people. I'll be overdressed, but you won't. You keep giving the hard eye to everybody. Nobody can stand up to your gaze anyway."

That's just what we did. We changed our clothes again. I had that four-in-hand tie that Melisande fixed on me. Then we put in the pin with the black thunderbird. It was just beautiful, and it fit the whole outfit, and I'd only paid about four bucks for it instead of several thousand. That's what Western aristocracy would wear, wouldn't they?

I kept telling Melisande we weren't faking nothing. We were Western aristocracy. Her folks come back way before the Forty-niners. They was in Utah as early as 1846 and, hell, I come out there pretty early. I was there in '67 hunting Comanches. What does the West produce besides Indians? Of course, they got them Indian chiefs, and I guess they're the real aristocracy, but they still live in a wickiup and she and I, we were in splendor.

Melisande held on to my arm when we entered the dining room, and she said, "When we get there the waiter will draw aside the seat and you must seat me and bow a little bit. Then you step over and wait until he draws out your chair and then you flip those tails up and sit down. Even though you don't know what you're doing, Brules, and I don't know what I'm doing, don't let on for one minute."

Well, we did just that. I want to tell you, you could see people turning around and talking about us. So we had a wonderful time playing Western aristocrats.

Then it come time to look at the menu and I looked at it just like I could read it, I wasn't gonna let on to nothing. I saw all those printed things on both sides of the menu and Melisande said, "Well, I'm reading this thing, but I don't quite understand it. It got something here that says there's an *Al* and then there is an *A* and then there is a *Carte*. I guess that it spells *Al A Carte* or something, I don't have any idea what that means. Let's see if we can figure it out.

"Now, over here on the right is a good meal. Oh, my gracious, there's some tomato soup, cream of tomato, and then here is something that you'd like. A rib roast of venison. Oh, yes, that's wonderful. Here they are saying a lot of fancy things with the way it's put together, but that doesn't make any difference. You'd like some mashed potatoes. How about some carrots or spinach or beans."

"Give me the beans."

So she ordered something, I don't remember what it was.

Then a salad, she ordered a special salad. She kept asking the waiter in a very clever way as if she knew all about what these things were. Before she got through, she did know all about them, 'cause she dragged it out of him and he didn't know that she was dumb about them things. In fact, she wasn't dumb, she was smarter than hell: she'd just been uninformed.

Well, we had a wonderful time. That was the greatest thing. She said, "You be awful careful, now, about eating this meal, that you don't spill anything on that beautiful outfit of yours. We wouldn't know how to clean it up very good. We'd have an awful time. I'd have to get some ether or something to clean it. So just be careful what you do."

I said, "Yeah, and how do you want me to eat?"

She said, "Well, what do you mean?"

I said, "I've got an idea. I can eat a square meal like I heard they do at West Point."

She said, "What do you mean?"

"Well, the cadets have to take their spoon and raise it up even to their chin, straight out, and then bring it in to their mouth and then back out straight—then down to their plate. They're always doing a right angle like that. Up, down, over, and out straight—then down to their plate—and that's supposed to be funny and what they call a square meal. Most of the time them poor guys is so damn hungry that they're willing to put up with that stuff. But, just between you and me and the gatepost, I ain't, and I think I'd look like a damn fool. I think that I'll just take this stuff in my hands."

She said, "You are not going to do anything like that, Mr. Brules. You're going to use your knife and fork. You're going to learn to use them and you're going to do a good job."

Well, that was about the end of that. We was all set.

We went to bed kinda early that night, because we was gonna have to take a train at eight o'clock in the morning that would put us into North Platte about three in the afternoon.

We was up at daybreak, had all this stuff repacked, and checked out of the hotel. I was giving dime tips here and there, just as if I was rich. We had a real good carriage that was taking us to the station for a buck, and when we got there, why, we had the porters take the things. Jesus, I had three different porters and I had to give three dimes to them. We purchased some big leather valises that took care of most of our belongings and made things much neater. I also had one long leather bag that took care of my rifle and rifle scabbard.

When the train come in, the porters helped us into our seats in the coach cars. Melisande had been smart enough to order some sandwiches from the hotel when we ate our early breakfast, so we had our lunch with us. The porters stacked all those bags up on the racks above the seats for us too.

I stepped out for a minute and walked down the length of the train to check the stall cars to make sure our family was there and okay. They was doing fine, eating hay, and didn't pay me no mind.

We had another exciting ride, out across the open country, north to Cheyenne.

30

A Command Performance

The arrival at North Platte was as good as all the rest of the wonderful things that had happened to us on that trip. We come pulling into the station there, the whistle blowing, movin' in pretty slow, and then at the platform it come to a stop.

When we stepped out on the platform, I was carrying as much of the stuff as I could, and so was Melisande. We knew that we wasn't gonna have any porters helping us in North Platte, and I had to go back and get the second bunch of bags. Standing right there to meet us was a captain of the cavalry who snapped to attention, gave us a salute, and extended his hand. "I am Captain Brown of General Crook's staff, and I'm your official greeter. There are some enlisted men here that will take care of your baggage, and it is my understanding that you have some horses in the stock car?"

I shook hands with him and said, "Yes, that's right, Captain, we do. We have a stallion and a mare there. I would like to be there when they off-load them. I sure want to be careful with my horses."

"Yes, sir, I understand that completely, Mr. Brules. I'll see that some of our men take care of them, but I'm sure that you will want to watch over it yourself."

Just about at that time we hear a damn whooping and yelling up the platform and here come a-trotting the damnedest-looking fellows you ever saw in your life. When I first looked at them, they was in scout outfits and all and big bushy beards, and one was a great big guy—and suddenly I seen who it was—it was Big Baptiste. He and Frank Girard had come to meet us. Old Bapt, boy, he rushed in there and give me a big bear hug that like to crush the ribs out of me. He pounded my chest and was so glad to see me. Then he turns to Melisande and he says, "So this is ze beautiful wife of ze scout Brules." He grabs her by the waist and lifts her right up over his head. "Boy, she is beautiful, beautiful."

I started laughing. "Put her down, Baptiste. Damn it all, she's my wife."

Of course, Melisande was laughing all the time and thought it was great. Old big Bapt put her back down. Then he took his coonskin hat off and backed away and made a sweeping bow, with his arms dragging the coonskin hat almost to the platform. "Welcome, madame, welcome."

Frank Girard, of course, was kind of different. He was pretty much of a gentleman, I guess. He just said, "How do you do, madam. We're glad to see you. Brules is one of our old friends and one of the top scouts."

Of course, Melisande was just beaming. She was just having more fun, you know. It was the greatest deal she ever saw.

The enlisted men had grabbed the luggage, and we introduced Baptiste and Girard to Captain Brown, and he shook hands with them and said, "Yes, I have heard of you fellows, and you all were great scouts in the campaign of '76."

There was a big receiving yard for horses and stock in them days. They just had to have it. The railroad went through the country, but when you left the railroad, like I done told you before, you were on your own. You better have some animals. So every one of these railroads had big stockyards and livery stables and everything necessary to take care of horses.

After we watched them unload the horses, we went out to meet the carriage that was gonna take us to Fort McPherson. While we was doing this, the conductor began yelling, "All aboard, all aboard." We stood there on the platform and watched that train pulling out. There was an observation car on the back with several folks standing there, as it chugged away.

Melisande said, "That's a different thing. We didn't have that on our train."

"I know, honey. Ours was just a branch line down to Denver. This is now transcontinental—they've got them observation cars, and the swells all sit out there and watch the country go by. Those cars come from Salt Lake or San Francisco, and have just been added to our train."

When we went through the station, there's this line of cavalry and infantry standing there. My God, there must have been four or five hundred of them, and there was a band. The band starts playing, and I said to Frank Girard, "This is, of course, the reception for us, ain't it?" and I winked.

"No, not exactly. The train from the east is down the tracks there a little ways. You can hear the whistle. It's got General Sheridan on board, and that's who it's for. They ain't looking for you, Brules."

"Well, that's a relief." Everybody laughed, and Girard said, "Come on, let's stand here and see what happens."

Pretty soon the train come in, and the band was playing all kinds of tunes, until finally the bandmaster stopped them. There was a moment of silence while the troops just waited and then, from out of the station, come a bunch of staff officers walking in good stride. Somebody yelled, "Attention," and the ranks closed and snapped to attention. Then the band struck up the "Battle Hymn of the Republic."

Well, Sheridan was a grand sight—not a very big fellow, but I guess that he was one hell of a cavalry leader. He never let up until the enemy was down. That was the same way he was with the Indians, you know. He just kept saying, "Keep after them, keep after them, and eventually they're gonna collapse." Of course, that's exactly what happened. He was plenty popular with the troops. There was some civilians, too, and they was cheering, and everybody was excited.

The band got through playing, and the officers went to an at-ease position. General Crook stepped up, standing at attention and saluting, and Sheridan returned the salute, and all his staff officers immediately fell into rank and snapped to attention. Then the generals shook hands cordial-like.

Crook had come with a carriage to take the general, and asked him, "Would you like to ride a horse, General, or would you . . ."

We scouts was standing over there by ourselves, at attention, but not like the soldier boys. Thrilled to see him again, I whispered to Melisande, "That's General Crook."

Melisande was jumping up and down with excitement. "Oh, what a wonderful-looking man."

Sheridan said something I couldn't hear, but I could see right away that he wasn't gonna ride in no carriage. Crook turned and spoke to one of his adjutants and they run back to the cavalry unit, and about two minutes later the sergeants returned leading some horses. General Sheridan picked a beautiful horse and mounted. He was a man who had to be well over fifty and he swung up on top of that horse just as nice as could be. Hell, he was an old cavalryman and you could tell it.

Course, General Crook had his favorite horse there too. He rode on General Sheridan's right side, being that Sheridan was his superior officer. Orders was given and the ranks all fell into place and then the band struck up the great Seventh Cavalry March, "Garryowen." It had a real rhythm, it just kept the horses prancing. Oh, it was a beautiful sight.

General Crook was greeting his superior officer, General Sheridan, one of the great men of the country, so he wasn't gonna be bothering with us scouts just now. He couldn't come over and speak to us, 'cause he would break up the formality and the troops would wonder what the hell he was doing with the scouts. But I knew him well enough to know that when we got out to the fort, we'd get a message to report to him.

Of course, Frank Girard said, "Well, Brules, would you and Mrs. Brules like to ride out to the fort on horseback or in the carriage?"

I turned to Melisande, who said, "Oh, let's ride horseback. Let's do that."

"Okay, that's fine. We'll ride."

"All right," he said, "we'll take all your luggage in the carriage here—matter of fact, what we got here is one of them regimental ambulances. We use it lots of times to carry baggage and stuff like that.''

So we piled them big leather bags into the ambulance, and I picked up my saddle and swung it over my shoulder and headed for the corrals. Baptiste picked up the saddle blankets and Melisande's saddle and carried them for us. We all marched together over to the stockyards.

There was a hell of a lot of animals in there, and it took a little time to get organized. Old Jupiter was standing a couple of hands higher than any of the other horses around, his head held up like he was saying, ''Boss, why have you abandoned me in this multitude? What have you done that for?''

I went up to him and kinda talked to him. I said, ''Never mind, you're looking good and we're going through town.''

We mounted and was soon on our way. Baptiste and them fellows was all ready to go, and in the distance we could hear the band playing, marching that whole column out. Jogging through town at a pretty fast pace we hit a nice, easy lope and soon caught up with them. We followed the parade through the rest of the town and on out to the fort. The band was a-playing away and everybody was shouting and waving. The scouts was a-laughing. There was other fellows that come in there, too, you know. They would break ranks in the parade and come up and shake my hand and everything, and kinda salute Melisande. Herendeen and Bill Hamilton was there.

Anyway, we paraded into the post and was taken over to some good quarters where the scouts was all together. Officers was quartered in another place and enlisted men had separate accommodations somewhere else. Some of the higher officers lived in houses on the post with their wives and families. The bachelors lived in the bachelor officers' quarters. They used to call the bachelor officers' quarters ''bedlam,'' and I guess that there was good reason.

Anyway, by the time we got out to the fort it was around four-thirty, and the staff officer, Captain Brown, who was following right with us, saw that we was well situated. He said, ''Mr. Brules, you are invited to a reception at the general's house at five-thirty this evening, and after that to some music and festivities and dancing at the fort armory.''

I turned to Baptiste, asking, ''You fellows going too?''

''You betcha. You betcha we go.''

I thanked Captain Brown, who said, ''Yes, sir, and we will be awaiting your presence. Is there anything further that I can do for you? Let me see that your luggage is placed in here properly.'' He done that and escorted us to our quarters, which was pretty nice. Kinda a two-room apartment: we had a bath-tub there, and it was our own. That was real unusual, and we had a sitting room and bedroom.

Captain Brown saluted, and I gave him a half-ass salute, and he departed. Baptiste and Girard still stayed around. ''Brules, you don't kill buffalo, you son of a gun, you. You not kill buffalo this time for troops, eh? No kill buffalo?'' Baptiste joked.

''Well, Baptiste, by God, I'd kill them if they was around here.''

''Ah, sad thing. Buffalo no more. Some way north, way north. Not many, they go fast. Indian come off reservation no more because nothing for him to eat. Buffalo gone, you know?''

''How are we supposed to dress for this?'' I asked.

''Oh, like you are now. That is a fine shirt you got. That an Indian shirt, huh? Bead work, beautiful. You wear that, maybe.''

Melisande kinda nudged me, and I thought that I'd better hold my tongue here. She might have something else planned. Anyway, we said to the fellows that we had to get settled in, and we'd meet them over there at the general's house.

So we parted from Baptiste with much laughing and back-slapping. He and Girard left to go to their quarters. As soon as Melisande shut the door, she explained, ''Brules, Baptiste and Girard have it right. We are to go to the reception at the general's house, then tonight we are simply going to a supper in the armory. The night they have the dance, that's when you're going to wear your black outfit. Right now I think what you do is, you just go in that handsome-looking buckskin shirt, and I'm going to put on one of my linen dresses."

"Honey, you look like a million dollars in your riding outfit."

"Yes, but I don't think I would go to a reception in a riding outfit. It's quite different for you, a scout. You're wearing a brand-new outfit, and it's in great shape. General Crook is going to be very pleased to see you. You'd better be all set up like that and ready for it."

"Let's see if we've got some hot water for a bath."

Well, there was hot water, all right, and it didn't take us near as long to get ready as I thought it was going to. Not near as long as it did in that luxury hotel, the Windsor, where everything was bowing and scraping but wasn't too much action.

Melisande put on one of her linen dresses and, my, she looked just beautiful in it. She had a smart-looking hat that went with it and told me, "I'm going to wear this over there, and then, if the other ladies don't have hats, why, I'll take mine off. I'll only need one quick look in the mirror to straighten up my hair."

"You're exactly right," I told her. "Heck, when you're the most mussed up that you can be and you have mud all over your face, you're better looking than anybody around. So you're gonna knock them dead, honey."

A young junior officer escorted us over to General Crook's home and the security guard there saw that we were properly brought in and ready to be introduced. There was quite a long line of officers and ladies working their way toward the reception group. The line was made up of all kinds of people, mostly officers and scouts and one or two civilians that had been chosen for some special reason. When we got up close to where the reception group was, we saw that there was some pretty important people there.

Of course, General Crook played the host, but he stood to the right of his superior officer, General Phil Sheridan, and next to him was a civilian, who I learned real quick-like was Secretary Schurtz. Sure struck a key with me, remembering Senator Adams and Count von Donhoff. I looked again and seen that there was another officer and, by Jove, it was Adams. He was standing in line, and we were about three or four places down the guest line when I seen this situation and I realized that we were in for something.

It would have been a wonder to me if any of them recognized me, when it finally came to my turn, with me in my scout outfit, and all clean shaven and all that. I kinda stood at a military attention, and bowed to him and said, "General Crook, Cat Brules, sir."

General Crook just burst out—"Why, Cat Brules! And, for heaven's sake, is this your beautiful bride? Why, how do you do, my dear? I see that you have exercised your delightful authority in having your husband shave for special occasions. I am surprised, indeed, to see what a really fine-looking man he is. He always hid behind a terrific beard when I saw him.

"Brules, how are you? It's just wonderful to see you. I was very pleased to learn that you were coming. Now, let me introduce you to one of the most famous people in the country. You have heard of General Sheridan?"

General Sheridan turned to me. He was a little guy, but he was right smart. He said, "Oh, Brules, Brules. I've heard of you. Brules, you're a fine scout, sir. It's very good to meet you and this delightful lady." Phil Sheridan was one of those old cavalry commanders, and was always "Mount and charge," and "Be nice to the ladies," you know.

Next to him, of course, was Senator—today General— Adams. Neither Crook nor Sheridan had his wife with him, I don't know why. I never did know exactly whether General Crook was married or not. He never spoke of it. I didn't ask nobody. General Adams, I knew, was married, and, sure enough, his wife was there with him.

Adams said, "Cat Brules, I hardly recognized you, young man. You're handsome without a beard. And this is your lovely young lady. Well, isn't she just delightful. What a lucky fellow you are, Brules. Now may I present Mrs. Adams."

Every time I introduced Melisande, she sorta curtsied, which I thought was kinda nice, 'cause all the women wasn't doing that, but some of them was. I was real proud of her.

She'd been taught to do that when she was a youngster, and she curtsied to Mrs. Adams.

"I'm so delighted to meet you, dear. I've heard of your husband so many times from the general. He spoke so highly of him during the Meeker campaign," Mrs. Adams said.

Adams asked, "How you been getting on, son? You're doing well, are you? This is going to be a great party and we're glad you're here."

It was things like that they was saying all along the line, you know. It was kinda fun, and of course, Melisande was on top of the world. She was laughing, blushing, and curtsying. We met some other people; there was an old Scotsman named Adair and then finally, two or three down the line, was Charlie Goodnight. He was an old man by this time, but then I kinda connected it up and I knew that he'd been a partner of Adair's, and they was the ones that went in 1868 down through the Comanche country, by God, with a couple of covered wagons and went to Palo Duro Canyon, which is in the heart of Comanche land, and started one of the great ranches in Texas.

When we finally got through the line there was a lot of mixing around, and people coming and speaking to us. Of course, old Baptiste was there and so was Girard and some of the other scouts. I shook hands with Captain Benteen and several others. Then there was some of the officers. There was Lieutenant Varnum, who was a captain now. Didn't see Bradley, and when I asked for him they said he'd been killed at McIntosh's assault at Dull Knife's village of the northern Cheyennes on the Tongue. That was right after Crook's campaign that ended in the Black Hills. That came as a real shock to me. What a hell of a shame for a young officer like that to lose his life right at the end of the Sioux campaign, when he had gone through so much. I would miss him.

My thoughts went back to the party. It was a whirlwind, the whole thing, you know. Then we all went over to the armory and they had tables out there for dinner. That was where they was gonna hold the dance the next evening.

We had dinner, but me and Melisande was kinda tired, so we went back to our quarters and went to bed early. I was out the next morning looking the whole fort over, seeing what was going on and meeting and seeing old friends. People was pretty much of the opinion that the fighting was over as far as anything really important in Indian affairs. The railroads had come in, and it was too easy to move troops. Most of them was just looking forward to the fun that was gonna be had.

I understood that we was going on an antelope hunt in the afternoon, and in the evening there was gonna be the big ball, and everybody was getting ready. Melisande and I—but particularly her—she was in seventh heaven.

I didn't get much of a chance that first evening to talk any further with General Crook, because he was so busy with all the guests. I made up my mind that I'd try to do it in the next evening, and try to see if I couldn't find out how he was thinking about things. See if he could ever make anything out of that deal of Bouyer having stole his orders. Maybe I could tell him a little about the things that I'd learned up in the headwaters of the Stillwater, when I'd visited the old Medicine Man up there and heard about that conference of Bouyer and the Sioux before the Little Big Horn.

That morning we had a fine time. We heard that there was gonna be some folks coming in on the train, and we ought to get down there at the railroad station and see it. By God, there was an honor guard there and a band, just like it had been the day before when General Sheridan had come in. This time it was no other than Tecumseh Sherman, Chief of Staff, and he just made the trip special. Of course, Crook and Sheridan both were old friends of his, and when Crook wanted to pull this last-of-the-Indian-Wars gathering, why, Sherman didn't want to miss it.

The big surprise came when everybody was crowded around waiting for the general to get off the train. As he come down the steps of the car, by God, after him come Bill Cody, old Buffalo Bill. He'd been back east setting up his Wild West Show, you know. He was getting ready to go to England, and they said that damned if he hadn't signed up old Sitting Bull. I didn't know that Sitting Bull had come back from Canada, but I understand that he agreed to go into the show.

I don't know how in hell Buffalo Bill could have pulled off such a stunt like that, but he was a master showman, and I imagine that he must have charmed the hell out of the old Medicine Man. God, the Medicine Man just hated the white folks—how would he go into something like this? Anyway, that's what they said he was gonna do. I was kinda wishing he'd be at the party, but that was too much to expect.

Anyway, the band struck up the same kind of tunes that they done before. It was a big celebration and lots of fun.

Later, one of the staff officers came to our quarters and said that General Crook would like us to sit at his table at lunch in the armory today. When we arrived there, General Crook greeted us real cordial like. He had a great big table of friends and, of course, all the high officers and important people were there. The tables was in a kind of U formation. The general sat in the middle and his honored guests on both sides of him. That's where we fitted in. I noticed he placed Melisande to his right, and me on the left. He was sure taken with Melisande's beauty, and so was the rest of them officers.

Well, I want to say that after lunch that antelope hunt in the afternoon was lots of fun. We rode out toward them Sand Hills that was northwest of the post, and damn if some of those guys, them officers, didn't have greyhounds along. I thought the greyhound's a hell of a fast animal. I mean, he's faster than a racehorse, but I don't think he's as fast as an antelope. It sure was an amazing sight to see them perform. We'd spot an antelope in a whole herd and turn the greyhounds loose. They called it "coursing" with the hounds, and it was exciting to see them run, but I never saw one of them take an antelope.

I do know that they was having trouble getting a shot, and I sorta separated myself a little bit from the company and rode up on a ridge. Before I topped the ridge, I was very careful to just peek over, and sure enough in the distance I saw an antelope herd. So I told Melisande to come along with me, we'd stay low on the ridge and get up-sun and downwind from them and come in that way.

The main party was going off with lots of shouting and yelling and the hounds was barking. We just got as close as we could within five hundred yards of the herd, and then I took off my cap. I told Melisande, "Keep down. Don't show at all on the ridge." I held that cap of mine on the gun barrel and stuck it up and waved it a little bit at the sentinel—all them antelope herds always have a sentinel up on the hill overlooking. He's always looking for trouble, and he's the one that gives the signal when there's danger, and they all go off—they go like the wind.

Another thing I knew about them was they were very curious animals. If they saw the image of a man, they was gonna run, because they had sense enough to know that he was their mortal enemy. On the other hand the antelopes were curious, so you could draw them to you if you knew how to do it. I done quite a lot of antelope hunting at one time or another, and I knew about putting that hat up there, waving it a little bit. That sentinel took a look at it and he must have made some sound—he was too far away for me to hear, about eight hundred yards when I first seen him—because I could see the whole herd lift their heads and turn to look where he was looking.

Then he and a couple of other bucks started slowly toward us. They'd take a few steps and look, then take a few more steps and look. I kept waving the hat and having it disappear and bringing it back up again. The way I done it drawed them down, but it took a while and Melisande was impatient. "Honey, don't you think that we ought to be getting in toward where the other hunters have gone?"

"We'll find them sure as anything, but I think it would be kinda nice to arrive with an antelope, don't you think?"

She laughed and said, "Yeah, I do believe that would be nice. Do you think that you're going to get somewhere with this?"

"I'm gonna try, girl. I'm gonna try and we'll see what happens."

Well, I drew that little old antelope down to within about five hundred yards. Now, that's a long shot at an antelope. It's even a long shot if you've got a telescope sight. Of course, we didn't have anything like that. Some of the buffalo hunters had them, but I never had any of them. That 1873 Winchester had a pretty good drop at five hundred yards. Anyhow, I drew down on him, and the trouble was, he was always looking straight at me, and a little creature like that, he was awful thin. My God, he's got a chest that's only about six inches wide, you know, at the most. You try to hit something like that five hundred yards out and it's not so easy.

Anyway, I kept working on it, and finally the little fellow came in and stood there and the cloud kinda moved off of the sun and he stood real bright. Still five hundred yards away, but when I squeezed off, he dropped instantly.

Melisande let out a scream and said, "You got him, you got him."

"That's right, honey, that was my intention. Let's get on our horses and get on over there."

Of course, as soon as the gun was fired, the herd, which was still eight hundred yards out there, started running away, and we never saw them again. You'd see them running and sailing over things, like birds. I pointed this out to Melisande. "They look like they are flying, don't they?"

It was a nice little antelope, and didn't take us long to dress him out and everything, and I hauled him up and put him in back of the saddle on Jupiter. Jupiter kinda shied around for a minute and didn't like that smelly thing being anywhere near him, but I got him calmed down, and we rode on in. We galloped for several miles in the direction that we'd last seen the hunting party, and sure enough came up on them. Some of the fellows had had some shots, missed, and they hadn't killed anything. When I came trotting in with the antelope on the back of the saddle, everyone was real surprised. Of course, there was a couple of remarks.

Baptiste said, "Oh, glory. He's the show-off again. Never he can do anything except show off. Damn Brules."

General Adams yelled out, "Thattaboy, Brules. You're the guy who could do it." Somebody else said the same thing. They all were real nice, and General Crook said, "Well, it's expected of you, Brules. Glad to see your trophy. Bring the wagon over, Sergeant, and we'll put the antelope carcass in it and get it off that fine racehorse. He doesn't like it.''

We had quite a time the rest of the day, and they finally did bag a couple of antelopes. Some of those fellows did some pretty good shooting and it was fun, but you could tell the folks all missed the buffalo.

That night we had that marvelous ball. Of course, Melisande made me shave again. I kinda scraped around and tried not to cut myself, using my hunting knife, which I always kept razor sharp. When I got through and I was all brushed up, she thought it was fine.

I put on that damn black suit that I had, that four-in-hand tie, and even Melisande had a hell of a time tying it for me. Then she stuck the pin in with the black figure of the thunderbird on it, against that white silk cloth. I looked in the mirror and thought, God, Brules, you almost look decent, you know.

I was all dressed up and standing there stiff at attention, and she was fussing with this and that, and she said, ''Brules, you're the most beautiful man that anybody ever laid eyes on. You can't know how proud I am of you. Why, when you start focusing those eyes on those girls, they are going to go crazy. I'd better stick pretty close to you, I'm holding on to you tight.''

''You've got a fat chance of losing me. We're going on and live together all the rest of our lives, aren't we? That was our deal, wasn't it?''

''Well, you know it was, sweetheart.'' She give me a nice long kiss and said, ''Now you've spoiled my makeup and I've got to get in front of the mirror again and get my lips fixed up.''

We went to the ball, escorted by a staff sergeant, and you never saw such a place—that armory was all decorated with flags and the band was up on a stand there, playing the most beautiful music. They played these waltzes, and there was laughter and everything and the champagne was flowing.

Melisande whispered, ''You know, I've never had champagne. If I fall down on the floor will you carry me out?''

''Honey, if you fall down on the floor, I'm gonna step on

you. You can't do that at a place like this. I'm just kidding, darling—one champagne glass isn't gonna hurt you. Just don't be like a lot of these damn fool girls that keep sipping champagne. They sip one glass after another, and then pretty soon they get to talking so damn silly, everybody's sick of them. I don't want you to do that."

"I won't. I'll just have one glass."

"Well, that's all I'm gonna have."

We took one glass each, and I said, "I'm gonna make a quiet toast here before we all sit down."

"What's that?"

"I'm gonna toast us. I think that we're the best couple in this place, and I love you beyond all things. I'm gonna be with you for the rest of your and my life. I'm gonna be with you whether you like it or not, when you're an old lady and I'm an old man."

"Maybe you won't like me when I'm an old lady. I'll be cross."

"No, you'll be beautiful always, as far as I'm concerned," I told her.

Well, we toasted each other, and then we started paying attention. People went nuts over Melisande. Lots of them seemed to think that I was handsome too. I was kinda having fun with some of those officers' wives. Course, they was used to all the uniforms, feathers and brass and the buttons and the epaulets, but they seemed to like me, though I was nothing but a scout with a dark suit with a white four-in-hand tie, nifty pin and all.

Well, it was lots of fun listening to the comments. You'd see people glancing over toward us, and I heard one lady say, "Why, that's General Crook's favorite scout." One of them said, "Well, I thought his favorite was Baptiste or Girard or one of them." Another one said, "Oh, no, that young man has done something wonderful for General Crook. I don't know what it was, but he went through the enemy lines, and there is a wonderful story I've heard George talk about it a number of times, but—" Other people would say, "Isn't she lovely?

Where did she come from? Do you suppose that she's from New York?"

Melisande was the most beautiful thing in that ball dress. It was a pink dress, very light pink, and then there was some little trim color. I can't remember quite what she wore, but a flower in her hair, and everything was very simple. When she curtsied, of course, she was very graceful. She was young and she could really do a curtsy down. She did it to all the older ladies, who would flick their fans around. It was cool in the evening there in North Platte, Nebraska, but they'd make their fans go faster showing approval. They bowed to her, and then they'd say, "Isn't she a nice girl? My, how attractive. That is the most attractive couple in the whole place."

Well, you know, by this time my chest was sticking out, and I was thinking, it's about time that you swells, you fast folks from back east, understood what us Western aristocracy is.

The officers was coming up to Melisande to fill out her dance card. She was a little bit confused, but she caught on real quick.

She said, "I have this around my wrist, but I don't know what to do."

"Oh," the officer said, "let me open it and see. I'll tell you what. I'll put my name in there first, and all the other officers can do it later."

Whoever this guy was, I was looking at him thinking, best of luck, fellow. You might dance with her, but I'm gonna take her home to bed.

Well, it didn't take very long before all them young bachelor officers had come over and asked her to dance. Of course, they tried to be a little skillful about it. You'd see them circling around and going by the old crows that they didn't want to dance with.

The band, they did play some wonderful waltzes and, you know, something about the Blue Danube. Another one I liked, and I asked, "What's that one?"

"I don't know, but I'll ask this lady across the table," Melisande said.

"Why, my dear, that's Strauss's 'Vienna Woods.' "

"Oh, yes, I thought that was probably so." She nodded.

I pushed her and said, "Don't talk like that, somebody is going to catch up on you. Just thank her for telling you."

Then they played the "Tennessee Waltz" and all kinds of different things. The ball lasted until almost three o'clock in the morning, and everybody had a hell of a time, including me and Melisande.

Finally I said to her, "Honey, we're gonna have to go home." When we'd stepped out and had walked a little ways in the dark toward our quarters, I just reached down and picked her up.

"This is nice, but you don't have to carry me," she said.

Then I threw her over my shoulder, beautiful dress and all.

"Let me down. Brules, let me down."

"Honey, you're just walking in this mud. It's been raining while we was in there."

"Raining?"

"Yeah, it's been raining a little bit, the grass is wet, and we're walking across the parade ground, and I think I'd better carry you."

"Well, smarty, you can carry me in your arms, but don't throw me over your shoulder. I'm no sack."

I swung her down and said, "Yes, ma'am. Give me a kiss."

She laughed and did. "But I'm not riding on your shoulder anymore."

Well, we were there at the fort for a whole week. There were all kinds of parties and all different things. Melisande and me said good-bye, very mournfully, to the people who had to leave.

Buffalo Bill talked to me a little about being in his show, but I told him I wasn't ready for any of that kind of stuff. "Well," he said, "if you ever are, Brules, why, you come with me, and we'll have a great time together."

I asked him about Sitting Bull. He said, "Yeah, I kinda talked the old man into it. He's quite a fellow, you know. I don't think he'll go to England with me, but if he stays on for a few shows in New York, Philadelphia, and Washington, and places like that, I'll get my money's worth out of him.''

''You're paying him pretty well?'' I asked.

He said, ''You bet I am. That's what's making him come. It sure ain't no love for me, you know.''

During that week we did one thing that was real important. We visited Buffalo Bill's ranch—Scout's Rest—which was about ten miles west of Fort McPherson. One day Buffalo Bill asked a few of the officers and some of the scouts and others to come out and see his place. He had a barbecue there, and it was a noontime deal, 'cause we was gonna have to ride out there and back on horseback, so he couldn't pull any night stuff.

He had a nice ranch house, rustic-like, and had a lot of rifles and trophy heads and paintings. Anyway, damned if he didn't have a lot of his Indian friends there that was connected with his show. He let them park their tepees on the ranch, alongside the North Platte River. Some northern Cheyenne was there, and some Sioux, some Pawnee, and a couple lodges of Blackfoot. He didn't have any Shoshone, I noticed, and I didn't see any Arikaree, but it was very picturesque.

Old Bill himself, with those flowing locks of blond hair, was a magnificent-looking man. A big fellow, he always wore a buckskin outfit, the kind of boots that come up to his hips, and lots of fringes on his shirts. He wore that big old scout's hat of his that was really something to look at. He was a good shot—he wasn't real tops, but he was a good shot—and he rode a horse like he was part of it. No doubt about him being a good horseman. He had a way with people, too, you know. That was the thing that I thought was real good. He was smart. Anyway, he had us all out there and it was a privilege to be there.

One morning toward the end of the week Crook sent a staff sergeant over to our quarters and asked if I could come over to his office, which I did. He greeted me very courteous-like.

''It's wonderful to see you again, Brules. I'm glad to see

you so happily married. That's a fine, fine young lady you have there, and you've got to take good care of her.''

"I sure as hell intend to, General."

"You know, I was wondering if you and your little bride would like to go hunting. I know that you brought your horses here. I've asked a couple of other couples and some friends of mine. Phil Sheridan, Charlie Goodnight, and Adair have other plans and can't go. Still, I would like to pull together an elk hunt. We might even see some buffalo, and I'd like to have you go with us.

"I thought that we would just take the railroad up to about Rock River and cross the Medicine Bow Range, then follow the North Platte River up to North Park. That's the open range. No one has started ranching in there yet. I think it's about eight thousand feet, most of that country. This time of year it ought to be wonderful. It's part of the Old West that still hasn't been touched.

"You know how I am about hunting, and I'd be very pleased if you'd come, along with that delightful lady that you have with you. We'll have plenty of tents, and I'm taking a few of the troops so that we'll be well taken care of. I can assign a striker to you, and I think that we'll be very comfortable. We'll have a good cook and mess tent."

"General, you don't have to go any further," I jumped in. "We'd be plumb honored to go with you, sir. You know, hunting is in my blood."

He looked at me again and laughed. "You don't have to tell me that, Brules. You're just a natural hunter."

"Well, thank you, sir. I know that Melisande would be tickled to death."

"Good. You tell her to pack her nice clothes and leave them here, because she'll only need some riding gear. She has that beautiful riding outfit, but maybe you could just get her some less fancy clothes. Does she have anything warm enough? It gets cold up there."

"I reckon that I can handle that all right. If there is a general store in North Platte, we'll get what we need. When do you figure on going, sir?"

"At the end of the week, Brules. I thought that we'd leave here on the Union Pacific. There's a westbound California train that comes through here about ten o'clock in the morning every day. We should be at Rock River in five or six hours, and this time of year we'll have plenty of daylight. We can head on in to the Medicine Bow the next morning."

"Oh, boy. That sounds wonderful," I said.

Of course, when I told Melisande about it she was jumping up and down, thinking what a great thing it was. I said, "Honey, aren't you glad you brought your .32-20?"

It was glorious hunting, and we had perfect weather. We rode into the Medicine Bow and done some shooting there: we found a band of elk. We had both whitetail and mule deer and there was lots of antelope around. Following the North Platte we went up into North Park, and, man, was that beautiful too. With them Big Horn Mountains there, you look southeast and see them Rockies, Long's Peak and some of the Arapahoes, and it's a hell of a sight.

It was a great trip. Then we made our way back out, picked up the railroad, and went back on into North Platte, like we'd planned.

By that time we'd been gone three weeks, and I'd only planned to be away for two. I told Melisande we'd better get the hell out of there, and get on back before we wore out our welcome. We got our clothes together and all our fancy stuff, but in them days they didn't have no way to transport meat or anything, so I couldn't take any backstraps from the hunt.

General Crook had us over to his house for dinner the night before we left. We talked about what was going on and I asked him, "Well, I guess that the Indian situation is pretty well settled down, isn't it?"

"I think it is, Brules," he agreed. "I think it is. There may be some outbreaks here and there. I know that the Sioux seem to be settled down all right, but with those fellows, I wouldn't know when they might start something again."

Anyway, his conversation that night took another turn, and he said, "They're having some trouble down in Arizona. You know that renegade Geronimo? There are a lot of Apaches that don't like him, but he's got others stirred up pretty badly. I don't know just where it stands now, but I do know that he ran off the reservation into the Sierra Madre in Mexico. He had a few warriors with him, and there were some terrible burnings of farms and ranches in Arizona. But that was last year. I think that there may be something going on now, and I'm going to make a prediction.''

''Yes, sir. What's that?'' I asked.

''If there is trouble down there again, I think that the high command will send me to Arizona to fix it up. It is beautiful country down there. Have you ever been there, Brules?''

''The only part of Arizona I've been in, sir, is the Navajo Reservation. I haven't been down in the south at all.''

''Well, that is a little bit different country. It's hotter than hell in the summertime, but very pleasant in the winter. I have a feeling something will happen there. I'm just making a guess''—and he winked and said, ''but if I ever go down into that country, I'm going to get hold of you, because I'll want you to go with me.''

I felt real honored by that, you know. I said, ''General, I'd sure be mighty honored to serve with you, sir. Wherever you are, that's where I'll be if you want me.''

He laughed. I was sitting next to him and he reached over and patted my shoulder. ''That's good news, Brules.''

Anyway, Melisande and me left the next afternoon on the train and went through Denver. We didn't stop in Denver except to change trains, and we went on down south and arrived back in Lamy the next morning. By that time it was mid-October. Both of us was real flushed from the wonderful time we'd had, and the fun of associating with those high-muck-a-mucks, you know, we being kinda wild people.

31

Don't Cry, Alfred

When we arrived at Lamy, we went through the usual drill of me going over and unloading Tina and Jupiter from the boxcars and putting them in a corral there, right back where the livery stable was. Once I got them straightened up, we crossed over to the Harvey House to get some breakfast. Of course, a lot of the girls knew Melisande real well, and greeted her with all kinds of hugs, asking, "Where have you been?"

"Well," she replied kinda highfalutin, "we were up in what's called North Platte, Nebraska. We were visiting General Crook and General Sherman and General Sheridan."

I kinda kicked her under the table and said, "Come on, quit putting on the dog, honey."

The girls said, "Yeah, I just bet you were."

"Well, Melisande likes to kid around a little bit every once in a while, but this time what she's saying is true," I told 'em.

They were bug-eyed. They were wanting to know all about it, and of course, Melisande played it like the queen of England. These girls thought that was the most wonderful thing. I noticed that they were looking at me with a little more favor than they had before, thinking that I must have some real connections. I was amused, but knowing the truth I was hoping that Melisande wouldn't overplay her hand.

Well, the girls asked her if she was going back to work here, and she said, "Just as soon as I get all my clothes."

"My, that is a pretty sporty traveling suit. Isn't she beautiful, Brules?" They looked at her, admiring her style.

"She sure is, girls. She sure is. She knocked 'em dead." Then I told her, "Honey, we're gonna have to go up to the house soon, but right now we've got to go see Alfred. We haven't seen him all this time."

"Of course. I want to see him before I do anything else."

"Well, come on. We're going back down to the stables."

I didn't see him out in the corral yard, and I guessed that maybe they'd put him in a stall or something. So we went down, and I looked around and I didn't see Alfred nowhere. Finally, I went into the stable and looked around, and, hell, I didn't see him in there either. Just about that time the stable owner come in, and I said, "Yeah, I've come to get my mule, Alfred."

"Well, buddy, you're just about five days too late."

"What do you mean? Is he dead or something?"

"Oh," he said. "Hell, no, he's not dead, but, by God, you said you were gonna be back here in two weeks. You just give me a two weeks' advanced payment, and I held him for three weeks. You didn't show up and I thought you was out of the country, so I sold him to somebody for his board."

I stepped up and took that guy by the collar and jammed him against the wall real hard. In a flash I had my gun out, cocked and shoved right up under his chin. "You scum-sucking pig. Make one wrong move and you're a dead man. I'm damn near ready to squeeze the trigger now."

Just thinking about it now I get the jitters, because if I'd just moved a little bit and squeezed, the bullet would have gone right up through the top of his head and there wouldn't have been nothing to it.

I was so damn mad, I couldn't see straight. I was practically holding him off the ground and against the wall. I was mad and he was scared. God, he was bug-eyed and twitching. He could hardly talk 'cause I had that barrel so hard against his throat.

He kept saying, "I—I—I . . ."

I eased down a little bit to let him talk.

"God, I didn't mean to do that, God, don't shoot, mister. Don't shoot."

"Whether I shoot or not depends upon what you're gonna tell me," I said. "You're life is hanging in the balance. Now, you tell me exactly what happened. Keep your hands away, Goddammit, or I'll pull this trigger and blow the fucking top of your head right off. Now, what happened?"

"Well," he said, "I didn't have no money. Nobody knew where you'd gone. I couldn't find out, and that mule was eating like crazy—he was a big mule, and he was taking a lot of hay, lot of feed. A guy come in here and offered to buy him, thought that he was a hell of an animal, and offered to buy him for the feed bill. So, by God, I sold him."

"How much was the feed bill?"

"It was about seventeen, eighteen dollars."

"Why, you son of a bitch. I mean, if you'd sold him for a thousand dollars, I would have felt a little better about it, but to sell my prize mule for that Goddamn feed bill. Now, who did you sell him to? Who did you sell him to? Quick! Before I kill ya!"

"He was a Gypsy."

"A Gypsy?"

"A Gypsy that come through here. He had a Goddamn big wagon and he'd done killed a mule that was pulling it. It was one of them mule-killer wagons, just got the two wheels and the shafts. It was awful hard on his little old mule, and the mule just died. He'd whipped him to death. He said that your big old mule would handle it fine."

Well, by this time I was shaking so much, I almost had tears in my eyes. Imagine taking my Alfred out and putting him onto some such Goddamn rig. I asked him, "Was it loaded heavy?"

"Oh, Christ," he said, "that thing was loaded so heavy that it was just a-groaning in the axle."

"Well, that's just like one of them damn Gypsies to do something like that," I said. "Where did he go?"

"I don't know."

"Was he alone?"

"Yes, he was alone."

"Well, where do you think he went?"

"Well, he done said something about Tucumcari. Said something about the Goodnight-Loving Trail. I don't know, following the Pecos or something like that."

"Well," I said, "you're gonna know. You're gonna know real good, mister. I'll tell you what, I think I'll kill you."

"Oh, God, don't do that, mister. Don't do that. Please don't pull that trigger."

"I'm gonna kill ya unless you do what I tell ya."

"I'll do anything. Anything that you want," he whined.

"You get your Goddamn horse, the best horse you got, get him now and get him saddled. Be ready to go with me. I'm going in fifteen minutes, and you're going with me," I told him.

"Where are we going?"

"We are gonna find that Gypsy, and you better get at it."

I eased the pressure off and took him down from the wall. I just shoved him down on the ground and said, "I should kick the shit out of ya, but I ain't gonna 'cause I want you to live long enough to find me that Gypsy."

"What are you gonna do, kill me after we find him?"

"No," I said, "if we find the Gypsy and the mule, and the mule ain't hurt, I'll let you go. But if I find anything wrong, if my mule has been worked to death or something like that, mister, you ain't gonna live."

He was just shaking with fright.

"Now, quit your shaking, Goddamn you. Go get your saddle and hurry up."

"Well, well, let's see. I—I—I guess maybe I'll take— maybe I'll take that old mare."

"She's not gonna be good enough. She can't travel. You get a good horse."

"Well, well, I'll take that gelding over there. He's real nice."

"He might last, all right," I answered. "You take the gelding and bring him in here and saddle him up, by God. I'll get my horse."

Meanwhile, all this time Melisande was standing there, and she said, "Be careful, Brules. Be careful." I didn't pay no attention to her at all. Well, she was mad as hell, too, you know, but she didn't want me to go killing this guy, especially 'cause he had the information where we could find Alfred.

"Listen, honey. I'll go get—"

I said, "You just get Jupiter, honey. See if you can saddle him. He's awful tall, but lead him alongside of that load platform, and maybe you can saddle him up while I watch this son of a bitch. I ain't gonna leave him. He ain't gonna run off now; he ain't going nowhere but to his grave if he don't find Alfred."

"Now, Brules. Don't talk that way."

"I mean it, honey. I mean it, I'm killing him if I can't find that mule."

"You'll find him, all right. You'll find him."

"Honey, just go get my saddle and put it on Jupiter and we'll get out of here. Get my bridle too. I'll need a bedroll and I need some equipment. You know how to fix it up."

"You bet I do," she said, and run out of the stable to go about her chores.

"Do you have any kind of bedroll or anything?" I asked the stable man.

"No, I haven't," he said.

"Well, there's a horse blanket over there. You can tie it on the back of your saddle. You'll need it, 'cause the nights will be cold, and don't try to leave me, 'cause I'm a hell of a tracker and if you leave me, that's your death sentence. I'll follow you to the ends of the earth, and I'll kill you. You only got one way to live, mister, one way to live, and that's for me to find that mule and get him back and get him back in good condition. Do you understand that?"

"Yes, sir, yes, sir. I've got to tell my—"

"You don't have to tell your wife a Goddamn thing. Don't talk to anybody. You're leaving now."

Well, he was just shaking all over and fumbling around with things that he could have done easy, like pulling the bridle over the nose of that gelding, but he was shaking like a dog shittin' peach stones. By God, he just couldn't get it over.

"Snap out of it. Snap out, for Christ sakes. Pull that thing on"—and I helped him a little bit. "What saddle do you want? Okay, get that one over there. Hurry up and put it on. Let's get out of here."

He did. He saddled that horse up in a hurry. Bridle and all that, got everything, but he was shaking so much that he could hardly get the bit in the animal's teeth. He finally did it okay and the animal could kinda smell him being afraid. Anytime you get around a horse and you start acting real afraid, the horse is apt to act up, and this gelding was giving him a little bit of trouble. I thought, well, shit, if the son of a bitch gets bucked off, it'll be good for him, then he'll ride with a broken ass or something wherever we're going. By God, he's going, he's not going anywhere else but with me.

I said, "Get you a coat. I see that duster over there. You wear that and we're on our way. How about some oats? Let's take some oats for these animals."

He said, "Well, I've got a couple of oat bags."

"Get them and I'll hold your horse for you. Get them, hurry up."

He run around there like he was a squirrel. Finally, he got everything, and we tied some oat bags on, and I said to the liveryman, "Now, mister, you get on your horse." I was holding the gun on him. "Get on him, Goddamn ya."

Boy, he scrambled on that horse quick.

I just stood by Jupiter and took ahold of the horn and was in the saddle in an instant. Melisande was starting to cry.

"Honey, don't cry about old Alfred."

"It's not only old Alfred, but it's my husband too," she said. "I better go with you. I'm going with you."

"No, you're not. You go right back to the Harvey House and go to work. You'll be in company with all those girls, that'll be good for you."

"Aren't you even gonna kiss me good-bye?"

I said, "This time I ain't gonna do that, honey. I'm just too damn bitter and I'd leave a lot of bitter taste in your mouth;

I might leave you with a bitter feeling. I ain't gonna do that, but I love you. I love Alfred too.''

''So do I, and you find him.'' Then she stepped up to that man. ''You're the worst man I've ever heard of. Selling that beautiful mule for his board.''

''All right on your way, boy,'' I said.

As the liveryman started going out of the gate of the corral, she said quiet to me, ''Don't kill him, Brules. Just scare the hell out of him.''

''He's already had that. The killing is coming later.''

''Oh, please.''

''Well, never mind. You go on back to the Harvey House and forget all about this.''

The two of us pushed along the Santa Fe trail, but I saw right away that we needn't follow it. Sure there were wagons coming and going on it, but it was real simple to figure out. That Gypsy had to sell to people who was in remote places. People along the railroad track weren't gonna buy any stuff from him, 'cause, Christ, they could get it off the railroad for much better and cheaper than he could sell it.

What he had to do was to load his wagon at the railroad and get out into the backcountry to sell people what they needed, from piss pots to porcelain. If I didn't miss my guess, that old boy weren't gonna spend his time foolish-like. So we was in Lamy, and picked up that little old track that run from Lamy down to Galisteo about five miles, something like that. Didn't seem like there was much traffic around, and after a while I could see several wagon-wheel tracks on that road. If we got into the town of Galisteo, I could speak enough Spanish to get by, and I asked the liveryman if he could. He said he was pretty fluent in it.

''Well,'' I said, ''you may need it. It may be the thing that saves your life.''

When we went into the little town of Galisteo, I knew the best damn thing was to ask some questions. Plenty of Mexican folks kinda sitting out on a bench, or standing, leaning against the wall, resting themselves in the afternoon sunshine in the shade of their own sombreros. I stepped up to one fellow and tried to question him, but he didn't quite understand me.

So I told the liveryman to ask the son of a bitch if he'd seen anything. The Mexican answered right away, *"Sí, sí, sí."*

Then I said, "Question him at length. Translate accurate, now. No matter what happens, I'm watching you. I know enough Spanish to pick up stuff, and I'll know whether you're short-changing me or not."

Then he started translating. "Yeah, he come through here, and, boy, that wagon was heavy loaded."

"Well, let's try to find those tracks, then, if that's the case."

The old peon sittin' against the wall was kinda laughing, and he said something about that gringo. "Man, he was using the whip a lot."

Well, that made my blood boil. We went on down the trail, headed toward Moriarty, and when we'd gone quite a ways I said, "I don't see any heavy wagon tracks here. What the hell's happened? Something is wrong."

Then I said, "Come on, we've got to go back into Galisteo," and we asked the guy again, "Where did you see the fellow go out?"

He just made a motion to the southwest. We went back again and looked over tracks. There were too many tracks going through Galisteo for us to pick up anything at all, but then we went down the road again a ways, and I saw a place where something had turned off to the west. I looked at it carefully and said, "By God, look at this. Look, this wagon track just turned off here. It's going through an old path down there."

It was going through rough country and, boy, those wheels were digging in. Sure enough, I found traces in the brush there of heavy, heavy animal tracks. Heavy mule tracks, by God, and by the size of them there weren't no doubt in my mind now we was on the trail of old Alfred.

It was obvious from what I'd seen that the Gypsy was getting off the road and was going down through the little towns, and would end up closer to the foot of the Sandias at Tijeras, where at last he would be on the main route to Tucumcari. There was a lot of small towns along that route, so that was his plan of going. It all fit.

We passed through several little towns, and we got the same message everywhere. I ain't gonna dwell on all the cruel problems that we heard about. I could see things was bad, because I was seeing drops of blood along the trail every now and then, and I thought maybe Alfred had hit something like barbwire or some kind of bushes, but I couldn't tell. I could tell the way he was using his feet that he was getting awful tired and he was being driven real hard.

Well, when we passed through Estancia, there again it was the same story, "Oh, yes, the Gypsy passed through here, and he'd sold a lot of goods. Yes, he had a very heavy wagon, very heavy, señor, very heavy. The mule was a big, big mule, but he was so tired and he was running with blood. Poor animal, you know. One of the men here, he go and get a bucket of water, and bring it out and mule just drink, and drink. Everybody in Estancia think that this man is so mean. He not give the poor mule something to drink, and he is all the time with the whip. Wagon, she is so heavy, so, so heavy. Well, the people they buy a few things from this man, and the poor mule have a chance to rest, but his head is down, he not feel good at all, you know. It is very bad. When the man is ready to go, he climb on the wagon and he use the whip. He do not lift the reins or ask the mule to start, he just hit with the whip. Many of the people shake their head and say this is very bad, very bad." He said, "That mule is not to go very much more, it is not to go. He lay down someplace for sure, for dead. Then this man, I know, he be mad and he keep a-whipping and the mule can't get up and it be very bad."

Well, I was just frantic, and I was galloping along the trail there and keeping a good eye out for signs. I wasn't losing track of that wagon and them heavy tracks of the mule, but I could tell the way old Alfred was putting them down, they was coming heavy and hard.

I remembered that the old man in the village had said, "It is a long way from Estancia to Tijeras, and there is but one small place to stop. It is a creek that is come through very heavy mud and a bad place to cross. There is no other way, and this poor mule, when he gets to that, he is going to have, oh, so much trouble.'' I remembered the old man shaking his head, and I thought, by God, if only we can get there on time!

The rate that old Jupiter was eating up the miles, it didn't take very damn long, maybe twenty or twenty-five minutes, to make that stretch to this little place on the creek. Then I noticed that there was something awful black maybe a mile out, there was a big black pile laying on the ground there. I thought, oh, God, he's killed Alfred.

I went racing ahead to see him, but when I got in close I found that it was a burned-up two-wheel cart and a pile of the goods that had been in it. It was a complete pile of ashes. You could see axles and spokes and the iron rims. The sideboards and floorboards, they was all burned down. There was nothing much left of it—just a wreckage. I seen a burnt handkerchief, a broken part of a bottle, all kinds of tin pans and stuff, all bent out of shape and everything.

It looked like it had been a hell of a hot fire, and there was parts of old logs that was just charred stumps. There was three or four sad-looking Mexican peons was sitting there, you know, just looking—not saying anything.

Of course, I quick looked on the other side, and I seen that there was mule tracks, old Alfred's big feet. By God, this time he wasn't straining. He was a-running. I thought, well, what in hell has happened here?

I picked some man tracks and the man tracks was running ones. You could see his tracks running after the mule, and something was trailing behind him, I could pick up on that. First of all I thought it was a snake track, but I looked real close and I seen what it was. He was trailing the big blacksnake whip as he was running after that mule.

I quickly turned around and said to the damn liveryman, ''Well, the son of a bitch's wagon burnt up, but why did it happen? You speak enough Spanish, let's ask these people.''

These Mexicans were just kinda standing around, and the liveryman asked questions in Spanish, and they talked back and forth. Finally one of them spoke out in English so I could understand. It was a fearful tale. "Well, the very tired mule, he comes through the creek and there is much mud and the wagon is so heavy, but the Gypsy, he is not to be stopped from going across the creek, so he whip and whip and whip the mule. Finally the mule starts up and goes all the way across, but the wagon is stuck way down in the mud and he is straining and pulling."

I looked at the tracks and that was exactly what had happened. It was right about where the burned area was, and I could see where Alfred's hindquarters had been just a-driving, driving, trying to get something pulled across the mud. You could see where the cart had been stuck in the water. The cart was so heavy, and you could make out the deep tracks in the bottom of the creek bed.

"Well, what happened?" I asked. "What caught fire?"

"Oh, the wagon catch fire."

"Yeah, but why was the wagon in the fire? It was stuck in the creek! What happened?"

"Oh," he say, "this man, he is so cruel, cruel, and he stand on this side of the creek and he whips the mule with a big blacksnake, and the mule was struggling and he bray, but the Gypsy he keep whipping and whipping all the time. It was just awful. Then there come by from the other way—some man."

"Was he a Spanish man?" I asked.

"No, maybe he work in the mine or something, I don't know, but he say, 'When you get a stubborn mule like that, don't do no good to whip him. What you want to do is build a big fire under him. By God, then he'll move.' And the Gypsy says, 'That is good idea.' Good idea, he move the lazy mule now!

"So he goes and takes the ax from the wagon, and goes out and cuts the brush along the creek and some juniper and piñon. Meanwhile the mule is resting and have head way down and not feel good at all. Then this man, he pile a big pile of wood underneath the mule. Then he puts some paper in there and he lights the pile and waits for what happens.

"Well, the fire he gets started, it burn and it pop and

everything, and the mule is feel this hot fire and it's underneath him and he must do something. He pull against the wagon, and he pull and the flames get higher and higher and they are burning his belly of the mule and you can hear it sizzling and smell the burn and the mule is braying. Finally the mule back up a little and, bang, he hit awful hard and he jerk that wagon right out of the creek and right over the middle of the fire, and then the mule stop.

"He can not go farther, he's too tired. The man, he walked around and said, 'What the matter now?' He look in front and he start to whip the mule again. The mule, he just hunched up and he's whip him and he just won't go nowhere. He not doing anything. The man, he is a-cursing and whipping. The damn fool should have kicked the fire out from under the wagon, but he so busy whipping the mule, he is too late and the wagon, he start catching fire too. See?

"Then the man is frantic, but the fire is coming up, and it gets to be a big fire, burns everything in the wagon. The whole works go up in smoke, and the man stands aside and he is saying, 'I am ruin, I am ruin, and all my money, all gone. Everything gone on account of this Goddamn mule.' Then he take out the lash and hit the mule again. This time the mule jump, and them reins that held them harness bust loose, 'cause the wagon shaft burned off. It was rotten.

"The mule started running and he run over that hills there, and we don't see him no more, but the man is run after him, and he's trying to catch him and he's trailing the blacksnake. Okay."

Well, by God, when I heard that, I thought, old Alfred is still alive and he got away from the son of a bitch. I'll bet he can run faster than that Goddamn Gypsy! I just thanked that fellow a lot and kicked up old Jupiter and we went out at a hell of a gallop. We traveled maybe three miles down around the hill, going like hell. Then we seen where the mule cut off toward the hills on the right. It was the foothills of the Sandias, you know. There was these piñons and all that kind of thing up there and I thought, man, old Alfred knows what he's doing, boy. He's hitting for grass, fresh water, and timber, and he's gonna leave that son-of-a-bitchin' Gypsy behind. He'll tire him out: that Gypsy won't catch him, unless he's so bad hurt now from all the beating and everything and from the fire that he can't run anymore.

Well, by that time I was feeling like I had when I come upon Pedro's body, laying there out in the open, and seen my friend had been dragged to death. I was gonna go back and I was gonna kill me a bunch of Comanches, which I done.

Now, I was only gonna kill one man. All the time I was plugging along, I wanted to be real careful. I slowed old Jupiter down, 'cause I didn't want to lose the track, and as we was weaving in and out, I kept thinking of things that I was gonna do to him. Maybe I'd give him the Apache torture and hang him upside down over a fire and let him boil himself up and burst his brains out.

I was thinking of every mean thing I could, but I thought, I probably won't do nothing like that. The first thing I'll do is go up and shoot him. He won't last thirty seconds after I get there. But then I come up to a flat place that was kinda grassy, and I seen something laying out there. It wasn't in the trail, but it was just where the hoofprints of the mule and the footprints of the man had made their own trail. I seen it was a man laying facedown. When I come up on him, I seen that it must have been that son-of-a-bitchin' Gypsy, although you couldn't see his face or the top of his head. Both were gone!

Then I knew that Alfred had saved me from doing the thing that had to be done. Alfred had killed that son of a bitch, and here's how he done it. You could see where this fellow had been running, jumping, and falling on his face, trying to catch those reins, them burnt reins that the mule was dragging behind him. Finally, he got hold of them, and you could see where that old mule was a-prancing and acting up, and then he hauled back and kicked that Goddamn Gypsy. His iron hoof hit that son of a bitch just between the eyes, and took the whole top of his head off, just like he'd done it with an ax.

There was the corpse a-laying there and what was left of the brains was oozing out. He was so Goddamn dead! But it was a death much too good for him. Christ, all the agony he put old Alfred through, and he probably died instantly. That ain't fair, but Alfred done it and done a nice clean job.

Well, then I seen Alfred's tracks where he trotted off, and I kept looking for him. He was bleeding and I knew he was in bad shape and I had to catch him. We started on up with hope, and then old Jupiter began to neigh a little bit. Then, far up on the side of the hill, I heard this "Hee-haw, hee-haw," or maybe it was "Ah, hell, ah, hell," I don't know which, but, by God, there was old Alfred. He was a-coming down off the mesa, just a-jumping between the piñon trees and weaving his way, to meet his old pal Jupiter.

I tell you, it brought the tears to your eyes to watch them two coming up to each other, prancing around and neighing and putting their noses together. Boy, I'm telling you if there was one glad man, it was that liveryman. He'd been following along dutiful-like. He hadn't tried to get away or anything, and he was so Goddamn glad to see old Alfred alive, he said, "Why, that beautiful mule."

"Beautiful, hell. Look at his belly!" I yelled. "He's all burned out, his chest, Christ, his whole belly, his pecker is all burned, inside of his legs—God, this poor fellow, he's gonna have a hell of an infection."

"I'm sure that we can do something about it, if we just get him to a veterinarian," he said.

"Veterinarian? My ass. This mule is in damn bad shape right now, and what he needs is bear grease. He needs some bear grease spread all over him. It will ease his pain, and that's what we're gonna do."

I turned to the liveryman, and said, "Now, Goddammit, you stay right here. Stay with Alfred and don't you move anywhere. You go ahead and get a fire started, so I can see you when I get back. There is bear in them Sandias. I know there is, because I've been here before. I'm gonna kill me a bear. It will take me about three to four hours, then I'll be back."

"God, you can't kill a bear without dogs and everything. How are you gonna do it? It's getting late in the afternoon."

"You ain't talking to no ordinary hunter. Now, you just

mind what I'm telling you. I'm going up on that mountain and I'll kill a bear. You be here with this mule when I get back."

I made quick work out of that bear hunt. I knew just how to do it. I hit up the mountain fast until I come to a chokecherry patch and then started casting around. It wasn't long until I found bear sign—a medium-size boar. I tracked him for about an hour, finally coming up on him while he was eating out of an anthill. I shot him the instant I saw him without him ever seeing me. I didn't waste no time skinning him out, 'cause I didn't want the hide, except to make a sack out of it, so I didn't have to be too careful.

I made two sacks out of that bear hide and took all the fat off that old bear and put it in them sacks. I laced 'em up, slung them on the saddle just in front of the horn, and they rested on Jupiter's withers. He didn't much like that, so I had a little rodeo all by myself up there on the mountain, but we finally made our way down okay. We got to the fire two hours after dark.

"Well," that stableman said, "about sundown, sure enough, I heard a shot. I thought perhaps you was gonna have to make two or three shots, and then remembered what everybody done told me, that you were Brules and you was a dead gun. You know I didn't wait for no other shot, 'cause I knew you had him right then. I also know I was sure stupid to sell that mule and I feel real bad about that."

"Too bad we don't have any pots here."

"Well, why don't we go back a ways and see if we can't find something out of that burned bunch?" he suggested.

We went back a ways to where that stream was, and where the burned-up stuff was, and looked around. There was nothing there, but we told the villagers what we wanted. One of them said, "Yeah, I got big pot you use."

We made camp just outside the village, got a good fire going again, and peeled off that bear fat. We dumped it into that pot and got it all heated up, stirred it, and let it cool. I dipped in with my hands and I plastered it all under the belly of that mule. I was a-packing him everywhere with bear grease, down his haunches and all that. I took care of everything and just greased him up good. It must have done him some good. He was stinking a little bit of burned flesh, but you get putting bear grease on like that and get it calmed down, and the pain goes out pretty good. It feels sore, all right, but the fiery pain of it is gone.

That old mule, he had big tears coming down his eyes, and he was looking at me. Every time I'd come around, he'd nuzzle me and nuzzle me. He didn't bray none, but nuzzled. I had some oats to feed him. I told Jupiter, "Jupiter, you got to be a gentleman this time and let Alfred have your share of the oats, honest to God. You're in great shape, fellow, with your slick hide."

Old Jupiter tossed his head as if to say, "That's really quite a matter of indifference to me." Well, you know them two. I'll tell you.

The next day I didn't want to travel none with the way the mule was feeling. The stableman kept saying, "I've got to get back to my wife."

"*Only maybe* you're gonna get back to your wife! We ain't through the mission yet," I told him.

He said, "Oh, all right. Yes, sir."

"You let them horses and mule eat a little bit and catch up here. We don't have too far to go, less than a hundred miles to ride—maybe seventy or eighty, what we done in the last two days. Let these animals graze."

About the third day I thought the mule was ready to travel. I think that most people would have shoved him out right away, and he probably would have made it just the same, but I kinda wanted him to have a rest. I was on the edge of tears most of the time over the poor damn mule. I kept checking his hide and he had terrible welts all over him. His sore burned-out belly, man, it was awful.

I sure was glad that he killed that son-of-a-bitch Gypsy, because I would have probably done something terrible to him. Then I got to thinking, maybe I'm sorry that he killed him and I didn't. But that was all over. No use talking about. Let's get on with life. And that's what we done.

On the way back when we went through them little towns,

like Madrid and Corrales, people was looking and nodding at me, knowing that we found the mule and we was taking him home. I didn't say nothing to anybody about what caused it or nothing. The stableman was relieved when I told him that he'd done his job, and I wouldn't kill him, but I sure as hell didn't ever want it to happen again.

The happiest of all was Melisande. She was down at the Harvey House when we got in, and she heard about it. We was kinda the talk of the town, how we went out and got this mule and brought him back. So she came over and threw her arms around me and kissed me, and dashed for the mule and put her arms around him. She just bawled as I told her what had happened, how he was beaten and all that. She could see it, where his hide was all cut and the result of the fire.

By mid-December old Alfred was looking pretty good again. The wounds had healed but his hide had quite a few scars on it, and I told Melisande, "I'm plumb ashamed to take that mule around anywhere, 'cause everybody will think I beat the hell out of him like that."

"Don't worry," she said. "I think that when he gets his winter coat on he's going to cover all that up and it will eventually be all right. If necessary we'll tell people what happened. That he was illegally sold to some awful man. Anybody that would treat an animal like that deserved to die," she said. "Alfred straightened it up, didn't he? Just killed him, that's all."

"Alfred has been tried and found innocent. He acted in self-defense," I said, and we both agreed and it was worked out.

That was a happy Christmas and winter in Lamy. We went up to Santa Fe all the time, only five miles away, 'cause Melisande just loved the Plaza there. The Governor's Palace and the big cathedral were impressive; the shops were filled with goods, and the Mexicans was always having a holiday. It seemed like every ten days something was happening or there was some Saint so-and-so's day.

There was snow on the ground, of course, and the Sangre

De Cristo towering behind us was snowcapped. We was plenty content.

About the middle of February 1882 I came home one day to the little house we had there in Lamy. I had been trading cattle and done pretty good. Melisande was back working at the Harvey House, 'cause there was always demand to take on girls, especially married girls. After she got through work that evening, she come from the post office, all excited, saying, "Look what you got. You got a letter from General Crook."

32

Apache Country

Melisande had a letter indeed. A letter that would change our lives forever. It wasn't a military order, but just a letter to me, kinda personal-like. Coming from the great general it was a real compliment, and both me and Melisande was thrilled to get it.

The letter went:

Friend Brules:

Greetings. I hope this finds you both in good health and enjoying life. The Santa Fe area is a wonderful place to live; beautiful scenery, lovely climate, and one of the most interesting historical places in America. All your friends here envy you.

Winter here in North Platte has been harsh, and we see no relief for at least two months to come. We have weathered it very well, though, because there have been no winter campaigns with their attendant suffering and hardship. All hostile activity in this area now seems to be a thing of the past. I certainly hope that this is the case.

The post has been very active socially and the long winter has at least been cheered by many dances and parties given by the post personnel and the civilian groups that join us on occasion. This has helped to pass the time and keep the people of both North Platte and Fort McPherson relatively happy.

You and your bride certainly were a great success with everybody who came to the reunion. I have heard very favorable comments from the officers and their wives here at the fort. I've some letters from General Sheridan and General Sherman in which you were both mentioned. Believe me, that's the equivalent of the Victoria Cross, as neither one of those gentlemen is apt to go out of his way to mention anyone.

Now to the business of this letter. Do you remember that I told you, when you were here, that I thought that my next military assignment would be in the Arizona Territory? As you may have heard, there is quite a bit of hostile activity in that territory now, and having been in campaigns there from the years 1871 to 1873, I have considerable experience with the various tribes and the nature of the country.

My best guess is that I will be ordered by the War Department to Arizona sometime during the summer. Because I believe the unrest will soon increase, I assume that I will have my hands full. With this thought in mind I have come to the conclusion that if I do go to Arizona, I shall be in need of first-class scouts. Desert tribes are far more assertive and unpredictable than their prairie cousins.

I have learned from experience that advance information, either with respect to days of unrest among the tribes or thorough knowledge of the territory, is absolutely essential for any success in military endeavors in the Southwest. During the last campaign years ago, I had some excellent scouts, men with great ability, integrity, and courage. I had men like Tom Horn and Al Sieber, who is quite old now. They were my chief-of-scouts—among the best men any commander could have along on any campaign. It is my hope that I will have the services of those men again.

In addition I am looking for the services of another type of scout. I want a man who has not been trained in the military environment, who has traveled and been by himself, without being associated with any force for long peri-

ods of time, who can support himself in the wild, a man who is able to defend himself on his own and can travel great distances, who is as good a tracker as any Indian, and who can survive under the most extreme circumstances.

In short, I want a civilian thinker with scout abilities who is able to discern from his own unique observation what the military in its mass movement with its—shall we say—head-down charge might never perceive. Such a man could put in proper order the information that he has gleaned, and determine its real part in a mission of perhaps four to ten thousand troops. Such a task, of course, is of tremendous difficulty and vast scope, and requires a particular capability that I know you possess.

Brules, this is not an order. I am not calling you back to active duty. The choice will be entirely yours. You must discuss this with your wife—after all, she should be your first consideration—then perhaps you will give me an answer as to whether you would accept such a position under my command in Arizona.

I suspect that we would conduct most operations either from Whipple Barracks at Prescott or Fort Apache in the White River Agency. I intend to make it the latter, if possible, as that White River area is among the most beautiful places on earth. Vast forests and mountains, lovely running streams, and perhaps the greatest elk hunting in the world. I know that this is dear to your heart, Brules, and it certainly is to mine. I don't know any man who likes to hunt more than I do except, perhaps, a fellow called Cat Brules.

Either at Prescott or at Fort Apache I can arrange to have you and your wife assigned to officers' quarters, which are very comfortable if you don't have a large family.

I wish you would think this over, and let me know at your earliest convenience. I can tell you that if your answer is in the affirmative it will be received by me as a great pleasure. The services of a great scout like you, a *crack shot, and more native instincts than the Indians themselves, is hard to come by and a great asset to any commander.*

Now that I've blown your praises out of the powder magazine, let me give you a few important details. Should you answer this offer in the affirmative, please write me a letter so stating, as it would not be advisable or in the interests of the War Department for you to use the telegraph, thus disclosing this matter to the public through prying reporters. If you agree, I will write you a long letter concerning the state of affairs in Arizona as I know them to be at present, together with information on the various tribes, their locations, nature, and present state of stability. Such information would be of great value in your future activities.

Let me hear from you as soon as possible, as many things depend on your decision. We will see that orders are cut for you and your "family" so that the shipping of the racehorse and mule and Mrs. Brules' saddle horse, is taken care of.

Kindly extend to your lovely lady my most admiring felicitations.

> *Your Friend,*
> *George Crook, Brigadier General*
> *Commanding Officer.*

Of course, when Melisande and I got through reading it, we were going, "Whoopie!" and hollering around. She kept thinking about what a wonderful time we would have at the military posts, and getting up into that beautiful country, and how much I would like doing the scouting and the hunting. She thought that maybe the cattle trading I was doing now was a little boring for me. Melisande was pretty pleased that the greatest Indian fighter in the world, General Crook, was calling on her husband to be a special scout for him.

Well, it was plumb overwhelming, and we hugged and kissed and danced around. The answer was pretty well decided in about five minutes, but we said we'd sleep on it for a while and we done just that.

About two days later I said to Melisande, "Come on, we better write a letter back to the general, unless you done changed your mind."

"You know that I haven't changed my mind. I just am looking forward so much to doing that. I've been thinking about it at the Harvey House—how tiresome everything is, waiting on passengers, and the eastern swells, and miners and roughnecks that have been coming through. Some of those fellows think they are wise and handsome and can do just about anything they want to with any girl they meet. I'm sick of that.

"I want to do something else. Let's write him back right away, and tell him that of course we'll accept. We need to find out just when we are supposed to be there. My gracious, I've got lots of packing and things to do. Here we are, just nicely settled here, and now we're going to get up and go. But that's the army way, isn't it?"

"Well, I've never been in the army too long," I reminded her, "but I reckon it is. In fact, when I was with them I never knew when we was gonna get orders or whether they were gonna be worth a damn or where we were going. But with General Crook, I can work with him easy, and he knows how to treat me. When I get upset about something I've seen as real stupid, something that don't make any sense, he's the guy to get me rearranged on it, so that I don't waste a lot of energy cussing the boob army."

Melisande sat down with pen and ink, and I kinda spoke out a message to the general that we would sure accept his offer. As I remember it ran something like this:

Friend General, Sir:

Your letter received. Was welcomed and filled with information regarding that wonderful country of Arizona and the things that you would like me and Melisande to be doing in it. Whipple at Prescott is fine, but I sure hope that we go with you to Fort Apache. That country sounds great to me, just my kind of doings. We could have a hunting competition between you and me as to who gets the biggest elk. If I know the army ways, I better let you win if I ever want to get a promotion. Ha ha.

  As for me, General, send me my orders and the information about the tribes and all. I will do what you say, and my lady will go along with me.

                              Your friend and loyal scout,
                              C. Brules

I declare, what them railroads can do at a time like this. To get back a reply in the old days, before the railroads come in, would have taken at least two months, but we had an answer back in five days. When the Silver Express from Denver come balling into Lamy five days later and all the mail was unloaded, there was a letter for me. It come in a kinda big packet.

Melisande could hardly wait to get it over to me, at the stockyards, when she seen it in our mailbox. "Let's open it, Cat. Let's see what it is. See what the general has for us."

That envelope held several different things. One was orders assigning me back in to the company of scouts, Third Cavalry, and special assignment as chief-of-scouts, reporting direct to the commanding general. That was damn good. The pay would be a little bit better than a middle-grade commissioned officer would be getting, maybe a major. Of course, I was right pleased with that.

Besides that there were some vouchers for transportation for ourselves and our stock, by our choice along the Atchison, Topeka and Santa Fe Railroad or the Southern Pacific. I didn't quite understand that, but it turned out real plain later.

In with the packet was a little short note from Crook and what it said was *Well done, Brules. We march to the same drum. Welcome.*

Then we seen there was this pretty lengthy letter, or rather information report, that Crook had promised to send us.

It started out:

As I promised, here is the information on the Apache nation. I've included as much information as I possibly could pertinent to the subject so that you may have a real background.

The Apache people were once buffalo hunters and were spread out over the plains, south of the Republican clear into Texas. When the Spaniards came they brought horses. Like all other Indian tribes their living conditions vastly improved with the use of the horse, and the buffalo supplied virtually all of their needs.

At first it was the Spanish and then the Comanches. What the Spanish started, the Comanches finished. They drove the Apache west into the country that's now northern and middle Arizona. There were no Apaches in southern Arizona during the days of the Spanish Occupation. Pressure from the Comanches, who are more vicious, stronger fighters than the Apaches, was overwhelming. I needn't describe to you what it meant to be the opponent of the Comanches.

The Apaches made a few sorties out into the plains very much like the Shoshone, to gather what buffalo hides and meat that they could procure without loss of life. As the buffalo herds began dying out because of the white buffalo hunters and the gradual encroachment of railroads, the hunting of buffalo became less and less an important feature of the Apache life.

The Navajo and the Apache are distantly related and have common language roots, being of Athapaskan stock. The Navajo have had an experience all their own, and in my opinion are now settled in such a fashion that they will never again fight the whites.

The Navajos were the terror of the western frontier for many years, particularly during the time of the early trappers. It was the Navajos that traded many slaves of other tribes in their visits to Taos. But in the early 1860s Kit Carson ventured into the very heart and stronghold of the Navajo nation, when he followed them into Canyon de

Chelly and Canyon del Muerto, the Canyon of Death, and virtually pounded them to pieces.

When they surrendered, they were taken under Carson's direction to the Bosque Redondo down on the Pecos. It was a miserable place, where they suffered greatly from starvation and disease and loss of pride. They continued there for several years until those interested in the Indian programs managed to arrange their return to their own reservations with the understanding that they would abandon the warpath forever.

The Navajos have kept this oath and have prospered well on sheep and cattle and do some farming. They live on a vast reservation that appears to be capable of supporting them for many years to come during the process of training their young people. I don't believe they will ever take the warpath again.

Now for the Apaches: the Lipans, the Mimbreños, the Chiricahuas, the Jicarillas, the Mojaves, the White River, the Tontos, and others.

The Lipan Apaches, who lived down in southwest Texas, no longer count. They were almost exterminated by a combination of the whites and the Comanches. I doubt if more than twoscore of that tribe is still alive, and they are lost somewhere in Mexico.

The Mescalero will not give us any trouble either. They are located in their mountain stronghold of the Capitan Mountains, which they call the Home of the Mountain Gods, a range providing very beautiful and productive country. I believe they're sufficiently enchanted with that area to want to stay there after their rough experience in the Bosque Redondo. As a matter of fact they were never really transferred to their present reservation. When the Navajos were finally moved back to Chinle and Window Rock, the Mescaleros just sneaked out and drifted quietly into the Capitan Mountains, and never emerged. Everybody, both Indian and white, considered this a blessing and have left well enough alone. Really, that has been one of the best solutions of the Apache problems.

As to the Chiricahuas, that is another story. They were originally in the area of southern Colorado, around Durango, in the four-corners country. They were relatively peaceful as far as the relationship with the whites was concerned, although of course they carried on their own Indian warfare with other tribes, particularly the Utes.

When mining operations developed in the mineral-rich mountain veins of southwestern Colorado, mining camps sprung up and the Jicarillas visited the camps often, to the consternation of the miners, who were distressed by them. Chief Mangas Coloradas, of the Jicarillas, was a magnificent warrior of tremendous proportions. He is reputed to have been well over six feet, with a massive frame that weighed some three hundred pounds. He evidently was a curious fellow and kept hanging around the sluice boxes and machinery of the mining camps like some wide-eyed child marveling at the techniques and activities of the whites.

However, some took a different view of this, feeling that he was somehow spying on their activities and that someday this would bear no good, that he would lead his warriors down on an utterly destructive raid.

They were annoyed by his presence and, to get rid of him, hit on the very unhappy plan of giving him a good flogging, which is not the treatment for an Indian. He was tied to a wagon wheel and lashed with bullwhips until his back was a mass of lacerations. When he was released he staggered out of the mining camp.

There was such a fierce hatred in his eyes that the frontier might well have shuddered. Indeed, he organized his warriors and, in retaliation for this torture and humiliation, proceeded to devastate the white settlements in the four-corners country. As one trooper sarcastically put it, "Well, the miners disciplined one Indian chief and the result was the murder and torture of several hundreds of whites. Hardly a good bargain."

The old chief died some years ago, still a bitter enemy of the whites, but at that time his younger followers began to split up and go into different ways. The Jicarillas have not been the threat they had been some twenty years ago. Many of them moved south and mingled with the Chiricahuas or the White River Apaches.

Farther to the west in Arizona are the Tontos, who lived beneath the Mogollon Rim, at times called the Tonto Rim. It was with this tribe that I was engaged from 1871 to 1873. They are good fighters, but not as good as their cousins the Chiricahuas, or the White Mountain Apaches, who, under their magnificent chief, Cochise, fought splendidly. It was with great difficulty that they were eventually defeated and sent back to their reservation.

At that time I held command at Whipple Barracks at Prescott, and in order to combat the Tontos and the Chiricahuas I had to resort to some rather complicated plans.

First, let me explain to you that there is a trail that comes from Mexico beginning almost way down in the country of the Yaquis, a tribe related to the Apaches. The trail crosses the border near Agua Prieta, Mexico, or Douglas, Arizona. It leads up past near where Fort Bowie and Fort Grant now exist and continues north past Fort Apache to top the Mogollon Rim and on to Window Rock on the Navajo Reservation. It is known as the Navajo-Apache Trail.

It has been used by many tribes, I would say much in the manner the Warrior Trail in the Appalachians a hundred years ago was used from Florida to Georgia, Kentucky, and Ohio. That trail got its name in the days of the dark and bloody ground of Kentucky—old Kantuck!

Of course, the fertility of the soil in those eastern areas and their consistent rainfall produced an environment that would support many, many more tribes of greater population than anything we are up against in the Southwest. In that respect and that respect only the Navajo-Apache Trail loses its comparison with the Warrior Trail of Appalachia. Nevertheless, it has many of the same qualities. It is a highway by which tribes travel back and forth from the high desert country of northern Arizona all the way to the *lower torrid regions, the Tierra Caliente and the Sierra environment of southern Arizona and northern Mexico.*

I had command of the Third Cavalry at that time, located, as I've said, at Fort Whipple–Prescott. It fell upon me to do most of the planning to stop the bloodshed and bring the Chiricahuas back to their reservation.

Let me explain here that the reservation of the Chiricahuas was first and foremost the third part of the whole San Carlos Reserve. It was known as the Fort Apache Reservation and contained the White River Apaches under a chief called Zele, who was subchief of the Chiricahuas.

The lower part of the reservation extended down to the very hot country of San Carlos, and its southern half was known as the San Carlos Indian Agency. The San Carlos Agency stood at the junction of the San Carlos and the Gila Rivers. It was the most forlorn, terrible part of Arizona or any other part of the United States.

I knew that if we had trouble with the Chiricahuas, we had to be able to move troops into the area very rapidly. It would, of course, be possible to bring whatever garrisons were stationed at Fort Bowie or at Fort Grant by passing them up the Navajo-Apache Trail, a fairly reasonable passage.

If I were stationed with troops over at Fort Whipple at Prescott, we would have a hard time reaching Fort Apache in time, in case of a difficulty. I therefore commenced building a military road that ran from the Whipple Barracks to Camp Verde and then on to Fort Apache, crossing the Navajo-Apache Trail. This gave us easy access in four directions and I think was a key element in the war with Cochise, which lasted two years, an extremely difficult and complex campaign that cost the lives of many troopers and Chiricahuas.

Now, ten years later, there are rumors of the Chiricahuas' dissatisfaction, and last year that thug named Geronimo, who is not a chief of any tribe at all, but only a big bully whose cohorts give him credit, led a few of the young men in various raids.

There's another group of Apaches I have not mentioned, a mixture of several tribes that live on the border, mostly in Mexico but raiding across into parts of southern Arizona when they choose. That is the gang Geronimo returned to last year. Geronimo himself has only the redeeming qualities of great courage and great tenacity. Otherwise he is a monstrous individual. He is cruel, treacherous, entirely uncontrollable, and to make matters worse, his word is worthless, as has been proven in a number of instances.

During the past few years most of the Apache tribes have lived in relative peace and cooperation, but there has been a great deal of unrest attached to the Chiricahua Apaches around the White River Agency. Let me give you an overview of this difficulty.

The reservation is probably the size of the state of Delaware but consists of two very different environments. The Fort Apache area, which I have mentioned before, is beautiful country, surrounded by high mountains and deep timber and lovely streams, great game country under the Mogollon Rim to the north. Beyond to the north the high desert stretches away at the elevation of six or seven thousand feet, flat and uninteresting all the way to the Navajo Reservation at Window Rock. It includes the Painted Desert and is pleasantly broken in the north by the Lukachukai Mountains.

To the south, as the land slopes away, the country becomes more and more desert. The beautiful grass parks and the whispering pines and the running streams are left behind when one enters the fierce environment of the Sonoran Desert. Here stand the paloverde trees, the barrel cactus, the tall, almost comical saguaro, yucca, and staghorn. The many varieties of thornbushes give the country the rather forbidding name of the "armed desert." It is beautiful but tough, and the Apaches, who know it from every ledge and valley, mountain and plain, are as tough as the country itself. They have the ability to fade into the environment and disappear.

They are not great horsemen, because the country in reality is too tough for horses, even for mules, but they travel on foot, often barefoot, with feet callused like boots, and appear and disappear in the most deceptive and startling manner. A few choose to be hostile, but of course, this only adds interest and spirit to our task.

The two posts of Fort Grant and Fort Bowie lie on the hardpan wild rock desert at the southern boundary of the reservation, and they are not considered attractive posts by any of the military personnel. Temperatures in the summer sometimes reach a hundred and twenty degrees in the shade. In winter the temperatures are in the seventies and eighties and it is pleasant enough, but in the summer it is hard to know which post is the more unpleasant. Troops say of Fort Bowie that it is forty acres of hell and of Fort Grant that they're in hell's forty acres. I suppose that Fort Grant is slightly better because it rests on top of a small hill.

San Carlos Indian Reservation is located some twenty miles from Fort Bowie and is situated at the junction of the San Carlos and Gila Rivers. This one agency has the responsibility of the entire so-called Chiricahua and White River Apache Indian Reservation.

Why several hundred Chiricahua Indians have been located here is beyond comprehension. It is impossible for them to farm anything in this area. There is insufficient water and bad soil, and trying to teach them to pick up the white man's ways in this location is the height of absurdity. There is unrest throughout the whole San Carlos Indian Reservation all the way from the White River Agency to the Gila River, and it is little wonder.

What is even more startling is to observe historically over the last twenty or thirty years the absolute incompetency of the Department of the Interior's Bureau of Indian Affairs and their management of reservations for all Indians throughout the United States.

Their mismanagement is particularly obvious in the manner in which the Chiricahuas and other Apache tribes

*have been treated. The Apache is a loyal friend and quite
an able and competent fellow in his own right, but if he
becomes your enemy he is a demon and nothing to trifle
with.*

*That we are continuing to force Indians into hostilities
with the whites is due to the incredible mismanagement of
these reservations. The regular allotment of their food,
which is only barely adequate to maintain them, has been
pilfered by dishonest contractors to the point the Indian
has been reduced to starvation, and exploited by all sorts
of white folks, who have cheated them right and left, and
sold them liquor and other dismal products.*

*The wonder of it all is that the vast majority of the
Apache have borne this with stoicism that is commendable
and remarkable, but of course there are a few discontents
in any society and these conditions only help the trouble-
makers to advance their cause.*

*Last year, in August or mid-September perhaps, when
we were all enjoying ourselves at Fort McPherson, a medicine man of the White Mountain tribe living near Fort
Apache began to stir up misconceptions in the vicinity
with all sorts of magical incantations to the point where
he was becoming an obvious menace and a problem that
had to be dealt with.*

*Let me tell you that it has been my experience during
the years of '71 to '73 that it is futile for cavalry troops of
the regular army to try to engage and defeat Apaches. It
has been done only on a few occasions and then by sheer
good fortune, but on the whole it cannot be done.*

*You must fight an Apache with an Apache. The standard
procedure for a hostile Apache band is to raid some particular place that is desirable and vulnerable—desirable
from the standpoint of horses, supplies, and ammunition
and vulnerable from the standpoint of inadequate defense.*

*When such a raid has been accomplished it usually
comes as a complete surprise to everyone in the area, and
then the culprits fade away like phantoms. For an ordinary American trooper to try to track them is virtually*

impossible. The band splits up like coveys of quail and the tracking becomes impossible.

For this reason I established a system of troops of friendly Apache scouts. They were sworn into the service, equipped with the best rifles and pistols available, and paid and supplied the same as our white troops. They took their new military duties very seriously and served with bravery and loyalty.

I assigned to each troop of cavalry a troop of scouts under the command of young, vigorous, and white intelligent officers. These troops of scouts required much more leadership than that necessary for a normal troop of cavalry. I chose my young officers with great care. In every case I assigned men just out of West Point, inbred with the honor and traditions of the service, and yet intelligent and educated enough to perceive the Apache problem in its entirety and understand the tremendous responsibilities with which they were entrusted, before they became too hardened and unpliable in the old army ways.

Many of them learned the Apache language and have, in their own right, learned to respect and appreciate the remarkable qualities of the Apache race. I have never known an Apache troop, or any member of it, once inducted into the service and pledged to duty, to indicate any disloyalty or cowardliness in the face of the enemy.

These young officers, too, even though they were complete novices at this type of campaign and had no practical experience, without exception rose to the task and performed wonders where perhaps a more experienced and skeptical older officer would not.

I suppose all things have their weaknesses. A man cannot be overburdened beyond his limitations. There have been many doubts expressed by older officers in Washington, and various headquarters throughout the country, that perhaps it was wrong to trust Apache scouts too far. But as I have said, in all this time up until now I have never seen any indication of disloyalty or treachery in the innumerable encounters that our troops of Apache scouts have had.

I say up until now, because, sadly, that great record has at last been broken. Of course, we all know that we can trust and believe men up to a certain point and then perhaps, when they are faced with a most unusual circumstance, even the best may crack and turn.

A young, able Captain Hentig of the Sixth Cavalry received orders to arrest the medicine man of the White Mountain tribe near Fort Apache, the one who had been stirring up all the trouble. Hentig's superiors felt that he could take a squad of Apache scouts and arrest this troublesome fellow. The scouts had been ordered to join in the attack on some of their own people who had turned hostile, and experience tells us they would have done so without the slightest hesitation and would have given their lives in the process in accordance with their military oath.

But perhaps to go beyond the realm of reality and to get into the spiritual realm was more of a strain than any of these young Apache fighters should be required to obey. In short, the Apache scouts who accompanied Captain Hentig and his white troopers, for the first time in history, suddenly, and without warning, turned on their comrades, mutinied, and slew Captain Hentig and all of his command. In other words, they demonstrated that they could not be ordered to arrest a man of God, a man of the Great Spirit.

How this condition came about I do not know. I have never seen it happen before and it comes to me with as great a surprise as it did to the poor fellows who must have realized, with horror, that they were about to die at the hands of their own scouts.

What is worse, this incident will certainly be used by many officers in the regular army who have disapproved and distrusted the use of Indian scouts. There was enough ruckus raised about this incident that the use of Apache scouts may be prohibited by order, in which case we will certainly lose whatever future military engagements we *may have with the Apache nation. I reiterate that we cannot possibly fight these Apaches without the allied help of their own nation.*

Unless we can reestablish the faith between the two races, being a young commander of a troop of scouts will no longer be a desirable assignment, and the hard task of pacifying the Apache nation will be impossible. The only alternative will be the policy of complete annihilation that has been practiced before in other parts of the country. It would be long and bloody and may in the end be nigh impossible. It is unthinkable that we should have to follow this course.

It is therefore with great concern that I have studied this problem. It is my desire to try a number of methods to see if we cannot reestablish a satisfactory relationship between the white man and the Apache nation. It will not be easy, particularly in the near future, because of this most unfortunate and bloody mutiny that killed Captain Hentig and his command. The fact is, the hostiles involved, some fifty or sixty in number, have scattered into the White Mountains, where they remain a constant menace to settlers near the border of the reservation. Pursued, of course they scatter, or take refuge among the peaceful Indians who feed and protect them.

At this time there are about six thousand Apache on the White Mountain Reservation, with headquarters at San Carlos. Should they all go on the warpath, we would have a hell of an Indian war to cope with.

As I have said before, about twenty-five miles up the Gila River from San Carlos is the abandoned Fort Godwin. Near it has been established a subagency under San Carlos for a few of the Chiricahua and Warm Springs bands who had made peace some time before, when they were living there with their principal chiefs, Loco, Nana, and Juh. I calculate that there are about three hundred seventy-five in number.

Many of these Chiricahua were among the scouts who killed Hentig and his white troopers. The same mutineers, apparently, a month later mingled with their Chiricahua hosts and decided to kill the agency chief of police, a fellow named Sterling and his subagent Hoag. Hoag escaped, but the mutineers, completely stirred up, headed for Mexico.

Just to show you how tough they are, a small number were intercepted on the Navajo-Apache Trail by two troops of the Sixth Cavalry that had been sent out from Fort Grant. In close combat they thoroughly whipped our troops, killing a sergeant and three men, and then had such dexterity in beating a retreat toward Mexico that our troopers never even came close to seeing them again.

The band consisted of about two hundred twenty-five people. One of the three Warm Springs or Chiricahua chiefs, the fellow named Juh, went with them. Loco and Nana, the two other chiefs in this group, and about one hundred fifty of the remaining Indians, refused to join and have stayed peacefully on the reservation.

That is how things now stand. I cannot help but believe that there will be other outbreaks, maybe some of them far more severe. I am concerned about the unrest in the Chiricahuas and, in fact, the whole San Carlos–Fort Apache Reservation.

Of course, what we must guard against is a complete unsettling of the six thousand Chiricahua people. It is necessary that we glean as much information as possible as to the conditions on the reservation, and it is to that end that I am asking you to come in with us.

I would like you to go immediately or as soon as possible with your horses and mule on the railroad to either Fort Bowie or Willcox, whichever you choose. I'm sure you are aware that just recently the efforts of a very influential New York financier, Endicott, brought about the completion of a southern transcontinental railroad line. Rather than trying to raise the necessary millions to advance the Atchison, Topeka and Santa Fe across northern Arizona through Gallup, Winslow, Flagstaff, and Kingman, his solution was to extend the road south rather than west, down through the valley of the Rio Grande from Albuquerque to Deming, New Mexico, and from there to join the Southern Pacific, which has come through from California and just in recent months arrived as far as El Paso. A move taking only about four months' track-laying time has given them a competitive transcontinental position with the well-established Union Pacific and its twelve- or thirteen-year head start.

In summation, Brules, I want to say that I see the situation about like this. The main activity is with the Chiricahuas, perhaps the Warm Springs or the Mimbreño branch of the Apaches, and perhaps the White River. Those are the tribes around which the whole problem revolves.

We see no trouble from the Mescaleros on their reservation in eastern New Mexico. The Jicarillas have long since left Colorado and what few of them survive are now mixed with the Warm Springs and Chiricahua peoples. The Tontos will in all probability go along with the Chiricahuas. The Mohave Apaches and the Yavapai are too far west, too small, and too unconcerned with the situation to be any threat.

Indeed our whole problem lies right there at San Carlos and north. It is for this reason that I would like you to take your household, your horses and mule, and after arriving at either Willcox or Fort Bowie, proceed to do the following things.

I would like you to visit Fort Bowie and get your own casual and informal impression of the present condition of that post and its capacity to withstand an attack.

I would like to know matters concerning the commanding officer and the troops as to quality, disposition, and present status.

It would also be well for you to move up the Gila to old Fort Godwin and the subagency there, and visit with Nana and Loco, to see how the remaining one hundred and fifty Chiricahua and Warm Springs Indians are doing.

Then it would be proper for you to go west to Fort

Grant, take a good look at that situation, and continue on up the Navajo-Apache Trail to Fort Apache, observing as you go along any situations, incidents, or conditions that you may feel will be pertinent to the whole problem of the San Carlos Indian Reservation unrest.

When you get to Fort Apache you will hand these accompanying orders to the commanding officer, Major Evans. You and your lovely lady will be housed in the officers quarters' and you will have all the privileges of the post.

Then I would like you to make a sort of lone scout, of the White Mountains, visiting perhaps lonely camps and other places where the tribesmen may be in small numbers.

I should arrive by midsummer and will come from Prescott by way of that military road to Camp Verde and meet you at Fort Apache.

I hope all goes well and that we may see each other again, at which time hopefully the whole Apache problem will be sufficiently restrained to where we can do a little hunting in that gorgeous country.

> *Godspeed to you both.*
> *Signed:*
> *George Crook,*
> *Brigadier General*

Well, when we got that last letter from the general, Melisande damn near went crazy. She was so happy, she couldn't see straight. She thought so much of the general and remembered all that stuff at North Platte, and she could see us at a military post again, out hunting with the general, and having a wonderful time.

Hoping to go hunting, too, she'd take that little rifle with her, that .32-20, and she'd ride Tina along with us and we'd have a great time. She never give any thought at all to the Indian troubles up there, thinking that was up to us, and if General Crook and me was around and a few other scouts, we would take care of everything, and we wouldn't have nothing to worry about.

In the excitement she started talking about another thing. "Isn't that amazing? I knew that the railroad went down to the south here and somehow joined up and that you could go clear out to Los Angeles on it, but I didn't know that Mr. Endicott was all that involved. He must have made a big financial deal with the Southern Pacific and the Atchison, Topeka and Santa Fe. Think how it only took two hundred fifty miles or so of track to join up those two railroads together and have it so that we had a transcontinental railroad going right through here at Lamy. Isn't that amazing?"

Well, to be real honest with you, I hadn't thought about it much myself. But I knew it was pretty smart figuring, and no doubt that Endicott had something to do with it, because that is what General Crook had said.

"Was that the same Endicott, that son of a bitch, that was paying all the attention to you?" I asked.

"Oh, don't call him that. He was a nice man. Yes, I'm sure that's the same fellow. He always had big deals with the railroads, and he was so very nice about everything and—"

"Yes, I know. You've been telling me how Goddamn nice the son of a bitch was. Too damn nice as far as I'm concerned."

Melisande laughed and came over to sit in my lap. She said, "Listen, why do you feel concerned about something like that? You don't have to worry. You're the most handsome man in the world, and what's more, you're my husband."

I said, kinda joking-like, you know, with a wink in my eye, but saying it stern-like, too, "Listen, Melisande, you start fooling around with someone like that and your husband is gonna give you a spanking. Now, just remember—keep a-going and behave yourself."

"Well, you're always talking about that kind of thing, Brules. Why are you always saying things like that?"

"Well, I kinda mean it, you know."

"Yeah, but you mean something else. Don't kid me. You'd like to give me a spanking right now?"

"Come to think of it, I would," I said. "But I would rather do something else."

"That's what I mean. Let's go!"

With that she jumped up and started tearing off her blouse and working with the waistband of her skirt. I was ripping off my shirt and trousers and everything as fast as they would go and we landed on the bed, both of us naked. We made love then, and we had no more trouble between us from that time on.

I don't suppose that we ever did fight. It may seem funny, may seem odd to some couples, to say that. They say that you've got to fight once in a while to find out how good it is to make up, but I never felt like that. Melisande and I just had a wonderful relationship, and that's the way we was gonna keep it. Why would we be so foolish as to get angry with each other? I looked at her and thought she was the most beautiful thing I ever saw and had the sweetest nature. I never knew her putting out a cross word. She seemed so clean and straight and honest, and what's more, she was looking out for me all the time. She was seeing that my clothes was right, and seeing that I got the right things to eat, and was always taking care of me. Then she would kiss me and tell me what a wonderful time we was gonna have on some adventure or other.

Well, we received that letter from Crook on a Tuesday and the next Saturday we was able to catch that morning train that come whooping through overnight, all the way from Denver the day before. And we had a real interesting ride through New Mexico.

About five o'clock the next morning we come a-whistling in to stop at Fort Bowie, in Arizona.

I guess the general's staff had wired ahead that we was a-coming on that train, because there was an enlisted man, a corporal, there to meet us and see that everything was arranged for us. We unloaded our stock, and I asked him how far the fort was from the station.

"Oh, about four miles," he replied.

"Well, hell. I ain't gonna lug this load four miles. I think I'll pack the mule," I said.

"That would be a very good idea, sir," he agreed. "I'll help you."

He was a right good hand too. We got the sweat cloth and pad on old Alfred just like I'd always done to take care of his back so he'd always be able to pack a load. You start wrecking his back and you've lost your mule. Hell, that pad I used weighed about fifty-five pounds, but it was a damn good thing to cushion the heavy load that he was always gonna be carrying. I must have had maybe three hundred pounds of stuff, which for Alfred wasn't nothing. On top of the pad went a couple of blankets and then the pack saddle. Then I packed them panniers and put them on the pack saddle, hooked them on the cross bars, and he was ready to go.

Of course, there was nothing to saddling Melisande's Tina in a big hurry, but she was having a little trouble saddling Jupiter, 'cause he was so damn tall. She could hardly reach up. Finally she figured out how to work him around to where there was a platform she could get on, and saddled him from there. She was a good gal, good with horses. Of course, she had been around horses all her life on the farm.

Well, the corporal mounted his horse and started leading us off. We remarked how pleasant the day was, warm and lovely. In Santa Fe it would be real sharp that time of morning and we'd have had to wear coats.

"It's real nice here this time of year. You can see for miles," he agreed.

As we got away from the station platform and began to look around, we sure as hell could see a long ways. It was a country of, seems to me, real sharp peaks. They were almost like pyramids, and the morning sun was shining on them. All the country around was desert, had all them desert plants that General Crook was a-talking about. To the southeast you could see Cochise Peak, the last stronghold where that old boy fought it out to the end.

The four-mile ride to the fort was a pleasure. We rode right in to the corrals, and then we seen that the stock was turned loose with the other horses in a kind of a big pasture, if you want to call it that. Weren't enough grass in it to make it any good, but there was lots of bales of hay around.

"You got to feed the horses in this country all the time, don't ya?" I asked the corporal.

"You bet your boots we do, sir. You know, there ain't enough stuff grows around here to feed a jackrabbit."

Well, we was shown around to our quarters, and they wasn't half bad. They was plain and simple; there was a little sitting room and a bedroom with a big old brass bed, a mattress with some blankets on it, and a couple of pictures hanging on the wall. One of the pictures was a fort and one of them was of some old general. There was a rocking chair and a table in the room and a washbasin and all. A pitcher, towel rack, and slop jar, and under the bed I seen a covered chamber pot. There was curtains around the room; I supposed they kept out the bright sun in the middle of the summer.

I asked the corporal, "I guess that it gets a little hot down here in the summertime?"

"Hot, sir? It gets to be real hell."

He said it with such enthusiasm that he kinda frightened Melisande a little bit. She looked at me and said, "Well, I suppose that it does get quite hot."

"Mr. Brules and Mrs. Brules, would you like to come over to the officers' mess? They are serving breakfast just about now and I think that the commandant of the fort is waiting for you," the corporal said.

"Yes, sir. We'll be right there," I answered, but Melisande said, "Well, we've got to wash up a little bit."

"Yes, ma'am, we thought of that. The pitcher is full of water and there's some soap." He pointed to the table.

"Oh, that's so thoughtful. Thank you. I'll just wash my hands and face, because we've been dealing with all the horses and everything."

A few minutes later he took us over to the officers' mess, which was a kinda nice place. When we walked in all the officers were there, and of course, when Melisande walked in, why, they all stood up, almost stiff at attention. I watched their faces very close, and, boy, they were bug-eyed. Some of those poor bastards hadn't seen nothing but Apache squaws and Tucson whores for a long time, and here come a real lovely girl that was an absolute knockout, and they sure brightened up. Of course, they stood very respectful-like, and Lieutenant Blake, chief of the post, said, "Brules, I presume?"

"Yes, sir."

"And Mrs. Brules."

I'd been about to introduce her, but he beat me to it.

"Mrs. Brules, how delighted we are to have you."

Boy, I could see Melisande was really pleased. She curtsied to him and he beamed and pulled his whiskers. Man, he was excited.

Then he done introduced all the young officers, and each one clicked his heels and bowed and murmured something like "Great pleasure, ma'am," or "Delighted to see you, ma'am," and all that kind of stuff.

I want to tell you, Melisande was eating it up. It was just what she'd expected, you know. She'd gotten a good portion of such attention out there at Fort McPherson on the North Platte. She knew just how to handle herself and was very much the lady.

I noticed one thing real plain. Normally a scout would not be included in commissioned officers' quarters or in their activities, but, by God, we was included and she was one of the reasons. I could see it just as clear as hell. In the first place Melisande was an absolute stunning beauty. She wasn't just a pretty girl and she wasn't just a hot-looking gal that would be waiting on tables somewhere. She was a beautiful lady and she acted like one. She'd had a pretty good education, you know, and she could hold her own.

She had no airs or anything. She'd just say that she'd been born of Mormon parents on a frontier ranch. That her family was a big one and very well known, with big ranches and properties, which was all damn true. She told me she'd been brought up very properly by old Hannah after her mother died. Hannah never hesitated to use a switch on any of the kids, girls or boys, if it was necessary. Melisande had a healthy respect for what was proper, and it stood her in damn good stead under these circumstances.

As for me, I'd never had much use for mixing with society people, nor with any kind of formal officers' mess, where all that politeness was drilled into them. But I'd seen quite a bit of it when we was at Fort McPherson, and I ain't slow in taking up things. Right away quick I knowed that I could handle the situation.

I once said to Melisande, "You know, I haven't had the training of all these gentlemen in that kind of thing."

But she told me, "Listen, my love. You are a natural gentleman. All there is to being a gentleman is having respect for somebody else and being courteous and polite. You're a natural that way. You don't have to be schooled. As far as your language is concerned, it's perfectly satisfactory. It's the language of a scout, and that's what you are, and the best in the world. So don't worry about it."

She was boosting my pride all the time and telling me how great I was. I sure needed it sometimes because, you know, I didn't have no background compared to people they called well-bred. I never understood what the hell they meant by well-bred. Was they linebred or inbred? I couldn't figure that one out, but that's the expression they was always using. So I didn't know what to do except to follow my instincts, and that's what Melisande done told me to do.

Well, I done everything I could and was nice to the ladies, and I guess that the major had done told his staff and all the commissioned officers and ladies that we was a-coming, and that he'd had a letter from General Crook. Some of the ladies told me later, "Mr. Brules, the general thinks so much of you, he just extolled your virtues to the sky." Now, I don't know just what that means, but I guess it's good. Anyway, my name as a scout had gone along and they was treating me like I was almost Buffalo Bill.

About one of those gals married to them skinny officers and pale-faced fellows that are always bowing and scraping, Melisande said, "She'd love to have a man like you, and what's more she's not going to get you because I've got you. You're mine.''

I said, ''Honey, you can say that again. You're just as right as rain. How did you get so correct all of a sudden?''

She come back, ''Well, don't be smart, now. You're just gonna get a big head because I've been telling you all these nice things. You're being a naughty boy. Maybe I'll have to do the same thing to you that you keep telling me that you're gonna do to me.''

I said, ''Well, what's that, honey?''

She said, ''Just keep still. You know exactly what I'm talking about.''

I kinda put a smile to her and said, ''Well, I done brought you up right, didn't I?''

She squeezed my hand and said, ''Now, let's pay attention to everybody.''

Well, we was all seated at three big tables, but, by Jove, the chief of the post had Melisande sitting on his right and me sitting on the left. The rest of the officers didn't seem to mind none. Apparently they thought we was in line with everything.

The chief of the post started out by saying how glad they was to see us, and all that. Then he begun asking me about being one of Crook's scouts in the Rosebud campaign. When I started telling him, his ears really perked up.

''I heard that you were supposed to have taken some very special message.''

''Well, sir, I don't know how special it was, 'cause I never read it.''

''Where did you take it from? Tell me about it.''

Just then one of them nice elderly matrons that was sitting next to me on the left could see that I was being flustered. So she leaned forward and said, ''Oh, sir, you know, Mr. and Mrs. Brules brought the most wonderful animals with them.''

She went on, trying to change the subject, and I was sure grateful to her. ''Yes, Mr. Brules has a marvelous seventeen-hands racing thoroughbred. Oh, he is such a magnificent animal. What's his name, Mr. Brules?''

''Name's Jupiter, ma'am.''

"That's a beautiful name for such a big beautiful horse."

The major said, "Mr. Brules, would that happen to be the horse that General Crook mounted you on when you were to take a special message to Terry?"

"Yes, sir, it was." I was getting uneasy again, but then breakfast was served. I was real grateful for that: it put an end to the questions.

We stayed at Fort Bowie for a few days and got our stock and tack in good order. I spent a little time looking around the fort, seeing what things was like. There was a few Indians that had camped around nearby, and I went around their lodges and kinda checked on them. They was mostly Chiricahua and perhaps some Warm Springs too.

I done what the general suggested I do. I packed up one day and headed for Fort Grant, where the commanding officer was Colonel Shafter. We went through the same procedure entirely. The colonel had heard from General Crook, and anything that General Crook wanted was the word of God. We was greeted in the same fashion, and had very similar conversations. You could tell Melisande was enjoying every bit, because it was the same kind of experiences we'd had down in the fort at North Platte, except not on such a grand scale.

The thing that I liked about it was, it was the kind of life that seemed to appeal to Melisande. She was a young woman that wanted to meet people and see things; she loved dances and being around educated folks, and it was something that suited her.

Anyway, Fort Grant was a different sort of location. It was up on a hill, pretty good height, and had some timber around it and wasn't too barren. They told me that the hill wasn't high enough to lessen the heat in the summer. It was still one hundred fifteen degrees in the shade and no place to be. Of course, that didn't bother us any in March.

I went to the San Carlos Agency and talked to the acting agent. The San Carlos Agency was just a little bit north, and at the top of a triangle from Fort Bowie and Fort Grant. It was situated where the San Carlos joined the Gila and it sure looked like hell. The forts at least had something of a military appearance about them, but this agency looked like a real dump. There was a lot of poor Indians hanging around there, half-naked kids, and they was all looking at you like you stole their mothers or something. They didn't trust you and they had a real resentful and mean look. God, you could hardly blame them, considering what kind of abuse they'd been through.

Anyway, the agent wasn't there. I had heard that he'd gone back to San Francisco on the railroad. He had said that it was a hell of a place for him to be, and the only reason that he ever had the job was 'cause he wanted the money and it was a political appointment. He'd left the handling of the agency to a nice old fellow, Wilson, who was an ex–army officer and needed the job. I suppose that Wilson had been around San Carlos, Bowie, or Grant for some time and knew what to do and was glad to have a job.

Like all the other army officers Wilson was just as furious as could be with the Department of the Interior and the Bureau of Indian Affairs. It was a stinking mess and they all knew it. Most of those fellows had a great sense of honor and training. Certainly they did if they were West Pointers. They'd had that drummed into them and it had to be a real crook that didn't get a sense of honor and honesty in the military. Here you could see corruption and fraud on every side. Everybody was talking about the Tucson Ring, which was a bunch of crooks, I guess, that were constantly stirring up problems with the Indians so the Indians would break out of the reservation and troops would have to be called in. That meant these merchants would have a lot of customers when the soldiers were brought in.

That fine old honest officer, Wilson, did talk to me a little bit. Without making any waves I asked whether he thought there was real dissatisfaction. He said, "There sure is dissatisfaction, but, you know, these Apaches are pretty good people, basically. There is a lot of grumbling and stuff going on up around the old Fort Godwin, up there at the subagency, twenty mile up the Gila River."

"What tribe's up there?" I asked.

"The Mimbreño—they call them the Warm Springs—and the Chiricahua."

"Do they get along?"

"Yeah, they're Apache tribes that do get along. They take up the same battle all the time. Of course, trying to train the Indian to be self-sufficient is not easy here. In order to be self-sufficient he's got to stop hunting for game, because that kind of game isn't left in the country—besides, this isn't game country down here.

"They tell him that he's got to run sheep or to farm. But, hell, you can't farm this. You've got to irrigate all this land, and look at it: it's mostly gravel and shale, and how in the hell are you gonna farm that? You know, it's just terrible—it's just awful stuff that they've done to these Indians, and I don't blame them for grumbling and raising hell. What the hell would you do?"

"Well, if it were me, you know, I'd take a lot of white scalps. That's what I'd do."

He looked at me and saw I had a grin on my face, so he laughed too. "Well, I guess maybe that's probably what you would do."

That night I told Melisande I thought we ought to pack up and move up the Gila to take a look at the conditions up there. After that maybe we'd swing around and hit the old Navajo-Apache Trail and just meander, slow-like, until we got to the high country. We were still gonna have a couple of good months; it was late in March, and about one hundred twenty or thirty miles up to Fort Apache from Grant. I thought we would make that easy enough in just a few days when we finally decided to go.

We did go up to the subagency, at Fort Godwin. That was a sorry situation. That old boy up there was just kinda an old whiskey bum that was left in charge, and again it was a sad sight.

I didn't see any immediate signs of anybody getting rambunctious or anything, but it was a poor place to camp, and we didn't stay but just a night or two down on the river. It was all cliffs and barren hills around and nothing that we wanted to mess with.

Anyhow, we drifted out of there and picked up the Navajo-Apache Trail. Hell, it wasn't like the Santa Fe Trail, which was wide and beautiful, but it was a trail that obviously had a lot of traffic on it. It had wagon tracks, even though it was a little rough for them, and there had been plenty of horsemen up through there.

Taking advantage of the terrain, we'd go off the trail, maybe a half mile or mile, and pick someplace to camp that we thought was reasonable and couldn't be surrounded—up on a hill or with a cliff back of us as our protection. We made very small fires. Nothing to attract anybody, and as a matter of fact, we did most of our camping preparations before sundown because that's the way to do it. When it got real dark, we put out the fire, didn't need any fire in that country 'cept for cooking. Course, I had my rifle and Melisande had hers, and we had plenty of ammunition.

I done a lot of training on Melisande. I had her so that she was a pretty good shot. She was kinda cool by nature, and I got her where she could handle a rifle pretty damn well. I did it in every damn army post we were in. The first thing we did was to go down to the rifle range and practice. Some of the soldiers was quite interested in having us shoot. They used to like to watch me shoot, and they'd ooh and aah, but the main thing was that they could see how Melisande was getting along.

I asked her one night when we were rolled up in a blanket together, "Honey, are you frightened out here? There's a lot of Indians around and things a little bit difficult and uncertain."

"No, I am not, Brules," she said. "I feel just fine, but that's because I'm with you. I want to tell you that if I were alone in a forest or these rock mountains, I would be absolutely terrified. Oh, it's like the Bible story of Ruth says, 'Whither thou goest, I will go.' I'm going to stick right with you. You are my strength. I am your wife. I want to live with you, but if I have to die with you, that's all right too. I just don't want to die alone."

Well, when she'd say something like that, I'd take her in my arms and we'd love each other until most of the stars would make their journey across the sky. Then we'd fall in a deep sleep, and at the crack of dawn we'd be up and alive and the world was bright.

We followed that Navajo-Apache Trail, which cut a little east of Globe, a mining town that was prosperous right about then, but like the Indians we didn't go anywhere near it— although I could see Melisande looking at it with curiosity. For me, I wasn't taking any woman of mine, especially a beautiful woman like Melisande, to any more mining towns. I didn't have to express myself on that. She knew just how I felt, and never said a word.

We just passed on east and headed on up the trail, climbing and climbing more and more into beautiful country, moving into open mountain meadows and pine trees.

It was the end of March by the time we got into that country, and in southern Arizona, even in the mountains, the snow is pretty well gone and it's green and beautiful.

It was a glorious day when we arrived at Fort Apache. By that time we'd traveled through so much beautiful forest and seen so much game that we weren't surprised at anything. I'll never forget, several days before we reached there, as the trail was winding through the forest country, I saw a herd of elk flick across the trail and then caught sight of them working their way up the mountain in a long line. Of course, it was the springtime, too early for the calves, but the bulls still had their racks. They wouldn't lose them for some time and there would be no calves until June.

The sight of Fort Apache made us real happy. It was even better than we'd expected. The country was just like General Crook had said it would be. It was forests all over, stretching way up the mountains to the east, the mountains called the White Rivers, and from the top of them you could see all the way east, maybe almost as far as the Rio Grande, and to the north or northeast you could see almost as far as Zuni. In the distant far northwest you could see the tip of San Francisco Peak.

We didn't get to see all that until we done some packing in the hills. Right then, from the post, you could see down the valley of the White for quite a few miles.

Fort Apache was on a shoulder of land a couple of hundred feet above the White River.

Everything was made out of logs, that being the material most handy. They didn't have much shipped in, and in them days shipping in was a long process. The railroad, being on down along the southern border of Arizona, hadn't yet affected very much all that country from Fort Whipple and Camp Verde through to Fort Apache.

There was some nice ladies at the post, wives of the officers that had been there for some time, perhaps from as far back as the Apache Wars of the past decade. They all took to Melisande in a hurry.

The last night out before we got to the fort, Melisande had made me shave, and I kinda bitched about it.

"No, I'm telling you," she said. "It's the thing to do, going to a new post. I want you to appear your very best. Brules, you're the handsomest man alive, I've told you that before, but you're not good looking with that beard. So just get it off your face and make me proud. You'll look like an officer, even though you're just a scout, but a chief-of-scouts is as good as any major. Everybody will be thinking that General Crook hadn't made any mistake."

That's just about the way it turned out. The ladies accepted Melisande right away; the officers sorta looked me over and made up their minds that I'd be all right with them. Melisande done told me that I was as handsome as any of them, and I sure knew that I could outshoot and outride any of them. The fact that I couldn't read or write was none of their damn business.

Major Evans was the commanding officer of Fort Apache and he gave us a hearty welcome, telling us that he'd had a letter from General Crook concerning us and he was mighty glad to have us aboard his command. He'd heard of my reputation as a scout, rifleman, and tracker, and knew that when I familiarized myself with these mountains I'd be a tremendous asset to the command.

As far as my lady was concerned, he said, he only had to

look at her to see that she would bring sunshine and distinction to any cavalry post in the country.

Well, he was laying it on mighty thick, but, you know, I think he was sincere. He was one of them southern gentlemen that could always carry on the most complimentary conversation and make everybody feel good and seem like he meant it. I sure hope he did, because both Melisande and I liked him real well.

His wife was a nice lady, too, as were most of the other ladies of the command. When we went to the officers' mess for dinner, we had a little libation before we sat down at the tables, and the young officers of the staff crowded around Melisande like bees in a flower bed.

As far as the women of the post were concerned, I could see they were asking questions of the older officers and then glancing over at me. I could see some shining eyes among those ladies, that was made even brighter by the candlelight.

After we were seated and a proper military toast was made by the commanding officer, dinner was served by Mexican personnel who seemed dressed for the occasion. It sure didn't appear to me like a frontier post, but like something that might be somewhere in Virginia. Officers, like Evans, who came from either Virginia or the Carolinas had that wonderful gentlemanly talk and manners that made everyone sit up and take notice.

After dinner I began talking with some of the young officers about hunting, and they told me some wonderful stories. Naturally, I was itching to go into the backcountry, and there were several of them that wanted to go with me, but I thought that it might be better if I went by myself.

I decided to take Melisande with me. She was riding Tina, and of course, we weren't gonna leave old Alfred behind, not only because we loved him, but because, by God, we needed a mule to pack our equipment.

The commanding officer, Major Evans, was a little bit disturbed about the idea of me going off with my wife alone in the mountains. He knew that there was some Apaches of that White River gang who were right at the edge of being renegades. As he explained to me, after all, it was only last August when young Captain Hentig and several of his men had been killed.

It was a deplorable situation, but he thought that the real key to it was, even though we could ask these Apaches to scout against their own people, and could count on their fidelity, it was another thing when we put them to the task of turning against a medicine man, a holy man.

He hoped that was the reason rather than the fact that the Apache scouts could not really be trusted in a crisis. In the whole time of using Apache scouts in the system that General Crook had set up, they had never shown a sign of betrayal. Naturally, the Washington armchair generals had said right along that it would be just a matter of time.

Evans did say that although I knew my business and had gone through Comanche country alone with no difficulty, I should remember that now I wasn't going on foot and keeping myself out of sight, but rather was packing up through the country with a splendid horse that would be the envy of any Indian and a mule who would be a prize.

In addition, he pointed out, I was taking a beautiful white girl with me who would make a fine squaw for some warrior, or she could be carried into Mexico and sold as a slave for a very high price somewhere among the Apaches of the Sierra Madre.

Well, all this kinda made me gulp a bit and feel a little bit shaky. I didn't know whether to talk to Melisande or whether to just let it go, but finally decided I would tell her that there was some risk.

When I talked to her in our log cabin that night, she was a brave girl. She said she didn't care, 'cause she'd feel more in danger around the post by herself than if she were with me in the mountains, and that if anything was gonna happen to us, it better happen to both of us together.

I must say my heart was overwhelmed at her devotion and her absolute conviction that she was gonna be with me no matter what happened.

One of the missions that I was instructed by Crook to

perform was the investigation in the backwoods area of Chiri-cahua and White River Apaches, and I planned to determine the status of things there.

I told Melisande that I couldn't be cringing around the fort here if I was gonna do General Crook justice. I had to get out in the timber and see what it was all about. Undoubtedly we'd run into some Indians, probably they'd be stalking us a long time before we ever saw them, and they'd be very interested in what we was doing, and maybe some of the terrible things Major Evans had suggested would be in their minds, but they would take some time and thought before they did anything to bring down the wrath of a whole damn U.S. Cavalry.

Another thing that I thought perhaps would be worthwhile was, since I was a legend among the tribes as the Cat Man whose rifle spoke with the tongue of death, I'd use that. I was known throughout all the tribes and held in great respect, and I got to thinking that maybe that respect would do us some good when it come to real safety. I remembered when the Blackfoot warriors come chasing Wesha and me for the horses we stole from 'em, how the Sign of the Cat turned them back, because of their superstitions. I intended to lay the Sign of the Cat around quite a few places, if I had to carve it in trees or mark it with some burnt stick on a rock. I needn't talk to any officers about it: I just talked about it to my wife, and we decided that was a darn good thing to do. Everywhere I went would be the Sign of the Cat, and Indians being as superstitious as they was, it might keep them from bothering us.

We went off on a sunshiny morning and headed southeast toward the highest part of the White River Mountains. We could see from what little snow there was on the ground occasionally that the place was full of game. There were all kinds of tracks, about everything you could imagine, elk, deer, bear, mountain lion. Of course, I didn't see no antelope tracks.

Before we started seeing game, I didn't think it was neces-sary to do any shooting. I just thought we'd camp out at one of the places, put the Sign of the Cat on a tree that was overlook-ing our fire, and if anybody wanted to come in and join us, they could. It would be stupid of us to think, for one minute, that we'd be traveling through Apache Reservation in the White River Forest and not be spotted. Of course they would spot us and would be following us and watching us. It was the Indian way; but we would be real nice to them if they came to see us.

On several occasions we saw warriors hanging around the outside of the camp in the middle of the day, and we invited them in. I had lots of ammunition and I give some of it away. That was one of the best presents you could give them. There was other things, of course, but I hadn't come to be a trader, so I mostly used ammunition, 'cause I knew I could get more. I checked that out at the post before I ever left. I knew that some of them fellows, when I went back to buy some more ammunition, would be kidding me about all the shots I'd missed, but I wouldn't tell them that I'd given them mostly to Apaches.

Several of them Apaches got to be real good friends of ours, least I thought they was. They seldom came to the camp at night, but they'd come in the middle of the day, sit and talk—tried to do everything in sign language, and I was fair in that. It wasn't long before they discovered the Sign of the Cat wherever we went, and that seemed to make a big difference.

Once they made friends with us, then they would come at night, although the first couple of times they did, it was kinda spooky seeing these armed warriors come out of the woods and into the circle of the firelight without saying a damn thing. First time it happened, Melisande almost screamed. I always carried my rifle right beside me, so I let it swing around on the intruder. When I seen who it was and that he was making the signs of peace, I remembered that he was a guy we had fed the day before. So I invited him in and things was very peaceful.

I'll tell you this, in all my wandering through Apache country I never once had anything stolen. The Apaches ain't thieves. Quite different than a lot of other tribes. I was glad to be told from General Crook's letter that they wasn't as fierce as the Comanches. They certainly weren't, although they didn't lack bravery when the time come. You could see in their faces that they were a different kind of people, not nearly so rough and brutal. I honestly felt that if the Apaches had a decent chance and could make the conversion to white man's ways, they'd be a real asset to the country. I haven't changed my mind any about that.

We was out about a month, and as we progressed along we seemed to make more and more friends who would come to see us. I remembered that there was some squaws that would come sometimes too. They was kinda shy, but they was excited about what they saw and always they'd point to the Sign of the Cat on every tree where we'd camp. I made a habit of carving it in there as one of the camp duties.

We did a little bit of trading. Melisande fell in love with a beaded shirt that was the best-looking thing I'd seen in a long time, especially on her. We got some other things, too, because the Apaches were beginning to work in silver.

They hadn't got so they could do the fine work they would later on, and they never did get as good at it as the Navajo. But some of that Apache stuff was damn nice looking, and seemed to catch Melisande's eye, and that's all I cared about. I traded for a necklace for her of silver beads made into little figures that you couldn't tell exactly what they was.

We stayed out about a month and came back to the fort in good time. We had killed some elk, just for food, and had plenty of staple supplies that carried us through fine. When we come back we was quite the objects of curiosity. There weren't many of them officers that would consider going out by themselves, or taking their wives with them, and wandering through the Fort Apache Indian Reservation the way we done.

I told Major Evans I hadn't seen no signs of unrest, and as a matter of fact I thought that the children down in San Carlos, half-starved, half-naked little creatures, was a lot more resentful of the white man than the Chiricahua warriors or their squaws up in the high country.

I told him about the warriors' visits to our camp, both in the daylight and the dark. Major Evans only shook his head. "Brules, it seems to me that you were taking some awful chances."

"Well," I said, "maybe I was, Major, but it didn't seem

like that to me. I get a feeling when things are about to happen—like the hair standing on the back of my neck. It's been my signal for many years, and I didn't feel none of it this time.''

Then I told him about how I'd put up the Sign of the Cat, and he listened very intently to that. He nodded and said, ''Yes, I heard about your doing that up there in the upper Yellowstone area, and how it had worked on several occasions. It seems that your idea has traveled ahead of you.

''Still, you were a sitting duck out there all by yourself with your wife, and that fine stock you had with you—if anything saved you from being in real deep trouble, perhaps it was that symbol. I hope that your guardian angel, that Sign of the Cat, continues to keep you out of trouble, Brules.'' He smiled and shook hands and said, ''We're glad to see you back. I suppose now you can just wait for General Crook—when he comes you'll be seeing a lot of things happen. Meanwhile, of course, you're perfectly free to do whatever you wish.''

Well, I started to make a few plans, but I didn't have long to wait. About mid-May the Jicarilla informed us that a war party of the Chiricahua had come up from Mexico and raided the subagency and forced the Indians there under Chief Loco to return with them to Mexico. The renegades had started straight south and proceeded with the usual slaughter of cattle and humans, and the burning of every ranch house in the way, leaving a trail of carnage on the road to Mexico. Troops from both Bowie and Grant and some from New Mexico raced over to cut them off. The American troops didn't suffer any casualties either time, for the simple reason that the Indians were so well mounted and moved with such speed that they escaped to Mexico with hardly no loss of their fighting men.

Just by chance, though, women traveling in advance of the rear guard of warriors did run into a Mexican military force. The Mexicans did a great deal of damage to the women and children in that group, but the warriors in the rear guard, hearing the firing up forward, come a-racing up, and it didn't take long for them to clean out the Mexican infantry. It was no match for a band of well-armed Apaches.

Feeling it a matter of duty I decided to make a quick trip down the Navajo-Apache Trail to San Carlos to inspect the area around Fort Godwin and the subagency, to see for myself what was left and what had happened. Melisande, no matter what I said, kept insisting on going with me, and so in the end I just shrugged my shoulders and took her along.

She was well armed. I had bought her a small revolver of .32 caliber, and had her spend more time with her .32-20 on the target range at Fort Apache. She had a good keen eye and natural instincts, and by that time was becoming a pretty fair rifleman. She knew how to clear a jam and clean her gun and handle the weapon in the same kinda natural way that was common to everything she did.

We wanted to travel fast, and for a short time had thought we'd leave Alfred, but then, remembering how we'd missed him in the past, I packed him with a light load of various things that we needed, plus plenty of ammunition, and we hit off at a good pace.

We rode damn near sixty miles the first day, and Melisande, even though she'd ridden all of her life, and a lot with me, was still a little saddle-sore at the end of that day's journey. She toughened up in a hurry, though, and we made it into San Carlos the second night.

We had a talk with the agent there, who didn't seem to know what had really happened. It all had come about so quick. The only thing that he was grateful for was that the Apaches didn't attack his agency—but made directly for Mexico.

There had to have been something like two hundred twenty-five people, of which a hundred were warriors. That weren't anything to fool with. As a matter of fact, Tom Horn, one of the great scouts, been hanging around the agency at the time. He wasn't there when I got there, so I didn't get the story from him. The agent told me that Horn saw that there was no way to defend San Carlos, so he retreated up to a spot of spiraled cathedrallike rocks and settled down there to make a last stand, if necessary.

Neither the Indians nor Tom Horn's group fired on each

other. The Indians would have had a very costly attack if they had rushed those riflemen up in the rocks, and the riflemen would have been courting disaster if they had fired on so many warriors. It was sort of a natural truce and everybody stood back.

I was sorry that Tom Horn was not there when I came in, 'cause I would have liked to talk to him about it. He had a very keen mind and was one of the most fearless men in the Southwest. He spoke very fine Apache, and in this way was superior to his teacher Al Sieber, who could only speak it in a halting, thoughtful sort of way. Later Horn went with Sieber several times into Mexico to have conferences with Geronimo, and Horn's command of Apache made the deal a lot easier.

The only thing that really got to Melisande was that it was now May and down there in the San Carlos country it was hotter than hell. It was ninety to one hundred a lot of the time. When she began complaining a little bit about it, I said, "Honey, how would you like to get stuck down here in this country in mid-July and August when it can be a hundred and twenty in the shade?"

She just shook her head and said nothing. I knew what the answer was.

Well, we hurried on back up to Fort Apache and were sure pleased to get up in that cool country, in the forest and the streams at five thousand feet altitude.

Major Evans seemed glad to see us back, as did many of the officers, and the ladies were certainly asking Melisande all kinds of questions, now that she'd been out on two Apache scoutings.

To be real honest with you most of them ladies was plumb scared to death to remain there at Fort Apache, if there was gonna be an uprising. You could hardly blame them, 'cause the way they looked at it was, my God, there are six thousand Apaches right here in this area. Course, we all knew that the only ones that would really rise, unless they were given some terrific reason to do so, would be the discontented, and they would only amount to about twenty percent of the nation, but still, twelve hundred Apaches on the warpath is an unpleasant thing to think about.

We was there at Fort Apache for another few weeks, not doing much, just staying around the post. As Melisande put it, "Kinda cooling off again." But it was great to just be with her and we had many wonderful nights in our officers' quarters.

33

Chaffee's Victory

Everything went along fine until the morning of the seventeenth of July, when a party of fifty-four White Mountain warriors from right around Fort Apache made a quick rush down a hundred and twenty-five miles to the San Carlos Agency, and killed Colvig, chief of the agency police. He'd succeeded the man who had been killed by Juh and Geronimo before they beat it for Mexico. The Indian gang had come clear from Fort Apache to smack the San Carlos Agency again, and not only killed Colvig, but seven of his Indian police that was loyal and stood with him. Seemed like being chief of Indian police at San Carlos or at the subagency was a damn unhealthy job.

Then, instead of going south to Mexico like Geronimo and Juh had done, which was a kinda traditional departing, they swung north again and raided through the San Carlos Valley, moved a little east of Globe, changed their direction northwest, and crossed the Salt River at the mouth of Tonto Creek.

You can imagine the hell that was raised at Fort Apache. The telegraph line to Whipple Barracks was a-humming, with a result that was kinda surprising to me. Within three or four hours of the outbreak the United States Cavalry in Arizona put into the field fourteen troops of cavalry from different positions, all to concentrate on the fleeing White River renegades. This was a hell of a good example of what the telegraph meant.

Two troops of the Sixth Cavalry, two troops of the Third Cavalry, and four White Mountain Apache scouts, all under Major Evans of the Third Cavalry, left Fort Apache almost immediately that morning. I rode right with Major Evans, at my suggestion and his hearty acceptance. I left Melisande behind in a flood of tears and protests. Having been out on two Apache scouts with me before, she couldn't understand why she couldn't go along on a full-fledged cavalry attack, but we kissed good-bye and I whirled my horse around and left her on the dead gallop.

At the same time we was working our way out of Fort Apache, one troop of the Third Cavalry and one of the Sixth had departed from Camp Verde under a Lieutenant Chase. They'd taken the Crook military road around the escarpment of Tonto Basin that cut the Navajo Trail, with the purpose of heading off the hostiles if they went that way, which they done. Besides that, four troops come out of Fort Thomas. Two troops of the Third Cavalry, two of the Sixth Cavalry, and eight Tonto scouts under Captain Chaffee, with that old best-of-all-scouts Al Sieber, left Whipple Barracks that day and made Camp Verde, forty-two miles, by night. By forced marches they reached Wild Rye on Tonto Creek two days later. Shortly after they had set up camp, one of the Bixby brothers, who owned a large ranch in Tonto Basin, rode in wounded and reported that their ranch had been burned and his brother killed.

Captain Chaffee, of the Whipple Barracks force, despite the exhausting marches of the last three days, immediately broke camp again, remounted one of his two companies, with the scouts under Sieber, and started for Tonto Basin. He left the rest of the command to follow.

A Lieutenant Morgan remained back to bring the pack train from Verde through Hardscrabble Canyon. He done this and cut across country alone and overtook Chaffee just before the fighting began.

Chaffee had hit the trail of the hostiles in Tonto Basin just ahead of us, and one of our patrols overtook Chaffee to advise him that help was near if needed. That night Chaffee sent word back to Major Evans that he was close in on the hostiles and needed reinforcements. Troop E of the Third Cavalry under Captain Converse, the lead troop with our command, was rushed ahead to join Chaffee the next morning. The rest of our troops followed close behind.

It was here that the inexperienced White Mountain chief, Na-ti-o-tish, made his fatal mistake. Chaffee's troop was a white-horse troop. The Apaches were watching Chaffee, and being the sharp observers they were, they knew the strength of Chaffee's troop to a man. They were sure that their own fire-power could stand up to one troop of the U.S. Cavalry. It was their plan to lead Chaffee's command into a trap and massacre the whole troop, which they could do easy, 'cause they out-numbered them by a hell of a lot.

The fact was that Captain Converse's troop was also a white-horse troop. No doubt that troop, rushing to Chaffee's aid, looked like the straggling rear of Chaffee's command, as it flickered through the trees. The Apaches had no idea that they were facing two troops instead of one, with several more troops not far behind.

The hostiles also didn't notice that Chaffee had with him some Tonto scouts from Fort McDowell, and some White Mountain scouts from Fort Apache that had come with Morgan when he'd made his incredible dash to be with Chaffee.

Yet the trap Chief Na-ti-o-tish had laid for the cavalry was pretty good. The Apache trail the troops were following led down into a canyon, a sort of steep cut in the earth about a thousand feet deep, with almost perpendicular sides, and maybe two thousand feet across at the top. It was called the Big Dry Wash Gulch, a tributary of Diablo Canyon.

The hostiles, with their stolen horses and the plunder from the ranches they had raided, crossed the canyon and ascended the opposite side to near the top. They sent their horses back out of sight on the level ground on top of the canyon, then built some good parapets of loose rock that would hide them and put them in a great position to fire on Chaffee and his command as they descended into the canyon. If their scheme had worked they would have wiped out Chaffee's command to a man.

Just figure what would have happened if Sieber and his Apache scouts hadn't spotted Chief Na-ti-o-tish's band across the canyon on the edge of the opposite cliffs, even as they was hiding behind the parapets.

The trail was real steep and straight down the side of the canyon, across the creek on the other side, and directly up on the opposite cliffs.

Well, the warriors laying behind them rocks would have just waited until the troopers was way down into the canyon, and then they would have started firing. There wasn't no place to hide down there, and them Indians up above would just empty their magazines on the troops.

The destruction would have been awful. All kinds of piling up and turning around and fellows trying to dash back up the trail, but the Apaches would have sat there and shot them off their horses or killed the horses as they was going up, just as easy as pie.

But Sieber done seen them. The whole command stopped short of the canyon wall and just waited. In a few minutes, as promised, Evans with his three troops come up and joined Chaffee. He, of course, outranked Chaffee—Evans was a major, Chaffee only a captain—and Chaffee turned to him and said, "All right, Major, the command is yours now, sir."

"The hell it is. You found them, you dogged them, it's your command now, Captain. You set up the battle plan and go to work," Evans insisted.

You know, that was one of the most unselfish and finest things that a superior officer could do for a subordinate. Evans could have took all the credit for it when in reality it was Chaffee that had gone for three hard days of tough riding and tracked them down to this position.

Well, Chaffee didn't mess around very much. Real quick he knew what he was gonna do. He ordered his own troop to advance into position and to dismount, keeping the horses back from the edge, lined out as if ready to set up a line of defense. Then he brought the other troops up and ordered us forward in a scrimmage line. It made us look like we was getting ready to cross the canyon—like we'd spotted Na-ti-o-tish's band and was gonna give covering fire.

I've got to explain that coming up to the edge of the canyon was a pine forest all around. There was no underbrush, and when the horses and men was dashing around, it kinda made a kaleidoscope of colors and changes and it was hard for the Indians on the other side of the canyon to decide just what the hell was going on.

Right away Chaffee ordered Lieutenants Kramer and Cruse with Troop E of the Sixth Cavalry and Chaffee's own Troop I, and part of the Indian scouts under Sieber, to go cautiously to the right of the trail, and work along the edge of the canyon, out of sight, and cross down below, possibly a mile or farther, but out of sight of the Indians on top of the ridge.

Troop K, Sixth Cavalry, and Troop E of the Third Cavalry, and the remainder of the Indian scouts under that fellow Morgan of the Third Cavalry, Chaffee sent to the west to go along the edge of the canyon to a spot way down where they couldn't be seen, and then to cross over. In other words, he saw the Indians had no idea that there was twelve troops of cavalry working at this thing instead of one. They was certain they outnumbered us, but instead it was the other way around.

Them Apaches was paying so much attention to the firing that Chaffee was keeping up all the time, that they didn't realize they was being surrounded by a vastly superior force.

Meanwhile the other cavalry troops crossed at their positions up and down the canyon, but out of sight of the present action, and then converged again on the trail where them Chiricahuas was sitting in ambush.

The action started around midafternoon I'd say, and the sun was shining bright.

Our battalion had finally found a place to the east where we could climb down the side of that chasm. It was tough, but we gained a beautiful stream that flowed at the bottom.

We did plenty of strenuous climbing on the other side and finally reached the crest and formed a scrimmage line. I Troop, on the right with Sieber and his scouts, moved rapidly forward. Just as we started, we heard the crash of several volleys and knew that the other encircling column was in action. Sieber and his Indians with I Troop ran into the Indian herd just then. The horse guards was distracted by the firing in the other direction, and our people soon wiped them out.

Then we rounded up them ponies and placed them behind our column with a guard, and moved on. Now we knew we had the ponies and the band that was supposed to be setting up the Apache withdrawal. They sure was gonna be surprised when they run for the big retreat and found out they was gonna have to keep on running and not riding.

Anyway, then we hear crashing and firing to the west— half our buddies had reached the top of the plateau and was fighting. They engaged a column of Indians that was trying to encircle our rear, and our guys caught them out there in front, coming down a trail, where they was all exposed. Our troops turned the ambush into an Indian massacre instead of a white massacre. They just cleaned them out, right there.

We had formed a scrimmage line and was moving west toward our buddies as they closed the trap.

A few Indians was left out of that massacre on the side of the canyon. They ran back to the main camp and the pony herd, which they didn't know we'd already captured. They were joined by them Indians that had been laying down, firing at our troops across the canyon. Every one of them Indians must have knowed by now that there was something wrong, but nobody could tell what it was. They just kept right on moving and gathering together, and the main body of them hostiles came sweeping through the wood right toward us. At first we thought they were trying to rush us and recapture their pony herd, but as a matter of fact they were unaware of our being there, until we fired directly into them, causing further casualties, and drove them back.

Meanwhile, Lieutenant Kramer had swept the right of his line across the Navajo Trail by this time, so that line of retreat was cut off. We then swung our line in a semicircle toward the hostile camp, driving the hostiles in front of us and penning them against the edge of the canyon.

The shadows was heavy in the dense forest. This time our

troop had come up so that we was within about two hundred yards of the main camp of the hostiles, and we could see plenty of scattered blankets and cooking utensils.

Sieber was on my right. We kept moving up the line and all of a sudden got a furious burst of fire from the hostiles. Young Morgan, that fine officer who had made the dash to catch up with Chaffee, was shot. God, he'd got real excited when he dropped one of the Indians and yelled, "I got him." In doing this he exposed his position to another Indian in the same nest, who fired and got him through the arm, into the side, and apparently through both lungs. Furious fire got the Indian that shot Morgan, but Morgan was in bad shape. We thought he'd die that night but, by God, he didn't. It turned out that the bullet going through his arm lost most of its force, struck a rib, then slid around the side and lodged in the muscles of his back. The surgeon dug it out and presented it to Morgan, but Morgan didn't do no fighting the rest of that campaign. He lived for a long time, though, God bless him. A fine man who sure had a lot of guts.

Meanwhile, I kept right along with Sieber, me thinking he was the guy to be with. A scout of his experience was the kind of shadow I wanted to follow, and I wasn't wrong. I seen him kill three hostiles as they was creeping to the edge of the canyon to drop over. He would say, "There he goes!" and then *bang* would go his rifle. The Indian that I'd never seen, strain my eyes as I might, would throw up his arms as if trying to seize some support, then, under the force of his own rush, plunge forward on his head and roll over several times. One shot near the brink caused a warrior to do the most perfect dive into the base of the canyon, which seemed to me to last about ten minutes. It was a hell of a drop.

When it was getting toward dusk, we got up real close to where the Indian camp was, only about seventy-five yards away. A little ravine about seven feet deep separated us from the Indians there. It seemed to me that, unless the camp was taken pretty quick, the Indians would escape under the cover of darkness. I guess that idea also came to Lieutenant Cruse, who was with us.

Cruse told Sieber that he was gonna rush across the ravine with his men and smash the camp. Sieber kept saying, "Don't do it, Lieutenant. Don't you do it. There are lots of Indians over there, and they will get you for sure. There are too damn many of them, you can't do that."

Cruse was funny as hell. He turned to Al Sieber and he says, "But, Al, I figured that you already killed every damn one of them."

The lieutenant didn't pay no attention to what Seiber had to say. He lined up his men and then give the order to advance at a run with their guns loaded and their cartridges in their hand. It was the damnedest thing: they suffered no casualties—I think partly because the rest of us were smothering the hostiles with our fire.

We also rushed forward to the other side of the ravine and soon discovered, as Seiber said, that there were a lot of Indians, and we was busy as hell. While all the action was going on, we seen Cruse stand up almost simultaneously with a great big Indian who wasn't six feet away from him. The Indian raised his gun level at him. It seemed to us he couldn't miss, and I thought for sure that Cruse was a goner like Sieber had predicted. Strange enough, that Indian missed him, but hit a young Scotchman named McClellan, who was on Cruse's left and probably a foot in the rear. McClellan fell. At the same time that damn Lieutenant Cruse threw himself down. By God, I thought both them fellows had been hit and killed. I didn't think there was any doubt about it.

Then, to my great surprise, Cruse got up and dragged McClellan back into a low ravine. While Cruse was dragging McClellan back to that small place of safety, we were all firing like hell to keep the hostiles back; but I'm not sure our bullets didn't come dangerously close to Cruse. He told us later that it sure as hell seemed that way to him.

I guess that there are lots of times that soldiers have been killed by what they call friendly fire. It ain't very friendly when that half-bit piece of lead traveling at two thousand feet a second hits you and spreads out and tears your guts away.

Cruse grabbed some blankets and made a nice bed for

McClellan, who had passed out by that time. McClellan just thought he was shot in the arm, but the bullet had smashed his ribs and gone through both lungs. He wasn't as near as lucky as Morgan. He died about an hour after the engagement.

That encounter had just about wiped out Na-ti-o-tish's whole band, and we didn't hear no more from them for the rest of the campaign. Later Lieutenant Cruse got the Congressional Medal of Honor for his action, and he Goddamn well deserved it.

After campaigning with the guys in Arizona I changed my mind a lot about them pony soldiers. They was dumb in the right direction—they forgot any fear and sure went into the fighting madder than hell and doing their part. With an army of them guys you got something done, and that is just what Crook was after.

We went back over the canyon in the dusk and got to our camp, a pretty exhausted bunch of men. A Lieutenant Hodgson had been left all night with a patrol on the other side of the canyon in an abandoned camp of the hostiles, to guard the horse herd and make sure that we'd protected both ends of the trail. During the night he heard some groans, and in the morning, with his patrol, made a kind of a cautious investigation. He thought maybe there might be some wounded Apaches left; a wounded Apache is a damn dangerous thing to come up on, worse than a maimed wolf.

It was a good thing that Hodgson was real cautious, because suddenly there was gunfire, and the men all dropped to the ground. It was just a single shot and it come from a little parapet of loose rocks. They spotted it by the powder smoke rising from the other side of the canyon.

Everybody took cover and fired on the parapet, and a shot and then another one replied to them. The men continued to fire for a few minutes and a few shots literally smashed the rocks around that particular place to pieces. After a while when there was no more shooting back, they was positive that they'd killed the Indian that was there.

They didn't want no further action from the parapet, and they spread out in order to charge it. They weren't shot at again. What they found behind the parapet was an eighteen-year-old girl, lying on the ground, shielding a six-month-old baby with her body. She drew a knife from her girdle and started fighting the men, until she was overpowered and disarmed. With her was an old squaw of sixty or more, who made no resistance at all. The younger woman had been firing the rifle. She'd had three cartridges, that was all, and the empty shells lay there beside her. When she ran out of ammunition there was nothing she could do.

The men noticed right away that the young woman's leg had been broken by a bullet just above the knee. They made her a makeshift stretcher of boughs right on the spot and brought her on over to our side of the canyon. It was a tough job because it took damn near two hours, and that girl must have suffered terribly, but the men said she didn't utter a groan.

Almost immediately after she reached our camp, one of those sudden hailstorms set in and lasted for more than ten minutes. We didn't have no shelter for our own wounded and could not quickly improvise anything for this wounded girl. In a second she and her baby were covered with hail and drenched to the skin with ice-cold water. Our surgeons were so busy with our wounded that they could not give her any attention clear up into the following day. By that time they decided the only thing they could do was amputate her leg.

There wasn't a drop of anesthetics to be had. The small supply brought by our surgeons had been used entirely in caring for our own men. There was not even a little whiskey to deaden the pain. That young squaw stood the amputation operation without making a sound.

I figured that I'd stay there and watch the operation. Maybe I'd learn something. But when them surgeons got their knives all ready, and I seen the expression in that poor girl's eyes, I decided to hell with it, I'd leave amputation to the surgeons, and walked away.

The next day I saddled one of the quietest pack mules with a cavalry saddle, covered it with several folds of a pack-train blanket, lifted the girl up on the mule, gave her her baby, and put the old woman to leading the mule. In this way she done "marched" with us through the mountains for the next week it took to get back to Fort Apache. Three or four months later I seen the girl at San Carlos running around with a home-made crutch, acting like nothing had happened at all. That's one thing about the Apache nation: you sure had to call them brave, and people that had that kind of courage somehow or other, if they was just given the chance to learn some of the white man's ways, by God, I thought they'd make out all right. I didn't feel about them like I did the Comanches, not at all, although I know they done some torturing and some unhappy stuff. Course, I never did see no excuse for torture of any kind for any reason.

Incidentally, this was the last time the cavalry ever faced the Apaches in open combat. After this battle all the fighting of the Apache Wars was done by troops of Apache scouts under the command of a white officer, usually a second lieu-tenant just out of West Point. They done wonders and brave service under the damnedest conditions, and was the finest officers in the world, and most of them was heroes in my book.

When I got back to Fort Apache, I found Melisande was almost crazy. I tell you, she seemed plumb frantic. When she come running to me and threw her arms around me, she was a-bawling like a baby. It was quite a while before I got her quieted down and took her to our cabin.

We had a little talk, and she told me, "Brules, I can't stand this. I just can't stand this."

"Hell, honey, I wasn't gone for more than a week or ten days, and we just had a small fight up there. Wasn't nothing like what went on up in the Yellowstone River country."

"I don't care what went on in the Yellowstone. All I care is what's happening to you and me right now. Brules, if any-thing happened to you, I would die. I couldn't stand it. I think of you all the time, I worry about you, I can't sleep at night, and when I do I get bad dreams of you being in the hands of the Indians and being tortured. I can't stand it. This army life is a terrible life."

"Now, wait a minute, baby. Let's take it easy here. This

was a small outbreak and it's all taken care of. Any more riding I do for all summer is just with you. I'll be with you."

With that she clung to me and started bawling again. I thought, man, she's hurt some. I'll take care of her. I've got to sort of nurse her along here, because I'm going to be going out with the other scouts. I can't be sitting around hugging my little wife all the time. It was hard for her and it was a long time before she got adjusted. I did everything I could to kinda ease the pressure. We went out hunting quite a lot, camping, did some fishing, and there was a few dances and she sure did like that, and finally I think she settled down and she was all right.

I didn't have to go out again that summer at all.

34

General Crook Brings Order

In August of 1882 Crook arrived at Fort Apache. Everybody was overjoyed to see him. It was kinda like he was a savior.

I must say, I personally sure felt glad to see him, because I knew what was gonna happen with him around. He spoke very formal-like with every one of the commanders, and he praised them fellows that had been in the action at the Dry Gulch of Diablo Canyon. Then he finally got around to shaking hands with the scouts, and of course, when he got to me he shook hands kinda vigorous-like, and said, "Glad to see you, Brules. Guess we've got to go hunting one of these days, don't we?"

"Yes, sir. Anything you say."

Well, we didn't go hunting right away, I can assure you of that. He had some business to do. He called all the chiefs in that was around there and discussed what was going on at the reservation and what would continue to go on.

He told them what was expected of them, and what would happen to them if they didn't behave themselves. Then he wanted to hear any complaints they had. Anything that he could do to straighten things up, he wanted them to know that he was gonna do it. The Indians had real confidence in Crook and it was great to see him work.

After he'd been there about two weeks, he called me to his office and told me that it was necessary for him to go down to San Carlos and have a visit with the Indians down there and look the situation over. He would make a decision on just what his policy would be, and he'd tell all the tribes.

As it turned out, what he had to say was going to be damn important, and I was lucky enough to go with him. He said he liked to have me go along, and of course, when the general says that, I couldn't hardly refuse.

I told Melisande I was going, and she almost had a fit again. But I told her, "Hell this is no war campaign. This is nothing. I'm just going down with the general, and have a council down there."

"Well, I want to go along," she insisted.

"Honey, I don't think you can. I'll talk to the general and see. Of course, this is a peaceful mission but—"

"No, I want to go down, I really do. I want to go. If I have to ride all alone—"

"No, you're not gonna do that. You're not going to be riding through Indian country by yourself. I'll talk to the general and see what he says."

Well, the funny part about it was, I didn't have to ask him at all. I was going by the headquarters building on the way to the corrals to check some equipment and check our stock, and the general come out and stopped me. "Brules, how are you?" he asked.

I stepped up and saluted and said, "I'm fine, sir. Sure glad to have you here, sir. Everything kinda snaps to when you come around."

He smiled. "Well, I suppose that's the way it works, but we're going to have to go hunting one of these days, Brules."

You know, every time he would say he wanted to go hunting I would answer, "Yes, sir. I'm ready. I made a trip up through there and I didn't kill nothing, but I seen two or three big bulls, with big imperial heads—they'd go seven points a side. Boy, they were big. Big thick horns at the base too."

"Yes," he said, "I know, and in another month or so they will be a bugling to beat hell."

"Before that, sir. They ought to start about the fifteenth of September."

"Well, maybe we can be back by that time. How's your little lady taking it here? Does she like it?"

"Oh, she just loves this post and loves the army life, but she gets awful upset when I go off."

"Well, I don't blame her. You've only been married a couple of years, haven't you?"

"Yes, sir. That's about right."

"So, she's lonesome and she hasn't got a family around and all that yet, but the women on the post like her very much. I've seen her riding a few times—she's a good horsewoman. She knows what she's doing, and that's a nice little mare you got for her."

"Yes, sir. She sure does love to ride it."

"You say that she's a little bit upset about your going away. That's too bad. As a matter of fact, I don't see any reason why she shouldn't come along."

Boy, I could hardly contain myself. "Oh, that would be wonderful. Yes, sir. Thank you, sir"—hoping to close it before he said anything more.

"Well, that's fine. You know we won't have any trouble, and we'll go with a couple of troops, so we'll be safe as if we were in church. One thing she'll learn is how lucky she is to be up here at Fort Apache instead of down there either at Grant or Bowie. Bowie is the worst, of course."

"Well, sir, she's seen that."

"Oh, she has?"

"Yes, but when we came up, it was the middle of March."

"Oh, that's a different story. Even now at the end of August, it's going to be a little hot down there. Anyway I think it would be wonderful to have her come along. You tell her that I extend the invitation myself."

"Yes, sir," I said, and snapped to salute. "She's gonna be real pleased, sir. Thank you so much." Boy, I could hardly wait till I got back to our quarters. There she was, sewing; she'd gotten herself a sewing machine from someplace, and she was trying to put something together. I guess she'd had a lot of practice on the farm as a kid, sewing with her mother.

Anyway, when she looked up, I said, "Hey, I've got good news for you!"

"What is it?"

"You're going to go with us."

"Oh, boy," she said. She jumped up in the air and threw her arms around me and kissed me. Her feet were about six inches off the ground.

"Gosh, isn't that great? Isn't that great?" I said.

"Yes, that's going to be wonderful. You know, that General Crook is a darling man."

"Now, wait a minute, honey. You sound like you're falling in love with him."

"Well, I am, kind of. When he does nice things like that for me."

I kinda patted her on the backside and said, "Well, you get your stuff ready now, because we're going to go at the crack of dawn tomorrow."

"Do you think we'll go in one day?"

"Well, he pushes the hell out of things, so be prepared. I'm glad you've been riding quite a bit around here and you've got yourself in shape, so you're not going to pick up saddle sores or something."

"I'm fine. I'm tough."

"Yeah, I know you're tough, but give me another kiss." And she did.

The next morning we was on our way. Melisande was all laughing and joking around, but she had sense enough when everything got going to kinda shut up and go along and not make a nuisance out of herself. She was pretty considerate of me too. She didn't want to do anything that would make me look silly, and I was grateful to her for that.

We camped at a little creek about halfway there the first night. It was about a fifty- to fifty-five-mile ride and then we had about the same the next day. A pretty good jaunt, and of course, we took old Alfred along with us. I was afraid that he'd raise such hell if I didn't, and this way he was just as happy as a lark. Little Tina was prancing along, too, and Melisande was riding her nice as pie. Boy, she sure had the admiring looks of a lot of the men.

I don't know how it affected some of the other young officers, 'cause their wives wasn't asked to go. I kinda felt funny about that, but, you know, there was one thing about it—I think that old General Crook really liked Melisande. I think he kinda had an eye for her.

Now, there weren't nothing at all like scandal in George Crook's life. He was a gentleman of the old school, but just the same he liked to have pretty ladies around, and there was no doubt about how pretty Melisande was. I think he just took a shine to her, and having this young couple, kinda like his personal friends, on this trip, made for something good. I don't suppose it sat too well with the other officers, but after all they were officers, and I was nothing but a scout, so I didn't have to worry about it.

We had old Alfred packed up real solid with a lot of damn equipment, and we had a good tent. So we did better than most of the officers on the trail. As for the troops, they all had the buddy system and they split their pup tents with the other fellow and slept head to foot and all that kind of thing—the old Army style.

We didn't sleep no head-to-foot. We had a damn nice tent and a big sleeping bag, and we slept face-to-face, believe me. I didn't exercise no restraint with kissing her and making love.

We arrived at Fort Grant first and ascended the mountain it was set on. Crook gathered all the officers together and give them a good lecture. That was the third day, and we stayed there in Grant that night and went on to Bowie the next day.

Well, I'll tell you when we got down in that flat country, even though it was late August, the temperatures was still about a hundred and ten.

Right away quick when Crook arrived at San Carlos, he started telling both whites and Indians how the cow ate the cabbage. He didn't mince no words, he just come right to the point. Called all the chiefs together and told them that he knew there had been some raw deals that they got and things weren't straight, and he was gonna do whatever he could to fix it up.

He told them what he expected of them, how they were gonna have to act, and he told them what would happen to them if they didn't.

Then he shared a piece of news that gave them a great cheer. He let them know they didn't have to stay around that San Carlos Reservation all tagged and numbered. He knew who they were and what tribes they were, and just wanted to know where they was. That was all there was to it: they could go out of that hardscrabble country and go on up Turkey Creek, and that's where most them elected to go. They could go anywhere they wanted, as long as they stayed on the reservation and didn't cause no trouble.

Well, that was a big help, because they had all been confined down there in that terrible country, being asked to farm when the ground wasn't any good and they didn't know how to farm anyway. They was a nomad people, and beside that, they knew that they were getting cheated right and left on rations and prices at the agency store. There was a lot of unrest.

Like I said, even the kids would go around looking at you as if you were some kind of animal, and that they would never believe anything you'd say. What we were doing was all wrong. It sure as hell was.

General Crook brought a lot of cheerful smiles, and they don't smile very much, them Apaches.

Then he went to work and started getting things straightened up. He was a good administrator, old Crook was. He put a Lieutenant Crawford in charge of the whole damn reservation, and he had Lieutenant Gatewood in charge of the White River Apaches up at Fort Apache, and a Lieutenant Britton Davis in charge of San Carlos.

Right quick, under his command they took a hard look at what was going on at the agency. The agency, of course, was under the Bureau of Indian Affairs, which was part of the Department of the Interior. It was the most corrupt setup that you could possibly imagine. The military soon found out what was going on around the place.

The agent was a political appointee, and he came down on the railroad from Denver to see what was going on. He made no bones about telling Crook and everybody else what Arizona was and that he had no use for Goddamn Apaches. He didn't care whether they lived or died. This was a political deal and he was going to be there at the reservation only enough time to hold his job, which turned out to be about three times in four years. He'd put a Colonel Beaumont in charge of the agency as the chief clerk, and he was going back up to Colorado to enjoy life.

Well, we didn't expect nothing less, the way the Department of the Interior was run in them days, so we thought it was probably the best thing in the world that the son of a bitch was out of there. If the government wanted to pay him for sitting on his ass up in Colorado, it was all right with us. Anything to keep him out of our hair.

One thing was certain, we sure liked Colonel Beaumont. He was a fine old southern gentleman. He'd been a Confederate officer and he was doing a damn good job, the best he could, to see that the Indians got a square deal. We all had a lot of respect for him.

First thing that Lieutenant Britt Davis done was find out just how bad the Indians was getting gypped out on the scales. He asked Beaumont if the meat scales had been tested, and Beaumont said, hell, he didn't know. Not since he'd been there. So Davis went and got him some marked weights and brought them in there and put them on the scale. He found out that every time the contractor had made a delivery of Indian beef to the reservation he was getting paid by the government for fifteen hundred pounds that wasn't there. Them scales was all off balance—on the profit side, of course.

Davis found out another thing: the cattle dealers would always drive the cattle to the San Carlos River and hold them on the other side before bringing them across to weigh them the next morning. Of course, the steers was plumb thirsty to death and when they put them into the river, they just drunk their fill and swelled up like balloons. Then they come in there and put them skinny son of a bitches on the scales and they weighed to beat hell for a while, so the crooked contractor collected on the water that was in them.

Davis stopped that in a hurry. They fired that contractor and got a good rancher nearby who was gonna play it straight. He was glad to have the contract. It made a hell of a change in things right away quick.

The officers had a nice building to live in. It had been built as a schoolhouse, and the year before they'd had a bunch of gals in from back east, who knew nothing about the West. The agency put them in there and let them start trying to teach the half-naked kids that was hanging around.

Well, that and the heat was too much for them gals, and they got the hell out of there. I don't know as you could blame them. Of course the Department of the Interior doesn't have any brains, but what they should have done was to have taken some good Kansas farm girls that was used to hot weather and ranching and a few things like that, and maybe they would have made good.

But it left a nice empty building that the officers could make themselves comfortable in, and they was glad to have it. As for me and Melisande, we had one end of a barracks that was given to us. It had about three or four rooms, and we was real comfortable.

Even that late it was pretty damn hot, but Melisande kept saying to me, "Can you imagine being in this hellhole in the summer?"

"Well, honey, it could happen to us, so let's not get too sore at it right now."

Lieutenant Gatewood paid a visit to the storekeeper of the agency store there. The man had been charging very high prices, and since the Indians wasn't allowed off the reservation, he had them by the short hairs. He could charge what he wanted to and was getting rich off them.

Well, Lieutenant Gatewood was one of them guys who was about six foot one and he had clear steel-gray eyes and wasn't afraid of nothing. Well-educated man, had the highest principles, and when he looked at you, you knew Goddamn well that what he was telling you was straight. He just had a little visit with the agency man, and I'm sure that he must have pointed out what had happened to the cattle contractor, and guess what? The next day all the prices in the store was half of what they'd been before.

Little bit of treatment like that, over three or four months, and, by God, the whole attitude of the four thousand Apache around San Carlos Agency changed. Instead of being kinda fearful, wondering, holding themselves back, distrustful as hell, and figuring that the next white man they'd talk to was gonna cheat them, they began to get friendly. Although I hadn't been around Apaches much, I began to see what kind of people they was.

You know, they are pretty good people. Everybody talked about the terrible Apache. Well, as a fighter he was terrible. He was aggressive and moved with great speed. One thing was, he never fought if he didn't have to, but if you cornered him to fight, he threw all caution to the winds. He didn't seem to give a damn about what the consequences were, he was coming at you. You better be prepared to meet him.

On a whole the Apache people were capable. They were pretty damn smart. Some of them went to farming; some of those who joined the scouts and served with us against their own people were loyal as hell, strangely.

To the fourteen troops of cavalry that Crook had available between Whipple, Camp Verde, Fort Apache, Fort Thomas, Camp Grant, and San Carlos he added about ten troops of scouts. About forty men in each. If Crook thought they was going into action somewhere, he'd usually double the number of sergeants and corporals to make sure that there was leadership in case they was engaged in heavy fire and suffered some losses.

Some of them scout battalions was drilled, though not so much like the regular infantry troops. They didn't have to go through that kind of drill, but they had a little taste of it to show them what it was like—mostly, they was drilled in rifle practice, signaling, and doing things that would be important. They served damn well in the field when they finally got there. It took the very finest kind of leadership to lead one of those troops; it was ten times as hard as leading a troop of whites, because you were dealing with different minds. It was a problem trying to get over what was wanted, and there was also a language barrier. So each troop had an interpreter. A second lieutenant, right out of West Point, was used as a commander for the scout troops.

I'll say this for them young fellows from West Point: They was all eager. They was eager to prove themselves, they was willing, and showed time and time again how they could stand up under the real tough stuff of a campaign against the Apaches.

When Crook got through with his organization efforts, he headed back to Fort Apache. Me and Melisande went along with him. We were glad to get back to that beautiful country, even though it was getting along in late October, early November, and we expected some snow. Like Melisande said, snow was one thing, heat and hell was another.

Crook took us back up the Navajo-Apache Trail to Fort Apache, and then he crossed over on his military road to Camp Verde and back to Whipple Barracks. He didn't ask us to go along, and for a while Melisande was a little downhearted. She was afraid that maybe we didn't get along with him so good or maybe he didn't like us so much.

I kept telling her, "Listen, honey, this is military organization. He's got a lot of things to think about besides a scout and his good-looking wife. You know why he has us around most of the time, don't you?"

"Yes, because he thinks that you're such a fine scout."

"No, ma'am," I said.

"Then what is it?"

"Because he likes a real beautiful girl like you around, that's why," I told her.

Sure enough, about three weeks later—it was before the first snowfall but there was getting to be a little twinge in the air—we got a letter from the general, and he wondered if we wanted to come over for a week or two to see what it was like at Fort Whipple.

He give us our choice. He asked, "Do you want to come now or would you like to come at Christmastime when everything looks like New England? It is quite different from Santa

Fe or Taos, but if you would like to come, I can arrange for you to have quarters here.''

Well, it didn't take us long. We thought, boy, that would be fun. Why not come about a week before Christmas and maybe stay through the New Year, and just have a fat time of it? Melisande said, ''There are going to be a lot of parties going on and all that.''

''Yes, there is, there is. I don't know how good the hunting is in that country this time of year, but, you know, I never had a chance to take the general hunting. That's a hell of a note. He's just been so busy.''

''You'll get your chance, don't worry, but let's do it that way,'' she said.

We made our arrangements, and a few days before Christmas me, Alfred, Jupiter, Tina, and my beautiful wife was ready to start out alone. Evans wanted to know if we wanted an escort, going through some Indian territory, up around the Tonto Basin where the military road goes through. There's not a lot of travel by various Indians in that country.

I said, ''Hell, I thought we'd go by ourselves.'' It was a kind suggestion, but I didn't want them fixing it so that personnel on the fort had to be at our service. It would be a pain in the ass for them that way to have to take care of us. I reckoned that I'd had as much experience in the region as these guys, and I'd get along.

Anyway, we made it through there all right, and we come past Camp Verde and everybody greeted us. They said, ''Yeah, we understand you're going to Fort Whipple for Christmastime. You're going to have a great time in Prescott. That's a nice town and a lot of nice people, it's a cattle town.''

General Crook sure was glad to see us, especially Melisande—he kept holding her hand, and he had us fixed up fine. He told us that he didn't have any space in the barracks that would be suitable. All of the officers' quarters had been taken, but he'd engaged a nice house in town for us, and thought that we'd be happy there. We were able to leave the stock out at the fort corrals, and so we done that.

''You know, General Crook is just like my uncle. He's just

the nicest fellow I've ever seen. I've got to get him a good Christmas present,'' Melisande told me.

"Well, I'll leave that up to you. I'm not gonna get mixed up in something like that."

"Maybe *you* ought to get him the present."

"Well, I can't think what the hell it would be."

"Wouldn't it be nice if you got him a bear rug?''

"That's a hell of an idea, but wait a minute. How far are we from bears? I know there's got to be bears up around the San Francisco Peaks. There's a lot of timber and all kinds of brush in there. But, Jesus, that's a good hard day's ride and then a day of hunting, and, hell, we've only got a few days before Christmas."

"Let's. I'll go with you." She got real enthusiastic.

That's just how it happened. We went on a bear hunt, but we didn't have to go as far as I thought we would. We just got to that country up above Oak Creek and Mormon Lake, north of where the town of Sedona now stands, and we come on some bear sign. It wasn't very long before I had me a nice black bear. He was a big fellow and I skinned him out. I had a hell of a time to get Alfred to pack him out of there, but we did. It would have been well if I coulda got a nice grizzly for the general. He would have really loved that, but there wasn't any grizzlies in that country—at least I hadn't heard of them. Maybe there was, but during all the time I campaigned in southern Arizona and northern Mexico I never seen no grizzly nor no sign of them.

Well, when the time came, we fleshed the hide as best we could and kinda fixed it up. At Christmas we gave it to the old general, and I thought he was gonna bawl. He was just so pleased, and I told him that Melisande was the one that suggested we do this, 'cause we didn't have much of a way of getting him a present, at least anything that he hadn't already got.

"This is about as fine a present as I could have. I'm going to give this girl a big hug and kiss," he said.

He sure done that. I could see just exactly how he felt about her.

We had a wonderful time there in Prescott that Christmas. We liked it so well that we stayed on awhile. It was incredible cattle country, and we'd ride up toward where we'd been doing the bear hunting and all around. Once in a while the general went with us, but most of it was just Melisande and me and maybe a scout or two that wanted to get out of town.

Sometime in late January, Crook told me that he was going to open a campaign into Mexico in the spring, as soon as things got straightened up.

He said he'd probably set up his headquarters at Willcox because that was about as near a point to the border as any place that was on the railroad. He planned to get started sometime in mid-February. I suggested going to Fort Apache so that we might go hunting. I told him that I knew where there was some big seven-point Imperial heads, and we really ought to make a try for them before those big bulls shed their horns in the spring.

He agreed to that, and so we crossed over by the old military road, same as we'd always done, through Camp Verde and on to Fort Apache. When we got there the general attended to a few things, and meanwhile I did some scouting up the mountain a ways toward the east and seen some tracks of big bulls in the snow. I come back and told the general, and he got so hot for it, he just knocked off all his hard work and we took out one day, just him and me.

Having good horses we moved fast, even though there was quite a bit of snow on the ground. It wasn't breakable crust or anything like that; it was dry packed snow, and we made our way on up the mountain. We soon picked up some elk trails and followed 'em out. Sure enough, we come out in a clearing and there was a big bunch of bulls. They'd separated themselves from the cows and was running in their kinda boys' club, which they always done every year after the rutting season.

Through his field glasses the general picked him a big bull. He asked me, "What about that one on the right?"

"No, General, he ain't as big as the one right in the center of the herd but toward the rear of it," I pointed out. "Do you

see him there—the one with two or three bulls around him?
Now, wait a minute, he's got his head up, now he is gonna
take a step—there he is. Do you see him?''

The general said, "I sure do. That's a dandy."

"I'll hold the horses, General."

Crook got off his horse and pulled his rifle out of the
scabbard. He had the same kind that Custer had. It was one of
them Springfield long-range hunting rifles with a scope, bolt
action. He started to kneel down and then he said, "Let me use
your shoulder as a rest, and I'll see what I can do, Brules.
Dammit, try to stand still, will you?"

I laughed and said, "Yes, sir. Can I breathe?"

"No. Hold your breath."

Well, he aimed real careful, and I was holding my breath.
God, I thought I was gonna burst. Holding reins in one hand, I
put my fingers in my ears, and finally the rifle crashed. By
God, that bull went down. The herd went off in a hell of a
rush, throwing lots of snow all over the place, and I said,
"Jesus. What a shot, General! What a shot!"

He grinned. He was real pleased, and he said, "When you
say a good shot, Brules, I believe it. I thank you for your
guiding. It's a privilege to hunt with a hunter like you."

"Yes, sir, and we better get on down with this pack mule,
'cause we're gonna have to dress that elk out and get the meat
back home."

"I'm glad you brought some good-sized panniers on old
Alfred."

"Well, he's a big mule and that bull probably weighs
eleven hundred pounds, but by the time we get him dressed
out, quartered up, and everything, I think he'll be down around
six or seven hundred—something like that.

"I tell you, General," I went on, "I don't think we should
try to skin out the hide here. It's all right, but it's not going to
do us much good—we ought to take the best meat, and what
you want to do is pack that head. That's a hell of a rack, and
we ought to pack that up and not get this mule so damn loaded
that he can't carry the rest of it."

"I agree with you," he said. "Let's do the best we can."

When we got over and measured him out, boy, that elk was a fine one. He had good tines, seven points on a side, with a couple tipped up there that would make eight points, if you wanted to cheat. A fine-looking animal, hide in good shape and everything.

It was such a big bull that the old gentleman was kinda hefting around, so I had to get over in the snow and yank a little bit, too, but we finally got the job done. I cut him up one side and then rolled him over to the other and skinned out that head and horns and, boy, it was a beauty. Big heavy base of his horns right near the skull, a fine-looking bull elk, as good as any I had seen. Of course, these were Merriam elk in Arizona at that time—I understand they got wiped out in later days. It's a breed of elk all to itself, a little bit smaller than the Yellowstone or Colorado elk, but, by God, looking at this bull you couldn't tell that it was any smaller.

We got the head up there and tied it on the back of the pack mule. We had to tie it upright, because otherwise the horns would stick Alfred in the side all the time and would have given him a fit. The thing I was afraid of was that some hunter might see that damn rack going through the woods and wouldn't see the mule and might unload on him. After we got the rack on, I tied a great big white rag on the top tine so that somebody would at least think that we was coming in peace, and wouldn't shoot.

Anyway, we packed the backstraps in the panniers, took a haunch, and let it go at that. I imagine that the coyotes and the bears took good care of the rest of that elk. We got back to Fort Apache down toward evening. I'll tell you, when we come in with that big rack on, it really stirred the place up. It was fun to watch the general trying to be modest, but swelling out with pride. Of course, all the officers come out and congratulated him, that's the army formality, you know. But then the Apache scouts come around and they started looking at it. They were clicking their teeth and smiling and clicking their teeth. That got to the old man, and he knew that he'd really done something.

He invited me to come over to the officers' club to have a

drink before I went home, and on the way over he put his arm on my shoulder and said, "Brules, I'm really grateful to you. That's the best elk head I've ever seen and I'm pleased. I know that I was with a real hunter."

"No, General. I'll admit that was just pure luck that we found him, but it doesn't take too much of a hunter to find elk in this country, and I'm here thanks to you, sir. You sure made a good shot."

"Yes, and you can stay here as long as you want, that's the way I feel about it."

"Thank you, sir." I saluted him, you know, and he kinda patted me on the shoulder and laughed.

"Well, we'll go hunting again, Brules."

"Anytime you want, General," I said.

"Well," he said, "the reason I like it is that it takes you away from the routine. Then I don't have to worry about all this paperwork. I'm having a hell of a time with the Arizona politicians and I'm having a hell of a time with the politicians in Washington, and the real sad part of this whole thing is that General Sheridan, my chief, has no idea about what's going on. He knows all about the Sioux, but he hasn't got the least idea of what it's like fighting Apaches.

"He still thinks that the country is the open plains and the Apache is a big force of Indians that will stand up to the cavalry, but he doesn't understand what it means when you get mixed up with these boys. I've got a hunch that Chaffee was real lucky when he came up on Na-ti-o-tish and those White River Apaches in Diablo Canyon and pretty well wiped out that bunch. It will surprise me a great deal if we ever see a situation like that again with the Apache. Every time they've done it, every time they have stood up and tried to fight the cavalry, they've had their heads knocked off. So they are not so stupid as to keep doing it.

"Their strong point is in guerrilla warfare, where they strike and retreat, strike and retreat. That's going to give us fits. Now, we've got about six thousand troops here in Arizona, but six thousand troops won't do any good if you can't find the enemy.

"Of course, the newspapers are all raising hell, and those contemptible fellows that constitute the whiskey patrols are always ready to fight the Apache and clean them out—but they never get more than half a mile away from the bar where they have been doing all their bragging. I don't want anything to do with those people, but they are always criticizing me, and have all through the campaign.

"You know, I wouldn't get anything at all done if I hadn't gone back to Washington before I came out here."

"Oh, I didn't know that, sir. Did you go there from Fort McPherson at North Platte?"

"Yes, I met with senators, with the Bureau of Indian Affairs, with the Chief of Staff. You remember him?"

"You mean General Sherman? Yes, sir, I do."

He said, "Well, I had a lot of meetings with him. Finally we poked something through Congress and through the State Department—a treaty with Mexico. They're being bothered with these Apaches just as much as we are. What Geronimo and his bunch are doing all the time is to run down south, crossing the border where we can't follow them. The same way with the Mexican troops: they'd come up this way and run smack into the barrier of the United States. Geronimo knew this and he was playing both ends against the middle.

"Well, I'll tell you, we've got permission now. There has been a treaty signed, and we can go into Mexico."

"Boy, that really is something, General. That's something. Now we knock the hell out of them."

"I don't know about that, old man. I'll tell you about that country south of the border—I've seen a little of it, and our Indian scouts have told me about it, and we've had a few white scouts in there, unbeknownst to the Mexicans. That Sierra Madre is the toughest kind of country. You really can't work cavalry in that country."

"Oh, is that so?"

"Yes, it's rough, beyond anything you can imagine," he said. "The wilderness is about two hundred miles wide by about three hundred miles long. It runs somewhere between ten and twelve thousand feet above sea level, and the Mexicans have just about given up trying to run the Apaches out of it. All that happens is they go in there and get themselves ambushed. As I say, if you get up close and start pressing them, why, then they run off and scatter like quail. Now, how do you get them?''

"I don't know, sir. How is it gonna work out?"

"I still think that the cavalry units can be used as a backup for the scouts and a protection for the pack trains," he said. "Now, you know, the pack trains are the main part of your army, because the army travels on its stomach. You've got to have food and you've got to have ammunition, and without them you're helpless.

"So I'm very particular about our pack trains, and sometime—if you want to—you can get some of those fellows like Al Sieber to tell you what we do with the pack trains. You know, we can't use the good old Missouri mule in that country. We use the little Indian donkeys. The mountain trails are unbelievably narrow, and when they go around a very sharp point, for instance, high up on a precipice, one of our Missouri mules would begin to drag his pack along the wall and shift his weight a little, and the first thing you know he's made a misstep, he slips, and he pitches over the cliff and falls a hundred, two hundred feet. It kills him and scatters his load all over the place, and then you've got the job of going down there with some other stock to pick up the wreckage and pack it back up to the trail.

"That happens several times on a campaign, and of course, the cavalry just can't go in there at all. You can't use a full-grown horse in there. It's almost all on foot. Brules, I remember you telling me that you used to hunt those Comanches on foot sometimes. I see that you still wear Comanche moccasins, and they are awfully handy things—they're good walking equipment and also make pretty good chaps when you're riding through some of this mesquite."

"Yes, sir, that's why I wear them."

"You keep right on, son. That's good footgear for that country," he said. "I think that you'll do well back in there, Brules. You know how to get around on your feet without having a horse under you all the time. You've proved that in the mesa country of New Mexico, but I want to point out to you the sharp edges of that Sierra Madre country—the high Sierra. The flattop mesas you were working with in New Mexico—even taking into consideration the problem of getting up through the cap rock and all—that's still not comparable to the Sierra Madre. No, sir, you're going to find this tough.''

"Well, I expect so. Geronimo wouldn't pick tough country, if he didn't know it was good defense.''

"Right, he's smart enough to do that. I haven't given up on the cavalry altogether—I want to use them as a rallying point for the scouts and a protection for the pack train, but I can't take them back in the high country, that's for sure.

"My advice to you, Brules, if you go into that country at all, you leave not only Jupiter behind—that's a given. A racehorse like him wouldn't last five minutes in that country. Such a beautiful animal, you don't want to put him at risk. Nor that mule of yours, old Alfred. He can't make the turns, or work those narrow precipice trails. As sure as hell he'll bump his pack against something, lose his balance, and you've lost the best friend you've got.''

I listened to him real intent, looking straight at him, and then I said, "Well, General, I will pay attention to that, and if I have to go across the border and down into the Sierra Madre, I hope that I get to go with you.''

"Oh, yes, you're going along, Brules.''

"Well," I said, "I'll just have to get used to something else. I used to walk when I was a young man, running around that Santa Fe Trail and mesa land. I'll get back into condition, and it won't take me long and I'll be right with you, sir.''

"That's fine, Brules.'' He nodded. "I think I'll go to Willcox, as I told you, and I expect that we'll go into Mexico sometime in late March or early April. That's secret information. Don't breathe a word of it around, because right now nobody knows what we're going to do. If word gets out, the newspapers will get hold of it and reconstruct it to suit themselves, and then you'll hear all kinds of hell from Washington from people who don't understand. If they just leave me alone, I'll handle this.

"Now, we're never, repeat never, going to capture Geronimo down there. He's too wily, too perceptive, and we can't catch him because he'll always stay out of our reach in his own country. Where we're going to get him is if he comes in to try to raid something, if he crosses the border this way and we get him in some open country. Or, better than that, what I'm going to try to do is to give him an idea how tough it is to stay out there without any goods. Get his people complaining to him, get his squaws all worried and tired.

"The scouts tell me that on these forced marches they lose their babies about half the time. The troops come up and find dead babies around, because even those Indian girls can't manage to stay with the pressure. When it's tough enough for an Indian woman not to stay with them, you can damn well believe that it's really tough."

"Yes, sir, I can believe that, considering what I've seen Indian women do."

"I'm going to push him. I'll never catch up with him and catch him in a camp or wipe him out or do anything like Chaffee and Evans did up here at Diablo Canyon," he said. "Geronimo is too cagey. But I'll keep rushing his camp. I'll come up on his camp while he's down raiding some villages or out hunting, and destroy all his supplies.

"After a while when I keep pounding him like that, he's going to get damn tired, and his followers are going to get damn tired, and they'll start coming back in twos and fours to the reservation. One chief after another will give up, and he'll find himself out there without a hell of a lot going for him. What we'll have to do then is to meet him someplace and negotiate with him, because he's going to have his dignity.

"If we try to capture him, that's crazy. We won't be able to do it. He'll always be a sore point to the United States, because he'll stay south of that border and be the center for malcontents who want to join him. We'll never have peace on this border, never as long as Geronimo is allowed to roam in Mexico.

"I'm going to make it damn hot for him, and I'll let him know if we have to fight him for fifty years, we're going to keep it up. Meanwhile, if he wants to come in, we'll treat him right and we'll take him back to the reservation, but this time he'll have to sit.

"Geronimo is really not a heredity chief. He's just sort of a war chief and has only a few of the warriors as a following. Most of the Apaches don't like him at all, and he doesn't begin to have the stature of Cochise or Victorio or Mangas Coloradas or any of those fine men. The thing about him is he's crafty and ruthless and he's proved time and time again that his word is totally worthless."

A few days later the general left Fort Apache for Willcox. He had Lieutenant Crawford, who was there at Fort Apache, go with him, and sent word to Lieutenant Davis and Lieutenant Gatewood, to meet him down there and to bring troops with them.

The general left about the end of February and I still hung around up at Fort Apache, 'cause I wanted to get a few things done, and I wanted to have a little time with Melisande before I went out on the expedition into Mexico. She didn't say much, but the tension was building up. She didn't cut loose or anything: she just seemed to bite her lip and go on, never wanting to talk about it.

Anyhow, I had to get my stock shod, and I was waiting for my turn at the post blacksmith shop. I took time to do that, because I wasn't going to be able to take Alfred and Jupiter. It was pretty much of a shock, come to think of it, you know. I had always had my family with me all the time, but I sure wasn't gonna risk them in a Mexican campaign—that would have been plumb crazy.

I didn't expect to be in Mexico any longer than about three months, but who in the hell could tell? I mentioned that in front of Melisande, and she said, "Good God, three months! If you're away for all that time, I just don't know what I'll do."

Well, she kinda went in a mood, and I had to talk to her a long time. It took a day or two to get her spirits back up. I could see what was happening, and I figured that someday there was gonna be an end to this business of me being a scout because of the absences all the time. I knew the wives of the officers felt the same way about it. One of them wrote a book called *Glittering Misery,* telling about how it seemed all fancy, with the dances and the fellows in uniform and everybody in excitement at being on the frontier, but in reality they never knew where they was gonna move, or they'd move at the wrong time, and if they had children to take care of it was bad, if a woman was pregnant it was bad. In fact, she wrote, it was the worst kind of life a woman could have.

I could see that, and a couple of times I got the idea about saying something to Melisande like ''Well, listen, honey, as soon as this campaign is over, next year at the latest, I'll take you back to the most beautiful ranch you every saw in your life and we'll make our home there.''

But I never said it to her. Now, that would have been a big step for me to take, because I'd always thought of that ranch as belonging to Wild Rose and me. To take another woman there was gonna be tough, but nevertheless, I'd been married to Melisande a lot longer than I had been to Wild Rose. Come to think of it, it was 1883, and we'd been married for four years. As for Wild Rose and me, we only had a year together, but that year was a lifetime.

I was still not at the point of wanting to tell Melisande about that ranch. I felt that the time would come and I would be settled down to where I wouldn't mind taking her there. So I didn't mention anything about it.

Anyway we stayed around Fort Apache, but we was always feeling on the edge of something when we was in the Apache Reservation. There were four thousand Apaches at San Carlos and about a thousand up at Fort Apache, and there was always something going on, somebody stirring up something, and of course crooked contractors made things pretty impossible. At least, since Crook had been there, that had started changing around. Fair prices was charged at the agency stores, and there was no gypping on the beef, and they began to get good beef and good rations.

You could notice it in the children and the women. They was wearing better clothes that they could buy at the agency stores. Their money was worth something, and they were getting their allowance on time, and they seemed to have some hope. Most of them, I found, were pretty fine people. They had a great sense of humor, and it's kinda been proven, 'cause they've come a long ways the last thirty years, I understand. I haven't been there in that long, but they tell me that those Apaches are real hard workers.

Nevertheless, it was the idea that you were a few white people in the sea of Indians who were really just working their way out of the Stone Age, and that anything that kinda upset them might get them wild, and we knew that when they did get excited they were like wolves. It was touchy business, and all you had to do was let a bad word get around, and somebody would start some crazy thing.

Another thing we was kinda on edge about was the possibility that those hostiles south of the border might make a raid up to the reservation, the way they had back in 1882, when Geronimo had forced old Nana and some of the other chiefs to join him south of the border. We never knew when that was gonna happen again.

It also stirred things up when we got a wire from General Crook, saying that a band of about fifty hostiles had broken across the border and up into New Mexico and were swinging around into the reservation. Just a few days after we got that first message, we heard that a bunch had hit the outskirts of Silver City, New Mexico, and had killed Judge McComas and his wife and stole his little son, Charlie. We learned later that the hostiles only numbered twenty-six and they was under the chiefs Chato and Benito.

To give you an idea of the kind of riding they did, I figured out that they'd ridden horseback some four to five hundred miles in the six days and nights they were in the United States.

I reckon that the first one to be aware of the hostiles coming into the reservation was Lieutenant Britton Davis. At that time he was with the Chiricahuas and Warm Springs that had gone up Turkey Creek. Davis was lying on his bed in camp before daybreak, and real quiet-like an Indian slipped through the tent flap with a revolver in his hand. Right then Davis must have felt the hair stand up on his head. He challenged the buck, but the Indian whispered back "Tar-gar-de-chuse." He was one of the very secret-service Apache scouts that Crook in his wisdom had set up.

There were only a few of them, maybe ten at the most. Nobody knew who they were, and they didn't know anybody else that was involved. There was even one or two women in the group. They was told to be quiet, keep out of the way, listen to anything that looked like it was dissension or anybody who was organizing anything, report always in a secret manner. Usually they threw a pebble at the tent of the controller, whoever it might be, which in this case was Lieutenant Davis. He'd crawl out under the side of the tent, and in the darkness go quietly maybe to a tree—fifty yards away. Then the secret-service brave would step out.

These people was highly paid, they was intelligent, brave, and, of course, they had to be nervy because you can imagine what would happen to them if their fellow Apaches ever discovered that they was spies. It was to Crook's great credit, and the sharp senses of these young lieutenants that was in contact with these spies, that they was never discovered.

Anyway, when Tar-gar-de-chuse was challenged after he had given his name, his message was "Chiricahua come." Hell, that was all Davis needed. He bounced out of his bed and headed for his white scout that was nearby, a fellow named Bowman.

Tar-gar-de-chuse reported that the Chiricahua were in the camp of White Mountain Apache up the San Carlos River, about twelve or fourteen miles from the agency. Britton Davis had about thirty scouts scattered around the camps that he could assemble in about half an hour. There were about five or six Tonto volunteers who scared the guts out of the Chiricahua, 'cause they didn't have any use for these renegades who were running off to Mexico and causing all the grief for the other Indians.

When they started out, they didn't know for sure what would be going on in the camp with the hostiles, but when they surrounded it and the Apache scouts began to call in, they discovered it was only one man. He was a White Mountain married to a Chiricahua, a member of the hostile gang that had done all the riding.

They brought him into the agency, and that's where I first seen him. He was a pretty brave young man because he didn't have the slightest idea what might happen to him, whether he'd be shot or hung, or what. He was a good-looking fellow, very light complexion, about twenty-three or twenty-four years old. His name was Tzoe, and he told us he'd left the hostiles near the eastern edge of the reservation and had come to this White Mountain camp to get news of his mother and other members of his family.

35

Hell in the High Sierras

We wired General Crook at Willcox, advising him of the capture, and asked him for instructions. Crook instructed Davis to remain on duty there, but to put Tzoe in the hands of a reliable scout, handcuffed and disarmed, and have him sent down to Willcox for questioning. The wisdom of that was pretty apparent: Tzoe would be able to tell the general where the hostiles were in Mexico, and how Geronimo was getting on. He'd know whether the rest of them was following, or if they were getting ready to break away from him, and what attacks were planned.

I could see that was pretty damn important, so I said to Davis, "Bowman is the only other white scout you got here, and you can't hardly spare him, so I'll volunteer to take this character in and deliver him to the general."

"It's quite a responsibility, Brules. You know that," Davis responded.

"Hell, yes, I know that, but he's gonna get there alive and happy and talking plenty, when I get through with him."

Davis laughed, and I think he pretty much trusted me.

"Brules, you've got a job," he agreed. "Saddle up right away and let's get going. I'd handcuff him to the saddle, and not take any chances. We don't want him to escape, and lose all the information we might get out of him. It won't do any good to shoot him, because the way you shoot, he won't talk much afterward."

Well, I took that with a grain of salt, but said, "You have him handcuffed and all, and I'll take a good rope to make sure he don't get too far from me."

Davis laughed.

Then I ran over and got Melisande and told her to get packed up. "We were going to pack up the mule and the horses and get started 'cause we were taking a prisoner down."

"Oh, that's terrible."

"Never mind how terrible it is, you better come along. You're going to see the general down there at Willcox."

"Well, I'd like to see General Crook."

"Yeah, I know you would."

In a few minutes we had everything all saddled up. They brought the prisoner out and we put him on a skinny Indian horse and handcuffed him with his hands behind his back. I put a rope around his waist and around my saddle horn. I figured that he wasn't going anywhere like that. I led the horse that he was on, so it wouldn't get away from him.

I thought about putting the rope around his neck, but then if the horse bolted I might hang him before we got him there. Anyway, that was the way Tzoe come into Willcox—handcuffed, rope around his waist, and the horse being led.

I'd picked up a few words of Apache, and I let him know that if he tried to escape, I'd kill him. It was pure bluff, because I couldn't bring him in dead—the general would have a fit. But we got there all right.

You know, just to show you what kind of bright guy Crook was and how he handled things, when we marched Tzoe inside, Crook took a look at him and told me to take the handcuffs off. He had his men give the Apache something to eat and drink, and let him relax a little bit. Then, through an interpreter, Crook told him that he was planning an expedition to go into Mexico and find Geronimo. He wanted to know whether Tzoe would guide him to Geronimo's secret place in the Sierra Madre.

The Apache volunteered in a hurry. I guess that he figured it was that or getting hanged, and like a lot of them other Indian fellows, he didn't have too damn much warmth for Geronimo. Most of them were afraid of him, they thought he was a big bully. A lot of them saw the stupidity of trying to fight the white people—there was too many of them and the hardship of campaigning was futile. Anyhow, he agreed.

Well, I'm getting ahead of my story here. When Crook finished talking to the prisoner, and made sure that he was properly locked up, he turned to me and said, "Brules, I want you to stick around here and help out with the preparations for my expedition into Mexico. It is a very important thrust we're going to make. Now that we have the treaty that lets us enter Mexico in pursuit of Apaches, it's going to be a big surprise to the Apache nation. And the way we handle it is what counts. If we do it right, it's going to be the showdown on these Indian Wars.

"My perception is that most of the Indians back at either San Carlos or Fort Apache reservations are doing fine since my men got in there and straightened things out. The best thing that we ever did was let them go up Turkey Creek, where they seemed to be happy now—it's beautiful country. These people have a lot of good qualities, but they've got a few real malcontents among them that stir up all the trouble.

"Anyway, stick around and help me a little bit with the preparations, and I think that you'll learn a lot."

Of course, as soon as the general said that, I had nothing to do but answer, "Yes, sir."

He said, "Well, as long as you have that attitude, Brules, you're gonna get along fine. Sit down a minute, son. I want to talk to you about some things that perhaps will help you."

Well, when the general wanted to talk like that to me private and all that, I tell you, that was a great honor, so I sat down and leaned forward eagerly and listened to what he had to say. What he done told me then, as he was sitting there talking to me, just an ignorant scout, was like getting a lesson from a professor at one of the great universities in the country. I swear, it was as if I was getting a private education, and that's just about what it amounted to. It wasn't full of all the subjects that you'd have in college, but it was full of a lot of practical stuff that I needed to know and didn't have any idea about. He started out and said, "Now, Brules, I want you to get involved in, and give good help to, the most important part of the whole army, and that's the pack outfits."

Of course, when he started saying that I thought, oh, my God, he's gonna have me handle mules, and I started getting depressed. Well, I listened to him a bit and I come around to seeing what the problems were and got kinda enthusiastic about trying to solve them.

Then he done said to me, "Brules, an army travels on its stomach. If troops don't eat, they don't live to fight—that's self-evident. They have to be fed every day."

I nodded.

"In addition, they have to have other supplies. They have to have spares for this and that, they have to have ammunition, medical supplies, all of which have to be transported. Now, it would be easy if we were fighting a war in Europe, but we're not. We're fighting a war in the roughest kind of primitive country that is still left in the United States, and the worst in Mexico. We can't get in there with wagons, we've got to get in with pack trains. The pack trains are of supreme importance for reasons I just mentioned. If a pack train fails for any reason—if the mules go lame, get sick or overworked, or lose their shoes and have their feet break up in the rough country, or Indians drive them off, or they die of thirst or exhaustion— any of these things—let me tell you, the whole army stops right there."

"Yes, sir," I agreed.

"The whole basis of this campaign is the pack outfit—the supplies that back up the troops. The troops will do the fighting if you will give them food and ammunition, but without that they can't do a thing. Maybe some of the other officers have told you that I have made a study of pack trains and the seriousness of this phase of military operations. If they haven't, I'll repeat it here.

"You see, pack trains are a hobby of mine. If you apply

yourself to a problem, you can usually solve it or solve a great part of it.

"I'll try to show you how I've gone about solving some of the biggest problems that we've had in transporting ammunition, food, and medical supplies to our troops to back them up.

"First of all let me explain to you about the Sierra Madre. As I told you, that's where the Apaches all run to. In Mexico they've got the protection of the border, and until this treaty we just worked out, they were perfectly safe back of the border. All they had to do was fight the Mexicans, and they found that much easier than fighting U.S. troops.

"On top of that, though, Geronimo knows that the northern part of the Sierra Madre Range is probably the greatest natural fortress in America. As I mentioned, it's about two hundred miles wide by three hundred miles long, and averages somewhere between eleven and thirteen thousand feet. In its upper part there are beautiful glades in the pine forests that skirt the slopes of the mountains that have the finest grass in America. There are clear, lovely running streams, abundance of game, and wild turkey galore. This is the area Geronimo likes to stay in.

"The important thing is that to get to that paradise up in those high mountains it is necessary for troops to approach from either the east or the west. The approach from the west, the drainage of the famous Yaquí River, consists of a whole group of ridges that run out westward of the high Sierra Madre. These ridges are very steep, but rather comfortable for walking or riding. The Mexican troops, time and time again, have pursued the Apaches when they raided Guaymas, Jiménez, Hidalgo, or Ciudad Obregón. The Apaches would come down Yaquí Valley, unseen and unheard, and strike Mexican villages and towns, and even the outskirts of some cities, to just wreak horrible chaos and carnage. They captured innumerable Mexican slaves, mostly women, and then retreated back to the Sierra Madre by the pathway of these sharp ridges.

"They always left a rear guard behind, carefully situated in fortified places. It was not possible for the Mexican troops to go up the gorges on either side of these ridges in order to circle the Apaches' position, for the going was not only too rough, it was totally impossible. It was necessary for them to work their way right up against the ridges, constantly exposed to ambuscade by the rear guard, which took a terrible toll. You know that the Apache is a good shot."

I sorta smiled slightly at that.

"Anyway their maintenance of this stronghold has been good for a hundred years, and served them well. As to the east, the land slopes away from the timber around the eight- or nine-thousand-foot level and one travels a long way before one comes to any Mexican villages. There are places like La Cuchilla City, Torréon, Parral, et cetera. There is a long, long ride in and out, and the Mexican troops are totally exhausted before they even get to the forest. There they have some steep climbing against the certainty of ambuscade. They consider the whole struggle not worth the candle and one can hardly blame them.

"The result of their refusal to face the problem for whatever reason has been a complete and unopposed destruction of all the little towns that run through the mountains, Vavispe, Bacerac, Estancia, Huachinera, and Oputo. Every family among these poor people has lost a male or two to the outrages of the Apaches, and so Geronimo feels secure in his mountain fastness.

"It is my intention to disturb that sense of security. You can imagine what panic will be forced into the Apache mind when he finds that United States troops can ride right to their most sacred inner fortress of the Sierra Madre. It's something that has never been done before. We intend to do it, though we will not be able to without a crack force of several first-class pack trains to follow the various military units.

"Brules, do you have any idea where pack trains originated?"

I just shook my head and said, "No, I don't, General."

"Well, would you give a guess?"

"Yes, sir. I suppose that they might have come from the

prospectors and miners of the high Sierra of California and up in the Colorado country and maybe in Peru.''

General Crook smiled and shook his head. ''No,'' he said, ''they come from the Spanish and the Arabs.''

I said, ''The Spanish and the Arabs?''

He said, ''Yes. Brules, have you ever heard of Columbus?''

''Yes, sir, I have. He discovered America. My mamma made me remember the date, it was 1492.''

Crook smiled and said, ''Good enough. Remember how Columbus got his ships to sail to America?''

''Yes, sir. I remember that there was a queen—what was her name, Isabella?''

He nodded that it was correct.

''Ferdinand and Isabella.''

''Do you know what she had to do with it?''

''General, the way I was told, Isabella give Columbus her jewels to go buy ships to make that trip.''

Crook said, ''Good enough, that's right. Do you know why she was happy enough to do that?''

''No, sir. I don't really know nothing about that. Maybe she liked Columbus or his idea.''

''There was a moment of great joy and celebration in Spain that year because the Spanish were finally able to drive the Moors out of the southern part of Spain and back across the Straits of Gibraltar to North Africa, where they came from. The Spanish captured Granada, the great stronghold of the Moors. That was the last foothold that the Moors ever had in Spain. They had occupied it for seven hundred and fifty years,'' Crook said.

I kept nodding, not really knowing what to say.

''Let me tell you, when Isabella's Spanish forces laid siege to Granada, they marched down there with a pack outfit of fifteen thousand mules.''

I let out a whistle. ''It must have been some job herding them mules along like that, General. Wow, what a job!''

He laughed and nodded and said, ''Indeed it was. It took the very finest packers to handle the job. The Arabs and the

Spanish learned so much about packing mules that it's lasted all through to our times. The conquistadores, going up into the high Andes where they found the gold, used mules, and they used them all through Mexico for years. Of course, we borrowed it clear up to Montana and everywhere else.

"We raise a lot of mules in Missouri too," he went on, "but we don't know how to pack them. Let me tell you something about that, Brules. Do you know what an aparejo is?"

I shook my head.

"Yes, you do. An aparejo is the pack cushion that is issued by the quartermaster department."

"Oh, yes, sir. I know that."

He said, "The Army aparejos are a joke. They have killed more mules than they have helped to carry their load. What a mule needs is the same thing that a soldier needs in carrying his pack outfit. It isn't good for a soldier if a thirty-five-pound pack doesn't fit his back and shoulders properly. You admit that, don't you?"

"I sure do, sir."

"Well, the same thing is true with an aparejo. It's got to be made to fit each animal, and each one is different. That's the way to keep the animal from getting back sores and from going out of business. Brules, do you know what a suader is?"

I shook my head again.

"It's a sweat cloth—a light cloth that extends from the withers to the loins to absorb the sweat off the mule, so it doesn't get into the aparejos. What you do is put the suader, the sweat cloth, on first, then two or three saddle blankets, and then the aparejo—a large mattress, stuffed with hay or straw."

"Oh," I said, "I've done some of that."

"Well, that's what it is. It's laid on to make the best distribution of the load on the mule's back. After that you put the pack load on, which is termed by the Spanish the cargo.

"Do you know what a shavetail is, Brules?"

"Yes, sir. It's a young officer just come out of West Point and don't know his ass from his elbow."

The general laughed. "Well, that's a familiar use of the term, but it's not the way it started. A shavetail is a mule that is new in the pack train. He's skittish, doesn't know where to stand, doesn't know what to do, doesn't follow the bell horse. You know, mules have a white horse at the head of the pack.''

"Yeah, I know that. I wondered what that was.''

"Oh, and another thing, Brules, never let a bunch of colts run anywhere near a pack train.''

"Well, General, I did hear somethin' about that, but I can't quite remember what it was.''

Crook answered, "When a bunch of colts come near a pack train, the mules will just go crazy wanting to play with them.''

"Well, I wonder why the hell they'd want to do—'' I asked.

"Maybe it has something to do with their not having any colts of their own. They play with the colts and they play rough and sometimes the colts get hurt. But whatever the reason, it can sure mess up a pack train. It's a good thing to remember. The art of packing and running a pack train is just the guts of an army,'' he said.

The general went on, "There are a few things that we've got to keep in mind. Remember that the successful stand you made in the middle of that little fracas up near Diablo Canyon, where you surrounded and virtually annihilated a band of the hostiles, was due to the clever way Captain Chaffee handled the command. The hostiles were totally ignorant of what was going on and tried to set up a trap for Chaffee.''

"Yes, sir, that's right. And if they'd ever pulled off that trap, and it hadn't been for Sieber and them scouts seeing it, the results would've been very bad.''

General Crook nodded. "Anytime you catch an enemy force down in a canyon with no cover, they are in a bad situation.''

"Yes, sir, they sure are. There's no doubt about that, but it was sure masterful the way Chaffee run that thing.''

"Brules, what do you think of those young officers?''

"I gotta tell you somethin', General. I use to think pony soldiers was a joke, but I don't think that anymore. You done told me about discipline when I was up there with you at

Cloud Peak Camp when that Major Nickerson run me through that Dead Man's Canyon. Now, I still think he's a stupid son of a bitch, but I understand something about the discipline. I'll say this: Crawford, Chaffee, Davis, and Gatewood are the finest young fellows you could find anywhere in the world.''

"I think so, too, Brules. As a matter of fact, I think they're the equivalent of the finest officers in any army anywhere you want to go. It's the roughest kind of fighting you will find—it's guerrilla warfare with a foe that knows a lot more about the country than you do and is better armed. I raise the devil in Washington about our troops having the single-shot Springfield carbine when the Indians have '73 Winchesters.''

"Well, General, there's one compensation.''

"What's that, Brules?''

"I got an 1873 Winchester, and I didn't get it from no Army. Nobody give it to me and I didn't buy it either.''

"Is that so, Brules? Then where did you get it?''

"I took it off a Blackfoot brave. It was when me and Wesha—you remember Wesha?''

"Oh, that fine Shoshone warrior who saved your life at the Rosebud?''

"Yes, sir. That's the man I mean. He is a great warrior.''

"What's happened to him since?''

"Oh, he went back to the reservation at Lander, Wyoming, and I think I'd a done the same thing, if I'd been in his shoes,'' I answered.

"How's that, Brules?''

"Well, he had a couple of the best-lookin' wives you ever saw in your life, General. They missed him and he missed them.''

The general laughed and said, "Well, you're quite right, Brules, that is a good reason. But you're pretty lucky that way too. You've got a beautiful wife. Is she your first wife, Brules?''

"No, sir.''

He seemed to be waiting for more, but I didn't say anything and he went on, "Well, the world is full of unpredictable things, Brules. I think I asked somebody once and they told me that you were married to a relative of Wesha's.''

''Yes, sir. I was married to his cousin.''

''Oh, she was a Shoshone girl, then?''

''Yes, sir,'' I said, ''that's exactly right.''

''Well, the Shoshone girls are certainly known for their beauty.''

''Yes, sir, that's true. She was more beautiful than any of 'em.'' I didn't say anything more and the general never pushed me—him being a real gentleman and knowing that if I wanted to talk to him I would and if I didn't, then let it alone.

Here it was the spring of 1883, and it had been seven years since it all happened. I was very much in love with the wife I now had, but the thought of Wild Rose brought a pain to my heart. I reckoned that was the way it would always be.

I said to the general, ''You sure got a great bunch of packers. That Tom Moore and them other fellows—you can't beat 'em.''

''No,'' he said, ''and I intend to divide the whole system into five pack trains with sixty mules to a train. We've got the best equipment that money can buy and we've culled out all the old mules, the ones that were sickly or couldn't make the grade, and the packers that weren't responsible men. The new mules we brought in, though they're skittish, are all good material, and working with the old-timers, they'll come out just fine.

''We're ready to go right straight through to the heart of the Sierra Madre and camp right in the stronghold of the Apaches, and that should put a panic in them. When they realize that we can come right into where their best place is— where they've never had anybody come before—they're going to be shaken up a little bit, and I think they'll be a little easier to deal with. In the end the white man has to win, but he can't do it the way he's been trying to do it.

''I want to tell you that I'm sure that your scuffle up there at Diablo Canyon under Captain Chaffee will be the last time that the Apache will ever meet a United States Cavalry troop head-on, regardless of the odds. Every time they've done it, it's been a disaster to them. Now they're going to go to guerrilla warfare. As a matter of fact, they seldom do any real harm even if they lay an ambush—they may kill a few people and animals and stir things up badly, but they'll never capture an entire cavalry outfit. There will never be another situation like Custer where there were thousands of Sioux hitting him head-on. That isn't going to happen. These fellows are going to strike and go, strike and go.

"In the end it means that they can't occupy territory. Remember, I told you that the military theory of warfare is to destroy the enemy force—meet it and destroy it. Then it is perfectly possible with what force you have left to occupy all the territory that your defeated force was protecting. There is no way the Indians can destroy the forces of the United States. It is true that we're going to have difficulty destroying them because we can't find them half of the time, and they are terrific guerrilla fighters. We are going to keep pushing them by finding one camp after another. They'll never have a moment of peace and they'll never know when we're sneaking up on them, surrounding them, and they are going to have some trouble. They can never go to sleep at night without the threat of an attack. Now, there is one thing that I'm concerned with and haven't yet decided how to handle."

I waited a minute. I was afraid he wasn't going to go on. Maybe it would be bad manners of me to ask him to continue.

He thought a few minutes and then said, "I'm using the cavalry in the Sierra Madre this time because I think they can be used as a rallying point for the scouts and as a protection for the baggage trains. It just may prove to be fallacious and it may be that the scouts will travel faster and could protect their own baggage train. I do know one thing—being Apaches they can hunt Apaches far better than any white man. Whether we can bring enough force to bear and cause the hostiles to surrender is another point. It is a gamble, Brules, but I feel it's a good one and we must take it. It's all we've really got."

Well, me being just a scout and having no education, I wasn't up to people like the general, but I sure as hell thought the world of him. And somehow he had a strange respect for me, or I figured he wouldn't be talkin' this way. Perhaps he knew that I had no political ambitions as far as the Army was concerned, and that I had a keen enough mind to follow what he was saying and understand it, yet would never be talking about it to anybody. He knew that for sure. Maybe he just liked to kick the idea around a little bit. Maybe he just liked to talk to me to kinda clarify his own thoughts, to see if he might come up with another angle. I don't know, but I just worshiped the fellow and I stayed right there. If he'd told me to go alone down into the hostile country and try to look for Geronimo by myself, damned if I wouldn't have done it. There were instances where men did go into the camp of Geronimo alone— Tom Horn did it and Gatewood did it.

With all this talking to me I was kinda anxious to go down into Mexico and see what I could do as a scout. I knew it was going to test everything, but I would learn a lot and have some fun. Then he kinda deviated from what we was just talking about and said, "Brules, did you ever hear of a corona?"

"A corona, sir? No, sir, I never heard of it."

"Well"—the general laughed—"you know, that's one more piece of equipment that the muleteer or the packer in the Spanish mountains always has with him. A piece of cloth with all kinds of fancy colors, each one different. He uses it for suspending over the cargo when he's packed his mules. He does this so he can look along the line of packloads and pick his own right away—go right to it—and if he's looking at a mule from a distance, he can tell it's his mule by the corona."

Then he burst out laughing and said, "Well, Brules, now that I've given you all that file of useless information, maybe you can have some fun with it."

I said, "General, there ain't nothing useless about that. It all just makes plain horse sense—or mule sense, I guess. I've been around mules and horses all my life but, I swear, sir, I know nothin' like what you just got through tellin' me. I feel like I just had a schoolin' course."

The general burst out laughing, roared, and clapped my back and said, "Well, Brules, we've got to be on our way. I think tomorrow we'll be shoving off for Mexico."

I said, "That just suits me fine, General. I'm ready to go."

At dawn on one of the last days of March 1883, General Crook's expedition into Mexico began, an expedition that was going to surprise and shake the roots of the Apache nation. Earlier, General Crook had ordered Crawford to take three companies of Indian scouts, Companies C, D, and E, to San Carlos, and proceed to Cloverdale, Arizona, right on the border. Crawford had been directed to send a few scouts across the border a month ahead of the expedition. The idea was that they could spread out ahead of the expedition as far as sixty miles south of the border and pick up any information that might be of use when the actual advance came. We rode out of Willcox that morning with two troops of scouts, picked up Crawford's three troops at Cloverdale, and crossed the border feeling like we were Cortez on his way to conquer Montezuma.

The night before my departure was spent with a very sad girl. Although several times during the night we made mad love, Melisande was in tears most of the time. Sometimes she would hug me, and I could feel her trembling all over. She really had an awful fear of Indian warfare and of letting her man go down into the very heart of the country of the hostiles. She told me that she had terrible nightmares about it, and the idea of our separation was almost more than she could bear.

We had a room in the boardinghouse there at Willcox, but now that I was going to be gone for maybe a month, she really found herself in a condition she called desperation. There were no officers' wives or anyone else she could visit at the forts on the San Carlos Reservation. The fact was that the living conditions at those forts were so terrible that few women could survive. Most of the officers' wives had taken off to go back to their homes, perhaps in Ohio or as far back east as Massachusetts or Connecticut. I remember one officer telling me his wife was back in Nantucket enjoying the wonderful weather they had there in the summer, while he had to sit around in 120° heat. He had realized it was no use dragging his wife into that hell when he'd be out campaigning most of the time.

Well, little Melisande couldn't go back to her home, that was for sure. We didn't have any children to take care of, and she found herself completely alone with no women friends around and nothing really to do. The glitter of army-post life had faded. She thought that maybe what she'd do was go into Tucson and get a job there. She mentioned there were two good restaurants—boardinghouse places, kinda like hotels, that everybody knew about. One was the Shoofly and the other was the Crystal Palace. She figured she might be able to take the train and stay there until I came home. She said she didn't know whether she'd go right away in case I came back in two or three weeks. If she left, she said, she would leave word where she was.

Well, of course, I thought about her all the way as we went down into Mexico. By the third day of the expedition, though, I had to come to terms with the situation. I knew I couldn't keep thinking of her all the time and do a good job of scouting. I had to be out ahead of the troops or out around on a swing somewhere, and I knew well that although we couldn't see them, Apaches were everywhere in the hills of the cactus-riddled, thorn-infested desert, which some well-informed writer had named the Armed Desert. It was now not only armed by cactus plants and thornbushes but also by the fierce, perceiving eyes of hundreds of hostile Apaches. It would be stupid to think anything else.

Geronimo would have his scouts out watching what the cavalry would do when they crossed the border. It must have been a hell of a surprise to them that the cavalry was coming across, but, still, Geronimo knew very well that he was hidden far back in the high country of the Sierra Madre, hundreds of miles south of the border, and the chances of this column of troops ever getting to him was remote. All this I'm sure he done figured, but he didn't figure on Tzoe.

Crook had sent out Crawford's troops of scouts far in advance of the column, but to no avail. They picked up almost no information. We kept following right along the route Tzoe told us to take, advancing for several days, until we finally halted about sixty miles northeast of the town of Nácori in

Sonora. The main body of the expedition halted, and Crawford and Gatewood, with forty or fifty of the scouts, were sent forward, along with Tzoe, to reconnoiter. I considered that a very smart move.

When they returned, they were in fine fettle. They had surprised the camp of the subchief Benito, while most of his warriors were away on a war party raiding villages on the eastern slope of the Sierra Madre. The remaining warriors, who stayed to fight, were killed, except for a very few who escaped. In the process several women and children were captured and brought back to the main command. There was one white child, about six years of age—a boy Crawford first thought was little Charlie McComas, the son of Judge and Mrs. McComas, who had been killed by the raiders three or four weeks earlier at Silver Springs, New Mexico. Unfortunately, it was not the case. The boy was identified as a Mexican boy who came from northern Mexico. He was restored to his family at the end of the expedition.

Some of the captured women turned out to be mighty valuable. There were two groups: One was Mexican women who had been captured in previous raids and were the slaves of the Apache warriors. These women were half crazed with fear and showed evidence of having lived an incredible life of agony and terror. They were restored to their Mexican families. The second group, of Indian women, were held captive in the headquarters camp, until they were finally employed on a very important mission. The most intelligent and most willing were picked as emissaries to proceed to the camps of the various chiefs hidden in that vast wilderness. Hostile camps were scattered over a large tract of mountainous country. I later scouted there for two years alone, and found the terrain would make a normal campaign totally impossible. These women were treated well, fed, clothed, and sent as emissaries to the chiefs of these various hostile camps. That ended up being mighty effective, 'cause it got the chiefs to come to the general's camp for a powwow.

The chiefs wanted peace and they wanted it bad—that was real plain. For over a hundred years the wilderness had been their fortress and no one, not even Mexicans, had dared enter it. Now a strong, armed force of cavalry was milling around right in the heart of it. They all allowed that they wanted to return to the reservation—that they'd always been good, never killed anybody, and were always the friend of the white man. It was one bunch of lies after another, which we took with a grain of salt, as part of somehow corralling these hostiles and getting them back into the reservation, where they could be disarmed and controlled. The chiefs were ready to go back immediately to San Carlos, but they said their other people were scattered throughout the mountains in dozens of camps and it would take time to get the word to them that peace had been declared. They said it was going to be even harder to get word to them now that the alarm had been given that the troops was in the Sierra Madres.

The end result was that it would take about two moons for them all to get together and go. It was finally agreed that the general would return to the United States and to the San Carlos Reservation, with as many Indians as could be gathered at the moment. That would include the women and children who could be assembled, along with the old men and the few warriors available. Others were to come as soon as word could be gotten to them at the various camps. They were to proceed immediately, following the trail back to San Carlos, and there lay down their arms.

The later group were to be met at the border by a protective force when they did come two moons hence, in order to keep the local ranchers, who had suffered so much at their hands, from seeking revenge.

The general started back, and I went with him. We brought with us three hundred and twenty-five Chiricahuas and Warm Springs Indians, of which there were fifty-two men and two hundred and seventy-three women and children. That meant that we'd left about two hundred Apaches in the Sierra Madre, most of them fighting men. They were left there to gather up the other families, but as it turned out, they really used the time to raid Mexican ranches for horses to trade to their own kin at the San Carlos or Fort Apache reservations. Geronimo, of course, was one of those who stayed out with the warriors.

36

How Long Is Forever?

Thus it was that Crook came back to San Carlos, arriving about the twenty-third of June. The temperature in the shade was around one hundred and ten, but was expected to go as high as one hundred and twenty or better in the next months. All the time we were going back, I kept thinking of Melisande and how much I wanted to see her. I was pretty sure that she wouldn't have stayed alone in the boardinghouse at Willcox— she'd go mad doing that. So I wasn't surprised, when I got leave from Crook and went down to Willcox, to find that there was a telegram waiting there for me saying that she had found work at the Shoofly Restaurant and Boardinghouse in Tucson, and to meet her there. The telegram was dated April twentieth, and was signed *Many hugs and kisses* with a sentence at the end saying, *Don't forget to bring your good clothes. They're hanging in the main closet of the boardinghouse.*

After he read me the telegram, I asked the stationmaster, "When's the next train to Tucson?"

"It's leaving here at two-thirty this afternoon."

"What time is it now," I asked.

"Twelve o'clock."

"When does it get into Tucson?"

"About five-thirty," he answered.

"Give me a ticket." I took the money from the oilskin side of my belt and paid him. "Another thing: I want to send a telegram to my wife."

"Sure, here's a pad and you can just write it out. It'll be ten cents a word."

"You write it," I said.

He smiled and said, "Okay."

I said, "Begin it, *'My love.'*"

"Okay," he said.

" 'I'm comin' on the five-thirty train to Tucson. Hope you can meet me. If you can't, I'll come to the Shoofly. I'm bringing my fancy duds. Sure love ya.' Sign it *'Brules.'*"

"How do you want this telegram addressed?"

"Why, I want it ta—let me see, ah—ah, Mrs. M. Brules—ah, care of the Shoofly Restaurant in Tucson, Arizona. That oughta get to her, yeah."

"If she's there, it'll get to her."

"What the hell ya mean? Of course she's there—she wired me from there."

I figured that since I had two hours before I had to catch that Goddamn train, I probably ought to go over and see my "family" in the Willcox military stockyard before I left. But, Jesus, there wasn't time. I ran over to the boardinghouse and seen the lady there about getting my clothes.

"Oh, yes, Mr. Brules, your wife left these for you. My gracious, it was a couple of months ago. Where have you been?"

"Well, lady, I've been down in Mexico with General Crook."

"Ohhh," she said, "my gracious, fighting Apaches!"

"Well, ma'am, there was more ridin' than there was fightin'. But I'm sure glad to be back, and I'm looking forward to seein' her."

"She's sure a nice girl, and she's written a couple of letters addressed to you, that I was told to give you when you arrived."

"Oh, fine—great, great. I'll take 'em right with me, and I thank you." I didn't want to ask her to read the letters and I didn't know how to read them.

I asked, "When did she send 'em?"

"One was about a week after she left here and then the

other one came about two or three weeks after. Let me see, that's dated May twenty-first, that last one. Yes, and both of them from Tucson.''

''Well, thank you, ma'am.'' I took them letters and put them in the pocket of my duster right close to my heart. I thought, when I get to Tucson I'll have Melisande read 'em to me, and it will be nice as it can be. After she reads them to me, I'll kiss her, and then I'm sure gonna make love to her. Hot damn! I'd been away a long time. I figured I ought to get a bath before I left, but then decided I didn't have time. I didn't dare take the chance—I had to catch the train. Hell, I was over there and must've waited forty minutes for that damn train to come in, but pretty soon I heard it whistling and seen it a long ways down the track. It was roaring along, and soon it came into the station. I waited about ten minutes while they was loadin' stuff on and passengers was gettin' in and out, and then I got on and sat down. I never used to smoke at all, but once in a while I would take a chaw, you know, but I didn't have nothin' to chaw, so I bought a cigar at a place right next to the boardinghouse. I stuck that in my jaw—didn't light it, but jawed on it a little bit, and kept thinking about Melisande.

The train finally pulled out of the station and began hummin' along over the tracks, and as I seen the desert going by like from a gallopin' horse, I got to thinking about how neat it all was. The world seemed good, the sun was going down in the west, and I looked out and seen all the country down by Tombstone. I seen that high mountain, Mount Lemmon, by Tucson layin' out there ahead of us and the Dragoon Mountains to the southwest. The time passed, and I was tired from so damn many hours in the saddle, and it kinda caught up with me. I was still a-dozin' off when I heard the whistle and, by God, that meant we was comin' into the Tucson station.

As we pulled in the station, I kept lookin' for Melisande—she'll be there with her parasol and her fine outfit and she'll be lookin' for me, I thought. Boy, I'm gonna grab her as soon as I see her—Jesus, how great it's gonna be. Well, everybody was pouring out of the cars, and I finally got out on the platform. I kept lookin' up and down to see where she'd be, but she wasn't anywhere. I had my good clothes in a kinda bag slung over my shoulder and wished that I'd shaved before I came, since I knew how she liked to have me shaved, but I couldn't take the risk of missin' the train. Jesus, I had three months' growth of beard, but I'd done the best I could.

She wasn't there, but I figured it was just a big rush hour at the Shoofly, and she couldn't make it. So I asked around a little bit about where the Shoofly was, and folks told me that it was about three blocks down the street. I headed that way with my heart poundin' to beat hell, and then I thought, you know, maybe she didn't get my telegram. Otherwise, I just knew she'd have been at the station to meet me. It didn't take me long to locate the place and I went in.

It was a mighty fine restaurant and boardinghouse, with a lot of nice girls in waitress-type dresses going back and forth. Everybody was real polite.

I asked someone, "Is Melisande around here?"

One of the girls looked up at me kinda strange and said, "No, no, she's not here now."

"Well, where would she be?" Nobody answered that, and so I said, "Well, she's gotta be around here someplace. She's boardin' here and waitin' on tables."

Finally a handsome, middle-aged lady came up and said, "Can I do something for you, sir?"

"Yes, I'm lookin' for my wife, Melisande."

"Oh, are you Mr. Brules?" she said.

"Yes, ma'am, I be he."

"Mr. Brules, I thought you knew."

"Knew what?" I said.

"Why, Melisande left here more than a month ago."

"Left here, left here! Where the hell did she go?"

"She told me that you'd probably be coming here, Mr. Brules. She sent me a letter saying you'd probably come because she had sent a wire to Willcox. Isn't that where you were going off on the campaign with General Crook?"

"That's right."

"In any case, she left a letter here for you, and then another one came a little bit later, and I have them both here."

"Where in the hell did she go?"

"Mr. Brules, I think probably you should let her explain that in her letter, because I'm not really sure. Just come in my parlor, won't you?"

I stepped into a real nice room with a lot of fine furniture. Of course, I had my hat off by that time, and I was a-bowin' and a-scrapin' and being a gentleman, but I could sure feel my blood pressure comin' up. Damn! Where in the hell was Melisande? I had this rising feelin'—a kinda fright that I'd never had before—like I was goin' into a bunch of Apaches all armed and ready to kill me and I didn't know where they was, like I was goin' up a narrow canyon and they was on all sides.

Then she said, "Here are the letters, Mr. Brules, and they should tell you what you want to know. I'm sure that Melisande would love to know that you've come back from Mexico."

"Ma'am, please tell me—where did she go?"

"Well, I believe she bought a ticket to San Francisco."

"San Francisco, Jesus Christ! Excuse me, ma'am, but what—why, do you suppose?"

"She said something about a job offer she had there. You see, about a month ago, a week or so before she left, a man came through here. He was a very nice, fine-looking man who was supposed to be very influential in building the railroad through here. His name was—I believe it was Endicott."

"Endicott!" I guess my eyes narrowed down to steel.

She said, hurriedly, "Oh, well, then, you know him?"

"No, ma'am, I ain't never met him, but my wife done told me about him a couple of times, and I'm lookin' forward to meetin' him."

She seemed a little flustered then and said, "I'm sorry, Mr. Brules, I don't know what I can do except give you these letters. Here they are. She took all of her clothes. She was a fine girl, though, and we were so sorry to see her leave. She worked so hard and she did everything just right. She was so charming, and Mr. Endicott seemed to think that too."

"Why the hell *wouldn't* he think so!"

She got more flustered and said, "Here are the letters, sir."

I took the letters and asked, "Do you mind, ma'am, if I sit down for a minute?"

"No, of course not, that's all right. Can I offer you some refreshment? Would you like a brandy or something?"

God, I guess I looked pale as a ghost. I don't know. I said, "No, ma'am, I think I'll be fine. I just need . . . to get . . . I got two letters here sent to me at Willcox and now you give me two, and I don't really know what to do."

"Well, I certainly would recommend, sir, that you start reading the letters. Why don't you read them in an orderly sequence and then you'll see."

"Yeah, I guess maybe I'd better." I took the first one and said, "Now, let me see, which one is the first one here?"

She looked at the letters and said, "This one—that's the first one that's addressed to you in Willcox and has the earliest date. Why don't you begin with that one?"

So I opened it and seen writing on the pages. I stared and stared but I couldn't make anything out of it. I shook my head, and then I looked up and seen that lovely lady looking at me with real kind eyes—maybe even a little misty.

"I know that you've been out there in the mountains and the deserts of Mexico and the sun there is very bright and bad for your eyes. And you haven't got your glasses with you," she said.

"No, I haven't got 'em. I lost 'em somewhere."

"Would you care to have me read the letters for you?"

"Yes, ma'am, I'd be most grateful." You know, I wouldn't have done that with just anybody, but she seemed like such a nice lady, so clean and decent, and she seemed to know the kind of trouble I was in. My wife was gone. Why the hell was she gone clear out to San Francisco? God Almighty! "Yes, ma'am, please open the letters."

"Shall I open the first one and read them in order?"

"Yes, I think that'd be a real good thing to do, ma'am, if you don't mind."

So she opened it and read:

" 'My Darling Boy.' Well, that starts out pretty nice," she said.

"Yeah, she used to call me that when she was gettin' frivolous and wanted to play around."

She said, "Oh well, I understand that." Then she continued:

"I waited here at Willcox for ten days, and of course, there's no word of the expedition and you are gone high up in the Sierra Madres, and it seems like it will be a long time. Geronimo, they say, is certainly a slippery character. I thought about it so long—sat around that boardinghouse with nothing to do, and I could feel the heat coming on with it being only the middle of April. With it getting so warm now, I could see what it would be like in July, and I'd have absolutely nothing to do—no children, no work to be had in Willcox. I finally decided that I'd go crazy worrying about you, so, dear heart, I packed my things and took the train to Tucson. I remembered you telling me about that nice lady Mrs. Wallen, who was well known in the territory."

Mrs. Wallen said, "Isn't that a nice thing for her to say? My, she remembered me."

She continued reading:

"I came directly to the Shoofly even though I knew the Crystal Palace was a nice place, too, but I rather thought that I would like Mrs. Wallen, and so I would come to the Shoofly and see if I couldn't get some work. She was kind enough to hire me as a waitress in the dining room, which I liked best. It's nice work and lots of nice people come in. And guess who showed up, of all the people you could imagine? It was Mr. Endicott. I guess he was out on some railroad business. He looked so handsome and pleasant. He's such a nice man—so pleasant to me—inquiring of me as to why I had moved down here. I told him my husband was a scout for General Crook. He asked what

my husband's name was and I answered that your name was Brules. He said that he remembered you were a scout—and that almost everybody in the West knew about Cat Brules. He was full of praises and said he hoped someday to meet you."

I thought to myself, well, that ain't half bad. Maybe the son of a bitch ain't a bad guy, I don't know.

Mrs. Wallen said, "Shall I continue?"

"Oh, yes, ma'am, please, please, keep reading on."

"He was coming through here to look over Tucson to see if it was a good place to put in another Harvey House, since there isn't one here."

Mrs. Wallen said, "Yes, I knew about that. I heard that's what he came for, but I hope that he doesn't do it, because if he does I'll have to close up my place and leave. We can't compete with a Harvey House."

"Oh," I said. "I hope he doesn't either." When she glanced at me and saw the look in my eye, she looked away. "Please read the rest of the letter," I begged.

"He was just so pleasant and he asked me to show him around part of the town, which I did. He was only here for twenty-four hours, and he asked me to join him for dinner, because he wanted to talk over the possibility of a Harvey House here and wondered if I would be interested in working in it. Of course, I told him I would, and he said I was just the kind of girl to head up something like this, and it would be a very good salary. Oh, Brules, I went for that. I thought it would be great, you know, if I could start making a little money, be busy, and have something to do while you were away. I can't wait for you, darling. I can hardly wait till you come back. Please take care of yourself, my darling.

"Mr. Endicott left and there hasn't been much to talk about since. There seems to be a lot of nice people here,

but also there's a group called the Tucson Ring that I think are maybe bad men. They are making trouble, I understand, up at the Indian reservation, and I really don't understand anything about it. I really don't care about that. God, I hope you come soon and it'll be just wonderful.

"Loads and loads of love, until I can hold you in my arms again."

I was kinda mad about Mr. Endicott, but I knew what she was saying was all right and I trusted her. I couldn't blame her for being interested in a good job, but I sure felt a little uncomfortable about that son of a bitch bein' around her. Then I said, "Well, that's the end of that letter, and that was dated when?"

Mrs. Wallen said it was dated the first of May.

"That's only about a week or so after she got here. Now, here's the second one, and what date does that have?" I asked.

Mrs. Wallen looked at it and said, "It's postmarked the twenty-first."

"Would you read it, ma'am?"

She said, "Yes. It begins:

"My Darling Husband,

"I have such great news for you. Just think. I must tell you of the wonderful opportunity that has come my way, and it's all on account of Mr. Endicott. Four days ago I got a wire from him saying that he is mailing me an important letter and he wanted me to consider everything in it very carefully. Well, I just couldn't wait, and when the letter came, it was all typewritten very nice. It came from his office in San Francisco. What he said was that he had enjoyed the short time that we had together because it gave him a chance to evaluate my character and personality and that he knew that I was a girl of fine breeding with a keen mind and very beautiful. Wasn't that nice of him to say that?

"Then he said that they had come to the conclusion in their San Francisco office and in the New York office that

they must open a Harvey House in Tucson, since it is going to be an important city in Arizona. He would like me to become the manager of that establishment and the pay would be very good. He said that it would be about three times as much as a waitress would make. Then he went on to say that in order for me to run an organization of that kind, I would need quite a bit of training. There were many things connected with ordering, hiring people, maintenance of the facility and equipment, and other things I had to know about. The only thing to be done was for me to go through a training school they have for managers. They have one in New York and one in San Francisco, and he presumed that San Francisco would be the nearest and best for me.

"The training course would take about three months, and I would have to come to San Francisco, but all my expenses would be paid and I would also be paid a very nice salary during my training period. Then I would return to Tucson and perhaps be involved in supervising part of the construction of the restaurant. He wanted to know in his letter if I would accept the proposition, and if so, could I report to San Francisco within a week to start training.

"Of course you know what happened, darling. I sent a wire stating that I would be there right away. I got packed very quickly, and caught a train in about three days. I'm counting on being finished before you get back, but if not, certainly soon after, and with all that extra income that I'll be making, we'll be in fine shape."

By this time I was getting a little hot under the collar but I asked Mrs. Wallen if she would read me the next letter. She said it was postmarked the first of June. Although I was grittin' my teeth and really didn't want to hear more about this same stuff, I was curious and trying to keep down my anger. I don't think I showed Mrs. Wallen anything but straight interest. So she began the third letter:

"My Darling Husband,

"You have no idea how beautiful the city of San Francisco is. It is built on hills overlooking a glorious bay on one side and the wide Pacific Ocean on the other. The water is blue and the hills are green, with the most beautiful houses you ever saw. Mr. Endicott has a very fine house on the top of a hill called Nob Hill. I also have visited the company's headquarters down near the railroad yards. They are very handsome, very new and clean. There is a wonderful Harvey House here, much bigger than anything else I've ever seen, and so well run. I'm sure it's about three times the size of anything that we would have back there in Tucson, but still the chance to run one of these famous Harvey Houses is a real challenge.

"Mr. Endicott has just been wonderful to me. He took me in his carriage all over San Francisco—my, it's a hilly place. He showed me the views across the bay and kept telling me what a wonderful place San Francisco harbor is—so big that it can anchor all of the fleets of all of the nations of the world. Then he took me down to the Yacht Club, which is a very fancy place, and we went out in his sailboat. He has a wonderful yacht with a couple of men to help him sail it. I think he said it was a sixty-footer, something like that. He seemed to know a lot about sailing and giving orders to the men, who were doing what he told them. The Yacht Club seems to be the center of a lot of social activity.

"I start my training course next week. Mr. Endicott said that he was going to stay around to see that I get started properly. We had a wonderful day, and he took me to dinner at one of the big hotels with a beautiful view from the dining room. It had an orchestra that played the same kind of music that we enjoyed at the Windsor Hotel in Denver, but much sweller.

"I can't get over how nice Mr. Endicott is to me, how beautiful this city is, and what a lovely climate. He lives in a truly gentlemanly manner, and is apparently a very

powerful and influential man in the business world all over the continent. He is a partner in a firm called Morgan and Company back in New York. They do a lot of financing for the railroads, and even handle the financing for some foreign countries. He never seems to lack for style and class and I must say, I am fascinated with all he knows.

"I do hope your campaign in Mexico turns out well and that nobody gets hurt. I don't know how long my course is going to take here. It seems that there's a lot of homework, and I only have about three hours of class a day. The rest of the time Mr. Endicott takes me around to make sure I'm not bored.

"Dearest husband, let me know when you get back from the campaign."

Mrs. Wallen began lookin' at me in a kind of a strange way, but I didn't pay no attention to her. I said, "Mrs. Wallen, would you be kind enough, please, to read the last letter? Now, when was that written?"

She said, "Well, it appears that it was written—let me see—the fifteenth of June.

"My Dear Husband,

"You cannot imagine what living in San Francisco is like. I am completely won over. You must come someday to see it, it is so beautiful. There is activity all the time. I have been sailing a lot with Mr. Endicott and his friends. He knows a lot of people here in San Francisco, and we have been asked to a number of parties by very attractive people who are very nice to me because Mr. Endicott has taken an interest in me.

"I am waiting to hear from you. I will expect to get a letter or telegram from you any day now telling me the campaign has been victorious and you are home safe and sound. I will need some time after my training course is over to get things in order before coming back to Tucson.

Please let me know as soon as you return—don't waste a minute.

"Your loving wife."

Them letters disturbed me, and I don't mean just a little. I couldn't wait till the next morning when the telegraph office opened. I had Mrs. Wallen write out a telegram for me and it read:

Dearest Wife,

I have managed to get home safely. Just yesterday. The campaign was tough but we had light casualties. I came to Tucson thinking you were here. But have read your letters and know all about your move to San Francisco. I'm here now on a pretty short leave.

Please come back to Tucson as quickly as possible. Let me know what train you will arrive on.

I got a wire back that afternoon:

Dearest Love,

So glad you came out of the campaign successfully and without many killed or wounded. I want to come and see you soon but there is no chance of my getting away from here for at least two or three more weeks. There are a number of parties I've agreed to attend with Mr. Endicott. Then he is giving a ball in my honor at the Palace Hotel two weeks from now. I can't possibly come until after that time. I will be in Tucson just as soon as I can. Even though I hate that awful heat.

I have a new address, which is 1000 California Street. The Union Pacific Railroad has a lovely home up on the top of the hill overlooking the harbor where the executives of the railroad stay. It's an enormous house that has been made up into private apartments. Mr. Endicott has arranged for me to have one. It's the smallest one in the house. But I'm very happy to have it because it is much better than the hotel. The hotel was all right but it was too

*far away and too inconvenient for the many different func-
tions we've had to attend.*

I went back to see Mrs. Wallen at the Shoofly and asked
her to read me the telegram. When she got through, she looked
at me kinda skeptical-like. I said, "Mrs. Wallen, would you
please get a pencil and let me send a telegram back to my
wife?"

"Certainly, just a minute until we get set. Now, what do
you want to say? I've written the address in here the way she
stated it in the telegram."

"All right, let's begin. Address it to Mrs. M. Brules.
Here's what I want to say: *'Get your ass on this afternoon's
train for Arizona! If you fail to make it, I will be on the train to
San Francisco in the morning. You can tell Endicott that I am
coming to kill him!'* Sign it: *'Your husband.'* "

Mrs. Wallen didn't do anything for a moment, then she
said, "Now, Mr. Brules, are you sure you want to send a
telegram like that? That sounds very threatening, and I don't
know if the telegraph service will send the vulgar word you've
put in this."

"Ma'am, I may have to drop that vulgar word, but I mean
every damn bit of that telegram. Now, please leave it the way it
is, and I'll take it over to the telegraph station."

Well, when I done that, the clerk read it over and burst out
laughing, but he said, "You know, sir, I don't think we can
send a word like that. There's all kinds of rules about vulgar
words going over the telegraph."

"Well," I said, "what about putting 'your butt'?"

"That's a little tough too."

"Well, all right, put 'your bottom'!"

It wasn't over an hour later that I got a telegram back. I
took it to Mrs. Wallen to read and it said:

*I am shocked and dismayed at your vulgar language
and your most ungentlemanly manner. Unfortunately I
know you are not joking. So I will be on the five o'clock
train out of San Francisco for Los Angeles, which makes*

*connections with the Southern Pacific. I will reach Tucson
the day after tomorrow at four P.M. Meet me.*

*Don't worry about Mr. Endicott. I showed him your
telegram and he is taking the next train for New York.*

I couldn't help but chuckle. You're Goddamn right that
son of a bitch is going to New York. He's got one of the
deadliest gunmen in the West coming after his ass. He knows
I'll hunt him down, no matter where he goes, if Melisande
isn't on that train.

Mrs. Wallen was great. She burst out laughing when she
saw that son of a bitch was taking the first train out of San
Francisco. We both got a good laugh out of that.

"But," she said, "saying something like that in a telegram is kind of a threat."

"I meant it to be a threat."

"You can't go out and kill a man just because he's fooling
with your wife."

"Oh, yes I can, and I'm the kind of guy who can kill him
fast too."

"But what about the consequences?"

"Never mind about the consequences. That has nothing to
do with it. Whether it's a big-shot financier or a Goddamn
sheepherder—I don't care who it is. If he starts fooling around
with my wife, he better know that he's damned apt to get
killed. Anyway, I don't think I'm gonna have too much trouble."

She looked at me real stern-like when I said it. She sure
was a fine woman of middle age and not half bad lookin'.

"Well, Mr. Brules, with your wife coming now, have you
got a room in town?" she asked.

"No, ma'am, I ain't got none right now."

"I have one for you here, if you'd like."

"I'd be very pleased to have it and, yes, that's exactly
right, I'll sure want one when my wife gets here."

She took me up to the room and told me it was five
dollars a night, which was damned steep, but I paid her for

four nights in advance. She seemed real pleased with that, and I brought my fancy clothes around.

"We do have a bath at the end of the hall. The hot water has to be brought up in buckets from the kitchen, but if you'll let us know, we'll get it up to you. I see you brought your nice clothes with you," she said.

"Yes ma'am, and I'm a-gonna have to shave."

"I'll bet when you shave and wear your best clothes, you're a good-looking man."

"Well, my wife tells me that, but you're the first lady to say so besides her. I thank you very much for the compliment."

"Not at all, Mr. Brules. Maybe your wife doesn't know it, but she's got a hell of a man, and they're hard to find. She's dazzled with this multimillionaire—and what girl wouldn't be?—but I think she'll get over it, and I think you'll handle her all right."

"Of course, I got a lot of ideas in mind."

She said, "Maybe you ought to give her a good spanking."

I said, "It's got past that. I'm not going to do anything like that. I don't feel that way about it—I'm more deep hurt than that. There was one morning in a mining town when she began swishing herself around a little bit and I told her I didn't want to have to kill somebody. Those miners were really looking at her and that time I did paddle her butt, but that was kinda in fun, and we was only kids then. She's supposed to be a grown-up lady now."

She looked at me kinda wryly and with a kinda one-sided smile and said, "Well, no woman is any older than she acts."

I said, "That may be, but I'll tell you what—no man's any older than he acts, and right now I'll tell you what I'm gonna do. I'm not gonna change my clothes, and I'm not gonna take a bath just yet. I'm gonna put my stuff in here and leave everything behind, 'cept my .38. I think I'll go out and get drunk!"

"My gracious, don't you think—"

But I seen the way she said it, she had a kinda twinkle in

her eye. "After all, you've just gotten off a campaign, and I know how tough that can be."

"Do ya?"

"My husband was quite a frontiersman, and I did a lot of riding with him in the Armed Desert," she said. "We had a couple of run-ins with Apaches some fifteen years ago. My husband was a dead shot, and I felt pretty safe when I was with him. But, Mr. Brules, no man can protect himself, no matter how good a shot he is, if he's bushwhacked. Out here in this country you never know what's going to happen."

I didn't ask no more questions, but I gathered that something like that happened to her husband. I did kick back with the remark, "Yeah, out here and sometimes in San Francisco too!"

She laughed.

I went out and just had a hell of a good time. I visited every saloon and listened to what everybody said. I usually don't hit the bottle very much, but I did that night. I didn't get out of control. Although I had to give up my gun several times going into bars and get a check for it, I never argued about that—if everybody was in the same condition, it was all right with me. Just going down the street, though, you needed to carry a persuader of some kind.

Sure enough, on the second day when the train come in, I was there to meet it. I'd got shaved and cleaned up and put on my best-lookin' Buffalo Bill clothes.

Mrs. Wallen took one look at me and said, "Wow, that girl ought to pay attention. She's got one hell of a man."

I smiled a little, 'cause that was kinda encouraging, and then went on down the street almost an hour before the train came in. I sat on the platform and seen the train way on down the track a-puffin' away and coming closer and closer. After what seemed an age, it come thunderin' into the station and wound to a stop. People started gettin' out of the cars. I just stood there and watched and waited—didn't know which car Melisande was in, but then I seen her. God, she was beautiful. She was wearin' that riding outfit that I'd bought for her in Denver, only this time she had a little light black veil that come down to about her chin, and it was sure fetchin'. I reckon it was a little something she picked up there in San Francisco to sorta give her style. Boy, she didn't need no style, though, she just had everything.

She saw me and waved, and I went toward her, and stopped in front of her for a minute. She stopped, too, and put her bag down and stood there lookin' at me, and I at her. I guess my heart was going a hundred thousand beats a minute. I must say, her cheeks were flushed a little too.

After she'd stood there a while, she said, "Brules, you look wonderful!"

"Honey, you look the same."

We stepped a little closer and then threw our arms around each other and I give her a long kiss. It kinda meant everything—maybe a truce, maybe I missed you a lot, maybe where have you been, maybe I can't wait to take you somewhere and really make love to you. It was all them different things. I picked up her bag, she hooked her arm in mine, and we walked off the platform and down the street to the Shoofly. Neither of us said nothin'—too hard to talk—too much had gone on.

It was about four o'clock in the afternoon, and I said as we went into the Shoofly, "You must be hungry and tired. Would you like to have a cup of tea before we go up to the room?"

Quietly she said, "Yes, yes, I'd like that very much."

We went into the dining room and there was a few people around, but it was kinda quiet. We took a table over to the side where we could speak quietly to each other and try to fill some terrible gaps.

"Brules, you know you really acted very badly," she began.

"Melisande, *you* really acted very badly."

She smiled a little and put her chin down in a coy way and looked up at me with her eyes, and said, "Well, maybe we both did, but you shouldn't have sent me a telegram like that. Why, when I showed it to Mr. Endicott, it scared the poor man to death."

I burst out laughin'. "He did some scrambling, didn't he!"

"He certainly did. He tore out of the house with the few things he grabbed, and caught the first train for New York."

"Sounds like a real courageous fellow, that guy."

"Well, you can hardly blame him. He knows about you, and when the deadliest gun in the West says he's coming to kill you, anybody would be scared."

"I hope so. You were a very wise girl to get on the train and come here, 'cause that son of a bitch would've been dead by now if you hadn't."

"Oh, Brules, you mustn't talk that way. I think really that you're sort of out of touch with a lot of things. San Francisco is a very civilized place. There are thousands and thousands of people who live there and there's no sign of Indians. There is a police force but nobody carries a gun. Those days were gone about twenty-five years ago. When a fellow like you comes around, ready to shoot up the place, why, it doesn't quite fit the scene."

"I'm aware of that, Melisande. Honey, I'm aware of that. I know I'm just a scout—a man of the mountains and plains. I don't fit in that society stuff. I understand that, but when somebody starts fooling with my wife, there's only one law I know of. It's either him or me, and I rather think it's going to be me."

"Really?"

"Really. Fooling with the wife of Cat Brules is dangerous business, and you ought to inform other men that this is so."

She looked wide-eyed and said, "Well, I thought I was your wife—I didn't know I was just a piece of property to be fought over."

"Honey, stop that kinda ridiculous talk. Of course you're not a piece of property. I honor you, and have from the day you and I first got together."

"Yes, that's true. I have to say you always treated me like a lady, and you were considerate and kind, except when you threatened to spank me."

"Well, I only did that once and that was when you got to

swishin' around up there in that mining camp, and got all those fellows testy. I thought we mighta had a little gunplay.''

"Oh," she said, "I didn't mean that.''

"I know you don't mean it, honey, but that's what comes of acting like that. Now you got this Endicott guy all in a froth and he's a-runnin' and a-prancin' around like an old goat, and I just run him off—scared him off, that's all.''

"Well," she said, "would you like a sandwich or have you had enough to eat?''

"Yes, I have.''

"Then why don't we go up to the room together?" she suggested.

"I've looked forward to this for months, and of course I'm going with ya.''

I carried her bag up to the room and put it in the closet. She looked around the place and said, "This is very nice, but not like San Francisco.''

"Hell, no, not like San Francisco! This is Tucson and it's the best there is in town.''

"It's very nice and I'm happy. I didn't mean to say that about San Francisco. I know it gets you upset a little bit.''

"Well, why the hell wouldn't it?''

"Come and sit down and talk to me now.''

So I did. I knew she had something on her mind, 'cause she wasn't actin' right and wasn't comin' clean all the way around. I needed to find out just how she felt. I thought I really knew already, but I wanted to hear it from her.

She started out, "You know, Brules, I loved you from the moment I first saw you. You're the most exciting man and a most handsome man. I look at you now and think that what I'm going to say is a little crazy, but I've thought a lot about it and I must say it.''

I stood up for a minute and she stood right up in front of me. She put her hands on my shoulders and said, "Brules, I must ask you for a divorce.''

Well, I'd had an idea something like this was comin', but I'd held it in the background of my mind and didn't dare really think about it. When it come it was still quite a shock, but I didn't show nothing.

I just said, "Oh, well, this is a sorta interestin' development. Why are you doin' this?"

"Because Mr. Endicott has asked me to marry him, and I think I would like to very much."

By that time I was cold steel. I was madder than hell, mad enough to kill her, but yet I kept my temper. I was real cool about it, 'cause I knew I wasn't gettin' the whole story, and there was something else behind all this.

"So you want a divorce? Supposin' I don't give you one?"

"Then I would have to take some other action. The State of California, being Catholic because of its Spanish background, doesn't recognize any marriage except one made in the church. Our marriage was performed by a missionary at the agency at Los Piños, and wouldn't stand up under California law. I've been informed I can get an annulment quite easily, but I thought it would be better for you to consent to a divorce."

I could see she was having trouble sayin' all this and she'd sorta recited it. Maybe that son of a bitch had worked her up to this thing and told her just what to say and how to say it. She didn't have complete conviction in her voice. I knew that anything could happen. She could change her mind in a flash. I could see that she'd forgotten a little bit what it was like being in my arms, and I knew that no matter what she asked for, she really still loved me. She just thought that we would have a different kind of life, and she was goin' a little crazy about the terrible heat in Arizona and my drifting ways as a scout. In the long run this was not the life for her, but she still felt a very strong passion for me.

"Let me think about it," I said. "I'll give you an answer soon. Right now you're here and I'm here, and I want to give you a kiss."

I stepped forward and kissed her just the way I always had when we was gonna start making love. She responded and started to gasp and burst into tears.

"Oh, Brules, oh, Brules, I really don't want to leave you—really I don't. I'm all mixed up and don't know what to do."

I went over and sat down on the bed. She was standing there wringin' her hands and beginning to sob.

"Melisande, I know what you should do."

She raised her head up for a minute and looked at me.

"Take off your clothes."

Right away quick she quit sobbing and looked at me for a minute in a kinda tempting way, and then a slow smile crossed her face. She reached up and started to unbutton her blouse. I sat and watched her strip as I had on a number of occasions, experiencing a rising rush of emotions as I saw the most beautiful girl in the world slowly revealing her exquisite self. She took off her blouse and her arms were long and bare and the undershift she had on came up above her breasts. Reaching down, she unbuttoned her skirt and slipped out of it. She had on pantaloons, but you could see the shadow of her legs and know they were perfection. She sat down, kicked off her shoes, and started to pull off her stockings. In another minute she slipped out of her shift, dropped her pantaloons, and unlaced a small corset and threw it onto a chair. Then she stood totally naked, leaving me gasping.

I hadn't been wastin' my time during the whole process. I'd kicked off my boots and pulled my shirt off. Stripped to the waist, I stood up for a minute. She stepped over to me, a beautiful naked girl, as lovely a thing as I've ever seen in my life—all warm and real and loving. She put her hands on my shoulders and ran them down over my chest.

"My God, Brules, what a man! You're the most beautiful man that ever walked. I don't want to leave you. I want you. I don't know what I'm talking about with this divorce business—that's crazy. What am I doing?"

With that she reached down and started to undo my trousers, and I gave her a big lot of help on that. I had 'em off in a minute. I kissed her again and said, "Slowly—come and sit down."

She started to sit down beside me on the bed, but I said,

"No, no, don't sit that way. Sit on my lap—sit across me, facing me."

She smiled and said, "We've done this so often, you don't have to tell me what to do. I love you so, and I'm so excited. Take me, take me."

"I will. I'm going to roll over on you, and you know what I'm going to do?"

She gasped as I went into her and answered, "Yes, I know what you're going to do."

"No, not quite. I've been in the mountains and desert a long time—too long without you, and knowing in my heart that something was wrong. Now you're back here with me, we're both naked, and now I'm gonna make love to you, so hard and long, you'll never forget it."

"Oh, I'll never forget, Brules, how can I? My God, how can I forget this? How can I? Oh, you're my man. Oh, oh, oh, yes." Then she was moaning.

Well, we were there for quite a while, and we made love three or four times. When we got through, we went to sleep in each other's arms. It was almost eight o'clock when we woke up, and we could hear the dining room downstairs going full blast and there was some music.

I said to her, "Come, honey, let's get up and get washed and dressed and we'll have dinner and dance together. How would you like that?"

"Brules, come here and give me a kiss."

I kissed her again.

"I'm your woman and you know that. I'm nobody else's woman, I'm yours."

"See to it that you remain that way. Now, get dressed and let's go downstairs."

When she got dressed, she looked so beautiful again, even more than before. Boy, I felt like a million dollars. I put on all my dress clothes, and we went down together. We walked into the dancing room and I took her in my arms. The music was playin' soft and beautiful and she was like a feather. She put her cheek next to mine, and then she turned and kissed me with her lips. We didn't say nothing, just danced very slowly and easily around and around. I felt great holdin' the prettiest girl in the world. She seemed to be feeling the same way, and told me I had a natural sense of rhythm whether I was on the dance floor or anywhere else.

We slept till late the next day, and then she told me that she wanted to see our family, old Alfred, Jupiter, and her little Tina. Sadly I explained that I had had to leave them at the corrals in Willcox, but we could take the train there and perhaps ride them down.

"But you haven't any riding clothes, have you?" I asked.

"No, I haven't, but I can get some new riding clothes here and maybe we can go up next week. When do you have to report back for duty?"

"Well, I got special leave from the general out of San Carlos. He was real pleased to give it to me when he heard I was coming down to see you."

"Still I have to get some clothes," she said.

"Did you leave some clothes here before you left?"

"Yes, I left quite a few things because I didn't think I'd need them in San Francisco."

"Did you leave a lot of clothes in San Francisco?"

"Yes, I did. I had to leave very quickly—you remember that, don't you?" She smiled.

"Yes, I do."

"You know, there is one thing about Arizona in July. Even here in the low country of Tucson, during the day in the summertime the heat is just oppressive. I can certainly feel it."

"So can I, but I've gotten used to it."

"Don't you think we could arrange to go up to Whipple Barracks? We could get off the train at Maricopa."

"First we'd better go back and get our stock."

"Sure," she said, "we could get our stock and bring it back through here, and then go on up to Maricopa and ride the stage road up to the Whipple Barracks."

"I think I can arrange that all right. I don't expect there's any more need for me to go back into Mexico for quite a while."

"When do you think you'd have to go again?"

"Well, I don't know—everybody's waitin' on Geronimo. He said he'd be out in two moons, but we don't have no idea."

"That should be August or September," she said.

"Yes, that would be about right. But you know, summers in Prescott are beautiful. There's nothing wrong with that."

"No, I know it. It is a lovely little town and I'm very fond of it. So I think that's perhaps what we ought to do—go back. The heat's too awful here."

We just didn't seem to know which way to go or what to do at that point, but we stayed together for two more days decidin' this way and that way. I made love to her a lot, and every time she swore she never wanted anybody else in the world.

On the third day I said, "Melisande, you told me you had an open-date return ticket. Is that right?"

"Yes, but I think I could turn it in and get a refund."

"I don't think you should turn it in. I'll go down and make a reservation for you for tomorrow afternoon and you can go back to San Francisco."

She looked at me and her jaw just dropped.

"Yes, I think it would be better, and I'll give you a written consent to a divorce, which I think is what you're gonna need."

"Well, Brules, I'm—I'm speechless. I thought we were going to—"

I began to shake my head, sitting there on the sofa. She suddenly ran to me, dropped to her knees, and when I leaned forward to hug her, she put her arms around my shoulders and her head against my chest.

"Oh, Brules, don't send me away. Don't send me away! I love you with all my heart."

"I love you, too, Melisande, with all my heart. But you and I both know better than that about our lives. You just *hate* it down here. You *hate* this Army life, you *hate* that we don't make much money and that we don't have nothin'. Here you've got a chance to marry a very rich man and travel all over the world. Just think, you can have steamship trips to Europe and you can go on yachting cruises. You can go anywhere you want to, even back here to Arizona, if you choose to. But with me we're gonna be tied down for a long time. I've really been thinking about it, my girl, and it's what I want for you. It breaks my heart to give you up, but I think you'd be better off that way."

She sat with her head down in silence for a while and didn't say a word. Then she said, "What would you do then?"

"I don't know," I said, "I've been thinkin' about it. I'd probably stick things out till we get this Apache War under our belt, 'cause I know Crook needs me. When that's through, I reckon I'll go on back to my old haunts in Colorado. I'll go back to my ranch and see what—"

"Your ranch? I didn't know you had a ranch!"

"Yeah, I got a ranch."

"Well, how big is it?" You could see the curiosity in her eyes starting to gleam.

"Oh, it's only about five thousand acres, but there's a lot of other acreage around that I can pick up. It's the most beautiful place you ever saw in your life."

Then I began to tell her all about the Broken Bow Ranch. I told her about all the great meadows enclosed by just puttin' up a few lodgepole pines. How there was a beautiful meadow with a winding stream in the middle, which, when you followed it far enough, ended in a waterfall that pitched down into the basin of the Dolores. From that point you could look out across one hundred and fifty miles and see the Lukachukai Mountains or the Blues. If you turned, lookin' way up northwest, you could see the La Sals, those mountains that had been towering over her own daddy's ranch ever since she was born.

She began to weep again, and said, "Oh, God, Brules, I don't know, that sounds so marvelous. It sounds so real. You know, why couldn't we go back there to your ranch and raise some kids and all?"

"Well, we've been trying like hell to make kids. We've sure been workin' at it for the last four years, and yet we ain't got anywhere, have we?"

"No, we haven't and I don't know why," she said. "You told me you had a child once?"

"Yes, I do. I have a daughter."

"You were married to a Shoshone girl?"

"Yes, that's right."

"Well, then, the trouble isn't with you, it's with me." She said that in a kinda desolate voice. "Why didn't you tell me you had a ranch? We could have gone there and settled down, and we'd be in none of this trouble. You wouldn't be in this terrible Army, doing this awful thing, and we wouldn't be here in Arizona where it's so *hot* you can't stand it—barren, hopeless, and full of Mexicans and Indians."

"I know, honey. I thought a lot about it, but that wouldn't have worked. You wouldn't have been happy up on that ranch. It's lonesome and far from anything. It's beautiful—more beautiful than any other spot in the world—but I know you have to have people around, and there wouldn't be any people—not anyone for miles and miles. It isn't like some of the ranching country where there are other ranch families all around and the wives can get together. This would be very lonely."

"Oh, if I'd only known you owned a ranch," she said. "That makes so much difference. I thought you were just a poor scout working for wages."

"I am working for wages."

"Yes, but there's a big difference between that and owning your own ranch."

I began to see the light all around, and said, "Honey, what we better do is to do the best thing for you. That may be the best thing for me too. If we lived together, and you were unhappy, you'd sure make me that way too. If I forced you to do something, and then later on you saw how it was gonna turn out—thought of the chances you could have had—you'd blame me for the rest of your life. I don't believe I could stand that. You better give me that ticket, and I'll take it down to the station and make your reservation on the train going back tomorrow afternoon."

She looked at me for a minute, the tears starting to slowly streak down her cheeks. I went over and sat beside her and gave her a kiss.

"I don't know," I said. "I thought it was a horrible thing when you got mixed up with this man, but maybe it's just gonna show us the way we have to go. You can't be happy with my way of life, and I'm too far along to suddenly change to yours. I couldn't be in with all those fancy people. I wouldn't know what to do—just like they wouldn't know what to do if they was trackin' grizzlies in the La Sals."

"No, I guess that's right."

We slept together in perfect harmony that night, making love before we went to sleep and again when we woke up later on in the morning. The train was to leave at two o'clock in the afternoon. We got dressed, had an early lunch, and I carried her bag down to the station. She was in her beautiful outfit, but somehow she looked very sad and lonely.

She kept saying, "I don't know whether we're doing right or not."

"I'm sure we're doing right, honey. I'm sure we are. It breaks my heart that you're goin'—you're my love, my life— but you've shown me the way and I know that it's right. You must go and live your kind of life and I must live my kind of life."

"How will we know about each other? Will you write me or what?"

"Honey, you know I'm not very good at writing, and it's very hard for me to ask someone else to write a letter to you and express the way I feel. I don't think I will, and I don't think you should write me. I think that we've had a wonderful time together. We've expressed ourselves in a thousand different ways with each other. There's been the physical side, there's been the mind side, and the spirit side. It's been wonderful, but I think you have a great opportunity here, and you can wire old Endicott to come back in. Tell him I said I ain't lookin' to kill him."

We both laughed, and she said, "I don't know, you've scared him so badly, he may never leave New York."

"With your charms, honey, he'll come out again, I know. I'll leave it this way: If anything goes bad with you—if life turns sour, you get a bum deal from somebody—you know where to reach me.''

''No, I don't know how to reach you. You'll be all over the place.''

''You can always try General Crook's command, wherever that would be, and they'd probably forward the letter on to me. If I'm not with him, I bet there's a post office in Telluride, and you could write to me in care of the Broken Bow Ranch. It ain't registered in no post office now, but when I get back there, I'll see that it is. Meanwhile, my love, let us be grateful for what life has given us, what we've had with each other— the great excitement, and the way we had such a ball anytime we went anywhere together or did anything together. Let's not forget that. You be a good girl now, go your way and play your game, and if you marry old man Endicott, make him a good wife. Just someday, when you're back amongst them New York swells, think about that old scout, that old mountain man, Brules, that used to love you so well and so hard that you almost lost your brains!''

At that she laughed a little and squeezed my hand, and said, ''Gosh, I feel like I haven't got any brains right now. Maybe that's the problem.''

''No, honey, you're just tired, exhausted with tryin' to figure out an impossible solution. You better go on back and you'll have a wonderful life. You love San Francisco and you'll like New York, I betcha. You'll go living out there on that Long Island with that fella and you'll have a fine time. Meanwhile, think of Old Brules just pluggin' along the best he can, lookin' over every horizon to see if he can see somethin' new.'' I took her down to the station and loaded her baggage on the train and saw that she got a good seat. I drew her up to me and give her one last long wonderful kiss, and told her that I loved her and would love her till the end of my days. She burst out crying.

''You're lucky, you're in the last car of the train,'' I told her. ''Let's go out to the observation platform now, honey, and dry your tears. I'll step off the platform when everything gets ready to leave and stand on the tracks lookin' at ya.''

She squeezed my hand, and between her sobs said, "Please do, Brules. Please do."

We must've stood there for fifteen minutes before the train started. Finally I heard the conductor yell, "All aboard, all aboard." I jumped down off the platform onto the tracks below, grabbed the railing, and pulled myself up to where she could reach down and kiss me. She took my face in both her hands and gave me another long, wonderful kiss. It was interrupted by the whistle of the train, and I eased myself back down to the ties of the track. I stood there lookin' up at her and she lookin' at me. I couldn't help it none, but the tears started comin' down the sides of my cheeks.

I knew this was the best thing for this girl, but I *hated like hell* to let her go. It had to be that way, for I could imagine her years later, being so unhappy in some damn Army camp, that "glittering misery," or us trying to plug along up there at the Broken Bow Ranch together—a ranch that she would know all the time never really belonged to her, but belonged to Wild Rose, and I wouldn't know what to do.

Suddenly there was a big clamor among the cars as the engine gave a thrust, and pretty soon it began its *chug, chug,* and slowly moved away. Melisande stood on the observation car's platform, tears streaming down her face. I was standin' below on the tracks just kinda stunned-like. As the train pulled away, I took my hat off and put it over my heart so she'd know how I felt. I stood there still, not caring what anybody around thought, and watched that train pullin' away. As it gained speed, it began to get smaller and smaller, going down the tracks till it looked like the tracks were gonna be comin' together.

I had the field glasses slung over my shoulder that General Crook had give me, when he wanted me to make that dash to Terry way up there in the Big Horn Basin years ago. I took them out, focused them, and seen that Melisande was still standin' there. She was lookin' straight back at me, but neither one of us was waving. There weren't no use to wave, though we were watchin' each other. The train was off in the far distance now, and I knew she was too far down the track to really see me, but she was still standin' there. I watched that train till it made a turn around a bend where the roadbed went down along the river—and Melisande was gone.

Special Advance Preview
from the new Harry Combs title

THE LEGEND OF THE PAINTED HORSE

Available October 1996 from Delacorte Press

Chapter One
Summer of 1950

Steven Cartwright poked the embers of the campfire and glanced at the young woman sitting on the log beside him. A pale shaft of moonlight penetrated the gently swaying tops of the mountain pines, bathing her in silver light. Somehow her loveliness stirred him. He rose and walked around the fire, nudging the ashes with his boot, then turned and looked out from the high mountainside at the moonlit valley below.

His mind drifted back to his youth, when life was bright and full of promise.

He had been born on this ranch in southwestern Colorado in 1898, almost the turn of the century. It was the last decade of the Old West. Even as a boy, he was well aware that the Indians had been gone from his part of the country fifteen years before he was born. There were no more colorful processions of the tribes, wandering through their hunting grounds. And far over the continental divide to the east, out on the Great Plains, the thundering sound of buffalo herds had been silenced forever. How he loved the West and its rich, colorful history.

He thought back to when he was a kid and rode the high country slopes of Lone Cone Peak, looking for stray cattle. He remembered how he used to pretend, as he came around each shoulder of the mountain, that he would see a band of hunting Utes or perhaps a fearsome war party of Arapahos in their colorful beaded shirts and feathered war bonnets.

He would look out across the vast distances to the southwest desert and try to imagine what was out there beyond those buttes and mountain ranges a hundred miles away. Someday, he vowed, he would find out. Those were the thoughts he had as a boy, long, long ago when all things seemed bright and clear.

But now he took a little different view of the world. The Old West was long gone, faded into the past. Nothing would ever be quite the same again. But he told himself there were many things about this beautiful land that were still the same. The snowcapped peaks, the green, green grasses of the upper ranges in the spring, the gold of the quaking aspens in the fall, the mighty towering blue spruce trees that gave the high country a character of its own. They were the same and so, too, were the big mule deer bucks who stealthily eased their way through the oak brush. And, of course, above all, there was that wild bugle call of a bull elk far off up on the mountainside on a September morning. These things were, even now, just as they had been in the Old West.

Now, so many years later, he could still vividly recall his childhood fantasies. He remembered growing up on this wonderful land, learning the ways of the cattlemen, horses, firearms, saddle gear, and long, dusty cattle drives. He recalled the sad songs of his cowboy friends, who seemed to know so much about life when the West was young.

He remembered his youth with his mother, that stately and beautiful lady with the flashing black eyes who had taught him so much. He smiled as he thought of her now, gray-haired and noble, still ruling the ranch from the ample headquarters in the green hay meadows far below at the foot of the mountain.

Than there was Brules, the wild mountain man with the catlike eyes and the lithe stride of a panther who lived far up on the southwestern side of Lone Cone Peak. In the old days, those who knew him, the buffalo hunters, the cavalrymen, the Indian scouts, the frontiersmen, called him Cat Brules. But that breed of man was long gone and by 1900, the local ranchers called him "that damned outlaw."

Steven first heard of Brules on his ninth birthday. He was strictly admonished by his mother never to go near him under any circumstances.

His father called him a mountain man but his mother

used more uncomplimentary terms. When he asked why, she simply said, "Steven, I forbid you to ever go near that man."

"But why, Ma? He's just an old mountain man."

"Steven, that man is a thief and a murderer. He has a terrible criminal record and lives like a savage. I don't want you to go anywhere near him."

"But, Ma, was he ever in jail? If he's so bad, why wasn't he hung?"

"Hanged, Steven. All I know is what I've heard. People say he was a very bad man when he was young and committed all sorts of crimes. I don't know if he was ever in jail. Perhaps he was too old to be caught, but the stories about him can't all be fiction; there has to be some basis for them."

After hearing all this, Steven, of course, decided that the one place he really wanted to go was up on the mountain to see old Brules.

When he was eleven years old, he finally had his chance. After all the calves had been branded at the fall roundup held high up on the mountain, the cowboys from neighboring ranches rode off on their separate ways. Steven then mounted his pony and loped around the side of the Lone Cone until he came to the southwest slope. There, just as he had been told, was a small cabin and running along a few yards to the south was a little stream. Beside it knelt an old man panning for gold. It was Brules.

Steven was so excited he forgot his manners and spoke before he was spoken to. "What ya' doing, mister?"

Brules looked up in anger and let it be known that he liked peace and quiet and didn't appreciate a young scamp blasting into his privacy. "I'm a mindin' my own business."

Steven rode away with mixed emotions. On the one hand, he was excited about having discovered Brules' home and on the other, he was chagrined at having been so gruffly dismissed. Still, he decided to try again. Over the years, he stopped to see old Brules whenever he could and gradually a deep friendship sprang up between the old man and the young boy.

Brules taught Steven many things, how to braid a rawhide lariat, how to build a figure-four bear trap, how to bore-sight a rifle, how to start a fire with fire steel, and many other things that a right-minded mountain boy should know.

Once when Brules was an old man of sixty-three, he put on an exhibition of shooting at his cabin site, just to show Steven what he could do.

At that time he had a shock of beard and a rather distinguished head of white hair that he partially contained under a black sombrero of unique character. The hat was old but obviously treasured, and it spoke of many things. It said here is the plainsman, the Indian fighter, the mountain man, the hunter. Even at his age his eyes were keen as fire and he moved with the speed and grace of a cat. His face, although weathered, was still handsome and he stood tall and straight.

Steven had been around men with guns all his life, both before and since, and had seen all kinds of shooting, both good and bad, but he'd never seen anything like Brules that afternoon. Brules fired many times at still or moving targets, with both pistol and rifle, and never missed.

He had an old 1873 lever-action Winchester. The stock at one time had evidently been badly cracked just back of the pistol grip, for it was bound tightly with shrunken buckskin so hard-used it appeared to be part of the wood. The stock itself was old and scratched in places, but the barrel was clean and bright and the lever action was slick and sound. His old .38 Smith & Wesson revolver was the same, worn with age and use, but still smooth and clean in action.

Not only was Brules' shooting unsurpassed, but the speed with which he fired his weapons was unbelievable. He was so fast it was difficult for the eye to follow his movements. He complained that his reflexes had slowed and his eyesight had dimmed since his youth. That may have been so, but Steven had never seen any shooting comparable to what Brules showed him that afternoon. He was convinced Brules was the best gunman who ever lived.

Once when Steven was about twelve, he let a word slip out to his mother about his visits on the mountain. She saw to it that when his father returned that evening, Steven got a painful lesson in the woodshed. After that, his visits with Brules were always very carefully guarded secrets.

Now, almost forty years later, on this late lovely summer evening, high up on the mountain, Steven was feeling strangely disturbed in the presence of this beautiful woman. He trembled as he watched the firelight play on her long auburn waves.

"Damn," he said to himself. "Damn me. I'm letting her make a fool of me. What the hell do I think I'm doing? Here I am, getting all upset about a woman who is really just a girl. She's only twenty-four years old, and I am an old man of fifty-two. I'm thinking things that I have no business thinking about.

"The truth is that I don't feel old. I can ride, shoot, and fly just as I always could. And God knows, I feel the same way about a woman as I did when I was a kid. On the other hand, in those days I wasn't mooning over somebody who was twenty-eight years younger than me. I must be crazy! I've got to stay away from this girl or she's liable to make even more of a fool of me than she's already done."

He began to busy himself by spreading out the bedrolls and covering the pack saddles with canvas tarps in case it rained. Then he went out and gathered some more firewood. Any damn thing to keep his mind off his rising feelings for this girl.

That afternoon they had come up the mountain trail, just as they had done several times earlier in the summer. This afternoon was no different. They always had a pack string with them if they were going to camp out for a day or two looking for strays.

As always, he was in the lead and she was following behind, herding the four mules and the two extra saddle horses. She'd been around the ranch long enough to be good at that sort of thing. He kept telling her that she was the best "hand" in the whole outfit. She would laugh and retort, "Now, there you go again, just trying to get more work out of me."

In a few minutes, he came back into the ring of firelight, knelt down and drew out an ember to his pipe. Becky watched him intently, her gray-green eyes sparkling. Despite his age, he seemd to move with catlike grace.

What an amazing man he is, she thought! His weather-beaten features testified to his rugged outdoor life, yet he was so educated and well-bred. True, he was older, fifty perhaps, but she told herself that he had the body of a much younger man, a man about thirty-five, she judged.

She had known him almost since she could first remember and he always looked the same. From the time she was a little girl, he had constantly fascinated her with tales of far-off times and places. It was as if she had known him in another life—a thousand years ago. She was never tired or bored in his company. He was always telling her something new and amazing.

Steven was so knowledgeable about all sorts of fascinating things about the world: history, geography, wars, and especially, airplanes and horses. Yes, that was another thing that she liked so much about him. The ease with which he handled horses, the way they responded to him, nudged up to him and obeyed all his commands. Right now she wanted to hear what he had to say about the wild horse herd they had seen earlier.

She looked toward him and said, "Oh, Steven, weren't those wild horses beautiful today! Especially that painted stallion! Where do you suppose they all came from—in the beginning?"

He looked up at her and grinned. She liked his grin. She always felt warm when he did that.

"Well," he said, "they came here in the beginning because my grandmother brought them here."

"Your grandmother!" she said.

"Yes, my maternal grandmother. You'll understand when I tell you the story. It is in many ways the story of my life."

She stood up for a minute and brushed a fire ash from her jeans, a slender, graceful figure, a young woman in full bloom.

His heart began to pound. "Oh, God," he groaned to himself, "just look at her."

"Do you remember when we first met?" he asked.

"Indeed I do," she said.

"What do you remember about it?"

"Well, I remember that you had been with Pan American Airways doing something out in the Pacific. You had to come home suddenly.''

"Yes, that was in the summer of 1938 when Father was dying,'' he said. "Mother sent me a wire and I caught the next clipper ship out of Wake Island, where I was checking on a seaplane base we had constructed two years earlier. Transportation was very poor back then and it was no easy feat to get from a remote island in the Pacific to a ranch in southwestern Colorado.

"When I got to the ranch, I found my father weak and dying, trying to convey a few last words to my mother. Mother was as stately and beautiful as I had always remembered.

"I turned my attention to my father. That great oak of a man whose power and character had dominated me for so long now lay on his death bed.

"The lump grew in my throat as I held my father's hand. My mother, her black eyes shining with tears, watched her husband, who had been the pillar of her life, passing away into the great beyond.

"My father died later that same day. His last few words directed at me expressed the wisdom of a great cattle rancher, "Remember, son, don't push the summer range too soon. Work the south side of the mountain first. Later, you can swing the herd around to the north. The north face of the mountain is our best summer range. Now, take care of your mother." He said that last sentence twice, then turned his face to the wall and died.

"I left the room fighting back the tears. I walked out of the ranch house and down the long lane that led to the gate from which I could look up at Lone Cone Peak and across the pleasant, irrigated meadows that were so green on that summer day. It was there that I first saw you: the little, gangly, twelve-year-old girl my parents had adopted four years before. You were sitting on the top rail of the gate to the corral with your long braids hanging out from under a cowboy hat. You were chewing on something and I was hoping it was licorice."

"I remember meeting you,'' she said, wide-eyed, ''in

your Pan American captain's uniform. You were the handsomest man I'd even seen."

He laughed and said, "I reckon that uniform was pretty crumpled by then but I didn't have time to worry about clothes. I just worried about getting here before Father died and I just made it. You were a freckled-faced skinny kid. I was not surprised to see you there. Mother had written me about you."

"Yes," she said. "I'm sure that she told you the whole thing. I was only eight when I came to the ranch with my mother and father in 1934."

"Yes," he said, "I remember something about that. They were archeologists. Weren't they looking for cliff dwellings and studying the Anasazi people?"

"Yes. They had done a lot of work at Mesa Verde and down on the Navajo Reservation at Chinlee and Betatikan as well as in southern Arizona. They had often heard that there were wonderful cliff dwellings down in the area of the 'goose necks' of the San Juan River. Even at that time, it was very wild country."

"I know it well. It was a damn wild area. I was a rod and chain man on a survey team down there in the summer of 1916."

"Were you really, Steven? Well, then you do know. Your dad's ranch was the only decent dwelling place in southwestern Colorado back in those days. Still, it was a hundred miles away from the San Juan River. But Mom and Dad had a Dodge power wagon and although the roads were only dirt they could still move around pretty well. It wasn't like riding horseback."

"No," he said, laughing, "that's absolutely true. I did it on horseback in 1916. It took two days of hard riding to get home."

She nodded. "Anyway, my dad and mom made a deal with your mother and father. They stayed at your ranch and drove the old dirt roads down to the San Juan when they were ready to go on their explorations. During the winter time, of course, we would go back to our home in Massachusetts. That arrangement worked just fine. We lived on your ranch during the summer months from 1934 to 1938.

That was when you were gone with Pan American. Many times I was left alone in the care of Aunt Rose. I grew to love her and I think she also cared for me. I never got to go with my parents on the river because they said the trip was too rough and dangerous. I'm sure they were right because, as you know, Daddy and Mother were lost on their last trip.''

"Yes, I know."

"It had always been their plan to raft in with all of their supplies and walk out when their work was done, but unfortunately that didn't happen in the summer of thirty-eight," she said, her voice cracking slightly.

"I remember the story. Didn't they send out several search parties to look for your parents? It seems to me that they did finally find the raft."

"Yes, they found the raft, but they didn't find any trace of Mom or Dad." She turned away and said nothing more.

Cartwright could see that it was time to drop the subject. A few minutes later he said, "I remember you vividly. You certainly were some gal. You had a lot of pep and were always mischievous as the dickens. You would rather ride a horse than eat."

"I certainly would," she said. "I loved the ranch then and always have. I had nowhere to go, and that's why Aunt Rose adopted me."

"Oh, you had a place to go, all right. You worked your way into Mother's heart and she wouldn't have dreamed of having you go anywhere else. As a matter of fact, when Mom wrote me about it, I thought it was a great idea too.

"When I got to know you, I discovered you would do some of the damnedest things. You weren't afraid to ride any of those unbroken broncs. I had a lot of admiration for you. I remember thinking, she's either got lots of guts or no brains."

She laughed and said, "Yes, I guess I did ride quite a few."

"I know you did. Did you ever get hurt at all?"

"Well, once I got my leg jammed against a corral post by a big stallion that had his head down and was bucking like mad. He crashed into the barrier and I limped around for a few days, but aside from that I never had any problems."

"Well," he said, "I've watched you coming up these trails many times now. You are a wonderful rider. You have great hands and a real way with horses."

"Coming from you, that's a real compliment."

"I mean it to be. You are about as good a horsewoman as I've ever seen. I'm really proud of you. You have done awfully well at the ranch. Of course, you have had the best of training," he finished, tongue in cheek.

"Yes," she said. "I remember a little about that training."

"What do you remember in particular?"

"Well, there was the time when I left the gate open to the alfalfa pasture."

"Oh," he said. "Yes, I remember that too." He laughed.

She blushed and stuck her tongue out at him.

"You know that was pretty serious business," he said. "You damn well know that cattle cannot be allowed to get into fresh alfalfa. They will bloat and die. We lost eight good mother cows because a little girl didn't bother closing the gate! Especially when she had been told to do so time and again."

"Yes, I remember that."

He said, "I'm sure you do. They were prime young cows—a loss of some four thousand dollars."

"Yes, but you didn't have to spank that hard."

"I didn't realize that it was any harder than ordinary. I just used my hand. Heck! I used to catch it with a paddle or a switch."

"I don't care how you caught it. You delivered it damn hard and it stung like the dickens," she said.

"Rebecca Stuart," he said slowly, "it's good business for little girls when they disobey, to have a first-class, 'A Number One,' bare-bottom spanking."

"Well, you certainly gave it to me and I guess that I deserved it, but I was pretty upset and angry with you for a long time."

"Have you gotten over it now?" he asked.

"Almost," she answered, "but don't call me Rebecca, it always makes me think of it."

He looked at her and grinned. "I know one thing, Becky," he said. "You never left that gate open again."

"No, never!" she said. "Never, ever."

"Well, if that is what it took, to my way of thinking, it turned out very satisfactorily."

She laughed. "Okay, Mr. Smart Aleck, it may take a long time to get even with you, but I will sometime."

He looked at her for quite a while and thought, "Lady, you don't know, you have long since gotten even with me. What I gave you was nothing to what you're putting me through now. I have a heartache for which there is no medicant. Here you are, the most beautiful thing I've ever seen, and I can't even touch you."

That was the truth. Here was this lovely woman beside him, someone he wanted to take in his arms, someone he wanted to kiss desperately, someone he wanted to hold, but someone he couldn't even touch. Not because she was too young, but because people would think he was too old.

He thought, "Hell, I'm not really old, I'm still youthful and strong in many ways, but I will be perceived as too old for her. I am too old by custom, by tradition, by convention, and so I must stand aside and see someone else take her away. When that happens, as it surely will, it's going to kill me. Maybe I'll shoot the son of a bitch before he gets off the ranch with her."

His mood was dark and there seemed to be nothing he could say to break the silence.

Finally Becky sat down beside him and he immediately felt comfortable. "Steven, why don't you tell me the story now that you promised to tell me when I was younger?"

"What one was that?" he asked.

"The one about the wild horses. Remember? It was the second time you came back from all your flying. I think it was about 1943, during World War II. You were all handsome in your naval aviator's uniform. It was even more dashing than the Pan Am outfit I had seen you in five years before. Steven that was seven years ago, don't you think it's about time you told me the story." She paused and looked at him intently. "Please stop worrying about a lot of things that neither you nor I can do anything about."

There was something in her voice and in her demeanor which he couldn't decipher. Did she have an inkling of how he felt?

He instinctively put his arm around her and gave her a hug. It was the same kind of hug that he had given her for many years when they were out together or kidding around at the corral. It was a hug that said, "I'm fond of you, you are one of the family, I love you, you are a good little girl." He would have liked to have made something else of it, but since that was impossible, he forced himself to think of other things.

"What do you mean about wild horses?" he asked.

"Don't you remember? We were standing on the porch of the ranch house watching some wild horses on the mountain through field glasses?"

"I was just seventeen then and you said to me, 'Someday when we have time, I'll tell you the story about wild horses, where they came from, and how they got to be the way they are.' You told me, it is a very strange and beautiful story and that most people didn't know much about it. That was seven years ago."

There was a moment of silence between them.

"Why don't you tell me now, please? I am still interested," she said.

Again, he looked at her for a long moment. "All right, young lady, now that you are the venerable age of twenty-four, I will tell you the story."

She smiled and snuggled close to him.

"Millions of years ago," he began, "the original wild horses ran loose across the great stretches first of North America and then on to the steppes of Asia. This was long, long before man existed. For some unknown reason the horse died out here in North America. Later when man came on the scene in the Old World—this would have been about six thousand years ago—he started domesticating the wild horse. That's when our story really begins."

Becky looked at him with those beautiful gray-green eyes.

"Less than a thousand years ago, horses were brought back to the New World and were caught and tamed by the Indians. Now, just look at the North American Indian and what the horse meant to him. To the Indian, the horses meant everything. They were the sign of wealth, a medium of exchange in trade. In short, they were a power to be worshiped. The Indian knew in his heart they had been sent to him by the Great Spirit to enrich his life. For that reason, somehow, in his mind they had mystical powers, strange and inexplicable, but nevertheless, real."

"Mystical powers?" Becky asked. "All kinds of horses?"

"No, to be honest, not all of them. Although all horses were to the Indians a manifestation of the Great Spirit's blessing, there was one breed of horse that was particularly dear to his heart, the painted ones.

"Just imagine what a dramatic sight it must have been. The Indian mounted on his pinto, with his war bonnet, long-feathered lance, war paint, and evil-eyed buffalo-hide shield. Somehow the pinto, in his brilliance and natural pageantry, seemed to embody the free spirit of the Plains Indian. The pinto set a perfect background for the savage's own colorful costume, and made him stand out like some sort of god. Indeed, while he rode his horse, perhaps he believed himself to be just that.

"When he rode, didn't he have the speed of the bird? Didn't he stand ten feet tall in the saddle? Yes, indeed it was the painted horse that held a special place in his heart.

"True, there were blacks and bays and duns and whites. Some of them had great speed and endurance, obedience and intelligence that were not to be scorned, but the paint stood above them all in the Indian's mind.

"He felt that the painted horse was somehow endowed with mystical powers. He could carry his rider through battle without harm and almost bear his master up into the sky to the arms of the Great Spirit. He was the Indian's link with the supernatural, a handhold on the toga of the Great Spirit. The paint was special that way, and was treated as such by the Indian.

"Now, here is a strange, strange matter. For four hundred years, we have been told that the first horses came to the New World with the Spanish, and that their descendants were runaways that became the wild mustangs which the Indians caught and tamed. I don't think that the painted horses came that way. Really, I don't. I have a different idea about where they came from and I think I'm right.''

''You mean someone else brought the paints to America, perhaps by another route?''

He nodded. ''Definitely by another route.''

''Steven Cartwright, that is the craziest thing that I've ever heard. Everyone knows that the Spanish were the first to introduce horses into the New World.''

''Well, Becky, now just how do you know that? Can you prove it?'' asked Steven. ''Think of this. From the mouth of the Columbia River in the west, all the way across the northern part of the North American continent to Nova Scotia, the distance is three thousand six hundred miles. It is full of forests, rivers, lakes, prairies, and mountains. A hell of a big territory. Just tell me, who was in that wilderness a thousand years ago to say whether or not Indians had horses in that part of the continent before the Spanish came? No one knows! People might say that you cannot prove they did, but by the same token, you cannot say they didn't.''

''Now, Steven,'' she said, ''that's just going around in circles, it's a bit ridiculous.''

''No, my dear, I don't think it is, because I think that I can prove that horses were there, at least in part of that vast country.''

She looked at him steadily as he began again.

''How is it that in 1805 when the Lewis and Clark expedition entered the valley of the Columbia they found so many beautiful painted horses owned by tribes like the Kutenai, Shoshone, Flatheads, and Blackfeet? Lewis was so impressed that he wrote in his diary that 'it is not uncommon for one warrior to own two hundred head.'

''Why were the painted horses all gathered there? Why weren't painted horses found far to the south? Why did the Comanche tribes along the Mexican border have to trade with the Shoshones, (the only northern Indians who spoke

heir language) for painted horses? Why didn't they have
ny of their own?

"The truth of the matter is that the painted horse didn't
ome with the Spaniards."

"Steven," she said, "how can you possibly say that!"

"One reason you can be sure the painted horse did not
ome from Mexico and Spain was because the Spanish
iorsemen had no use for paints. Let's take just a moment
ind look at the origin of the Spanish horses.

"The original horses of Spain were of Iberian stock,
imilar to European saddle horses, bays or blacks, sorrels,
vhite, grays or duns.

"Sometime during the early seven hundreds the Islamic
iulture spread into Spain. It was at this time that the Arabs
prought their famous horses into Spain and superimposed
he Arab stock on the Iberian horse.

"The Arabs, it must be remembered, had no use for
painted horses either. Traditionally they destroyed painted
oals at birth.

"Curiously, the first introduction of paints into Spain
ame as a result of the subjugation of the Spanish Nether-
ands in the War of the Spanish Succession.

"The importance of this, is that the Spanish Nether-
ands was close to Friesland and the Scandinavian countries,
vhich had many painted horses.

"The painted horses were introduced into Spain from
he North. In fact, the first artist's pictures we have of them
lated from 1650 (one hundred sixty years after the Spanish
iad entered the New World). So, as you can see, the paints
vere never included in the first Spanish horse shipments to
Mexico, or Central and South America.

"The Spanish, like the Arabs, always ridiculed the paint
ind continued to do so, even after their introduction. We see
his demonstrated in the story of Don Quixote, whose
painted steed, Rozinante, reflected his master's comical air.

"Yet, mysteriously, the Indian, particularly the northern
mountain Indians, had obtained paints in considerable num-
ers."

Becky could contain herself no longer. "Now, wait a
minute, Steven, let me ask the obvious. If the northern In-

dian tribes had so many paints, where did they come from? Where, when, and how?"

"My dear lady, that is just the question. The mysterious source of the beautiful painted horse of the northern Indian tribes is a secret of history and a legend. It is a beautiful legend and very, very old."

"How old?" she asked.

"Oh, perhaps as old as thirty thousand years."

"You mean thirty thousand years ago they came to this country?"

"No, no that is not what I mean. I mean thirty thousand years ago is more like the beginning of the painted horse in the world."

"Well, where did that happen?" she asked, raising her eyebrows.

"I believe the first traces of the painted horse can be found in the brown, rocky, snow-flecked Khingan Mountains of northeastern China. This would have been during the last glacial age of the Pleistocene. Its legend runs like a rainbow curve westward across the mountain ranges of the Mongolian Altai to the Tibetan Himalayas and Carpathians, the Urals and into the mountains of Scandinavia—even across the Northern Sea to Iceland and the fjords of Greenland, and on to the western shores of Hudson Bay, and finally, to the open prairies and the Shining Mountains of northwestern America.

"The migration ends approximately eight hundred years ago in a blaze of beautiful painted horses. It ends in the hollow of a basin—the basin of the great Columbia River."